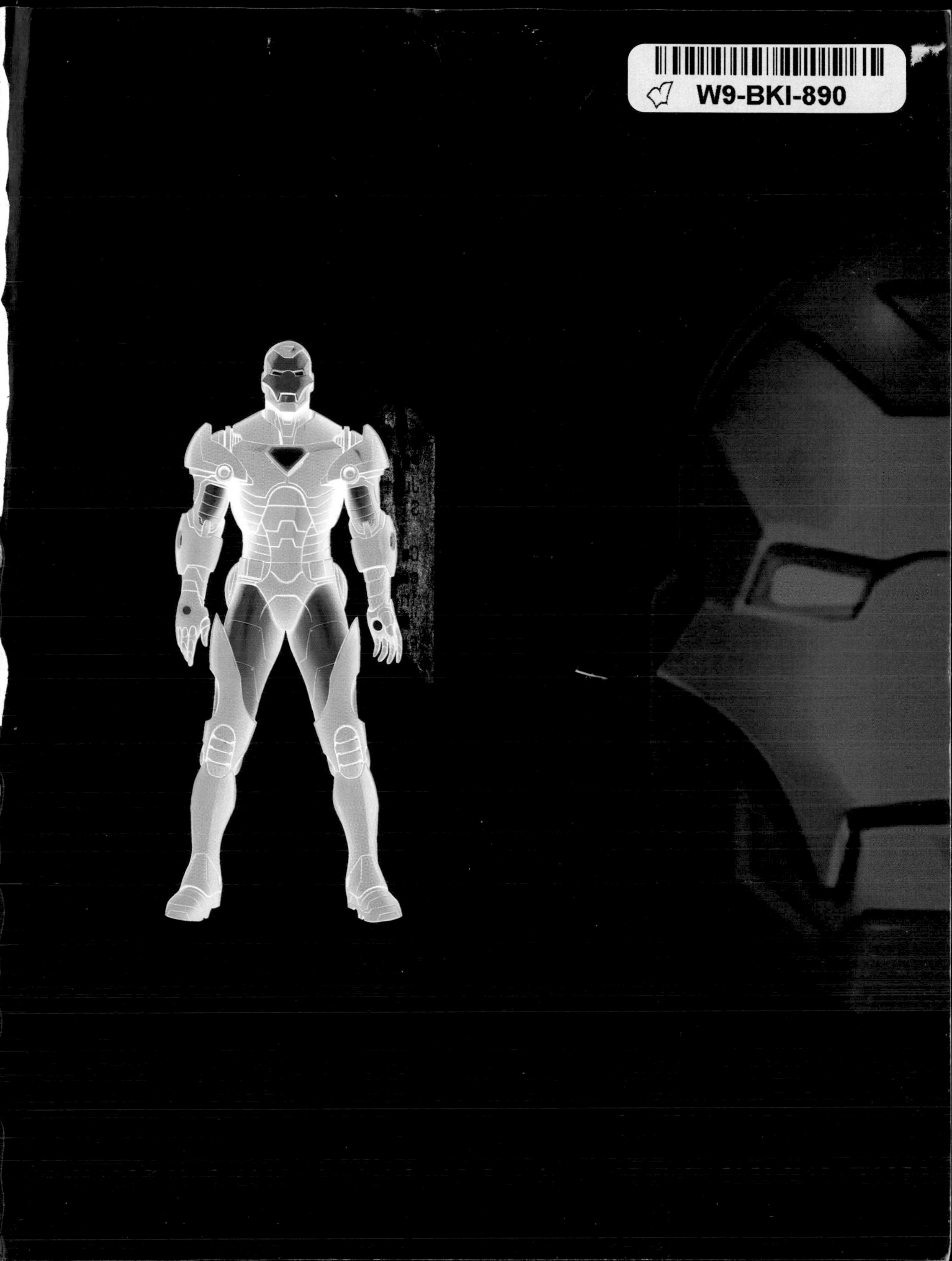

IRON.

BENEATH
THE
ARMOR

ANDY MANGELS

BALLANTINE BOOKS · NEW YORK

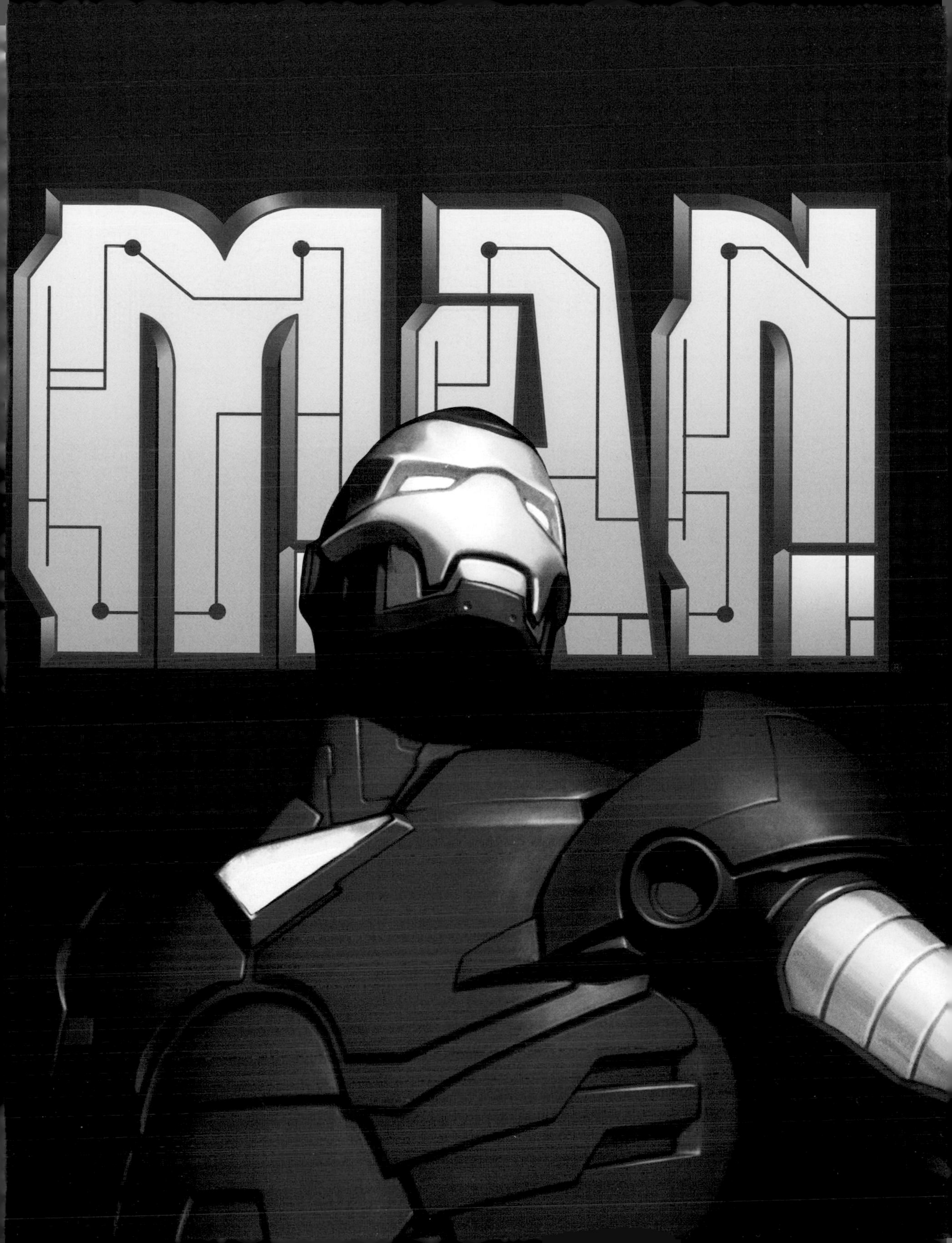
MAN

A Del Rey Books Trade Paperback Original

Published in the United States by Del Rey Books, an imprint of The Random House Publishing Group, a division of Random House, Inc., New York.

Del Rey is a registered trademark and the Del Rey colophon is a trademark of Random House, Inc.

Library of Congress Cataloging-in-Publication Data

Mangels, Andy.
Iron Man : beneath the armor / Andy Mangels.
p. cm.
ISBN: 978-0-345-50615-3 (pbk.)
1. Iron Man 2. Iron Man (Fictitious character) I. Title.
PN1997.2.I76M36 2008
791.43'72—dc22 2007052644

Printed in the United States of America

www.marvel.com
www.delreybooks.com

9 8 7 6 5 4 3 2 1

Book design by Foltz Design

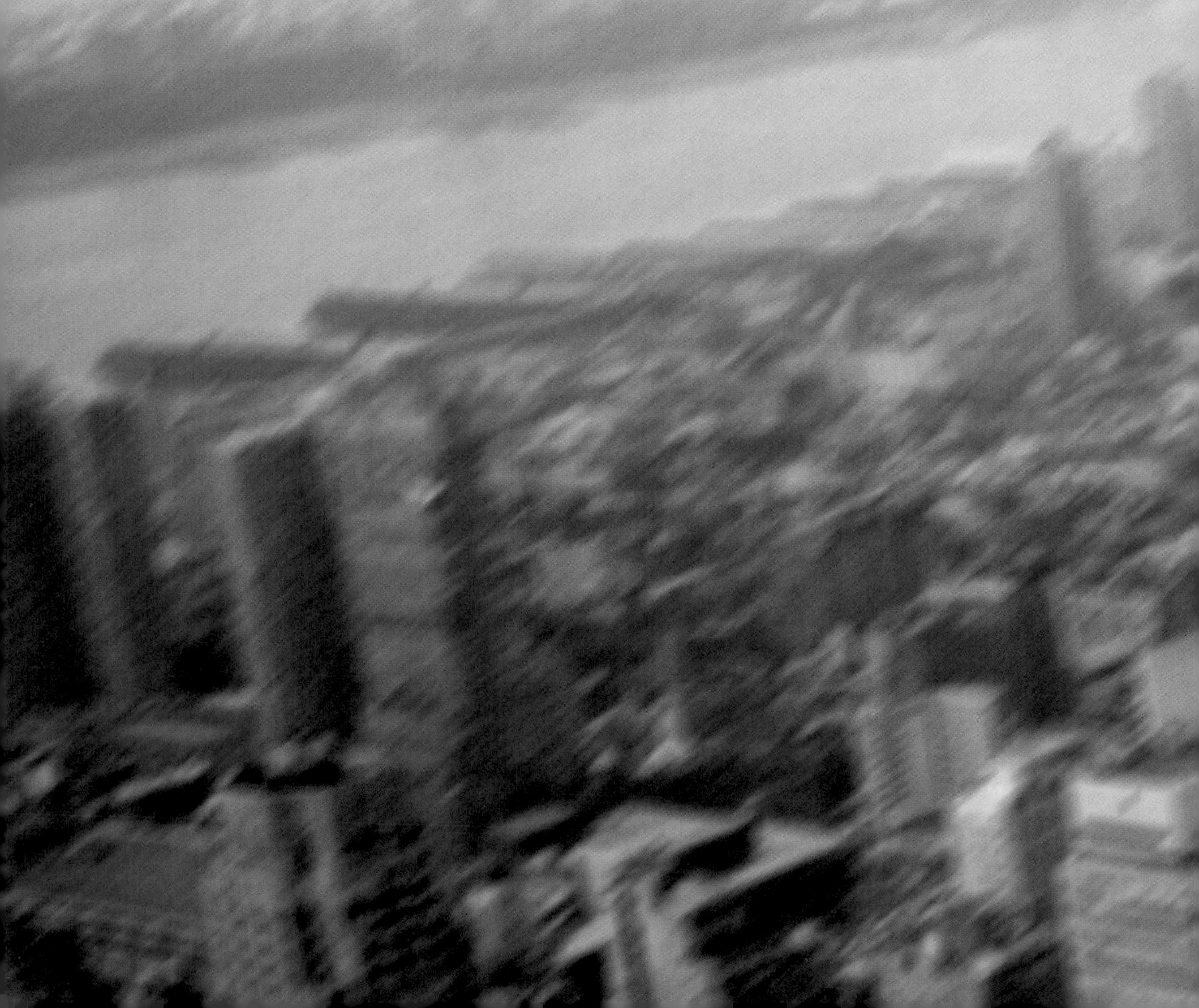

This book is dedicated to **Don Hood**, my partner of twelve plus years, and my close friends **Thom Butts**, **Mike Ryan**, **Jeff Cone**, and **Dale Nader**. They provided strength for me during a very difficult time in my life, and were the heroes I needed.

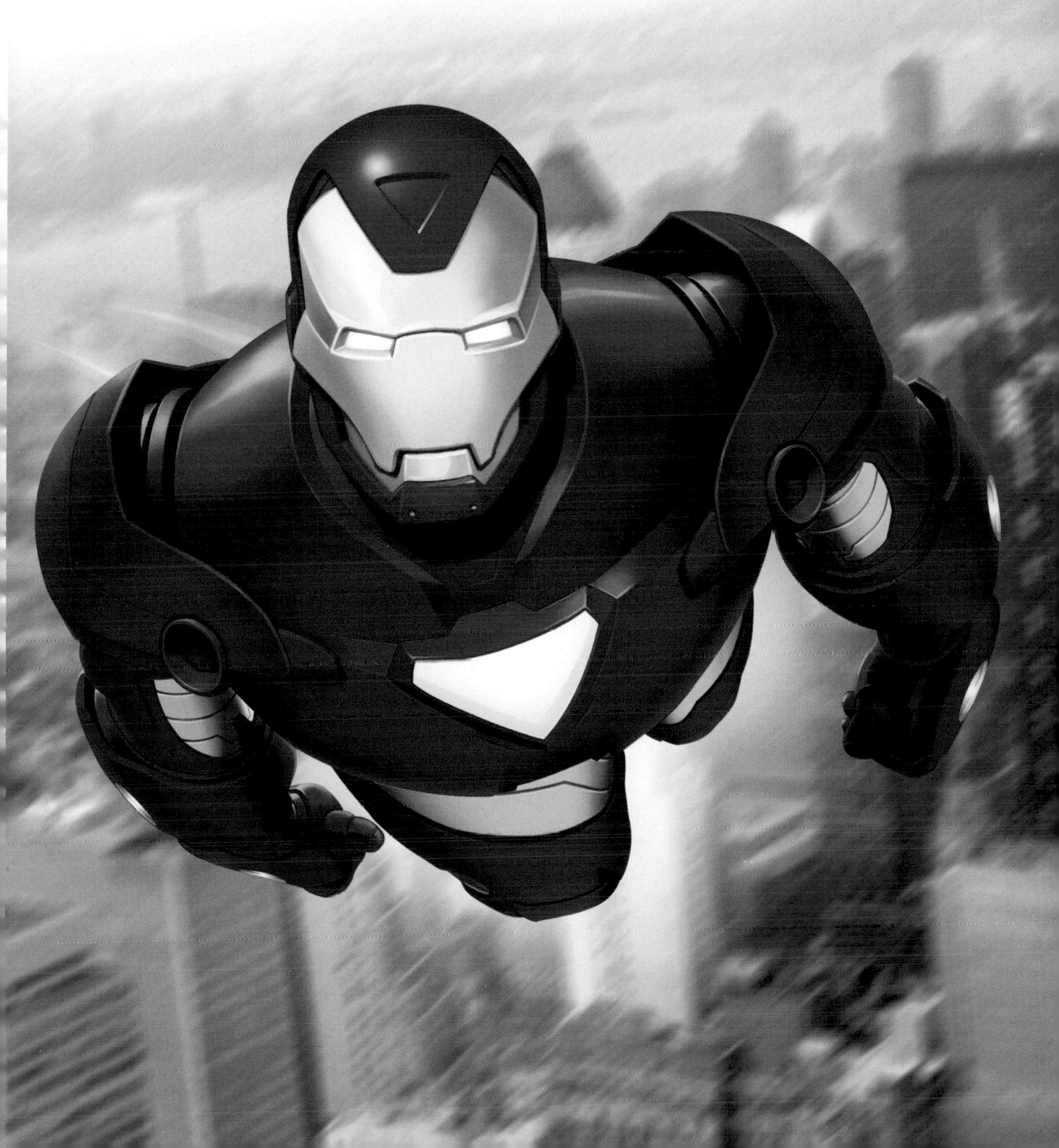

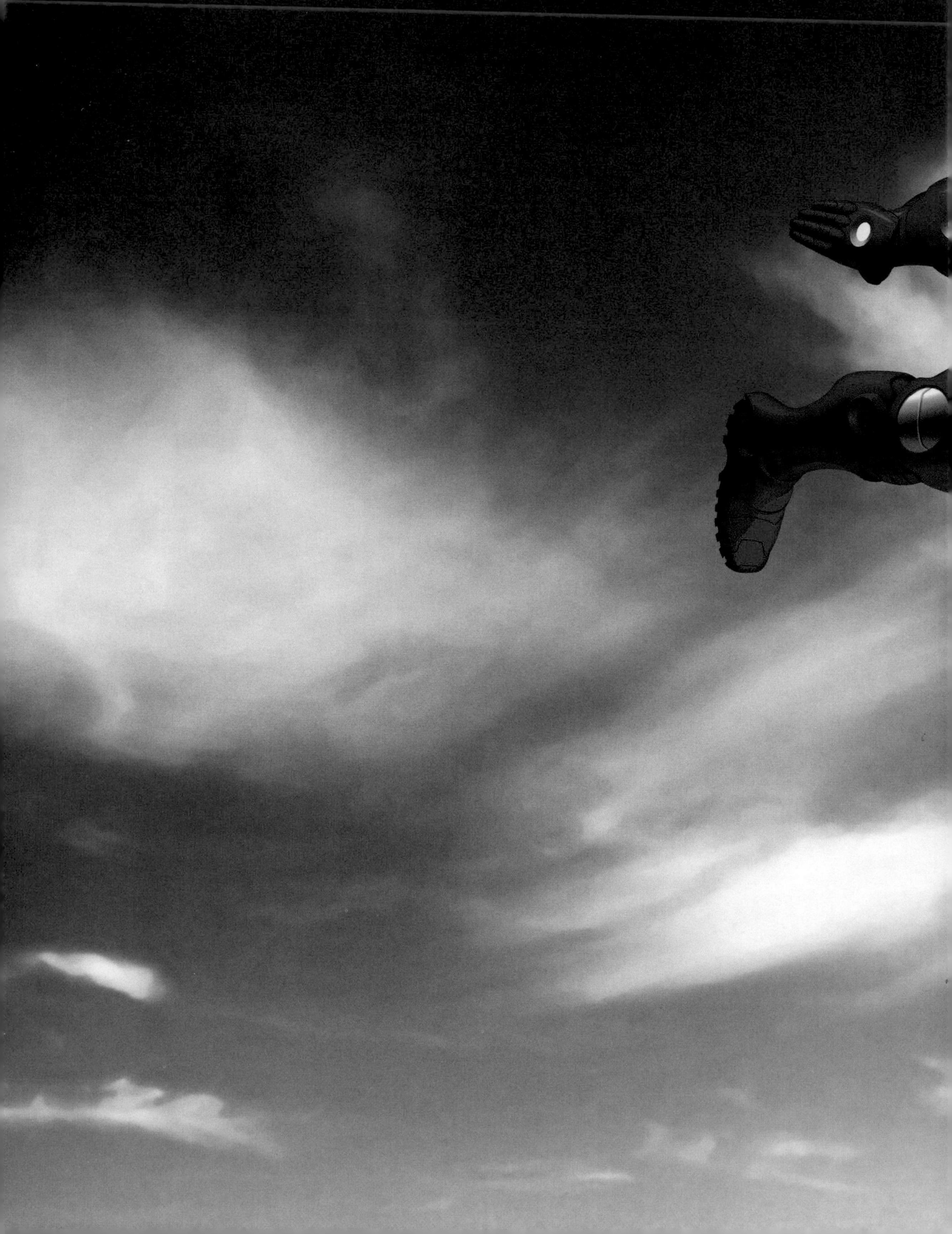

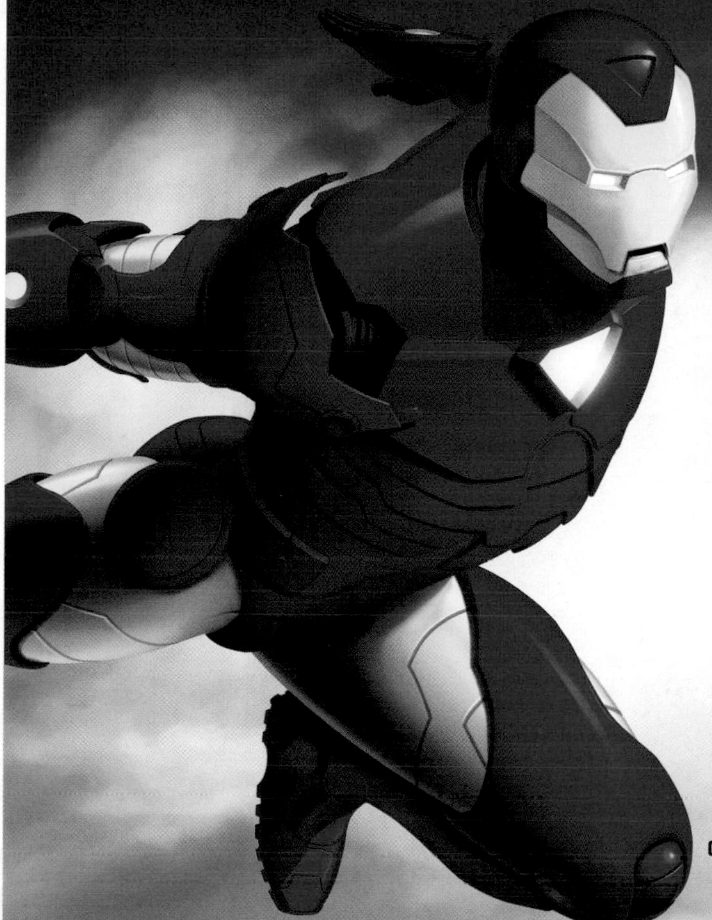

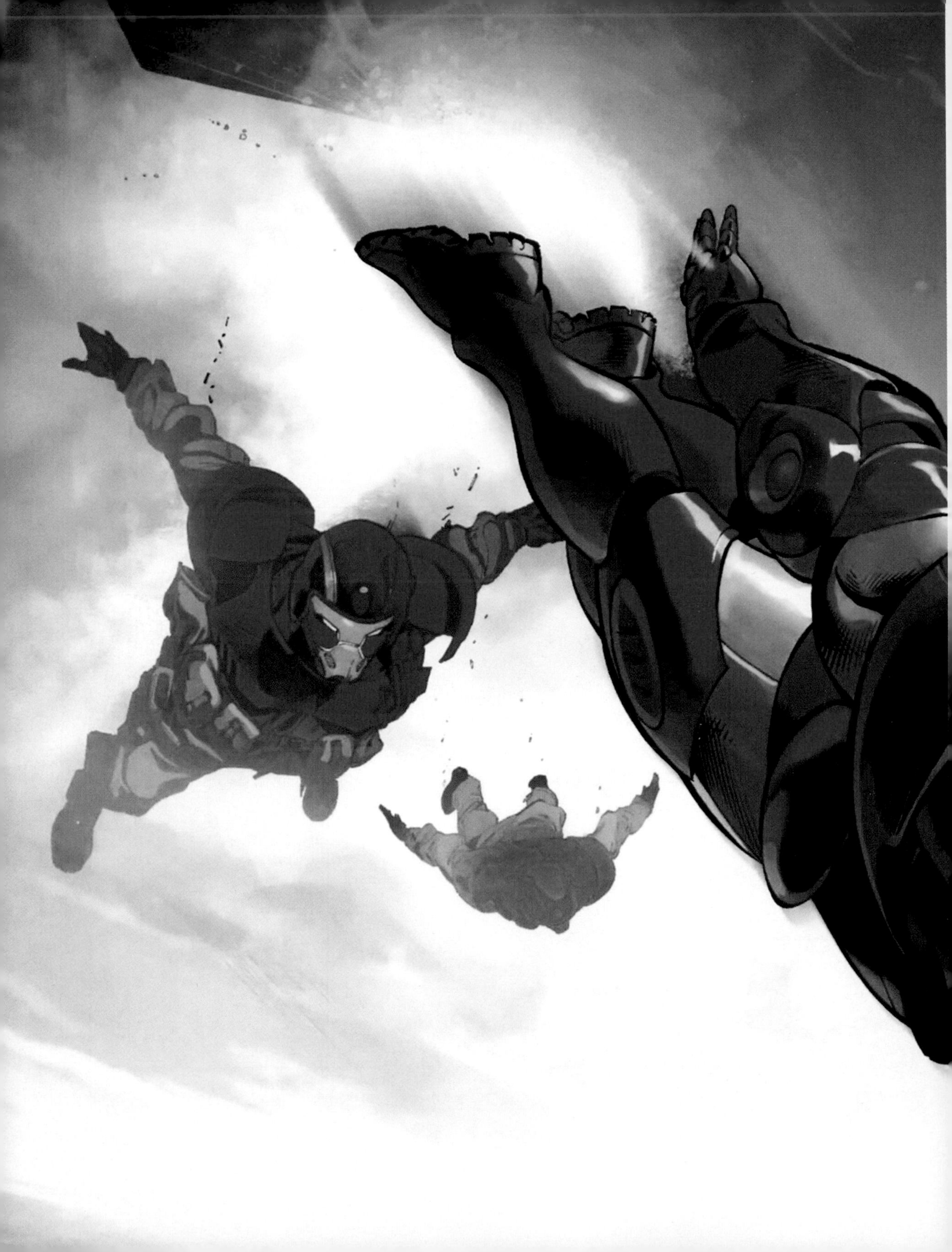

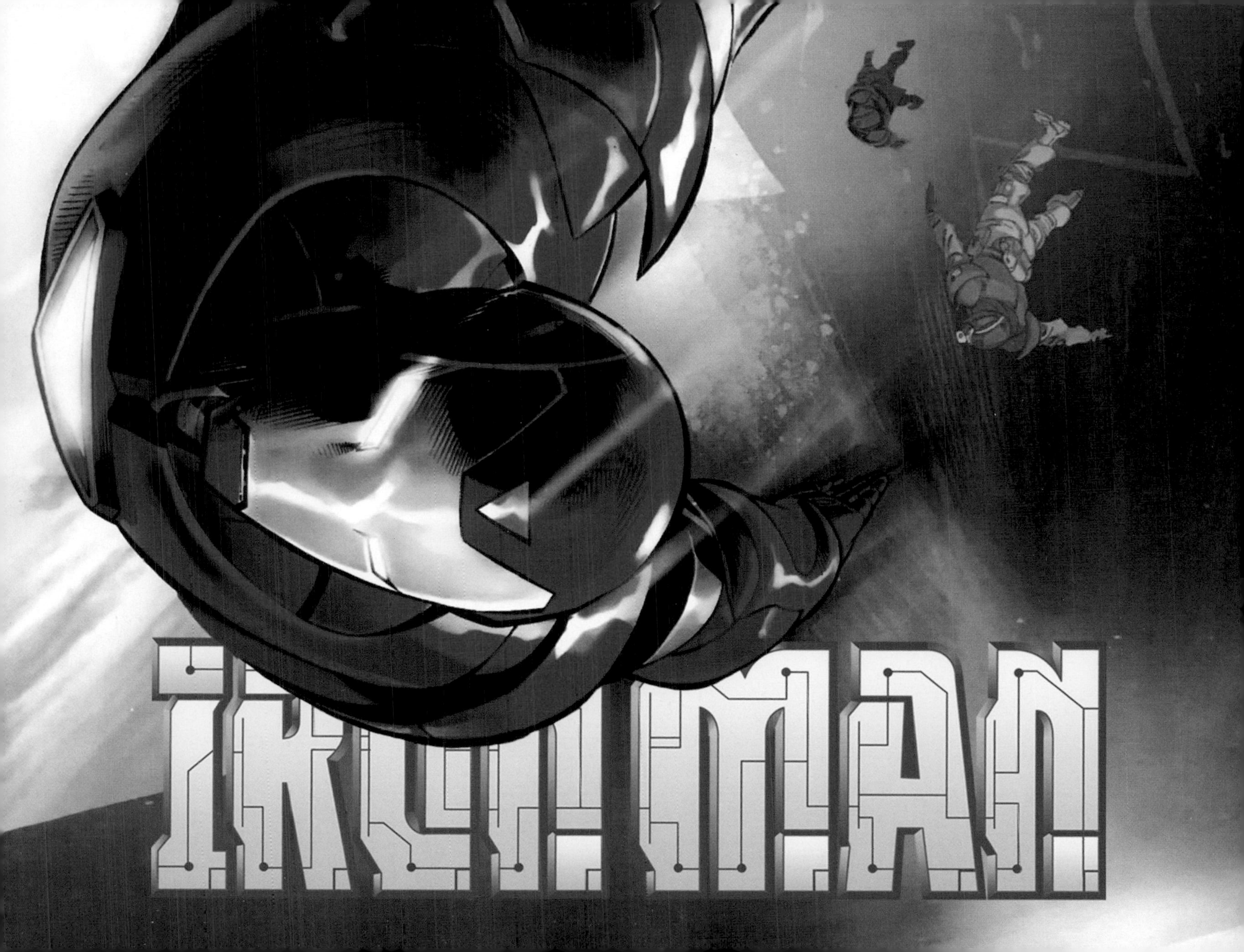
IRON MAN

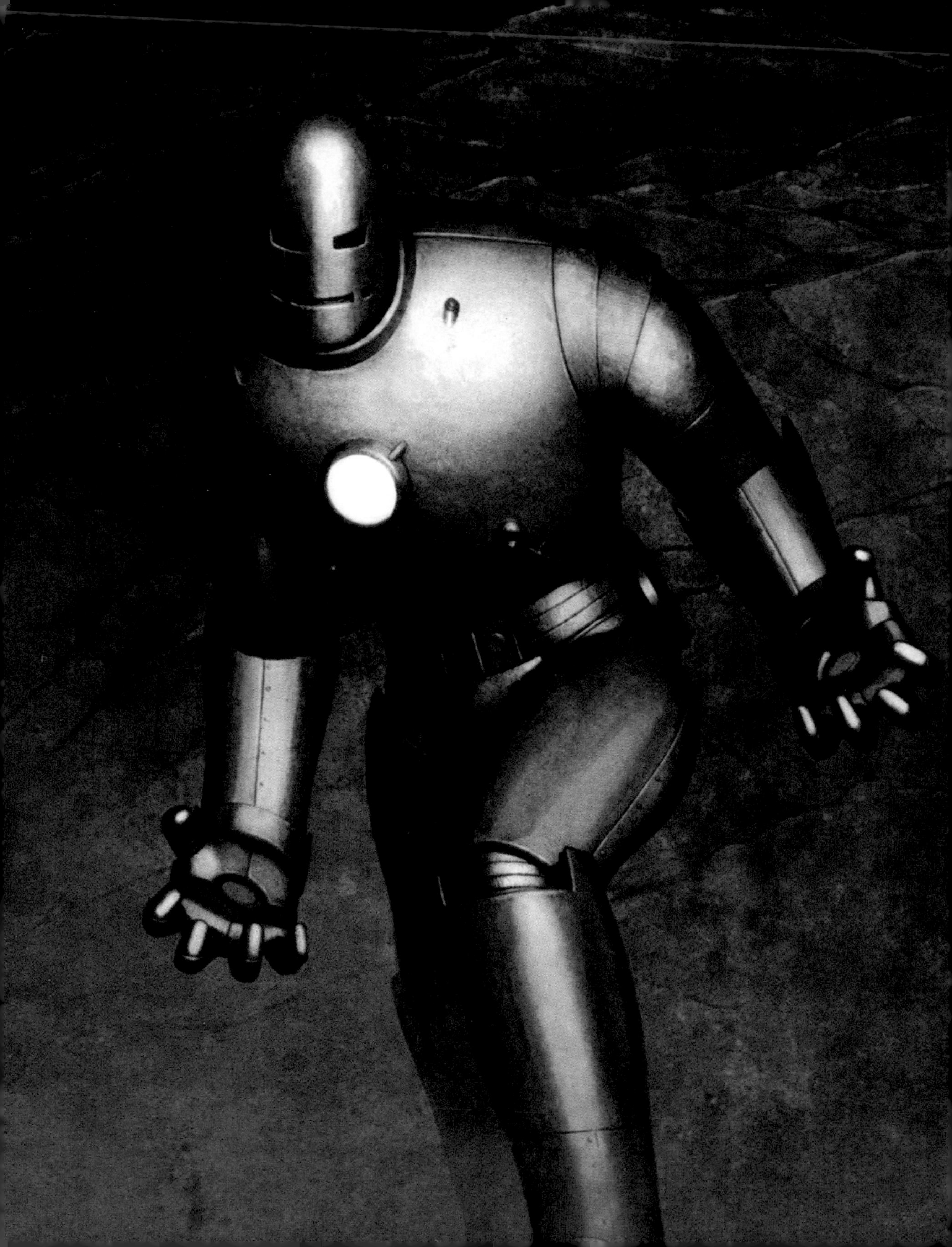

CHAPTER 1

THE MAN IN THE IRON MASK

As 1963 dawned, the world was in the midst of politi-cal—and scientific—upheaval. John F. Kennedy was president, and segregation was being supported, debated, and debunked across America. An unknown band named the Beatles were about to release their first record, while literary super-spy James Bond was being readied to make his big-screen debut. Conflict growing in Vietnam threat-ened to become international in scope, and—as the Soviet Union continued an unprecedented military buildup—the Cold War had Americans fearful of Communists in their own backyards, ready to betray American ideals. The process of cloning was conceived, while NASA's Mercury program put humans into orbit and was readying the first geosynchronous communications satellite.

The world of comic books was also going through changes. The post–World War II dip in sales, combined with attacks on the industry from psychologists and even senators who found little artistic merit in the four-color periodicals, had almost killed the comic book market. With distribution also tight, few publishers remained, and most were struggling to stay afloat . . . including Marvel Comics, led by editor in chief Stan Lee.

Marvel had evolved from the Timely Comics, estab-lished by Martin Goodman in 1939, and its later incarnation Atlas Comics from 1950 to 1961. The majority of its books

were science fiction, "space fantasy," female-centric humor or romance titles, westerns, or B-movie monster tales, until Goodman instructed Lee to take stock of the growing business that rival publisher DC Comics was doing with its Super Hero revivals. Timely had published tales of Captain America, the Human Torch, Sub-Mariner, and others in the past, but those characters had been dormant for several years.

In late 1961, Stan Lee and Jack Kirby created the Fantastic Four and gave rise to the new Marvel Age of Comics, in which Super Heroes were contemporary and mortal, coping with human foibles and relatable con-cerns even as they fought costumed Super Villains. The Incredible Hulk followed in the spring of 1962, while sum-mertime saw the debut of a teenage wall-crawler known as Spider-Man, a lame doctor with the power to turn into the heroic Norse god Thor, and the insect-commanding shrinking hero Ant-Man.

"Our Super Heroes were selling pretty well," says Stan Lee today. "I was a salaried employee at the mercy of my publisher, who said to me, 'Let's do another Super Hero, Stan. What can you do that's different?' We had already done a green-skinned monster; we had done a wall-crawling spider and all those different characters, and I was trying to think, *What can be different?*"

Despite some theories that link Lee's inspiration to the many robots appearing in B-movies of the time, he insists that his concept was much more old-fashioned. "I thought, *Well, what if a guy had a suit of armor, but it was a* modern *suit of armor—not like years ago in the days of King Arthur—and what if that suit of armor made him as strong as any Super Hero?*" I wasn't thinking robot at all; I was thinking of armor, a man wearing twentieth-century armor that would give him great power."

Although DC Comics' first Robotman from 1942 had been a robotic character with a transplanted human brain, and some armored characters populated DC's four-color tales—Shining Knight and futuristic Atomic Knights among them—a man donning a metal suit of armor to gain powers was *not* a common comic book sight . . . although there had been at least one such hero.

In August 1939, Quality Comics had published *Smash Comics* #1, which included a series called "Hugh Hazzard & His Iron Man," the first in a set of stories by Wayne Reid in which a heroic Hugh Hazzard climbed inside (or controlled from the outside) the gray-bodied Bozo the Robot to fight crime. The series was renamed "Bozo the Robot" with *Smash Comics* #12 (July 1940). Despite appearing in several dozen stories, Bozo disappeared in issue #41 (March 1943) and was never heard from again. Stan Lee has allowed Bozo to remain an obscurity, never stating that Bozo—or his original *Iron Man* designation—afforded any inspiration to the more famous armored hero's creators.

Indeed, just prior to the rise of the Marvel heroes, the comic company had published what many consider to be a predecessor to Iron Man in *Tales of Suspense* #16 (April 1961). In the story "The Thing Called Metallo!," drawn by Jack Kirby and Dick Ayers, a criminal volunteers to don an experimental red-and-gray lead suit that is built to withstand an atomic blast and give its wearer incredible strength. Due to his actions, the criminal is forced to stay in the suit, but a "malignant disease" will kill him if he doesn't discard it. As the story ends, the ironclad man clanks off into the desert to face his death.

Almost two years later, in December 1962's *Tales of Suspense* #39 (cover-dated March 1963, months ahead due to distribution guidelines), readers were greeted with another cover by Marvel mainstay Jack Kirby that showcased a man in gray clunky armor. The cover's headline blared a set of questions designed to pique reader suspense: WHO? OR WHAT, IS THE NEWEST, MOST BREATH-TAKING, MOST SENSATIONAL SUPER HERO OF ALL . . . ? IRON MAN! HE LIVES! HE WALKS! HE CONQUERS!

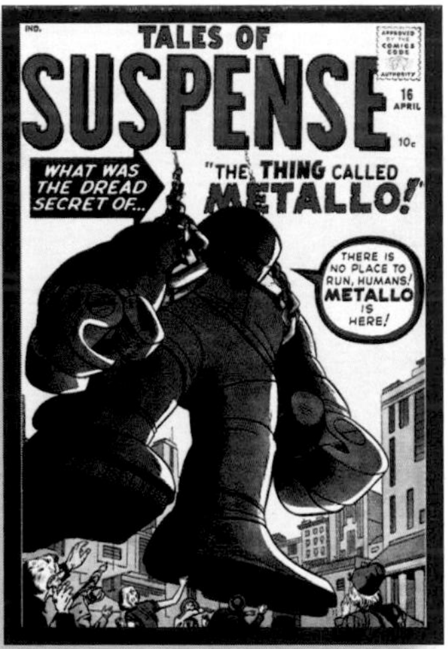
TALES OF
SUSPENSE
16
APRIL
10¢
WHAT WAS THE DREAD SECRET OF...
"THE THING CALLED METALLO!"
THERE IS NO PLACE TO RUN, HUMANS! METALLO IS HERE!

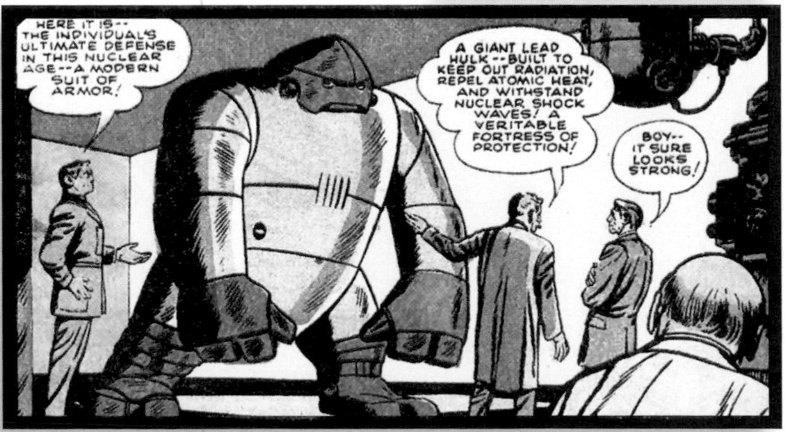
HERE IT IS-- THE INDIVIDUAL'S ULTIMATE DEFENSE IN THIS NUCLEAR AGE--A MODERN SUIT OF ARMOR!
A GIANT LEAD HULK--BUILT TO KEEP OUT RADIATION, REPEL ATOMIC HEAT, AND WITHSTAND NUCLEAR SHOCK WAVES! A VERITABLE FORTRESS OF PROTECTION!
BOY-- IT SURE LOOKS STRONG!

Metallo was Marvel's conceptual ▲ predecessor to Iron Man.

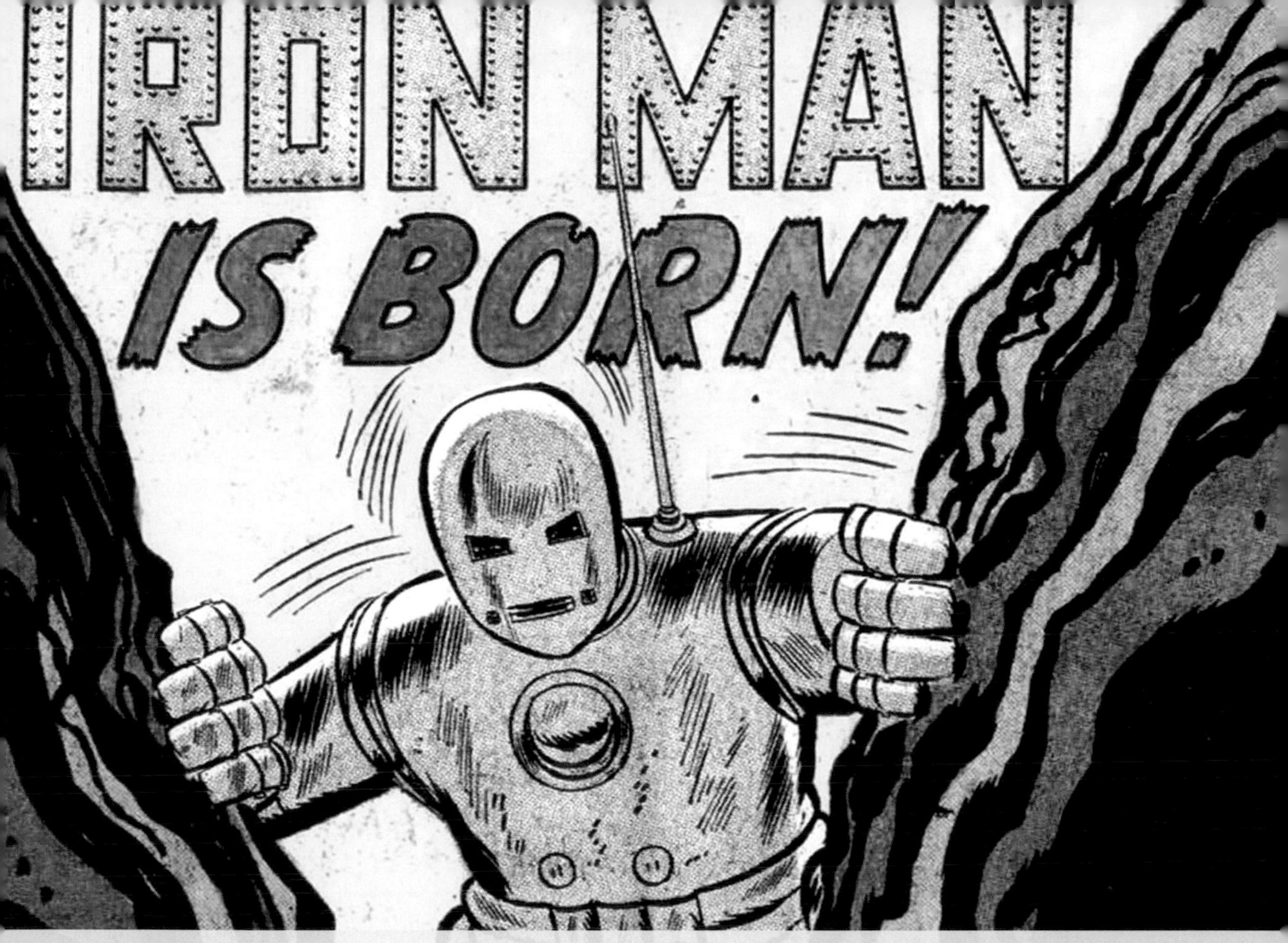
IRON MAN
IS BORN!

Inside the slick cover, the pulpy newsprint pages offered readers the story "Iron Man Is Born!," with a plot by Stan Lee, a script by Larry Lieber (Lee's brother), art by Don Heck, and lettering by Art Simek. In the thirteen-page tale, readers were quickly introduced to Anthony "Tony" Stark, a handsome millionaire bachelor and top scientist who designed weapons for the government to combat the "Red guerillas" in South Vietnam.

Stark's invention of a midget transistor device enabled US soldiers to transport artillery more easily through Vietnamese jungles, but when the dashing playboy visited these jungles, he fell prey to a booby trap. Shrapnel from the bomb lodged close to his heart, and "Red terrorist" warlord Wong-Chu offered Stark a lifesaving proposition: If the scientist would create a powerful new weapon for Wong-Chu, the warlord would have a surgeon save Stark's life. Stark agreed, but he secretly planned to double-cross the Communist villain.

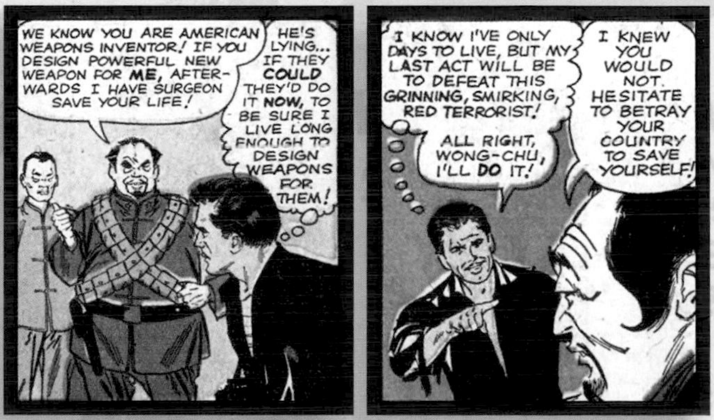
WE KNOW YOU ARE AMERICAN WEAPONS INVENTOR! IF YOU DESIGN POWERFUL NEW WEAPON FOR ME, AFTERWARDS I HAVE SURGEON SAVE YOUR LIFE!
HE'S LYING... IF THEY COULD THEY'D DO IT NOW, TO BE SURE I LIVE LONG ENOUGH TO DESIGN WEAPONS FOR THEM!
I KNOW I'VE ONLY DAYS TO LIVE, BUT MY LAST ACT WILL BE TO DEFEAT THIS GRINNING, SMIRKING, RED TERRORIST!
ALL RIGHT, WONG-CHU, I'LL DO IT!
I KNEW YOU WOULD NOT HESITATE TO BETRAY YOUR COUNTRY TO SAVE YOURSELF!

▲ The first Iron Man splash page (top) and Tony Stark confronts Wong-Chu (bottom).

Aided by the captured physicist Professor Yinsen, Stark created an iron suit powered by transistors, which magnified the strength and speed of any action Stark performed while keeping his heart beating despite the encroaching shrapnel. To stop Wong-Chu from discovering the Iron Man suit before Stark could be fully charged, Yinsen sacrificed his own life by charging toward the armed guards in an outer corridor.

Swearing vengeance against those responsible for Yinsen's death, Iron Man quickly mastered his suit's defensive capabilities, which included powerful hand-mounted suction cups for clinging to walls or ceilings, transistor-powered air pressure boot jets for short flights, tremendous strength, finger-mounted buzz saws and flamethrowers, and more. Setting off an explosion that engulfed Wong-Chu, Iron Man routed the Reds and set off to resume his life . . . albeit a life now forever tinged with the shadow of death: If he ever removed his metal chest plate, his heart would stop.

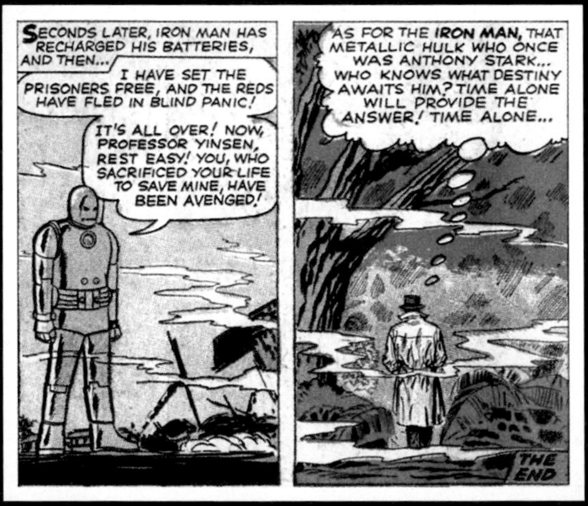
SECONDS LATER, IRON MAN HAS RECHARGED HIS BATTERIES, AND THEN...
I HAVE SET THE PRISONERS FREE, AND THE REDS HAVE FLED IN BLIND PANIC!
IT'S ALL OVER! NOW, PROFESSOR YINSEN, REST EASY! YOU, WHO SACRIFICED YOUR LIFE TO SAVE MINE, HAVE BEEN AVENGED!
AS FOR THE IRON MAN, THAT METALLIC HULK WHO ONCE WAS ANTHONY STARK... WHO KNOWS WHAT DESTINY AWAITS HIM? TIME ALONE WILL PROVIDE THE ANSWER! TIME ALONE...
THE END

The direct political and weapons-designer elements of the Iron Man mythos weren't as shocking for 1960s audiences as they might be for modern readers. The US comics of the 1940s had been fiercely patriotic, propagandizing against the Nazis and the Japanese aggressors, while war-based comics of the 1950s dealt not only with these older wars but with Korea as well. Still, while Americans were inundated with anti-Communist messages, comics had done little to directly address Vietnam. Tony Stark's occupation was a new wrinkle.

"I never for a minute thought, *Can we?* or *Should we?*" recalls Lee. "It seemed like the logical thing to do in those days. The Communists were the bad guys." But with a chuckle, he also admits that with Stark he was trying to do something different. "I was drunk with success and power, because our other characters were doing so well. Once I decided I wanted a guy in a suit of armor that would be able to do almost anything, I figured, *I'm gonna make him the kind of guy that normally young people would hate.* Obviously, young people hated war—and I don't blame them—they were all in favor of peace. So I figured, *I'm gonna make the hero a guy who manufactures war materials and weapons, and things like that. On top of which, I'm gonna make him a member of the military industrial complex. He's a big businessman, he's a multimillionaire.* And I said, *I'm gonna make them like him!* Because he'll still be brave and inventive and we'll make him likable."

Of the initial politics of the villains, Iron Man debut writer Larry Lieber says, "During World War II, it was the Nazis, so naturally they were the villains. During the Cold War, they would just pick somebody and make them a Communist or something like that. I don't think it was in any way bold, or daring, or trying to make a political statement. They weren't out to take chances. They were just trying to sell books."

As of the second Iron Man story, readers learned not only that Stark was forced to wear his iron chest plate under his clothes at all times, but that he also had to regularly recharge the device or risk coronary failure. Lee introduced this element to bring further audience sympathy and likability to Stark. "To make sure they liked him, and

Iron Man faces an uncertain future ▲
as his first story concludes.

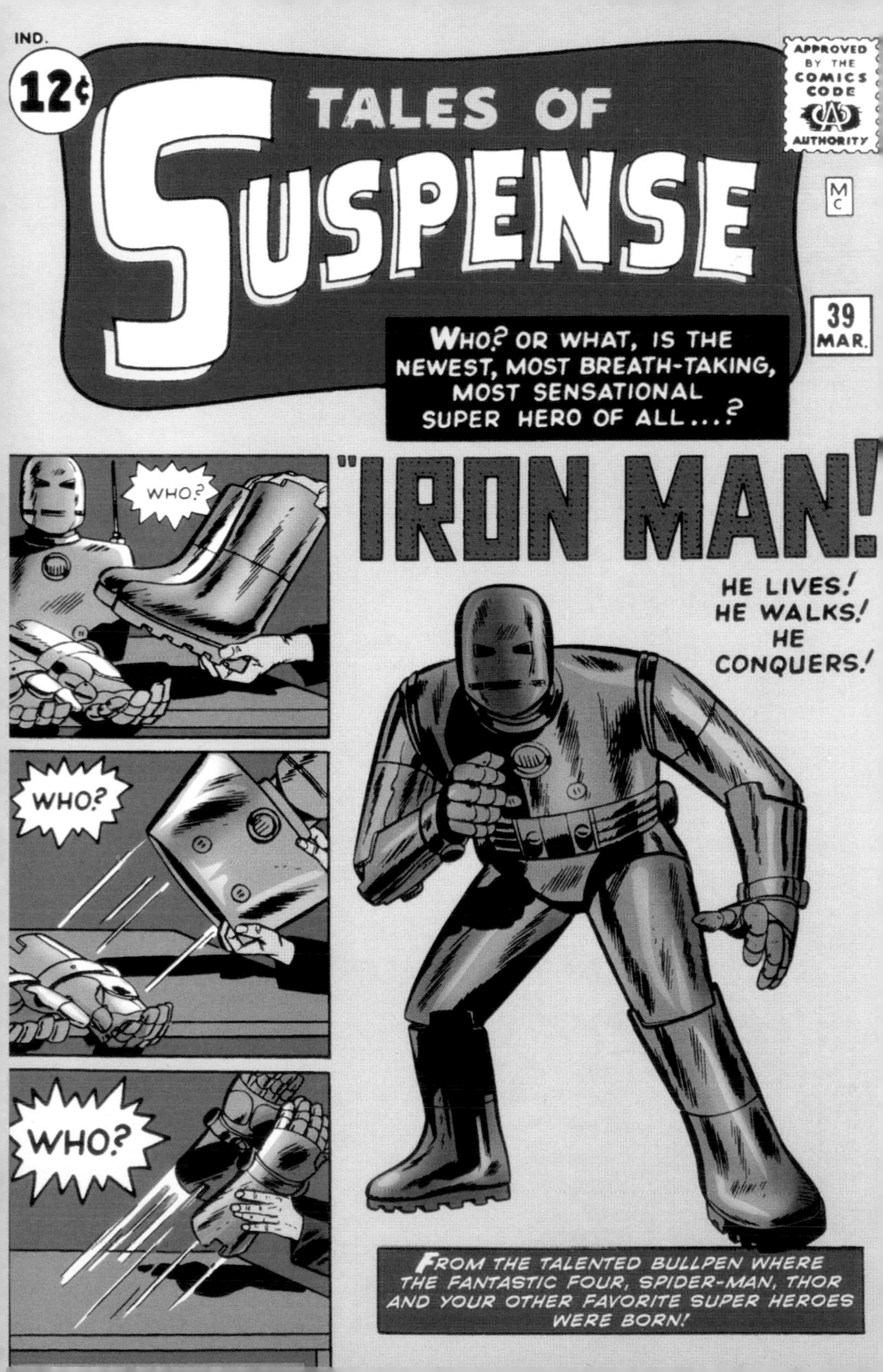
IND.
12¢
TALES OF
SUSPENSE
APPROVED BY THE COMICS CODE AUTHORITY
MC
39
MAR.
WHO? OR WHAT, IS THE NEWEST, MOST BREATH-TAKING, MOST SENSATIONAL SUPER HERO OF ALL...?
WHO?
WHO?
WHO?
"IRON MAN!
HE LIVES! HE WALKS! HE CONQUERS!
FROM THE TALENTED BULLPEN WHERE THE FANTASTIC FOUR, SPIDER-MAN, THOR AND YOUR OTHER FAVORITE SUPER HEROES WERE BORN!

Tony Stark takes time to recharge so ▼ he can keep going...and going...

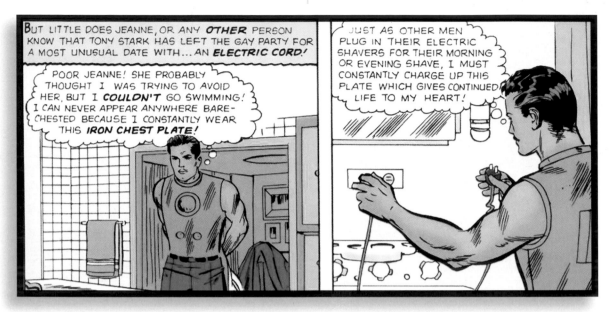

BUT LITTLE DOES JEANNE, OR ANY OTHER PERSON KNOW THAT TONY STARK HAS LEFT THE GAY PARTY FOR A MOST UNUSUAL DATE WITH... AN ELECTRIC CORD!
POOR JEANNE! SHE PROBABLY THOUGHT I WAS TRYING TO AVOID HER, BUT I COULDN'T GO SWIMMING! I CAN NEVER APPEAR ANYWHERE BARE-CHESTED BECAUSE I CONSTANTLY WEAR THIS IRON CHEST PLATE!
JUST AS OTHER MEN PLUG IN THEIR ELECTRIC SHAVERS FOR THEIR MORNING OR EVENING SHAVE, I MUST CONSTANTLY CHARGE UP THIS PLATE WHICH GIVES CONTINUED LIFE TO MY HEART!

so that he wouldn't seem to be all-powerful, I said, *We'll get a bullet or something to lodge near his heart and it'll be inoperable, but at any time it might kill him. So there'll be a tragic element to his life also. Here he will become one of the strongest of men when he puts on this armor, but at the same time he never knows when a heart attack will kill him.*

"There was an interesting result of that that I had never expected, an unexpected result," Lee notes. "We later learned that, of all our Super Heroes, Iron Man got the most fan mail from females, and I am convinced it's because (a) he was wealthy, and (b) he was glamorous, and (c) because he had that weak heart and was a tragic figure, and I think most girls who are romantically inclined would be thinking, *I bet I could nurse him back to health. I could take care of him. I wouldn't care that he has a weak heart; somehow his many millions would make up for it.*"

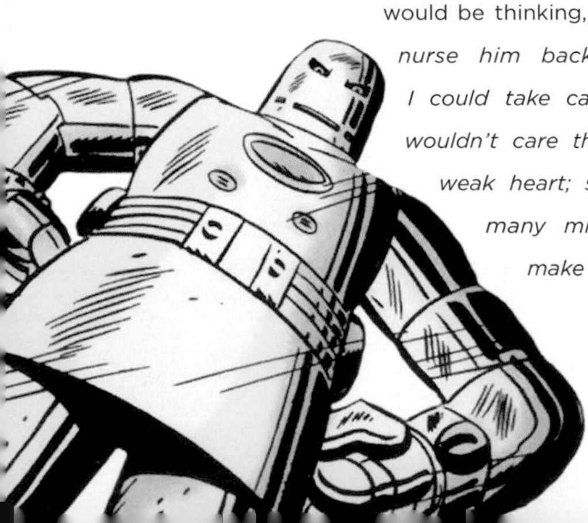

While Tony Stark was conceptualized by Stan Lee, it was his brother, Larry Lieber, who actually named the playboy inventor. Lieber had been writing comics since 1958 for Atlas and Marvel, though most of his work had been on westerns and monster stories. By 1962, he was also scripting stories over plots by Stan Lee (and occasionally Jack Kirby), including the first appearances and early adventures of Thor and Ant-Man. He also scripted the first Iron Man tale.

Of that initial story, Lieber recalls, "This was at the beginning of the Super Heroes, and I had been writing the monster books before the Super Heroes. When my brother made up Iron Man, he gave me the plot, and I had to write the story. What I *did* make up was his civilian name, Tony Stark. I was pretty good at making up names, or at least my brother liked the way I did it, and I made up the name of the guy in *Ant-Man*—Henry Pym—and also *Thor*, Don Blake." Lieber chuckles, noting, "The important things were their names as the *Super Hero* character. That I didn't make up."

Lee, however, thinks that the secret identities of the heroes are just as important, and credits Lieber for his contribution while revealing a secret of his own. "I would have made the first letter of the first name and last name the same," Lee says. "I would have probably called him Tony Thomas, or Sam Stark, or something like that, because I always did that. I have a bad memory, so if I forgot the name of a character, if I could somehow remember one name, then I would know that the other name began with the first letter, so that would make it easier for me to think of it. That's the reason why I used Peter Parker, and Bruce Banner, and Reed Richards, and on and on."

The specific creator of Iron Man's original armored look was cover artist Jack "King" Kirby, though some sources mistakenly also give him credit for layouts on the book's story—which was completely the work of interior artist Don Heck. In an interview prior to his death, Heck made certain that Kirby got credit for the armor design. "He designed the costume because he was doing the cover. The covers were always done first. But I created the look of characters like Tony Stark."

As envisioned by Heck, Tony Stark's mustachioed appearance was a rarity in comics. "I just told Don Heck, 'Make him handsome,' " recalls Lee today. "I was thinking of him really as a Howard Hughes type of guy, but I said I wanted him handsome, and that's the way he drew him, a little bit like Errol Flynn, which is great. I was a big fan of Errol Flynn's."

Indeed, comparing photos of Hughes (or Flynn) to Heck's drawings of Tony Stark reveals a remarkable and undeniable artistic

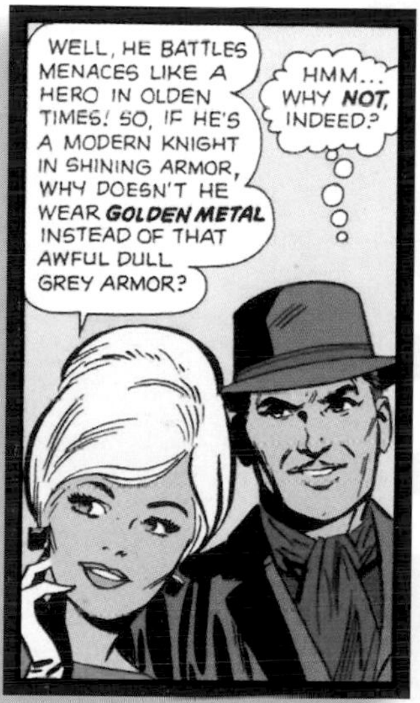

WELL, HE BATTLES MENACES LIKE A HERO IN OLDEN TIMES! SO, IF HE'S A MODERN KNIGHT IN SHINING ARMOR, WHY DOESN'T HE WEAR **GOLDEN METAL** INSTEAD OF THAT AWFUL DULL GREY ARMOR?
HMM... WHY **NOT**, INDEED?

▲ Stark's date gives him a golden idea.

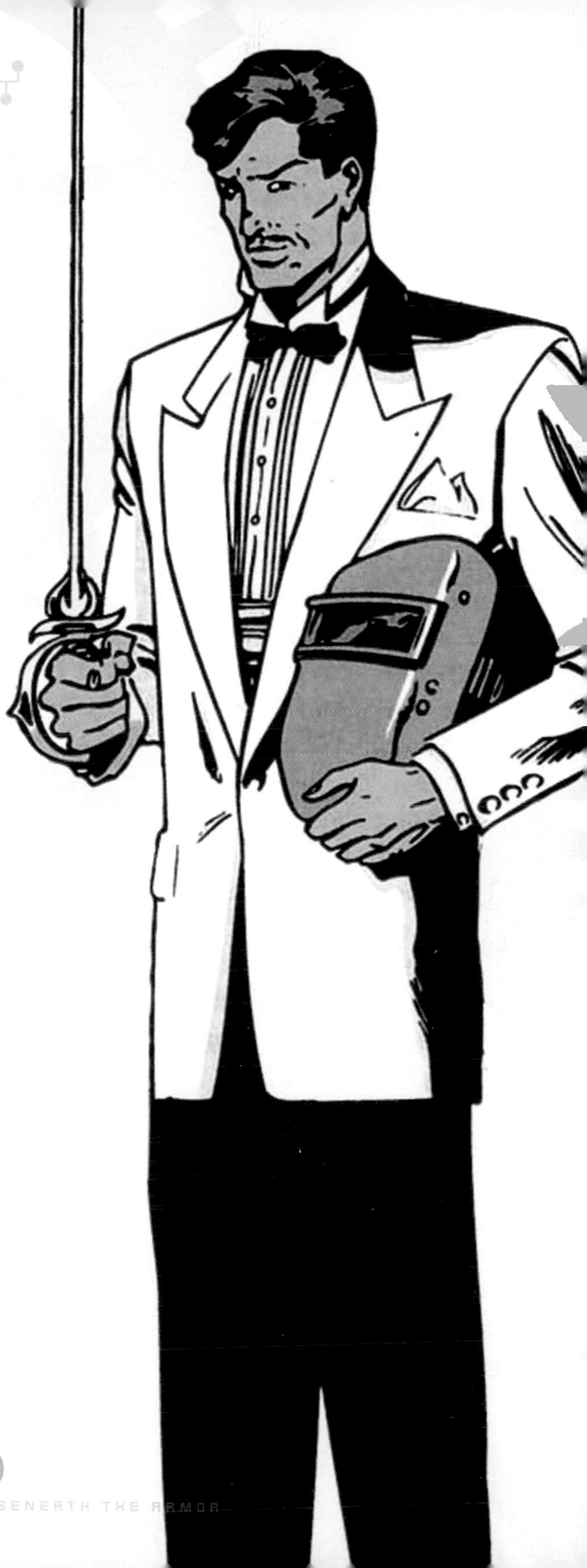

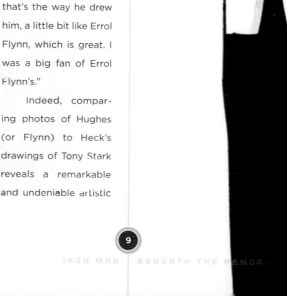

influence. But the comparison of Stark to Hughes was apt in multiple ways. The American billionaire had been an aviator, engineer, industrialist, and movie producer and director, though by the 1960s, his eccentricities—and burgeoning mental illnesses—had found him removing himself from the public eye.

•

Over the first several Iron Man stories in *Tales of Suspense,* the creative team was juggled a bit. Lieber lasted only one issue, moving off to write—and sometimes draw—Marvel's *Rawhide Kid* comic. "Jack Kirby had been drawing a western strip called *The Rawhide Kid,* and Stan I think was writing it, and when the Super Heroes started to be popular, that became much more important than a western. So Jack Kirby left the western, and Stan offered it to me. He said, 'Look, I'll let you write it, too. You can write it, you can make up the plot yourself. They don't sell that much, it almost doesn't matter what you do.'" Lieber laughs, recalling, "He was safe with me. I couldn't ruin it. I enjoyed *The Rawhide Kid* because I could write it and draw it. I did it for seven years."

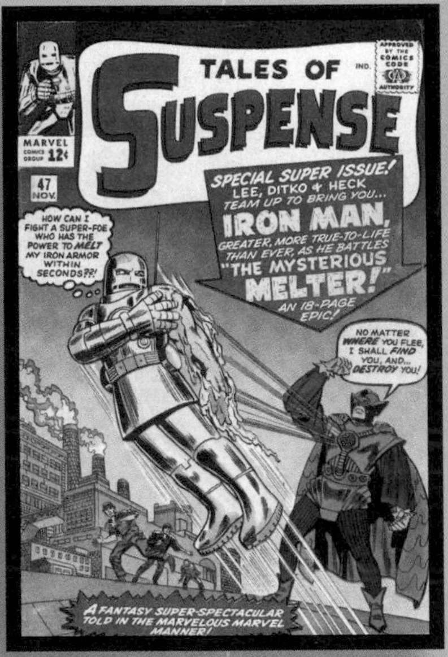
TALES OF SUSPENSE
IND.
APPROVED BY THE COMICS CODE AUTHORITY
MARVEL COMICS GROUP 12¢
47 NOV.
SPECIAL SUPER ISSUE! LEE, DITKO + HECK TEAM UP TO BRING YOU... IRON MAN, GREATER, MORE TRUE-TO-LIFE THAN EVER, AS HE BATTLES "THE MYSTERIOUS MELTER!" AN 18-PAGE EPIC!
HOW CAN I FIGHT A SUPER-FOE WHO HAS THE POWER TO MELT MY IRON ARMOR WITHIN SECONDS?!?
NO MATTER WHERE YOU FLEE, I SHALL FIND YOU, AND... DESTROY YOU!
A FANTASY SUPER-SPECTACULAR TOLD IN THE MARVELOUS MARVEL MANNER!

Overcommitted at the time, Lee would next bring on Robert Bernstein (credited as "R. Berns") to script over his plots. "At the time Iron Man was created, I was heavily involved in writing *The Fantastic Four, Spider-Man, The Incredible Hulk,* and others," recalls Lee. "As Larry returned to his own regular assignments, my friend Bob Bernstein also came to the rescue and scripted the next adventures, by which time I was finally able to take up the scripting chores and write the balance of the tales myself." With *Tales of Suspense* #47 (November 1963), Lee would write the Iron Man stories (mostly) solo for the next several years, helped for a few issues by Don Rico (who used the nom de plume N. Korok).

The scripting was done in an unusual style for the comic book industry . . . a style that eventually became known in industry parlance as Marvel Style or Marvel Method. Although other companies had writers produce "full scripts" describing each panel and each bit of dialogue before the artist ever drew them, thanks to his small staff and low budgets Stan Lee didn't work that way. The stories were plotted loosely then given to the artist to pencil; once drawn, they would then be scripted by the writer for lettering, and finally sent to an inker to finish. "Stan would call me up," Heck revealed in an interview, "and he'd give me the first couple of pages over the phone, and the last page. I'd say, 'What about the stuff in between?' and he'd say, 'Fill it in.' "

Until decades later, only Larry Lieber's initial *Iron Man* script had been done traditionally. "I always gave the artists a full script," Lieber says, "so I got the plot, wrote a little story, whatever it was, and gave it to the artist. Because I was an artist, I used to break down the stories panel by panel before I wrote the script. Like storyboards, I guess you'd call them. I lived in Tudor City at that time, and they had a park there, and I'd sit in the park with a clipboard and some paper and I'd say, *All right, let's see, page one, panel one,* and I'd sketch it out for myself. And then I go into my room and I had a typewriter and I typed it up."

The early *Iron Man* stories were mostly drawn by Don Heck, though Jack Kirby and Steve Ditko both contributed a trio of early issues. For his collaborators—who were staples of almost every book Marvel produced at the time—Lee has effusive praise. "I'm the luckiest guy in the world. I worked with the greatest comic book artists you could ever find. I never worked with one that was less than terrific. The first one on *Iron Man* was Don Heck. He had a nice sophisticated style, which I thought was perfect for *Iron Man.* He just did a great job and he was always a joy to work with."

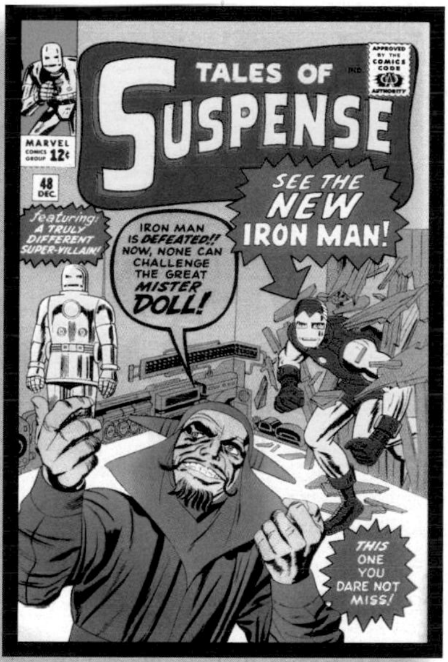
TALES OF SUSPENSE
MARVEL COMICS GROUP 12¢
48 DEC.
APPROVED BY THE COMICS CODE AUTHORITY
SEE THE NEW IRON MAN!
Featuring: A TRULY DIFFERENT SUPER-VILLAIN!
IRON MAN IS DEFEATED!! NOW, NONE CAN CHALLENGE THE GREAT MISTER DOLL!
THIS ONE YOU DARE NOT MISS!

Heck had begun working in the comic industry in 1949 and drew for various publishers before landing at Atlas in 1954, where he worked with Stan Lee on war books, westerns, jungle stories, and more. His delicate line work and beautiful women also made him invaluable to a few of the early Atlas/Marvel romance titles. "I was glad when I was given a regular character like Iron Man," Heck once said. "It was fun to do, especially in the beginning. . . . Tony was the man-about-town type."

Stan Lee's longest collaborations had been with Kirby, with whom he co-created the Fantastic Four and many other memorable comic characters. In addition to the initial covers, Kirby drew *Tales of Suspense* #40–41 and #43. "Jack was the king," says Lee. "He was the greatest. I was so glad that I was able to put him on *Iron Man.* I tried to give Jack almost any strip I was working on, because whatever it was, he could make it as good as it could possibly be."

Between stories for *The Amazing Spider-Man,* Steve Ditko rendered *Tales of Suspense* #47–49. "Steve was another Jack Kirby," says Lee. "He was one of the greatest. He still is. He could tell a story in pictures as well as any artist, living or dead." Ditko would later co-create Dr. Strange with Lee, another character who is still popular with comic readers today.

One of the stories Ditko drew also established an important aspect of the Iron Man mythos: the ever-adaptable classic red-and-gold armor. Iron Man's original gray armor had lasted all of an issue and a half before Stark painted it gold, ostensibly because the gray armor frightened people. "I was never happy with Iron Man's costume," reveals Lee. "I hated the first one; it was just big and clunky." The solution was to give the artists free rein to change the suit when necessary. "I don't know how many times I had the artist change it. Almost every new artist designed a different suit, and many of them even designed different suits while they were still drawing the strip. I think the artists didn't mind, because when a new guy takes over a strip he'd like to feel that he's redesigning it anyway."

The gold-armored Iron Man only made a few early appearances, in *Tales of Suspense* #40–48 and *The Avengers* #1–2, but it was in *Tales of Suspense* #48 (December 1963) that the familiar red-and-gold look emerged, as designed by Ditko. Following a battle against the mysterious villain Mr. Doll, Tony Stark completely refashioned and redesigned his armor to create the more lightweight flexible suit with more powerful attachments, more weaponry, and extra power units. "I found it easier than draw-

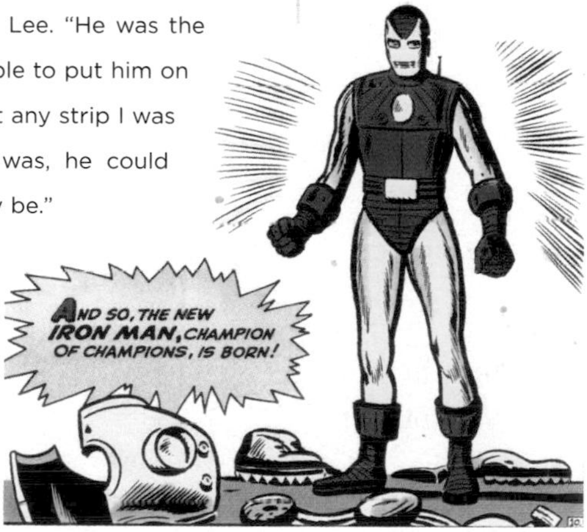
AND SO, THE NEW IRON MAN, CHAMPION OF CHAMPIONS, IS BORN!

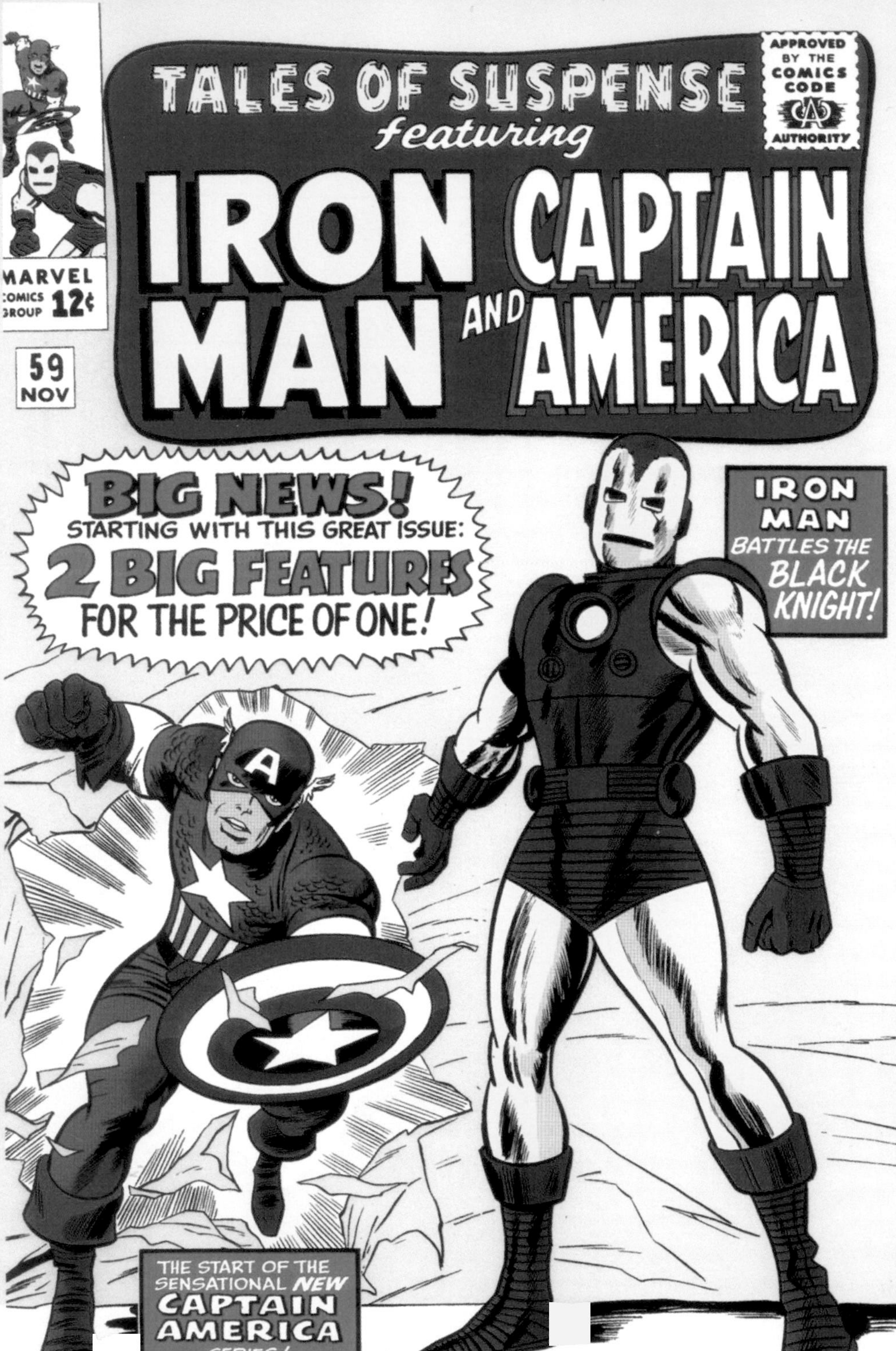

TALES OF SUSPENSE featuring
IRON MAN AND CAPTAIN AMERICA
APPROVED BY THE COMICS CODE AUTHORITY
MARVEL COMICS GROUP 12¢
59 NOV
BIG NEWS! STARTING WITH THIS GREAT ISSUE: 2 BIG FEATURES FOR THE PRICE OF ONE!
IRON MAN BATTLES THE BLACK KNIGHT!
THE START OF THE SENSATIONAL NEW CAPTAIN AMERICA SERIES!

ing that bulky thing," artist Don Heck once revealed. "The early design, the robot-looking one, was more Kirbyish." Variations on—and upgrades to—the red-and-gold armor would continue from 1963 to the modern day, with a few stops along the way to return to the original armor in certain storylines.

Although the science of the early Iron Man comics is quaint by today's standards, Tony Stark's inventions were relatively cutting-edge in their day—a time when the transistor was new. Still, Stan Lee jokes that he didn't do an extraordinary amount of research into real science as he wrote the stories. "I am not the world's greatest research guy," he says with a chuckle. "Did you ever read *Thor*? Well, you can see how scientific I am. When he wants to fly, he swings his hammer around and then he lets go of it and since it's attached to his wrist it pulls him along into the air. That's about as scientific as I can get."

•

Also introduced in the first year of Iron Man's adventures were two recurring cast members for the strip: Harold "Happy" Hogan, an ex-boxer who would become Tony Stark's chauffeur, and Virginia "Pepper" Potts, Stark's freckle-faced secretary. "I liked them both," says Stan Lee. "I wanted her to be beautiful, but you wouldn't know it until later on . . . the type of girl that, once she dressed up and did her hair the right way, she'd be gorgeous. I liked the name Pepper Potts, and what I wanted was she would be Tony's secretary, and she would be in love with him, and she's so close that he can't recognize the fact that she loves him. Probably he'd love her if he thought about it, but he didn't think about it. I thought it was a nice dramatic little situation, the two of them."

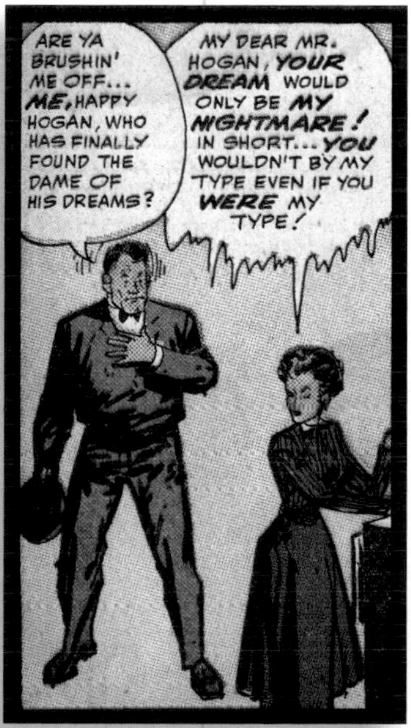
ARE YA BRUSHIN' ME OFF... ME, HAPPY HOGAN, WHO HAS FINALLY FOUND THE DAME OF HIS DREAMS?
MY DEAR MR. HOGAN, YOUR DREAM WOULD ONLY BE MY NIGHTMARE! IN SHORT... YOU WOULDN'T BY MY TYPE EVEN IF YOU WERE MY TYPE!

▲ Pepper Potts gives Happy Hogan a chilling welcome.

The rough-edged Happy Hogan was a popular blue-collar outsider to Tony's sophisticated world. "Happy was in love with Pepper, and resented the fact that she loved Tony," says Lee. "Happy was Tony's best friend, and he was eternally grateful to Tony for something Tony had done, and Tony would never have done anything to hurt Happy. And Tony had no idea that there was this problem with Happy and Pepper. I like situations like that. All three of them are good guys, but who are you going to vote for, who are you going to care about the most? It was an interesting triangle, and that made the story a little more mature, and a little more realistic than just a hero fighting bad guys."

Millennial-era *Iron Man* writer Kurt Busiek recalls learning from the late Don Heck the origin of Pepper's look. "Early on, Pepper Potts was played as the homely, Coney Island secretary gal and Happy was an ex-boxer, [a] scar-faced, broken-nosed, cauliflower-eared pug called Happy because he never smiled. He was a diamond in the rough. They provided so much contrast to the jet-set world that Tony wandered around in that it grounded the series. Pepper was based on a character who was on *The Bob Cummings Show* [1955–1959, also called *Love That Bob*]. Bob Cummings was a professional photographer who was always taking pictures of gorgeous gals, and his secretary Schultzy was this freckled girl who'd dress up pretty, but she was in love with her boss, who couldn't see her because there were all these gorgeous girls around. When Don Heck drew the character of Pepper, he based her on Schultzy, who was played by Ann B. Davis, twelve years before she played Alice on *The Brady Bunch*. So there's the secret origin of Pepper Potts. She's really Alice from *The Brady Bunch*!"

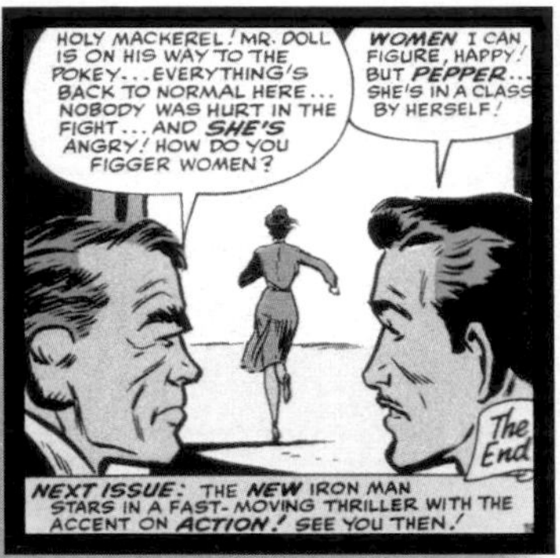
HOLY MACKEREL! MR. DOLL IS ON HIS WAY TO THE POKEY... EVERYTHING'S BACK TO NORMAL HERE... NOBODY WAS HURT IN THE FIGHT... AND SHE'S ANGRY! HOW DO YOU FIGGER WOMEN?
WOMEN I CAN FIGURE, HAPPY! BUT PEPPER... SHE'S IN A CLASS BY HERSELF!
The End
NEXT ISSUE: THE NEW IRON MAN STARS IN A FAST-MOVING THRILLER WITH THE ACCENT ON ACTION! SEE YOU THEN!

One aspect of Iron Man was entirely revolutionary in the comic industry: The armored man was the first Super Hero employed by a private corporation. To keep the secret of his ailing health safe, Tony Stark led the world, his employees, and his friends to believe that Iron Man served as his hired, personal bodyguard at Stark Industries. The ruse would be both a blessing and a curse over the next forty-five years. It did, however, give Tony a reason why Iron Man was around every time a Stark Industries plant was attacked or industrial sabotage against Stark was under way . . . elements that were common to almost every Iron Man story.

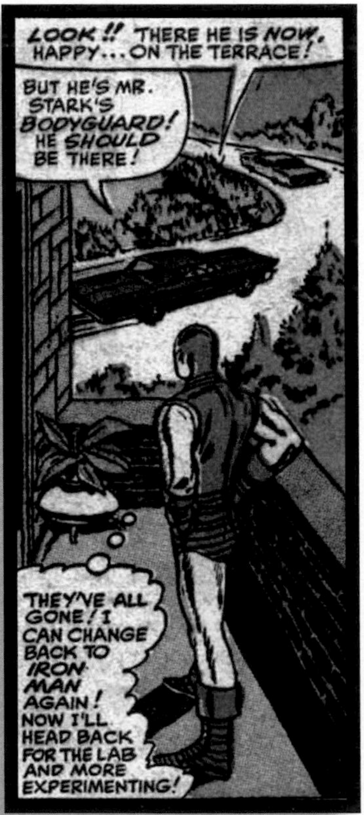
LOOK!! THERE HE IS NOW, HAPPY... ON THE TERRACE!
BUT HE'S MR. STARK'S BODYGUARD! HE SHOULD BE THERE!
THEY'VE ALL GONE! I CAN CHANGE BACK TO IRON MAN AGAIN! NOW I'LL HEAD BACK FOR THE LAB AND MORE EXPERIMENTING!

Being Tony Stark's bodyguard ▲ complicates life for Iron Man.

Even as his adventures proved popular in *Tales of Suspense,* Iron Man became the co-star of a second new Marvel comic. *The Avengers* #1 debuted in

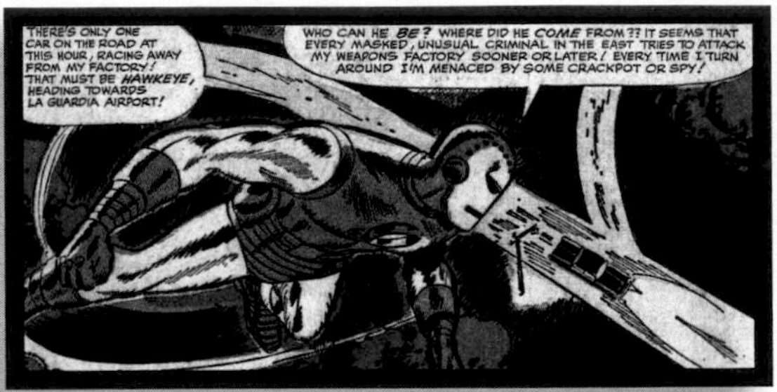
THERE'S ONLY ONE CAR ON THE ROAD AT THIS HOUR, RACING AWAY FROM MY FACTORY! THAT MUST BE HAWKEYE, HEADING TOWARDS LA GUARDIA AIRPORT!
WHO CAN HE BE? WHERE DID HE COME FROM?? IT SEEMS THAT EVERY MASKED, UNUSUAL CRIMINAL IN THE EAST TRIES TO ATTACK MY WEAPONS FACTORY SOONER OR LATER! EVERY TIME I TURN AROUND I'M MENACED BY SOME CRACKPOT OR SPY!

September 1963, teaming the metallic hero with Thor, the Hulk, Ant-Man, and the Wasp. By the fourth issue of *The Avengers,* a revived Captain America would join the group, shortly before sharing top billing with Iron Man in dual stories beginning with *Tales of Suspense* #59 (November 1964).

Writing about the creation of the Avengers team, Stan Lee said, "Iron Man's alter ego, the wealthy industrialist Tony Stark, was a natural leader. Don Blake, in the persona of Thor, Son of Odin, provided the necessary color and contrast as well as a fabulous sense of fantasy. Henry Pym and his lady love, Jan, were so totally different from the others that they rounded out the team beautifully. As for the Hulk, any group of do-gooders that included a not-so-jolly green giant would never have a dull moment." Lee was supported for the first eight issues of *The Avengers* by the powerful art of Jack Kirby, but with issue #9 (October 1964), Don Heck took over the art duties, meaning that he handled Iron Man's adventures in two regularly published books!

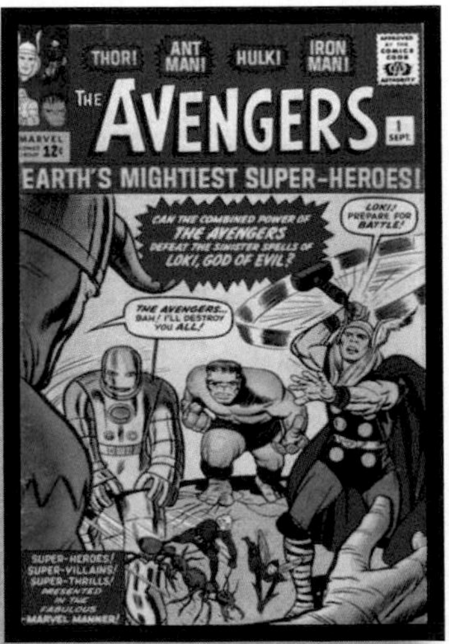
THOR!
ANT MAN!
HULK!
IRON MAN!
THE AVENGERS
1 SEPT.
MARVEL 12¢
EARTH'S MIGHTIEST SUPER-HEROES!
CAN THE COMBINED POWER OF THE AVENGERS DEFEAT THE SINISTER SPELLS OF LOKI, GOD OF EVIL?
LOKI!! PREPARE FOR BATTLE!
THE AVENGERS... BAH! I'LL DESTROY YOU ALL!
SUPER-HEROES! SUPER-VILLAINS! SUPER-THRILLS! PRESENTED IN THE FABULOUS MARVEL MANNER!

In the pages of *The Avengers,* not only did Iron Man take on the role of team leader, but Tony Stark (who hadn't yet revealed his secret identity to the others) was the team's financier. The Avengers were soon operating in headquarters set in Stark's own family mansion; eventually, they began utilizing the services of Stark's faithful family butler, an Englishman named Edwin Jarvis. As the Marvel Universe began to expand, the interplay between Iron Man's stories and those of the Avengers continued to grow. Villains from *The Avengers* would attack Stark's industrial plants in *Tales of Suspense,* while Iron Man foe Hawkeye, an exceptional archer, would eventually reform and become one of the long-term members of the Avengers. And even though Iron Man left *The Avengers* in issue #16 (May 1965), he would return to the team he co-founded many times over the next four decades.

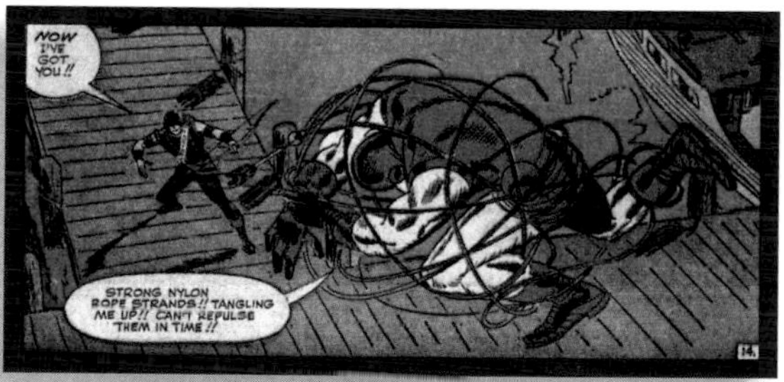
NOW I'VE GOT YOU!!
STRONG NYLON ROPE STRANDS!! TANGLING ME UP!! CAN'T REPULSE THEM IN TIME!!
14.

The reformation—or moral ambivalence—of villains in *Iron Man* was a recurring thread, beginning with the introduction of Russia's armored spy the Crimson Dynamo in *Tales of Suspense* #46 (October 1963). In that story, Iron Man faced his counterpart, Russian scientist Professor Anton Vanko, who used his electrically powered armor to sabotage and destroy multiple industrial plants owned by Stark Industries. Tricking Vanko with a doctored recording, Iron Man got the scientist to defect and begin working for Stark. "That seemed to me to be a nice way to end the story," says Lee. "I thought that would make Stark a real good hero if he tried to do that as much as

▼ Villain turned hero Hawkeye (left) and the Soviet-armored Crimson Dynamo (right) were two of Iron Man's earliest villains.

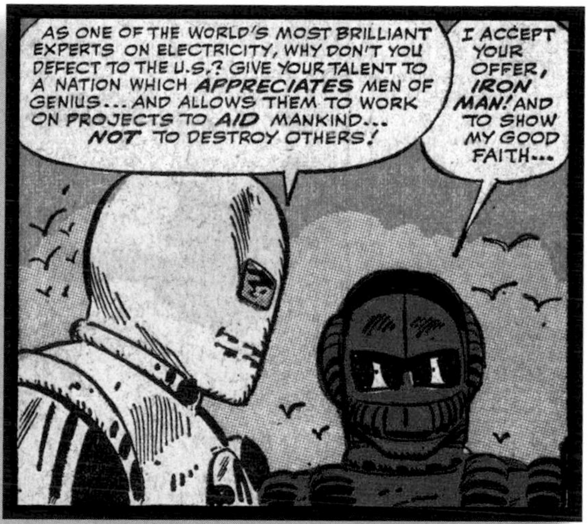
AS ONE OF THE WORLD'S MOST BRILLIANT EXPERTS ON ELECTRICITY, WHY DON'T YOU DEFECT TO THE U.S.? GIVE YOUR TALENT TO A NATION WHICH APPRECIATES MEN OF GENIUS... AND ALLOWS THEM TO WORK ON PROJECTS TO AID MANKIND... NOT TO DESTROY OTHERS!
I ACCEPT YOUR OFFER, IRON MAN! AND TO SHOW MY GOOD FAITH...

he could. Instead of sending a guy to jail, he made him a useful citizen."

Vanko's loyalty to Stark was so strong that he sacrificed himself to stop the second Crimson Dynamo in *Tales of Suspense* #52 (April 1964) in a story that introduced another conflicted character: the beautiful but deadly Russian spy Madame Natasha, also known as the Black Widow. In her multiple appearances, even as she gassed or double-crossed Tony Stark, Natasha felt an undeniable attraction to the industrialist. Black Widow would herself

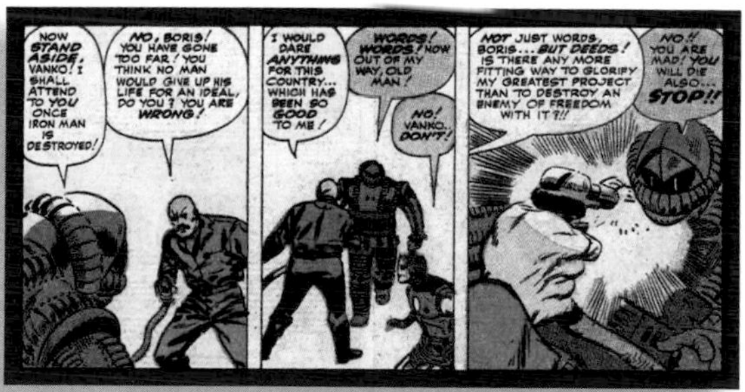
NOW STAND ASIDE, VANKO! I SHALL ATTEND TO YOU ONCE IRON MAN IS DESTROYED!
NO, BORIS! YOU HAVE GONE TOO FAR! YOU THINK NO MAN WOULD GIVE UP HIS LIFE FOR AN IDEAL, DO YOU? YOU ARE WRONG!
I WOULD DARE ANYTHING FOR THIS COUNTRY... WHICH HAS BEEN SO GOOD TO ME!
WORDS! WORDS! NOW OUT OF MY WAY, OLD MAN!
NO! VANKO.. DON'T!
NOT JUST WORDS, BORIS... BUT DEEDS! IS THERE ANY MORE FITTING WAY TO GLORIFY MY GREATEST PROJECT THAN TO DESTROY AN ENEMY OF FREEDOM WITH IT?!!
NO!! YOU ARE MAD! YOU WILL DIE ALSO... STOP!!

eventually fight alongside the Avengers, even if she wasn't politically in the same realm.

One villain with no such ambivalence was the

Black Widow (top left), Mandarin ▼ (bottom left), and Titanium Man (top right) bedeviled the golden Avenger.

LATER, AT A SWANK SUPPER CLUB...
IT IS STRANGE TO FIND A MAN LIKE YOU SO DEDICATED TO SCIENCE, YET SO SOPHISTICATED AND CHARMING!!
IF THERE'S A MOON OUT, LADY, YOU'LL FIND OUT HOW I FEEL ABOUT YOU, TOO!
RIGHT THIS WAY, MR. STARK!

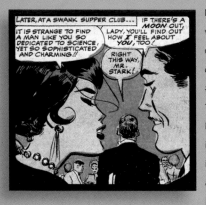

Mandarin, who was introduced in *Tales of Suspense* #50 (February 1964). The Mandarin was inspired by the infamous book and film villain Fu Manchu and the 1956 Atlas comic villain the Yellow Claw, and had similar goals. Although the Chinese villain was based in a castle in "the remote vastness of Red China," Mandarin made it clear early on that he cared little about helping any Communist leaders. Instead, he was content to use his scientific genius—and ten Rings of Power, salvaged from an alien spacecraft and each imbued with a different ability—to wreak havoc in America for his own goal of world domination by creating a new Chinese empire. But after Tony Stark and Iron Man invaded his castle, Mandarin vowed to cause the death of both men. With each successive appearance, the Mandarin seemed closer to realizing his megalomaniacal dreams.

WHAT??! YOU DARE ASK ME TO REVEAL MY SECRETS TO YOU??! DO YOU THINK THE MANDARIN CARES TO HELP YOU OR YOUR RED MASTERS? THE MANDARIN HELPS NOBODY! SOON, THE ENTIRE WORLD WILL GROVEL AT MY FEET!

Over the next several years, Iron Man would find himself facing the undersea Atlantean warlord Attuma, the illusion-casting Count Nefaria, the Mad Thinker and his Awesome Android, and another armored villain known as the Titanium Man. He also had to don his original armor to fight back against a thief who had stolen his Iron Man armor, as well as coping with Happy Hogan, who had learned Stark's dual identity just prior to being near-mortally wounded while helping Iron Man fight his foes.

•

The popularity and sales of Marvel comic books had continued to grow. By the mid-1960s, the company was both comfortably publishing more titles, and—with its more sophisticated storylines—was also commanding interest from older fans in addition to the younger readers. Indeed, the very concept of comic book fandom was also in a startling growth period, with readers connecting with one another through letter columns ("Mails of Suspense" was the name of *Tales*' reader-contributed page) and back issues being traded and sold.

I DON'T EVEN NEED THEM! WITH MY GREAT STRENGTH, I CAN MOVE AS EASILY AS IF I'M WEARING AN ORDINARY OVERCOAT!
IT'S UNBELIEVABLE! IRON MAN WILL HAVE NO CHANCE AGAINST HIM!

HOW BULKY, HEAVY, AND CUMBERSOME THIS ARMOR FEELS COMPARED TO MY NEW, FLEXIBLE GARB! I HOPE MY INJURED HEART CAN WITHSTAND THE STRAIN OF THE ADDED WEIGHT!
BUT, I'VE NO OTHER CHOICE! A NEW, TERRIBLE MENACE HAS BEEN UNLEASHED BECAUSE OF MY OWN CARELESSNESS...AND I'VE GOT TO DESTROY IT...EVEN IF IT COSTS ME MY LIFE!
"MY LIFE"! WHAT A HOLLOW MOCKERY! WITH A PIECE OF SHRAPNEL FROM VIET NAM HOPELESSLY LODGED NEAR MY HEART, MY LIFE CAN END AT ANY SECOND!
BUT I'VE GOT TO FORGET ABOUT THAT NOW...
ALL MY THOUGHTS, ALL MY TALENTS, ALL MY STRENGTH MUST BE DEDICATED TO ONLY ONE AIM...THE DEFEAT OF THE ONE WHO DARES TO WEAR IRON MAN'S ARMOR!

Marvel took full advantage of the rise in fandom,

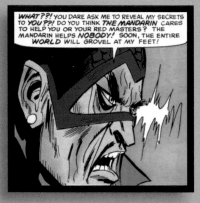

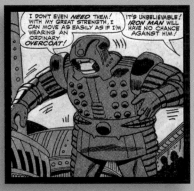

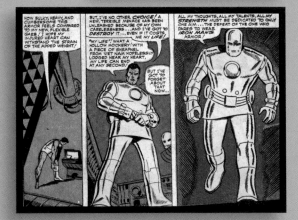

▼ The plastic Marx figure, trading cards, stickers, and Marvel memorabilia made Iron Man a 1960s favorite!

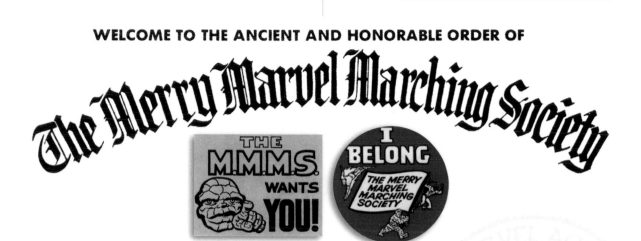

WELCOME TO THE ANCIENT AND HONORABLE ORDER OF

The Merry Marvel Marching Society

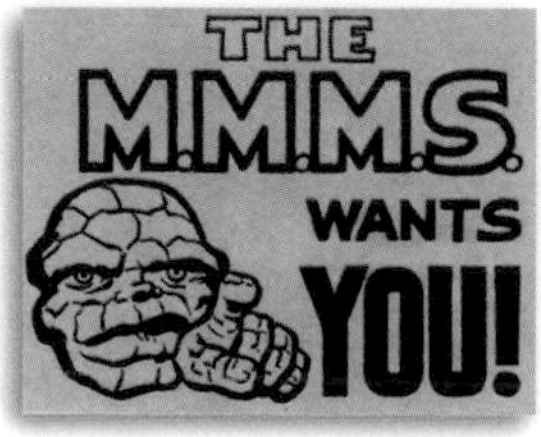
THE
M.M.M.S.
WANTS
YOU!

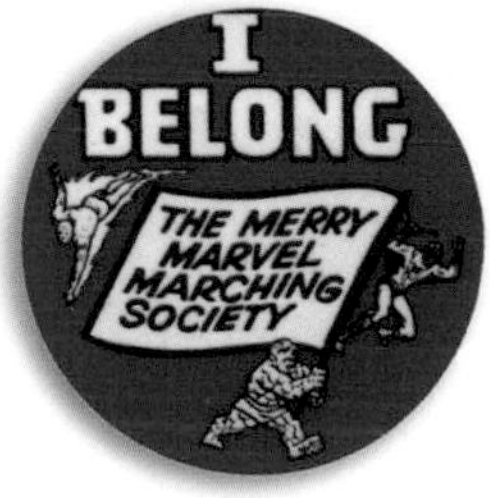
I
BELONG
THE MERRY MARVEL MARCHING SOCIETY

creating an organization just for enthusiasts in 1964: the Merry Marvel Marching Society, or MMMS, as it was more commonly known in the promotions. For a dollar, members could join and receive newsletters, buttons, stickers, and even flexi-disc recordings of Marvel staff members. Though the 1965 membership kit was a bit low on Iron Man, he showed up on the 1967 members' button and on a sticker, which urged fans to HELP RESIST RUST!

MMMS members were also able to buy merchandise including stickers, posters, and a set of "blowmold" plastic figurines made by Marx. One of these "Super Hero models" was Iron Man, using his strength to break a chain. The six-inch figures came in sets of three for two dollars: Iron Man, Spider-Man, and Hulk; or Daredevil, Thor, and Captain America. Although MMMS members were able to get gray figures (which, due to their limited membership-only distribution, are today the most desirable color for Marvel's armored avenger), the heroes were available in a multitude of colors for later retail sale. Other early Iron Man merchandise included a pennant from RNS Sales (1966), a SUPER HERO CLUB button from Button World (1966), trading cards by Donruss (1966), a green rubber gumball figure (1966), a Marvel "Flyer" gliding toy from Topps (1966), a bizarre kid's Halloween costume from Ben Cooper (1966), and a Marvel T-shirt in 1968. Iron Man also appeared in the first-ever Marvel novel, *The Avengers Battle the Earth-Wrecker,* written by Otto Binder (June 1967).

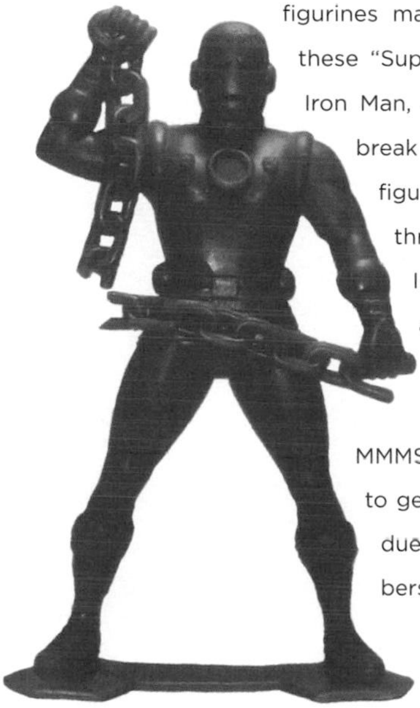

The biggest public pro-

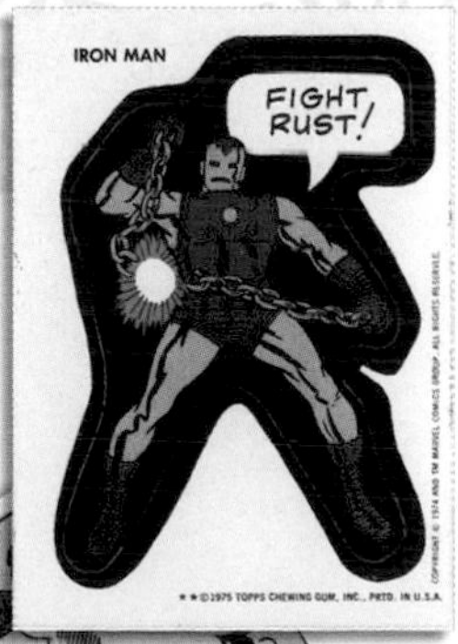
IRON MAN
FIGHT RUST!

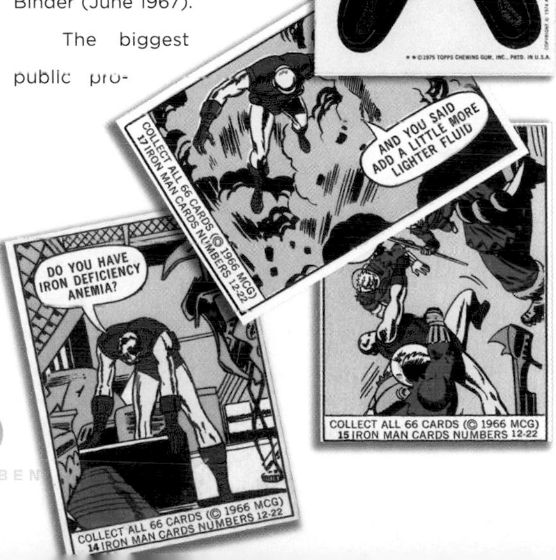
AND YOU SAID ADD A LITTLE MORE LIGHTER FLUID
COLLECT ALL 66 CARDS (© 1966 MCG)
17 IRON MAN CARDS NUMBERS 12-22
DO YOU HAVE IRON DEFICIENCY ANEMIA?
COLLECT ALL 66 CARDS (© 1966 MCG)
14 IRON MAN CARDS NUMBERS 12-22
COLLECT ALL 66 CARDS (© 1966 MCG)
15 IRON MAN CARDS NUMBERS 12-22

Storyboards for an *Iron Man* episode, ▶
with Stan Lee's handwritten notes!

motion that *Iron Man* got in the 1960s came during September 1966. The previous year, animators Grant Simmons, Ray Patterson, and Robert Lawrence of Grantray-Lawrence Animation had contracted for the license to produce the animated adventures of *The Marvel Super Heroes.* The team planned to do stories for five of Marvel's biggest heroes (excluding Spider-Man, which was in preparation for ABC; and Fantastic Four, which had been licensed elsewhere) for weekday syndication.

The cartoons utilized limited animation, produced through a process called xerography. Artwork was transferred directly from Marvel Comics onto the animation cels—with minimal redrawing required—and then given a slight movement by jiggling the cel or sliding it across a background. Lips and eyes were sometimes animated, as well an occasional appendage. The result looked exactly like a Marvel comic—if vocals, sound effects, and music had replaced the word balloons.

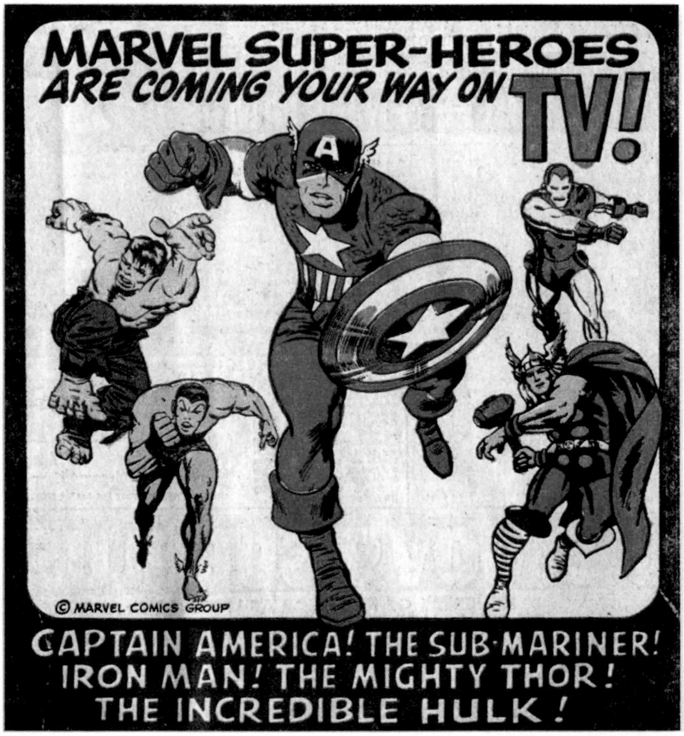
MARVEL SUPER-HEROES
ARE COMING YOUR WAY ON TV!
© MARVEL COMICS GROUP
CAPTAIN AMERICA! THE SUB-MARINER!
IRON MAN! THE MIGHTY THOR!
THE INCREDIBLE HULK!

▲ An advertisement for the *Marvel Super Heroes* show appeared in marvel comic books.

The Marvel Super Heroes debuted as a Saturday show on September 2, 1966, in Los Angeles, but was picked up as a daily show on the twelfth in Chicago and many other stations throughout the country. *Captain America* was Monday, *The Incredible Hulk* was Tuesday, *Iron Man* was Wednesday, *Mighty Thor* was Thursday (naturally), and *Sub-Mariner* was Friday. Each hero had thirteen three-chapter episodes. Each chapter had its own title and was six to seven minutes long.

The *Iron Man* stories were all taken from *Tales of Suspense* stories drawn by Don Heck and Gene Colan, from issues #45–46, #50–78, and #81–88. Some episodes found elements from multiple stories put together to create a more cohesive whole, with initial scripts by June Patterson and rewrites and additional dialogue by Stan Lee. Iron Man also appeared in other *Marvel Super Heroes* cartoons, most notably in the *Captain America, Hulk,* and *Thor* stories, all of which adapted some stories from *The Avengers.*

Voices . and music for the series were recorded in June 1966. John Vernon was the voice of Iron Man and Tony Stark—using a Styrofoam cup over his mouth when speaking as the Super Hero—while Marg Griffin played Pepper Potts. Although they also played miscellaneous bit or one-shot characters, four men provided the other recurring roles: Bernard "Bunny" Cowan was the narrator; Tom Harvey was Happy Hogan; Henry Ramer was Mandarin; and Ed McNamara was Titanium Man.

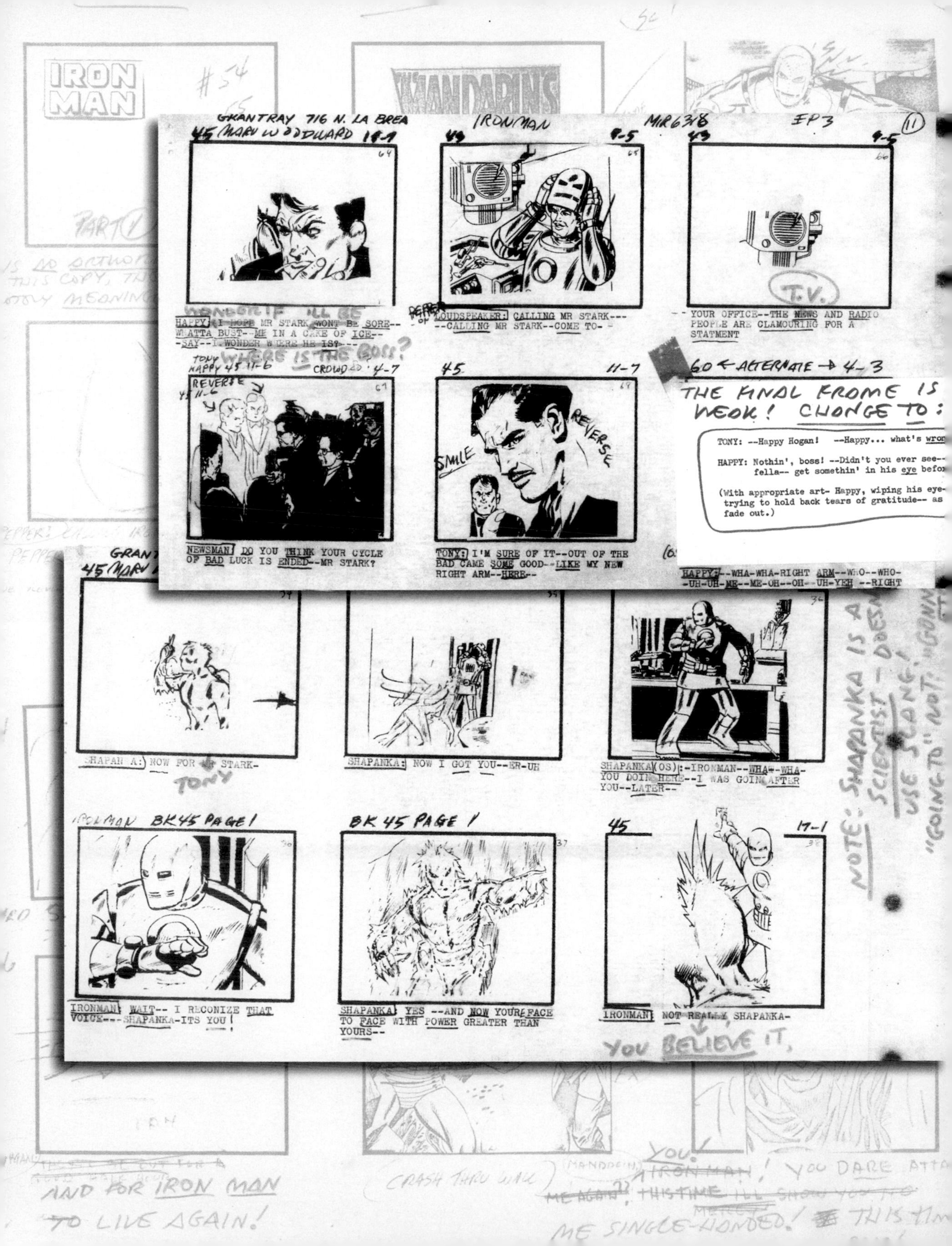

IRON MAN
#54
THE MANDARINS
GRANTRAY 716 N. LA BREA
IRONMAN
MIR 6318
EP3
45 MARV WOODWARD
HAPPY: I HOPE MR STARK WONT BE SORE--WHATTA BUST--ME IN A CAKE OF ICE--SAY--I WONDER WHERE HE IS?--
WONDER IF I'LL BE
WHERE IS THE BOSS?
PEPPER
LOUDSPEAKER: CALLING MR STARK----CALLING MR STARK--COME TO--
--YOUR OFFICE--THE NEWS AND RADIO PEOPLE ARE CLAMOURING FOR A STATMENT
T.V.
TONY HAPPY 45 11-6
CROWD 4-7
REVERSE
NEWSMAN: DO YOU THINK YOUR CYCLE OF BAD LUCK IS ENDED--MR STARK?
45 11-7
SMILE
REVERSE
TONY: I'M SURE OF IT--OUT OF THE BAD CAME SOME GOOD--LIKE MY NEW RIGHT ARM--HERE--
60 ← ALTERNATE → 4-3
THE FINAL FROME IS WEOK! CHONGE TO:
TONY: --Happy Hogan! --Happy... what's wron
HAPPY: Nothin', boss! --Didn't you ever see-- fella-- get somethin' in his eye befor
(With appropriate art- Happy, wiping his eye- trying to hold back tears of gratitude-- as fade out.)
HAPPY:--WHA-WHA-RIGHT ARM--WHO--WHO--UH-UH-ME--ME-OH--OH--UH-YEH --RIGHT
SHAPANKA: NOW FOR MR STARK-
TONY
SHAPANKA: NOW I GOT YOU--ER-UH
SHAPANKA(OS):-IRONMAN--WHA--WHA-YOU DOIN HERE--I WAS GOIN AFTER YOU--LATER--
IRONMAN BK45 PAGE 1
IRONMAN: WAIT-- I RECONIZE THAT VOICE---SHAPANKA-ITS YOU!
BK 45 PAGE 1
SHAPANKA: YES --AND NOW YOUR FACE TO FACE WITH POWER GREATER THAN YOURS--
45 17-1
IRONMAN: NOT REALLY SHAPANKA-
YOU BELIEVE IT,
NOTE: SHAPANKA IS A SCIENTIST - DOESN'T USE SLANG! "GOING TO" NOT "GONNA"
AND FOR IRON MAN TO LIVE AGAIN!
CRASH THRU WALL
YOU! IRON MAN! YOU DARE ATTA
ME SINGLE-HANDED!

While Iron Man's mask offered the animators a chance to avoid animating mouths, the fact that his armor changed in the midst of some storylines made more work for them, and made stock animation difficult to produce. Nevertheless, *The Marvel Super Heroes* became a long-running hit in syndication; it was still aired around the world up until the 1990s. Perhaps the most memorable part of the series for many fans though is the theme song for *Iron Man,* written by Jacques Urbont, which starts with:

Tony Stark makes you feel,

He's a cool exec with a heart of steel.

Back in the realm of comics, *Iron Man* gained a new artist in Gene Colan, whose first work for Marvel had been on 1950's *Captain America* #75. Colan had moved back and forth among comic publishers over the subsequent decade, and was working for rival publisher DC when he was tapped to draw the adventures of Iron Man. Because working for competitors was frowned on by some editors in the industry, Colan chose a new name: Adam Austin.

"There was a lot of competition," says Colan, "and at that time the companies were signing artists up with contracts to make sure that the work they did get was from their company. I didn't want DC to know that I was still working for Marvel. So Stan came up with this fictitious name for me, but I learned very quickly that artwork is very similar to handwriting and can't really be disguised. Anyone that follows your work would know right off that this wasn't anybody but me. So I just dropped it, and DC never made any comment about it."

Colan's first issue of *Tales of Suspense* was #73 (January 1966), in a story co-written by Stan Lee and his then-assistant, Roy Thomas. With a penchant for drawing moody shadows and fabric-draped characters and objects, Colan might have seemed an odd fit, but his work enhanced the series in a way different from that of his predecessors. "All the artwork that I did, I took very seriously," says Colan. "None of it was a comic to me, in any funny way. It was a serious story, and so I took Iron Man as seriously as I took anything else—Batman, or Captain America, or any other book that I did. I was always attracted to the lights and the darks. It set the figure firmly on the ground, there was a lot of drama in it, and that's where I really thoroughly enjoyed it. I grew up in the age of black-and-white movies, and that's where I got most of my information from."

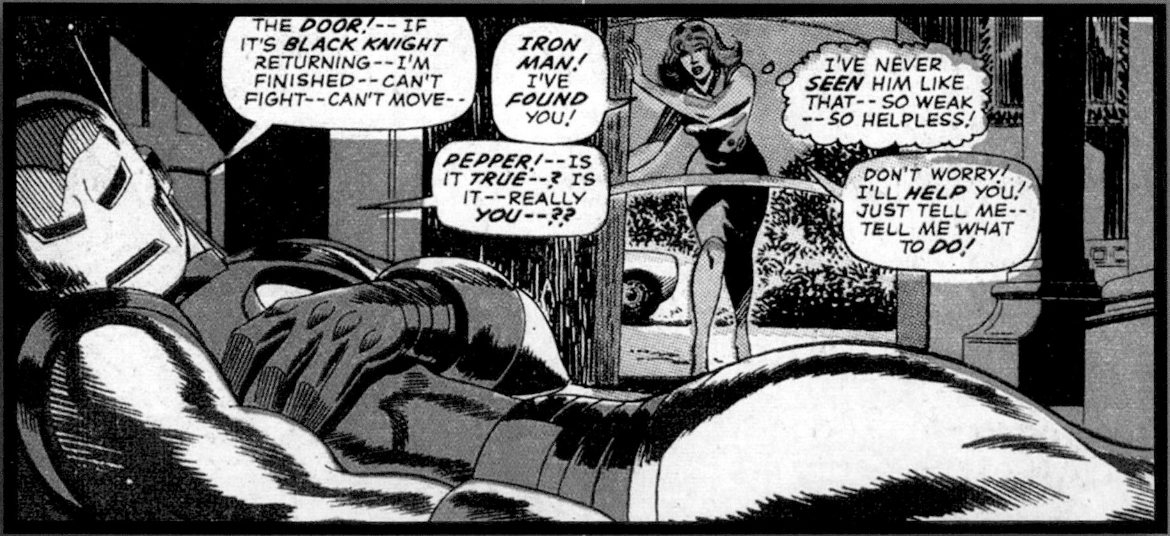
THE DOOR!-- IF IT'S BLACK KNIGHT RETURNING--I'M FINISHED--CAN'T FIGHT--CAN'T MOVE--
IRON MAN! I'VE FOUND YOU!
PEPPER!--IS IT TRUE--? IS IT--REALLY YOU--??
I'VE NEVER SEEN HIM LIKE THAT--SO WEAK --SO HELPLESS!
DON'T WORRY! I'LL HELP YOU! JUST TELL ME--TELL ME WHAT TO DO!

Gene Colan drew a ▲ moody Iron Man.

Colan also tweaked the armor slightly, making it more formfitting and slimmer, and adding a touch of emotional movability to Iron Man's armored faceplate. "To be able to do the things that he could do—fly around, get into fights, all that stuff—he had to be pretty athletic. To carry around this tonnage of weight would not be in keeping with the character. I picked up where Don Heck left off." As for the faceplate, Colan recalls, "I did that so that in some small way, I was hoping the reader would pick up on sadness, or fear, or anger. It just required a few lines put in or taken out to do that. I assumed that his armor that he did have was flexible enough for him to show some expressions. It could have been much lighter, more elastic, and that's how I thought of it in my mind. It didn't take much to show the moods of Iron Man."

The *Iron Man* stories became increasingly serialized over the following months. Rarely did an adventure end before another had begun simultaneously. "Marvel was the first comic book company to feature continued stories," Stan Lee once explained, noting that continued stories were a necessary shortcut for a writer who handled as many books as he did. "I saved a ton of time by taking one plot and stretching it out over many issues. Instead of spending so much time making up different plots, I could be spending that time completing the stories . . . Of course, what started out as a time-saving device turned out to be a good idea, quality-wise. We found that the continued stories, being longer, gave us more room for character development, and the addition of subplots helped to round out the stories so they read more like mini motion pictures."

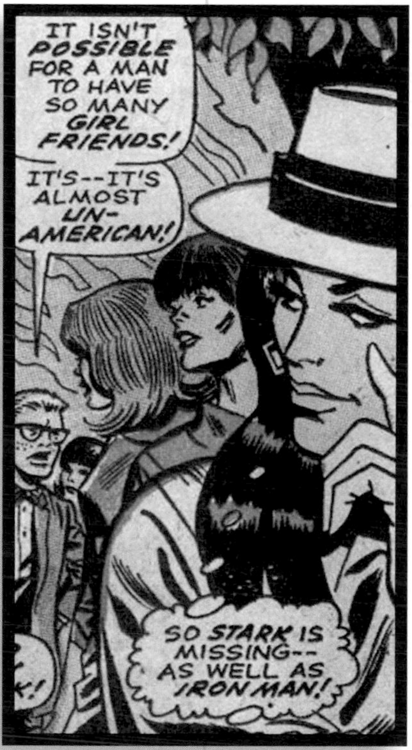
IT ISN'T POSSIBLE FOR A MAN TO HAVE SO MANY GIRL FRIENDS!
IT'S--IT'S ALMOST UN-AMERICAN!
SO STARK IS MISSING-- AS WELL AS IRON MAN!

▲ Femme fatale Whitney Frost schemes.

The continuing stories and Marvel Style plots would sometimes throw Gene Colan for a loop. The artist liked to be expansive in his storytelling, and he notes that "very often, I got involved with the story and didn't pace it properly on several different occasions, and then it would be jammed up at the end, trying to finish off what normally would require maybe five extra pages, would have to maybe finish it off in one, or two." Still, he felt that the serialization allowed the story to carry forward if necessary, in an exciting manner. "There's a cliff-hanger on the last panel, more to come, to entice the reader to come back. That's the way the old serials in films were done. They'd have this flaming wagon going off a cliff. Did the Lone Ranger make it? Did he jump in time, or didn't he?"

•

Colan drew many major moments in Iron Man's formative years, including the first time anyone substituted for Iron Man in the armor (Happy Hogan, in #84–86), the introduction of Stark's involvement with the government super-spy group S.H.I.E.L.D., a governmental investigation of Tony Stark resulting in his heart condition becoming public knowledge, plus epic battles against the Sub-Mariner, the Titanium Man, the subterranean Mole Man, the Grey Gargoyle, Whiplash, and the return of previous villains such as the Mandarin and the Melter. Additionally, the crime cartel known as the Maggia began plotting against Iron Man, with femme fatale Whitney Frost as its sexy leader. And in issue #91, Happy Hogan and Pepper Potts eloped and were married (off screen), ending the long-running love triangle and any messiness for bachelor Tony Stark.

In March 1968, *Tales of Suspense* ended with its ninety-ninth issue, but Iron Man wasn't gone from the stands for long, thanks partially to a better deal with distribution companies that allowed Marvel to expand its output. Following a one-shot *Iron Man and Sub-Mariner* special in April (created because Marvel didn't want four new series debuting in one month), *The Invincible Iron Man* #1 debuted on newsstands in May. Stan Lee had scripted all but the final *Tales of Suspense* story, but writer Archie Goodwin came aboard to take over the new series. The book's title and scripts weren't the only changes, however; Gene Colan left the art chores after the first issue to work on later Marvel books such as *Daredevil, Tomb of Dracula,* and *Howard the Duck.*

But as the decade ended, more changes were brewing for Marvel's armored hero . . .

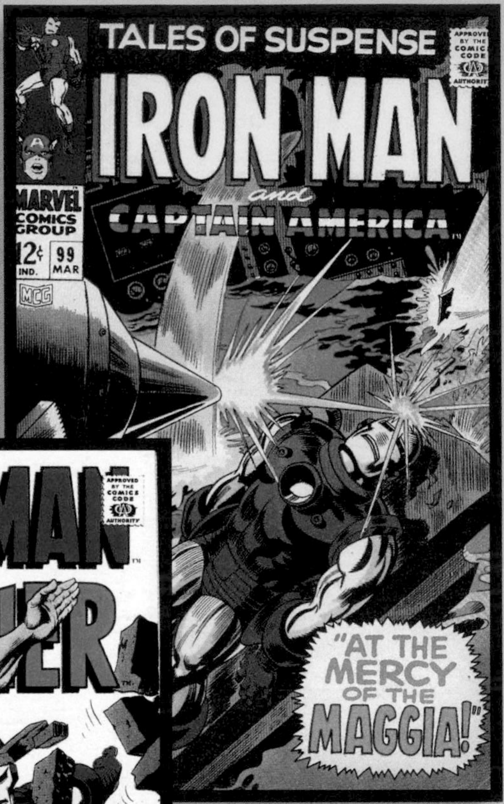
TALES OF SUSPENSE
IRON MAN
and
CAPTAIN AMERICA
MARVEL COMICS GROUP
12¢ 99 MAR IND.
MCG
"AT THE MERCY OF THE MAGGIA!"

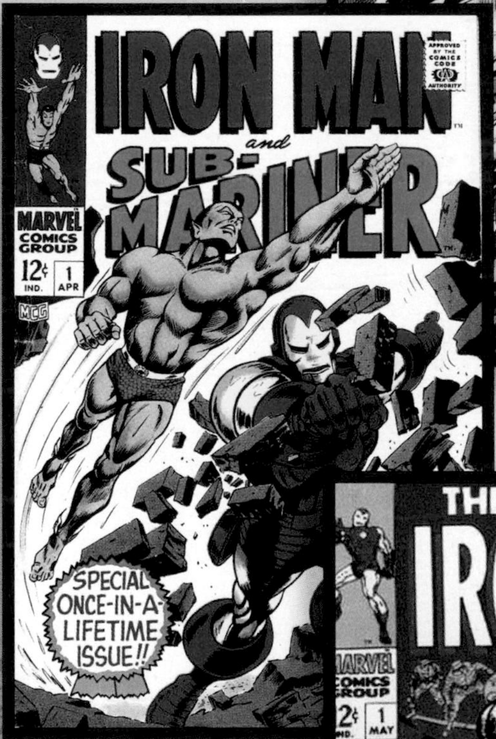
IRON MAN
and
SUB-MARINER
MARVEL COMICS GROUP
12¢ 1 APR IND.
MCG
SPECIAL ONCE-IN-A-LIFETIME ISSUE!!

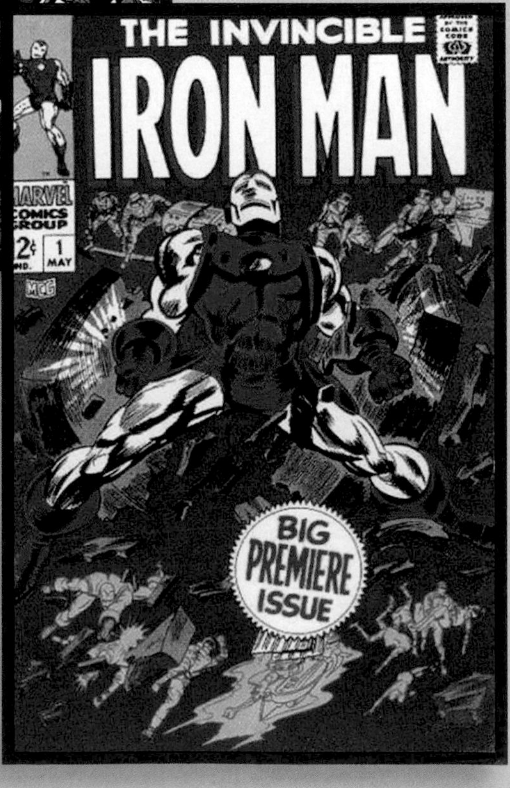
THE INVINCIBLE
IRON MAN
MARVEL COMICS GROUP
12¢ 1 MAY IND.
MCG
BIG PREMIERE ISSUE

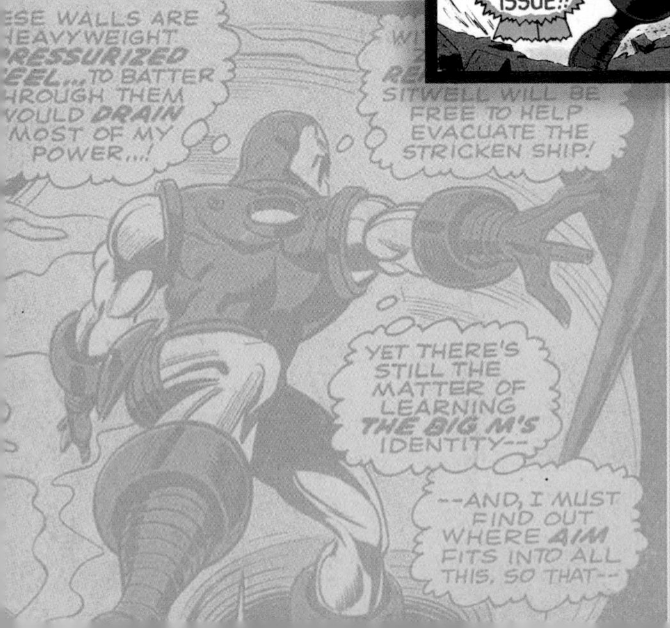
ESE WALLS ARE HEAVYWEIGHT PRESSURIZED EEL... TO BATTER HROUGH THEM VOULD DRAIN MOST OF MY POWER...!
SITWELL WILL BE FREE TO HELP EVACUATE THE STRICKEN SHIP!
YET THERE'S STILL THE MATTER OF LEARNING THE BIG M'S IDENTITY--
--AND, I MUST FIND OUT WHERE AIM FITS INTO ALL THIS, SO THAT--

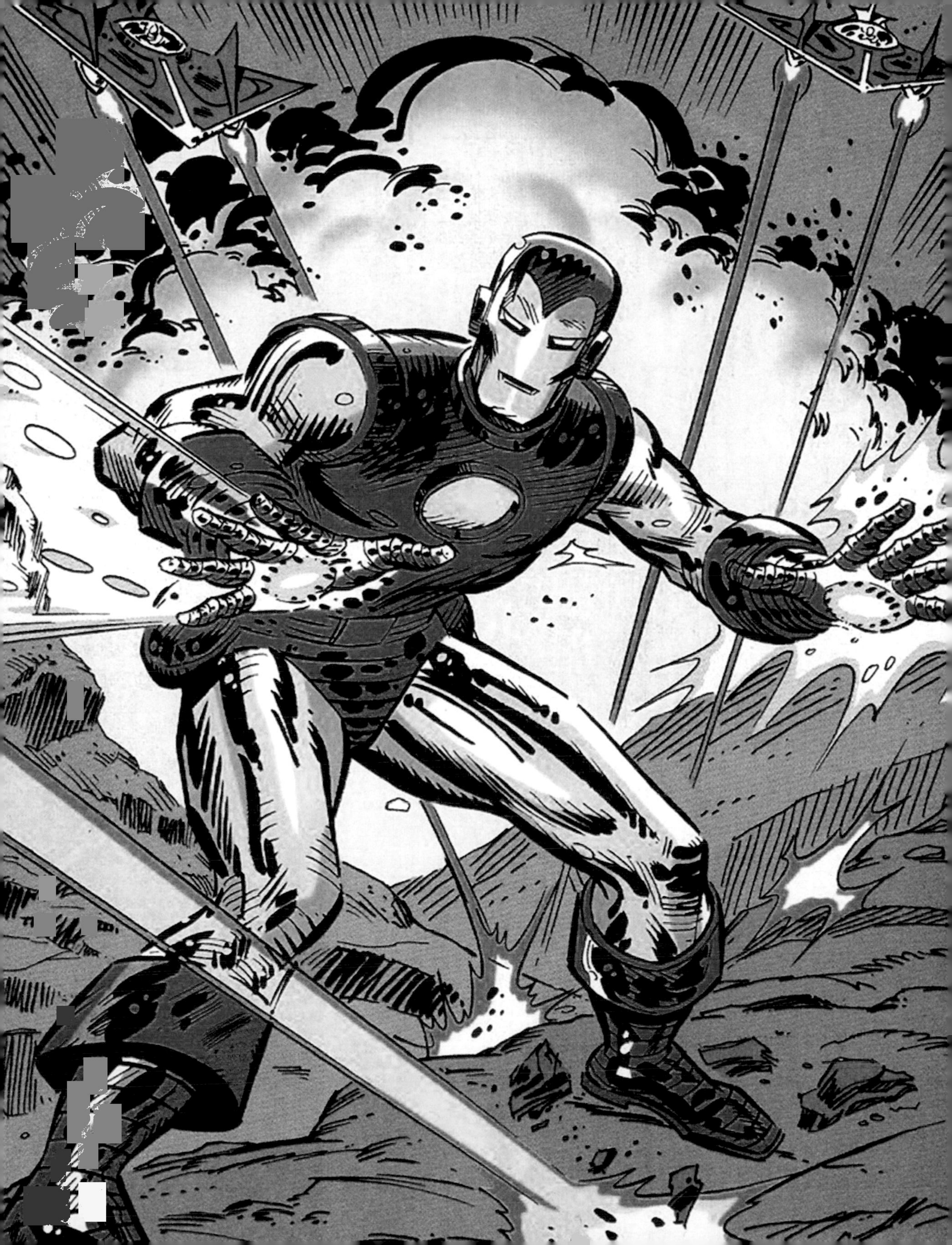

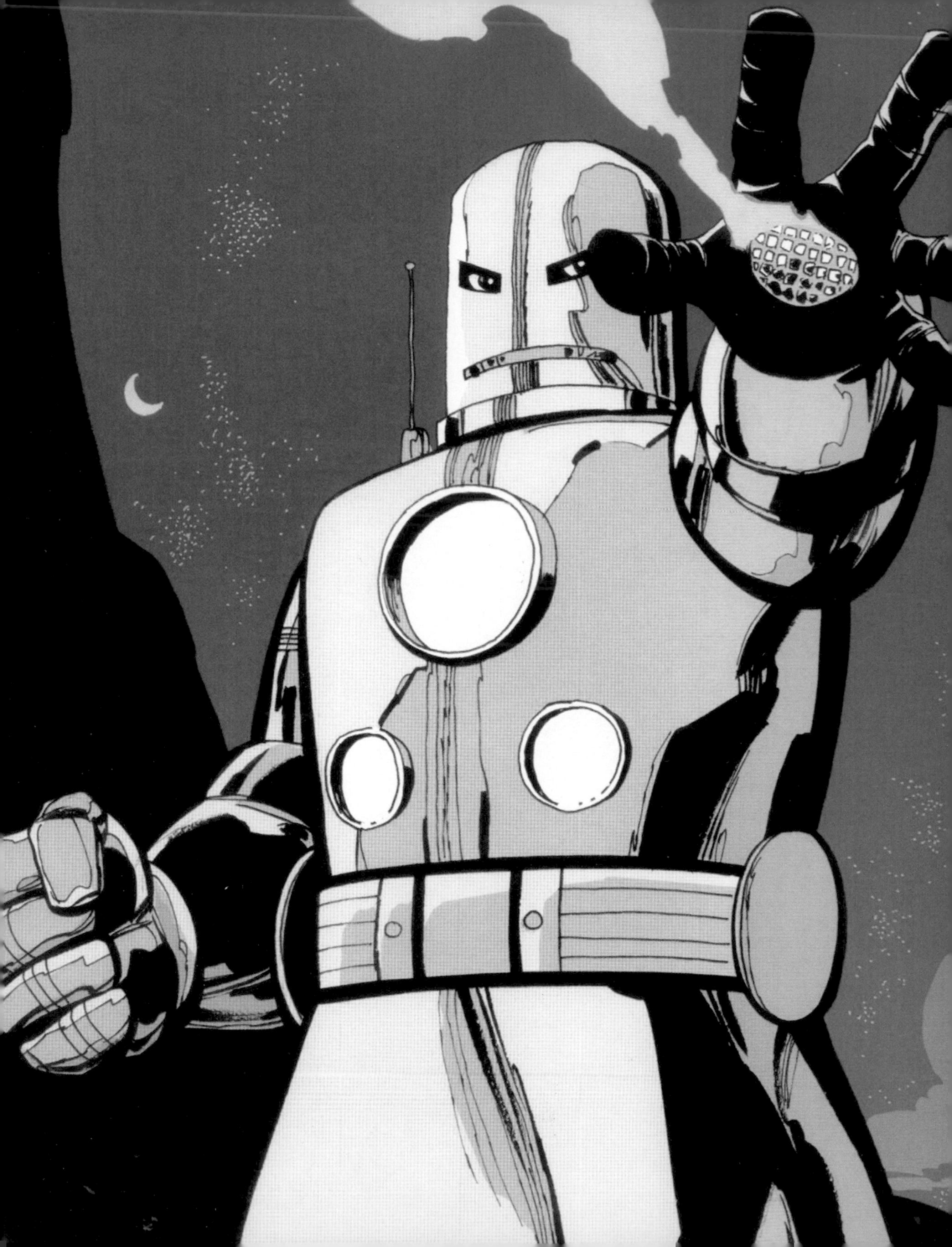

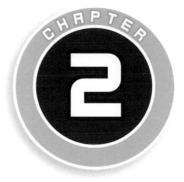

CHAPTER 2

A KNIGHT IN TURBULENT TIMES

Iron Man had been back to Vietnam in the pages of *Tales of Suspense,* but by the cusp of the decade's turn, politics, war, and even Communist enemies were a polarizing—and, frankly, too-familiar—subject. *Iron Man*'s new writer, Archie Goodwin, had come up from Warren Publishing's more adult horror and war magazines such as *Creepy, Eerie,* and *Blazing Combat.* He began to steer the stories away from politics and into new realms: organized crime and super-spies.

The international crime cartel known as the Maggia took forefront in many stories of the early *Iron Man.* The group was a fictional counterpart to the Mafia, but under the control of the seductive Whitney Frost—daughter of *The Avengers* and *Iron Man* villain Count Nefaria—the group began employing Super Villains and mad scientists to further its goals. Frost eventually donned a metal faceplate of her own when

SPARE ME TONY STARK'S PLAYBOY HOMILIES... BEHIND THIS MASK IS ONLY HORROR!
MIDAS' MEN RESCUED ME FROM A PLANE CRASH... A SURGEON HE HIRED SAVED MY LIFE... BUT NOT BEFORE CHEMICALS ON BOARD PLAYED A MACABRE JOKE WITH MY FEATURES!

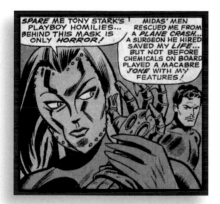

she was disfigured by chemicals; as Madame Masque, she would begin an ongoing love-hate relationship with Tony Stark and Iron Man that lasted for decades.

Even as Tony faced investigations and harassment from S.H.I.E.L.D. about his political loyalties, Goodwin brought back more villains, including the Unicorn, the Mandarin, and the Freak; created new villains such as the mind-grabbing Controller and ecoterrorist Firebrand; and guest-starred other Marvel characters including the Hulk, the Avengers, and the Sub-Mariner. For a short time, Tony was also replaced by one of his own creations—a Life Model Decoy (LMD) he had used to fool the Mandarin after the villain deduced his secret identity.

...AND BECOME THE CONTROLLER!!
BASIL! YOU'RE UP... WALKING, MOVING...
A MEDICAL IMPOSSI-BILITY! UNLESS...
BUT...YOU PROMISED YOU WOULDN'T DO IT...!
...IT'S SO INHUMAN... SO AWFUL!

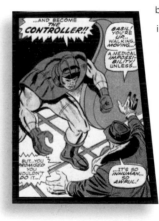

The battle against his doppelgänger led to a major development in Tony Stark's story: In a crossover tale between *Avengers* #68 and *Iron Man* #19 (November 1969), Stark underwent a heart transplant operation in which Dr. Jose Santini used synthetic tissue to repair the

▲ Madame Masque (left) and the Controller (right) repeatedly clashed with Iron Man.

The robotic Life Model Decoy of ▼
Tony Stark thinks it's the real deal.

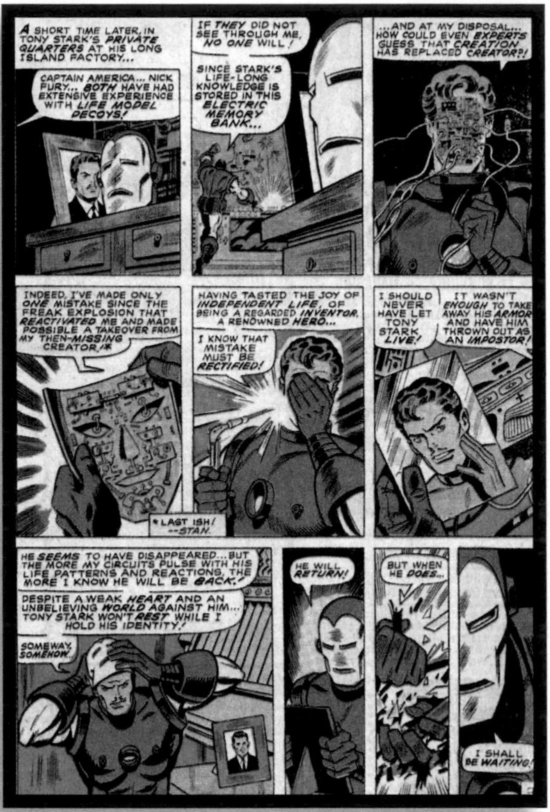
A SHORT TIME LATER, IN TONY STARK'S PRIVATE QUARTERS AT HIS LONG ISLAND FACTORY...
CAPTAIN AMERICA... NICK FURY... BOTH HAVE HAD EXTENSIVE EXPERIENCE WITH LIFE MODEL DECOYS!
IF THEY DID NOT SEE THROUGH ME, NO ONE WILL!
SINCE STARK'S LIFE-LONG KNOWLEDGE IS STORED IN THIS ELECTRIC MEMORY BANK...
...AND AT MY DISPOSAL... HOW COULD EVEN EXPERTS GUESS THAT CREATION HAS REPLACED CREATOR?!
INDEED, I'VE MADE ONLY ONE MISTAKE SINCE THE FREAK EXPLOSION THAT REACTIVATED ME AND MADE POSSIBLE A TAKEOVER FROM MY THEN-MISSING CREATOR!*
*LAST ISH! --STAN.
HAVING TASTED THE JOY OF INDEPENDENT LIFE, OF BEING A REGARDED INVENTOR, A RENOWNED HERO...
I KNOW THAT MISTAKE MUST BE RECTIFIED!
I SHOULD NEVER HAVE LET TONY STARK LIVE!
IT WASN'T ENOUGH TO TAKE AWAY HIS ARMOR AND HAVE HIM THROWN OUT AS AN IMPOSTOR!
HE SEEMS TO HAVE DISAPPEARED... BUT THE MORE MY CIRCUITS PULSE WITH HIS LIFE PATTERNS AND REACTIONS, THE MORE I KNOW HE WILL BE BACK!
DESPITE A WEAK HEART AND AN UNBELIEVING WORLD AGAINST HIM... TONY STARK WON'T REST WHILE I HOLD HIS IDENTITY!
SOMEWAY, SOMEHOW...
HE WILL RETURN!
BUT WHEN HE DOES...
I SHALL BE WAITING!

damaged organ. The constant threats of his weak heart would seem to have been over, but Tony still wasn't supposed to overstress himself or risk a rupture, so the recurring plot element didn't immediately disappear.

Artistically, *Iron Man* had settled into a new groove. After a few issues drawn by past EC Comics artist Johnny Craig, penciller George Tuska took up the reins with *Iron Man* #5 (September 1968). Tuska had worked on comic strips and comic books since 1939, including stretches on such series as Fawcett's *Captain Marvel Adventures,* Lev Gleason Publications' *Crime Does Not Pay,* and the newspaper strips "Scorchy Smith" and "Buck Rogers." Coming to Marvel in 1964, Tuska was another favorite of Stan Lee's, and he eventually took on the *Iron Man* book. With a few interruptions and fill-ins, Tuska would become the series' longest-lasting artist, pencilling more than seventy of Shellhead's adventures up to *Iron Man* #106 (January 1978).

"I didn't ask Stan or anybody for what I wanted to do," Tuska said in an interview for his book-length biography. "I took what they gave me. But somehow, I got another script for *Iron Man.* [Stan] must have liked it, the way I did it. I didn't question it. I had *Iron Man* all those years, a long time." Like Colan before him, Tuska tried to humanize the character. "When I draw Iron Man, I don't like to make it metallic, like a robot," he said. "I put a little human form into it. Add a little touch to the armor, sometimes laugh, sometimes sigh."

While Johnny Craig inked many of Tuska's early issues, later stories were often inked by Mike Esposito, under both his own name and—due to restrictions given his work at DC—his pseudonym, Joe Gaudioso. Esposito was a fan of Tuska's for his 1940s work on *Crime Does Not Pay,* and the younger artist would also eventually work at Lev Gleason before coming to Timely/Atlas in the late 1940s. Although he had inked a handful of earlier *Tales of Suspense* issues over Don Heck (then using the earlier pseudonym Mickey Demeo), Tuska was quite happy to ink Tuska on *Iron Man.* "I loved it because he was as clean as can be," the artist said in an interview for Tuska's biography. "He didn't make me have to worry about adding something that wasn't there. It was all there."

Before Goodwin left the series with issue #28 (August 1970), he had established information about Tony Stark's parents (Howard and Maria), introduced the death of Tony's girlfriend (Janice Cord, the first in a long line of doomed girlfriends), and written the first legitimate Iron Man replacement. In issues #21–22 (January–February 1970), Tony hand-picked Eddie March to be the new Iron Man, but the ex-boxer was hiding a secret about his health and didn't make it out of his first adventure unscathed. March was African American and became comicdom's first black successor

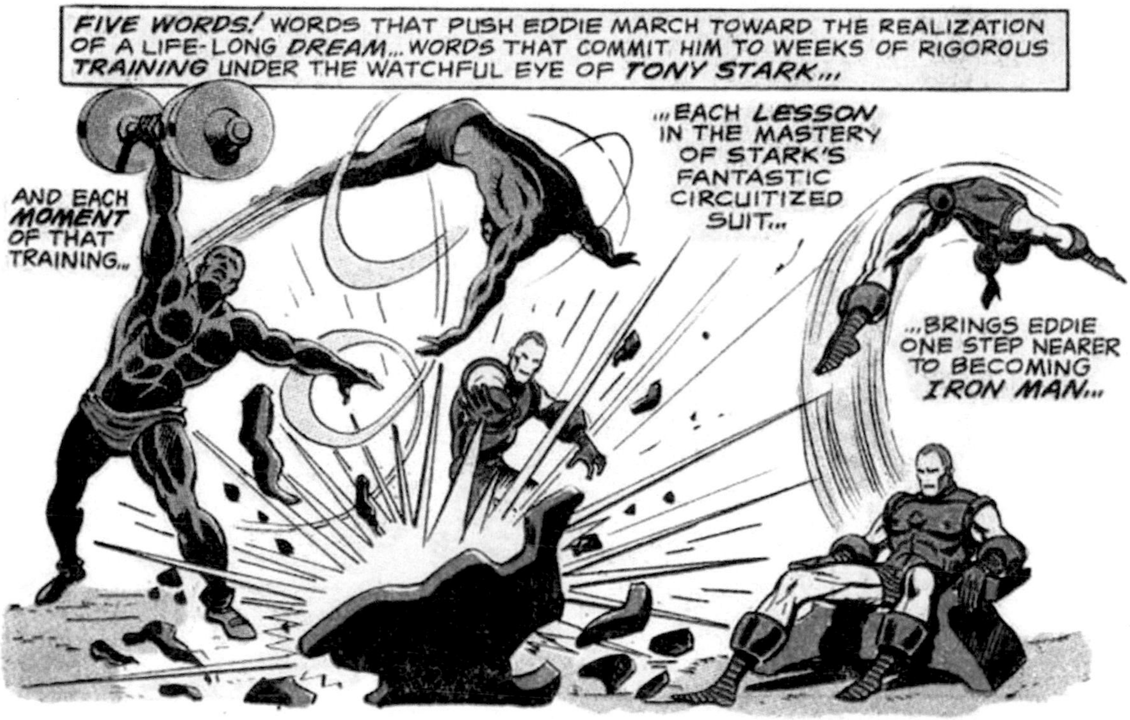
FIVE WORDS! WORDS THAT PUSH EDDIE MARCH TOWARD THE REALIZATION OF A LIFE-LONG DREAM... WORDS THAT COMMIT HIM TO WEEKS OF RIGOROUS TRAINING UNDER THE WATCHFUL EYE OF TONY STARK...
AND EACH MOMENT OF THAT TRAINING...
...EACH LESSON IN THE MASTERY OF STARK'S FANTASTIC CIRCUITIZED SUIT...
...BRINGS EDDIE ONE STEP NEARER TO BECOMING IRON MAN...

to a white hero; DC's replacement Green Lantern, John Stewart, wouldn't appear until December 1971!

Following a few fill-ins and some poorly received stories by Allyn Brodsky, *Iron Man* gained a new writer with issue #35 (March 1971) in Gerry Conway, but his ten issues were hardly fan favorites, either, mixing in plots from Conway's *Daredevil* and mystical fantasy elements that didn't sit well in the series' real-world/science-fiction milieu. The Brodsky and Conway issues did introduce to the series both Marianne Rodgers, Tony's psychic girlfriend who learned his secret, and Kevin O'Brien—aka Guardsman—the first armored character who wasn't created by Stark or the Communists. Sales on *Iron Man* began to slip, however, and the book was demoted to bimonthly status at the end of 1971.

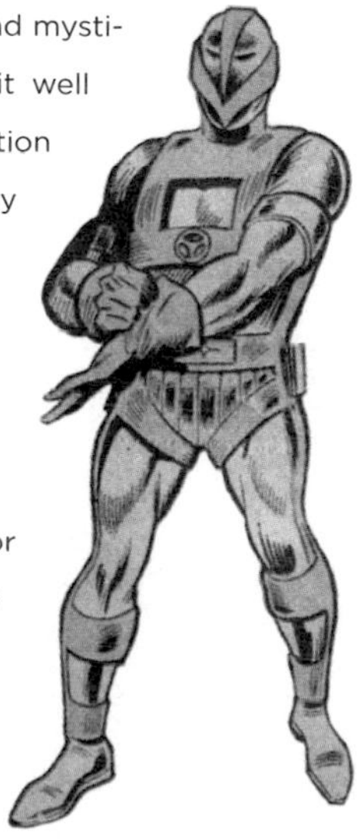

▲ Eddie March became Iron Man's short-lived replacement (top) while foe Guardsman (bottom) would cause armored havoc.

Writer Gary Friedrich came onboard with *Iron Man* #45 (March 1972), and Tony Stark was quickly faced with both a hostile takeover of Stark Industries and a battle-to-the-death with the Guardsman. "I accepted an offer of full-time work at Marvel in December of 1971 from then-assistant-editor Roy Thomas," says Friedrich, who had written titles for DC as far ranging as *Justice League of America* and *The Witching Hour*. "*Iron Man* was the first title assigned to me. I had read all of the issues and was a moderate fan." He felt he understood the fan appeal of Tony and his gadgets. "We don't call things boy-toys for nothing," he jokes. "A large percentage of American boys, by the time they are reading Marvel Comics, are fascinated by machinery and technology. *Iron Man* symbolizes that fascination."

Friedrich brought with him some political background, and it had some effect on how he wrote Tony Stark's adventures. "My politics were quite opposed to the Cold War approach of the original character. I tended to just ignore that aspect of the character and instead focused on Tony Stark taking his company's efforts in more socially productive directions. Unlike my earlier DC work, though, political issues took a significant backseat to the Super Hero/Super Villain conflict each issue. My political perspective was never discouraged at Marvel, I was just told it had to fit in the background, not the foreground." Interestingly enough, a fill-in story in issue #47 (June 1972) *would* broach politics: In a retelling of Iron Man's origin by Roy Thomas, now editor-in-chief, the armored hero began to have doubts about being a weapons designer.

--WEAPONS THAT CAN BE USED TO KILL ONE PEOPLE--TO SAVE ANOTHER.
SOMETIMES I'M OUT IN A CROWD, AND I HEAR SOMEBODY'S SCORNFUL WHISPER:
"MUNITIONS-MAKER!"
AND I FIND MYSELF PONDERING EVERY ACTION I EVER MADE.
BUT MAYBE THAT'S ALL TO THE GOOD.

Following issues that introduced Marvel über-villain Thanos, showcased Green Lantern doppelgänger Doctor Spectrum, and gave Pepper Potts the secret of Tony's dual identity, Friedrich kicked off a yearlong multipart storyline called "The Battle of the Super Villains," using Mandarin, Yellow Claw, Sunfire, Ultimo, the Mad Thinker, Modok, Black Lama, and many others. "I remember creating a scenario among Marvel villains where they were battling each other and Iron Man was caught in the middle," Friedrich says. "I had hopes of it becoming a companywide project, but I was only able to produce my little piece." Unfortunately, the author has negative memories of the story as well. "I'm afraid I handled the Mandarin poorly, by actively denying the racism it perpetuated. Even when confronted with Chinese American fans like Bill Wu—who eloquently described the sadness and bitterness of having the only Chinese character in my comics be a Super Villain—I refused to recognize what I was being told. I'm ashamed still."

Friedrich would stay on the series until issue #81 (December 1975), though a handful of fill-ins (and a reprint) would spell him when the series became monthly again and deadlines threatened. In one of his stories, *Iron Man* #72 (January 1975), Tony Stark attended the San Diego Comic-Con while dressed in his Iron Man armor. The issue is full of in-jokes, including appearances by real Marvel writers and artists, a reference to a *Star Trek* petition, and nasty comments about Iron Man's new faceplate . . . which, since issue #68, had featured an armored nosepiece.

The nose was perhaps the most controversial change to Iron Man's armor ever instituted, and even as fans complained about it in the series' letter column, "Sock It to Shell Head," the blame was laid squarely at the feet of Marvel's head honcho, Stan Lee. Years later, then-editor-in-chief Jim Shooter would explain the nose: "Stan had an incredible reputation. I think people were always in awe of him, and if he would say anything, just some little remark in passing, you know it would become *law.* I remember one time there was a situation . . . where Stan looked at a picture of Iron Man and said, 'Shouldn't he have a

AND THEN...THE DRAMATIC RESULTS!
FORTUNATELY THE RAW MATERIALS ARE HERE AT MY FINGERTIPS...
I CAN EASILY MOLD A NEW MASK OUT OF REINFORCED STEEL MESH, LIKE THE REST OF MY ARMOR--
--THEN TO ADD THE LATEST IN INTEGRATED-CIRCUITRY, I'LL BE ABLE TO TRANSLATE MY BRAIN WAVES INTO USABLE ELECTRICITY...
SO THAT I CAN MENTALLY COMMAND MY SUIT'S EQUIPMENT AND WEAPONRY AND THIS TIME I'VE FASHIONED INCREASED-STRENGTH PLEXIGLASS-LIKE EYE-AND-MOUTH SHIELDS THAT WILL WITHSTAND THE DEEPEST OCEANS--
AND I'LL FINISH THE ARMOR'S CHANGES WITH A SLIGHTLY MODIFIED APPEARANCE... TO ALLOW A BIT MORE EXPRESSION TO SHOW--
--AND SO PERHAPS INCREASE THE FEARSOME ASPECTS OF MY CHARACTER TO THOSE WHO OPPOSE ME!

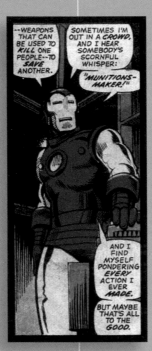

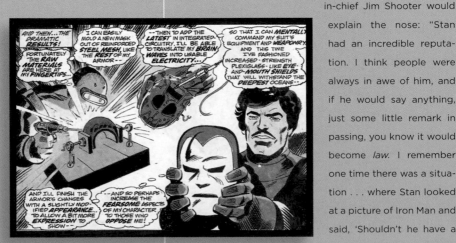

▲ Tony Stark considers fundamental changes in his career (top), and a less noteworthy change to his mask (bottom).

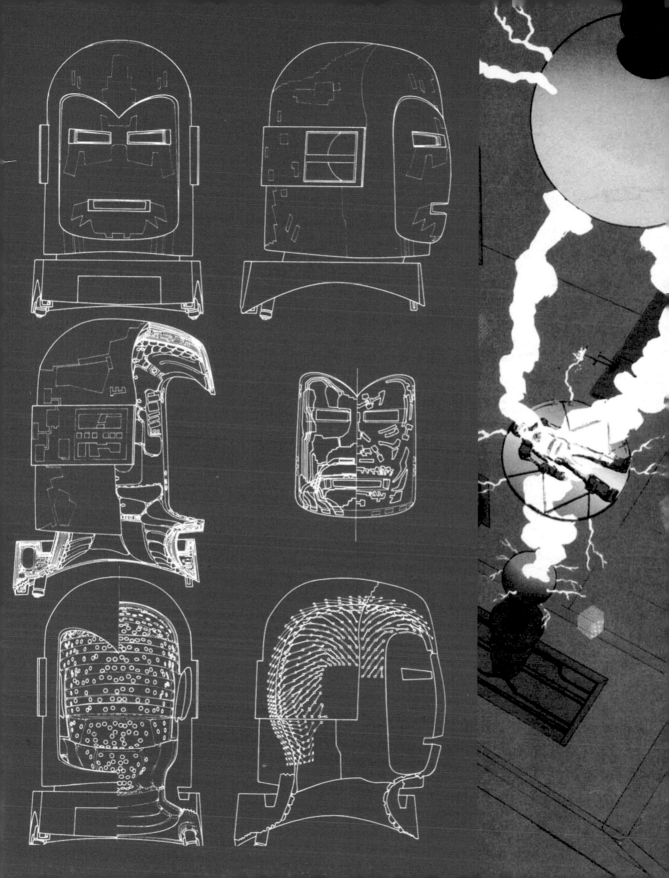

nose?' I know exactly what he meant. What he meant was the guy had drawn the mask so flat that it looked like there couldn't be a nose under there. All he wanted was a little room for the guy to have a nose, right? Immediately they went out and drew a triangular nose on Iron Man's costume and it was there for a year or so. Then later, Stan saw this picture of Iron Man with this triangular nose on his face and he said, 'What's this, why is this here?' And they said, 'Oh, you don't want that?' 'Well, it looks kind of strange, doesn't it?' They took *that* as an edict, too— 'No nose on Iron Man.' Then they all walked around saying, 'Gee, he changes his mind a lot.' "

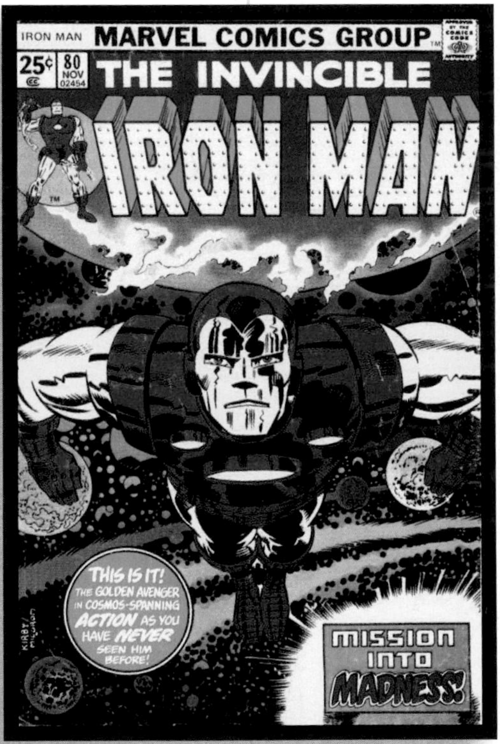
IRON MAN
MARVEL COMICS GROUP
25¢
80
NOV
02454
THE INVINCIBLE
IRON MAN
THIS IS IT!
THE GOLDEN AVENGER IN COSMOS-SPANNING ACTION AS YOU HAVE NEVER SEEN HIM BEFORE!
MISSION INTO MADNESS!

Leaving the book after four years with a bizarre story featuring an alternate-dimensional President Gerald Ford ("King Jerald"), Friedrich felt hampered by some of the artists he had worked with, and today believes his stories could have been better served. "I didn't have the imagination to work around this challenge, and the stories suffered because of it." Still, he counts the stories as a positive element of his writing career. "*Iron Man* provided a steady source of income and a dependable avenue of creative expression, both of which I lacked at DC earlier. My next career move was into publishing, which led me into the business and marketing side of comics, where I had more fun and more success than I did writing." Friedrich would go on to publish pioneering alternative comics such as *Star*Reach* and *Quack,* co-found the popular WonderCon, and function as agent/business manager for some of the most popular comic artists in the business. Today he is a political and union organizer, and a "smart growth" urban land-use advocate.

•

As America celebrated its bicentennial, *Iron Man* began a year of multiple writers, including Len Wein, Bill Mantlo, Gerry Conway, and Jim Shooter, and a returning gig for Archie Goodwin. Longtime craftsman Herb Trimpe filled in on several issues with art but wasn't well received by some fans. While Tony Stark's story progressed somewhat—he was reunited with Happy and Pepper briefly, and finally did away with his armored nose—the stories were haphazard and lazy about continuity from issue to issue.

Despite his travails in the comics, Iron Man was becoming immortalized in more and more merchandising throughout the 1970s. The most famous toy was an eight-inch action figure/doll from Mego in a cloth costume with a plastic helmet. Part of the "World's Greatest Super Heroes" line, Iron Man was available boxed or on a card from 1975 to 1978, alongside Spider-Man, Hulk, Captain America, and Conan, among others. Iron Man also appeared on a Marvel Super Heroes lunchbox from Aladdin (1976), on 7-Eleven Slurpee cups (1975 and 1977), View-Master reels (1977), and in calendars and games featuring Marvel's do-gooders. In 1979, Marvel produced a novel series through Pocket Books, and two featured Shellhead: *Iron Man: And Call my*

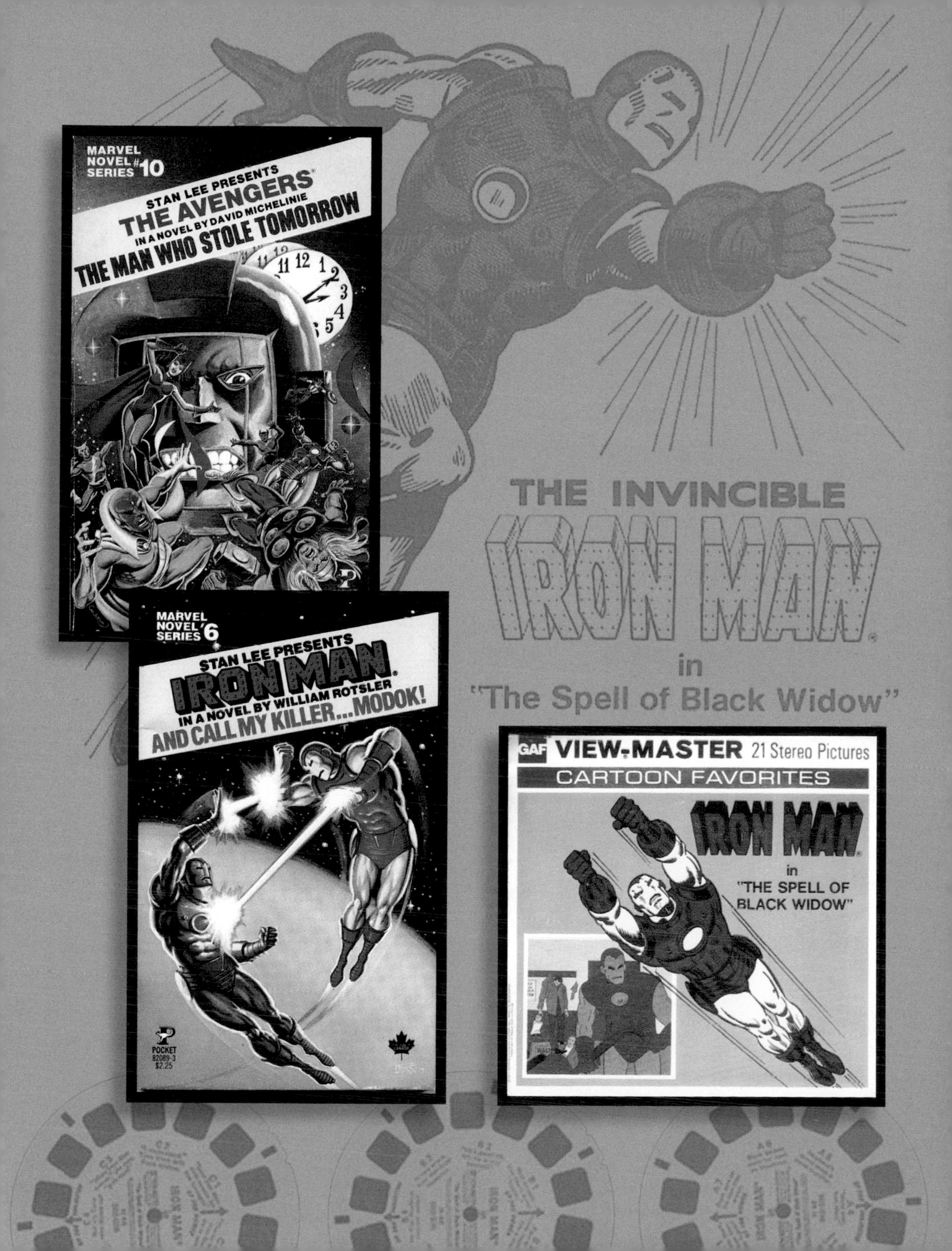

MARVEL NOVEL SERIES #10
STAN LEE PRESENTS
THE AVENGERS
IN A NOVEL BY DAVID MICHELINIE
THE MAN WHO STOLE TOMORROW
MARVEL NOVEL SERIES #6
STAN LEE PRESENTS
IRON MAN
IN A NOVEL BY WILLIAM ROTSLER
AND CALL MY KILLER...MODOK!
POCKET
82089-3
$2.25
THE INVINCIBLE
IRON MAN
in
"The Spell of Black Widow"
GAF VIEW-MASTER 21 Stereo Pictures
CARTOON FAVORITES
IRON MAN
in
"THE SPELL OF BLACK WIDOW"

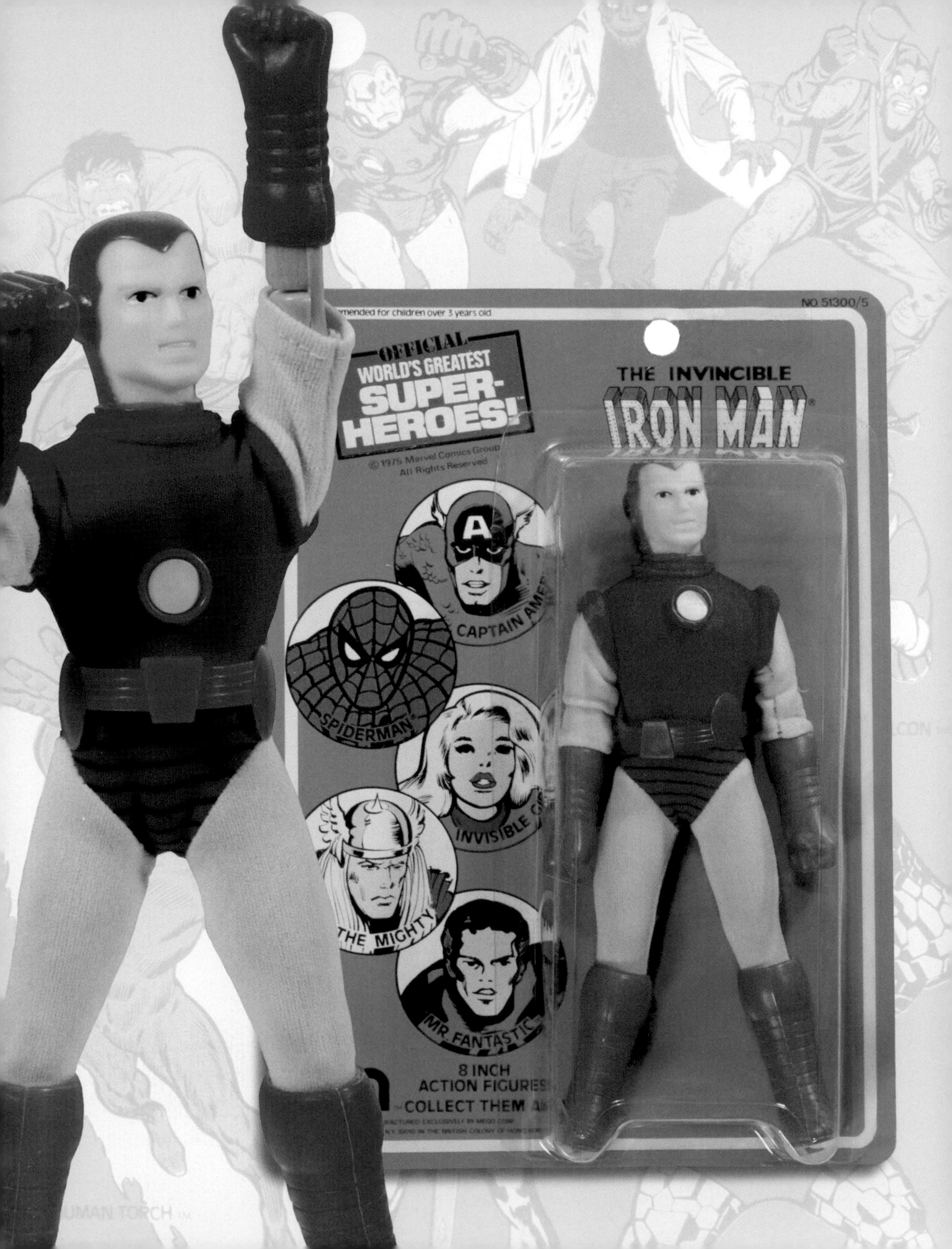

NO. 51300/5
OFFICIAL
WORLD'S GREATEST
SUPER-
HEROES!
© 1975 Marvel Comics Group
All Rights Reserved
THE INVINCIBLE
IRON MAN®
SPIDERMAN
THE MIGHTY
MR. FANTASTIC
8 INCH
ACTION FIGURES
COLLECT THEM

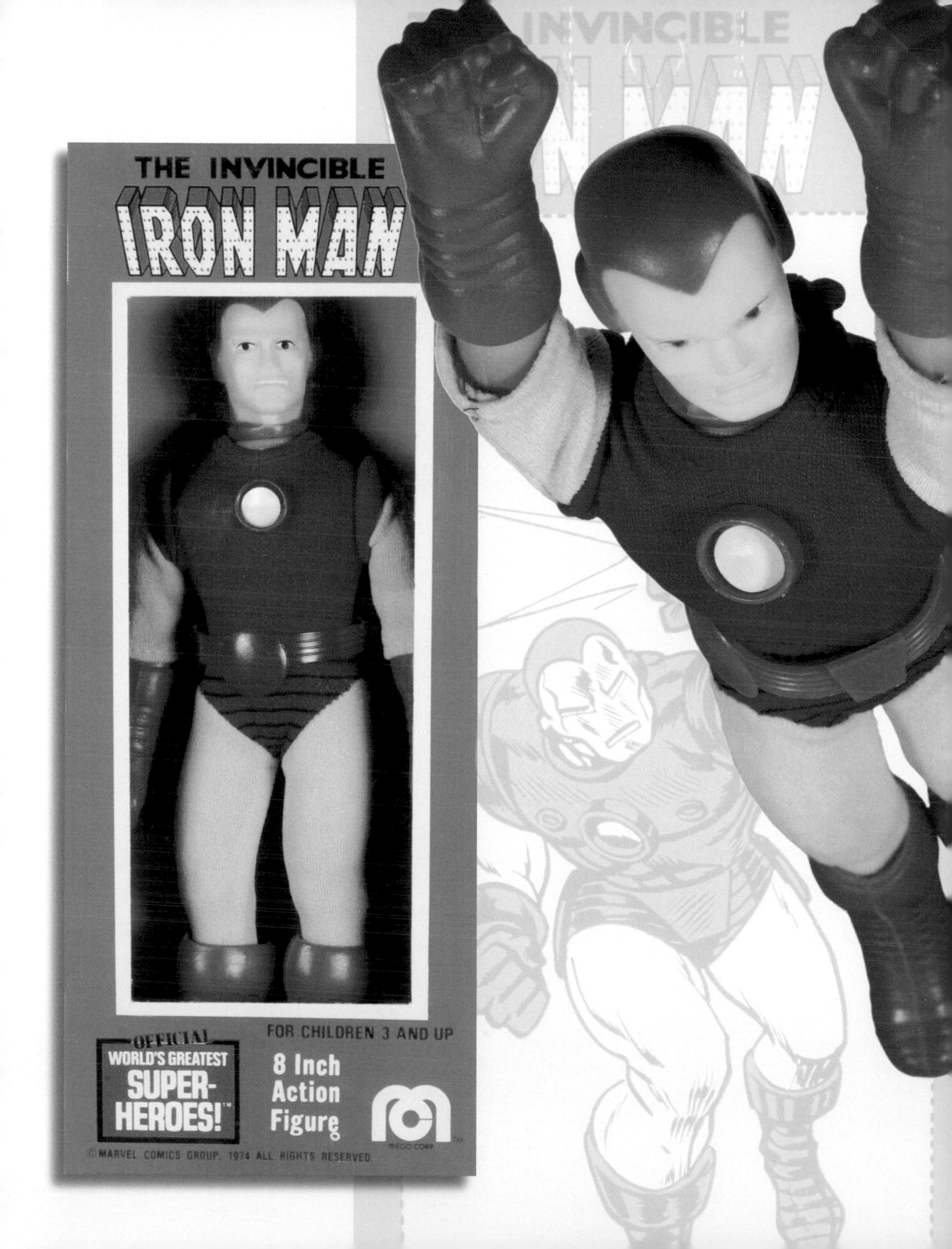
THE INVINCIBLE
IRON MAN
FOR CHILDREN 3 AND UP
OFFICIAL
WORLD'S GREATEST
SUPER-HEROES!™
8 Inch
Action
Figure
MEGO CORP
©MARVEL COMICS GROUP, 1974 ALL RIGHTS RESERVED.
INVINCIBLE

Killer . . . Modok! by William Rotsler, and *Avengers: The Man Who Stole Tomorrow* by David Michelinie.

Meanwhile, back in comic-land, the arrival of writer Bill Mantlo with *Iron Man* #95 (February 1977) heralded some stability for the series. Iron Man battled Ultimo and Sunfire again, then—after facing off against the vengeful brother of the Guardsman—donned the Guardsman armor himself and discovered that the Mandarin was still alive. "It was on *Iron Man,* my first regular feature with a character whose destiny I could control, that I really began to learn how to plot," Bill Mantlo said. "I tried to take a sagging character out of Marvel limbo and build him back up to greatness . . . I wanted to make Stark more human, because there's nothing more boring than a cardboard character to script every issue."

Mantlo had created a Super Hero named Jack of Hearts in another Marvel series, and he brought the character over to *Iron Man* for a multipart epic in 1977–1978's issues #103–108. In the tale, Midas attempted to take over Stark International, leading Iron Man to team up with Jack of Hearts, the Guardsman, the Wraith, Madame Masque, and S.H.I.E.L.D. agents to keep the company from being gilded by the corpulent Super Villain. In the process of the story, Mantlo also got a wish fulfilled: He had disliked Tuska's pencilling and lobbied for a new artist. He got a number of them over his next year's worth of stories, including Keith Giffen, DC mainstay Carmine Infantino, and newcomer Keith Pollard. Mantlo's final story in *Iron Man* #115 (October 1978) would bring aboard new regular penciller—and son of Marvel art giant—John Romita Jr.

Mantlo was actually replaced on the book due to the plans of new editor-in-chief Jim Shooter, who took over the job from Archie Goodwin in 1978. "The reader reaction was incredibly, overwhelmingly positive, for both Shellhead and Jack of Hearts . . . but Jim Shooter became editor at that time and, like anywhere else, an editor has his own ideas about how things should be," Mantlo said.

As Mantlo shuttled off to other Marvel assignments, his replacements on *Iron Man* would become one of the most influential storytelling teams in the character's history.

•

David Michelinie had worked at a film production company, writing commercial and educational film scripts, prior to writing for DC Comics on titles such as *The Unknown Soldier, Swamp Thing, Aquaman,* and *Superboy.* When he switched companies to work at Marvel, he quickly got control of two books. "Jim Shooter had given me the writing assignment on *The Avengers* when I first came over to Marvel from DC," Michelinie says. "I've always found two regular monthly titles to be a comfortable workload, so I was looking for another series to write. When *Iron Man* was offered it seemed like a natural choice, since Iron Man was also in *The Avengers* at that time, so I would have total control over the character."

Michelinie was not alone in taking on the new assignment, though. "I'd never read an Iron Man story before I took on that writing assignment, which I think worked to the book's advantage. My co-plotter, Bob Layton, was a longtime Shellhead fan and knew the character's history backward and forward. I had no knowledge of the character whatsoever, and so could bring a fresh perspective to the plots, a viewpoint uninfluenced by what had gone before."

Along with later Marvel editor-writer Roger Stern, Bob Layton had co-published a comics-oriented fanzine in the 1970s called *CPL* (Contemporary Pictorial Literature), which garnered him work at Charlton Comics and an apprenticeship with legendary artist Wally Wood. Layton inked Wood for several Marvel and DC jobs on *X-Men, The Champions,* and *All-Star Comics.* With Michelinie, he had previously co-created the science-fiction book *Star Hunters* for DC, and when his creative partner went to Marvel, he did as well.

"Together we went to Marvel and interviewed with Jim Shooter to work as a team there," says Layton. "We

James "Rhodey" Rhodes would become ▶ a major player in *Iron Man* history.

were given a choice of three lower-end books to work on, and I jumped out of my seat when I realized that *Iron Man* was one of those choices. That was the one book in the entire industry that I wanted to do more than any other. At the time we took it over, sales were lackluster and the book was in desperate need of revitalizing. Together we retooled the series into the way I had always imagined it could be. David Michelinie was never a hard-core Marvel fan in his youth. David's lack of a personal history with Iron Man's mythology proved to be a tremendous asset—translating into his fresher approach to the character. We had a fifty-fifty relationship on the plots, with both of us contributing equally to the story and character development."

Layton worked as co-plotter with Michelinie from *Iron Man* #116–154, and also worked as the inker/finish artist over a variety of pencil artists during the long stint on the book. John Romita Jr. would pencil the book for an original baker's dozen issues, returning late in 1980 for a second run. Other issues were pencilled by fan favorite John Byrne, Carmine Infantino, Jerry Bingham, Alan Weiss, and Luke McDonnell, while Layton would also fully illustrate many issues himself.

Two major changes were made to the series during the Michelinie/Layton run: The supporting cast was increased and solidified, and the adaptability of the armor was increasingly explored. "I have a great deal of affection for most of the supporting cast members Bob and I created during our first run on the book," says Michelinie. "We didn't go out of our way to create characters, but came up with new ones when there was a need. That way the characters always seemed to matter, to have a purpose rather than just being thrown in for comic relief or to serve a particular story. Probably my three favorite supporting characters were Jim Rhodes, Bethany Cabe, and Bambi Arbogast."

Of the three new characters, Rhodes would become the most important over time. "Rhodey came about when we realized that Tony needed to get places fast, but

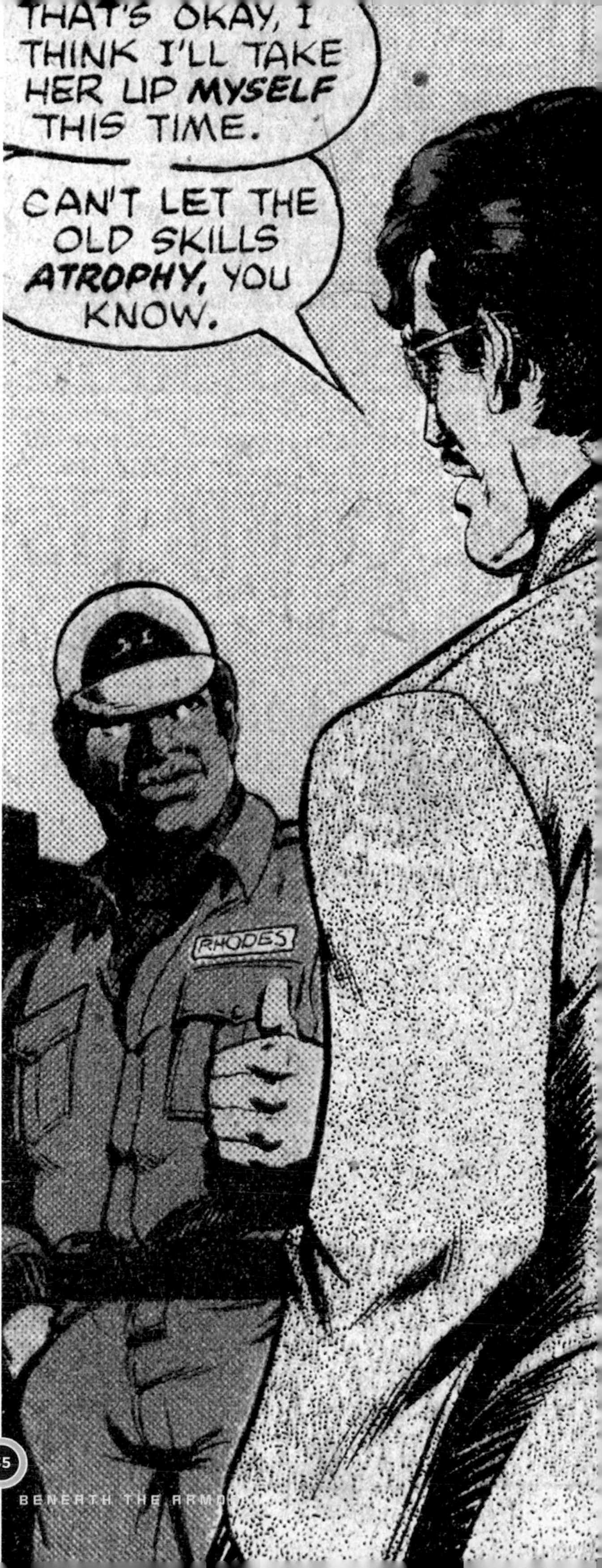
THAT'S OKAY, I THINK I'LL TAKE HER UP *MYSELF* THIS TIME.
CAN'T LET THE OLD SKILLS *ATROPHY,* YOU KNOW.
RHODES

couldn't always fly to destinations in his armor. He was rich and surely had at least one private jet, but how many millionaires fly their own planes? So we invented Rhodey, gave him a background as an ex-soldier and ex-mercenary, and made him Tony's pilot. But we also made him Tony's friend. Most Super Heroes have other costumed types as friends, but Tony isn't superpowered, and we wanted to surround him with other human beings because it would help him remain grounded when caught up in wild and dangerous adventures. Rhodey knew how to fight, but he wasn't a Super Hero. And that seemed more appropriate for a central character who, himself, had no innate powers."

John Byrne guest-drew the issue that introduced Rhodes, *Iron Man* #118 (January 1979). Although comics had featured some racial diversity, even by the start of the 1980s, non-Caucasian lead or supporting characters were still a relative rarity. "I was a kind of midwife in the creation of Rhodey, so he is somewhat near and dear," says Byrne. "I actually drew it sitting at a tiny drawing board tucked into the corner of Roger Stern's office. I came to the page Jim Rhodes first appeared on and I looked over at Rog and said, 'Any reason this guy shouldn't be black?' Rog liked the idea, so I drew Rhodey as a black man."

As for the two new women in Tony Stark's life, Michelinie says, "Bethany Cabe was another chapter out of that same book. When we took over the series, Tony had a tendency to date other costumed characters; I believe Madame Masque was his squeeze at the time. We wanted to show a more believable relationship with a strong woman who didn't shout, *I'm a strong woman! Hear me roar!* but instead showed her strength—both physical and emotional—through her actions and choices."

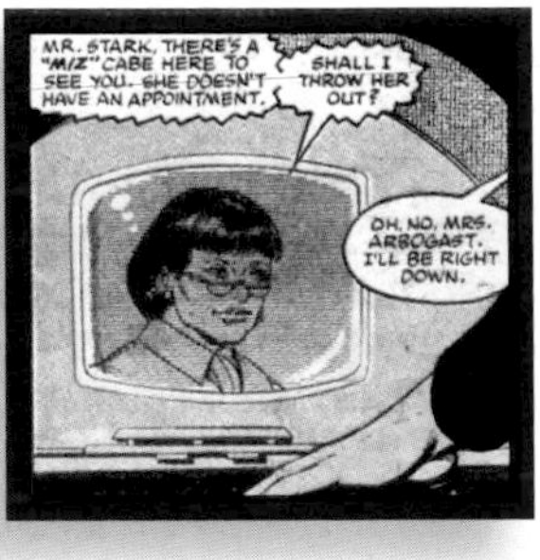
MR. STARK, THERE'S A "MIZ" CABE HERE TO SEE YOU--SHE DOESN'T HAVE AN APPOINTMENT.
SHALL I THROW HER OUT?
OH, NO, MRS. ARBOGAST. I'LL BE RIGHT DOWN.

With Pepper Potts long gone, "Mrs. Arbogast resulted from a need for Tony to have a secretary," says Michelinie. "We didn't want to do the usual thing and have her be a hot babe who drooled over the boss every time he walked by. So we made her a tough and protective den mother type who didn't take any crap from anyone. Including Tony." Layton concurs: "Mrs. Arbogast was particularly funny to do because of her acerbic wit and her immunity to Tony's charm."

As for the armor, "the one innovation I'm mostly credited for is of turning Iron Man into a metallic-looking hero," says Layton. "Prior to my being on the book, he was pretty much rendered like any other costume. I took the rule-of-thumb techniques I had learned from my mentors and applied them to rendering the armor so it looked like a suit of metal rather than just another spandex Super Hero outfit." As a child, Layton had loved Stan Lee's scripting and Iron Man as a character. "I even created my own Iron Man stories when I was young and dreamed up concepts for variant specialty armors. So when I actually got to Marvel and fulfilled my dream of being able to work on *Iron Man,* I was able to inculcate those stories and designs that I dreamed up as a kid into the regular series. The now classic Camelot Saga and the

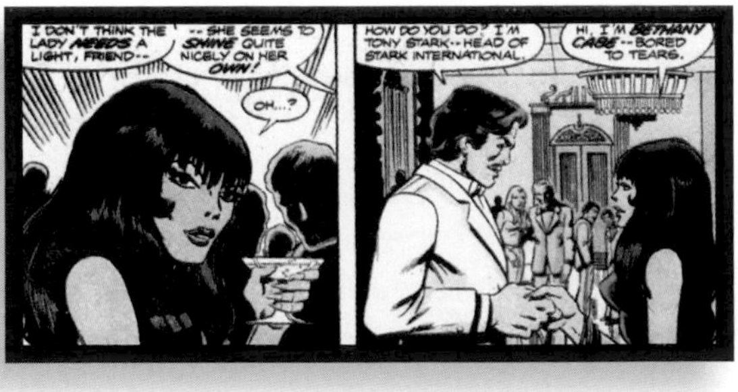
I DON'T THINK THE LADY NEEDS A LIGHT, FRIEND--
--SHE SEEMS TO SHINE QUITE NICELY ON HER OWN!
OH...?
HOW DO YOU DO? I'M TONY STARK--HEAD OF STARK INTERNATIONAL.
HI, I'M BETHANY CABE--BORED TO TEARS.

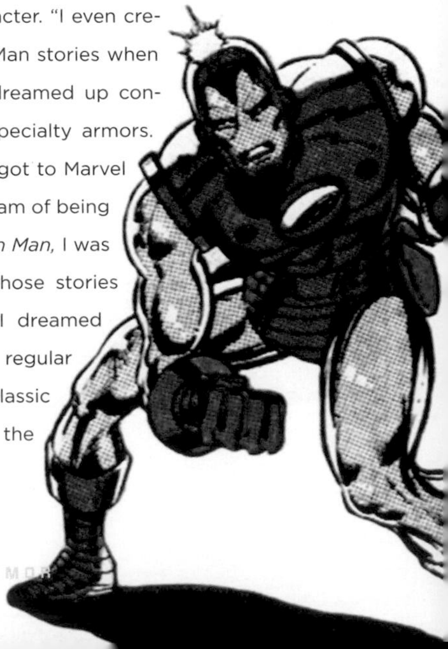

Bethany Cabe (bottom left) and Mrs. Arbogast ▲ (top right) supported Tony Stark in different ways.

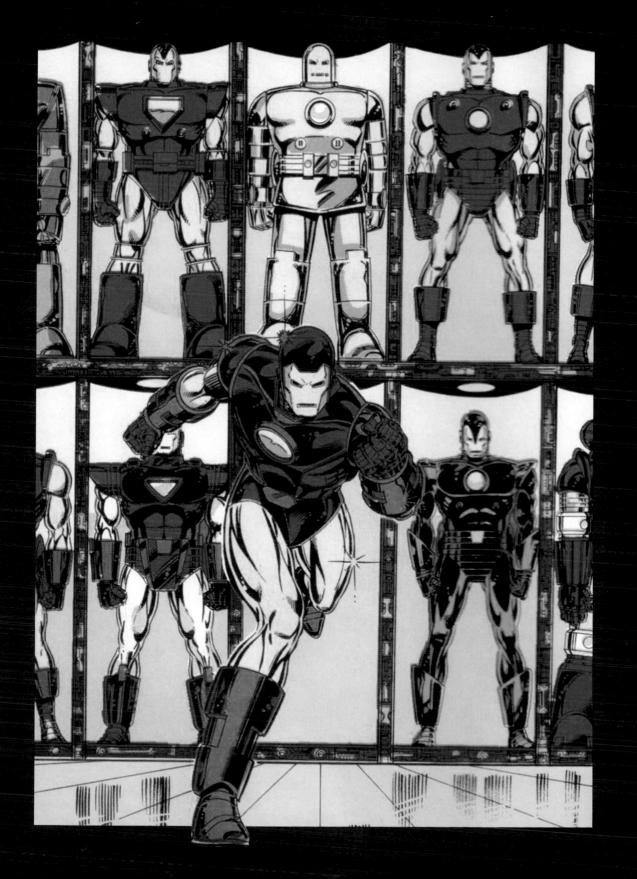

introduction of Iron Man specialty armors were a direct result of those childhood fantasies."

Specialty armors created by Layton included a Space Armor for non-Earthly adventures, Stealth Armor for spy missions, and even Deep Sea Armor for pressurized underwater battles. "It added a lot of opportunities to do neat stuff, both visually and story-wise," says Michelinie. "The Stealth Armor was practical, since it helped Iron Man get into the Soviet Union and other restricted areas undetected. But it also looked pretty damn cool. And with things like the specialized underwater armor, we had the opportunity to put Iron Man in new conflicts that grew out of specific situations—like having his eye slits pop open unexpectedly when he's several fathoms down and his armor starts filling with water!"

"What was cutting-edge ten years ago is totally obsolete today," says Layton. "Technology is constantly evolving, and so should Iron Man. That was my thinking when I originally created the concept of the specialty armors. There's a huge difference between a stock car and an Indy car. Each is designed for specific tasks, and *that* was our thinking when approaching the Iron Man armor. It's unrealistic to presume that one device can adapt to all situations and environments. Making this fictional technology believable is the key to making the entire premise work."

Layton cites an aptitude for science as a child for helping him devise new armors—which, he notes, "is something of a contradiction for someone with an artistic leaning. I've continued to read scientific journals and such to this day. That's probably why David usually left the scientific stuff to me when we worked on stories together. I've always been fascinated with certain aspects of science and I love applying what I read to my work. I really want my contemporary stories, which have science as a theme, to be on the cutting edge of the technological frontier."

Although the team utilized some traditional—or reimagined—villains, one creation would bring significant problems down on Tony Stark. "Of the villains we created, Justin Hammer is my favorite," says Michelinie. "His creation arose from a realization that there was a gap in Marvel continuity that needed to be filled. It seemed that new costumed villains popped up every month, each with amazing weapons or vehicles or other such hardware. Which begged the question: Where did they get the money for all those wonderful toys? The answer was Justin Hammer, a businessman who financed super-crooks for a cut of their take. His debut solved a problem while also serving to give Tony Stark a counterpart in the business world, one who challenged him in his role of hero as well. The character was based, both physically and personality-wise, on one of my favorite actors of all time, Peter Cushing. I always heard Cushing's smooth and impeccably focused delivery whenever I wrote dialogue for Justin Hammer. The name Hammer was, of course, an homage to Cushing's many portrayals in the horror movies from Hammer studios."

"As benevolent as Tony was portrayed in our series, Hammer represented the other side of that coin," says Layton. "They were two men essentially in the same line of work, but with diametrically opposed moral views."

Morality played a tricky element in Michelinie and Layton's most famous storyline, "Demon in a Bottle," encompassing *Iron Man* #121–128. In the decades since it

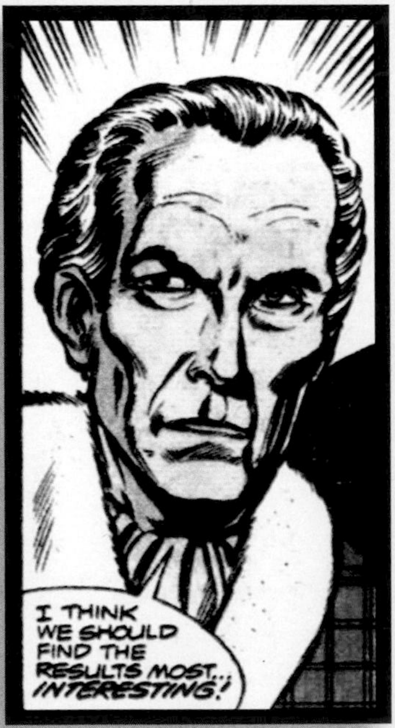
I THINK WE SHOULD FIND THE RESULTS MOST... INTERESTING!

▲ Justin Hammer proved to be an *Iron Man* foe for the ages.

first appeared, "Demon" has been collected into multiple trades, issue #128's iconic cover has been re-created as a Marvel statue, and the story has become one of the defining elements of Tony Stark's personality. In the saga, playboy Tony Stark had been drinking more and more frequently as his problems mounted, from being framed for murder by Hammer remote-controlling one of his armors, to facing an army of Super Villains with the help of Captain America and the new Ant-Man, to relationship issues with Bethany Cabe. By the tale's sweat-drenched denouement, Stark realized that he was an alcoholic and began to face his demons head-on.

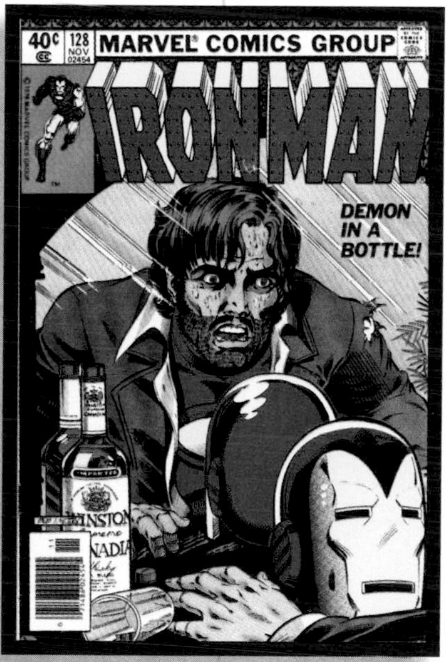

40¢
128 NOV 02454
MARVEL COMICS GROUP
IRON MAN
DEMON IN A BOTTLE!

Michelinie says that the story is one of his favorites. "When I first started researching the character after I was given the *Iron Man* writing assignment, I realized that this guy's world was really beginning to fray around the edges. His 'friends' at S.H.I.E.L.D. were trying to take over his company, his girlfriend was plotting to have him assassinated, and the government was trying to force him and his fellow Avengers to be licensed and regulated or else close up shop. A real person under that kind of pressure would have to find some sort of release valve or have a breakdown. So it seemed natural to have Tony Stark, who had previously been established as a social drinker, start to hit the bottle, hard. Some readers thought it made Tony less of a hero to succumb to alcoholism, but we felt just the opposite. Giving Tony a real-world problem, one that has likely touched the lives of many readers in one way or another, and then having him find the courage to face and conquer that problem, made him even more of a hero to us. 'Demon in a Bottle' was certainly controversial, but the only guideline we were given by Marvel was, 'Just do it well.' They were very good at trusting us and giving us a lot of rope."

Groundbreaking due to its treatment of a Super Hero with a chemical addiction, "Demon" garnered attention from the mainstream media, was written up by the Department of Health, Education and Welfare, and issue #128 won an international Eagle Award for best single comic book. Even finicky comic literary magazine *The Comics Journal* raved that it tackled a "powerfully depicted social problem" and that the story showed "a great deal of maturity and sophistication."

Editor Roger Stern recalls that the self-regulatory censorship committee, the Comics Code Authority, whose stamp of approval appeared on most newsstand comics from the mid-1950s to the present, considered the story, "a little controversial . . . They warned us that the Alcohol Information & Media Study Foundation would be all over us for 'trivializing something as serious as alcoholism.' What the Code didn't realize was that we already had that foundation's blessing. When it was all over, the AIMS Foundation gave us awards for 'highest achievement in teaching youth about alcohol and its proper use in society.' So much for the wisdom of the Comics Code Authority."

"That story is now considered a milestone event by most comic book historians," says Layton. "David and I felt that we needed to create a personal problem for Tony Stark that fit the world of corporate business that we set him in. Given his passions and somewhat compulsive behaviors at times, the alcohol story seemed somewhat to be a natural. We wanted to create a weakness for Stark that wasn't the 'heart attack of the month.' His alcoholism was one thing the armor couldn't fix. I think that worked out well as his personal demon."

As a long-term *Iron Man* fan, Layton feels that the story is perfectly in keeping with the character of Tony Stark and his role as the armored avenger. "Tony doesn't play [a] Super Hero role as other comic book heroes do. I believe he uses the Iron Man persona for two reasons: to protect his various business interests globally, and to ground himself to the real world. Keep in mind, as Tony Stark, he lives in an ivory tower, surrounded by people who tell him what they *think* he wants to hear. He has a celebrity status equal to a movie or rock star. This guy does *not* live in the real world. In many ways, his being Iron Man is like the Prince and the Pauper. Strangely enough, as Iron Man, he becomes a hands-on guy, interacting one-on-one with people and using that anonymous identity to maintain perspective of how he's [Tony Stark] perceived by the world at large. It's fair to say that it's another aspect of the obsessive-compulsive personality that led to his alcoholism. Iron Man is a fix that he needs to maintain his stability. In that story, we took that release valve away from him, which drove the character into a downward spiral."

Michelinie feels that what makes Tony Stark an interesting character and hero is that "he's a Super Hero with no superpowers. Any abilities he has are abilities that he makes, that he imagines and then invents. Prime among those, of course, is his amazing suit of electronic armor. Without the armor, he's just a man. A man with a huge brain and a few billion dollars, but still just a human being. Not an alien, not a mutant, not a Hero Born. He's simply a guy, and I think that makes him a lot more interesting than many heroes, as well as making him easier for the average reader to identify with. He could be you or me, if we had the money and inventiveness. And the courage. And the willpower."

Layton agrees that getting into Stark's head was the most important element of the stories they were telling. "In my opinion, when we took over the series, Tony Stark was little more than a vehicle used to get the armor on him and go into action. David and I felt that it was more important to concentrate on the man inside the suit than the suit itself. Remember that the man on the inside is what makes him special, not the electronic gadget he dons. That's why we introduced an entire cast of new supporting characters and changed the emphasis of the series to the world of corporate intrigue. Also, from an artistic level, I had to learn tricks in order to show emotion in a face mask that is static and inflexible. I learned various techniques as I went along of angling the head and intensifying the detail in the eyes in order to show expression."

As three years of tenure on *Iron Man* came to an end in 1981, and Layton and Michelinie prepared to move on to other books, they produced a saga in issues #149–150 that would not only hark back to the genesis of Stan Lee's conceptualization of Iron Man but also lay the groundwork for several future storylines of their own. In this adventure, Iron Man and armored Super Villain Doctor Doom become trapped in ancient Camelot, and Stark allies himself with King Arthur and his knights even as Doom plots evil with Morgana le Fey.

"Of the villains I didn't have a hand in creating, Doctor Doom is my all-time favorite," says Michelinie. "He's Tony's reflection in a dark mirror. He wears armor, he's a genius, and he wields great power. But the uses to which he puts that power are self-serving and threaten innocent lives, just the opposite of Tony Stark's efforts to improve the world . . . while still realizing a reasonable profit on his investments, of course."

"I was a huge fan of the Arthurian legends growing up," says Layton. "I had conceived of this Iron Man/Doom/Camelot storyline when I was a kid. We actually took Iron Man back to the days of King Arthur. The fans reacted to it so positively." Indeed, the duo would return Iron Man and Doom to the days of knights in armor for two sequel stories: *Iron Man* #249–250 in 1989 and the 2008 mini series *Iron Man: Legacy of Doom.*

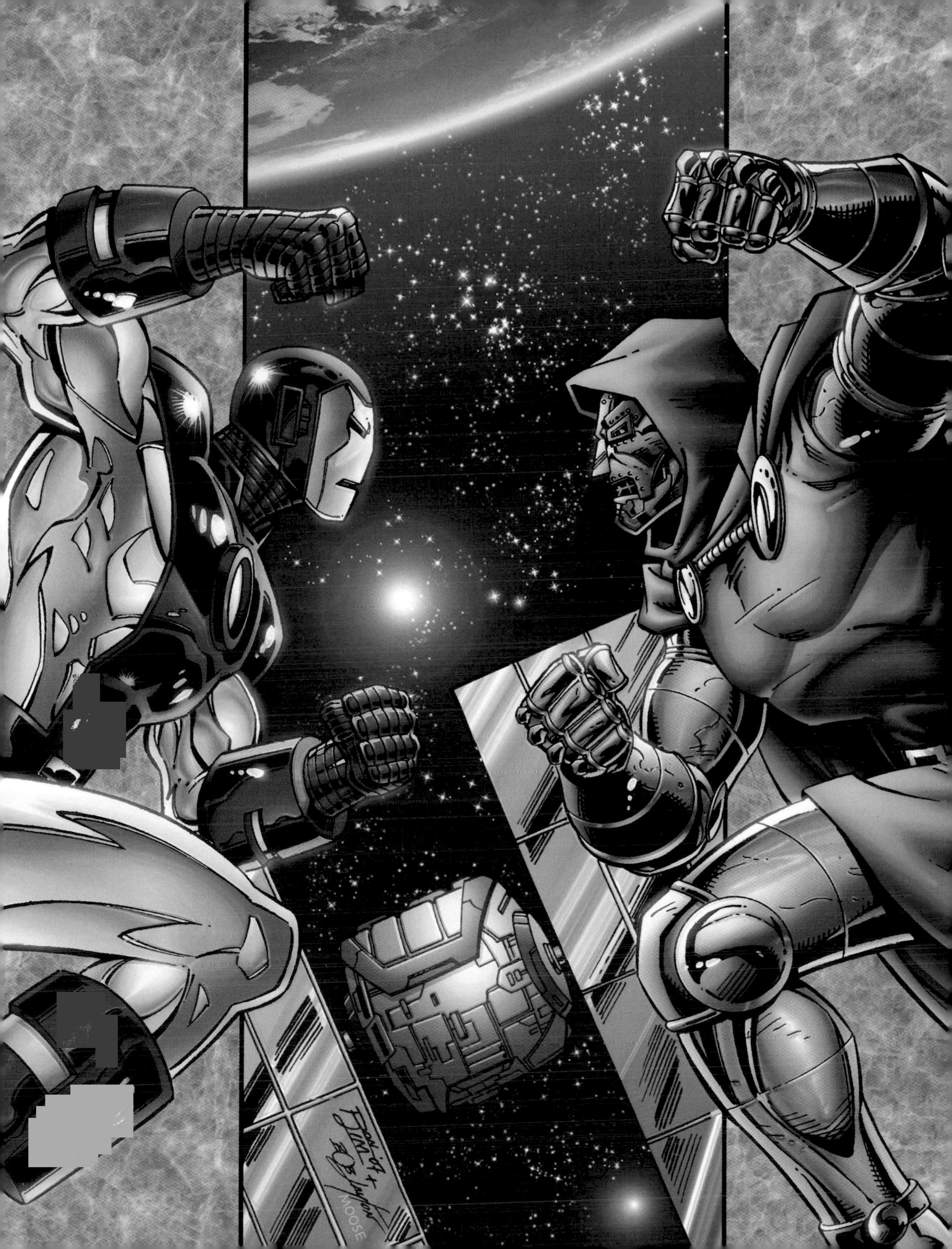
MOOSE

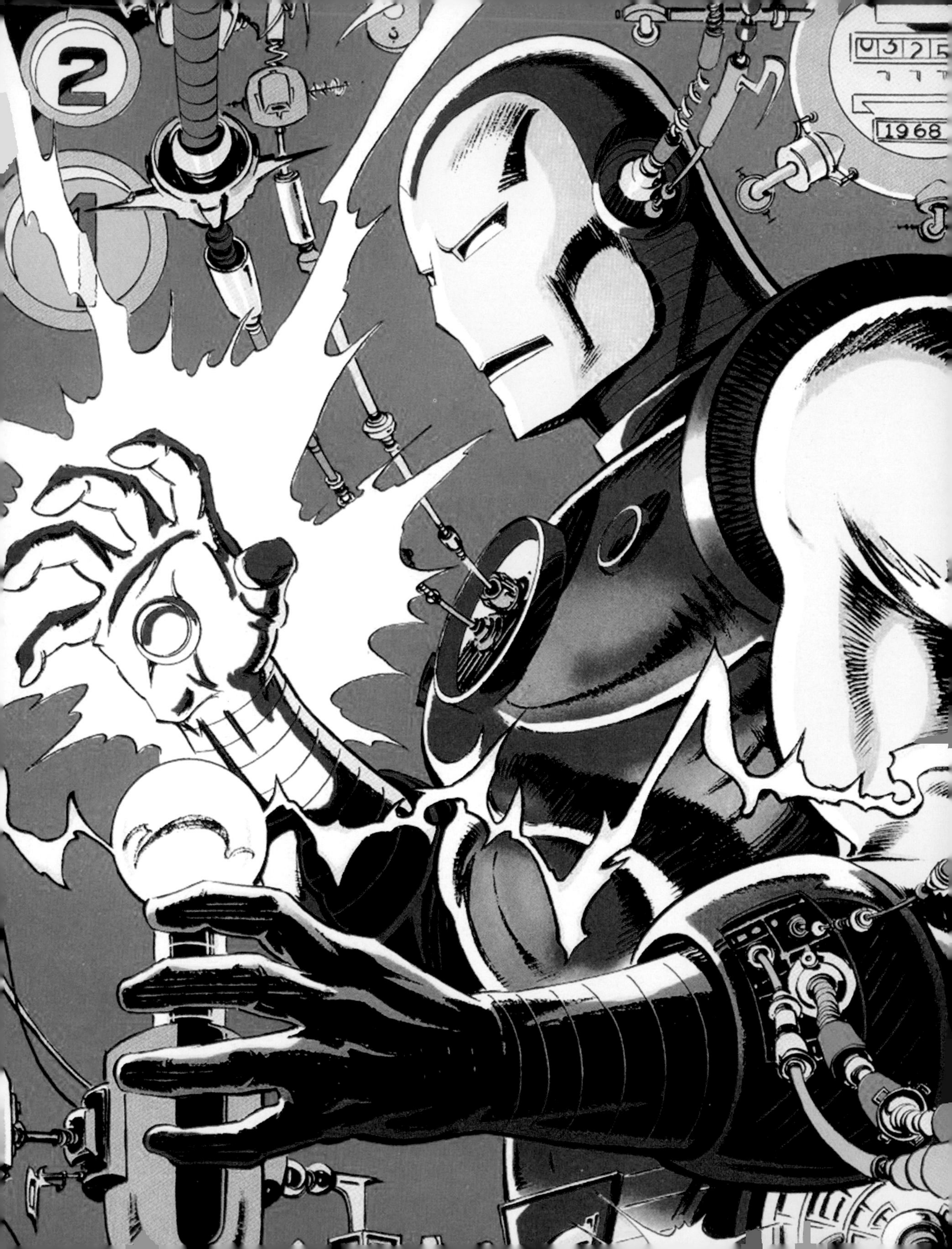
2
0325
1968

CHAPTER 3

CHANGING FORTUNES, CHANGING ARMOR

The 1980s were a time of economic liberalization, as the rise of the upper middle class gave birth to "yuppies" and President Ronald Reagan's conservative attitudes pushed religion to the forefront of politics. It was in this decade of pop culture and materialistic focus that the "Me Generation" readers were exposed to a Tony Stark, billionaire and Super Hero, who would soon lose not only his fortunes but his heroic alter ego as well.

Following the departures of Michelinie and Layton from *Iron Man* in 1982, current editor Mark Gruenwald asked writer Denny O'Neil to take over the job. O'Neil had begun his comic career at Marvel in the 1970s after Roy Thomas suggested he do some samples and Stan Lee liked them. He wrote *Dr. Strange* for a short time and some *Spider-Man* issues, but was soon at rival Charlton and then DC Comics, where his "socially relevant" run on *Green Lantern/Green Arrow* was the talk of the industry. He did other work on *Wonder Woman, Superman, Shazam!,* and *Batman* before returning to Marvel.

From his time as a Marvel editor, O'Neil was familiar with the series. He filled in on *Iron Man* #158 (May 1982) and was made regular writer on the series with #160 (July 1982), a position that he held for nearly fifty issues, mostly aided by the artistic team of Luke McDonnell and Steve Mitchell, and later newcomer Mark Bright and inkers Ian Akin & Brian Garvey.

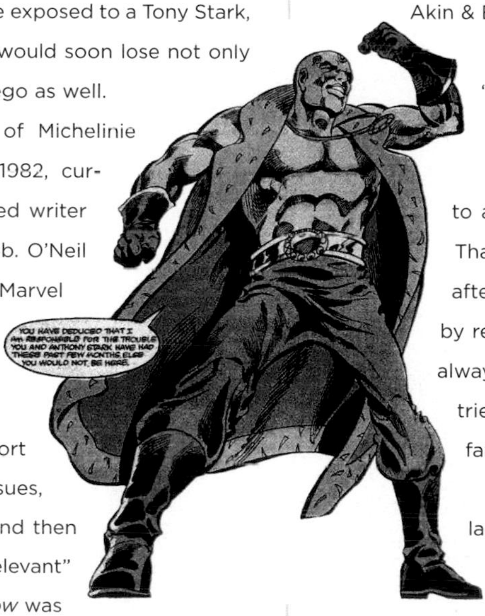
YOU HAVE DEDUCED THAT I AM RESPONSIBLE FOR THE TROUBLE YOU AND ANTHONY STARK HAVE HAD THESE PAST FEW MONTHS ELSE YOU WOULD NOT BE HERE.

As a character, O'Neil found Tony Stark "deeply flawed," and he saw Iron Man as "a walking icon of modern technology. The technology bore little, if any resemblance, to anything in the real world, and never did. That's not a knock. This is fantasy melodrama, after all, and shouldn't necessarily be bound by real-life considerations. So we did what we always do when dealing with super-guys . . . tried to be consistent within the rules of our fantasy world."

Evident in the first several stories is a lack of specific direction, but O'Neil soon established where he was going with the storyline by introducing multimillionaire munitions dealer Obadiah Stane. Like Justin Hammer, Stane was ruthless in his ambitions, but his evil plans were less about Iron Man than they were about destroying Tony Stark on a psychological and financial level. Making Stane

▲ Obadiah Stane hated Tony Stark almost as much as he hated good fashion.

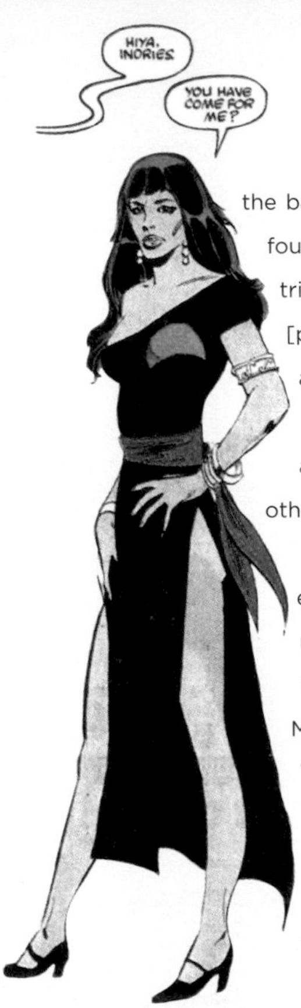
HIYA, INDRIES.
YOU HAVE COME FOR ME?

the bad guy was easier for O'Neil, who found Stark's past politics troubling. "I tried to duck politics because of the [past] elements," he says. "I have a hard time equating *hero* with *arms dealer,* and I'm pretty much an antiwar liberal, so I focused on other aspects of Tony's character."

Those other aspects included Stark's alcoholism, which was revisited by O'Neil. In his stories, lovely Stane employee Indries Moomji manipulated and seduced Tony and then betrayed him, thus sending Tony back to the solace of liquor. "Dave Michelinie gave Tony his weakness," O'Neil recalls. "Mark [Gruenwald] and I thought we might get more story mileage from it." Mileage indeed: Tony's slide into the bottle lasted almost two years of the book's continuity, during which Stark lost everything to Stane in a hostile takeover—even ignominiously being forced to watch the renaming of his own company to Stane International—before he ended up a homeless vagrant in the Bowery. "Fan reaction was overwhelmingly positive," says O'Neil, "but not every one of our colleagues shared that enthusiasm, a fact Mark protected me from."

Luke McDonnell was pencilling the book during Stark's battle with the bottle, a job the artist says he got because "I was in the office and the editor, Mark Gruenwald, needed a script done in a hurry. I did it and they continued to go with me." McDonnell had been a longtime fan of the character. "I was a fan, especially of the Gene Colan/George Tuska issues. *Iron Man* seemed very cool to me, starting with the look of the armor, the high-techiness of the concept, the swinger alter ego who drove around in a Corvette, the sexy girlfriend. I remember really digging [this was the 1960s] the hipster letter column title 'Sock It to Shell-Head'!"

"Tony Stark has a vulnerability–invulnerability diametric going on," continues McDonnell. "He has a bad heart and addictive personality, but when he puts on the suit, he becomes nearly impervious to harm. Iron Man is the whole thing in reverse: invulnerability covering over the vulnerable." The addictive personality led to a downward spiral for Stark, and the artist recalls some chilling research he did. "Since I had to depict the ravages of alcoholism, I remember spending a night in New York City, sleeping on the street, to research the grunge of Tony's *Lost Weekend* life. Not the coziest way to spend twelve hours," McDonnell says with a grim chuckle. "I think it helped a lot in depicting the grime of the down-and-out sequences. I suppose I could have tried drinking myself into a stupor as well, but that would have been taking it a little too far."

Even as Tony Stark's relapse destroyed him, his

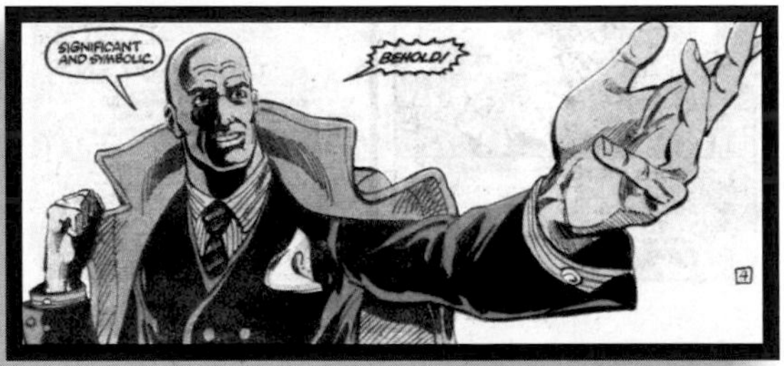
SIGNIFICANT AND SYMBOLIC.
BEHOLD!

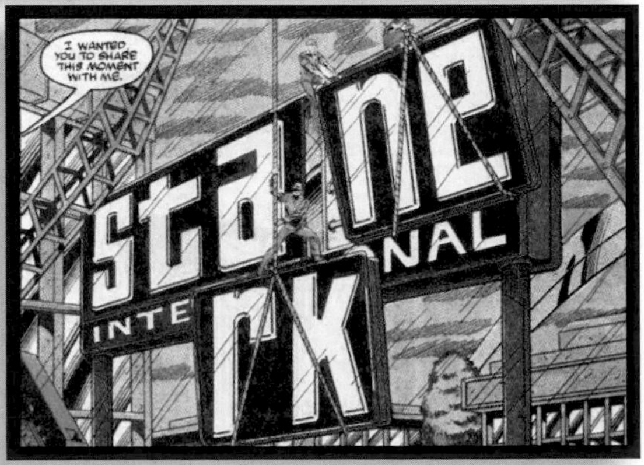
I WANTED YOU TO SHARE THIS MOMENT WITH ME.

Stane dismantled Stark Enterprises with ▲ the help of Indries Moomji (top).

faithful friend and employee Jim Rhodes, who now knew of Tony's dual identity, had made a fateful decision. The world needed an Iron Man, and in issue #169 (April 1983) Rhodey donned the red-and-gold armor to save the day.

I JUST REALIZED... I'M PUTTING ON THE SUIT. ME-- JIM RHODES!
SOON AS I DROP THIS HELMET ON I'LL ACTUALLY BE IRON MAN!
THEN WHAT?
TO BE CONTINUED.

THIS... THIS QUIETS THE SCREAMS, DULLS THE PAIN...
...HURRIES ALONG THE SLOW DYING...

▼ James Rhodes becomes Iron Man for the first time (left) and Tony Stark hits bottom (upper right).

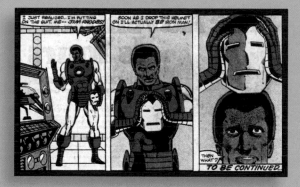

For O'Neil, who had created John Stewart as the African American replacement Green Lantern at DC a decade prior, the decision to create a minority hero wasn't even a question. "Rhodes was the most logical candidate to don the suit when Stark became incapacitated," O'Neil says. "His ethnicity was never any kind of issue."

McDonnell agrees with O'Neil's assessment. "I'm not sure if his being black was really much of a point in the story. It was more an issue of personality—Rhodes being a hothead, compared to Stark's cool rationalism, and how that affected things when they put on the tin suit." Eventually, Rhodes's anger became a story point as he became more aggressive, paranoid, and resentful of Stark. Although the temper problems were initially blamed on the armor's cerebral interfaces—which had been designed for Stark's brain—later stories would show that Rhodes was psychologically aggressive.

In *Iron Man* #182 (May 1984), Stark finally hit bottom after helping a pregnant woman deliver her baby in a snow-swept alley. Determined to rebuild his life and his fortunes, Stark went to the Silicon Valley in California with Rhodes—and siblings Clytemnestra and Morley Erwin—to found a new electronics company, named Circuits Maximus. Iron Man was now a member of the West Coast Avengers, but as his behavior became more violent and aggressive, Stark knew he would have to confront his friend. In issue #191 (February 1985), Stark donned a new set of armor that closely resembled his first gray suit, in order to take on Rhodey.

The following issue saw the battle royale of Iron Man versus Iron Man, but the two heroes eventually found their way to a reconciliation. Obadiah Stane

BLANG

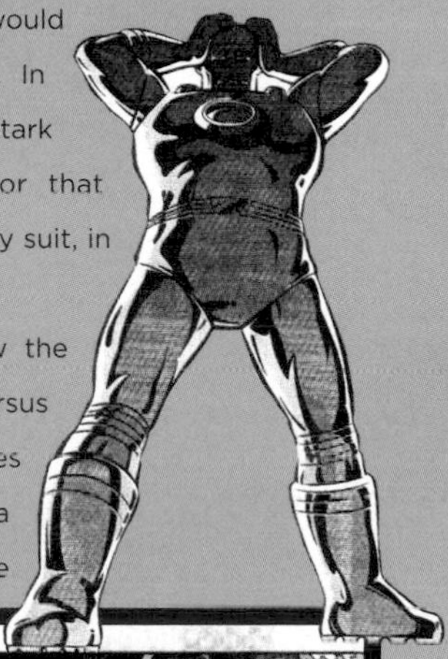

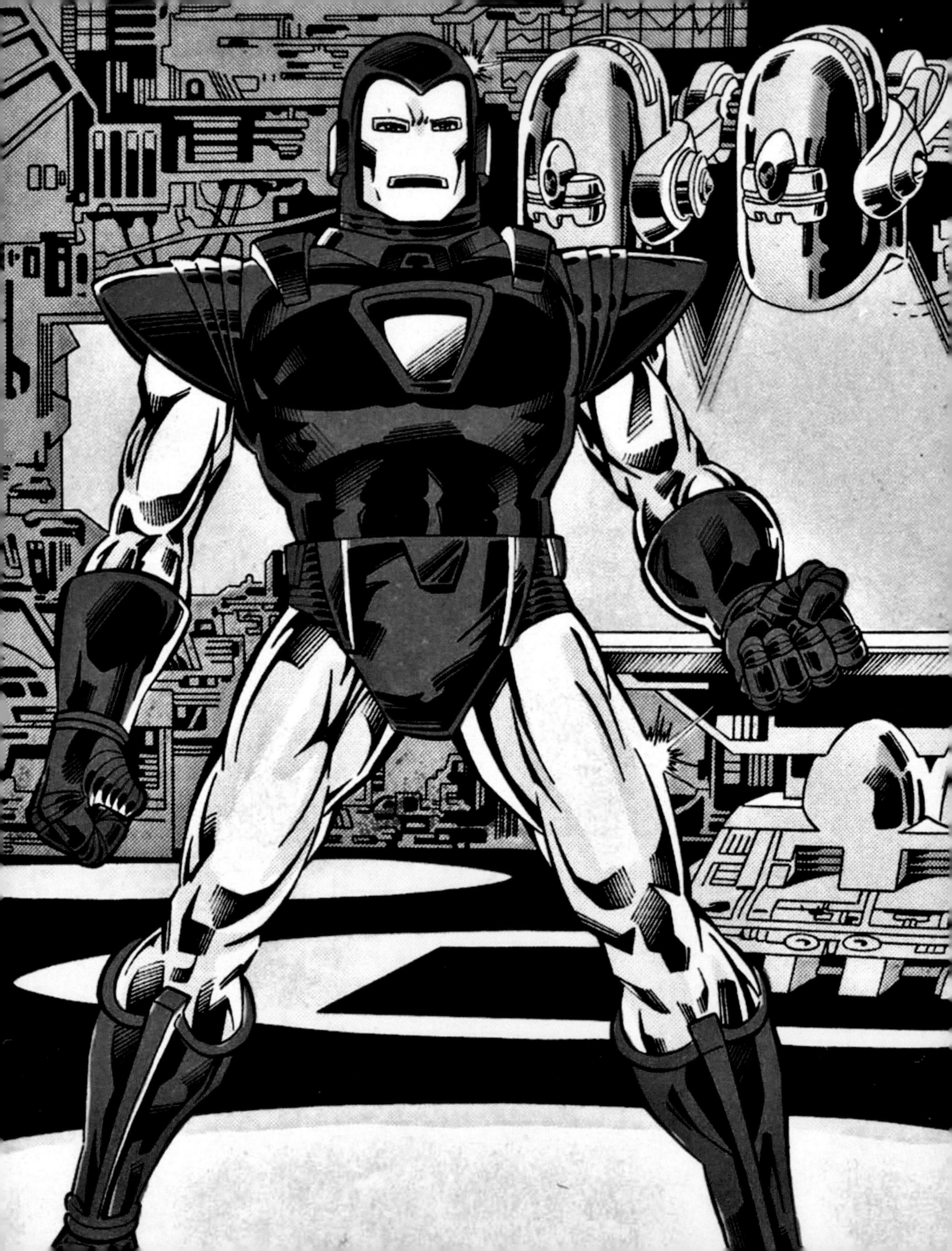

▼ Iron Monger looks good in blue (left), but the villains of A.I.M. (right) stood out in a crowd more.

waited in the wings, allying himself with the again villainous Madame Masque. By issue #200 (November 1985), Stane had destroyed Circuits Maximus, killed Morley Erwin, temporarily crippled Rhodes, and donned his own dark-colored suit of superpowered armor. The double-sized story saw Stark don an all-new set of Iron Man armor—dubbed the Silver Centurion armor due to its silver-and-red color scheme—and engage Stane as Iron Monger in mortal combat.

The anniversary issue was seen by fans as a major turning point in the saga of Tony Stark. Stane's martyrdom has haunted Stark for decades since, and their battle represented the hero literally—and allegorically—confronting his dark side. And the elements of stolen armor tech would come back to bedevil Tony in a major way.

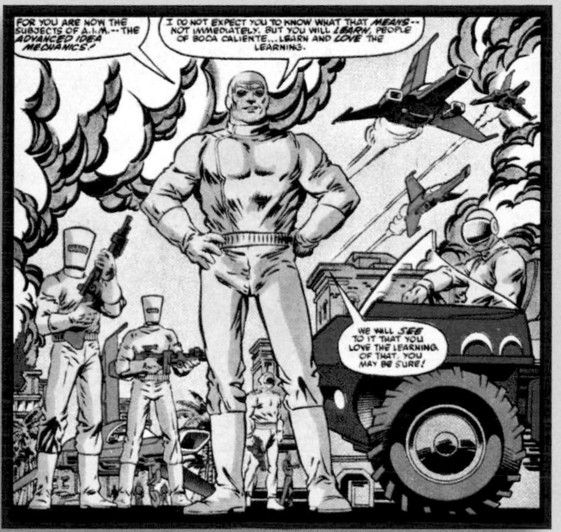

FOR YOU ARE NOW THE SUBJECTS OF A.I.M.-- THE ADVANCED IDEA MECHANICS!
I DO NOT EXPECT YOU TO KNOW WHAT THAT MEANS-- NOT IMMEDIATELY. BUT YOU WILL LEARN, PEOPLE OF BOCA CALIENTE... LEARN AND LOVE THE LEARNING.
WE WILL SEE TO IT THAT YOU LOVE THE LEARNING. OF THAT, YOU MAY BE SURE!

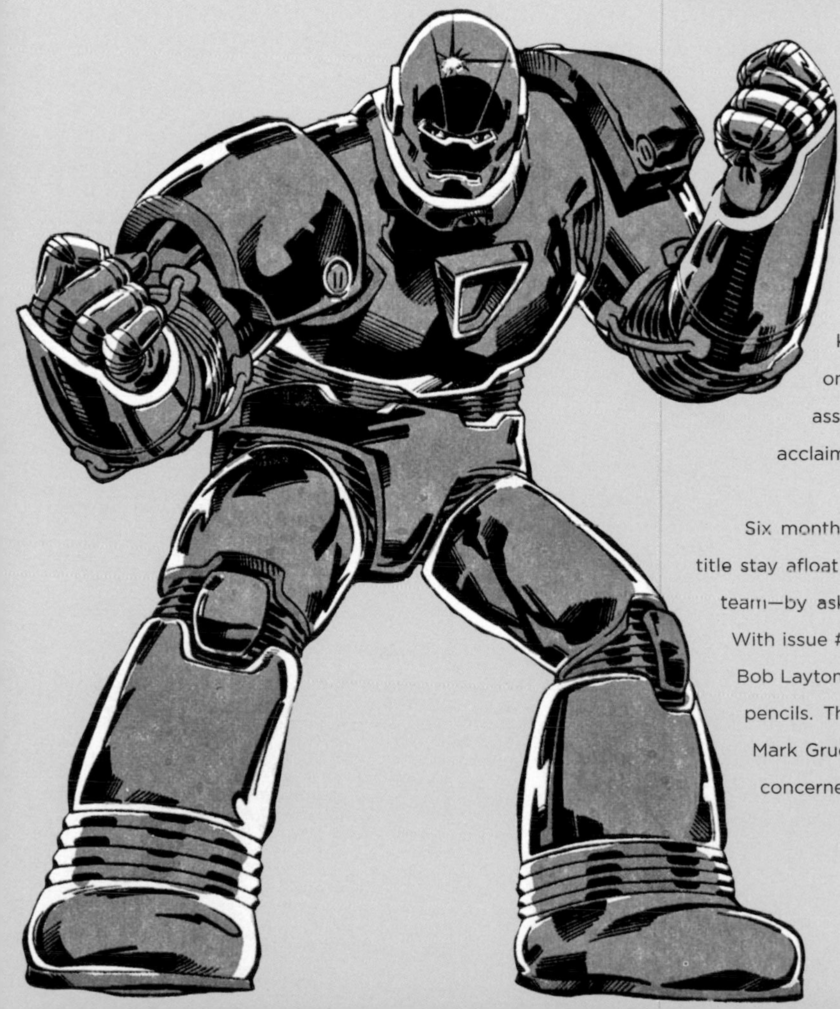

Following the literally mind-blowing conclusion of the Stane saga, O'Neil tied adventures in closely with *West Coast Avengers,* had Tony recover his fortunes from the late Stane, and put Iron Man in battle against A.I.M. (Advanced Idea Mechanics), Madame Masque, and giant-head-in-a-hoverchair Modok (Mental Organism Designed Only for Killing). Then, after more than four years on *Iron Man,* the writer moved on to other assignments at DC Comics, including critically acclaimed runs on *Batman* and *The Question.*

•

Six months of fill-in stories on *Iron Man* helped the title stay afloat until the editor could find a new creative team—by asking an older team to return to the fold! With issue #215 (February 1987), David Michelinie and Bob Layton returned to *Iron Man,* with Mark Bright on pencils. The pair made some decisions with editor Mark Gruenwald, including that as far as they were concerned, Tony Stark was now going to be a teetotaler and not drink any longer. Indicative of their positive new direction, they also established that Stark was going to build the new Stark Enterprises as a scientific think tank, absorbing smaller companies and their technologies and inventions.

The first ten issues of Michelinie and Layton's efforts saw Tony back in the armor and Rhodey out of the Super Hero game. "We had no idea that Jim Rhodes would be such a mainstay when David and I created him back in *Iron Man* #118," says Layton. "He evolved from a small supporting role into a large role in our storylines. I don't think Dave or I knew at the time how big he would become in the series. Remember, there weren't a lot of strong African American characters in the Marvel Universe at that time, and David and I wanted to give Tony a foil with a dissimilar background from his own. One of the biggest problems with comics in general is that few are couched in the real world these days. Everyone is a mutant or alien or cyborg. The supporting characters exist to ground the reader in a sense of reality. Through their eyes, we witness the fantastic and react in a believable manner. Rhodey was created by David and me to ground Tony Stark's fantastic exploits in some degree of reality. It was a mistake, in my opinion, to turn him [in later years] into War Machine. That dilutes his primary role by making him no different than the character he was created to support."

As expected, Layton also had some design and technological changes for Shellhead's armor. "My philosophy has been that the Iron Man technology should continue to evolve and streamline," says Layton, who admits that later, bulkier Iron Man armor "drives me nuts! I believe that the next twenty years is going to open up new avenues of scientific exploration that have only been dreamed of in the past. Tony Stark should always be on the cutting edge of that frontier."

With the behind-the-scenes return of Justin Hammer and Spymaster, an increasing number of older Iron Man foes began showing up. Many of them were armored, including Force, who was—in a throwback to Stan Lee's "reform a villain" scenario—welcomed to Stark Enterprises as an employee after his reformation. But these issues were all a precursor to the eight-part "Stark Wars" storyline in *Iron Man* #225–232, a tale that the promotions and later trade paperback collections would more specifically call "The Armor Wars."

"In 'The Armor Wars,' based on a suggestion by Jim Shooter, we had Tony discover that his technology had been stolen and used for weaponry by various Super Villains," says Michelinie. "We were thus able to explore how Tony felt when his inventions, which he had developed to improve life, were instead being used to destroy life. [He was forced to ask,] 'How many have drawn blood with my sword?' Unable to deal with delays caused by following procedure or by going through channels, Tony decides to take back the stolen tech on his own, breaking laws and crossing borders and lines he never thought he'd have to. And each choice gave us more insight into his character."

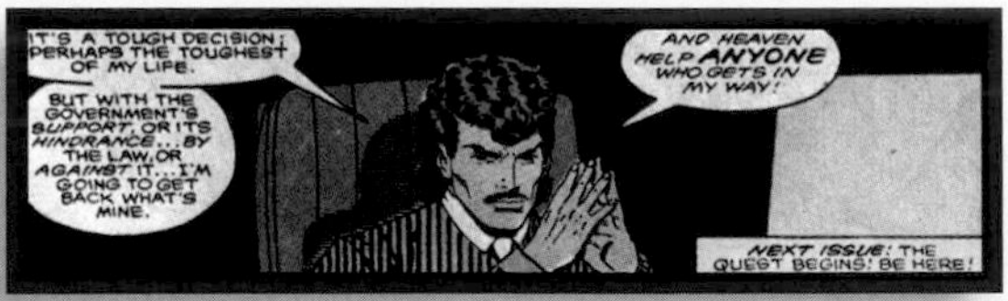

IT'S A TOUGH DECISION; PERHAPS THE TOUGHEST OF MY LIFE.
BUT WITH THE GOVERNMENT'S SUPPORT, OR ITS HINDRANCE... BY THE LAW, OR AGAINST IT... I'M GOING TO GET BACK WHAT'S MINE.
AND HEAVEN HELP ANYONE WHO GETS IN MY WAY!
NEXT ISSUE: THE QUEST BEGINS! BE HERE!

"The elements that make a good Iron Man story are the conflicts that create change in Tony Stark," says Layton. "Not unlike his armor, Tony is a work in progress, constantly adapting to challenges that life throws at him while trying to control the inner demons that sometimes push him down unexpected roads. Tony has an obsessive-compulsive personality—that is his kryptonite. The 'Armor War' saga that David and I did is a prime example of that compulsion that drives him to endanger everything he's built in order to do what he believes to be the right thing."

Over the course of the story, Iron Man hunted down

Tony Stark decides to get ▲ back what's rightfully his.

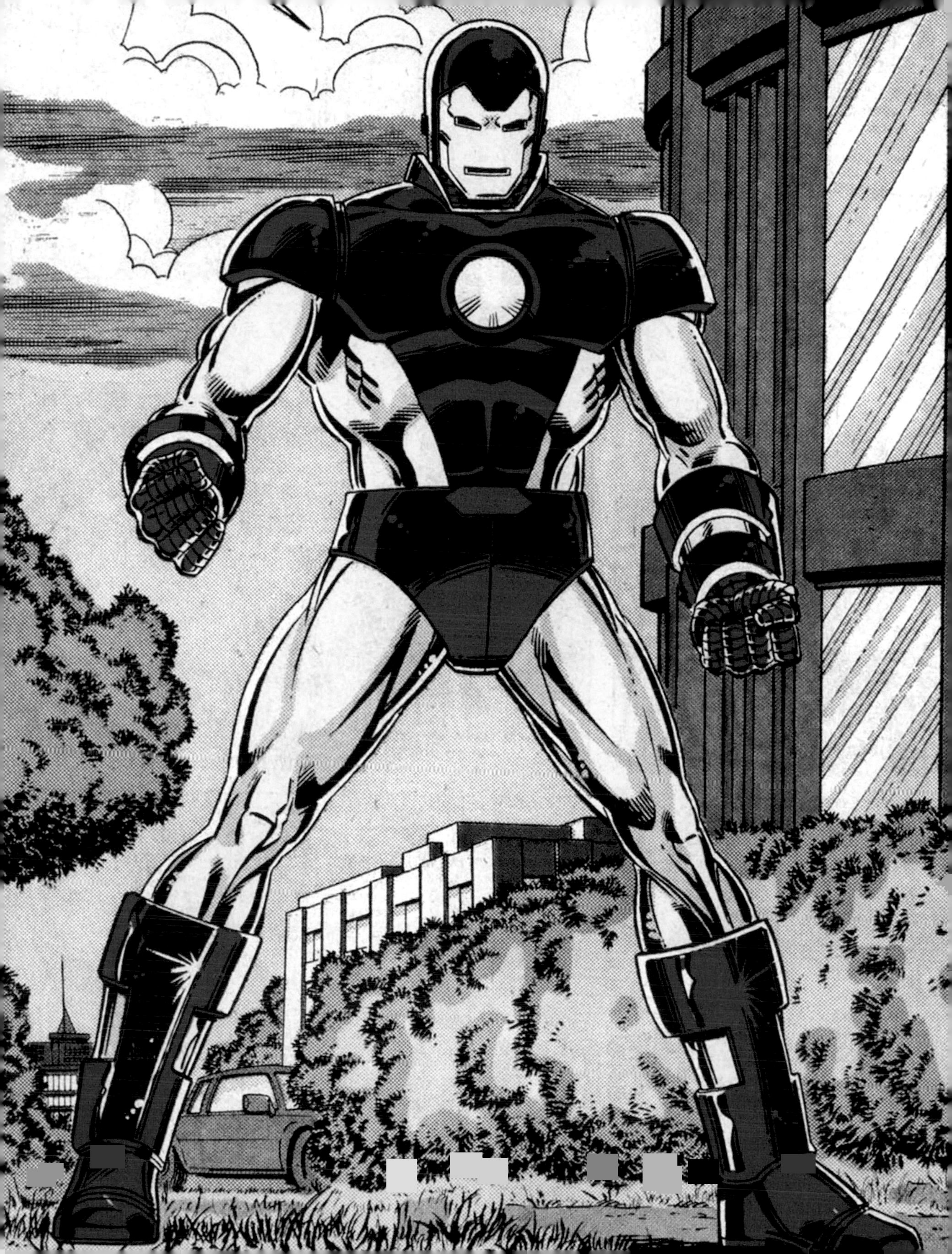

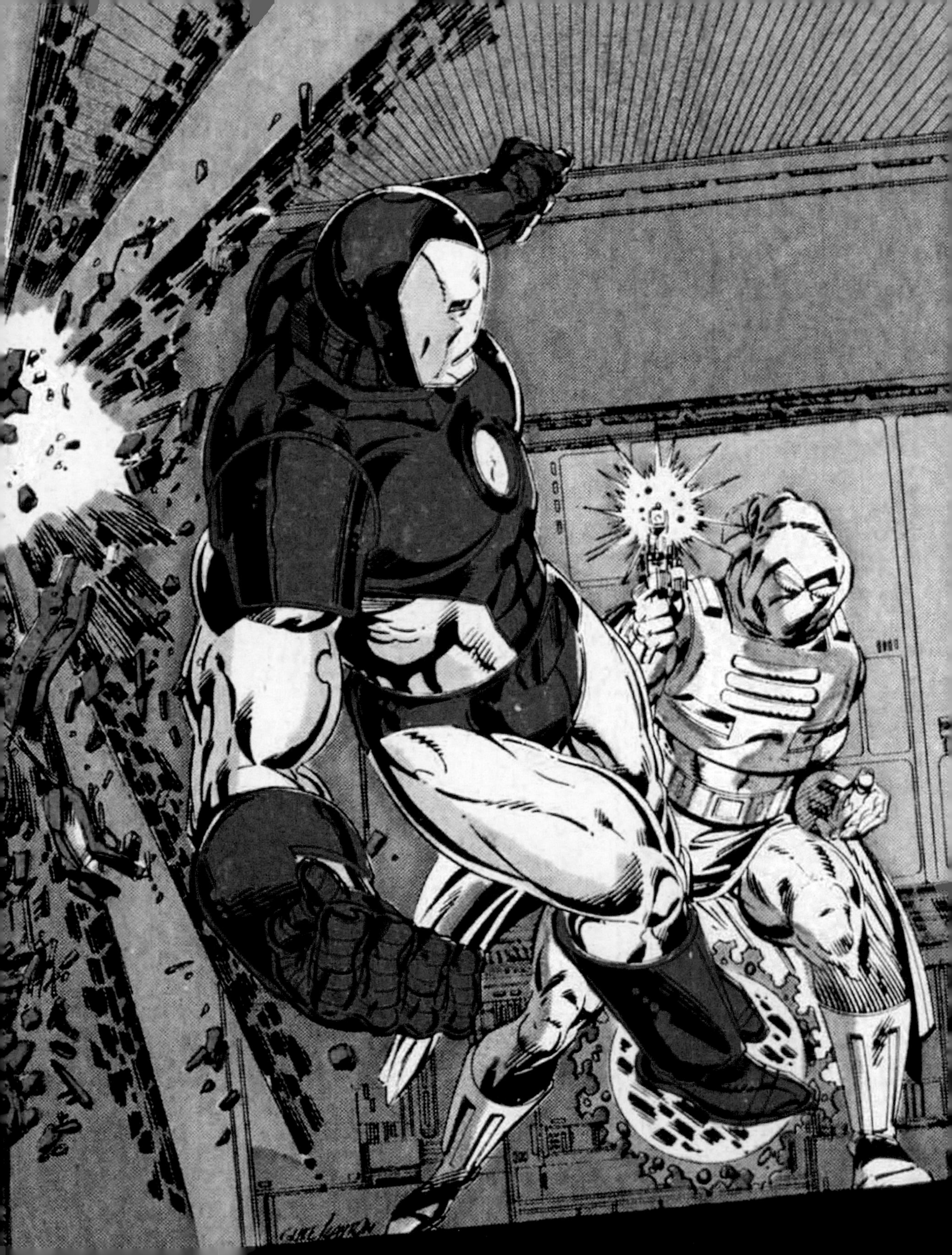

▼ The Armor Wars brought Iron Man into conflict with Titanium Man (top left) and Guardsman and Captain America (lower left), before he faced a refined Mandarin (right).

dozens of villains—and a few heroes—whose armors utilize stolen Stark technology. Unfortunately, Stark's crusade caused an international incident with the death of the Soviet Titanium Man, a double cross against S.H.I.E.L.D.,

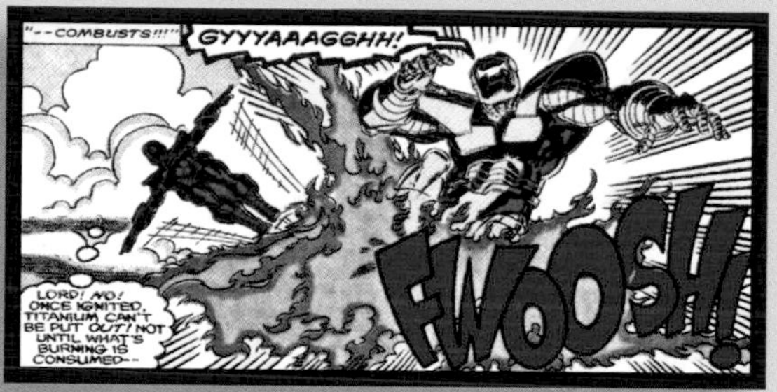
"--COMBUSTS!!!"
GYYYAAAGGHH!
LORD! NO! ONCE IGNITED, TITANIUM CAN'T BE PUT OUT! NOT UNTIL WHAT'S BURNING IS CONSUMED--
FWOOSH!

and a fight with underwater hero and former ally Stingray. Iron Man's negation of the Guardsmen armors also caused conflict at the Super Villain detention center known as The Vault, and created an ethical and philosophical rift between Iron Man and his Avenger compatriot Captain

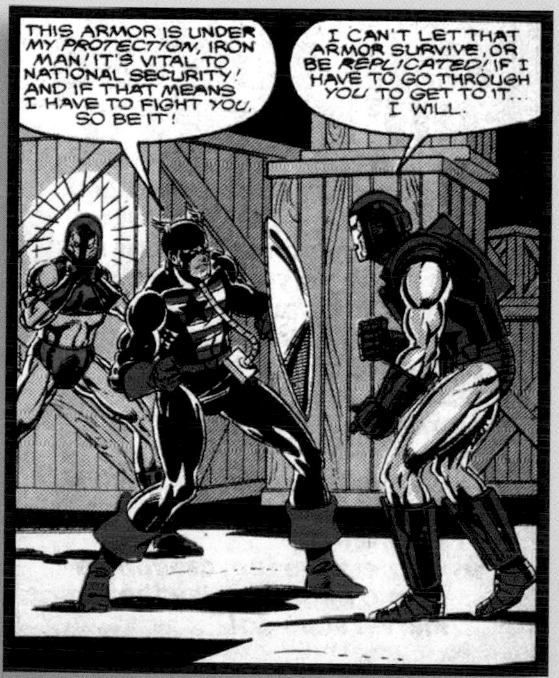
THIS ARMOR IS UNDER MY PROTECTION, IRON MAN! IT'S VITAL TO NATIONAL SECURITY! AND IF THAT MEANS I HAVE TO FIGHT YOU, SO BE IT!
I CAN'T LET THAT ARMOR SURVIVE, OR BE REPLICATED! IF I HAVE TO GO THROUGH YOU TO GET TO IT... I WILL.

America. In the end, Stark was forced to fake Iron Man's death (cue the destruction of the Silver Centurion armor) and debut the "new" Iron Man, a "new employee" wearing a shining red-and-gold set of armor.

Following the conclusion of the multipart epic, artist Jackson "Butch" Guice came aboard for pencilling duties, and half a dozen shorter stories found Tony foiling the plans of the Ghost . . . and even assisting Justin Hammer and teaming up with a trio of villains. Another familiar foe reappeared for a two-part story in issues #241–242: the Mandarin. Michelinie and Layton hadn't used the controversial villain in either of their runs prior to this, and tried to keep him stereotype-free.

"David and I avoided him entirely in our first run of the series for that very reason," admits Layton. "However, when we came back in the 'eighties for our second tour of duty, we decided to give the Mandarin a makeover. In our story, he was a Southeast Asian businessman, with a pri-

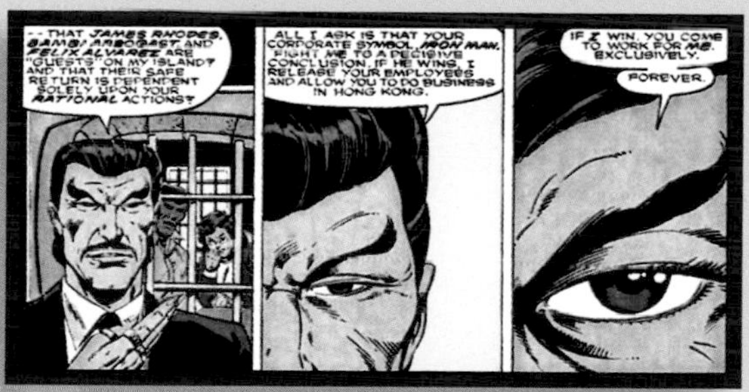
--THAT JAMES RHODES, BAMBI ARBOGAST AND FELIX ALVAREZ ARE "GUESTS" ON MY ISLAND? AND THAT THEIR SAFE RETURN IS DEPENDENT SOLELY UPON YOUR RATIONAL ACTIONS?
ALL I ASK IS THAT YOUR CORPORATE SYMBOL, IRON MAN, FIGHT ME TO A DECISIVE CONCLUSION. IF HE WINS, I RELEASE YOUR EMPLOYEES AND ALLOW YOU TO DO BUSINESS IN HONG KONG.
IF I WIN, YOU COME TO WORK FOR ME. EXCLUSIVELY.
FOREVER.

vate agenda of power grabbing. He wore modern clothing and lived in present-day society. Strangely enough, that didn't go over too well with some of the fans, who preferred the Fu Manchu mustache and flowing robes."

Michelinie concurs. "We tried to handle villains and heroes the same: as real people with real traits, both admirable and questionable. As for the Mandarin, we tried to show him as a patriot, a man who wanted to secure China's position of power in the world, to get his country the respect that it deserved. He did this through crime and terror, but his heart was in the right place. *Sort of.* That way his racial position could be understood and accepted without making him a stereotype or blanderizing him into a generic villain who happened to have yellow skin."

In the background of their second run of stories, the creative team was pushing Stark's latest flame, the obsessive Kathy Dare, closer to the edge of sanity, and she finally stepped over the line in *Iron Man* #242 (May 1989), with far-reaching consequences. "Another controversy we created was when we had Tony's current psycho-chicken girlfriend, Kathy Dare, go all *Basic Instinct* and shoot Tony in a fit of jealousy," says Michelinie of the issue's high-caliber finale. "That put Tony in a wheelchair and caused him to reevaluate a lot of things he'd taken for granted. We were going to do a riff on the old 'Spider-Man No More!' bit [a now classic Marvel story in which Spider-Man quit], but instead of having the civilian give up his hero identity, we were going to have Tony Stark start being Iron Man all the time, since he had normal mobility while wearing his armor. He eventually would have realized that his human side was truly the more important one."

BLAM

Although editorial supported the decision, Michelinie notes that "Marvel was a little leery of keeping Tony in a wheelchair, and asked us to limit the storyline to six issues. Ironically, when sales figures started coming in they asked us if we could extend the story to a year, but we'd already plotted the thing out. So we didn't get to go as far with it as we'd hoped." Indeed, by the second Doctor Doom story of issues #249–250, Tony was walking again, thanks to an experimental microchip implanted in his spine.

As the 1980s closed, Michelinie and Layton had departed *Iron Man* again, though Layton was planning on taking the reins as both writer and artist after a trio of fill-in issues got the schedule on track. However, the chance to become an integral part of new start-up comic publisher called Valiant had Layton jumping ship prior to beginning a second planned "Armor Wars" epic, though he laid ground for it in issues #254 (March 1990) and #256 (May 1990).

One other creator put armor on Iron Man in a cutting-edge way: In the original graphic novel *Iron Man: Crash* (April 1988), writer-artist Mike Saenz used an early Apple II computer and programs he and others created to illustrate the graphic novel nearly completely

IRON MAN
CRASH
THE FIRST COMPUTER GENERATED GRAPHIC NOVEL
BY MIKE SAENZ

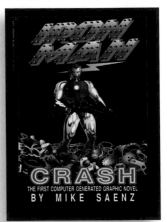

Kathy Dare shoots Tony Stark. ▲

on computer. Though it seems a bit crude by today's computer-art standards, the technique in *Crash* was revolutionary at the time, and matching technological hero Iron Man to a computer-generated graphic novel, in a story about the rise of modern technology, was a marriage made in twenty-four-bit color heaven.

•

As of *Iron Man* #258 (July 1990), John Byrne took over the writing duties on the series, with John Romita Jr. and Bob Wiacek on art. As both an artist and writer, Byrne had been blazing a trail through Marvel since the mid-1970s, after working at Charlton. His work on *X-Men* won awards and fans by the score, revitalizing the title into a powerhouse; his later critically acclaimed runs with the Canadian super-team he created for Marvel, Alpha Flight, and Marvel's premier team, the Fantastic Four, were tour de forces. Following his relaunch of *Superman* for DC Comics in 1986–1987, he had returned to Marvel to tell tales in *Avengers West Coast* and *The Sensational She-Hulk*.

"I had not followed Iron Man in his own magazine for years, but I enjoyed his presence in *The Avengers*," Byrne says, adding that while he feels Iron Man is most interesting due to his technology, Tony Stark succeeds as a character who is "a classic example of someone who is doing the right thing for the right reason."

Byrne recalls that he got the job because "Howard Mackie, then the editor, called me one day and asked if I had any *Iron Man* stories I'd like to tell. At the time, I had none. By the end of the day, I had three or four. The first arc I wrote was dictated by the title. Marvel had already solicited 'Armor Wars II' when the team before me left, so I had to come up with something that fit the title." The resulting storyline—which included few similarities with its predecessor—saw the return of the Living Laser, Rhodes's return to wearing armor, and a mysterious villain named Kearson DeWitt who had quite a grudge against Stark. And the main hero? Pains in his recovery caused

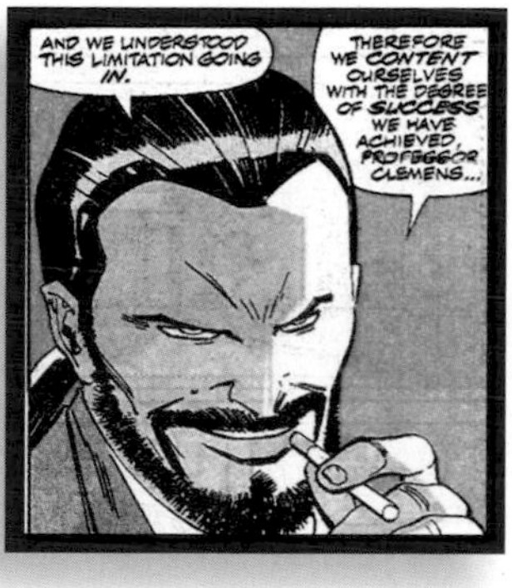
AND WE UNDERSTOOD THIS LIMITATION GOING IN.
THEREFORE WE CONTENT OURSELVES WITH THE DEGREE OF SUCCESS WE HAVE ACHIEVED, PROFESSOR CLEMENS...

Tony to use "encephalo" circuitry to make his armor function via remote control! Now no one was in the Iron Man suit, and Tony could control it from afar.

Having created the visual look of Rhodes when he guest-drew *Iron Man* #118 (January 1979), Byrne enjoyed coming back to the character. He wasn't as keen on the villains, however. "I was largely unimpressed with Iron Man's Rogues Gallery when I started, but JR [Romita] did such a spectacular job of drawing, and in some instances reimagining, them—the Living Laser, for instance—that I was blown away. Those pages were a joy to script."

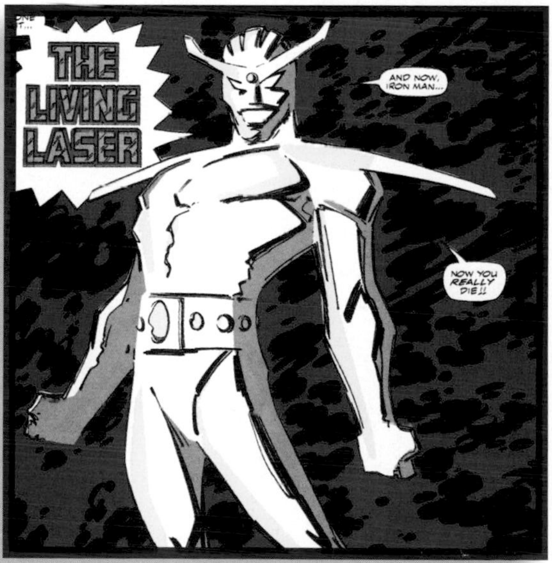
THE LIVING LASER
AND NOW, IRON MAN...
NOW YOU REALLY DIE!!

Even in the midst of "Armor Wars II," Byrne was planting a subplot to bring back the one villain he felt was integral to Iron Man's past. He didn't feel politically hampered

▲ Old villains with new looks included the Living Laser.

by charges some fans had made about the Mandarin. "Calling the Mandarin a racial stereotype is like calling Captain America a racial stereotype," Byrne says. "The Mandarin is representative of a particular part of Chinese culture. He's also the meanest mother in the valley. That's how I played him." Indeed, many Iron Man fans contend that Byrne's Mandarin was probably the best version of Stark's archnemesis ever portrayed in the comics.

Byrne also made Mandarin a part of Iron Man's origin, revealing that Wong-Chu had been an agent working for the Mandarin in "Southeast Asia" (not specifically Vietnam). "These days, my work is watched closely by many fans, looking for me to slip up," says Byrne. "When I did *Iron Man,* I seemed not to be under such close scrutiny. I eliminated the Vietnam War from his origin and made the Mandarin a part of it, and I guess I did it with such sleight of hand that no one noticed!"

During the revised origin, Byrne got a new artist for the book in Paul Ryan, who had previously worked on *Avengers West Coast* (with Byrne), *Avengers, Quasar, Squadron Supreme,* and others for Marvel. "When John Romita Jr. decided to leave, John Byrne called me and asked if I would like to draw *Iron Man,*" Ryan says. "I had been following Iron Man since his first appearance in *Tales of Suspense*. I just loved that character. A real self-made man both in his civilian identity and in his more heroic role . . . We know that he is a tragic figure. With all his money, charm, looks, and intelligence, he is a prisoner of a metal chest plate that keeps his heart beating. Yet despite his circumstances he chooses to don this amazing suit of armor, of his own invention, and fight for justice."

As for Iron Man himself, Ryan compares him to another famous hero. "Iron Man is a unique character in that he is constantly reinventing himself, improving his armor and its ancillary devices and weapons. Superman, once he reached maturity, has limits to his abilities . . . pretty far-reaching limits, but limits nonetheless. Batman is always upgrading his arsenal in the war against crime. I guess you could say that Iron Man is similar to Batman, in that respect, but on a grander, more powerful scale."

Like Byrne, Ryan was happy to take on the Mandarin. "The Mandarin is, in my mind, the perfect archvillain for Iron Man. Intelligent, charismatic, and aristocratic . . . Descended from Chinese royalty, he sees himself as above everyone he meets. His Rings of Power seem almost mystical. He's an interesting counterpoint to the technological power harnessed by Tony Stark."

The redesigns for the villain were in place by the time Ryan debuted. "All the heavy lifting was done for me," Ryan says with a laugh. "John Byrne and my pencilling predecessor, John Romita Jr., came up with the look and feel of the Mandarin for the subplot that would eventually culminate in the 'Dragonseed Saga.' The Mandarin's look was revamped to make him look more like a highborn Chinese lord. He was treated with respect and dignity. Gone was the scale-plated headpiece with the mask or the stripped-down, bare-chested Super Villain costume that followed."

The "Dragonseed Saga" in *Iron Man* #272–275 resurrected a past Marvel monster character, Fin Fang Foom, and tied him in to the Mandarin's revised origin. Ryan recalls it as his favorite

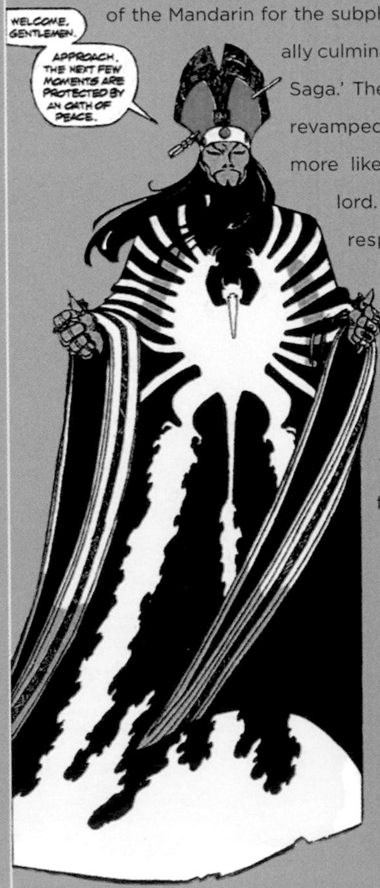
WELCOME, GENTLEMEN.
APPROACH. THE NEXT FEW MOMENTS ARE PROTECTED BY AN OATH OF PEACE.

▲ The Mandarin rises like a phoenix from the ashes.

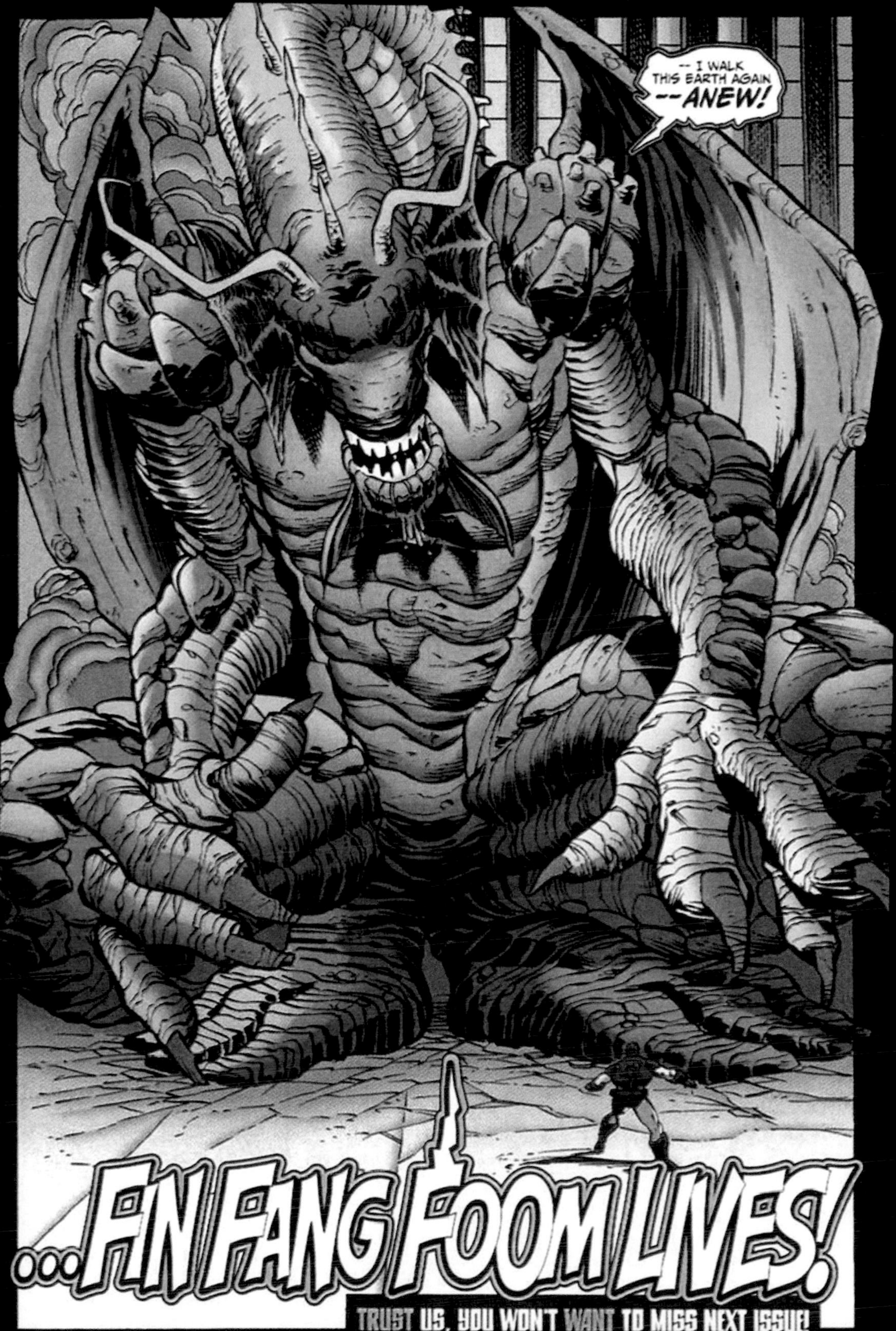
-- I WALK THIS EARTH AGAIN --ANEW!
...FIN FANG FOOM LIVES!
TRUST US, YOU WON'T WANT TO MISS NEXT ISSUE!

storyline. "I got a chance to add a little more than graphite to the project. John took Tony Stark to China where Tony sought a cure for nerve damage to his spinal column. While in China, Tony ran up against the Mandarin, an old wizard, Fin Fang Foom, *and* his brothers. John set up eight pages of exposition in each issue and let me run with the remaining fourteen pages where Iron Man, in various incarnations, battled the aforementioned bad guys!"

Byrne's final two issues, #276–277, saw Iron Man teaming up with Black Widow in Russia, a return to themes from the *Tales of Suspense* days. Ryan remembers that the story "involved the Black Widow and a Russian plot to start a nuclear war. These stories seemed natural for the Iron Man character who, in his earliest adventures, was always at odds with the Reds."

Recalling his time on the series, Byrne praises his artists, and says, "Writing *Iron Man* was one of the more pleasant gigs I have had . . . then there was an editorial change and the last few issues have a bit of a sour taste." Byrne didn't have to dwell on the taste for long, however; he soon created his own series called *Next Men* for Dark Horse, and he has since worked on popular titles including *Spider-Man, Namor the Sub-Mariner, X-Men, Superman & Batman,* and *Justice League.*

A STRANGE SENSATION...
...TO ADD TO A LIFE INCREASINGLY DOMINATED BY STRANGE SENSATIONS.
DID I HAVE THE LEAST IDEA, I WONDER, WHAT I WAS GETTING INTO THAT DAY IN THE JUNGLE WHEN I FIRST PUT ON THE ARMOR OF IRON MAN?
I CAME BACK TO THE STATES. I MADE MY MODIFICATIONS. MANY MODIFICATIONS, IN FACT.
AND FOUND THAT I NO LONGER HAD A LIFE TO ENTIRELY CALL MY OWN.
I WAS A MILLIONAIRE INDUSTRIALIST WHEN I WENT INTO THAT JUNGLE.

Iron Man changed his armor often... ▲

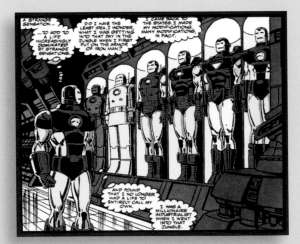

Ryan stayed on for a few more issues that featured an editorially mandated crossover story, but recalls the *Iron Man* run with fondness, even though he found it "challenging. I was working on two books a month. If I had to name one challenge I guess it would have to be the technology. Having to design backgrounds, gadgets, weapons and different armor that looked a little beyond cutting-edge . . .

"The fact that Iron Man was not relegated to one armor design was fun. It brought a little variety to the art chores." Still, Ryan recalls one contribution he made in his stories to the armor that took a bit to live down. "The only thing I designed was a suit of Space Armor. It got beat up a

EASY, EASY... LET THE SYSTEM THINK I'M JUST ANOTHER SENSOR GRID AT FIRST...
...THEN SWITCH OVER--TRICK IT INTO CLASSIFYING ME AS PART OF SELF-DIAGNOSTIC...

little around the Marvel Bullpen. Some compared the helmet design to the then-current hairstyle of Mary Tyler Moore. It became known as the Mary Tyler Moore helmet."

Having followed *Iron Man* with a mammoth run on *Fantastic Four,* plus the adventures of Batman, Flash, and Spider-Man in comics and the Phantom for newspaper syndication, Ryan sums up his feelings for the armored Avenger by noting that the concept works "on several levels. There are elements of the human condition in the premise that adults can relate to. There are gadgets, Super Villains, action, adventure, and power that the teens can appreciate. Tony Stark was everything little boys wanted to be. He had money, toys, and beautiful women. What more could little testosterone-charged adolescents ask for? For that matter, what grown man wouldn't envy Mr. Stark?"

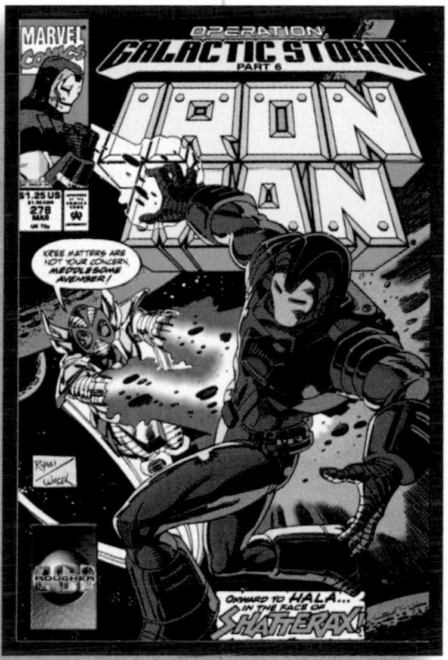
MARVEL COMICS
OPERATION: GALACTIC STORM PART 6
IRON MAN
KREE MATTERS ARE NOT YOUR CONCERN, MEDDLESOME AVENGER!
ONWARD TO HALA... IN THE FACE OF SHATTERAX!

•

Crossovers between comic book titles were not a common occurrence prior to Stan Lee's Marvel renaissance of the 1960s. Although teams of company-owned Super Heroes had gathered together as far back as DC's 1940s *All Star Comics* super-team, and the Justice Society of America and many Fawcett heroes would guest-star in each others' stories, the concept of one book "crossing over" into another was mostly created by—and certainly perfected by—Lee and his Marvel creators. Spider-Man appeared in *Fantastic Four,* the X-Men appeared in *Iron Man,* Thor appeared in *Hulk . . .* it sometimes seemed that the Marvel Universe was really only a neighborhood where everyone knew everyone and costume-clad battles were as common as a backyard barbecue.

By the 1980s, comic book crossovers were not only commonplace industrywide but often preceded a clear spikes in sales. This led to the idea of the companywide crossover "event" in which most of Marvel's heroes (or DC's) would gather for one giant multipart story that had tie-in issues in the regular series' books. The first *Marvel Superheroes Secret Wars* series in 1984 had been the industry's first major series of this sort, and while it presented major changes for some (such as Spider-Man's troublesome black costume), it had affected Iron Man (James Rhodes) mostly by giving him some armor upgrades. A resulting toy line from Mattel *did* give Iron Man a new hand-sized plastic action figure, however. Iron Man's involvement in several subsequent crossover events of the 1980s was even less important to the series' forward momentum.

With *Iron Man* #278 (March 1992), the book was brought into a major Marvel crossover called *Operation: Galactic Storm,* a nineteen-part three-month storyline that included all of Marvel's "Avengers family" series: *Avengers, Avengers West Coast, Captain America, Iron Man, Thor, Wonder Man,* and *Quasar.* In the sprawling story, the alien races Kree and Shi'ar were at war, and when the conflict threatened Earth, the world's Avengers rallied to the defense. The *Iron Man* issue saw the debut of writer Len Kaminski, while new regular penciller Kevin Hopgood would take over the art with #280 (May 1992), bringing a strong, edgy line work that pleased fans.

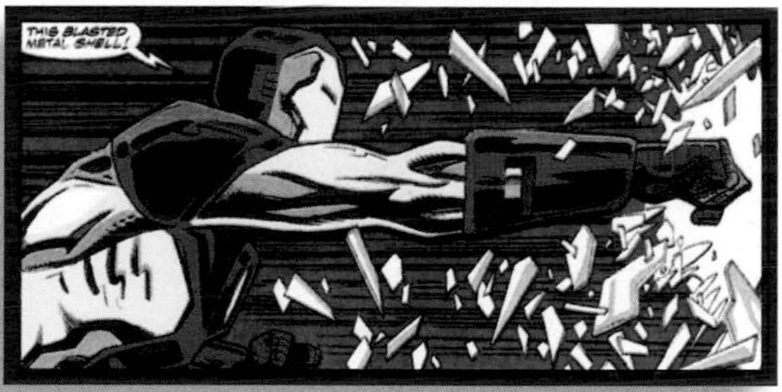
THIS BLASTED METAL SHELL!

▲ ...but Tony Stark wasn't always happy in the suit.

Kaminski's strong suits were science and technology, so his first storyline assignment was fortuitous, allowing him to introduce Stark's upgraded Space Armor. In a past interview, the author emphasized that the confluence and interaction of humanity and technology were of major importance, given the rise of computerized nervous system interfaces, biological engineering, and mapping the

Doctor Doom toasts a fallen ▼
foe he respected.

human genome. "I think Iron Man is a very good character to examine these things through, not just because he's a Super Hero with a technological base, but because Tony Stark is the type of person who's making these kinds of decisions in the world right now. He's in charge of a company that deals with biotechnology, that deals with electronics and computers, hardware and software, pretty much all things on the cutting edge of science . . . All in all, Tony Stark is probably more powerful than Iron Man is."

Unfortunately, by the end of *Operation: Galactic Storm,* Stark's health was ever-more problematic, and the following several issues would see it worsen. Tony developed a new set of black-and-silver armor known as War Machine, designed as a militaristic full-combat prototype armor with ultradestructive capabilities and firepower. Although the War Machine armor was a popular visual with fans and editorial, the concept itself wasn't consistent with Stark's philosophies—since it was designed for rampant destruction and durability—or his acknowledged engineering genius. Nevertheless, in the new armor Stark went on the offense against the troublesome Justin Hammer yet again, even as his health precipitously declined.

"When I took over the book, for the past year's worth of stories, John Byrne had kept talking about Tony Stark dying," said Kaminski. " 'Tony Stark is dying, he's definitely, definitely dying. There's no chance he's going to survive.' Byrne had had Stark himself accept this. It seemed like the best thing to do was to have him die." Thus, in *Iron Man* #284 (September 1992), Tony Stark appeared to die, while James Rhodes took over full-time both the job of running Stark Enterprises and the donning of the War Machine armor.

As the thirtieth anniversary of Iron Man's creation appeared on the horizon, Tony Stark may have been "dead," but the world of Marvel's armored adventurer was about to expand light-years beyond his original creators' wildest dreams.

LET US NOW DRINK TO THE MEMORY OF A WORTHY OPPONENT.
WE DECREE A DAY OF MOURNING THROUGHOUT THE LAND.

DAILY BUGLE TUESDAY, JULY 21, 1992

OBITUARIES

ANTHONY E. "TONY" STARK

STARK — Anthony Edward, died Saturday, July 11 at St. Matthew's hospital in Palo Alto, California after a long illness. Humanitarian, inventor, and financial genius, Mr. Stark was the son of Howard Stark, the founder of Stark Industries, a company known for weapons and munitions manufacturing during World War II. Inheriting the company at age 21 and renaming it Stark International, Anthony Stark transformed it into a multimillion dollar conglomerate. After losing control of the company in a hostile takeover, he eventually founded Stark Enterprises, one of the nation's leading manufacturers of high-tech computers and electronics. An acknowledged scientific and financial genius, Stark will long be remembered as one of the greatest minds of our time, whose accomplishments rival those of Thomas Edison, Albert Einstein and Reed Richards. A renowned philanthropist, his many charitable contributions included technological and financial support of the super hero and peace keeping groups including SHIELD, The Avengers and Avengers West Coast. Memorial services will be held for close friends only at an undisclosed location.

STARK ENTERPRISES PRICES PLUMMET

The business world was rocked yesterday by the announcement of the death of Anthony Stark, founder, chairman and CEO of Stark Enterprises. On the heels of the announcement, the Stock Exchange reported a 15 point drop in the price fo Stark Enterprises common stock as nervous investors panicked over the unsure future of the industrial giant. The stock listed a closing price of only $22.50 per share: the lowest price in the company's history.

In a hastily called press conference, board members assured the financial community that Mr. Stark's death will in no way change daily operations. Spokewoman Marcy Pearson said, "It'll be business as usual." But to many investors who saw Stark as not only the head, but mind, body and soul of the company, Stark Enterprises may well be destined for the same fate as its founder. Says one industry insider, "SE is a solid company, but, with the falling stock price, the burden of the recently acquired Stane International, and without Stark at the helm, it could easily fall prey to a hostile takeover. Corporate buzzards are already circling overhead."

Anonymous reports indicate that one well-known corporate raider has already expressed such interest — Stark's old adversary, Justin Hammer. A spokesman for Hammer denies the rumor. Said the spokesman, "Mr. Hammer is greatly saddened by the loss of Mr. Stark and at the present time has no plans for a leveraged buy-out of his company." Another raider with a possible interest in SE is business man Edwin Chord.

(cont. on p. 45, col. 2)

Friends Mourn

The untimely death of wealthy financier and international jet-setter Anthony "Tony" Stark has brought forth an outpouring of sympathy from his friends in the super hero community.

Gathering at both East and West Coast locations of Avengers' Mansion, super-powered mourners of Stark were devastated by the grim news. On hand was the USAgent, who commented, "Yeah, he was an okay guy, suppyling the government with munitions and that sort of thing. But he seemed to go a little soft as time went on. Tough guy to figure, I guess."

Iron Man, an Avenger and Stark's own bodyguard, was unavailable for comment.

On the east coast, Avengers leader Captain America told reporters, "Without Tony's help, there never could have been an Avengers. The world owes him a debt of gratitude that can never be repaid." Stark's close friend and confidant, James Rhodes, was reportedly in seclusion and not available for comment. SHIELD Director Col. Nicholas Fury, who openly disagreed with Stark when the millionaire announced that he would cease munitions production, also declined comment.

A bachelor his whole life, Stark leaves behind a vast fortune with no close relatives as heirs. This has led to widespread speculation that

(continued on page 48)

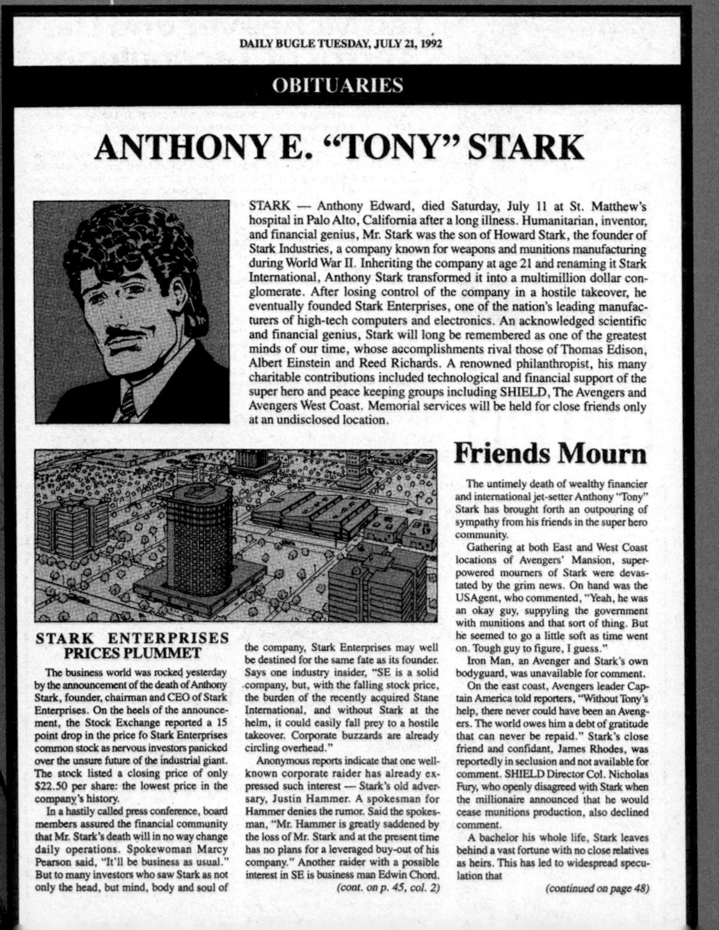

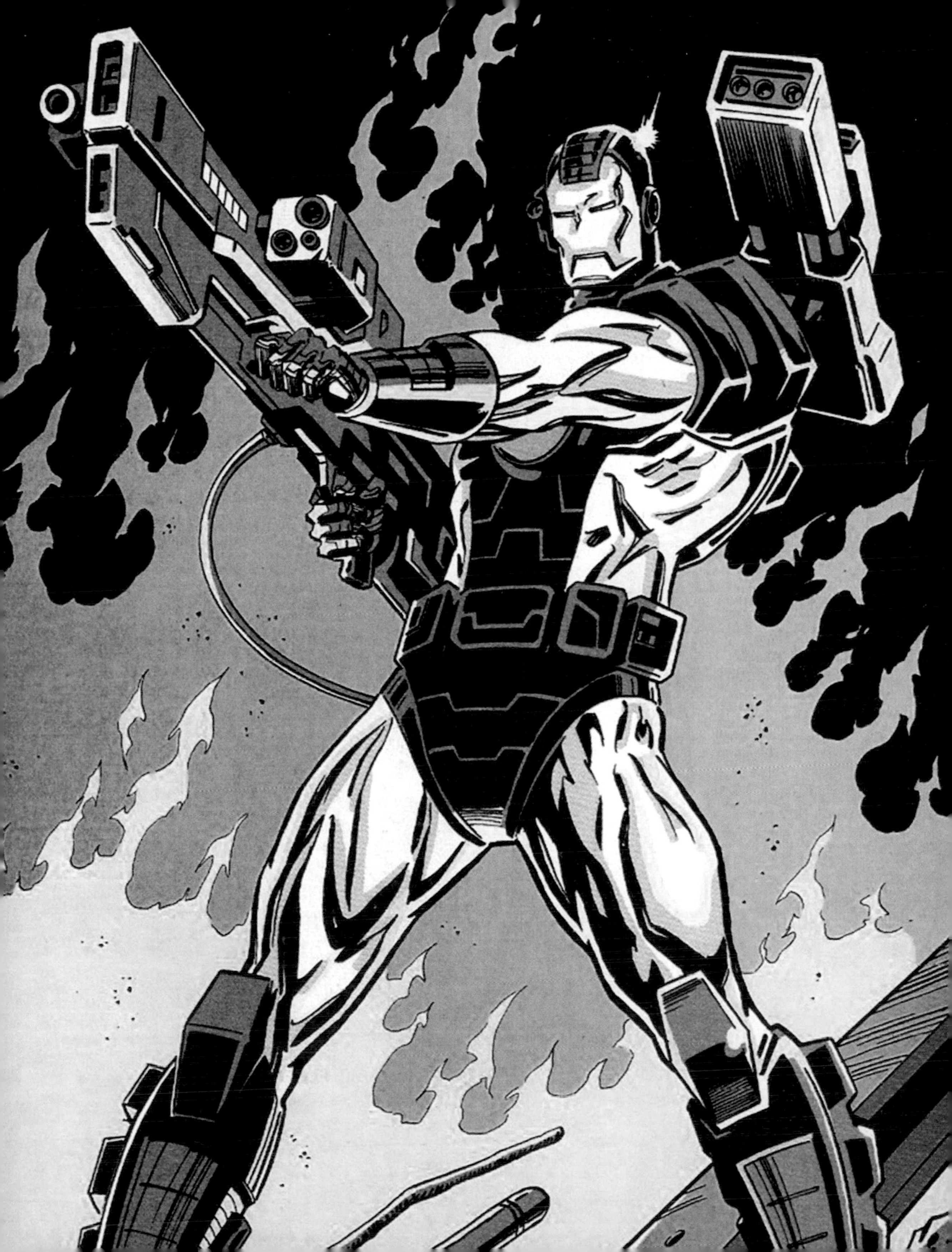

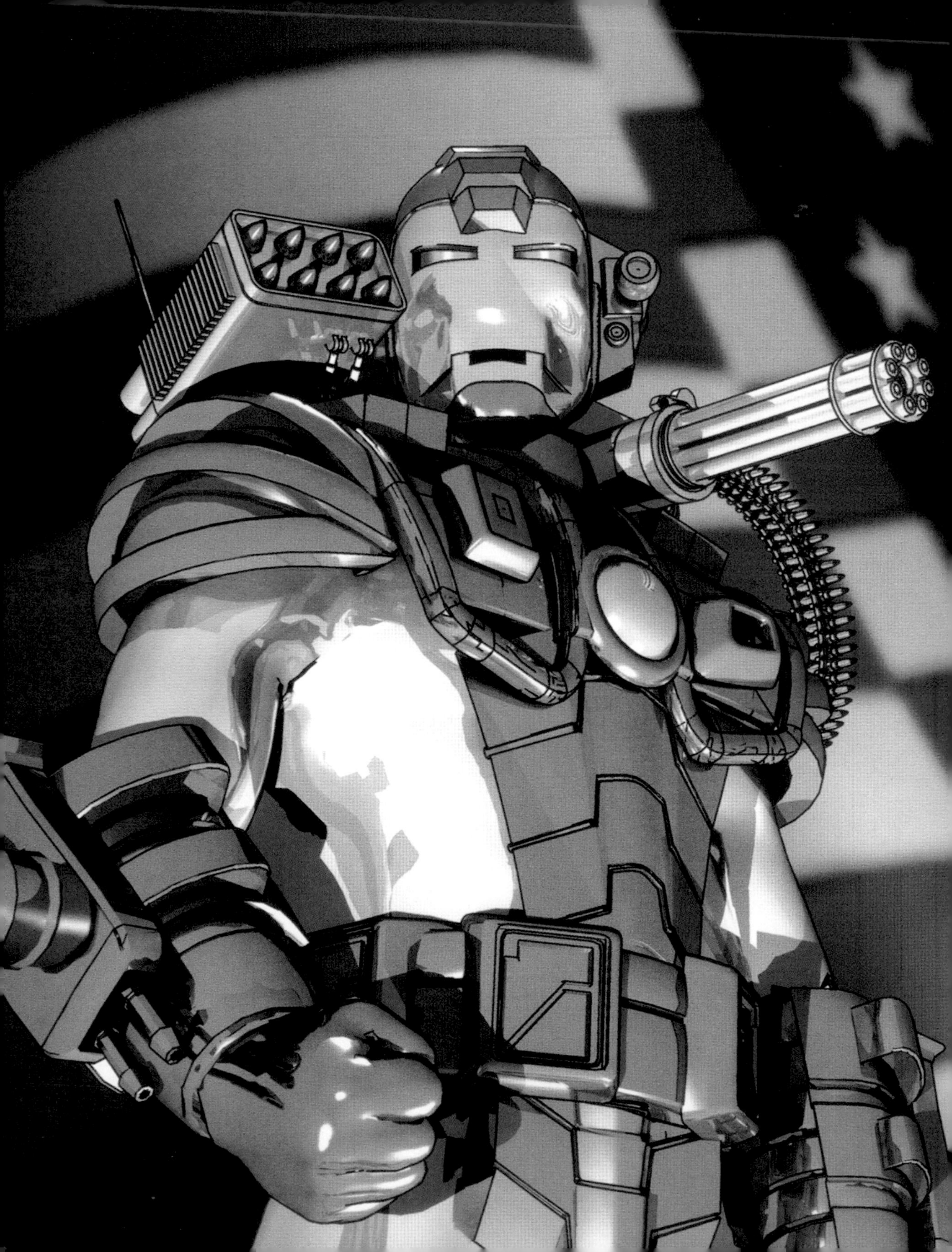

CHAPTER 4

DEATH AND REBIRTH AND DEATH AND REBIRTH AND . . .

In the pages of *Iron Man* #284 (September 1992), writer Len Kaminski knew that readers wouldn't believe that Marvel was really killing off an old-line hero—especially given that the character was about to face his thirtieth anniversary—so he let readers in on the truth immediately. Tony wasn't really dead, just in cryogenic suspended animation; the work of Stark scientists—and Tony's own "rebooting" of his mind and central nervous system using technological enhancements—allowed Stark to heal himself.

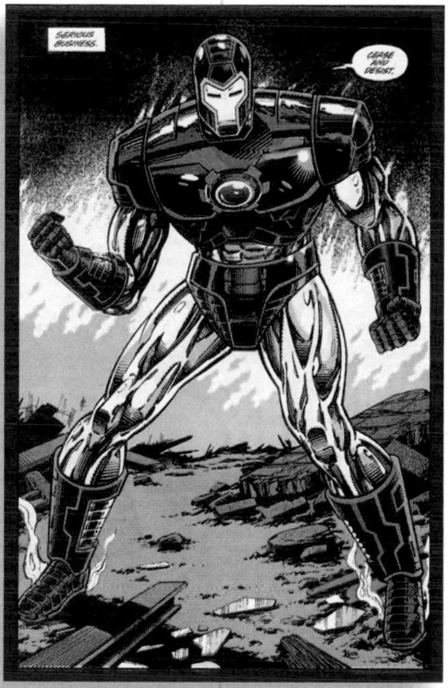
SERIOUS BUSINESS.
CEASE AND DESIST.

Unfortunately, Stark had made very few others aware of his plans, and James Rhodes was one of those out of the loop. When Stark was "reborn," in issues #289–290 (February–March 1993), the old friends acrimoniously parted ways, with Rhodes taking the War Machine armor and a still-incapacitated Tony using a special headset to use a virtual-reality-like remote control on a brand-new red-and-gold Telepresence Armor for Iron Man. Artist Kevin Hopgood has said that he enjoyed "drawing all the technology surrounding Iron Man and Stark Enterprises. In my own head, I was drawing a science-fiction comic and not a Super Hero comic . . . I'm a big manga fan, so a lot of my inspiration came from things like *Appleseed* and *Akira*. Big Japanese robot stuff generally. Also movies that were out at the time like *Terminator* and *Aliens*." It was another film that inspired Hopgood's take on War Machine, however. "The basic idea for War Machine was that he's a walking tank. I had *Robocop* at the back of my mind. The black-and-silver color scheme is what made the design take off, I think."

In April 1993, Marvel published *The Iron Manual*, a comic written as if by Tony Stark himself, that featured technical schematics of the Iron Man armors by Eliot R. Brown. "Tony Stark, Iron Man, will never let us forget that a balance can, indeed must be, struck between technology and humanity," Brown wrote in the *Manual's* afterword. "For a suit of armor, standing alone without a person inside, as formidable and beautiful as

▲ As War Machine takes flight, Tony Stark develops a new armor.

Marvel had big plans for Iron Man's anniversary (left), ▼ which included an Iron Legion (upper right) and a split between Tony and Rhodey (lower right).

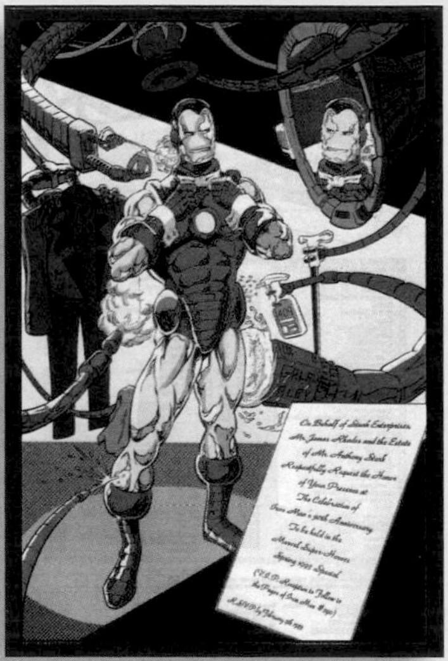

it may be, is a hollow, empty shell. So too is technology without the presence of humanity." The book was welcomed by fans, as it was the first close-up look at Stark's technological marvels.

The remainder of Iron Man's third decade celebration was contained mostly within his own series. Stark continued to rebuild his strength and use the virtual-reality-like Telepresence Iron Man Armor, while Rhodes joined *Avengers West Coast* as War Machine. Stark Enterprise's space station was revisited as Iron Man stopped the nanotechnological villain Technovore, and an attempt to recover nuclear matériel from A.I.M. (Advanced Idea Mechanics) put the hero in conflict with MODAM, ugly sister to Modok, and *X-Men* villain Omega Red. Unfortunately, a battle against the geothermally powered Earth Mover set free long-absent villain Ultimo (who had last appeared in *Iron Man* #96 in March 1977), who was determined to take his revenge against Shellhead.

Unfortunately for the armored hero, Ultimo made short work of the Telepresence Iron Man, putting Tony in a neural-feedback-induced coma. By the beginning of the double-sized issue #300 (January 1994), Jim Rhodes had returned to service and called on an army of Stark's friends to help. All those who had previously worn Iron Man armor—Happy Hogan, Eddie March, Mike O'Brien, and Carl Walker—were joined by Bethany Cabe as they all suited up to take down Ultimo as the six-member Iron

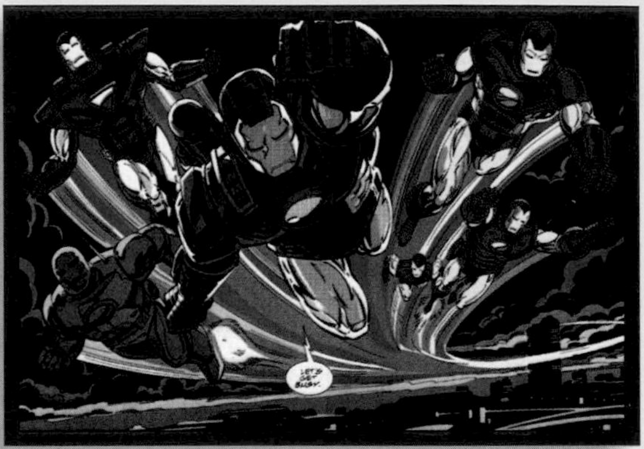
LET'S GET BUSY.

Legion. Although Stark came out of his coma, regained his mobility, and donned a new set of modular armor, the story forced the split between Rhodes and Stark to a complete breaking point.

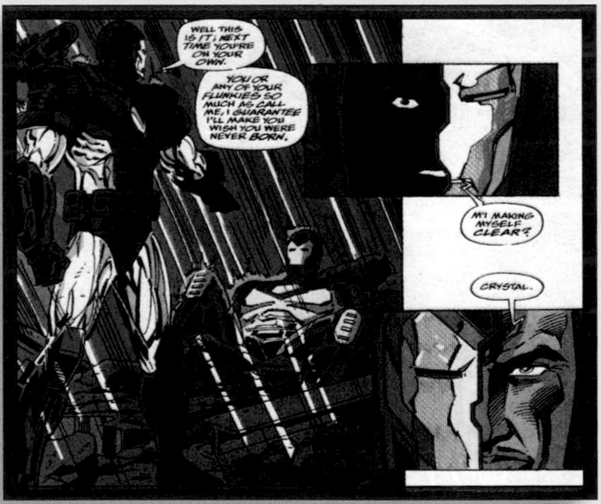
WELL THIS IS IT; NEXT TIME YOU'RE ON YOUR OWN.
YOU OR ANY OF YOUR FLUNKIES SO MUCH AS CALL ME, I GUARANTEE I'LL MAKE YOU WISH YOU WERE NEVER BORN.
AM I MAKING MYSELF CLEAR?
CRYSTAL.

Having explored cutting-edge science and technology for nearly twenty issues, Kaminski next began a six-issue arc called "Crash and Burn," designed to deal with some of Stark's past as a weapons manufacturer. When a mole within Stark Enterprises worked with a computer hacker to uncover the dark secrets and shady dealings of the company past, Tony Stark had to scramble to retain the good work his company was doing in scientific research. Even as Iron Man faced off against guest stars Deathlok (a cyborg), *Spider-Man* villain Venom, teen heroes the New Warriors, Thunderstrike, and the Hulk, Tony proved himself to be an ideal corporate leader for the 1990s. For many fans, the complete reorganization of Stark Enterprises wasn't nearly as exciting as the überbulky Hulkbuster armor Iron Man was forced to don, but either way, the world of *Iron Man* was set on a new course.

Meanwhile, James Rhodes garnered a solo title—and Iron Man's first-ever spin-off series—with *War Machine* #1 (April 1994). In this series, he initially worked with WorldWatch Incorporated, an organization dedicated to political peacekeeping, an element that put War Machine into global politics that S.H.I.E.L.D. or the Avengers wouldn't touch. The West Coast Avengers had already disbanded in January 1994, and eventually Stark worked alongside several of the WCA members and some newcomers to found a new Super Hero team called Force Works. Their series of the same name lasted twenty-two issues (July 1994–April 1996), while *War Machine* would best it with twenty-five issues, ending in April 1996.

While those two series were in their prime in the fall of 1994, Kaminski had instituted a multipart crossover among *Iron Man, War Machine,* and *Force Works* that dealt not only with the conflict between Rhodes and Stark coming to a boil, but also with the return of the evil Mandarin—now backed up by a gang of superpowered Asian warlords known as the Avatars.

Aided by *Force Works* writers Dan Abnett and Andy Lanning, Kaminski wanted "to turn Mandarin more in a mystical direction; to have him be less of a technologically oriented character . . . to reinforce the dichotomy between him and Iron Man," he said in a promotional interview. "You not only have Tony Stark and the Mandarin, but you have East and West, and science and magic. Another thing about the Mandarin . . . what his primary goals are in this crossover . . . he wants to turn back the tide of progress. He's looking back to the past and saying those were the glory days, that was the golden age, we want to go back to that. Whereas Tony Stark is always looking into the future, wanting to improve on things, wanting to improve the pace of progress . . . a very sharp contrast between the two."

Rather than being a fortuitous coincidence, the timing of the crossover and the use of Mandarin were planned by Marvel. The newest incarnation of Iron Man and his archfoe were about to hit fans . . . on television!

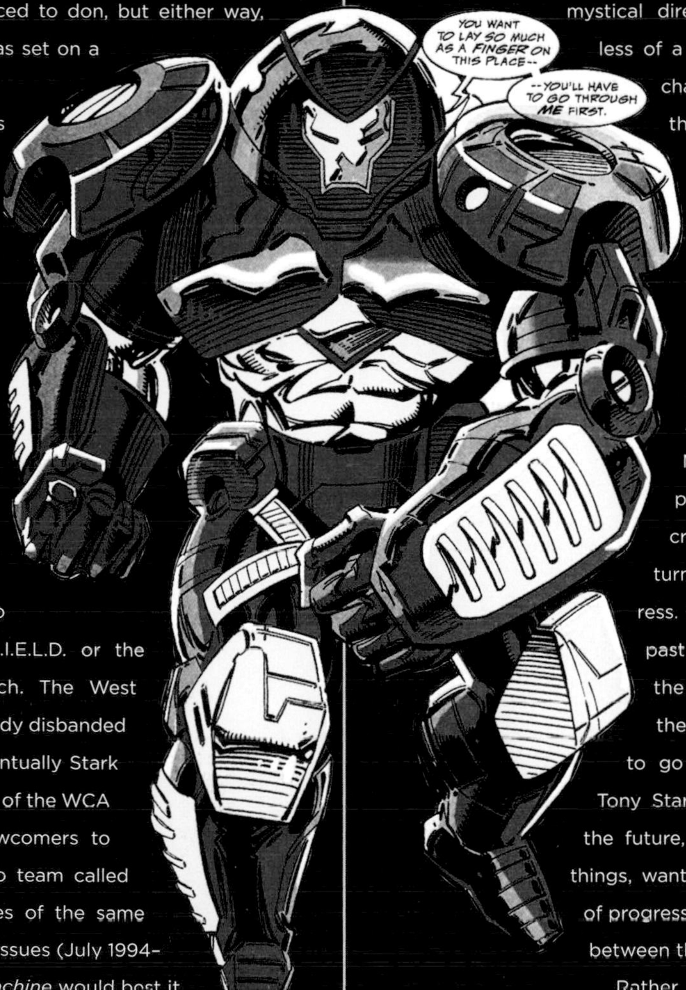
YOU WANT TO LAY SO MUCH AS A FINGER ON THIS PLACE--
--YOU'LL HAVE TO GO THROUGH ME FIRST.

▲ Who could stop the Hulkbuster armor?

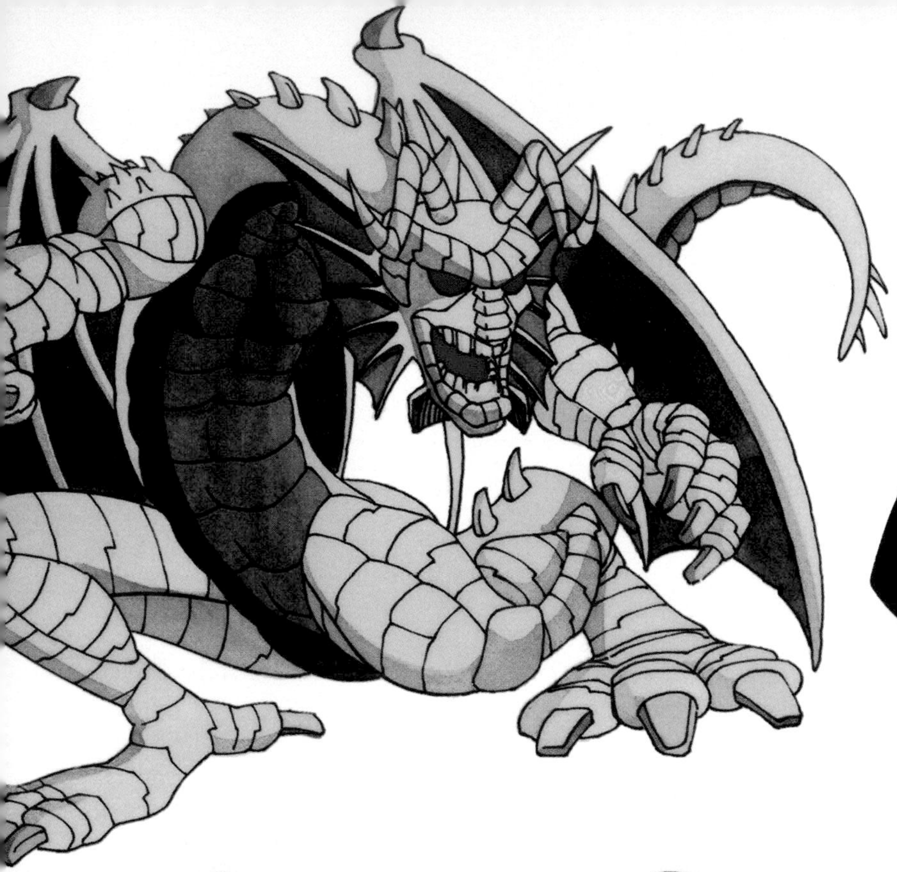
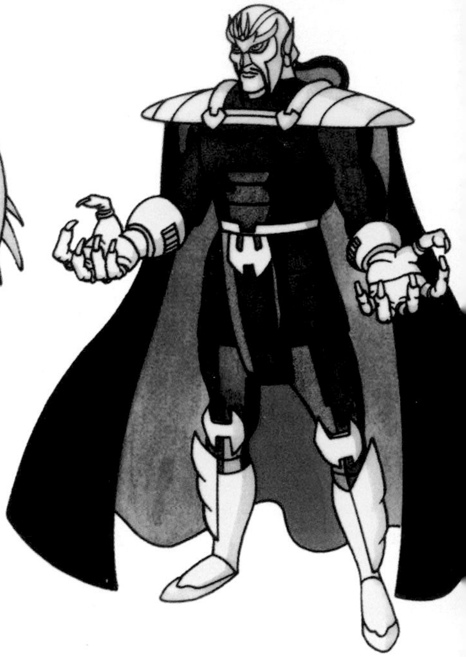
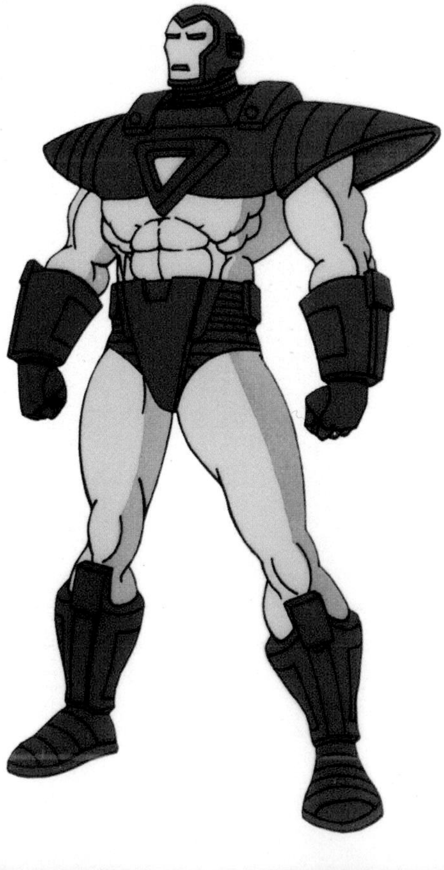
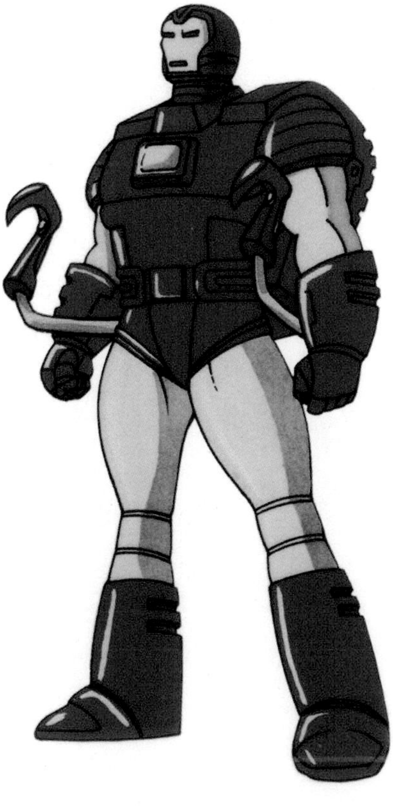
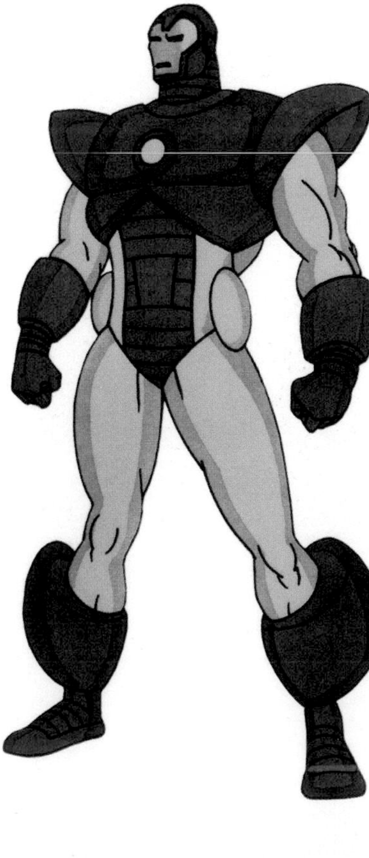

The early 1980s had seen an immense change for animation on television when Filmation debuted *He-Man and the Masters of the Universe* in syndication. Based on a popular toy line, that series was a huge hit, and dozens of toy-based syndicated toons soon followed, from *G.I. Joe* and *Transformers* to *My Little Pony* and *Jem.* By the 1990s, the realm of syndicated animation was a bit more streamlined, and obvious toy-commercial shows were a bit less welcome on the landscape. Almost all animation was now done overseas as well, and even the style of creating animation was changing: Three-dimensional CGI (computer-generated imagery) was being mixed with traditional two-dimensional hand-drawn art.

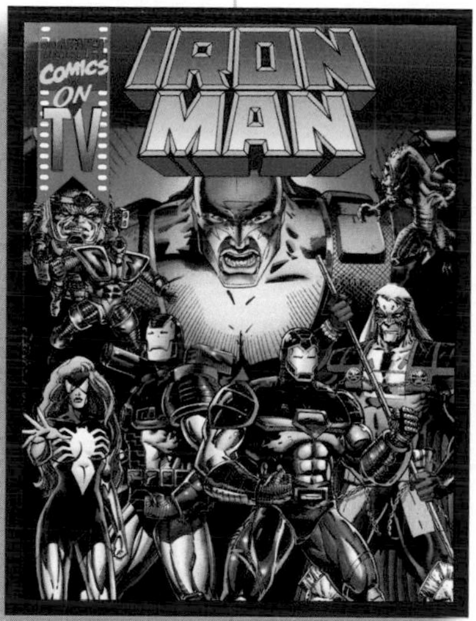
COMICS ON TV
IRON MAN

By 1994, Marvel was a co-owner of Toy Biz, and Avi Arad, past chief executive officer of the toy company, was now CEO of Marvel Films. Arad had a fondness for Iron Man, and when the opportunity came to develop him as both a toy line and a syndicated adventures series, he pushed for it. "Because I have always liked *Iron Man,* this was one of the projects I wanted to get into right away," Arad said in a promotional interview. "*Iron Man* has a lot of what I call 'the sign of the times.' It's going to be a science-based show, a technology-based show. Stark Industries is like Hughes Aircraft or United Technologies. The idea is [much like] the story of Howard Hughes—who was inventive and flamboyant and had an exciting life. Stark Industries is a company that is in the business of creating new technology—satellites, weapons, communications, chemicals—therefore it has allowed us to do stories that are *very* different."

As for the toy line, Arad noted, "When you design action figures, *versatility* is the key and every so often you have an opportunity to make something really different. If you look at the Marvel Super Hero universe, they are terrifically interesting and attractive, but basically men in tights . . . With Iron Man you have a figure of Tony Stark covered with an armor for every mission, straight from his Hall of Armors. So you have an undersea armor, a stealth armor, a space armor, a solar armor . . . and all of a sudden you have these *incredible*-looking figures; you can actually exchange the [armor] pieces among the different Iron Man/Tony Stark figures and role-play different missions."

Producing and story-editing/writing the *Iron Man* series—and a concurrently created counterpart *Fantastic Four* show—was industry veteran Ron Friedman, no stranger to armored heroes after producing sixty-five episodes of *Transformers,* along with series such as *G.I. Joe* and *Defenders of the Earth.* In a publicity interview, Friedman said, "*Iron Man* has been continuously successful through all the kinds of mutations that take place when a comic book has been running for thirty-some years. We felt that, with proper positioning and proper accentuation of what we felt were the strong points of the character and his team, *Iron Man* would be extremely appealing and have a cutting-edge, high-tech contemporary feel."

Although the writing, designs, and storyboard/production work was all done in California, *Iron Man* was hand-animated in Korea by Rainbow Animation Group, who were Emmy-nominated for their work on *Where on Earth Is Carmen Sandiego?* Their animation was combined in certain spots with CGI "morphs" for Iron Man's armored transformations, as well as realistic outer-space imagery—provided by NASA—for some adventures, in lieu of traditional painted backgrounds and environments.

◀ Character designs for the *Iron Man* animated series included Fin Fang Foom and Mandarin (top) and multiple armors for the hero (bottom).

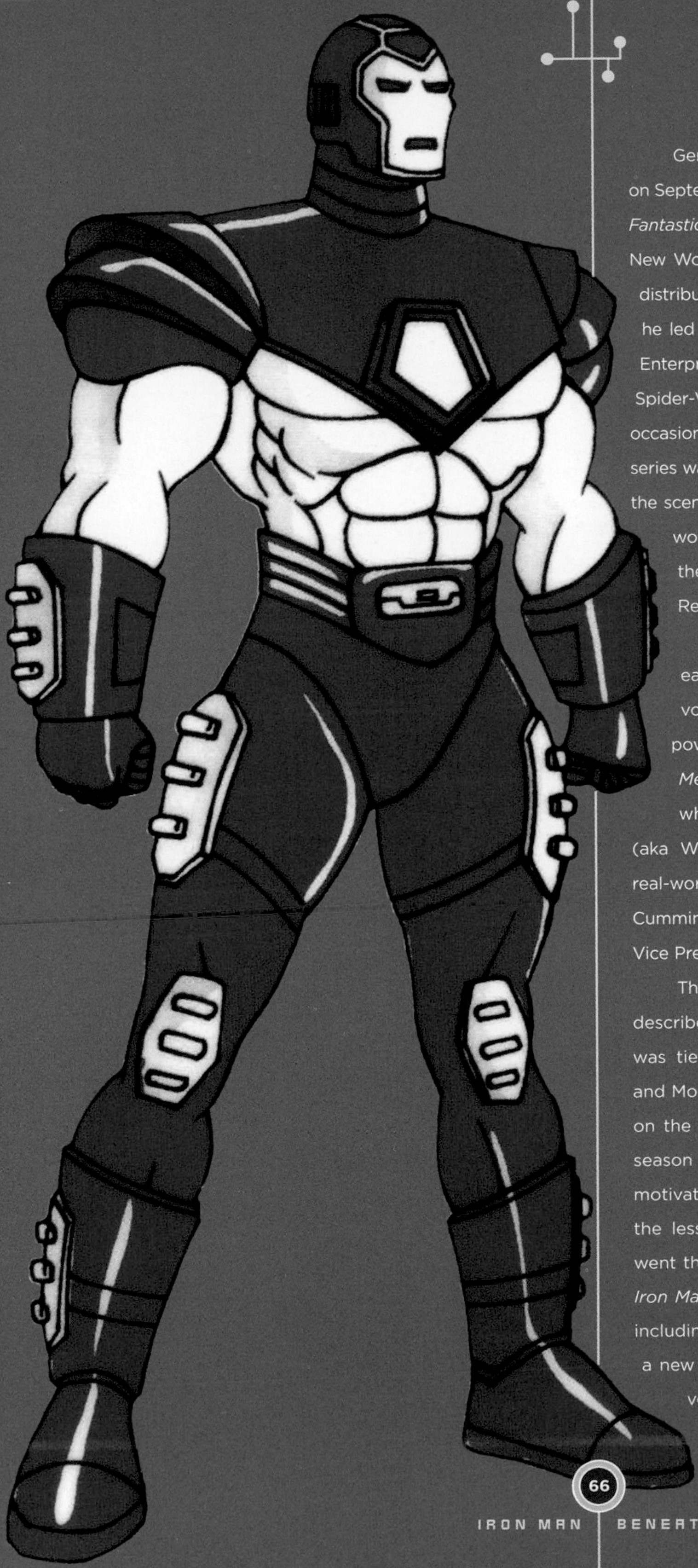

Genesis Entertainment launched *Marvel Action Hour* on September 24–25, 1994, with thirteen initial *Iron Man* and *Fantastic Four* episodes airing on 145 channels countrywide; New World Entertainment took the series for international distribution. In the series, Tony Stark was Iron Man, and he led the team of heroes known as Force Works: Stark Enterprises employees War Machine, Scarlet Witch, and Spider-Woman, as well as time-traveling alien Century and occasional guest star Hawkeye. The overarching villain of the series was Mandarin, who controlled many elements behind the scenes and had put Earth into a "secret war." Whether working for Mandarin or not, bad guys abounded in the forms of Justin Hammer, Ultimo, Modok, the Grim Reaper, and even Fin Fang Foom!

Stan Lee provided opening introductions to each episode in his inimitable style, but it was the voice cast for the series that really poured on the star power. *Airplane*'s Robert Hays was Tony Stark and *Full Metal Jacket*'s Dorian Harewood was James Rhodes, while Ed Gilbert was Mandarin and Jim Cummings (aka Winnie-the-Pooh *and* Tigger) was Modok. A few real-world guest stars also appeared (though voiced by Cummings or Gilbert) in the forms of President Bill Clinton, Vice President Al Gore, and opera star Luciano Pavarotti!

The first season of *Iron Man* worked best when it described the origins of characters; Tony Stark's tale was tied in to the Mandarin, and both the Mandarin's and Modok's pasts were shown. Ratings were strong, but on the emerging Internet, fans were vocal that the first season wasn't what they wanted, citing weak character motivation and repetitive stories. Perhaps because of the less-than-stellar reaction, the production personnel went through a major overhaul for the second season of *Iron Man* in 1995. Brought on board were more writers—including comic scripters Len Wein and Jan Strnad—and a new supervising producer/story editor in top industry veteran Tom Tataranowicz.

For its second year, *Marvel Action Hour* added a third component—*Biker Mice From Mars*—and became *Marvel Action Universe.* The thirteen new *Iron Man* episodes focused more on its star and less on the Force Works characters, and adapted more plots from the comics. Tony Stark faking his death, Mandarin losing his powerful rings, and encounters with Firebrand, A.I.M., and Madame Masque were only a setup for the two-part "Armor Wars," which followed its comic book counterpart as closely as the storyline allowed. The season ender, the two-part "Hands of the Mandarin," loosely adapted the more recent *Iron Man* comics by Kaminski and Hopgood.

Although *Iron Man* did not get renewed for a third season, the Toy Biz toy line did make it through four sets of releases. The five-inch action figures consisted mainly of Iron Man variations on nonarmored heroes and foes. The Iron Man armors were modular and "vac-metallized," giving them a metallic sheen; their modular element meant that they could be used interchangeably on other Iron Man figures to create new suits of armor. Twenty-five figures were released, with thirteen of them being some variation on Iron Man or War Machine. A fifth line was sculpted and announced but never released; the figures were later repainted and sculpted for release in Spider-Man and X-Men toy lines.

Back in the realm of comics, December 1994 saw the debut of *Iron Man*'s second spin-off series, *Marvel Action Hour: Iron Man.* The first three of the eight-part series adapted the scripts for season one into comic book form; after this, the stories were new but set in the animated continuity. The first issue of *Marvel Action Hour: Iron Man* also came poly-bagged with a preview of both *Marvel Action Hour* shows and one of three imitation animation cels that featured either Iron Man and Mandarin, three variations on the Iron Man armor, or Fin Fang Foom and Century. The cels were also available in *Iron Man* #310, *War Machine* #8, and *Force Works* #5, all dated November 1994.

▼ Tony attends an AA meeting.

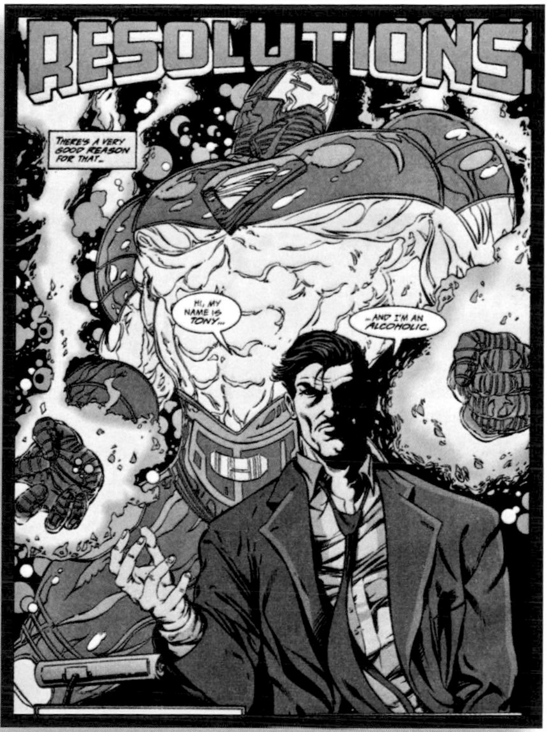
RESOLUTIONS
THERE'S A VERY GOOD REASON FOR THAT...
HI, MY NAME IS TONY...
...AND I'M AN ALCOHOLIC.

Meanwhile, in the series that started it all, following stories in which the media-friendly Iron Man teamed up with Captain America and Black Widow, and Tony Stark attended his first Alcoholics Anonymous meeting and faced down a former teacher and mentor, Len Kaminski left *Iron Man* with #318 (July 1995), after writing forty-one issues of the series. His replacement was a Marvel writer named Terry Kavanaugh, who had to contend with a dizzying number of artists on his fourteen-issue run . . . and a convoluted shift in character.

Following the stability Tony Stark had finally found with Stark Enterprises and his relationships, Kavanaugh dropped Stark into a mystery that was leading into a twenty-six-part crossover *Avengers* story Marvel was planning called "The Crossing." Tony's behavior became stranger and stranger; even he didn't understand it. Readers soon

Tony Stark turns evil (left) then faces ▼ an alternate reality Iron Man (right).

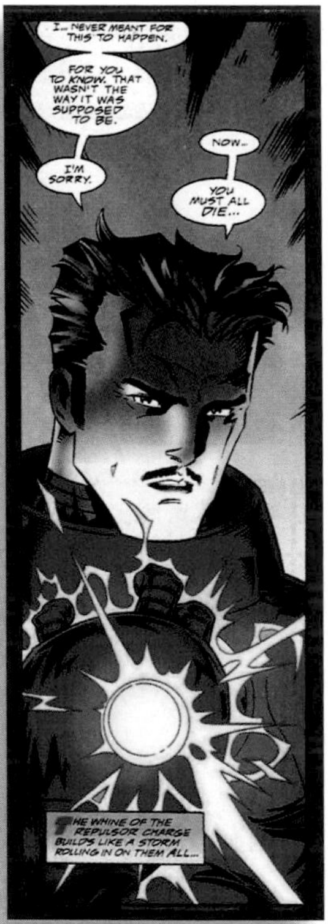
I... NEVER MEANT FOR THIS TO HAPPEN.
FOR YOU TO KNOW. THAT WASN'T THE WAY IT WAS SUPPOSED TO BE.
I'M SORRY.
NOW...
YOU MUST ALL DIE...
THE WHINE OF THE REPULSOR CHARGE BUILDS LIKE A STORM ROLLING IN ON THEM ALL...

found out, however, that an immortal time traveler named Kang the Conqueror—a long-time *Avengers* villain—had been manipulating Tony for years. By *Iron Man* #323, it appeared that Tony was responsible for several murders, and a deadly confrontation with the Avengers was imminent.

Over the course of the crossover, the Avengers traveled back in time and recruited a *teenage* Tony Stark from an alternate time line to help them. "Teen Tony" returned with them to their present and donned one of the Iron Man suits of armor to battle against his older self. In *Avengers* #395 (February 1996), Tony Stark regained control over his mind and body and sacrificed himself to stop Kang, dying a hero. This time, the old Tony Stark was dead for real, but in his place stood the teen Tony Stark. A special issue, *Age of Innocence: The Rebirth of Iron Man* (February 1996), told the new Tony's tale . . . as far as it was known.

Iron Man #326–332 comprised one of the most controversial set of stories in the book's history, as the young Tony Stark navigated college, girls, and fraternity keggers, in addition to fighting villains while wearing armor (that changed from issue to issue) and battling to gain legal control of Stark International. Finally, the new teen Iron Man joined the Fantastic Four, Hulk, and many Avengers to face the mutant villain Onslaught in New York City's famed Central Park. In the battle, as shown in *Onslaught: Marvel*

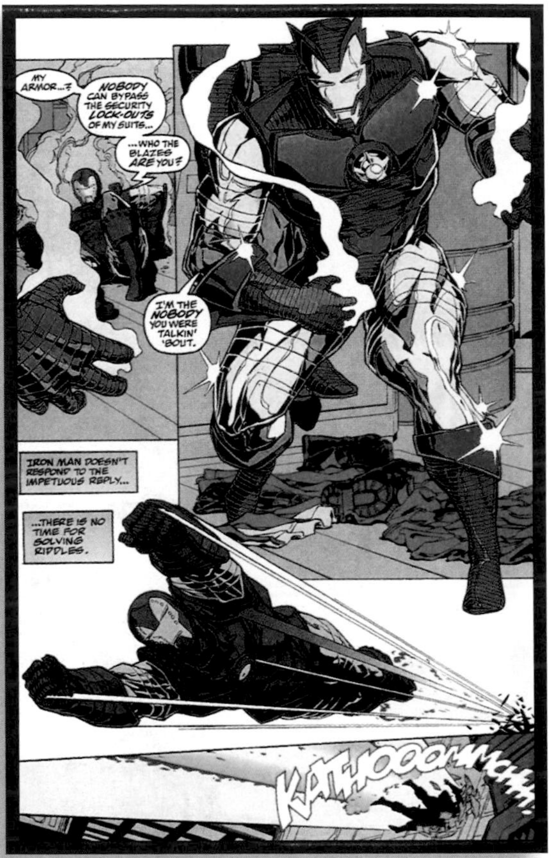
MY ARMOR...?
NOBODY CAN BYPASS THE SECURITY LOCK-OUTS OF MY SUITS...
...WHO THE BLAZES ARE YOU?
I'M THE NOBODY YOU WERE TALKIN' 'BOUT.
IRON MAN DOESN'T RESPOND TO THE IMPETUOUS REPLY...
...THERE IS NO TIME FOR SOLVING RIDDLES.

Universe, the heroes all appeared to lose their lives.

By the fall of 1996, Iron Man's fortunes seemed dim. His long-running series had been canceled with #332 (September 1996), as had his television series and toy line, and his character had been killed twice . . . *neither* time in his own series. But Iron Man *was* the hero of a new video game (along with Valiant Comics' armored character X-O Manowar); he was the star of one kids' adventure novel and one adult novel (with a second on the way), and he had guest-starred on UPN's *The Incredible Hulk* cartoon and Fox's *Spider-Man: The Animated Series.* To count out Marvel's armored avenger at this point would not be a good idea.

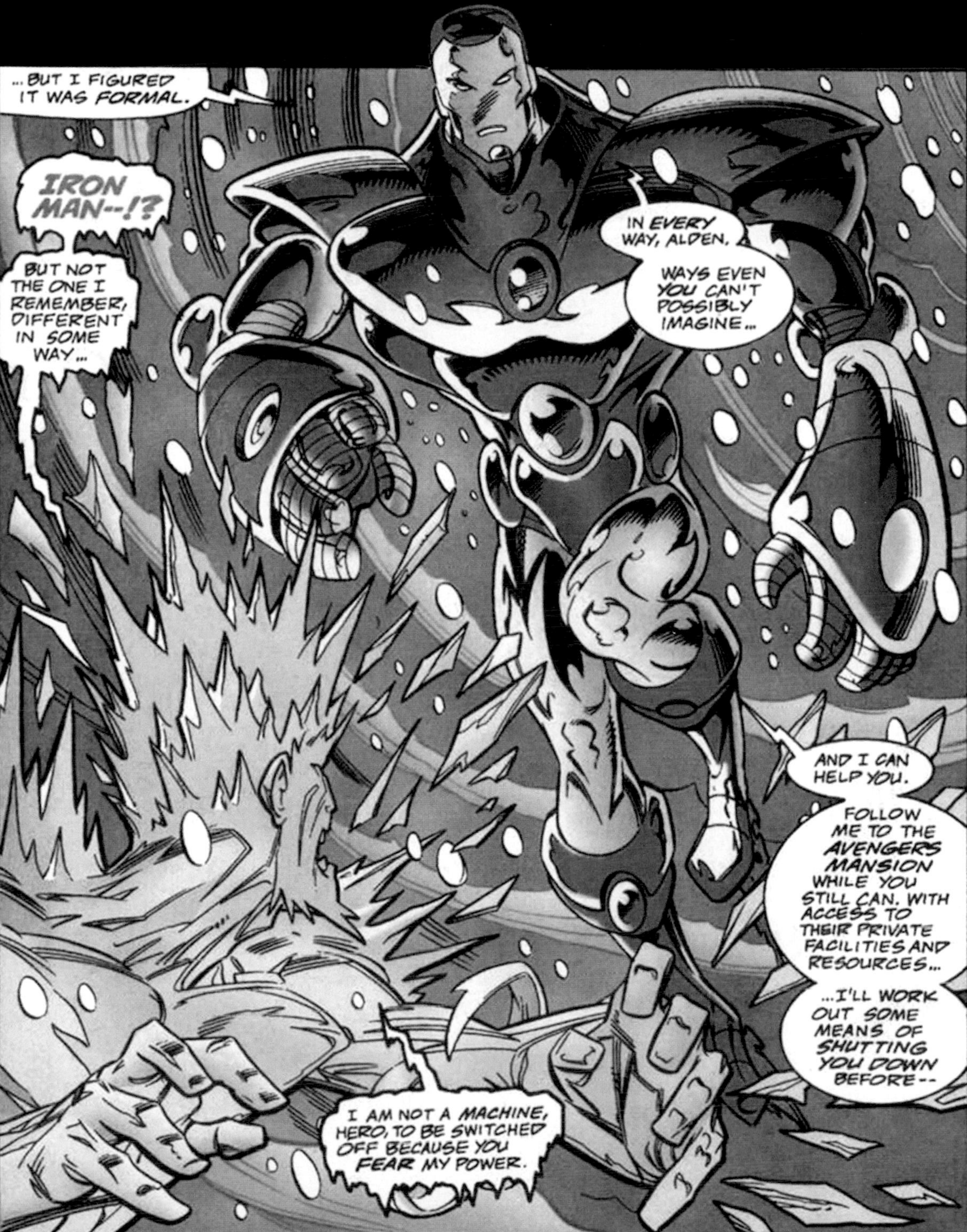
...BUT I FIGURED IT WAS FORMAL.
IRON MAN--!?
BUT NOT THE ONE I REMEMBER, DIFFERENT IN SOME WAY...
IN EVERY WAY, ALDEN.
WAYS EVEN YOU CAN'T POSSIBLY IMAGINE...
AND I CAN HELP YOU.
FOLLOW ME TO THE AVENGERS MANSION WHILE YOU STILL CAN. WITH ACCESS TO THEIR PRIVATE FACILITIES AND RESOURCES...
...I'LL WORK OUT SOME MEANS OF SHUTTING YOU DOWN BEFORE--
I AM NOT A MACHINE, HERO, TO BE SWITCHED OFF BECAUSE YOU FEAR MY POWER.

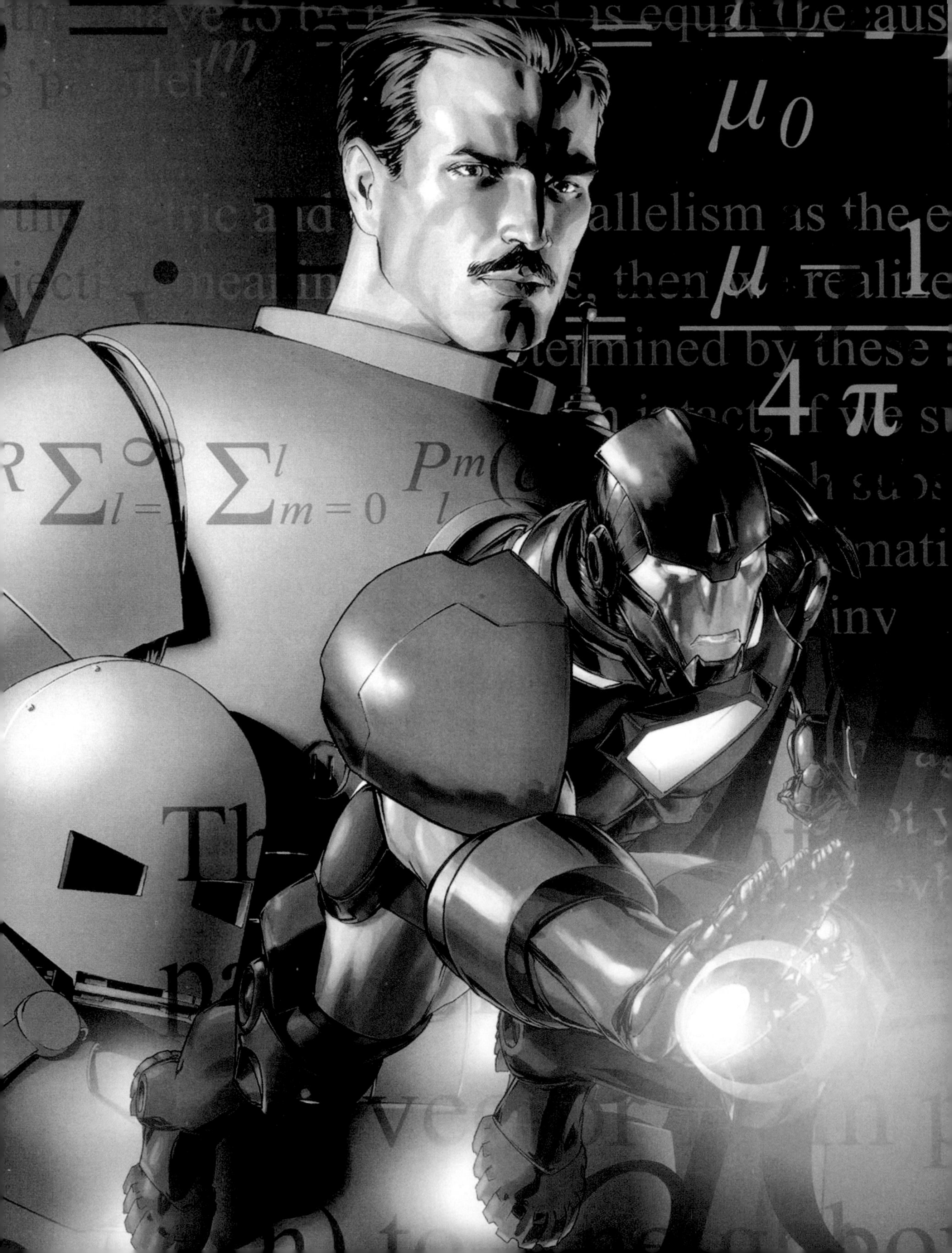

FORGED ANEW...

The comic book marketplace had become significantly different between the start of Iron Man's career in 1963 and the end of his first series in September 1996. Over the years, comics had gone from being distributed and sold exclusively through newsstands and grocery stores to being distributed largely through privately owned comic stores. The Merry Marvel Marching Society of the past had been a mild precursor to the hard-core fans who were in place by the 1990s. They didn't just communicate their fandom through letter columns or even self-produced fanzines, but had entire magazines devoted to their hobbies, and countless webpages and chat arenas on which to endlessly debate the merits of the latest comics.

The changes in comic book distribution had led to another major change in comics: the rise of "independent," creator-owned series. Early companies such as Pacific, Comico, Eclipse, First, and Dark Horse allowed their creators complete—or at least partial—ownership of their characters and stories. This gave talented creators not only control over the destiny of their own creations but also a much larger cut of the profits. Marvel and DC responded by giving stronger contracts and more royalties to their creators. The profits for everyone expanded as speculators began buying more books as future investments.

By the mid-1990s, comic book fan-favorite creators were better off than ever: Their names guaranteed sales; their original art sold for high figures; and their profile in the media outside the comics realm was significantly higher. In 1992, seven of Marvel's top artists left the company to form Image Comics, giving them a chance to control everything about their own characters and rake in the money themselves. Critics contended that Image lived up to its name, with the art and style of many of the books superseding storytelling structures, plot, and dialogue. Indeed, some of the Image founders were dismissive of writers in general, though others knew their value and hired on scribes to help craft their visions.

Marvel's fortunes were less strong by the mid-1990s, however, mostly due to a slump in industrywide sales from the speculators who bought extra copies of issues they hoped would become hot, as well as from a misguided attempt at self-distribution that Marvel made. "The speculator bubble had burst, and the entire industry was experiencing a dramatic sales downturn," said Marvel editor Tom Brevoort in an interview. "Simultaneously, the decision to distribute Marvel books exclusively through Heroes World wound up backfiring, and caused the consolidation of the direct market system down to one provider, Diamond."

In 1996, after significant successes with their own series, two of Image's top artists, Jim Lee and Rob Liefeld, accepted a one-year outsourcing deal with Marvel. They would revamp four of the company's titles—including *Iron Man*—into hoped-for bestselling status, with no editorial control from Marvel whatsoever. "This decision to reboot those four titles was part and parcel of the 'Unfinished Business' deal, in which Marvel's then-upper-echelon decided to license these books out to Jim Lee and Rob Liefeld to package and produce," said Brevoort. "The hope was that their involvement would bring some cachet and heat back to those characters."

This deal (originally code-named Unfinished Business) had led to the Onslaught storyline, which allowed Marvel to shuffle the Fantastic Four, Iron Man, Captain America, and the Avengers off into a "pocket universe" where the alternate time lines and stories would not affect mainstream Marvel continuity; its characters and plots continued on as if the heroes had sacrificed their lives. The universe-birthing event would be known as *Heroes Reborn.*

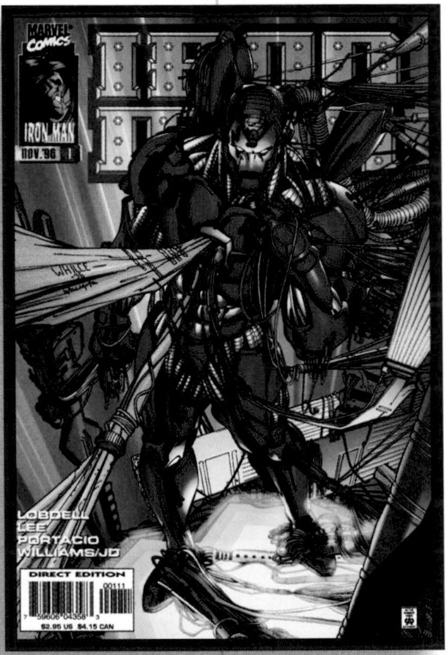
MARVEL COMICS
IRON MAN
NOV.'96
LOBDELL
LEE
PORTACIO
WILLIAMS/JD
DIRECT EDITION

The relaunch of *Iron Man* was complete when a new first issue debuted in November 1996. Co-written by Scott Lobdell and Jim Lee, the new series was drawn by Whilce Portacio and Scott Williams. The team immediately established that their Tony Stark was an adult, though he wasn't universally loved. Indeed, as a ruthless corporate raider, Stark had enemies; as the story opened, he had just been acquitted of charges of corporate espionage and insider trading. While testing a powerful suit of weaponized armor known as the Prometheum Armor, Stark employee Rebel O'Reilly was killed, but after a surprise confrontation with the Hulk resulted in heart damage, Stark himself was forced to don the armor to save his own life.

Over the next several issues, the new Iron Man battled the Hulk, had his life saved by fired former executive assistant Pepper Potts—who came up with the idea that Iron Man was Stark's personal bodyguard—met the Fantastic Four, fought the Living Laser, and joined the Avengers in stopping Hulk . . . again. With *Iron Man* #7 (May 1997), Lobdell and Lee left scripting the series in the hands of Jeph Loeb. The talented scripter hadn't yet reached his award-winning status in comics—he would go on to greater fame in the 2000s on the writing and production staff for *Smallville, Lost,* and *Heroes*—but he dove into Stark's story headlong.

Loeb had already been writing the *Avengers* and *Captain America* relaunches for Liefeld, so *Iron Man* was an easy fit for him. The first storyline wrapped up the fate of pre–Iron Man armor wearer Rebel O'Reilly. Afterward, Loeb and a rotating crop of artists—which included Ryan Benjamin, Terry Shoemaker, and others—reimagined such past Shellhead villains as Titanium Man, Crimson Dynamo, Madame Hydra, Mandarin, and Doctor Doom. This latter villain was also revealed to be a past college friend of Stark's.

As the yearlong *Heroes Reborn* contract reached its midway point, however, the writing was on the wall that it would not be continued. "Once it became apparent that the *Heroes Reborn* deal wasn't going to be renewed for a second year," Brevoort said, "Bob Harras and the rest of editorial met to determine how to bring the characters back and reintegrate them into the Marvel Universe once again." The last handful of *Iron Man* issues saw poor continuity, confusing time-travel elements, and the heroes

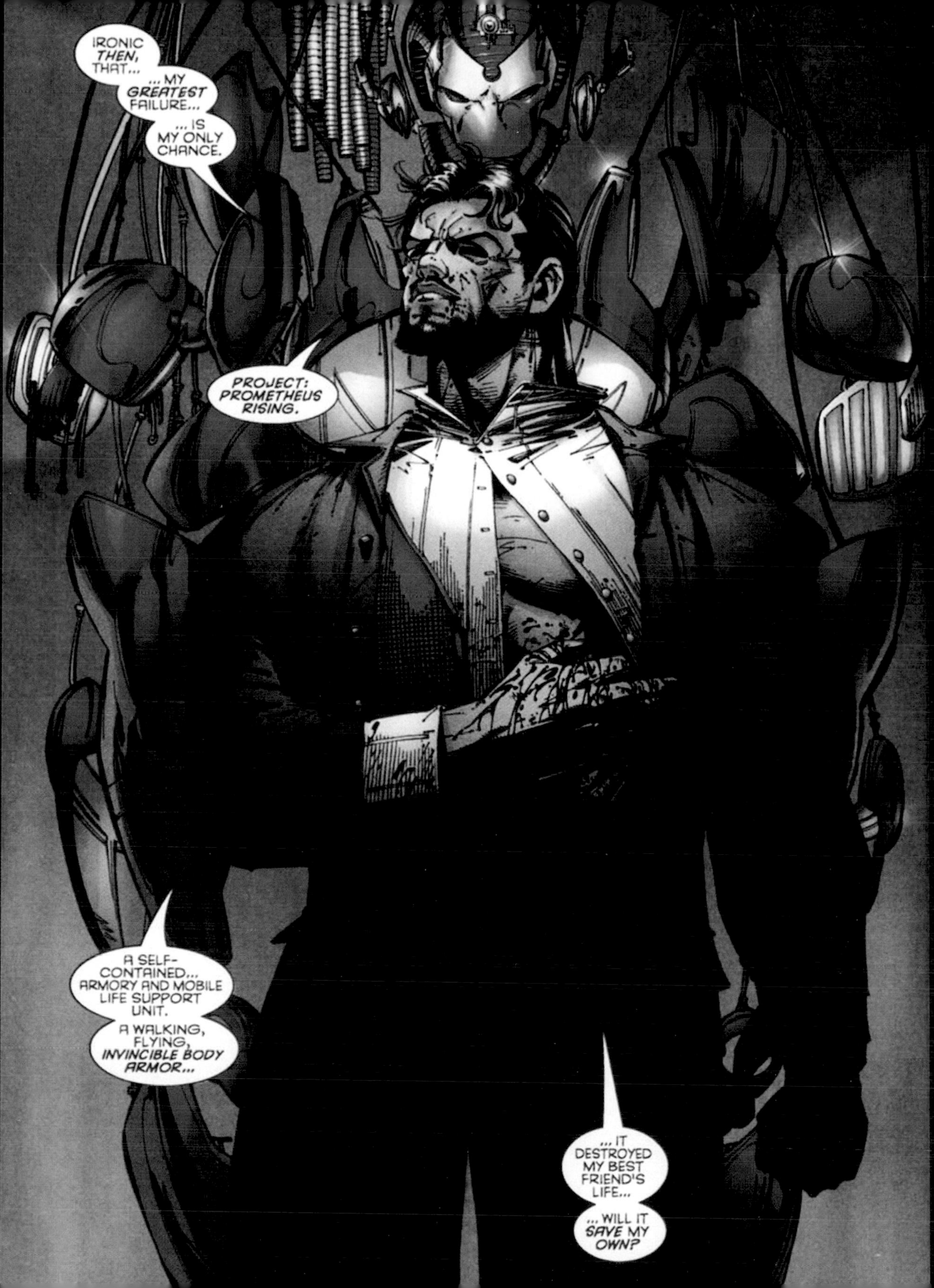

IRONIC *THEN,* THAT...
... MY *GREATEST* FAILURE...
... IS MY ONLY CHANCE.
PROJECT: PROMETHEUS RISING.
A SELF-CONTAINED... ARMORY AND MOBILE LIFE SUPPORT UNIT.
A WALKING, FLYING, *INVINCIBLE BODY ARMOR...*
... IT DESTROYED MY BEST FRIEND'S LIFE...
... WILL IT *SAVE* MY *OWN?*

of that universe realizing that they didn't quite "belong" where they were. The thirteenth and final issue of *Iron Man* volume II was released in November 1997, as part three of a storyline that crossed the *Heroes Reborn* characters over with Jim Lee's Image/Wildstorm characters. Ignominiously, Iron Man didn't even *appear* in his own final issue until the fourteenth page . . . and even then, he was revealed to be a shape-shifting alien Skrull.

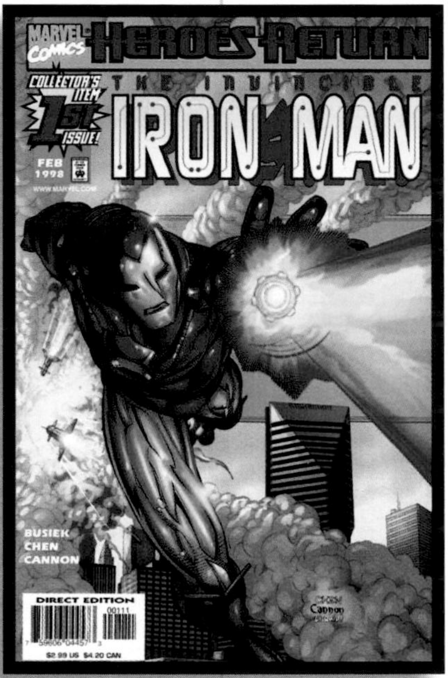
MARVEL COMICS
HEROES RETURN
THE INVINCIBLE
IRON MAN
COLLECTOR'S ITEM
1st ISSUE!
FEB 1998
BUSIEK
CHEN
CANNON
DIRECT EDITION
$2.99 US $4.20 CAN

The foûr-part *Heroes Reborn: The Return* was released weekly in winter 1997, written by Peter David and drawn by Salvador Larroca. In it, young Franklin Richards, the son of the Fantastic Four's Reed and Sue Richards and the possessor of awesome reality-warping mutant powers, was revealed to have "caused" the pocket universe. At the tale's end, all of Marvel's characters were returned to their original universe, to resume all-new series with new debut issues.

•

The third *Iron Man* #1 (February 1998) welcomed a new creative team onto the series: writer Kurt Busiek and artist Sean Chen. The back cover promised, "It's business as usual for dashing, multimillionaire Tony Stark and his armored alter ego, Iron Man, now that he's returned to the Marvel Universe—or is it? Tony must decide whether to wrest control of the Stark/Fujikawa corporation from his business 'partners' or seek to increase his vast fortune in other ways." From the first page announcing that Tony Stark, once thought dead, was alive, and a double-page spread showing Iron Man's new armor, the book was clearly off into classic *Iron Man* territory with nary a look back at the previous two years' worth of continuity nightmares. This new course was steered by Busiek, whose work in the field often built on what had gone before instead of reinvention.

Having begun his career in 1982 at DC Comics, Busiek had been a solid craftsman on books such as *Power Man & Iron Fist, What If?,* and his creator-owned Eclipse series *The Liberty Project*. But it was his realistic "ordinary man" take on Super Heroes in the *Marvels* mini series and his own *Astro City* project that brought Busiek acclaim, awards, and his pick of books. Despite those successes, the writer believes it was another Marvel title that got him the *Iron Man* gig. "I don't think it was *Marvels* so much as *Untold Tales of Spider-Man* that said, *This guy can write Super Hero comics every month,* instead of, *He can do some weird but successful mini series.*"

Busiek cops to being a longtime fan of the armored avenger, but he'd been able to work on the book only once, for a DC-Marvel crossover book called *Amalgam* that merged their characters. "*Iron Man* was the one long-running Marvel series that I wanted to write more than any other, and I have never disguised that fact. When they were doing the second round of *Amalgam* titles, I called Mark Gruenwald, who was the Marvel side of things, and said, 'Hi there, it's Kurt Busiek,' and he said, 'Let me guess, you want to write *Iron Lantern*?' And that's how I got that assignment. Basically, it was generally known throughout the Marvel editorial core that Kurt Busiek wants to write *Iron Man.* So when they brought Iron Man back from the *Heroes Reborn* thing, I got the call and I got offered the book. I didn't need to chase them down because they knew already that I wanted to do it. I did have to audition to the point where I had to write up

▼ A new series and a new company for Tony Stark.

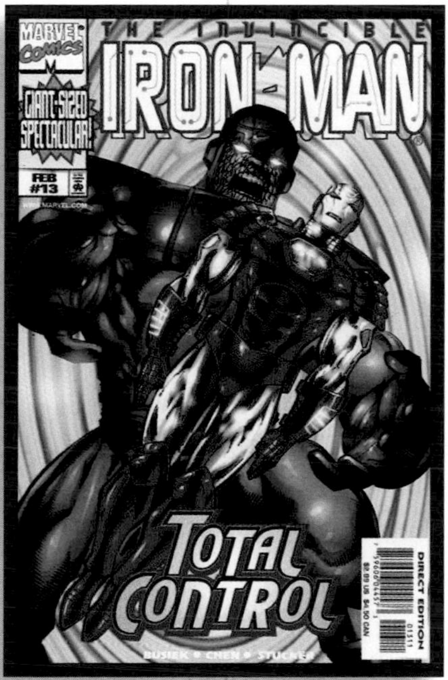
MARVEL COMICS
THE INVINCIBLE
IRON MAN
GIANT-SIZED SPECTACULAR!
FEB #13
TOTAL CONTROL
DIRECT EDITION
BUSIEK • CHEN • STUCKER

a pitch on what I would want to do in the series, and I think there were a few others guys who did that, but they chose me."

In the 1990s, when John Byrne was exiting the original *Iron Man* series, Busiek had written a proposal for the title, with sketches by a then-unknown artist named Alex Ross (years before his award-winning success on *Marvels* and DC's *Kingdom Come*). "I wrote up a pitch for a launch series with what I would want to do with *Iron Man,* and Alex did sketches for it. There were notes on what would come next and all that, and I sent it in, and as far as I know, nobody ever read it. If anybody at Marvel did, I don't know about it. The one thing we did get out of that—when I did get the book, I didn't write any of the stories that were in that pitch—the armor that we put Iron Man in with Sean Chen drawing the book was partially based on the armor that Alex had designed for that proposal."

Ross was credited in the first issue, along with fan artist Allen Bujak, who had created a cool design in an *Iron Man* fanzine called *Advanced Iron.* "Once they heard I was going to be writing *Iron Man,* they started sending me issues," recalls Busiek. "I was impressed that a bunch of Allen Bujak's armor designs—Guardsman designs and Crimson Dynamo—had this piping to them here and there that glowed. I saw it and said, *That's a cool element.* I asked if I could steal that from him, with appropriate credit, and he said sure. So we put that in the mix and added little glowing bits here and there to Iron Man's armor. It really said, *Modern! New! Crisp!* Since some of the other elements of the armor we put in were harking back to 1963, having an element that said, *Modern! Modern!* to balance out the elements that said, *Old! Old!* I thought worked really well."

In addition to the new armor, Busiek gave Stark a new raison d'être at the end of the first issue. "We made Tony a consultant. His company was Stark Solutions, and you bring him in to fix whatever business problems there were. I think that our reasoning for this was his company, while he had been gone, had been taken over by other people, and he *could* have a big fight with them, and get all destructive and tear stuff down, but in the wake of Onslaught, he wanted to *rebuild* things. He wanted to make the world *better.* So what he was doing was keeping a very stripped-down company that made a whole lot of money that he could pump into charitable projects."

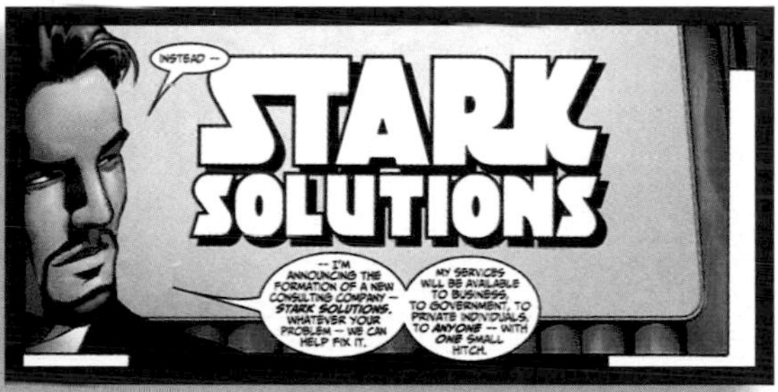
INSTEAD --
STARK SOLUTIONS
-- I'M ANNOUNCING THE FORMATION OF A NEW CONSULTING COMPANY -- STARK SOLUTIONS. WHATEVER YOUR PROBLEM -- WE CAN HELP FIX IT.
MY SERVICES WILL BE AVAILABLE TO BUSINESS, TO GOVERNMENT, TO PRIVATE INDIVIDUALS, TO ANYONE -- WITH ONE SMALL HITCH.

Busiek fully sees Tony Stark as being a more interesting character than his alter ego. "Tony Stark is the character that I was attracted to. The fact that he's Tony is the part that I like so much, because most Super Hero secret identities are, 'They do X, this is their shtick.' Clark Kent, newscaster, or reporter. Spider-Man, photographer. But Iron Man is just a story engine. Tony Stark has four different facets: He's a brilliant inventor, and that's a source of stories. He's an attractive ladies' man, which is a source of stories. He runs a business, and that's a source of stories. And he's a superpowered hero, and that's a source of stories. So whatever direction you go in, he's just gonna be generating stories. He's met a new girl and he's swept her off her feet, and she's in trouble, and *Bam!* You've got an *Iron Man* story. He's running his business and somebody's trying to take it down a peg and Bam! You've got an *Iron Man* story: corporate espionage. He's invented a new space shuttle engine and the bad guys wanna steal it. *Bam!* You've got an *Iron Man* story. He's such a versatile character because he can do so many different things and do them well."

As for Iron Man himself, Busiek says, "One of the things I've always liked about Iron Man is that he and Tony Stark pretend to be different people in the same setting. Iron Man is supposedly an employee of Tony Stark, which means he's walking around with a wall in front of his face, seeing people talk about him as if he's not there. That's got to be not only uncomfortable, but revealing. He's a spy among his own associates and friends, sort of unwillingly. I always thought that was a fascinating aspect of the character. But on a purely Super Hero basis, there's two things I really like about Iron Man. One of them is, he's the Swiss Army knife of Super Heroes. He needs a new superpower, he's gonna go invent it. He's got fire extinguishers in his boot pods, he's got GPS systems and built-in cell phones, and—for pete's sake—he's got pop-out roller skates in his boots. He's the Super Hero that's always improving himself, because if he gets a new idea—*Hey, in-flight movies in the helmet!*—he can just put it in. So he's modular and improvable, and that means that the character can change and grow and emphasize different things. I find that to be a unique and interesting part of the character.

"There's also the fact that because his armor is his power, you can take it away from him," Busiek continues.

"You can make Superman powerless, but you can't take his powers away and give them to somebody else, unless you're doing a weird story with Mxyzptlk or somebody like that. You trap Bruce Wayne somewhere and you've trapped Batman. But Iron Man, if he doesn't have his briefcase or whatever else he's carrying his armor in, he's just Tony Stark. He's completely powerless. He's brilliant and he's clever, and all that, so you gotta deal with that, but the power is separable and can be given to somebody else, which means that what makes Iron Man, Iron Man, has to be something *other* than the suit. Because if it's just the suit, you can give it to anybody, and they've done that from time to time. But it always comes back to it being Tony as Iron Man, and the reason is because it's the combination of that multifaceted character with that Swiss Army Knife exoskeleton that makes him so interesting."

Even as far back as Iron Man's origin, which Busiek recapped early on (keeping John Byrne's earlier non-time-specific non-Vietnam retconning), the character is one who, according to the writer, "is one of the few Super Hero characters who does not have a *motivating event*. Spider-Man feels responsibility for what happened to his uncle Ben. Batman is over and over again fighting against the guy who killed his parents. Over and over through Super Hero history, you see the thing that motivates them to be a Super Hero is tied in to their origin. Iron Man, he's got a motivating event that gave him the powers—the injury to his heart that made him wear the chest plate—but from that point on it's like, *Well, I'm wearing this chestplate and I can connect armor to it, so why not? It enables me to help out my company, and it enables me to do good.* It makes it possible for him to be a Super Hero. But the reason he is a Super Hero, recent years notwithstanding, is because he's a nice guy. Because he feels that he *should* do these things. When I was writing the book, I played him like a Rockefeller, like somebody who felt that the health of the world, the health of the United States, the health of the people out there is what put him in the position he's in. If it weren't for all those people out there, living and dying and spending money, working for him or working for other people and buying things that he makes, he wouldn't be a super-wealthy millionaire. So it's in his best interests and the world's best interests for Iron Man to keep it healthy. And that's, I think, a more nuanced, more complicated motivation than 'criminals killed my parents.' 'Criminals killed my parents' is simple and powerful, but Iron Man is nuanced and complicated because he doesn't *have* to do it. He could hire it out. It's about his character and not about any one specific event."

In Busiek's first six issues, he brought back Countess Stephanie de la Spirosa from *Tales of Suspense* #69 (September 1965), as well as civilian-again James Rhodes (whose War Machine armor had been destroyed in another Marvel book), and had his hero face off against the Dreadnoughts and the new Firebrand, plus conspire with the Black Widow to get himself abducted.

Iron Man #7 (August 1998) saw the book cross over with *Avengers,* which Kurt Busiek was also writing. He had begun a subplot there with Carol Danvers, a superheroine with multiple past code names—Ms. Marvel, Binary, Warbird—and a very convoluted past. "I wanted to do something with her that gave her a new source of emotional turmoil," says Busiek, "so that you could say once, *This is connected to the fact that she didn't used to have any emotional connection to her past, and she got it back, and she's messed up in a way that's easier to understand and now she's getting over that.*

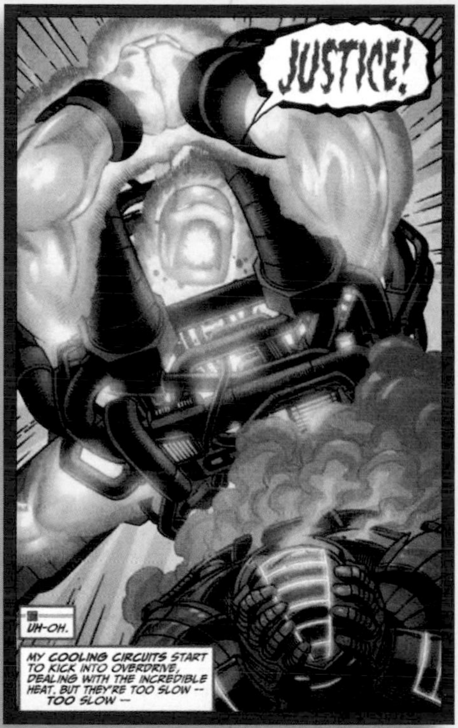
JUSTICE!
UH-OH.
MY COOLING CIRCUITS START TO KICK INTO OVERDRIVE, DEALING WITH THE INCREDIBLE HEAT. BUT THEY'RE TOO SLOW -- TOO SLOW --

▲ Iron Man's new armor glows, even when he's under attack.

You deal with the getting over it, rather than the constant re-explication of this complicated science-fiction situation that's very dry and technical. At the same time, I wanted to deal with Iron Man's alcoholism, but I wanted to deal with it in a different way. If you're an alcoholic, you're an alcoholic for life. The question is: Are you drinking or are you not drinking? That's the only way it had been done in an Iron Man story. Is he drinking? Is he not drinking?

"But alcoholism is more complicated than that, and it struck me that if Tony is going to Alcoholics Anonymous meetings, the next step for him should be to be somebody's sponsor, to sponsor someone else who's an alcoholic, and help them get through it. Trouble is, it's a Super Hero comic. You gotta hit people in a Super Hero comic. So if Tony is just mentoring an alcoholic—sponsoring an alcoholic, rather—it's not gonna suit the drama unless the alcoholic is another Super Hero, in which case you immediately got the visual aspect of all the stuff Iron Man went through but now he's seeing it from a different side. Now he's seeing it from the outside. I asked who could I have be an alcoholic, who I can make Iron Man their sponsor, and I was told, 'You can use Ms. Marvel, or you can use She-Hulk.' We discussed She-Hulk for a little bit, but we just decided She-Hulk is too fun. She-Hulk is actually reasonably well adjusted and she has an upbeat attitude toward life, and if we make her an alcoholic, that's such a downer that it breaks what works about the character.

"Ms. Marvel, on the other hand, Binary/Carol Danvers/whoever she was at the time, she's already struggling with emotional difficulties, so if we decide that her struggle with those emotional difficulties tips her over the edge into alcoholism, that fits the character, that enhances the character, and that gives us that simple, easily approachable explanation for what we do going forward where we don't have to mention over and over again that science-fiction backstory. So it seemed to be a natural fit there, and we had Warbird introduced in *Avengers,* then we could introduce the fact that she was an alcoholic and have her lose her place on the team as a result, knowing that we were then going to bring her over into *Iron Man*, and have the two alcoholics—one of them the recovering alcoholic, the other the still-in-denial alcoholic—play off each other and see what drama we got out of that."

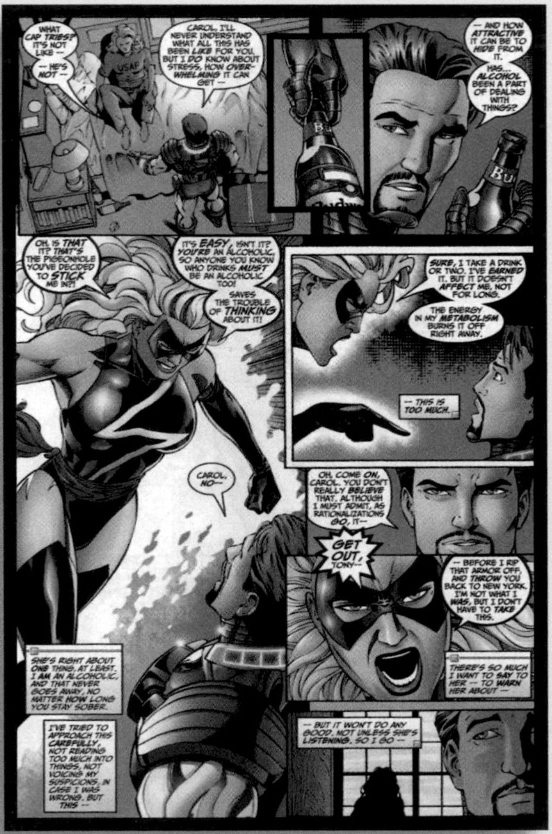

WHAT CAP TRIBS? IT'S NOT LIKE —
— HE'S NOT —
CAROL, I'LL NEVER UNDERSTAND WHAT ALL THIS HAS BEEN LIKE FOR YOU, BUT I DO KNOW ABOUT STRESS, HOW OVER-WHELMING IT CAN GET —
— AND HOW ATTRACTIVE IT CAN BE TO HIDE FROM IT.
HAS... ALCOHOL BEEN A PART OF DEALING WITH THINGS?
OH, IS THAT IT? THAT'S THE PIGEONHOLE YOU'VE DECIDED TO STICK ME IN?!
IT'S EASY, ISN'T IT? YOU'RE AN ALCOHOLIC, SO ANYONE YOU KNOW WHO DRINKS MUST BE AN ALCOHOLIC TOO!
SAVES THE TROUBLE OF THINKING ABOUT IT!
SURE, I TAKE A DRINK OR TWO. I'VE EARNED IT. BUT IT DOESN'T AFFECT ME, NOT FOR LONG.
THE ENERGY IN MY METABOLISM BURNS IT OFF RIGHT AWAY.
— THIS IS TOO MUCH.
CAROL, NO—
OH, COME ON, CAROL. YOU DON'T REALLY BELIEVE THAT. ALTHOUGH I MUST ADMIT, AS RATIONALIZATIONS GO, IT—
GET OUT, TONY—
— BEFORE I RIP THAT ARMOR OFF, AND THROW YOU BACK TO NEW YORK. I'M NOT WHAT I WAS, BUT I DON'T HAVE TO TAKE THIS.
SHE'S RIGHT ABOUT ONE THING, AT LEAST. I AM AN ALCOHOLIC, AND THAT NEVER GOES AWAY, NO MATTER HOW LONG YOU STAY SOBER.
I'VE TRIED TO APPROACH THIS CAREFULLY, NOT READING TOO MUCH INTO THINGS, NOT VOICING MY SUSPICIONS, IN CASE I WAS WRONG. BUT THIS —
THERE'S SO MUCH I WANT TO SAY TO HER — TO WARN HER ABOUT —
— BUT IT WON'T DO ANY GOOD. NOT UNLESS SHE'S LISTENING. SO I GO —

Warbird faces her own demons with ▲ Tony's help (left) and the villain Whiplash gets a makeover (right).

The remainder of Busiek's first year saw the return of Whiplash, Spymaster, and ultimately the Mandarin. "We brought back Whiplash. His name had been changed from Whiplash to Blacklash, and I don't know about you, but to me Blacklash is a mascara. It's a terrible name. It's not a tough guy with a whip. So we brought him back as Whiplash, and juiced him up so that he actually had the

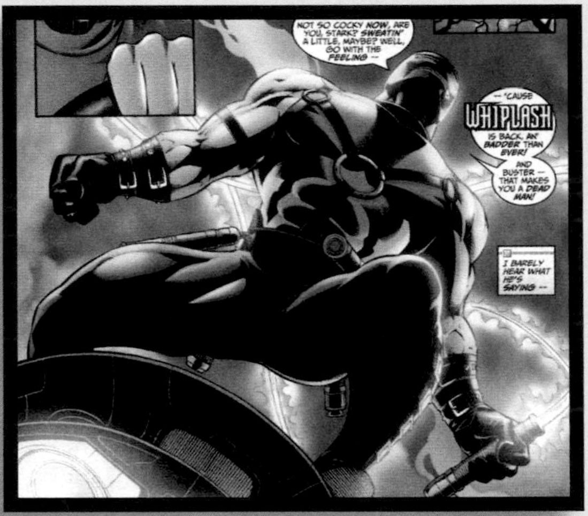

NOT SO COCKY NOW, ARE YOU, STARK? SWEATIN' A LITTLE, MAYBE? WELL, GO WITH THE FEELING —
— 'CAUSE WHIPLASH IS BACK, AN' BADDER THAN EVER!
AND BUSTER — THAT MAKES YOU A DEAD MAN!
I BARELY HEAR WHAT HE'S SAYING —

ability to fight Iron Man, and then somebody else immediately killed him. We'd also brought back the Spymaster and his Espionage Elite. I always liked the Spymaster because he works in that James Bondian corporate espionage world that Iron Man inhabits so well. And there was one story back in the 1970s where he had a team of crack agents—the explosives expert, the communications expert, the infiltration expert—and they were the Espionage Elite."

As for Mandarin, Busiek again refashioned the villain from previous versions. "We decided to play off the fact that the Mandarin believed in feudalism. He believed in the lords and serfs, and he believed in the idea that the elite of the world should rule, and the non-elite of the world serve the elite, and that's the way things functioned well. That's what he wanted to bring back. Not specifically, *I want to*

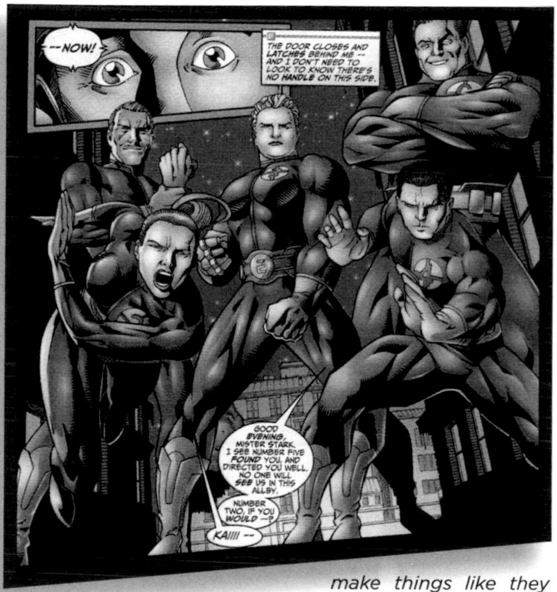
--NOW!
THE DOOR CLOSES AND LATCHES BEHIND ME -- AND I DON'T NEED TO LOOK TO KNOW THERE'S NO HANDLE ON THIS SIDE.
GOOD EVENING, MISTER STARK. I SEE NUMBER FIVE FOUND YOU, AND DIRECTED YOU WELL. NO ONE WILL SEE US IN THIS ALLEY.
NUMBER TWO, IF YOU WOULD --?
KAIIII --

make things like they were in ancient China, but, *I believe in the power of the elite.* Which plays into *Iron Man* because Iron Man is the modern equivalent of a feudal lord; he's the head of an international business. So he's got lots and lots of ordinary people working for him, and the value of their labor flows upward and outward, and as a result he feels protective of them . . . The laws and rules are a bit different, but the essential relationship of a CEO to the company he owns, [compared] to a feudal lord and his serfs and peasants and warriors, isn't all that structurally different."

In *Iron Man* volume III's second year, due to his workload and some health issues, Busiek took on Roger Stern as his co-writer. Stern had written just about every character at Marvel in the past, as well as DC's flagship character, Superman, but he had never written *Iron Man.* He had, however, edited first series issues #113–133 (including the infamous "Demon in a Bottle" storyline), and had followed the series as a fan since *Tales of Suspense* #56 (August 1964).

Like Busiek, Stern admired Stark as a character. "He's fabulously wealthy, but he's no slacker. In fact, he took a family business and made it greater than ever. And lost it all. And started a new business, and made that wildly successful. And lost control of the new business. And started yet another, wildly successful business. Tony Stark is an industrialist, but he's not a nasty bastard . . . at least, he wasn't while I was connected with the book. He funds more charitable foundations than most people know exist. And, of course, he bankrolls the Avengers, which he helped found. He's been seen with more glamorous women than James Bond and Bruce Wayne combined, and yet he's been unlucky in love. Tony Stark is a modern, sane Howard Hughes. And as Iron Man, he is the self-made Super Hero, a modern-day knight in shining armor."

Speaking of armor, the pair of writers brought back the War Machine armor, though this time there was a mystery attached as to where the armor came from and who was in it. "We got to take War Machine and make him a villain," says Busiek. "I always thought that *War Machine* is not the name of a hero. *War Machine* is the name of an antagonist, a guy who's gonna fight your hero. I wanted to go back to the design everybody liked, and make it a villain, and the only real problem we had with it was one point where the editorial people decided, 'Well, if you're bringing back War Machine, we've gotta update him and we've gotta make him cooler, we've gotta put him in a

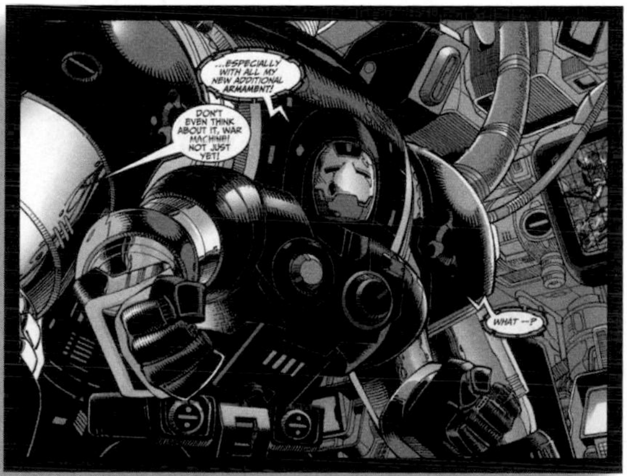
...ESPECIALLY WITH ALL MY NEW ADDITIONAL ARMAMENT!
DON'T EVEN THINK ABOUT IT, WAR MACHINE! NOT JUST YET!
WHAT --?

▲ Iron Man faced Spymaster's Espionage Elite (left) and a deadly new War Machine (right).

new armor suit,' and I was just going, 'No, no, no no! The armor is what people like! This armor design—the black and gray—this is what people like. If you're gonna change it, they're not gonna like it anymore. They never do.' And so I think we got to do two issues with War Machine in the classic armor, and then we had to upgrade the armor, and it turned him into this hulking, monstrous thing, and nobody liked it."

Other stories saw the return of the Controller and Fin Fang Foom, plus some new villains, but Busiek and Stern ended their run with the three-part Ultimo storyline in *Iron Man* #23–25 (December 1999–February 2000). Of his time on *Iron Man* in the 1970s *and* the 1990s, Stern says he's happy that "I got to work with a lot of wonderfully creative people, and we all got to show readers that Iron Man was, in fact, cool. I think that a good *Iron Man* series should have a lot of action and visual excitement, while dealing with themes of interest to an older reader. It should be handled in a way that doesn't alienate the younger readers or their parents. Like all good Marvel Comics—or all good Warner Bros. cartoons—*Iron Man* should appeal to all ages."

WIZARD
1/2
THE INVINCIBLE
IRON MAN
MARVEL COMICS

Busiek laments that he had some difficulties with Marvel editorial personnel, which he feels hampered telling the stories he believed were best. Combined with his health and scheduling problems, the aggravation finally forced him to leave. "It wasn't everything I wanted it to be," Busiek says. "I think we did good comics. I think we did a respectable job, and the reactions from Iron Man fans seemed to indicate that we didn't screw anything up too bad. But Iron Man was a dream character for me to write, and I had very high aspirations for it, and it didn't quite come together the way I wanted it to come together. I don't think it matched my dream of what it could have been. I wouldn't mind writing the character again someday to figure out how I can make it what I would want to make it."

Neither author would hurt for work post-*Iron Man.* Busiek continued on *Avengers* for some time, as well as his critically acclaimed *Astro City,* and did fan-favorite work on both *Superman* and *Conan.* Stern, meanwhile, wrote further adventures of the Avengers and Spider-Man, as well as *Justice League of America* and both a *Smallville* and a *Superman* novel.

•

With *Iron Man* #26 (March 2000), new writer Joe Quesada would come aboard, with major changes in store. Quesada had largely been an artist in the 1990s on books for Valiant and DC, and eventually formed a company, Event Comics, to publish the adventures of a superpowered firefighter in Ash. In 1998, the Event creators had contracted to do several more adult-themed comics in a sub-imprint of Marvel called Marvel Knights, and by 2000, Quesada's star was rising with meteoric speed.

Also rising were the sales of comic books collected into trade paperback form. Although neither Marvel nor DC has said it has a dictum that stories be written "for trade," the new millennium saw most storylines plotted as five- or six-issue "arcs," which coincidentally fit nicely into trade paperbacks. In Quesada's first five-part story, following a battle with Whiplash and the introduction of a new technological concept named S.K.I.N. (Synth Kinetic Interfacing Nanofluid),

▼ A new look for Spymaster (left) and an older look for Justin Hammer (right).

Stark was astonished to find his secret identity splashed on newspaper headlines.

Things got dicier in the next issue with the arrival of the Mandarin, and Tony getting stinking drunk, but the truth was soon revealed: In the last issue, Tony'd had a heart attack, and he'd hallucinated his "outing" and the resulting fighting and drinking binge. More disturbing was the revelation that the Iron Man armor was now . . . alive! By the final part of the story, the armor had captured and tortured Tony in an attempt to become "one." Tony resisted and had a massive heart attack, but the armor gave Tony its own artificial heart and "died."

"It's quite a daunting task to write a character that has as much history as Iron Man has," Quesada said in a past interview. "The trick I believe with characters like him is to tip your hat to continuity but try not to become reverent to it. It's a tough trap not to try to fall into . . . I just took all those years of emotional baggage that the character has been carrying around and looked to see what resonated with me, or what was common with experiences in my life. This allowed me to get into the character's head as best as I could."

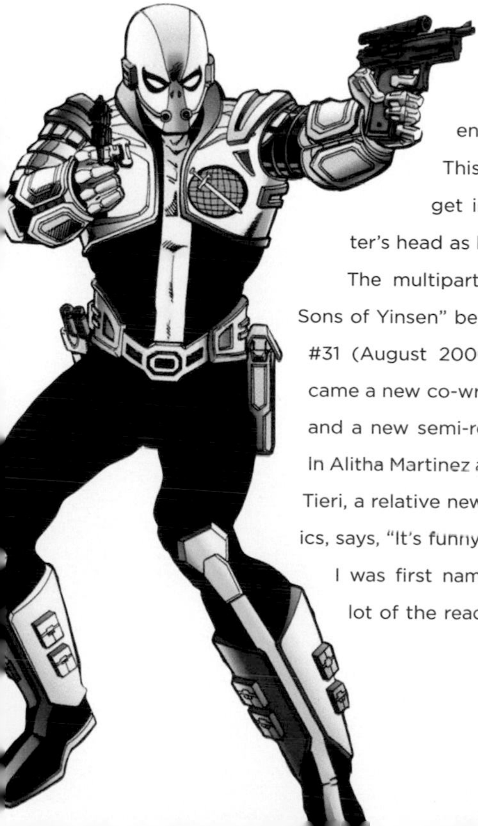

The multipart storyline "The Sons of Yinsen" began in *Iron Man* #31 (August 2000), and with it came a new co-writer, Frank Tieri, and a new semi-regular art team in Alitha Martinez and Rob Hunter. Tieri, a relative newcomer to comics, says, "It's funny, because when I was first named co-writer, a lot of the reaction was, 'Who the hell is Frank Tieri and why is he on my book?' And I sort of understood it because here I was coming out of nowhere and suddenly I'm co-writing a Marvel mainstay like *Iron Man.* But what those people really didn't get was that I was one of those overnight successes that, in reality, was years in the making. I worked at Marvel on staff for a number of years—most notably as an editor at Marvel.com—and pitched away every chance I got for what seemed like forever, until Joe Quesada came along. Joe and I knew each other from some work he did for Marvel.com and he knew I was looking to break in, so when the responsibilities at Marvel Knights became too much and he needed a co-writer on *Iron Man* to help with the load, he gave me a shot. It was the break that every aspiring comic book writer is looking for, and I was certainly going to make the most of it."

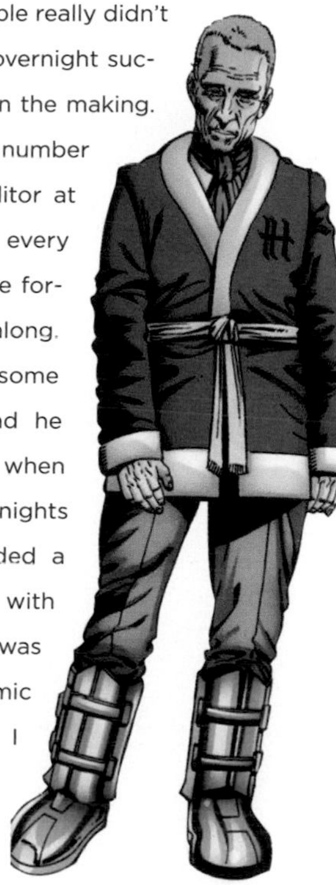

In the new team's story—which concluded in that year's double-sized *Iron Man Annual*—not only did Tony Stark don his classic red-and-gold armor from the 1970s and 1980s, but he also discovered that the two men most responsible for him being Iron Man—Professor Yinsen and warlord Wong-Chu—were both still alive. The storyline would have repercussions farther down the road.

Concurrent with the regular series, Marvel published *Iron Man: Bad Blood,* a four-issue mini series by David Michelinie and Bob Layton, in fall 2000. The story found Tony Stark acting very unlike himself, and saw the return of Justin Hammer and Spymaster, plus the debut of all-new Space Armor. "It had been quite a few years since we had originally tackled the character," says Layton, "and during

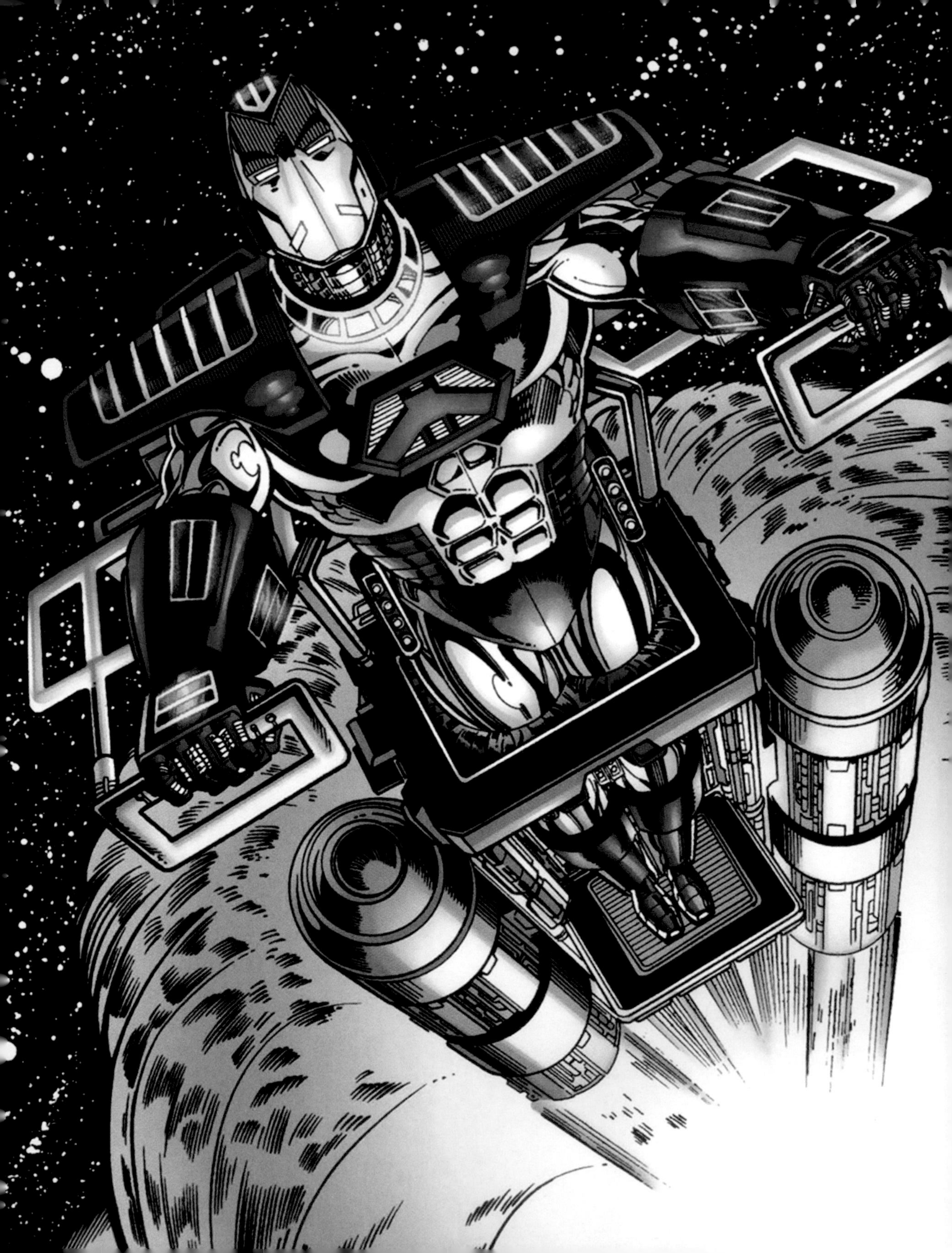

our absence, the editorial powers had succeeded in making Tony Stark incredibly Politically Correct. He was no longer a playboy, his business had become totally altruistic and nonprofit . . . Those elements made it a lot different and a little more difficult to portray him the way we saw him, creatively."

Meanwhile, Quesada's last issue as co-writer was #35 (December 2000), which was no surprise: He had just accepted the job as Marvel's editor-in-chief. Frank Tieri's next story, in *Iron Man* #37–41, found Stark adding a teleportation device to the armor, the debut of childhood rival Tiberius Stone, a lot of virtual-reality/dream-like scenes,

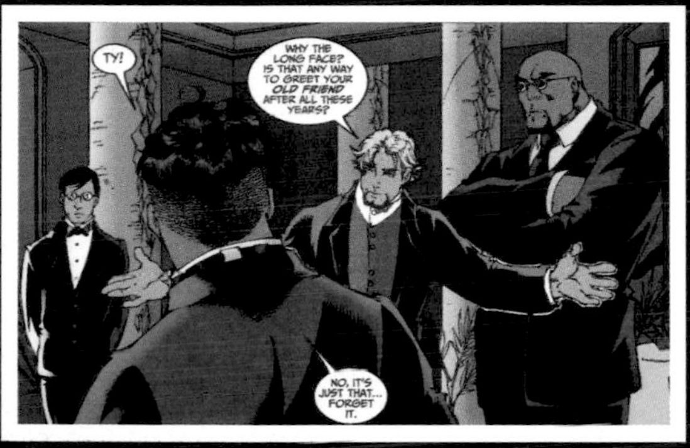
TY!
WHY THE LONG FACE? IS THAT ANY WAY TO GREET YOUR OLD FRIEND AFTER ALL THESE YEARS?
NO, IT'S JUST THAT... FORGET IT.

and the possible end to Stark Solutions. "This may have been my first solo arc on *Iron Man,*" Tieri says, "but the genesis actually came from plans Joe and I had before he had to leave the book. With the creation of Tiberius Stone, we wanted to introduce someone who could play on Tony's level—rich, smart, good looking, powerful. But if Tony was originally created by Stan to be Marvel's Howard Hughes, we had intended Stone to be a media mogul à la Rupert Murdoch or Ted Turner. And there was also something else about Stone—a very dangerous something else. While Tony always considered him to be a close childhood friend, Stone secretly harbored this insane, personal rivalry with Tony—so insane, in fact, that when Tony gained his fortune due to the death of his parents, Stone murdered his own parents for the money in order to keep up. Talk about being committed to a rivalry!"

Tieri notes that the storyline did have some problems editorially. "I guess the closest thing to compare it to is to say this was like a rookie pitcher getting his first start in baseball. Let's just say with me being so green, I hadn't fully earned the manager's trust yet, and as a result, the ending of the storyline was greatly affected. In our original pitch, Joe and I were going to have Stone 'out' Tony as Iron Man at the end of the arc. Editorial at the time got cold feet at the last minute, deciding they couldn't allow a rookie writer to pull off such an important development in the character's history. The ending comes off a bit flat as a result, in my opinion, and it was a decision on their part that I regret to this day. All the more compounded by the fact Marvel would reveal his identity within a year *anyway.* Oh well . . ."

During the following storyline, "The Big Bang Theory" (issues #42–45), Tieri got a new penciller in Keron Grant, had Tony pose as a blue-collar tech worker named Hogan Potts,

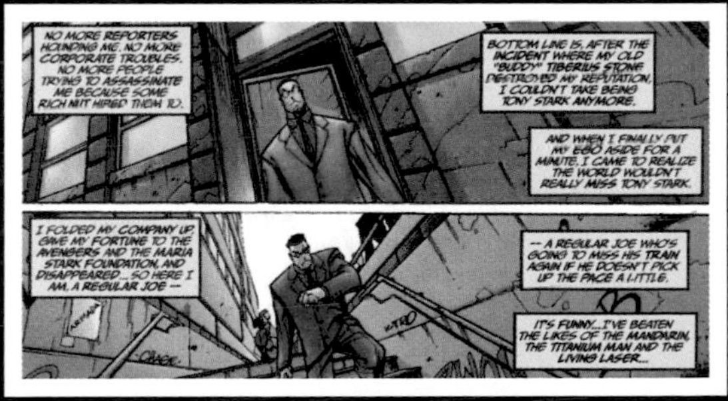
NO MORE REPORTERS HOUNDING ME. NO MORE CORPORATE TROUBLES. NO MORE PEOPLE TRYING TO ASSASSINATE ME BECAUSE SOME RICH NUT HIRED THEM TO.
BOTTOM LINE IS, AFTER THE INCIDENT WHERE MY OLD "BUDDY" TIBERIUS STONE DESTROYED MY REPUTATION, I COULDN'T TAKE BEING TONY STARK ANYMORE.
AND WHEN I FINALLY PUT MY EGO ASIDE FOR A MINUTE, I CAME TO REALIZE THE WORLD WOULDN'T REALLY MISS TONY STARK.
I FOLDED MY COMPANY UP, GAVE MY FORTUNE TO THE AVENGERS AND THE MARIA STARK FOUNDATION, AND DISAPPEARED... SO HERE I AM, A REGULAR JOE --
-- A REGULAR JOE WHO'S GOING TO MISS HIS TRAIN AGAIN IF HE DOESN'T PICK UP THE PACE A LITTLE.
IT'S FUNNY... I'VE BEATEN THE LIKES OF THE MANDARIN, THE TITANIUM MAN AND THE LIVING LASER...

and finally gave Iron Man a new armor composed of the S.K.I.N. and external components that would attach to it.

"The grand idea behind 'Big Bang Theory' with Tony giving away his wealth was to show the reader who I really thought Tony Stark was," Tieri says. "Tony Stark is not the money, the women, the cars, and not even the armor itself. Those are things we associate with *Iron Man* stories, but

▲ Business rival Ty Stone reappears (left) and Tony Stark makes some fundamental changes (right).

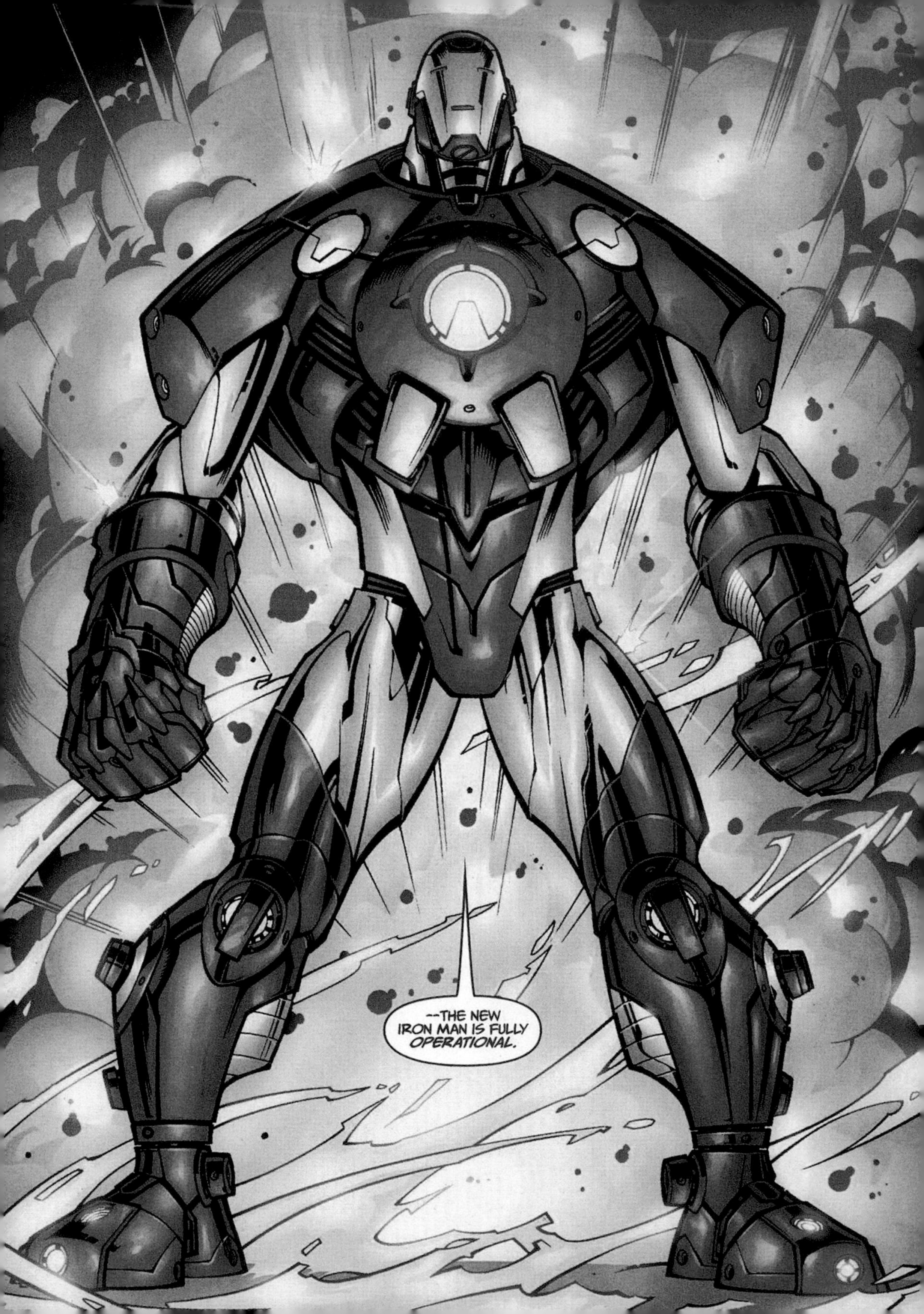
--THE NEW IRON MAN IS FULLY OPERATIONAL.

that's not necessarily who he is. To me, at his core, Tony Stark is an inventor, plain and simple. And no matter where he is or what happens to him, that's what he'll come back to. And that's what happens here."

The story also saw the return of two vintage *Iron Man* villains, the Ghost and Modok. Tieri says, "The longtime fans of the book had been clamoring for the return of some of the more classic *Iron Man* foes, and I saw this story as the opportunity to give them just that. In addition to bringing back Modok and the Ghost, this arc also has two other classic Marvel villains in it: the Blizzard and Mr. Hyde. Both those issues were really fun to do—the Blizzard one has Tony being forced to use an older armor to fight the Blizzard on Coney Island, and the Hyde issue finds Tony not only having to face Hyde but also having to contend with his belief that his armor is about to detonate. What was really different about that issue was, we did it in real time—fifteen minutes to be precise, the time we calculated it took the average fan to read a comic."

The sentient armor and the Sons of Yinsen made a significant reappearance in Tieri's next arc—"The Frankenstein Syndrome," issues #46–48—in a storyline that also used the sentient robotic Avengers super-foe Ultron and his onetime "bride," Jocasta. "I think 'The Frankenstein Syndrome' is the arc where I really started to come into my own as a writer," says Tieri, "and as a result, it's probably my favorite storyline from my time on the book. My idea came from Joe's 'Man in the Iron Mask' arc. Joe had taken a chance and set up that Iron Man's armor had become sentient largely due to Y2K. Well, as we all now know, Y2K wasn't nearly all it was cracked up to be, so something *else* had to be the culprit. Then it hit me . . . Ultron. Tony had downloaded Jocasta in his armor—and who had created Jocasta? Ultron fit like a glove—the only trouble was, he had just been used over in *Avengers*. But new editor Tom Brevoort gave me a shot—a long shot, but a shot nonetheless. All I had to do was convince *Avengers* writer Kurt

▼ Avengers villain Ultron means trouble for Iron Man.

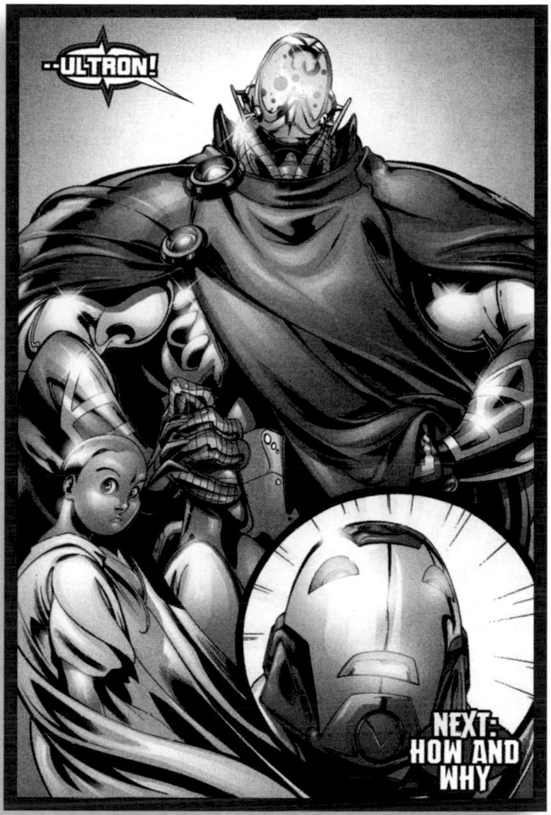
--ULTRON!
NEXT: HOW AND WHY

Busiek to let me use Ultron . . .

"So here I was, this newbie writer having to convince one of the biggest stars in the industry—who I didn't know from a hole in the wall, by the way—to let me use his character. And you know what? Kurt couldn't have been nicer about it. What he proposed was a trade—I could use Ultron if I agreed to have Jocasta downloaded out of Iron Man's armor and into another of his characters, Antigone. And you know what the funny part of all this is? If I remember correctly, Kurt left *Avengers* before his plans for Antigone and Jocasta had a chance to come to fruition."

Tieri's final *Iron Man* story was issue #49 (February 2002), which was presented completely silently—without word balloons or text. Tieri explains, "Marvel was doing a companywide event that month where every issue had

The Titanium Man doesn't need ▼ words to make his point.

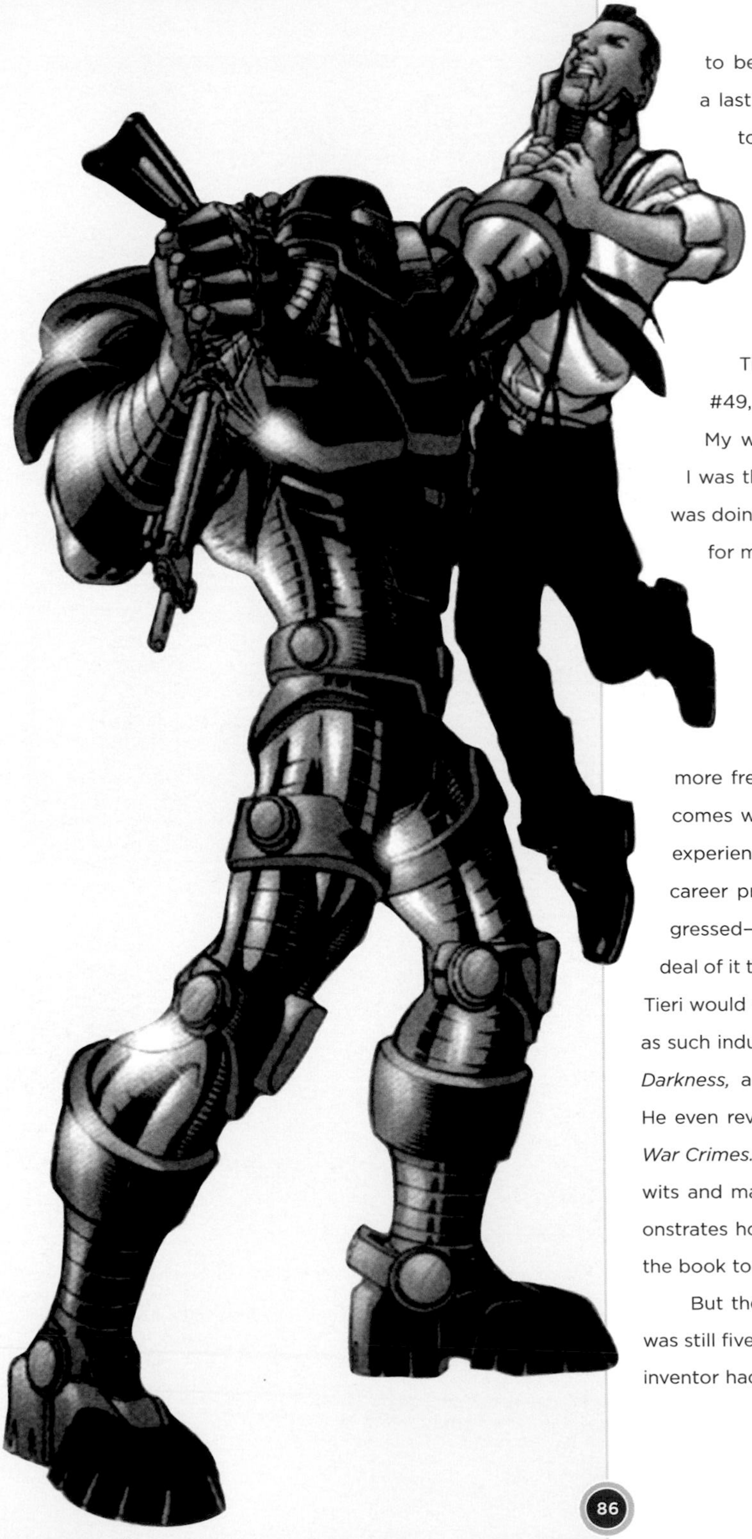

to be dialogue-less—which really wasn't ideal for a last issue since I couldn't do a proper good-bye to Tony without words. Instead, I opted to do what most people did that month: Do a big fight scene! In my case, I used an all-time favorite Iron Man villain of mine as the combatant, the Titanium Man."

Leaving the book was a necessity, Tieri reveals. "By the time it came time to write #49, I had already decided I was leaving the book. My workload had just become too overwhelming. I was the regular writer on *Wolverine* by then, plus I was doing an arc on *Deadpool,* and Marvel was looking for me to do a spin-off book from *Wolverine* called *Weapon X.*"

Tieri has mixed feelings about his time with the armored avenger. "I definitely feel there are things that I would have done differently and wish I had been given some more freedom in those earlier issues, but that's what comes with the territory of being a new writer; it's all experiences you learn from and use to grow as your career progresses. And my career thankfully has progressed—pretty nicely, in fact . . . And I owe a great deal of it to *Iron Man,* because that's where it all started." Tieri would go on to write *Wolverine* for two years, as well as such industry standards as *Hulk, Hercules, Dracula, The Darkness,* and most recently *Batman* and *The Punisher.* He even revisited Tony Stark in early 2007 for *Civil War: War Crimes.* "It has Tony getting down and dirty, matching wits and making deals with the Kingpin, and really demonstrates how I would write the character if I was writing the book today."

But the much-changed Tony Stark seen in *Civil War* was still five years in the future. Before that, the millionaire inventor had some real-world problems to face.

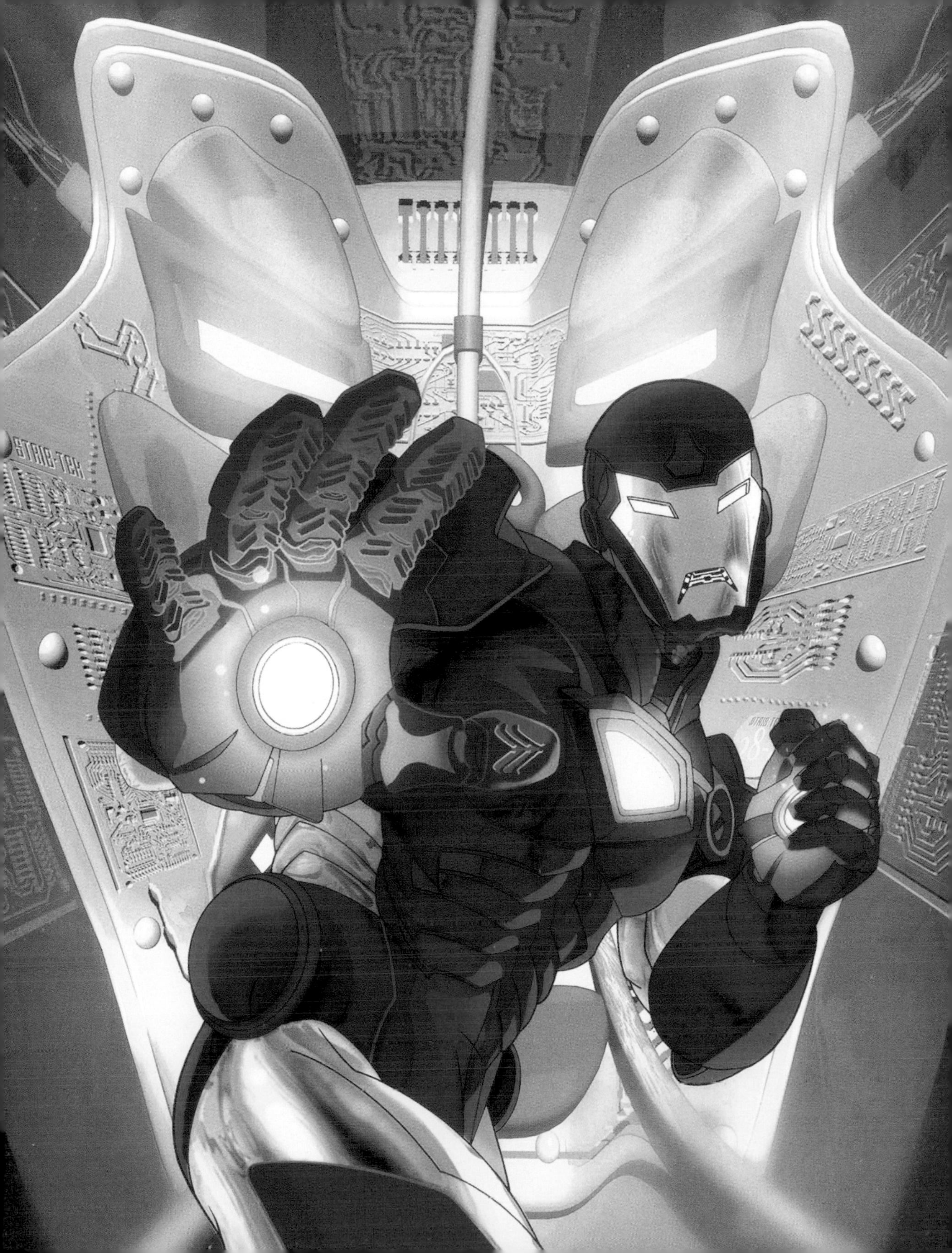

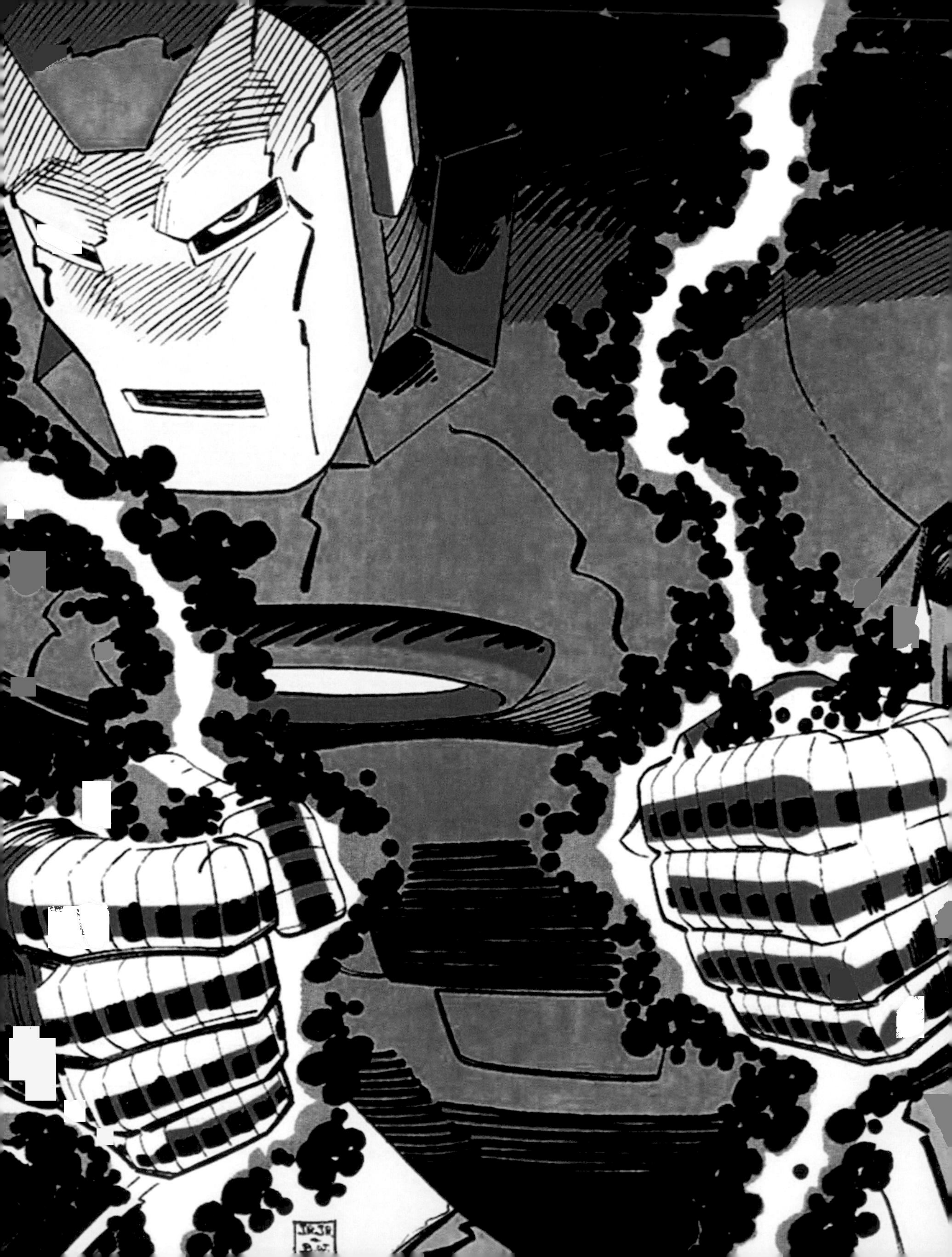

CHAPTER 6

A DARK AND
STORMY KNIGHT...

The world of 2002 was considerably different politically from anything seen in the nearly four decades since *Iron Man* had been created. "Ethnic cleansing," the attacks of September 11, 2001, and schoolyard massacres were a part of the public zeitgeist. The world of comics had changed as well, to a similarly darker and more dangerous realm. Stories about chemical dependency or racism or governmental subterfuge had once pushed the envelope, but since the 1986 publication of industry milestones *Batman: The Dark Knight Returns* and *Watchmen*, comics had entered a dark age, where grim and gritty heroes were sometimes as violent as their foes, and moral uncertainty was rife.

Part of the change in comics had come from their changing audience. Older readers who had followed their heroes from the 1960s and 1970s demanded stories that held their interest, while younger readers—if they read comics at all—had grown up in an age where video games, television, the Internet, and other pop-culture media not only competed for their interest but also exposed them to more adult concepts at ever-younger ages.

Iron Man editor Tom Brevoort took all these elements in mind as he chose the creative team that followed Frank Tieri's departure. He selected writer-artist Mike Grell to script the series, with a new art team of Michael Ryan and Sean Parsons. "The reason I turned to Mike to write *Iron Man* was, he had a long history—going back to the work he did elsewhere with characters like *Green Arrow* for DC and *Warlord* and so forth—of writing sophisticated adult characters, not sort of simplified or stripped-down sorts of things," says Brevoort. "And *real-world* characters. He always seemed more comfortable with characters who—in the case of those two—carried a bow and arrow or an actual pistol, than guys that shot beams from their hands or made tornadoes and such. I figured Mike could relate to Tony Stark and the idea that this is a guy inside a suit of armor, and could place him in context to the real world, and bring a little bit of an espionage feel to the series, which to me was always sort of one of the hallmarks of *Iron Man*, whether it was Cold War espionage in the '60s or corporate espionage in the '80s."

Grell had made a stellar name for himself in the comic industry since the 1970s, whether drawing the fan favorite *Legion of Super Heroes*, or creating, writing, and drawing DC's *Warlord* or his creator-owned series *Jon Sable, Freelance, Starslayer*, and *Shaman's Tears*. His run on DC's *Green Arrow* mixed Eastern influences with street-level crime noir to critical acclaim

A jet explodes over a city. ▼

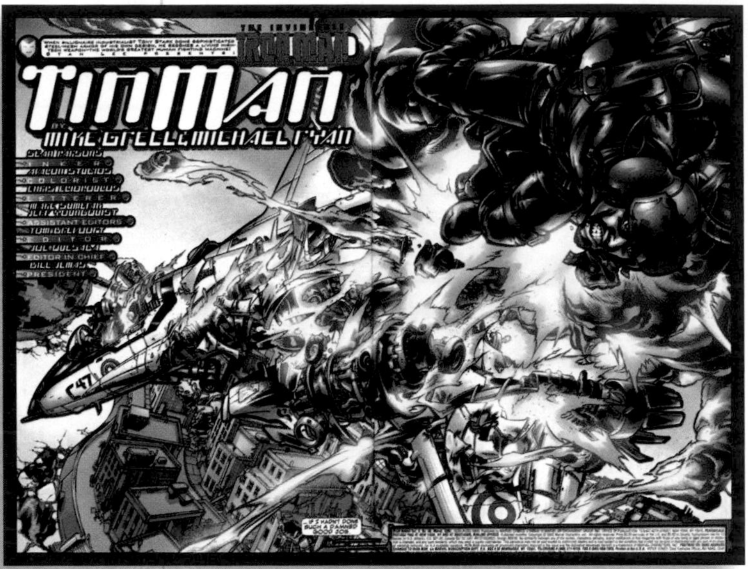
TIN MAN
BY
MIKE GRELL & MICHAEL RYAN
COLORIST
LETTERER
ASSISTANT EDITORS
EDITOR IN CHIEF
BILL JEMAS
PRESIDENT

"I did read *Iron Man* when it first started in comics, when it first came out," says Grell. "As far as a personal relationship with *Iron Man* goes, it wasn't so much something that made me want to work on it as it was a job that came along at the right time. I definitely felt that there was a particular connection there, because I like the character of Tony Stark. I like the approach that I was able to do, which was to focus more on the man inside the armor than the armor itself. As opposed to doing a strictly tech-oriented story, I tried to focus my stories on sort of a Tom Clancy techno-thriller kind of an aspect but really delve inside Tony Stark himself. That, to me, is the really interesting part of the character. I always liked the original concept that here's this guy who's got a piece of shrapnel slicing its way toward his heart and the only thing that's keeping him going is this machine and that he finds a way to turn that weakness into an amazing strength . . . The man inside the armor was the most important point to me, and I geared my stories that way. Everything that he got involved in had an emotional link and an impact on him in some fashion or another."

Working with penciller Michael Ryan was a pleasure for Grell. "When we began, I'd been accustomed to writing and drawing my own material for so long, and it's one thing to have a picture in your mind when you write it down on the page, and another things to see it brought to life as vividly as Michael did. In the first few issues, I think he saw that I was going for that sensitivity and humanity, and Michael seemed to go from the broad strokes of exaggerated super-action to some very good soft subtlety that was really nice on the page. And then it was just a kick in the pants to have written a scene where an airplane explodes over the city, and then open the book and see this airplane actually exploding over the city in about a million parts that really look like airplane parts."

As with most new teams on *Iron Man,* the pair established another new set of armor for the lead hero. "I get about half the credit on that one," says Grell. "I did the first design on it, and Michael did his as a refinement of mine, and in point of fact he added a lot more detail to it, and I remember writing and suggesting that he may have drawn himself into a corner—'cause remember, he was going to have to draw this every single time. Didn't faze him a bit. As I saw it, it was bits and pieces of armor that were put on over the top. The plate armor went over the top of what in real-world armor would probably have been chain mail. But we decided to make it the sort of banded steel tubing kind of thing. It's great graphics and it looks really good. The concept was that all the flexible parts would have that treatment to it, and then all the hard-edge parts, like the breastplate and shoulders, the lower arms and legs, would be done as shiny plate."

Grell's first issue was set in a foreign country where ethnic cleansing was taking place; a part of the story was a flashback to Iron Man's origin that altered elements of the

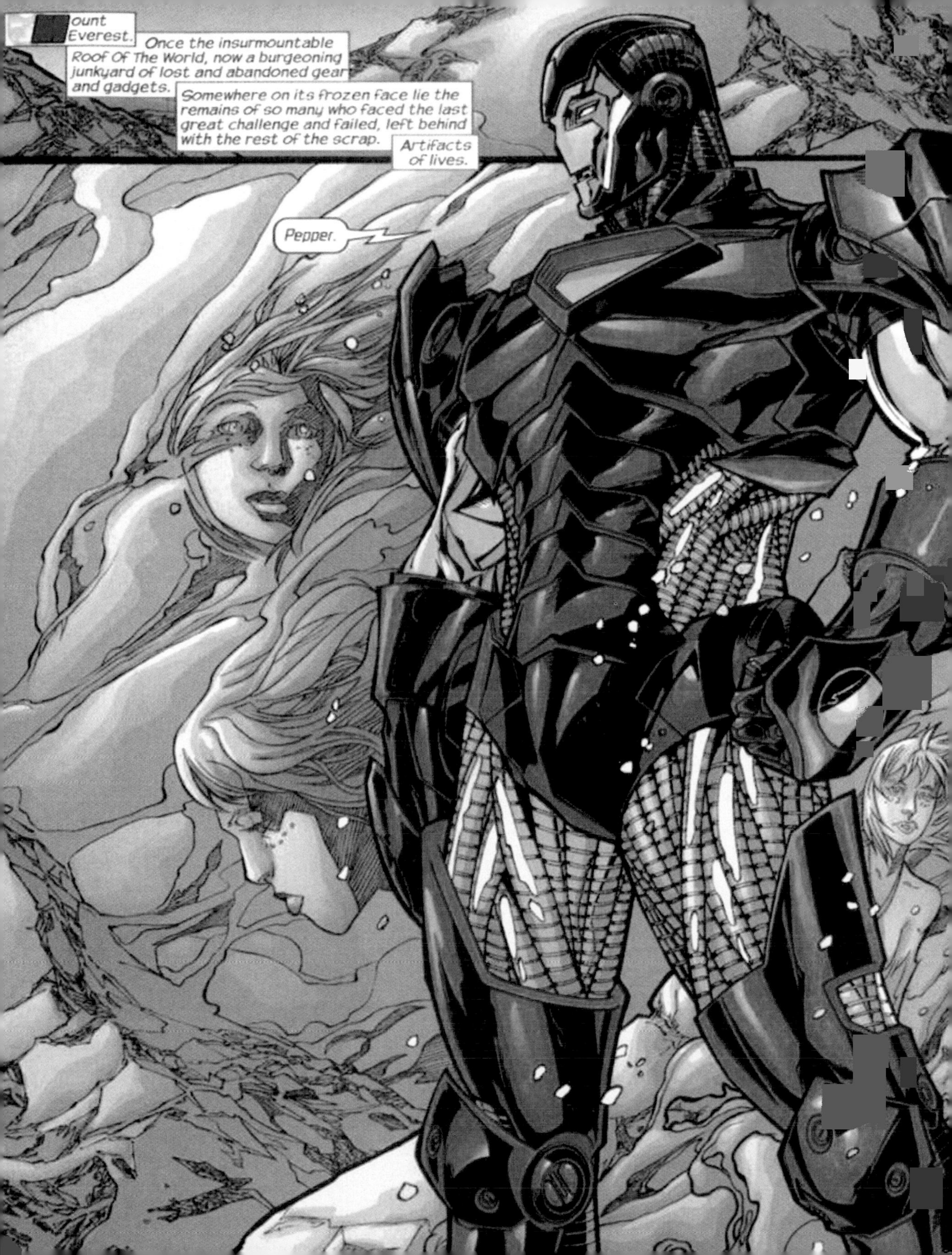

ount Everest.
Once the insurmountable Roof Of The World, now a burgeoning junkyard of lost and abandoned gear and gadgets.
Somewhere on its frozen face lie the remains of so many who faced the last great challenge and failed, left behind with the rest of the scrap.
Artifacts of lives.
Pepper.

traditional story. "One of the mandates that I had was that, as has been done periodically with *Iron Man* over the years, every decade or so, they re-create his origin, and update it to fit more with the modern times," Grell explains. "I was able to take the essence of the Iron Man origin, twist it around, and expand on it a bit, but keep the basics of it. In my version of this, Stark had developed a battle suit for the US military, and the suit was designed specifically to keep a soldier going no matter what happened; that included being wounded and included painkillers to block the pain, and drug stimulants to keep the body going long past the point of exhaustion or collapse. But they had neglected to take into consideration the human inside the armor, which drew my focus back to Tony.

"What I was doing with Tony Stark was taking the character, who approaches this weapons-design system as an intellectual exercise. He treats it as a mental challenge for himself—*Can I do this, can I build it?*—without giving any thought to how it's going to be used, and, of course, there are repercussions that come back on him very seriously, which is not unlike what happens in the real world. There have been numerous cases where people have approached designs of super-weapons . . . if you want to go as far back as the atomic bomb and say they did it because they could, not because it was really necessary, but they could do it, so they did do it, and sure enough they wound up using it."

The story also introduced a tough survivor of the foreign battle. "My very first story, I got into the question of war crimes in Eastern Europe," says Grell. "I made one of the key characters in the early stories Ayisha—she's a Muslim woman. She then becomes a very sympathetic character and a moderately romantic interest for Tony Stark when he's basically blown out of the airplane over the city while he's being shown around by this general, to whom he has actually supplied weapons. Stark has designed a lot of the stuff that is being used over there, and now that he's getting a look at what the actual aftermath is, he's getting involved. In order to fight against the forces that are coming to destroy her people, Ayisha puts on one of these battle suits that Stark knows is deadly. You can't wear it. It'll *kill* you, eventually, or it'll keep you going long after you should be dead. She becomes sort of a Frankenstein character as a result of that and essentially Tony Stark's own personal Frankenstein because she comes back to haunt him again."

In issues #53–55, Grell not only brought the Ayisha story to the forefront but also introduced the son of the Mandarin. But that wasn't what the story was *meant* to be, as Grell explains. "The Mandarin story was originally designed to explore different aspects of Tony Stark. My approach to it always was—and this did not come out in the storyline at the last minute; the editorial powers-that-be decided that couldn't be it—but I had approached this new Mandarin as a very mystical character that had highly developed martial arts capabilities. He'd grown up in a monastery. Basically, he was a supreme master of the martial arts and a Zen master, if you will, and capable of doing things physically that were beyond the realm of most people anyway, and then it turns out that he discovers that his father is the original Mandarin. He's passed this legacy of vengeance and hate against Tony Stark. My origi-

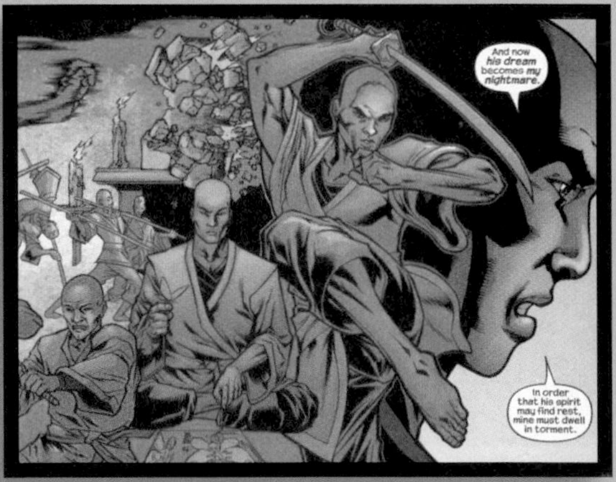

And now his dream becomes my nightmare.
In order that his spirit may find rest, mine must dwell in torment.

The Mandarin's origins are further explored. ▲

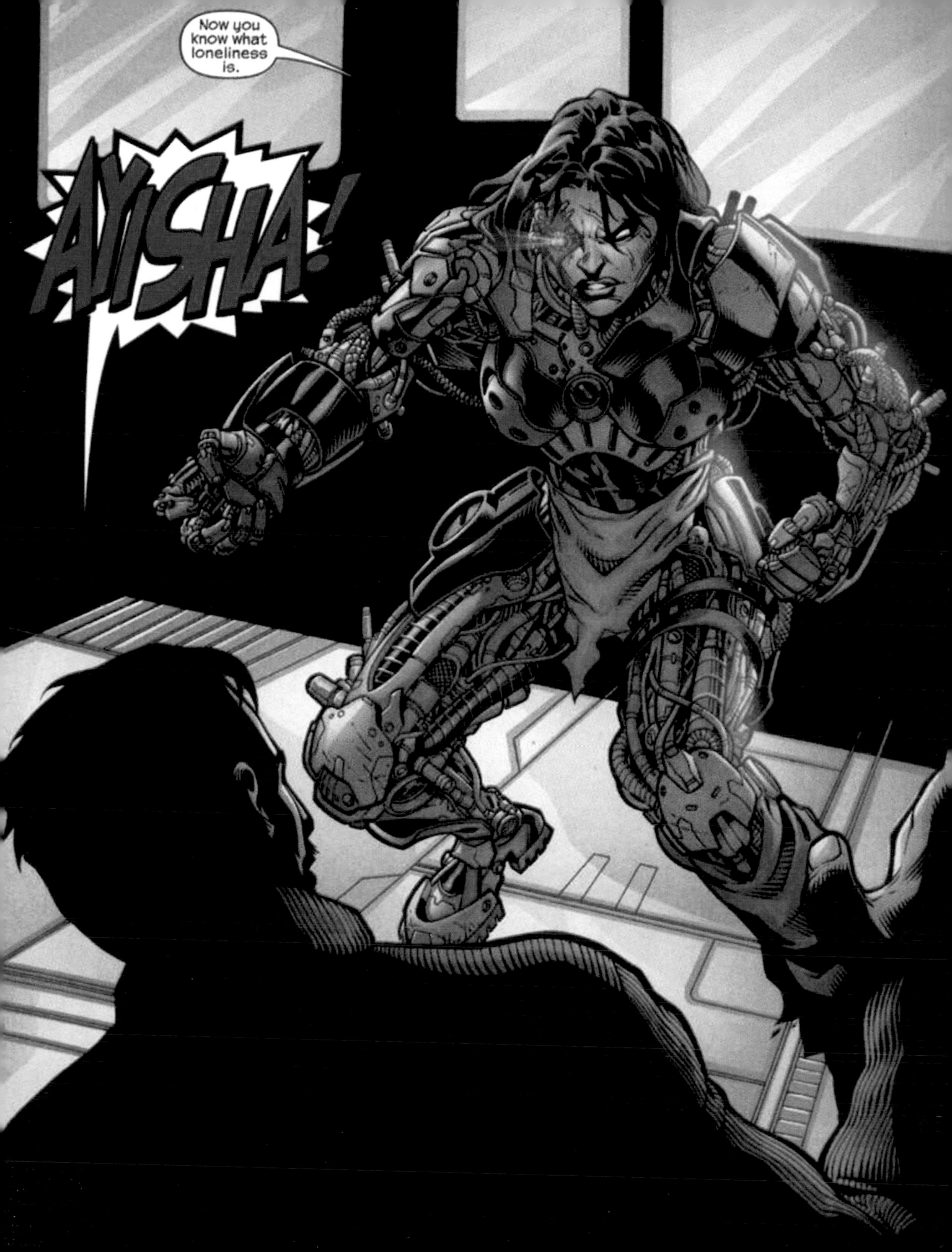
Now you know what loneliness is.
AYISHA!

nal approach to it was that ultimately it turns out that the Mandarin was not his father at all; *Tony Stark* is his father. If you read the stories with that in mind, suddenly everything takes on a different shape."

Brevoort says that the Mandarin reimagining was one of his favorite elements of Grell's run. "I also liked, quite a bit, his updating and reimagining of the Mandarin concept, moving from the father to the son, and sort of building a Mandarin who was steeped a little more in Eastern philosophy than Yellow Peril rhetoric, and who was, for lack of a better term, the honorable foe, the guy whose point of view and value system wasn't necessarily evil and was relatable, but happened to be in conflict with your own."

At the end of *Iron Man* #55 (August 2002), in an issue that was the four hundredth comic named *Iron Man,* Tony Stark revealed his identity to the world in an unexpected way . . . by saving the life of a puppy. "I think there was a large amount of confusion as to whether or not it would be a good idea to actually have him reveal his secret identity, although I had the complete approval of everybody on editorial with that before I did it," says Grell. "That's not the sort of thing that you do lightly. I wanted to do that in the way that I did it to show that sometimes a very simple thing can be the turning point for you. Of course, everybody resented him for having kept the secret from them as he had done, and then revealing it in such a fashion. What happens is there's a little boy's dog about to be run over in the street and Tony has a choice of either standing by and letting it happen, or stopping it from happening and revealing his secret identity in front of the news cameras and everyone else. He made that choice, but the reason that he does has to do with his relationship with Pepper and Happy. After all of this time of the two of them being back and forth in the relationship—Pepper and Tony Stark—of course she's happily married to Happy Hogan and there's still this bittersweet relationship between them that's never come to fruition. At the point where one of

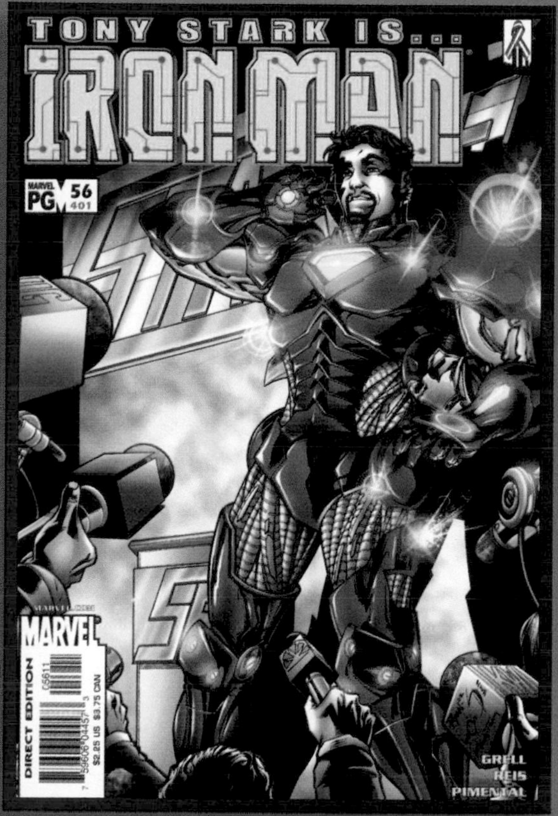
TONY STARK IS...
IRON MAN
PG 56 401
MARVEL
DIRECT EDITION
$2.25 US $3.75 CAN
GRELL
REIS
PIMENTAL

Tony's enemies puts Pepper in serious physical jeopardy, it turns out that she had been pregnant. Tony sees that as the child that *could* have been his, and it's *that* thing, that bittersweet hint of what might have been, that leads him to reveal his identity. Yeah, he's doing it for this little boy in the street, but in truth he's thinking about the child that could have been his own son."

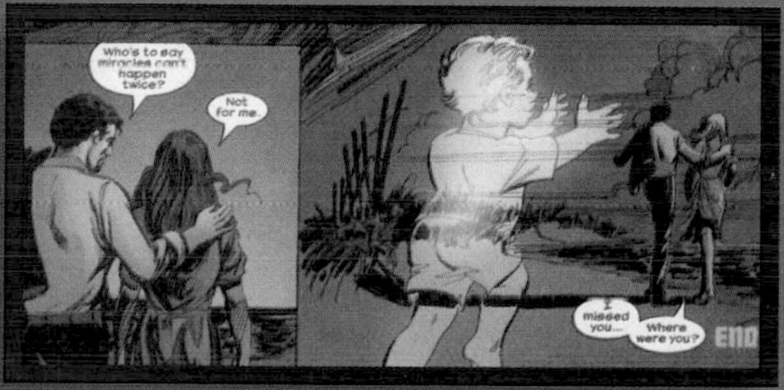
Who's to say miracles can't happen twice?
Not for me.
I missed you...
Where were you?
END

▲ Pepper Potts and Tony discuss the child that could have been.

Brevoort reveals that the decision to "out" Stark as Iron Man was not an easy one, but a necessary one. "The secret identity in comics generally is a conceit more than anything else. These characters maintain a double life because that makes the fiction good, rather than really making a lot of sense given the amount of effort that they spend, the amount of alienation that they create to their loved ones and the people around them. As we talked about Iron Man, it ultimately didn't make a heck of a lot of sense that Tony keeps his identity as Iron Man a secret. For one thing, he's in the public eye 24/7. It's gotta be next to impossible, just the physics of being able to hide the fact that you run off, you put on a suit of armor, you pretend to be your own bodyguard, and nobody ever photographs you together . . . it doesn't really carry a lot of weight. The idea that, in doing so, he was somehow protecting his friends and loved ones? His friends and loved ones all worked for him at the *same* plants that would be attacked by people that were coming to attack Iron Man because he worked there. It doesn't really make a lot of sense.

"It was a holdover from an era where Super Heroes had secret identities *because* Super Heroes had secret identities. To a certain degree, I can even buy it with Tony when he had the heart condition, because it wasn't even so much, *I can't tell them I'm Iron Man because they'll know I'm Iron Man*, it's *I can't tell them I'm Iron Man because they'll know I have a heart condition and I'll lose my defense contracts, and my wealth will be gone, and all my plant workers will be out of work, and this is my responsibility and this is the thing I have to maintain.* But once that sort of went away, the amount of effort you have to go through to conceal that for Tony Stark . . . is just beyond the pale of plausibility that this would work. Tony Stark is a billionaire playboy. People are following him, paparazzi are around him 24/7, people are checking out what this guy is doing." Revealing him as Iron Man "opened up some new avenues, some new places you could take *Iron Man* stories that you hadn't before that. So, we went ahead, we did the identity reveal."

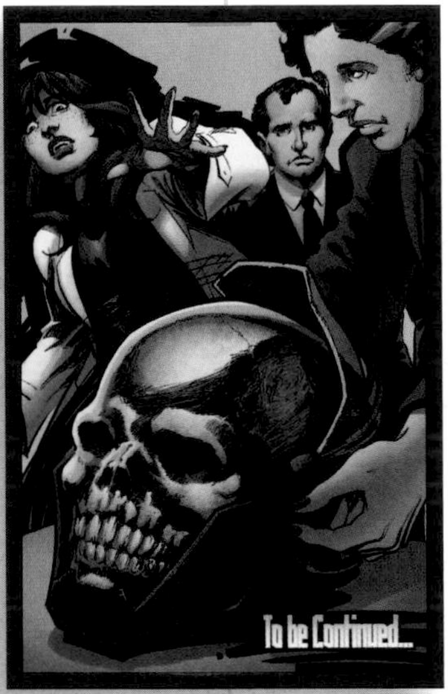
To be Continued...
An archaeological find shows a medieval ▼ skull in an Iron Man helmet.

Grell's next story saw the return of Ty Stone and Stark getting his controlling interest in Stark Industries back. The following three-parter, "In Shining Iron" in issues #59–61, saw Tony traveling back in time thanks to a time machine he had invented, to investigate why Iron Man's helmet was found—with a thousand-year-old skull in it—on an archaeological dig. Grell illustrated the story as well, and the plot was close to his heart. "The thing that I do like about *Iron Man,* and of course I have an affinity for it, is that he's a modern knight in armor," Grell says. "I perform with a group called the Seattle Knights, and my wife and I sword-fight and joust and we wear armor and clang and bang around and I fall off my horse all the time, on purpose. But there is something about the knight in shining armor, the guy who puts on this outer shell to protect him while he goes off and fights the battles . . . but you have to remember that it's what's inside that counts, too. Over the last ten or fifteen years, there's been a broader knowledge of things like the Renaissance fairs and festivals where people can go and watch knights performing and things like that, so it's more part of the pop culture than it has been in the past."

Once Stark returned to the present day, Grell continued to deal with the politics of the time. "Because 9/11 happened, we spun that into the storylines that actually dealt with terrorism and potential terrorist attacks on New York, and what would you do if you were a guy like Tony Stark? How far would you go to defend your people, your city, your country, the people that you loved? I had a story that brought it home on a really personal basis where he was the only one who could stop this, but he wasn't about to let it go public. He basically destroyed a submarine that had come up the river and was going to detonate a nuke in the heart of New York City. He destroyed it and jammed all their signals so they couldn't broadcast their message or anything else."

Fan reaction to Grell's run on *Iron Man* was mixed, as seen in Marvel's letters column for the book, but behind the scenes there were more problems. "I do know that there were editorial disagreements," says Grell. "I wasn't party to them, and it was never dis-

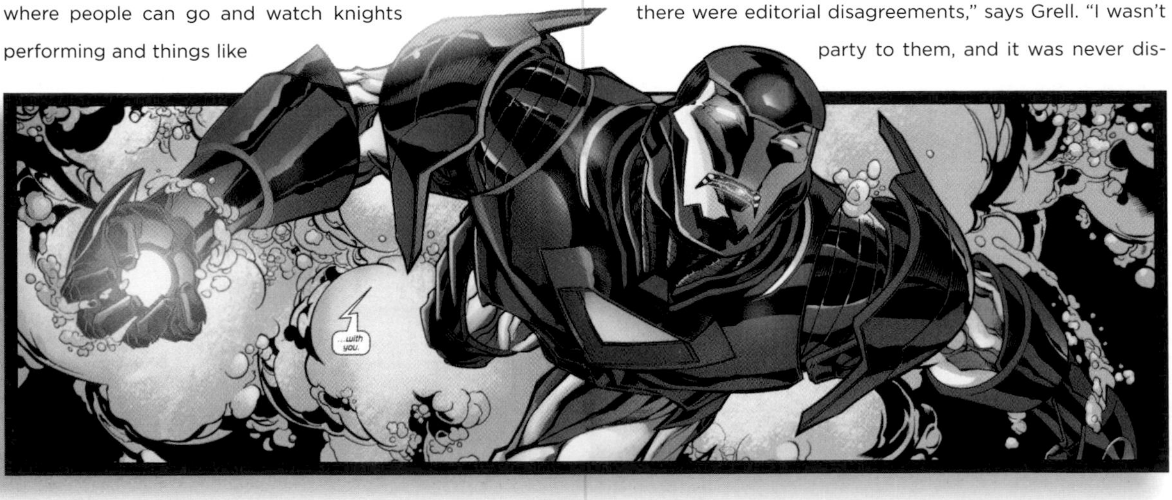
...with you.

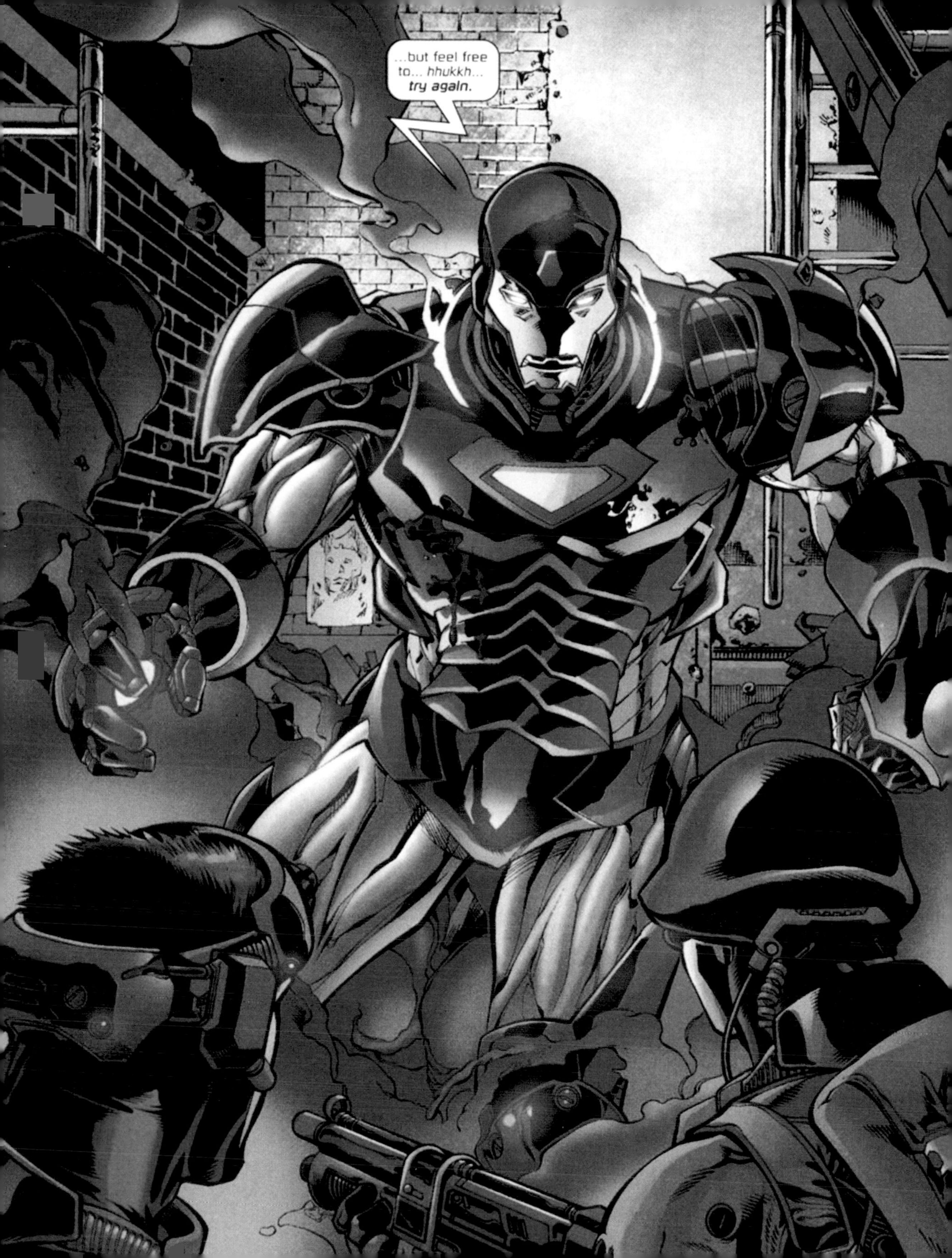
...but feel free to... hhukkh... try again.

cussed with me. But as far as I know, there were some disagreements [about] the direction that the book was taking. All I know is that the people that I had been dealing with had been totally supportive of the direction that I was going, and I understood that someone disagreed and they decided to pull the pin and go in a different direction."

Grell's final solo issue was *Iron Man* #64 (March 2003), a crossover with *Thor,* but he would contribute plot and some script to the following two issues. Since leaving *Iron Man,* Grell has returned to his street-level adventure hero, *Jon Sable, Freelance,* and is working on a new graphic novel called *The Pilgrim* with actor Mark Ryan.

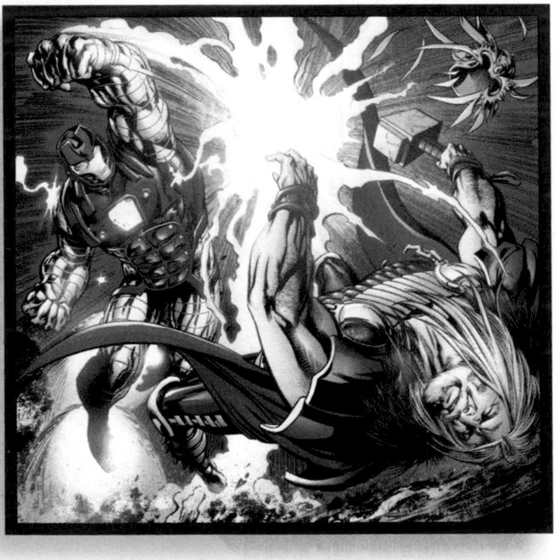

•

Iron Man #65–69 saw a new writer come aboard to finish the five-part "Manhunt" storyline, which found Tony under fire by snipers, Happy Hogan shot, the return of the new Mandarin, and peril for Pepper. Robin D. Laws was a popular designer of role-playing games including *Feng Shui, HeroQuest, Dying Earth,* and *Gumshoe,* but it was his novel, *Pierced Heart,* that brought him to the attention of Marvel's then-publisher Bill Jemas. He was assigned a project called *Hulk: Nightmerica,* then was called in to work on *Iron Man* for most of a year.

"I was a big fan of the comic as a kid, in the 1970s. This was the era when Iron Man had a nose on his mask, which I remember not liking so much," Laws says. "Iron Man is the ultimate gearhead's dream, a figure of gleaming technological fantasy. A well-written *Iron Man* sequence gives the reader the feeling of being in the suit, of being able to tap into that enormous power . . . and to imagine that you *could* be responsible for building it all. Stark is extremely intelligent and very driven, two qualities which offer enormous opportunities to a writer. Many of the Marvel characters are reluctant heroes, who want to be left alone but do their thing out of a sense of obligation or duty. Stark wants things and goes after them, meaning that he's a character who's easy to strongly motivate."

In "Manhunt," Laws expanded upon the story of the son of the Mandarin. "The storyline I joined in progress concerned Temugin, who was conceived to evoke his father, the Mandarin, in a more modern and sensitive way," says Laws. "The Mandarin owes his lineage to the way old pulps and serials dealt with Asian characters. These days, you look back on that source material and shudder at its corrosive racism. To write Temugin was a matter of finding his distinguishing drives as a person: in this case, his conflict between his sense of personal virtue, and his desire to be seen as a dutiful son, carrying on his father's legacy. Like any

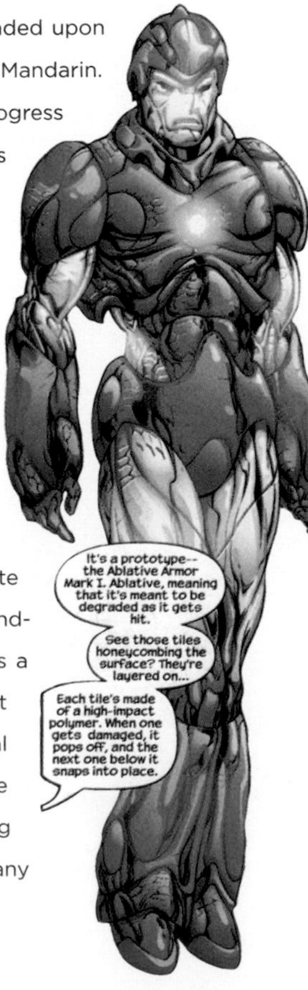
It's a prototype--the Ablative Armor Mark I. Ablative, meaning that it's meant to be degraded as it gets hit.
See those tiles honeycombing the surface? They're layered on...
Each tile's made of a high-impact polymer. When one gets damaged, it pops off, and the next one below it snaps into place.

Iron Man fights Thor (left) and develops ▲ his ablative armor (right).

character, he is the sum of his intentions. Being Chinese is not an intention, so if you're making that his defining trait, you're creating a stereotype, even if you're trying to do it in an admiring way."

By the storyline's end, readers saw a very different side to Temugin than they had anticipated. "The helpful thing in this instance was that he turned out not to be the villain of the piece," says Laws. "The real bad guy was a henchman who thought he wasn't being evil enough, and framed Tony Stark in an effort to provoke a confrontation between the two of them. So I got to emphasize Temugin's nobility, which seemed refreshing."

Laws' next pair of stories, "Vegas Bleeds Neon" in *Iron Man* #70–72, were, as Laws admits, "a tip of the hat to Stark's original model, Howard Hughes. He battles a fellow tycoon who's contracted Hughes's madness, and we get to see that for all of Stark's darkness, he also has the strength to avoid the depths that consumed his original inspiration."

The storyline also saw a new armor for Tony, this one known as the Ablative Armor, which was infected with a mysterious alien "nanoplasm" that Stark had to overcome. "It's extremely hard to come up with situations that put Iron Man in credible jeopardy," Laws says. "Other heroes can get kicked around a lot without violating their core defining traits. With Iron Man, you're walking an incredibly thin line. If you damage the suit, you interfere with the reader's power-fantasy attachment to the character. If you don't damage the suit, it's hard to fear for his safety or present him with obstacles that seem difficult to overcome."

JOHN JACKSON MILLER
STEVE ELLIS
THOMAS MASON
MARVEL
EPIC
PSR 1
CRIMSON
DYNAMO
DIRECT EDITION

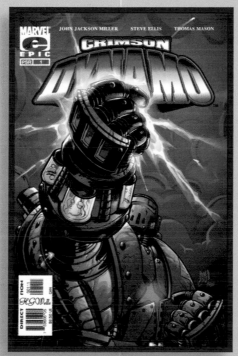

Laws left *Iron Man* with #72 (November 2003) and returned to the world of creating novels and role-playing games. "My brief stint on the book occurred at a time of competing creative visions at Marvel," he says. "I think it's fair to say that this was frustrating for all concerned." Thankfully, fans who were also frustrated with the changing creative roster were about to get some stability.

•

"He's always been our nation's best defense . . . This October we make it official!" So touted the ads for *Iron Man* #73 (cover-dated December 2003). It would be difficult for any reader to have anticipated what happened in this issue, and yet new writer John Jackson Miller and new artist Jorge Lucas fit the story seamlessly into continuity, acknowledging what had come before but taking a huge step forward into the millennial—and political—zeitgeist.

Miller was known by comic fans, having not only worked for years writing books and editing collectibles magazines for Krause Publications, publisher of *Comics Buyer's Guide,* but also having produced the scripts for the Marvel's *Crimson Dynamo* mini series for the Epic imprint in the fall of 2003. "That was the second incarnation of that line, created by Marvel as a kind of new talent program," says Miller. "For my proposal, I drew upon my background in Soviet studies, writing a new, post-Soviet variation on Iron Man's Cold War nemesis. Along the way, I elaborated on the character's origin, putting what Stan Lee had written into a larger geopolitical context. That series wound up being the flagship title of the imprint—not because it was any kind of blockbuster, but because we were the first ones out of the gate with a completed first issue. That put me in the loop to propose for some of Marvel's regular series. Discovering Marvel was in the market for *Iron Man* stories, I proposed a story arc."

The resulting storyline was put into the hands of Lucas, an Argentinean artist. In South America, he was famous for his own creation, *The Hunter,* published from 1993 to 1999. For Marvel, he soon drew *Inhumans, X-Force, Mystique, Wolverine: X-Isle, Avengers Ultron Imperative, Black Panther,* and other special projects. "Because I had worked on other Marvel titles, when Tom Brevoort wrote me to see if I wanted to work on *Iron Man,* my immediate answer was 'Yes!,' " Lucas recalls. "I had the chance to work on a legend, and one of my favorite characters."

Lucas continues, "I always read and was a fan of Marvel of the '60s and '70s. I used to watch the old TV cartoon shows, with all those marvelous illustrations made by Jack Kirby, Gene Colan, Don Heck, Dick Ayers, Ditko, Chic Stone, et cetera. When I was a child, *Iron Man* was one of my favorite comics, basically because it was one of those that appeared on animated TV shows, and I liked a lot to watch the comics I used to read."

Miller had also been a longtime fan of *Iron Man.* "I had been a Marvel reader for years, and my first *Iron Man* issue was #128's 'Demon in a Bottle,' " he says. "When I got the first issue of the series from a generous older cousin getting rid of his comics, I decided I would try to collect the entire series. It took several years, but I finally got everything all the way back to the beginning."

Tony Stark reminded Miller of "gifted students" when he was in school. "Really, in his case, 'scary-gifted.' He does all these amazing things not to show off but because he has the talent and the ability to do things that interest him. The flip side of that is that when he fails at something, it's a really big deal—because he so rarely encountered failure before, he doesn't have the coping mechanisms. Hence the alcoholism. I tried never to look at the alcoholism in isolation, but as a symptom of other issues in his personality."

As for the armored avenger, Miller notes that, "Unlike, say, Spider-Man, who is a much more extroverted character than his alter ego, I think Iron Man really is pretty interchangeable with Tony in terms of characterization. Iron Man rarely says a line that Tony would not say, for example. That made it easy in my arcs, where it had already been established that the world knew that Tony Stark was Iron Man. The armor became just another change of clothes for him."

Speaking of changes of clothes, another new set of armor was on tap from Lucas. "I believe that each artist wants to draw his own version of the armor—that is why there are so many and different ones," he says. "In fact, this

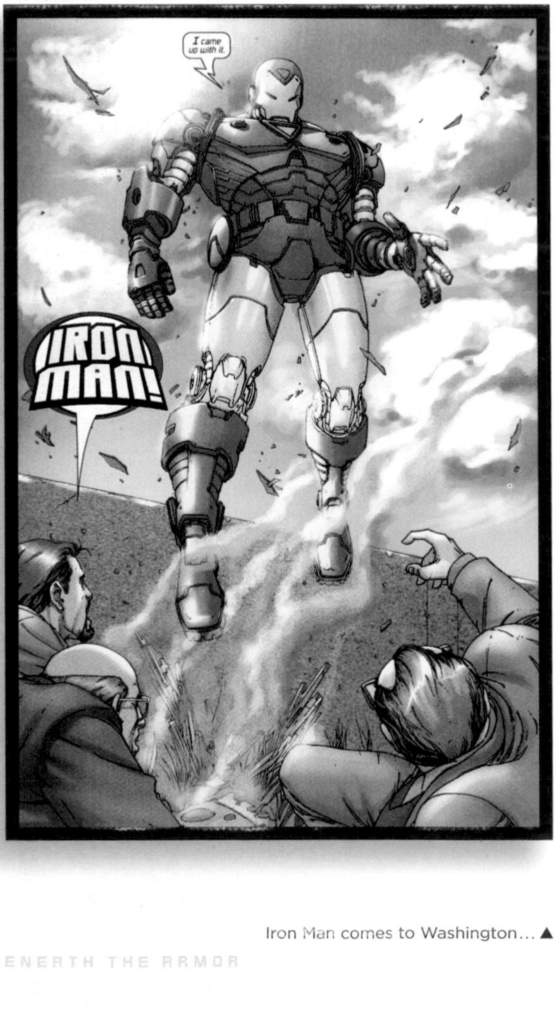
I came up with it.
IRON MAN!

Iron Man comes to Washington... ▲

▼ ...and Tony Stark gets political.

is what I liked most; its design was a kind of challenge for me. I always drew it keeping the original design in mind. As issues passed by, I tried to make it more similar to Don Heck's design, except for more technological details, and always tried to respect the original design. In fact, when I had to draw the character of Tony Stark, I [also] made the classical one, with a thin mustache and looking like the Howard Hughes of the '50s. For me, that is Stark. And I

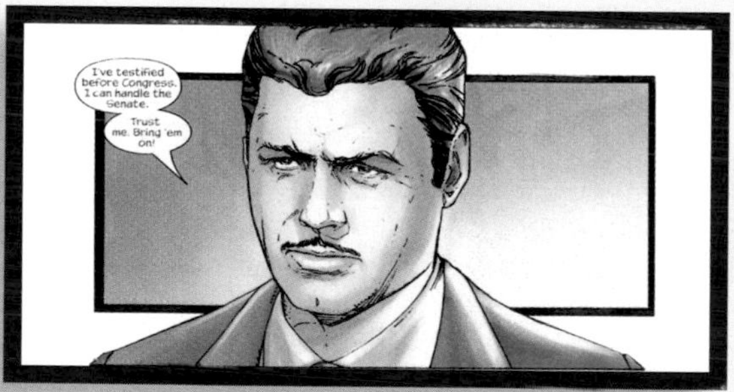
I've testified before Congress. I can handle the Senate.
Trust me. Bring 'em on!

read a comment from a fan who said, 'At last, Stark is looking like the real Stark!' When I read that message, I felt that someone had caught what I wanted to transmit."

Miller and Lucas's six-part storyline in *Iron Man* #73–78 was called "The Best Defense," and it revisited an element of Tony's history that had been pushed aside for years: his past as a munitions maker. With superpowered technology rampant, Stark was asked by the president's chief of staff to come on board as a technical adviser to the military. Although Stark at first dismissed the offer, later consideration and discussion found him meeting with President George W. Bush . . . to petition for the job as the new secretary of defense!

"Coming from *Crimson Dynamo,* I had kind of cultivated some Tom Clancy real-world themes into my stories," says Miller. "I looked at Iron Man as a chance to do that in spades. I recalled Tony's old stature as a Howard Hughes type, manufacturing weapons for the government, and real ized that since he gave up weapons manufacturing in the 1970s there really hadn't been much more done on those themes. But with 9/11 in the recent past, I saw a chance to revisit some of these themes from a new angle."

Miller set about refashioning the 1960s milieu from *Tales of Suspense,* only now setting it in the post-9/11 world. "I concocted a scenario in which Tony had no choice but to get back involved again. The Pentagon threatens to begin using Tony's Iron Man technology in its weapons—

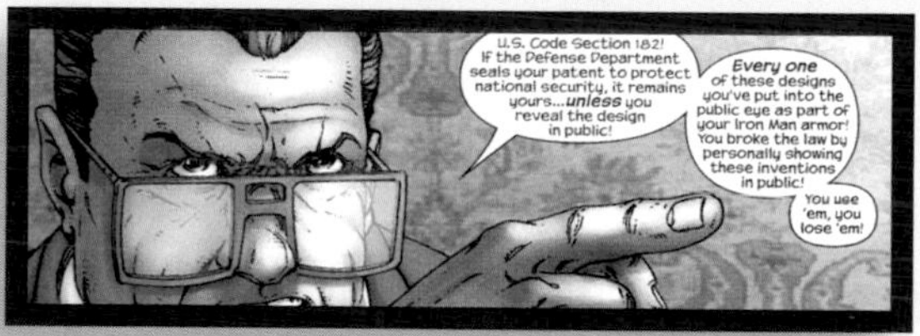
U.S. Code Section 182! If the Defense Department seals your patent to protect national security, it remains yours...unless you reveal the design in public!
Every one of these designs you've put into the public eye as part of your Iron Man armor! You broke the law by personally showing these inventions in public!
You use 'em, you lose 'em!

purely legally, as it happens. But they're unable to handle what they're using, and people are getting hurt. So Tony, thinking laterally, suggests a daring solution: Rather than steal back his technology, he agrees to help in its humane use, but only as secretary of defense. Instead of fighting the Pentagon—he was bidding to take it over! The nomination process that followed was a major element. The world knew by now that Tony was Iron Man, but that just made things more difficult. People on both sides of the aisle had reasons to be upset by things that both Tony and Iron Man had done. But Tony resists the temptation to run away, and in the end convinces everyone he's worthy of their trust."

The idea that a Super Hero could join the president's cabinet was outlandish, a fact that Miller didn't avoid. "We were very much trying to make *Iron Man* as real-world as possible during my storylines. If the thought of a Super Hero in the cabinet was outlandish, we engaged that. How would people react? How could he make it work? How soon would it be before he realized that the problems he found in the job were not conducive to Super Hero solutions? We took that all on directly. It necessarily meant Tony would spend more time on-panel than Iron Man—which was entirely the point: Instead of Iron Man solving a problem Tony had created, Tony took the Pentagon job to solve a problem Iron Man created. That last element may have been the most controversial, in the long run; if you were looking for a lot of fight scenes, this wasn't the sequence for you. But there were a lot of fans who were into the thought experiment, imagining how a real Tony Stark would interface with a real-world political system and military."

One surprising element to the already politically edgy story was the use of real-life political figures, who could legally be depicted in the series because they were public figures. Miller admits, "I was prepared *not* to depict an American president, but Marvel told me that 'our universe is the Marvel Universe,' and so we wound up not only with George W. Bush in a speaking role, but we also depicted members of the Senate Armed Services Committee and Bush's cabinet. Again, I tried to play it straight down the middle with these depictions. You could either interpret Bush's support of Tony for the job as a brilliant, outside-the-box decision . . . or as reckless and poorly thought out." Miller deliberately kept Stark's own politics private. "I worked to keep his own politics ambiguous. His pacifistic turn was a given, and I made a plot point of that. But it was also a plot point that both conservatives and liberals found things in his past they disagreed with."

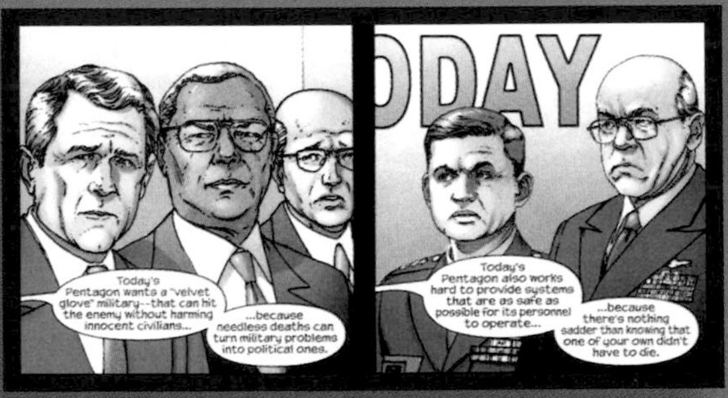
Today's Pentagon wants a "velvet glove" military--that can hit the enemy without harming innocent civilians...
...because needless deaths can turn military problems into political ones.
ODAY
Today's Pentagon also works hard to provide systems that are as safe as possible for its personnel to operate...
...because there's nothing sadder than knowing that one of your own didn't have to die.

Real politicians face Iron Man! ▲

The real-world elements proved a challenge for Lucas; the Argentinean artist had to find lots of reference for Washington, DC, as well as "Congress and the governmental buildings surrounding it . . . very common places to the American public and where I have never been personally. I had to get maps and many pictures of the Washington district, and satellite pictures, in order to be well oriented and so that the characters moved within the scenario correctly. That was very hard work for me, though I liked it, since I had to achieve the realism required by the storyline."

Although there was armor action as the story progressed, "The Best Defense" was largely a complex Tony Stark story, full of the behind-the-scenes maneuverings in Washington, DC, that readers might have been familiar with from another form of media. Editor Tom Brevoort notes that he enjoyed the fact that Miller "really came at this [as] sort of *Iron Man as an Aaron Sorkin drama,* which is very easy to think of at the time when *The West Wing* was one of the biggest shows around. Taking Iron Man out of the corporate boardroom and putting him more on the political world stage, moving him into new areas and different areas, but allowing him to touch back on some of the same issues, both as a guy who ran a multinational company and now is responsible for this particular division and branch of government, [and as] a guy who could bring technological innovations to that, and who could play on the world platform. I quite enjoyed most of John's run, and the fact that he kind of came to the character with something new and somewhere different to take him."

Following a contentious and even explosive nomination process, by the end of "The Best Defense" storyline, Stark was indeed named secretary of defense. But of *Iron Man* #79–82, Miller says, "At that point, there was no choice but to deal with the elephant in the room: Iraq. The Iraq War had started just when I was developing 'The Best Defense'; by the time I got to 'The Deep End,' Secretary Stark's first assignment, the occupation had begun. So we showed Tony dealing with supply and security issues . . . and while there is a Super Villainess in the arc, we tied her directly to Iraq's past."

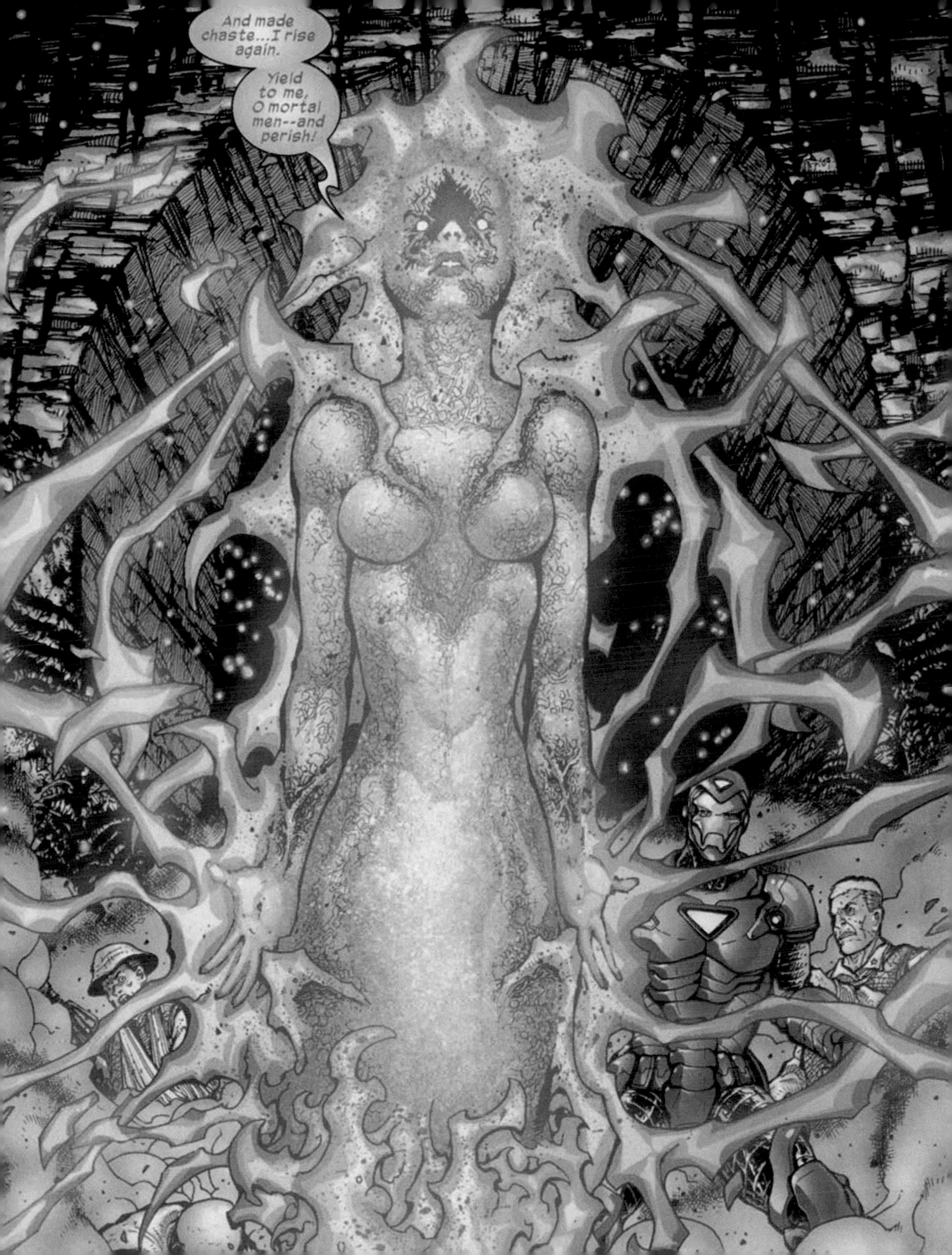
And made chaste...I rise again.
Yield to me, O mortal men--and perish!

The four-part story was guest-drawn by Philip Tan. "We tried to be as accurate as possible with the technology in the book," says Miller. "So much of it was military, so I got advice from air force and army personnel on military procedures and weaponry. I put behind-the-scenes pages on my website, noting what the real-world stuff was in each issue. That was appreciated by a lot of military readers . . . that, and our approach to depicting soldiers as humans with jobs rather than as faceless figures. The military in a lot of comics is set up to be the villain, and where there are times when that can be the case, in our arc Tony was really trying to understand the problems the professional military dealt with . . . So while I wouldn't say the Secretary Stark sequence is jingoistic, it does make the effort to treat the military fairly—and I heard from a lot of people in uniform that they appreciated it."

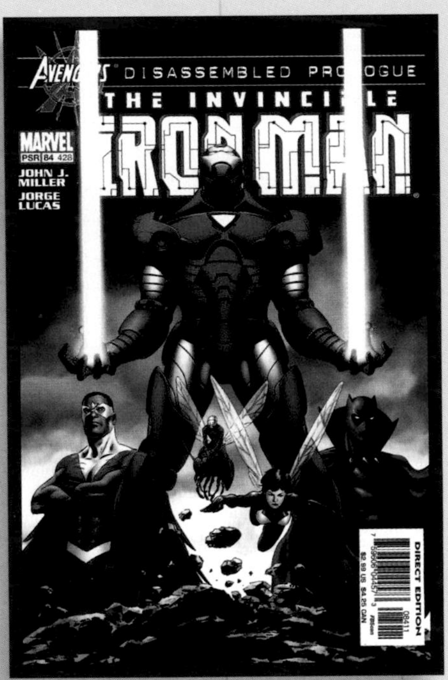
AVENGERS DISASSEMBLED PROLOGUE
THE INVINCIBLE
IRON MAN
MARVEL
PSR 84 428
JOHN J. MILLER
JORGE LUCAS
DIRECT EDITION

Jorge Lucas returned to the art duties with *Iron Man* #83 (July 2004); he would remain at the visual helm through issue #85 (December 2004), alongside scripter Miller. Before their departure, the creative team brought back Titanium Man and, later, *Avengers* foe Arsenal in a tale that pushed Iron Man more directly to an intersection with the Avengers and set up future story threads. "My idea had always been to 'return the character to his upright and locked position' afterward, as they say on the airplanes," Miller jokes. "By resolving Tony Stark's issues with government work, we helped to open up a number of possibilities in the comics again. The [future] *Civil War* crossover brought Tony into close coordination with the government again, and while that was after my time, I've heard from readers who found that his stint as secretary helped smooth the way for that characterization."

Miller found that his work on *Iron Man* opened doors for him in the industry. "I developed the ongoing *Star Wars: Knights of the Old Republic* comic book series for Dark Horse," he says, "and am writing the graphic novelization for *Indiana Jones and the Kingdom of the Crystal Skull*. But *Iron Man* was my first big series, and I'll always be thankful for that opportunity." Meanwhile, Jorge Lucas moved on to illustrate the *Hulk: House of M* storyline, *Ronan*, *Colossus: Bloodline*, and stories for *Avengers Classic*.

•

As *Iron Man*'s forty-first year drew to a close, a Marvel crossover event called "Avengers Disassembled" came calling, and Iron Man was disassembling right alongside his longtime cohorts. The four-part "The Singularity," written by Mark Ricketts and drawn by multiple artists, found someone in Iron Man's armor slaughtering Stark Enterprise's board of directors and killing Tony's ex-girlfriend, Rumiko Fujikawa. A battle to the end with the arms dealer posing as Iron Man helped Tony come to a decision. In *Iron Man* #89 (December 2004), Stark announced to the world that not only was he retiring as secretary of defense *and* as an Avenger, but he was retiring as Iron Man and would devote himself to scientific research. He warned the public that there would always be an Iron Man, however, even if it wasn't him.

Iron Man volume III ended its run with issue #89, the 434th comic to bear the title. Thankfully for fans of Tony Stark, a new beginning was coming with the turn of a calendar page.

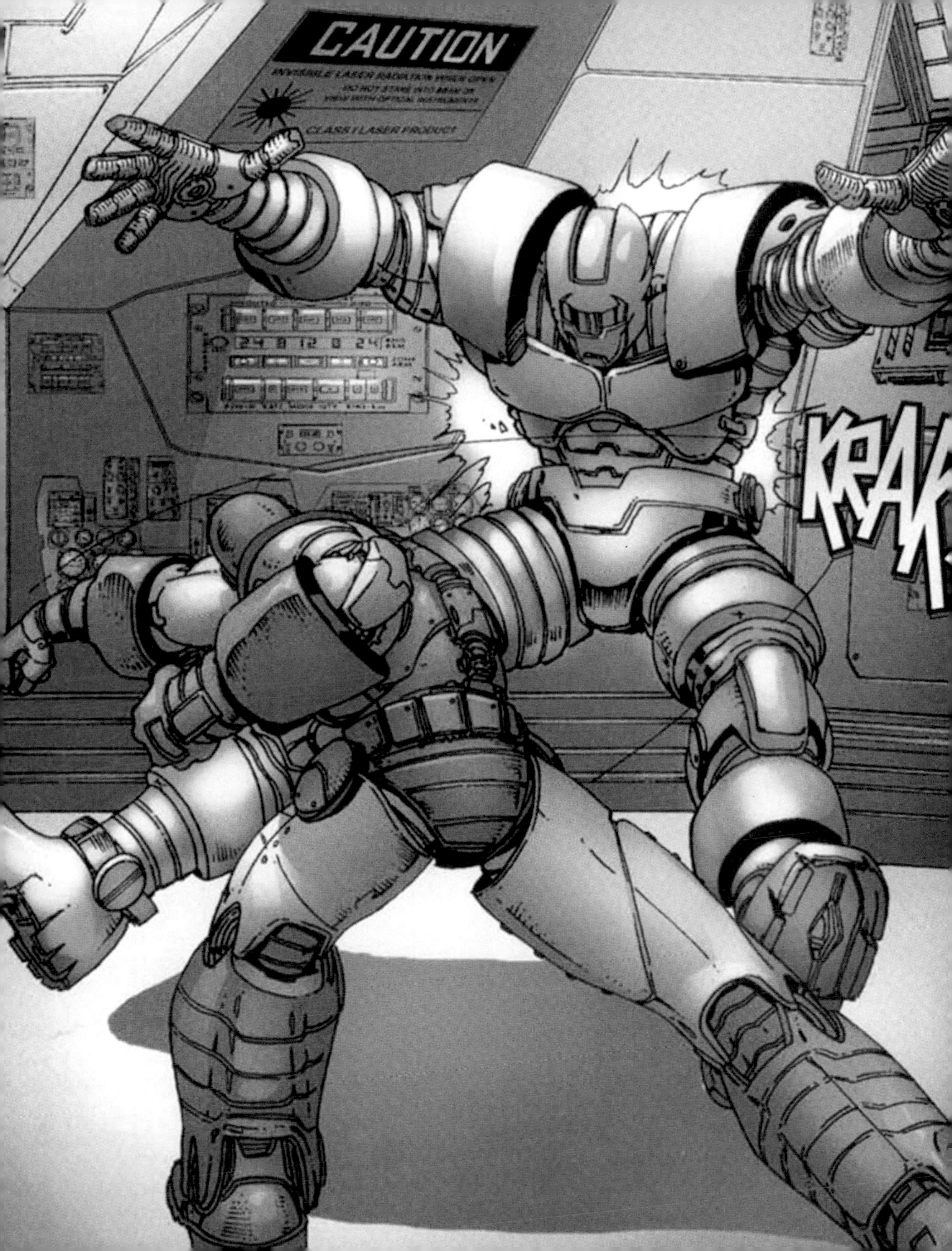
CAUTION
CLASS I LASER PRODUCT
KRAK

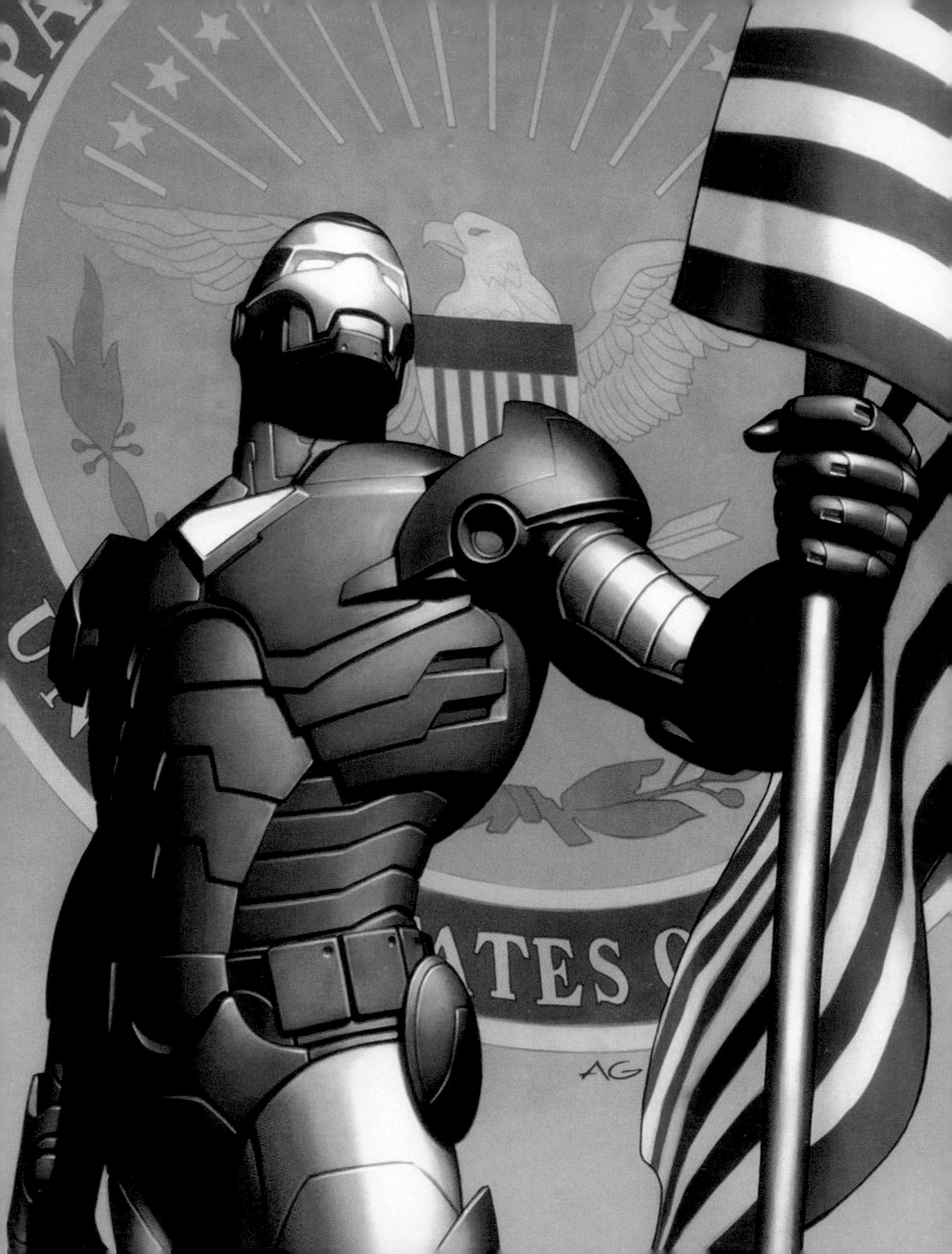
ATES
AG

CHAPTER 7

EXTREME . . . ULTIMATE . . . AND CINEMATIC

The renaissance for Iron Man would clearly begin in 2005. Not only would the fourth volume of his solo series begin, but so would a trio of mini series: *Ultimate Iron Man, Iron Man: House of M,* and *Fantastic Four/Iron Man: Big in Japan.* As January dawned, fans clamored for a new *Iron Man* #1 from the creative team of popular writer Warren Ellis and past *Iron Man* volume III cover artist Adi Granov.

Ellis was a British comic writer whose US career had begun inauspiciously at Marvel with runs on *Hellstorm,* the Marvel 2099 books, and *Excalibur.* When he left Marvel, he began to gain attention even as he broke Super Hero taboos in *The Authority* for Wildstorm and explored a dystopian future in *Transmetropolitan* for DC imprint Vertigo. Ellis became known for his sociopolitical and sociocultural commentary, as well as his propensity to pen stories that rode the razor's edge of scientific advancements.

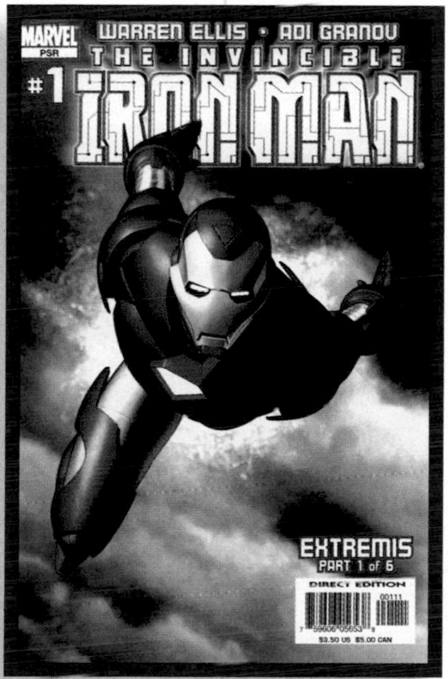
MARVEL
PSR
WARREN ELLIS • ADI GRANOV
THE INVINCIBLE
#1
IRON MAN
EXTREMIS
PART 1 of 6
DIRECT EDITION
$3.50 US $5.00 CAN

Bosnian-born Adi Granov was a concept artist at Nintendo before he came to Marvel in 2004, where he soon did covers on books such as *She-Hulk, Inhumans,* and *Silver Surfer,* as well as *Iron Man* volume III #75–83. His digitally painted artwork was gritty and three-dimensional, and applauded by fans and Marvel editorial alike. Granov says that *Iron Man* "was the first assignment editor Tom Brevoort offered me when I joined Marvel. He thought my style would suit the character, and I agreed."

The first six issues of *Iron Man*'s fourth series told the "Extremis" story. In it, Tony Stark's origin was retrofitted yet again, to the 1990s, and specific continuity from the past was either ignored or unaddressed. Still a brilliant inventor, Stark was also an arms dealer who was injured during the first Gulf War. He now used the Iron Man armor he created to enforce the law. When a rogue scientist created a powerful techno-organic virus-like compound known as Extremis, a terrorist named Mallen became a near-indestructible living weapon. Injured while trying to stop Mallen, Stark infected himself with Extremis, allowing it to rewrite his DNA. The resulting improvements to Tony allowed him to excrete an armored undersheath from the Extremis stored in his bones, atop which the newly enhanced pieces of the Iron Man armor could attach. As the story ended, Stark was now no longer a man in armor . . . the armor had integrated into his biological systems!

"Warren Ellis's first arc is all about using technology, using nanomachines and pharmaceuticals and gene tampering and DNA splicing to evolve and upgrade the human body," says *Iron Man* editor Tom Brevoort. "Warren's a guy who reads every contemporary science journal coming out and likes to be on the cutting edge of whatever the current theory is, so this was a very contemporary sort of an issue, where in the '60s it was all transistors and such, and then by the '70s and '80s you got Iron Man being solar-powered and so forth. These are issues now that can have some relevance to what we're hearing about in the world today, and allow you to bring [in] an antagonist that can stand in opposition of that, can give you a different point of view on the sociological issues, can give you a different point of view on the physiological issues of dealing with how we are going to relate to our technology and how we're going to relate to the world that's coming, and the fact that there's about a million times more information out there squirreling around everybody's head now than there was even ten years ago. *Iron Man* kind of gets to be the avatar of all that because, at its heart, one of the things that series is about, is about man and technology."

Granov says that, "the story in 'Extremis' came from Marvel's desire to update the character for a new age and give him some fresher and interesting qualities and flaws. Warren Ellis created a very dark sci-fi type of environment for Tony Stark, which I really enjoy, and which I think fits my style very well. After reading the script, I was really motivated to do as good a job as possible to try and match what Warren had written. The 'Extremis' story was created out of a need to give Iron Man a new technological edge reflecting the fast-developing technology of today. It only made sense to try to keep Iron Man current and not let him become a retro-style character with outdated designs and technology. Iron Man adapts and upgrades with the times; it keeps him relevant and modern. I think it's one of the biggest strengths Iron Man has over other Super Heroes. It's logical for him to change to reflect the specific uses and/or times the story throws at him."

In addition to Ellis's writing, Brevoort credits Granov with an equal part of the success of the "Extremis" storyline. "Adi had been doing covers for *Iron Man* during the John Miller era. He came on to do the entire book in a painted style—while it's not completely a digital style, it is painted and hand-done as much as it is digital—which had a much stronger digital component and digital look to it. Beyond the big ideas and the broad-strokes approach to Tony Stark that Warren brought, I think what Adi brought was the look, the sheen, that really propelled *Iron Man* into the future, into today and beyond today. He really made Iron Man feel as plausible or more plausible than he ever had before, because the technology of graphics had finally caught up with the technology of imagination."

The "Extremis" story was not without controversies: It altered the armored avenger's origin story; the final three issues took more than a year to release; and Marvel had to give the book an older audience rating on the covers due to some extreme violence.

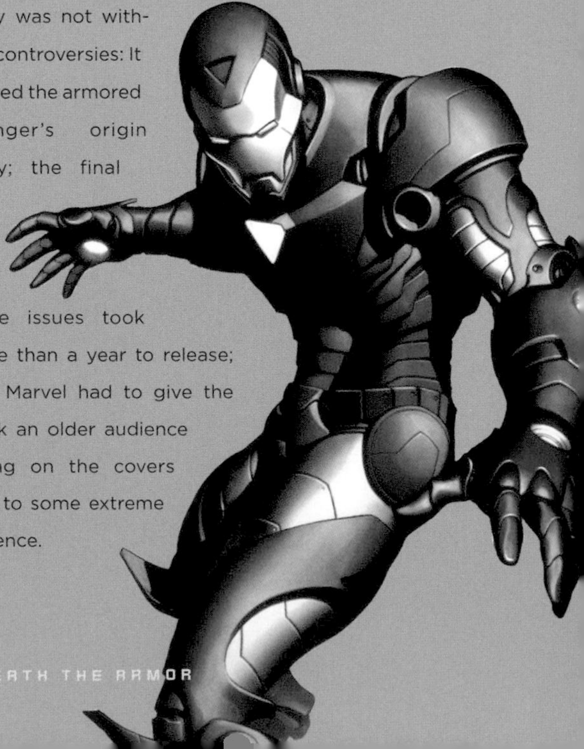

"The story of Iron Man has been rebooted a few times to make him more relevant to the times," says Granov. "Unfortunately, the political climate in the world has always been able to suit the threat that originally served as the backdrop for the comic. Weapons and those who design them seem as controversial and relevant *today* as they were during Cold War, so it's not too much of a stretch to transpose Tony Stark from the '60s into today."

As for the violence, Granov notes, "I really liked Mallen from 'Extremis' because he was genuinely scary in a very unsettling, violent, and realistic way." The artist also notes that "some scenes were fairly graphic, which prompted Marvel to up the suggested rating of the book, as well as request some color changes to subdue some of the violence."

The schedule for the series was a concern for fans and editorial, but each issue was released as soon as it was completed. "Warren did six issues and it took those six issues *awhile* to come out," Brevoort deadpans, adding that although he pushed the envelope, the writer was respectful of Marvel's armored hero. "I think Warren very clearly understands, acknowledges, and respects the difference between something that's creator-owned—and he can roam where he will and so forth—and a character like Iron Man, who is owned by a company, and who has a forty-year history and some expectation behind that. Whether he wants to confound expectations by going left when everybody else thinks he's going to go right—or where every previous writer had gone right—he sort of knows and understands and respects the boundaries beyond which you're just not going to be able to push something like that. That said, within those boundaries, he had pretty [much] carte-blanche freedom to take the character wherever he would.

"Warren changed one of the most fundamental aspects about Iron Man in the course of those six issues," Brevoort continues. "Before he started, Iron Man was a guy who had no powers and put on a suit, and when he

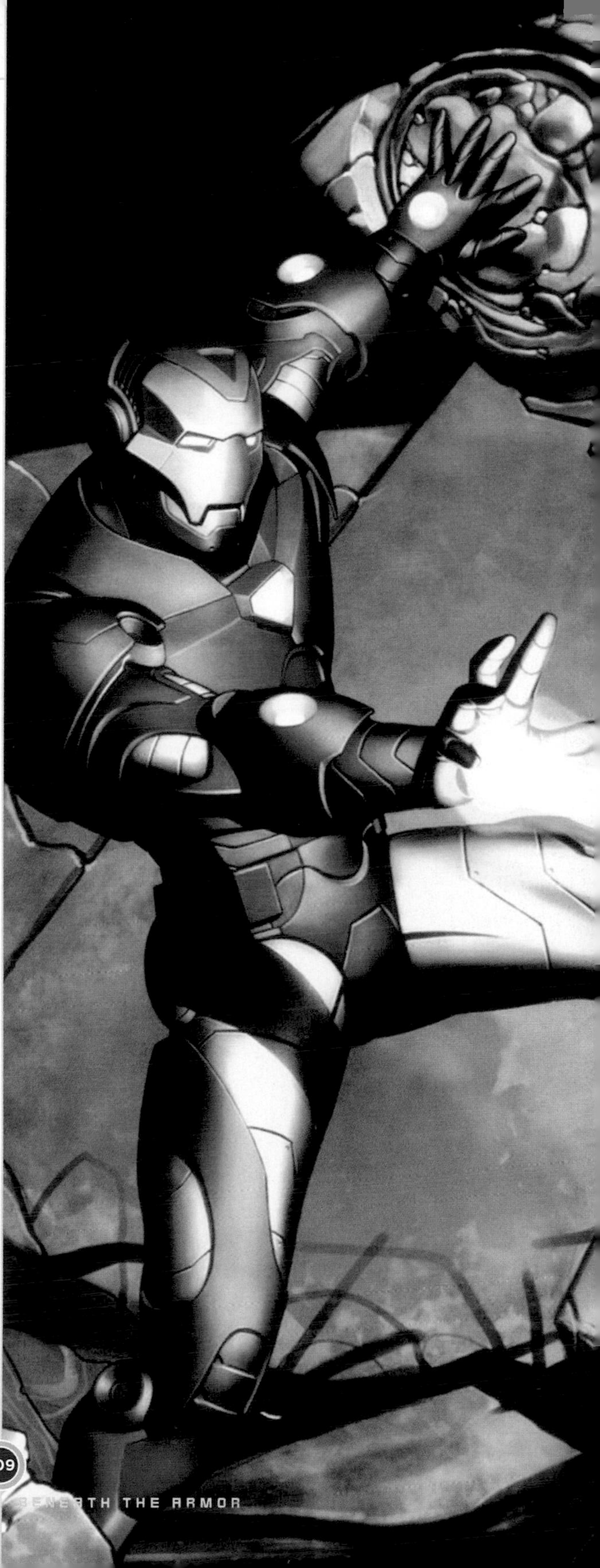

was done, Iron Man was a guy that *absolutely* had some measure of powers outside of the armor, because the technology has become so integrated into him. In a very real way, that's a colossal change, but there was not a lot of hand-wringing about letting him do that."

No hand-wringing was necessary: Iron Man sales became stronger. And if fans didn't respond to one set of stories, the next two years gave them *many* options for Shellhead's adventures . . . in comics, animation, and a live-action feature film.

•

In 2000, Marvel had reimagined one of its flagship characters for the millennium in *Ultimate Spider-Man.* The series was completely modern and written for teen-or-older audiences. *Ultimate X-Men* soon followed, then *Ultimate Marvel Team-Up,* which saw Spider-Man joining forces with other heroes of the Ultimate Universe, including Iron Man. In March 2002, *The Ultimates* debuted, with writer Mark Millar and artist Bryan Hitch refashioning the Avengers in a darker milieu. This series was definitely for mature audiences with violence, semi-nudity, and profanity.

Millar's Tony Stark was a womanizing drunk who had exceptional intelligence . . . and an inoperable brain tumor. Using the Iron Man armor, he pursued his own goals, which sometimes intersected with those of S.H.I.E.L.D. or the Super Hero team known as the Ultimates. Defending America from superpowered menaces and alien invasions—and controversial missteps in US foreign policy—the Ultimates charged through two thirteen-part critically acclaimed and high-selling series.

Ultimate Iron Man was announced by Marvel in 2004, and the five-part series debuted in May 2005. Writing the series was bestselling science fiction author Orson Scott Card, while Andy Kubert (son of legendary comic artist Joe Kubert) provided the art. The story drastically altered Iron Man's origin, showcasing young Tony Stark as a genetic accident whose body was infused with abundant neural tissue . . . essentially making the boy a living brain. The tremendous neural activity was agony for Stark, but between an innate regenerative ability and an experimental biotechnological armor invented by his father, he was able to contain and control the pain. Later issues focused on Stark's maturity to adulthood, as he developed a prototype power-armor, befriended fellow student James Rhodes, found that alcohol dulled the chronic pain he felt, and faced both terrorists and the deadly and devious Obadiah Stane.

With the successful sales of the first series, *Ultimate Iron Man II* debuted in December 2007 for a four-issue run, again written by Card, but with art this time by Pasqual Ferry. The story picked up immediately after the first series ended and saw the debut of Ultimate War Machine.

Related to the *Ultimate* line, and also announced in July 2004, was a pact for direct-to-DVD animated feature films, to be produced by Marvel Entertainment in Los Angeles and released by Lionsgate. The first from the studio was *Ultimate Avengers,* on February 21, 2006. The film loosely adapted the first *Ultimates* series, although it cleared out many of the more mature elements. *Ultimate Avengers 2* was released on August 8, 2006, continuing the story. Marc Worden gave voice to the role of Tony Stark and Iron Man in both projects.

The third film in Marvel's pact with Lionsgate was *The Invincible Iron Man,* released on January 23, 2007, directed by Patrick Archibald, Jay Oliva, and Frank D. Paur, and written by Greg

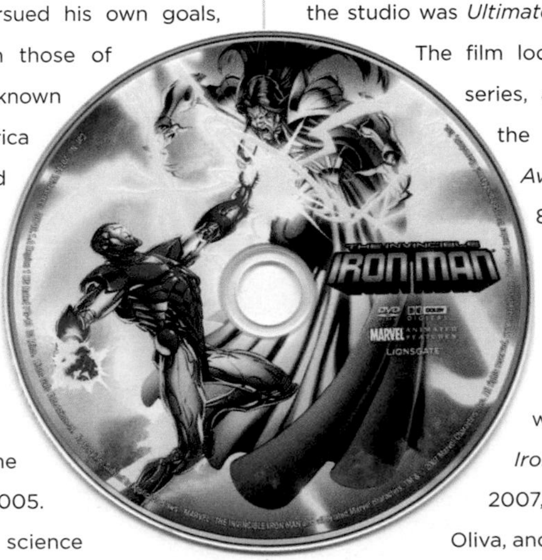
IRON MAN
MARVEL
LIONSGATE

▲ *The Invincible Iron Man* DVD

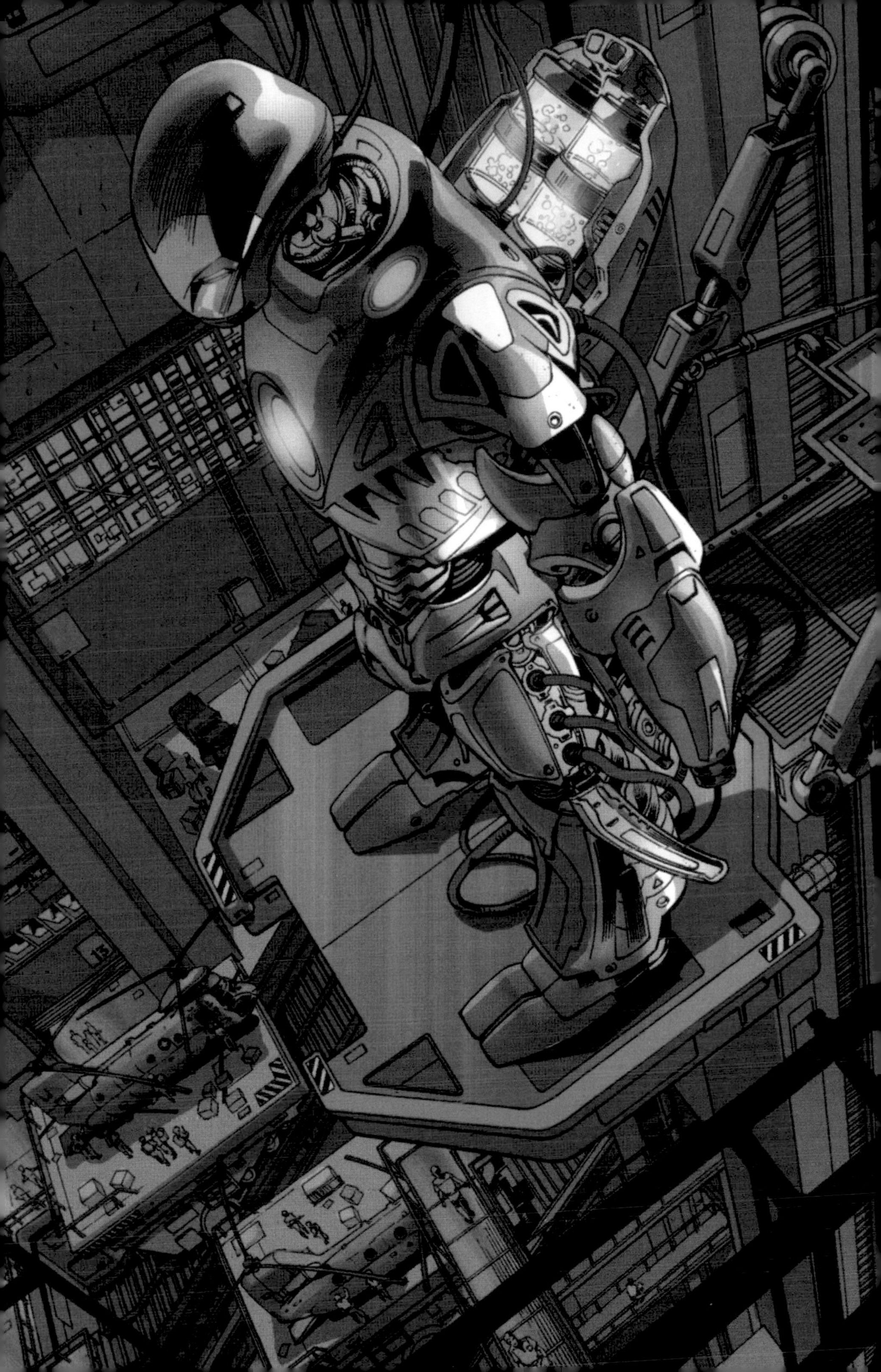

Johnson from a story developed by Johnson, Avi Arad, and Craig Kyle. The plot utilized elements from many versions of Iron Man's origins, but almost completely removed any aspect of politics, despite its PG-13 rating. Instead, Stark was attempting to raise an ancient Chinese city that was buried deep underground, but in doing so, he unleashed four elemental spirits . . . which set in motion the resurrection of the three-thousand-year-old evil ruler known as the Mandarin! In the complicated story, Tony had already secretly developed suits of armor, but now he was forced to use them to try to stop the evil spirits and clear his own name from S.H.I.E.L.D. charges of illegal arms dealing to the Chinese. By the film's end, it was clear that the story was showing an early version of the *Ultimate Avengers'* animated universe Iron Man.

Marc Worden returned to the role of Tony Stark/Iron Man for the animated film. In past interviews, he noted that when he first got the role, he had to research the character. "A friend of mine passed along the first few issues of *The Ultimates,* as well as *Essential Iron Man,* for me to wrap my head around. The graphic novels by Mark Millar and Bryan Hitch are spectacular, the perfect introduction to the genre. Being able to read their work next to some of the original comics from the '60s was a blast! Stan Lee created this character before I was even born and Iron Man has been kicking ass, breaking hearts, and nursing a hangover for over forty years."

As to how he sees Stark, Worden noted that "he's a suave, sophisticated, cultured gentleman who uses his intellect to save himself and the world from imminent disaster. Without the technology he created, he could not survive, and fortunately for the world, he is constantly refining his inventions and upgrading his suits to be one step ahead of whatever's next. He's like James Bond, Bruce Wayne, and Nikola Tesla rolled into one."

While no further direct-to-DVD adventures of Iron Man or Ultimate Avengers have been announced, Lionsgate is definitely not abandoning Marvel's most famous inventor. July 2008 will see the release of the fifth DVD film (following *Dr. Strange*), a more kid-friendly adventure called *Next Avengers*. Written by Craig Yost and directed by Gary Hartle, *Next Avengers* (once known as "Teen Avengers" and "Avengers Reborn") is set several decades from the present and will feature an older Tony Stark mentoring a new group of teen heroes—including a female Thor, a male Wasp, and new versions of Black Panther, Hawkeye, Quicksilver, and Captain America—as they battle against Ultron. Tom Kane, who had previously voiced some characters on the 1994–1995 *Iron Man* animated series, is reportedly voicing both Tony Stark and Ultron.

The film begins with the Avengers' final stand against the familiar, robotic foe . . . but the battle becomes a bloodbath. "It's this beautiful, tragic story," producer Craig Kyle said in a PR interview, "where Tony is forced to leave the battlefield and gather the children and usher them away to safety, before Ultron cuts his way through the parents to the last that remains of the Age of Heroes . . . What happens over time is the playboy has become the father. Now, these kids are his responsibility, and he fell in love with them, but all the love in the world and all the great technology that Tony still had couldn't protect them from the deaths that collide with them in this story."

•

From the fall of 2005 to today, Marvel has published more *Iron Man* comics per month than at any time in the characters' history. Even if the regular series missed a month, fans were treated to some special mini series, all aimed at expanding both the past and the present of the armored avenger.

"With any character who's popular, there are usually more stories and more creators who want to write those stories, or draw those stories, than could be fitted to any monthly comic book," says Tom Brevoort, who, as one of Marvel's two executive editors, oversees almost all of the

Avengers-related titles. "When these opportunities present themselves, we sort of evaluate whether there's a good story reason or a good publishing reason to do an ancillary *Iron Man* project of one sort or another, in the same way we do with *Spider-Man* or *Captain America* or whomever, and then we go ahead and choose to produce that series or not based on that merit. And that merit can be any number of avenues. Certainly from a continuity standpoint it's simpler to set things in the past."

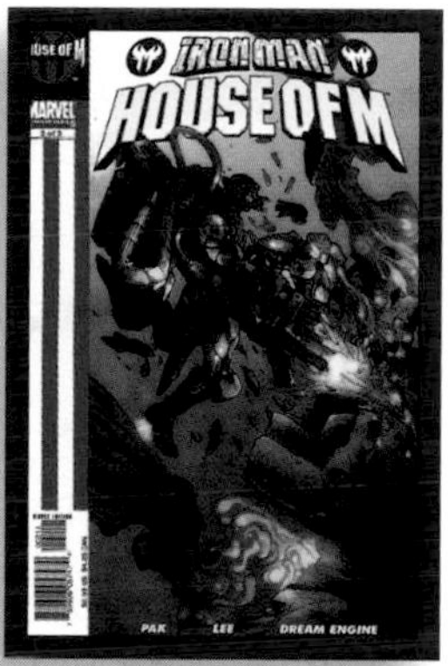

IRON MAN
HOUSE OF M
PAK LEE DREAM ENGINE

Iron Man: House of M was a three-issue series in September-November 2005, written by Greg Pak and drawn by Pat Lee. Tying in to a massive company-wide crossover in which the Scarlet Witch warped reality, *Iron Man: House of M* saw an alternate Earth on which Tony Stark invented super-armor to battle on the TV show *Sapien Death Match!* Stark later ended up using the battle suit to fight for the rights of nonmutants.

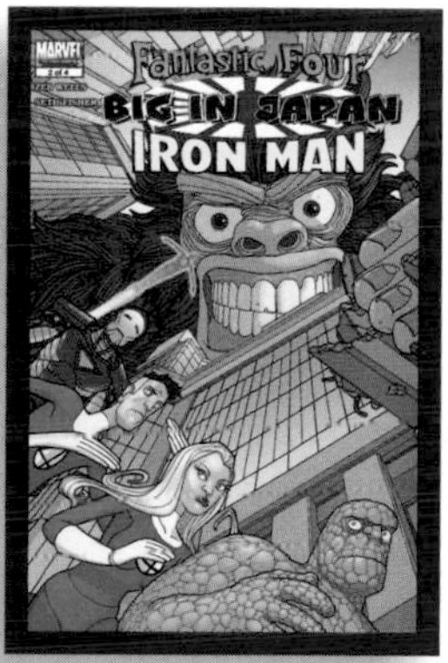

Fantastic Four
BIG IN JAPAN
IRON MAN

Fantastic Four/Iron Man: Big in Japan was a more lighthearted four-issue romp, published December 2005–March 2006, written by Zeb Wells, and drawn by Seth Fisher. This manga-inspired pop-culture story played the FF and Iron Man as celebrities beloved by the Japanese, especially when giant city-destroying monsters (*kaiju*) such as Droom, Giganto, and Eerok the giant ape arrived to trample the grand opening of Tokyo's first-ever Giant Monster Museum and Expo Hall! With giant robots and Kirbyesque monster "gods" running amok, *Big in Japan* was a popular—and intentionally bizarre—series, made more fun by Fisher's intricate artwork.

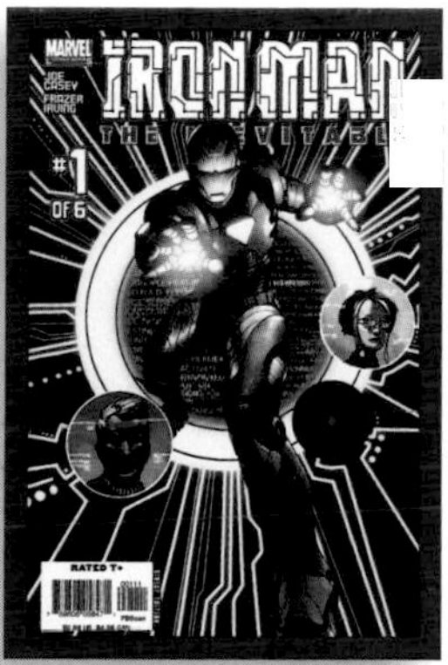

IRON MAN
#1 OF 6

Iron Man: The Inevitable was a six-issue series, written by Joe Casey and illustrated by Frazer Irving, published February–July 2006. The plot found Tony Stark—while trying his best to rehabilitate the Living Laser—being besieged by industrial saboteur-villains the Ghost and Spymaster. Casey's story referenced past continuity while keeping up with the new Extremis-armored Iron Man, and fans were grateful to get a dose of "classic" Marvel-style heroes-versus-villains action.

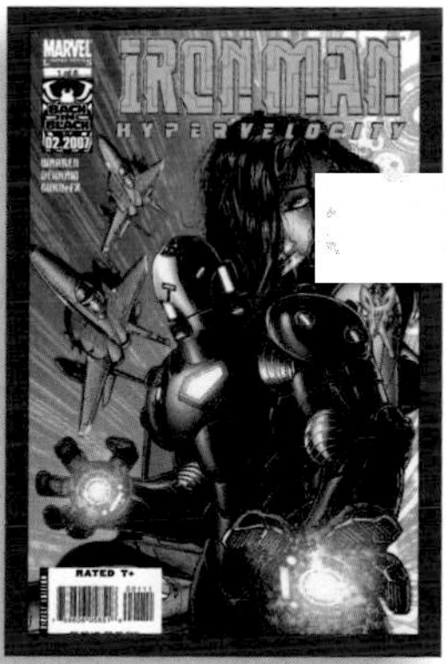

IRON MAN
HYPERVELOCITY

Iron Man: Hypervelocity was another six-issue series, released by Marvel in March–August 2007, and set in a pre-volume-IV time period. While artist Brian Denham rendered the realistic-style art (completely on computer using Adobe Illustrator), writer Adam Warren brought a hyperkinetic manga flavor to the story, which found Tony developing another new set of armor into which he could "upload" a digital form of his own consciousness. Caught between the bleeding-edge mecha technology controlled by a mysterious tattooed woman named Absynthe, and the hardware of S.H.I.E.L.D.'s elite Special Response Unit Alpha team, Iron Man was forced to use his own ultratech to survive a series of attacks that could erase him completely from the physical and techno-virtual realms.

Iron Man: Enter the Mandarin was a chance to get retro with Shellhead's most infamous villain. The six-issue series ran November 2007–April 2008, created by returning writer Joe Casey and artist Eric Canete, whose streamlined covers recalled art-deco-esque Cold War propaganda posters. To tell his tale, Casey greatly expanded upon elements mostly from *Tales of Suspense* #50–55 while connecting the 1964 story to modern continuity through a surprise character.

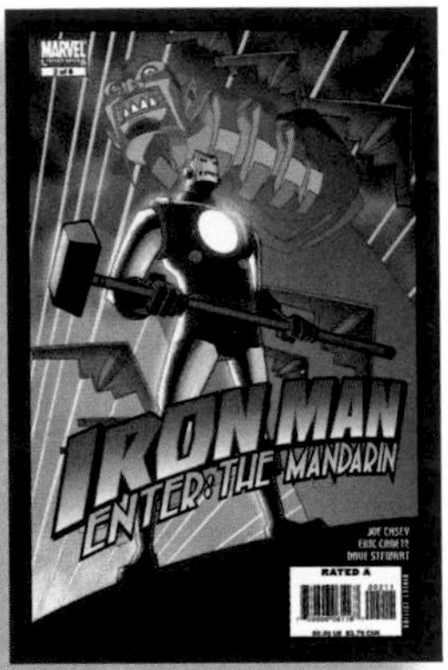
IRON MAN
ENTER THE MANDARIN

"The *Iron Man: Enter the Mandarin* limited series was set in the earliest days of *Iron Man,*" says Brevoort, "but really that was an attempt to sort of take the '60s interpretation of the Mandarin and try to build him some relevance in 2008, apart from his Yellow Peril Cold War sort of roots . . . to try to not really change the broad details of those stories from 1964 and 1965, but to *contextualize* them, to kind of squint and erase the things that were very much tied to that specific year and that specific era, and replace them with things that would allow that character to retain his appeal now and grow on it going forward."

Iron Man and Power Pack offered something for younger readers—and those older fans who wanted more "classic" Marvel storytelling—teaming Shellhead with Marvel's youngest Super Heroes, a quartet of siblings known as Power Pack. The four-issue series ran January–April 2008, from the creative team of writer Marc Sumerak and artist Marcelo Dichiara. In the non-continuity-heavy tale, Tony Stark engaged in both boardroom drama and philanthropy while working alongside the young heroes to battle Ultimo in New York, as well as villains such as the Ghost, Speed Demon, Blizzard, Titanium Man, Puppet Master, and even a host of Iron Man armors.

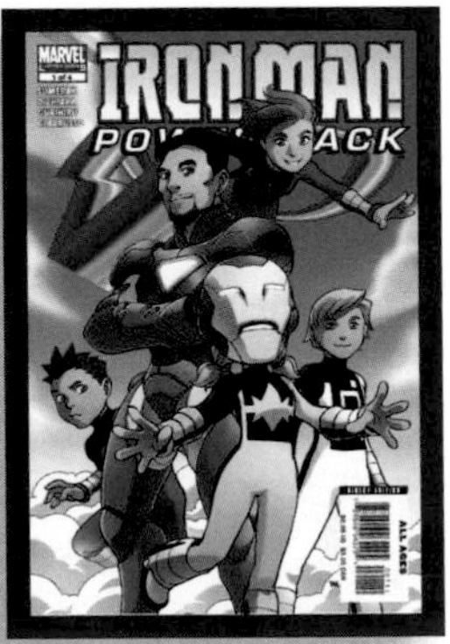
IRON MAN

That latter mini series was far from the only younger-skewing *Iron Man* title released by Marvel. Previewed in a June 2007 giveaway comic released for the nationwide Free Comic Book Day, the new series *Marvel Adventures: Iron Man* debuted in July. The regular series is set in modern times but does not follow set Marvel continuity; a new origin for Iron Man revealed that Tony was abducted by A.I.M. to create an electromagnetic pulse generator to destroy the stability of foreign governments. Fred Van Lente wrote the series, with pencils by James Cordeiro and others. In an arc that explored the various armors Stark had created, early issues saw reinventions of the Mandarin, PlantMan, Spymaster, Commander Kraken, the Living Laser, and Doctor Doom. The next arc, in issues #9–12, found Tony searching for his long-lost father . . . and finding out family secrets in the process.

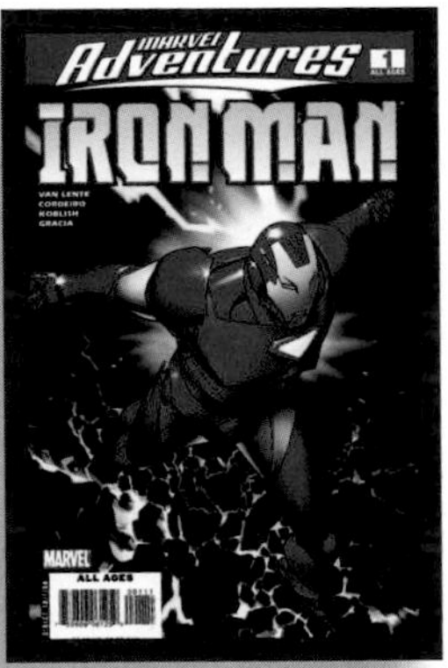
Marvel Adventures
IRON MAN

Brevoort says that for Marvel, "It's worth doing *Marvel Adventures: Iron Man* as an entry-level book for a younger reader who's maybe not as ready for some of the political sophistication or some of the content issues that you might get in the regular *Iron Man* book, but wants a good crackin' adventure of Iron Man, the guy in armor with all sorts of toys and weapons, fighting evil and so forth."

•

While Marvel's spate of *Iron Man* mini series offered diversity, fans of Super Hero conflict set "in continuity" found it in the regular *Iron Man* series. With issue #7 (June

2006), the father-son team of Daniel and Charles Knauf took over the writing duties, with Patrick Zircher and Scott Hanna on the art for their first six-part arc, "Execute Program." In the story, a mysterious hacker with ties to Tony's past is able to control the Iron Man armor, putting Shellhead on a collision course with the Avengers and Sentry.

"During Warren Ellis's run, Tony sort of rewrote his own biology with this Extremis enhancile to make himself more in sync and more simpatico with his armor," says editor Tom Brevoort. "What we've played with in the background going forward from that is the fact that now Tony is in a very real way connected to—or can connect to—all of the technology on the planet, which includes the Internet, the computers, the satellites overhead, the microwave transmissions, everything. We're all surrounded by all this information and all this high-speed go-go-go flow of info every day, but Tony is immersed in that 24/7, and what is that going to do to him? How does he deal with it? How does he cope with that? What this says about Tony's persona, his emotional makeup, his mental makeup, how he thinks, and what he's likely to do in any given situation informs the stories that we tell moving forward."

Daniel Knauf was wrapping up production on his HBO TV series *Carnivale* when one of his producers told him

that Marvel wanted to work with him. A short time later, Daniel was on board, bringing his son—a longtime comics fan—along with him. Editor Brevoort recalls, "I took what was my first, maybe my second phone call with them, and they said, 'Okay, let me break our story for you,' and they pretty much had their entire first six-issue arc completely mapped out, every beat, every character thing, every note. It all held together, it all made sense, it all held water, so we went ahead and did it. Anytime you have a writer who switches from one medium to the next, there's always a learning curve in terms of learning what the medium can and can't do and how it works versus another thing. Even out of the gate, they knew how to structure a story, they knew how to reveal character through action, they knew how to have incident build on incident, and they had a pretty good understanding of Tony Stark."

Due to scheduling snafus with the earlier Ellis issues, Marvel was in the midst of its huge *Civil War* crossover—which featured Iron Man as one of the main characters—by the time the Knauf-written *Iron Man* series caught up with it. "That was just an unfortunate fluke of publishing," says Brevoort. "They were stuck in a tricky situation in that Warren had left the *Iron Man* status quo in a particular place, and Mark Millar and the other Marvel writers were writing Iron Man in a particular place [in *Civil War*], and the Knaufs

▲ Iron Man faced Captain America for the final time in a Civil War.

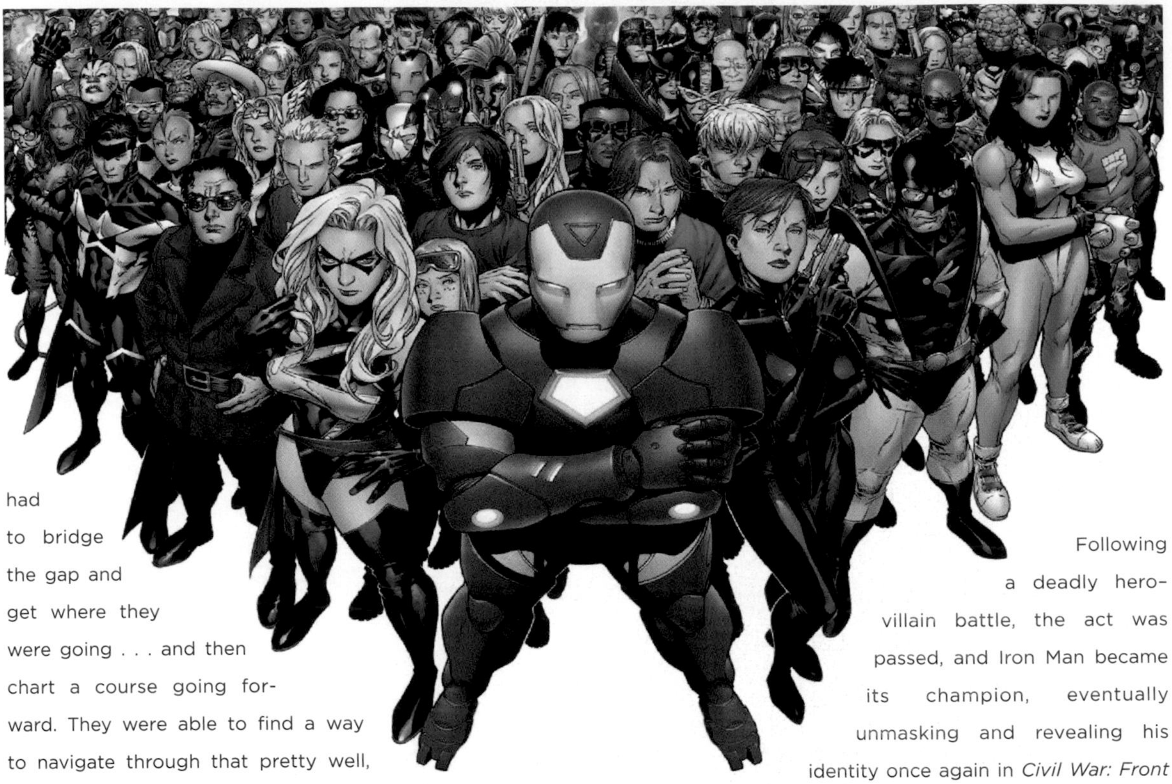

had to bridge the gap and get where they were going . . . and then chart a course going forward. They were able to find a way to navigate through that pretty well, emphasizing the humanity of Tony Stark, empathizing the burden he carries, the hard choices that he makes, and the price he's paid and continues to pay for the course he set out for himself."

Some of that course had been revealed in *New Avengers: Illuminati* #1 (June 2006), where a continuity "retrofit" showed Stark—years ago—organizing a meeting of powerful Super Heroes (Professor X, Mister Fantastic, Black Bolt, Dr. Strange, and Namor) in an effort to form a clandestine group that could govern Super Heroes and devise strategies on how to deal with major superpowered conflicts. The *Civil War* mini series that followed showed that in the present, a worried government was about to enact a Superhuman Registration Act, intended to force Super Heroes to reveal their identities to the government and become "licensed." Although he initially opposed the act—and even attempted to sabotage the government hearings—Iron Man changed his mind and supported the idea of registration.

Following a deadly hero-villain battle, the act was passed, and Iron Man became its champion, eventually unmasking and revealing his identity once again in *Civil War: Front Line* #1 (August 2006) while convincing younger hero Spider-Man to do the same. Throughout the seven-part *Civil War* mini series and a huge spate of crossovers, Stark stood by his decision to support the act, even though it put him in direct conflict with many of his former allies, including longtime friend Captain America.

Although many fans felt that Tony Stark was acting out of character (a point many characters in the books themselves brought up), Brevoort disagrees. "Tony Stark has fairly consistently been portrayed as a guy who will do whatever he thinks is necessary when he believes himself to be right. This goes back at least as far as the 'Armor Wars' story of the '80s where, having learned that nefarious parties had pirated his technology and dispersed it across the globe, selling it illegally, both to villains and to legitimate concerns, he went rogue and decided he was going to take it all down and get it all back and regardless of whatever international law he had to break, and

▲ Marvel heroes either backed the Initiative, or had to face this crowd...

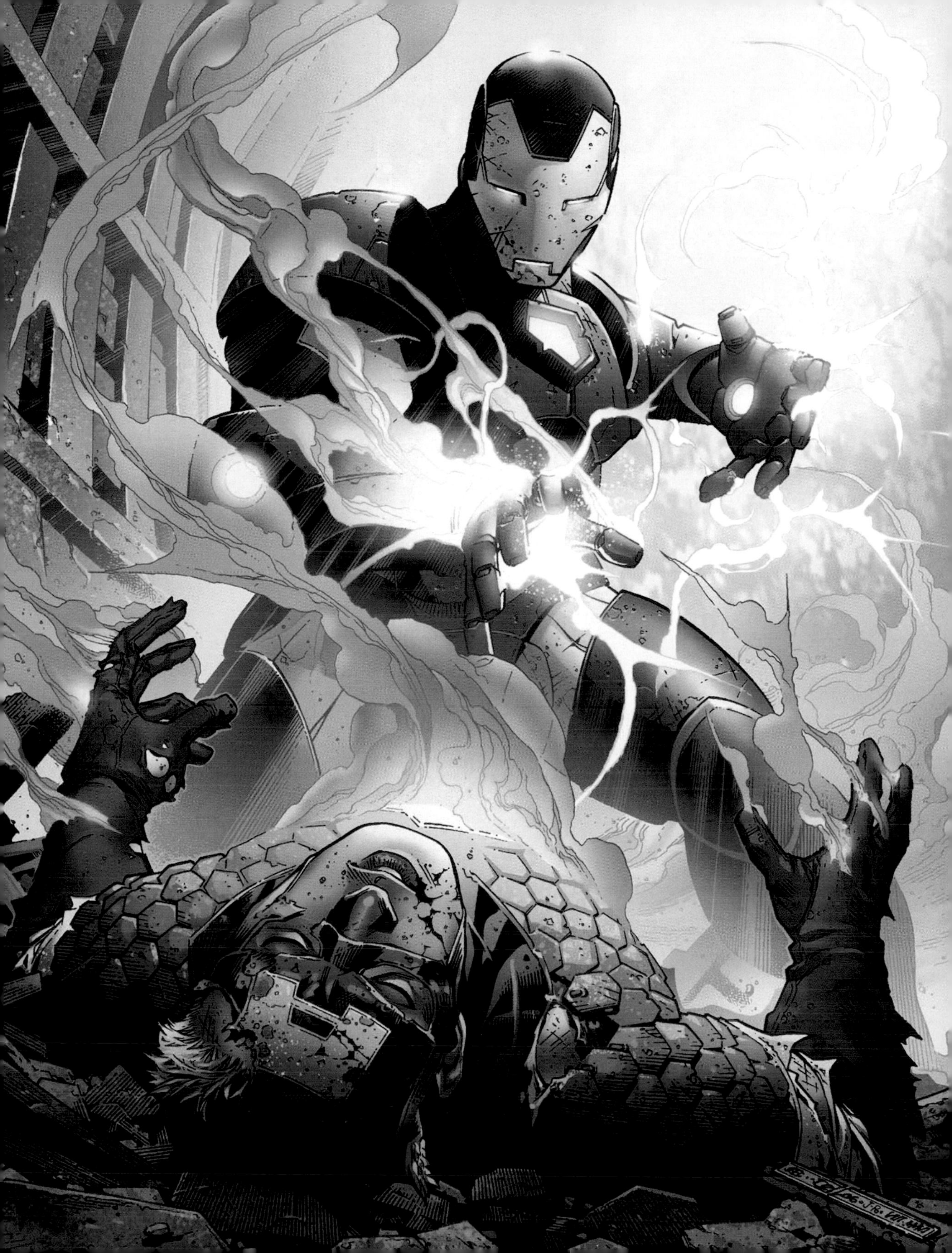

The new Hulk Buster armor ▶ in *World War Hulk*.

whatever he had to do, this was the greater good and he was going to do it, and he would carry that weight and he would pay that price. To me, that's very consistent with the position he takes during *Civil War*."

Brevoort notes that during the crossover, Iron Man was appearing "in dozens of titles because of the tie-ins," and that all the writers brought a bit of their own political stances to the characterization. "As far as Mark Millar, who wrote the main *Civil War* book, was concerned, Tony was the guy who was much more in the right in this situation. He saw the problem, there is a legitimacy to it. I think particularly for comic book readers who've been with the character for years, and have read ten or twenty years of Iron Man adventures, and really connected with this character and this fictional world, it's a tough thing to kind of step back and view it from the outside."

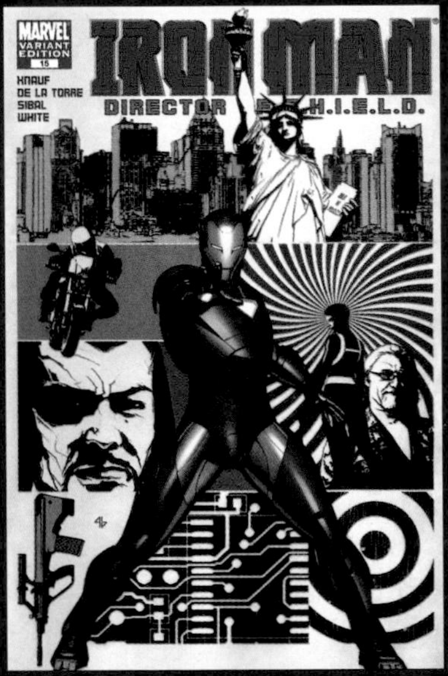
MARVEL
VARIANT EDITION 15
KNAUF
DE LA TORRE
SIBAL
WHITE
IRON MAN
DIRECTOR

To explain the thinking behind the concept, Brevoort notes that he lives in Manhattan. "I was here for 9/11, and I was here in the city for all the months and years that followed, and to this day, we have guards—National Guardsman or police officers, armed guards—all throughout Penn Station that I pass every day. They're there for reasons of security and maintaining public order and making sure nothing bad happens. They're honorable guys and they're doing a tough job, but there is something very uneasy about the fact that there are guys standing in my train station who have enormous guns. Extrapolating from that, if there were guys running around Manhattan who could *knock down buildings* with a beam from their hands, and then on top of that they were masked—nobody knew who they were or what they represented, nobody had any oversight or control over them . . . I would be petrified if I lived in a Manhattan like that, and you bet I'd want to know who the heck they were and I'd want to know that there was some oversight on them. That's a tough thing for a readership that have really connected with these characters to wrap their heads around, because instinctively you want the characters to share your beliefs, and you instinctively want to root for the underdog."

Continuing, Brevoort notes, "It's always easier to write a story where your guy is pushing against the omnipresent evil oppressive government than it is to push for your guy out there following what amounts to the rule of law in an unpopular situation. That was the balancing act that we tried to maintain throughout *Civil War,* and in some books we did it better than others . . . I certainly see where there have been readers who have been put off of this, and how on the simplest level you could think, *Tony Stark should be the maverick and Cap should be the guy who toes the line*. In point of fact, when we started the very first discussion about *Civil War,* that was where the initial instinct was to place them. Within twenty minutes of talking back and forth, and story building and throwing ideas around, we realized that really didn't work or make sense with who these characters are and what they believed and where they'd been all through the years. What we ended up doing was a little closer to what rang true for these guys."

In *Civil War* #7 (early 2007), Stark was appointed the new director of S.H.I.E.L.D. (now an acronym for "Strategic Hazard Intervention Espionage Logistics Directorate"). The new office was reflected on the cover of *Iron Man* #15 (April 2007), where the series gained the subtitle

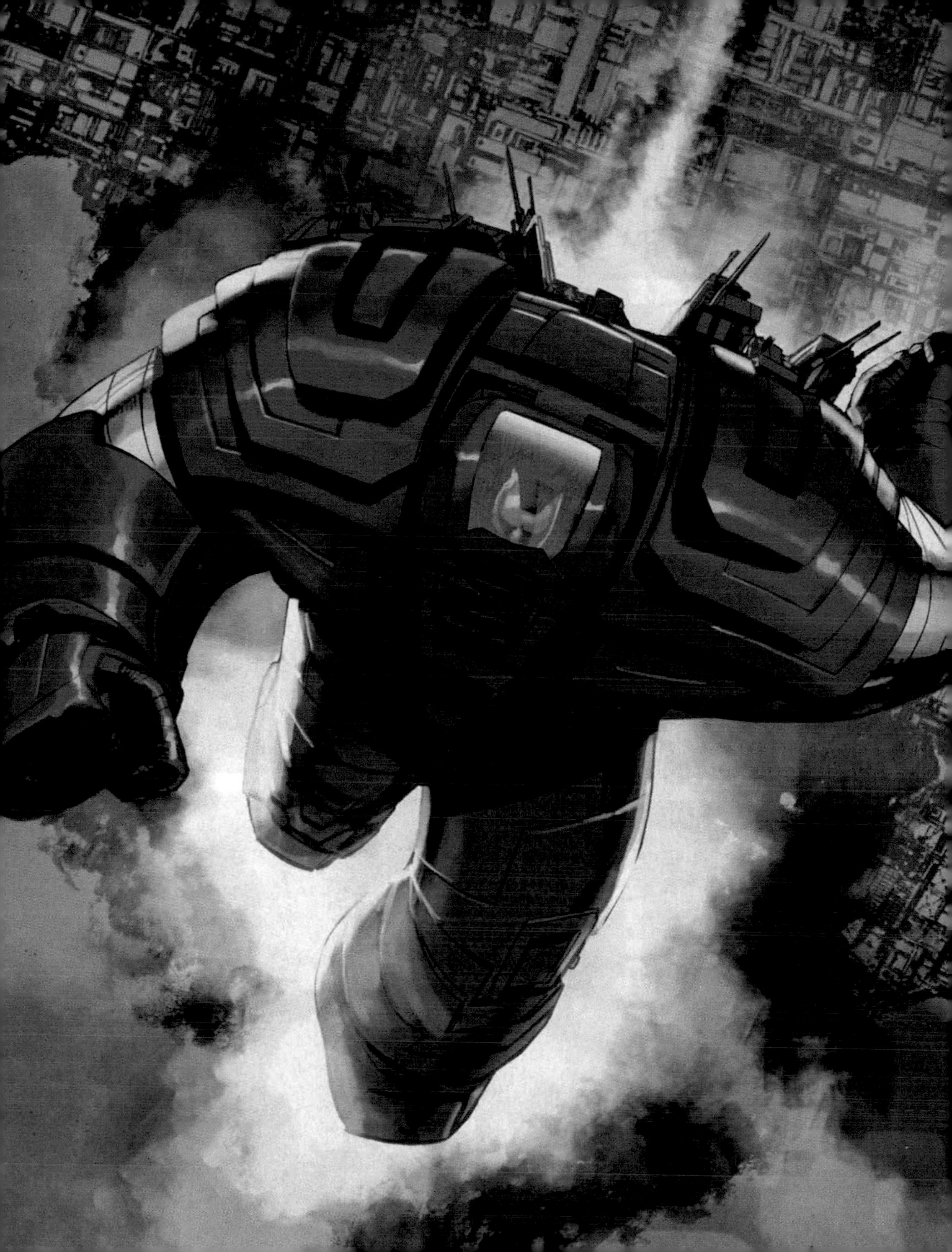

Director of S.H.I.E.L.D. In a multipart storyline that followed, Tony balanced his interests in science with his new militaryesque responsibilities.

"I think if people read *Iron Man* the book, even divorced from the rest of the Marvel line," says Brevoort, "Tony comes across as a terribly sympathetic character and as a guy who really does have the weight of the world on his shoulders in the way that only a great statesman or a 'watchman on the walls of the fortress that protects us from barbarism' can have. I think the Knaufs are very good at playing that. I think they're also good at being able to balance the sort of larger-than-life melodrama of elements of superheroic fantasy with a depiction that has that feeling of plausibility. Particularly moving into the *Director of S.H.I.E.L.D.* era, *Iron Man* is a strip that's got a little bit more of a military flavor to it. It's got a lot more hardware, it's got soldiers, it's got guys out there doing the job and beating back the bad guys. I think they're very facile at being able to balance all that stuff without losing sight of the characters, or the human beings who are carrying ordnance or wearing their highly polished suits of armor and going out and doing this stuff.

"I find that Tony and the problems he's dealing with are more interesting and relatable to me as the head of S.H.I.E.L.D. than when he was running a multinational company," Brevoort continues. "And part of that is the issues he's dealing with as the head of S.H.I.E.L.D. are issues of national and international security and elements that have some, even if it's really tertiary, relationship to my daily life . . . Tony as head of S.H.I.E.L.D. to me is really no different in its own way than Iron Man fighting the Cold War in the '60s. It's just the opponents have changed, the world landscape has changed, the players have changed."

What about the future of Tony Stark and *Iron Man*? For 2008, Brevoort notes, "Tony will be the director of S.H.I.E.L.D., he'll still be overseeing their peacekeeping operations across the globe, he'll still be sort of a removed administrative head, but brain-trust guy for the initiative, the program to put a Super Hero team in every one of the fifty states and provide the local law enforcement an oversight of superhuman activities. He'll still be part of the Mighty Avengers, the public-sanctioned aboveboard super-team. He'll have been rooting out the Skrull conspiracy, having become aware of it. There may be some questions he'll be dealing with in terms of his own identity, whether or not he himself might be a Skrull sleeper agent that is buried so deep that even he doesn't realize that that's who he actually is, and that'll be a thing he'll be grappling with through the course of this.

"How long Tony will remain director of S.H.I.E.L.D. remains to be seen, and what he'll do next after that is also somewhat up in the air," Brevoort concludes. "These are constantly ongoing soap operas of these characters and their lives, and different writers, different creators get involved and they have different ideas. Opportunities present themselves. At least at the moment, particularly because of his position among all the other Marvel characters, there's more interest and more buzz and more talk and more chatter about Tony Stark and Iron Man now than any time in the last ten years. And that's even before the film got under way and people started seeing the pictures and the trailers and such, all of which are going to excite people and so forth. Just by putting him in that prominent a position within the Marvel mythos, he takes on importance. He takes on weight. He's a character you have to acknowledge and you have to have an opinion of, whether you like him or you don't like him based on his position and what he's doing."

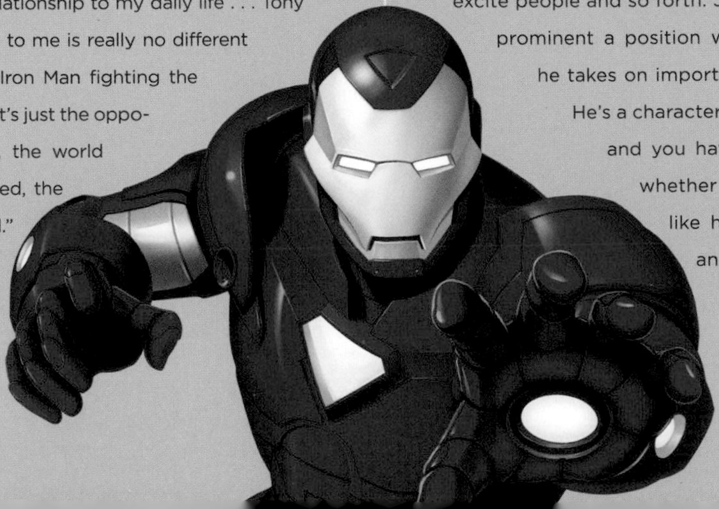

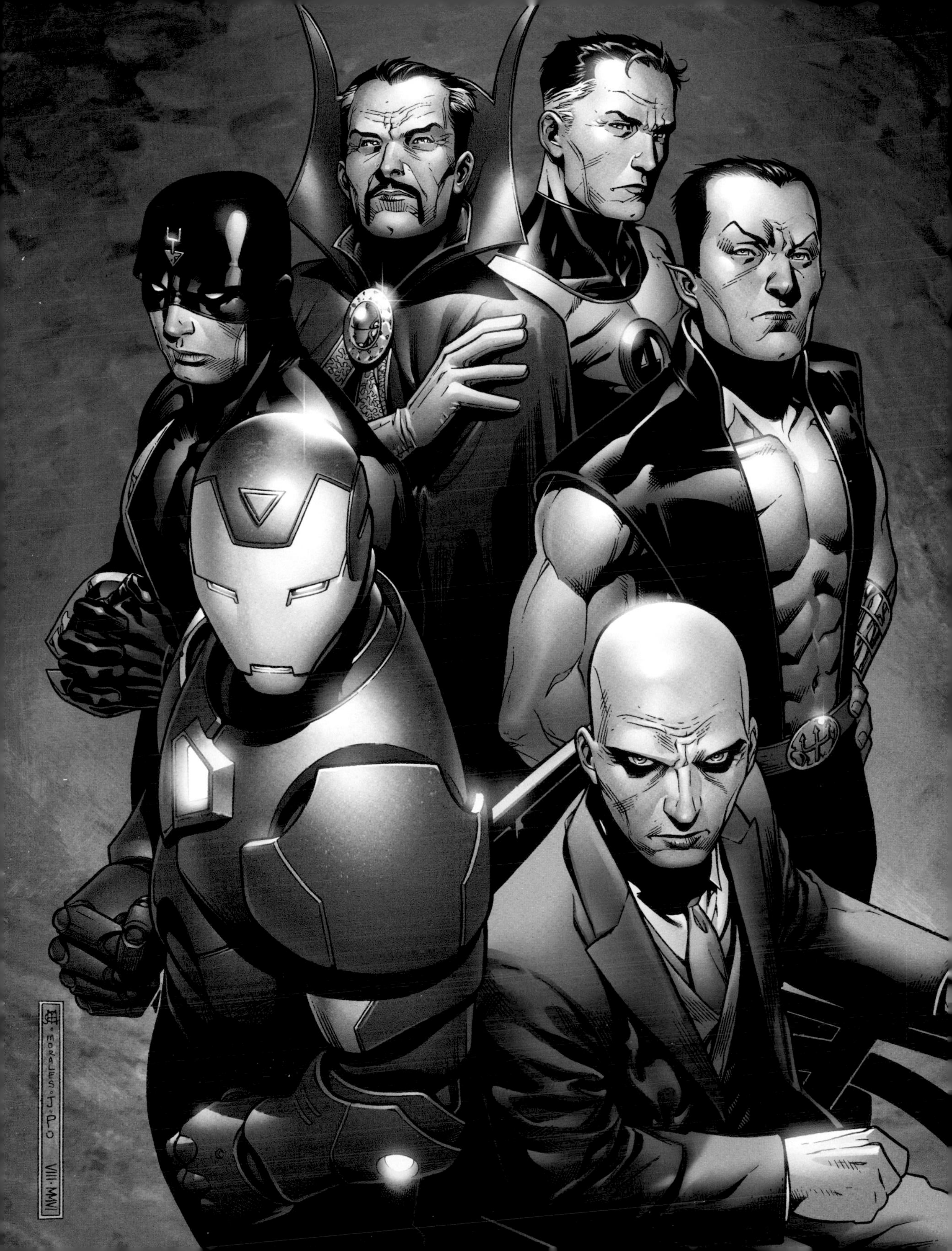
MORALES • J • D • O
VIII • MMVI

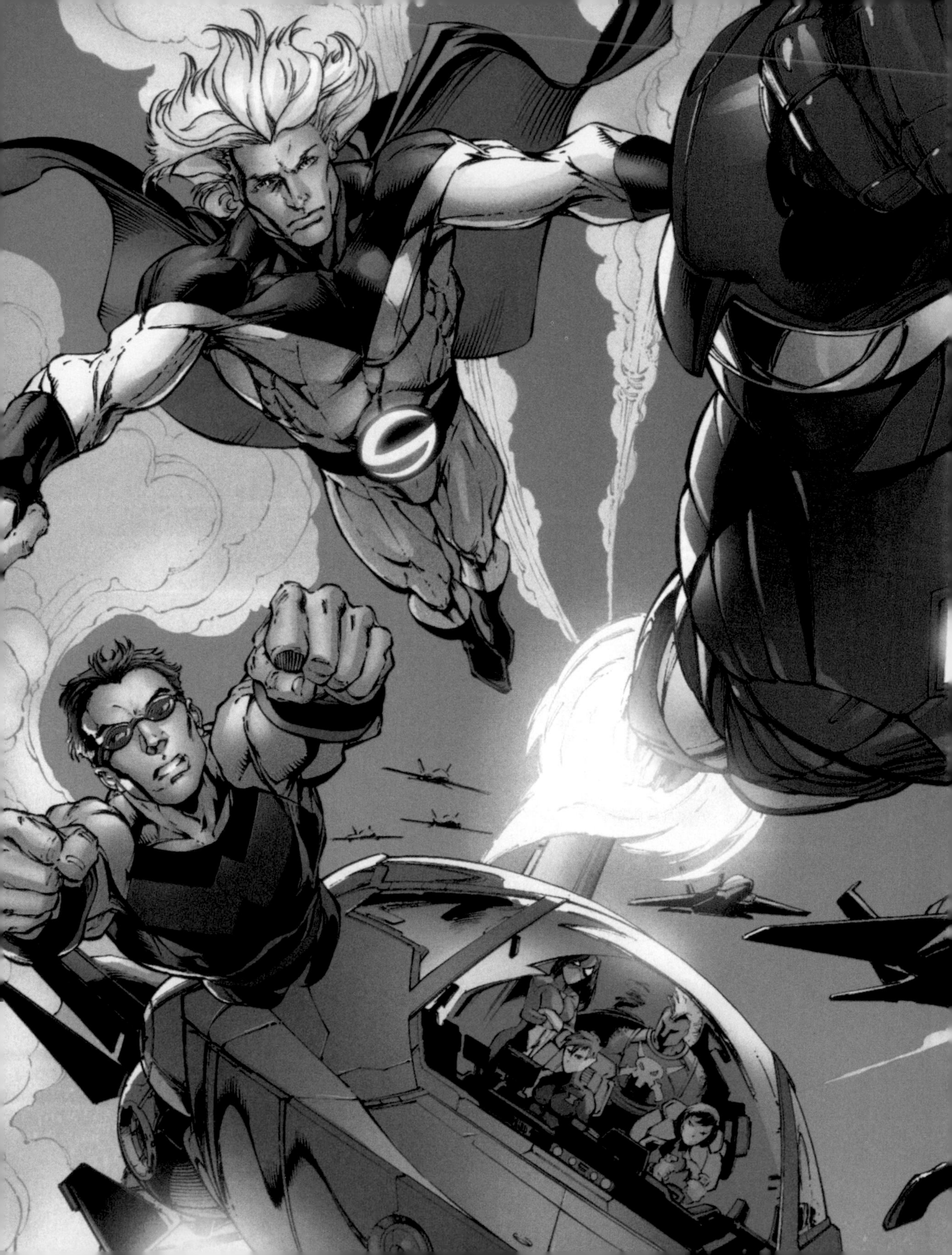

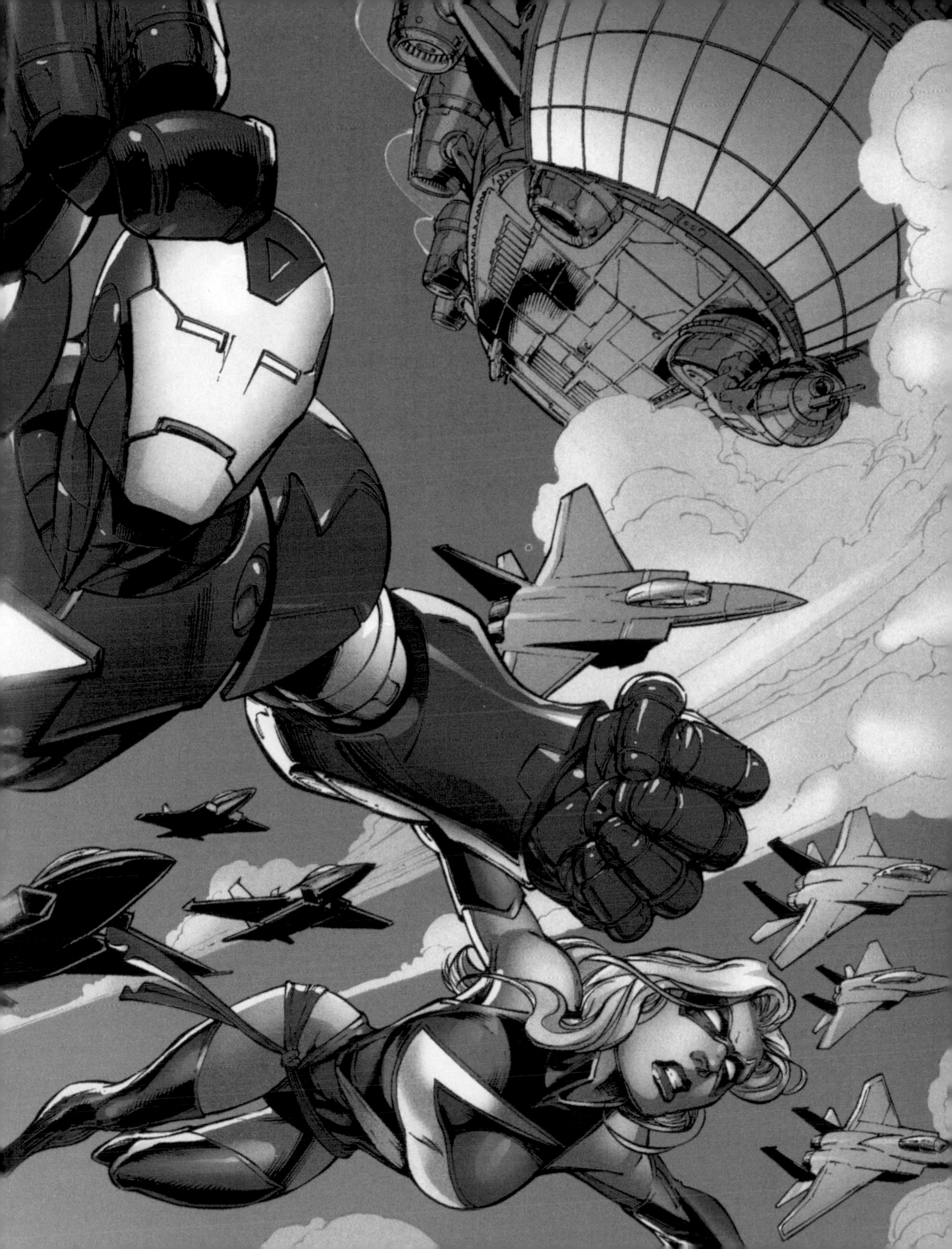

The *Iron Man* film of spring 2008 will not only position Iron Man in a brighter spotlight than he's ever faced before but also launch a number of side projects for the high-profile hero, from more comic series to video games, from animation to licensed full-scale pieces of Stark's armor!

The road to the Iron Man live-action movie has been a long one. Stan Lee first announced talk of an Iron Man feature film in the spring of 1988, but during the short time that New World Pictures owned Marvel, the decision was made to create a Hulk telefilm guest-starring Iron Man in 1989. After two other Hulk telefilms serving as "backdoor pilots" failed to ignite interest in series for Daredevil or Thor, the Iron Man telefilm was scrapped. By December 1989, Stan Lee would announce that *Iron Man* was now a go as a feature film, with Stuart Gordon (*The Reanimator*) at the helm, and Dan Bilson and Paul DeMeo scripting. Universal bought the rights to the film in April 1990.

That version was eventually abandoned, but by February 1996, *Iron Man* was at Twentieth Century Fox, with Nicolas Cage set to star as Tony Stark, from a script by Jeff Vintar (after an earlier draft by Andrew Chapman). The producers were to be John Langley, Stephen Chao, and Jeff Levine. Later reports linked Tom Cruise to the role, while an army of screenwriters took turns at the keyboard to hammer out Stark's story, including Tim McCanlies; Terry Rossio & Ted Elliott; Jeffrey Caine; Miles Millar & Alfred Gough; and Joss Whedon. By late 2004, the project was at New Line Cinema, to be directed by Nick Cassavetes and produced by Marvel Studios and Angry Films, from a screenplay by David Hayter. Eventually, New Line released the film rights back to Marvel, which started independent development of the film. Shortly thereafter, Marvel made a deal with Paramount Pictures to distribute ten feature films . . . with *Iron Man* as the first.

On April 28, 2006, Avi Arad, chairman of Marvel Studios, announced that Jon Favreau would direct *Iron Man,* with Paramount Pictures distributing. As an actor, Favreau had already played Foggy Nelson in the 2003 *Daredevil* film, but he had campaigned heavily to direct *Iron Man.* Given the previous films he had directed, such as *Made, Elf,* and *Zathura*—in addition to writing the cult hit *Swingers*—Favreau was an unusual choice, but his passion and talent won him the job.

Editor Tom Brevoort notes that Favreau met with several Marvel Comics staffers as development began in earnest. "A bunch of us from Marvel editorial, and a bunch of creators, flew out to California relatively early in the process while they were still playing with the screenplay, after the point at which Jon Favreau had come forward as director. We spent a day out there, talking about the story, reading whatever draft of the screenplay they were on at that point, speaking with Jon, throwing ideas around, and so forth. I think in the case of *Iron Man,* perhaps more so than other films, there's more connection between the movie that's being made and the creators. Very early on, they conscripted Adi Granov to come in and design a lot of the look and feel of Iron Man himself and the world in which Iron Man lives. So you can look at [the film], and particularly once you get to the red-and-gold Iron Man, that's clearly Adi Granov's Iron Man created in three dimensions."

Over the next several months, a talented cast would emerge. Respected actor Robert Downey Jr. was cast as Anthony Edward "Tony" Stark and Iron Man. "We didn't want to just go with a safe choice," Favreau told *USA Today.* "The best and worst moments of Robert's life have been in the public eye. He had to find an inner balance to overcome obstacles that went far beyond his career. That's Tony Stark. Robert brings a depth that goes beyond a comic book character who is having trouble in high school, or can't get the girl. Plus, he's simply one of the best actors around."

Academy Award nominee Terrence Howard was cast as Lieutenant Colonel James "Rhodey" Rhodes, now a pilot who aids Tony Stark, and a liaison between the military and Stark Enterprises. Howard told the press at 2007's Comic-Con, "I discovered *Iron Man* in like 1978, 1979. I was like nine, ten years old. My father gave it to me because I said, 'There's no black Super Heroes,' and that's why I didn't like them. And he goes, 'Well look, here's one right here: James Rhodes.' . . . I was formed by James Rhodes because I've been a rebel my entire life. A rebel with a cause. We need to be more socially conscious and hold ourselves more accountable to what's taking place in the world now."

Gwyneth Paltrow was announced as Virginia "Pepper" Potts, and she told the press, "She's his assistant, his confidante. She's really the closest person to him. He's a womanizer and kind of a loose cannon and she's sort of his center, in a way." Of working with Downey, she notes that "it had always been like a dream of mine to work with him and I was so happy to have had the opportunity because he's just amazing."

Shaving his head for the role of Stark's mentor Obadiah Stane was actor Jeff Bridges. Iron Man fans might recall that Stane had a second identity himself, as Iron Monger. About working with Jeff Bridges, Howard told the press that the actor is "just beyond brilliant. His instinct toward truth in the character was only matched by Robert."

Other members of the cast include Shaun Toub as Yinsen as well as cameo appearances by Hilary Swank, rapper and Iron Man fan Ghostface Killah, and Favreau himself (wearing a wig). But one cameo appearance might sweep the others off the screen: Iron Man's creator, Stan Lee, makes a brief appearance.

"I had to be very well dressed," says Lee. "Actually tuxedo pants and a tuxedo shirt and a smoking jacket. And I was puffing a pipe, and I looked somewhat like Hugh Hefner. Not only that, but I have my arms around three gorgeous, sexy-looking blondes. I said to them, 'You don't even have to pay me for this, guys.' I filmed for about an hour. It worked out beautifully, and Robert Downey Jr. is in the take with me. He and I exchange a few words." With a hearty laugh and a wink, Lee adds, "I told him not to be nervous, just to take his lead from me, and if he stumbled I would support him."

Having filmed cameos in almost all of the Marvel movies, Lee jokes that his nickname is One-Take Lee. But his Iron Man scene threw a hitch in that reputation. "While I'm standing with my arms around these girls, and we're all very close, and I've got the pipe in my mouth, and Robert Downey Jr. taps me on the shoulder from behind, so I turn my head to speak to him. Now, I'm so close to these girls—and I've got the pipe in my mouth—that when I turned my head the first time, I hit the girl next to me in the face with the pipe. Even though I'm known as One-Take Lee, I had to do that one again."

Filming for Iron Man began on March 12, 2007, showing Stark's captivity in Afghanistan (the Middle East was now the setting instead of Vietnam). With most of the movie shot at Edwards Air Force Base and other locations in California, filming wrapped on June 25, 2007, at Caesars Palace in Las Vegas, Nevada.

Though CGI work was produced by ILM, producing many of the Iron Man stunts with a "real" suit was a key element in the film's believability, according to Favreau. But while Stan Winston Studios created the actual suits, the designs were based on the work of comic artist Adi Granov and finalized by

designer Phil Saunders. Granov was brought aboard the film by Favreau, who liked his covers and armor work. "I worked on the designs and art direction," Granov says. "Both the hero and the villain in the story, as well as various scenes. I really enjoyed designing the armor and putting it to good use in both the comics and film. There is a great amount of satisfaction from seeing something I helped design come to life on a comic page or the big screen."

Iron Man's plot will be familiar to comic fans, as it retells the origin of Stark's decision to don the armor. Changes have been made to update the story, bringing it in line with not only the modern military and US operations in the Middle East but also the celebrity-obsessed media culture of the millennial era. Downey told the press at Comic-Con '07 that Tony Stark "just starts off as a guy who is desperate to save his own life and is very surprised that he was put in a position where he has to do so. I don't think he had a sheltered life. I think he was just probably in a lot of denial about the ramifications of what he did for a living. I don't think it's a film about someone's conscience getting the better of them. I think it's a film about survival and being conflicted. I think it's a pretty apt metaphor for the twenty-first-century human being."

During pre-production, filming, and post-production, Favreau has maintained high visibility on the Internet, promoting the film regularly on his MySpace page and appearing at San Diego's Comic-Con International in both 2006 and 2007. At a press conference at the '07 Comic-Con, Favreau said, "With movies of this kind there's a real dialogue between the fans and the filmmakers. If you don't accept it, it backfires . . . When you're dealing with a character like Iron Man, and you're coming in without a body of work that would suggest you can do a good job with this movie, of this genre, you have to make your case for yourself . . . Also, the fans are a tremendous resource and you'll learn what people expect of this character."

The Iron Man film will be reflected in other mediums as well. Sega Corporation will be releasing a highly anticipated Iron Man video game featuring scenes and dialogue re-created from the film. Hasbro has a toy line with not only multiple forms of Stark's armored hero but the villainous Iron Monger as well. And a new animated Iron Man television series is being created for debut later in 2008, produced by Marvel Studios' Eric S. Rollman, story-edited by Christopher Yost, and animated by France's Method Films.

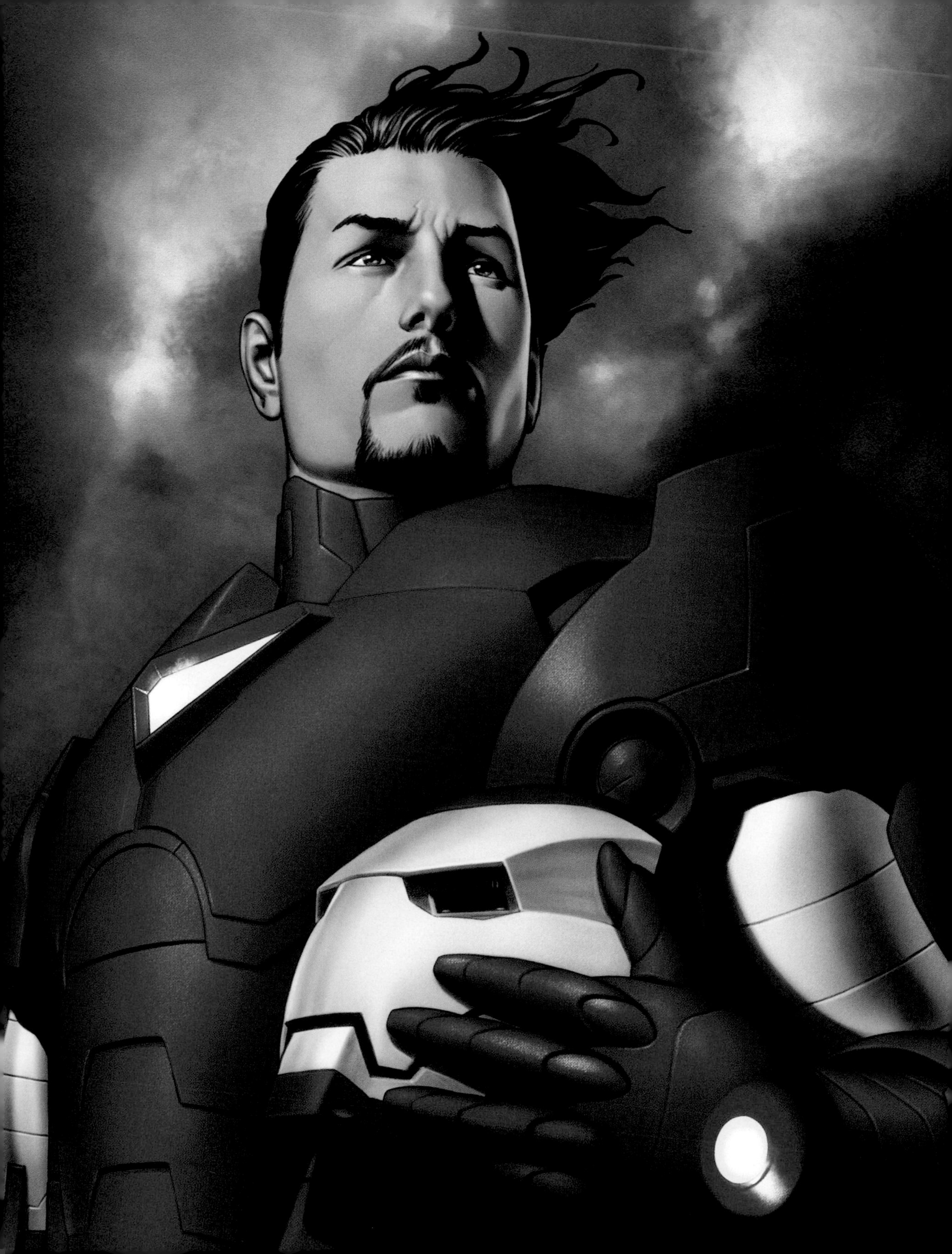

As 2008 dawned, the world was again in the midst of political upheaval, though science and technology, thankfully, were advancing every day. It was the year Tony Stark turned forty-five, and the year that nobody would be asking "Who? Or what, is the newest, most breathtaking, most sensational Super Hero of all . . . ?" because they know that the answer is *Iron Man.*

What has kept the character enduring, and what is his legacy? Why has Iron Man thrived as a hero for so long? Is it the James Bond–like espionage wish fulfillment? The high-tech gadgets? The knight in shining armor? The visual appeal of the character?

"There are certainly fans who love the shiny armor, and those who get a big kick out of all the gadgets," says writer Dave Michelinie. "But I think the bottom line is like I said earlier: Tony Stark is basically just a human being. Readers can identify with him because they could *be* him . . . as opposed to the likelihood of being bitten by a radioactive spider or being bathed in gamma radiation."

Artist Bob Layton agrees that there are many elements to Iron Man enduring, but says that "the primary appeal is that modern-day knight in armor. Iron Man is the modern-day representation of those Arthurian ideals,

which has thrived in literature for centuries. He is the king of his own empire; he wields power judiciously and punishes those who seek to destroy what he has built."

"Most of the characters created back then in the days of Marvel from 1961 through 1964 all endured: Spider-Man, Thor, the Hulk, Daredevil, Captain America," says writer Kurt Busiek, noting that *Iron Man* has endured as a book due to "the sleek, shiny technology aspect of it. It's a book that it's easy to put gorgeous gals in, it's got lots of adventure, and exoticism, high-society flash and flare, and it's one of the easiest books out there to modernize because Iron Man is supposed to be cutting-edge all the time . . . *Iron Man*'s got all of that flash and glamour, and the tricky part is to get that moral center into it somehow . . . I tried to play him as a Rockefeller Democrat, as somebody who felt noblesse oblige, who felt that his position in the world was the result of all these other people working and struggling. He depended on them for his privileged position, and therefore they had to be able to depend on him."

Artist Jorge Lucas calls Iron Man "the first political Super Hero. From being a bodyguard and a man who designs weapons, he has made a large variety of enemies, from the classical enemies to those who hate Stark Industries—politicians, et cetera. All these dramatic qualities make him very special; he is like . . . a knight under brilliant armor who must fight against the dragons of the modern world: arms wars, ideological wars, religious wars."

Writer-artist Mike Grell believes that it's the evolution of the character that has kept Iron Man fresh. "The character has evolved over the years. He's been skillfully and carefully reinvented every decade or so to fit the times. We're approaching a time right now where the stuff we used to dream about back in the '60s is already reality. An exoskeleton suit of armor is here. The Bionic Man was interesting fiction back in the day when it was first created, but . . . today, when you talk about computers and nanotech, we're just scratching the surface. It's an easy leap of logic for the audience to accept that something like this *could* be very real and very possible. The other thing that keeps the character going is that they've managed to populate the series with interesting and compelling characters, good storylines by solid writers, and they tap into the current culture and the current news while at the same time, I think it's very deeply humanizing, the character of Tony Stark himself. At the point where he was his most powerful was also at the point where he was his weakest, when he was a serious alcoholic . . . having that hovering in the background with Tony Stark is one of the things that sets him apart and above Bruce Wayne in terms of who's the more human character. If you break it down to the difference between the two, particularly the movie version of Bruce Wayne, it's not that different from the comic book version of Tony Stark. Big industrialist, lots of power, all the tech support he needs to create the gadgets that he needs in order to do the things that he does. We keep coming

back to the man inside the suit. It's the human inside the Iron Man that makes it."

Editor Tom Brevoort agrees with Grell. "He's the ultimate guy with high-tech toys, all of the gadgets and money and wealth and fame that you could ever want. But while fans like the thrill and the wish fulfillment of the armor, and all the stuff that it can do, what really engages them long-term, and what creates their sympathy and empathy and their connection, is the guy inside the armor. It's Tony, and his problems and his life and the battles he wages, internal and external."

"Iron Man is as much of a weapon as he is a Super Hero, [using] technology [that] turns an ordinary man into a very powerful force. It's a rather scary concept as it implies that anyone, good or bad, could gain control of this power," says artist Adi Granov. "He's very much a multidimensional character with a lot of conflicting traits, but he builds and dons this awesome piece of technology which helps him redeem himself in his own eyes. That's a pretty fantastic premise for great stories."

Displaying the kind of enthusiasm he's known for, Iron Man's creator, Stan Lee, gets in the last word: "There's never been a hero like this. He's so unique, and in today's world, if you can come up with something that's original and unique, you're already halfway home . . . There's something very different about Iron Man, and certainly you may have seen robots, but you've never seen a guy in a modern suit of iron armor doing what he does."

Thankfully for fans of heroic adventure, Iron Man will likely keep "doing what he does" for many years—and many suits of armor—to come.

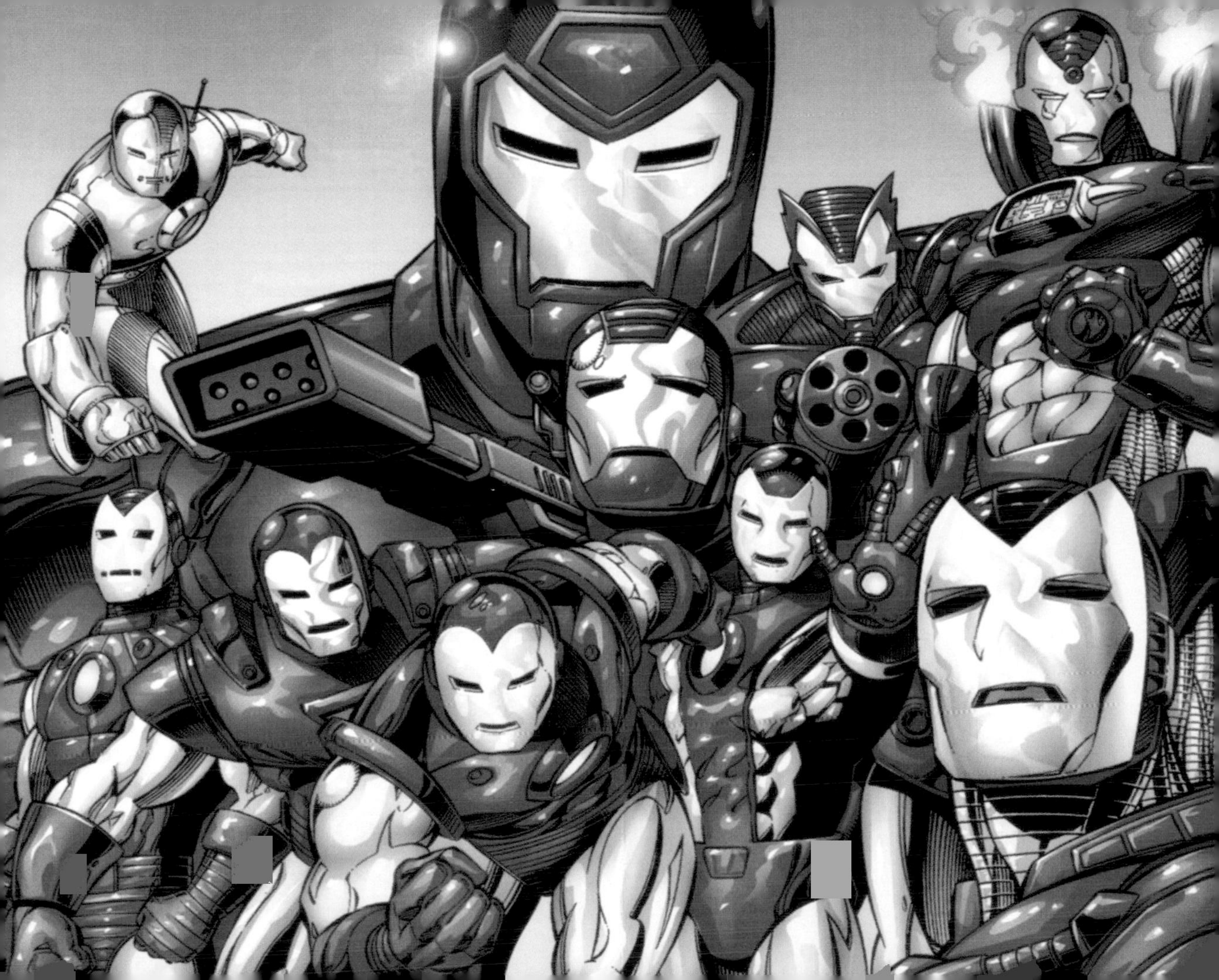

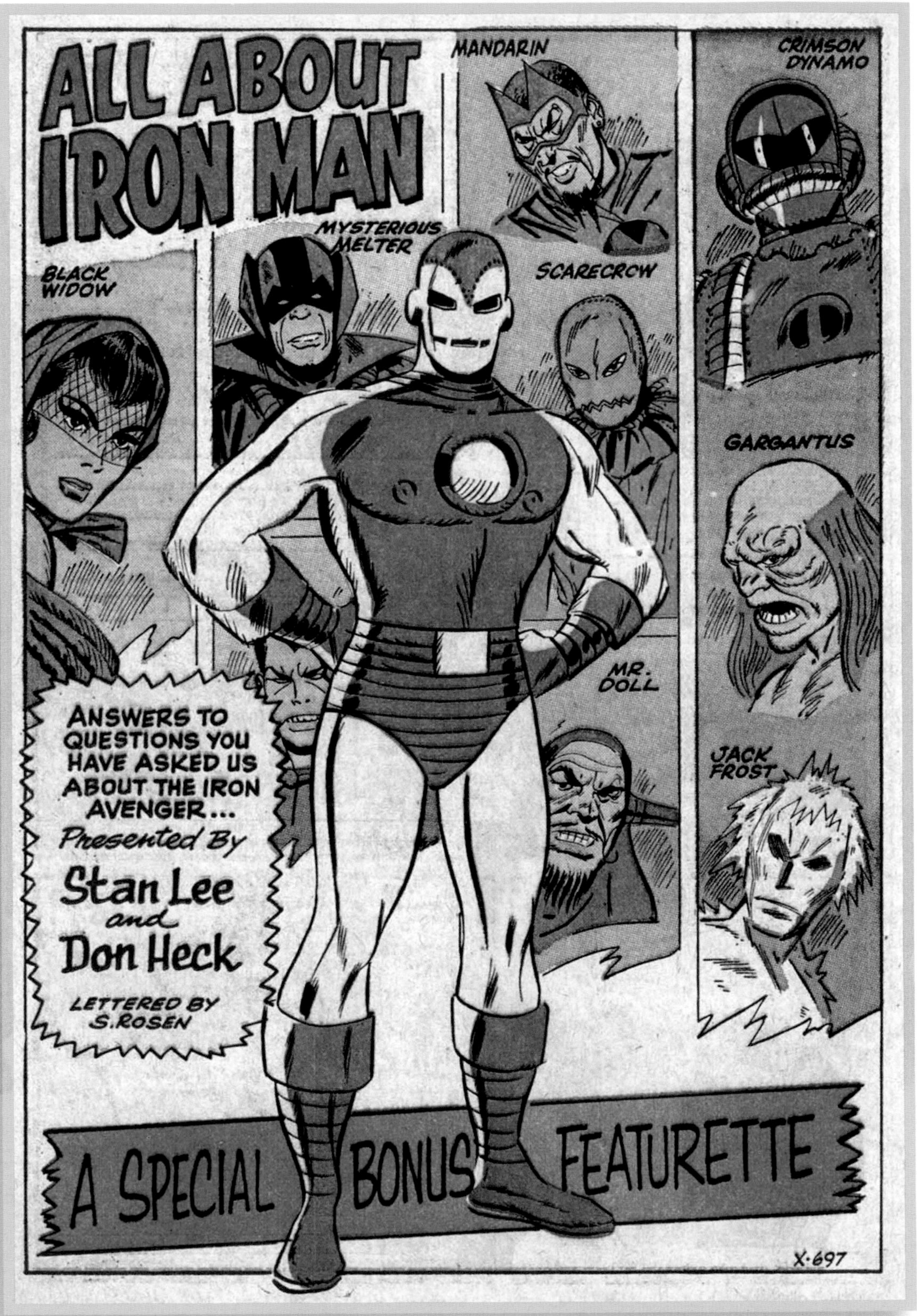

ALL ABOUT IRON MAN
MANDARIN
CRIMSON DYNAMO
MYSTERIOUS MELTER
BLACK WIDOW
SCARECROW
GARGANTUS
MR. DOLL
JACK FROST
ANSWERS TO QUESTIONS YOU HAVE ASKED US ABOUT THE IRON AVENGER... Presented By Stan Lee and Don Heck
LETTERED BY S.ROSEN
A SPECIAL BONUS FEATURETTE
X-697

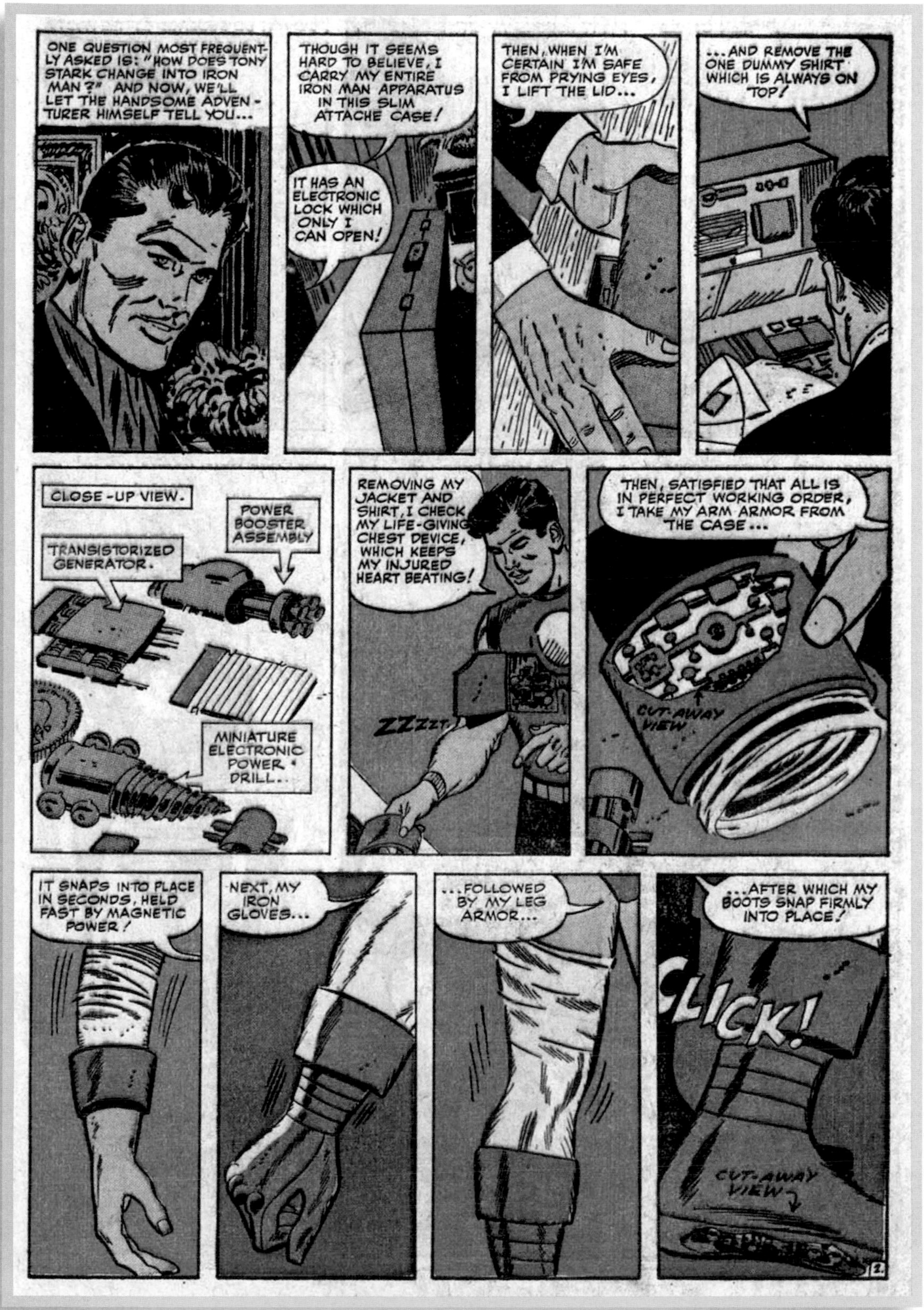
ONE QUESTION MOST FREQUENTLY ASKED IS: "HOW DOES TONY STARK CHANGE INTO IRON MAN?" AND NOW, WE'LL LET THE HANDSOME ADVENTURER HIMSELF TELL YOU...
THOUGH IT SEEMS HARD TO BELIEVE, I CARRY MY ENTIRE IRON MAN APPARATUS IN THIS SLIM ATTACHE CASE!
IT HAS AN ELECTRONIC LOCK WHICH ONLY I CAN OPEN!
THEN, WHEN I'M CERTAIN I'M SAFE FROM PRYING EYES, I LIFT THE LID...
...AND REMOVE THE ONE DUMMY SHIRT WHICH IS ALWAYS ON TOP!
CLOSE-UP VIEW.
POWER BOOSTER ASSEMBLY
TRANSISTORIZED GENERATOR.
MINIATURE ELECTRONIC POWER DRILL..
REMOVING MY JACKET AND SHIRT, I CHECK MY LIFE-GIVING CHEST DEVICE, WHICH KEEPS MY INJURED HEART BEATING!
ZZZZT.
THEN, SATISFIED THAT ALL IS IN PERFECT WORKING ORDER, I TAKE MY ARM ARMOR FROM THE CASE...
CUT-AWAY VIEW
IT SNAPS INTO PLACE IN SECONDS, HELD FAST BY MAGNETIC POWER!
NEXT, MY IRON GLOVES...
...FOLLOWED BY MY LEG ARMOR...
...AFTER WHICH MY BOOTS SNAP FIRMLY INTO PLACE!
CLICK!
CUT-AWAY VIEW
2.

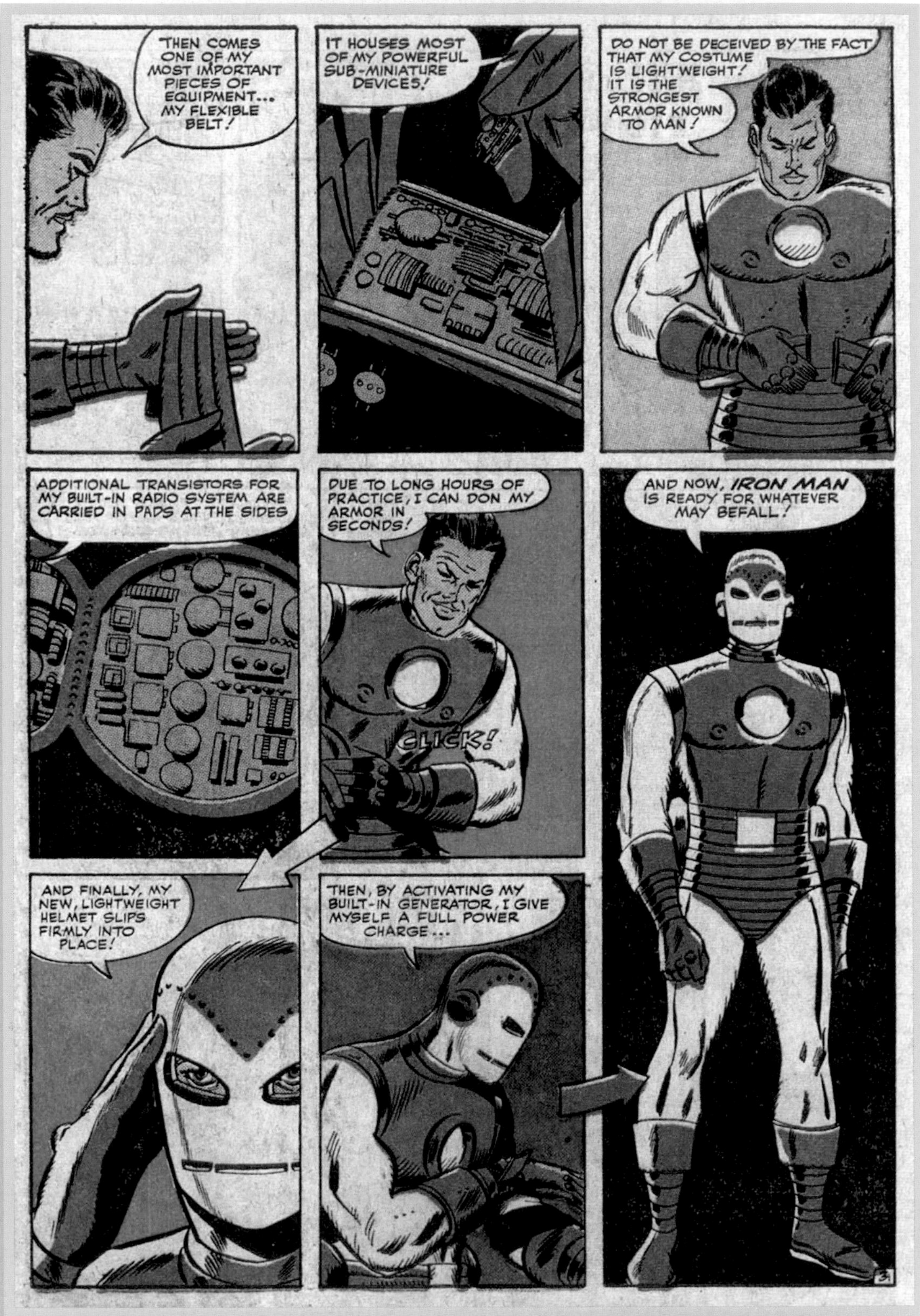
THEN COMES ONE OF MY MOST IMPORTANT PIECES OF EQUIPMENT... MY FLEXIBLE BELT!
IT HOUSES MOST OF MY POWERFUL SUB-MINIATURE DEVICES!
DO NOT BE DECEIVED BY THE FACT THAT MY COSTUME IS LIGHTWEIGHT! IT IS THE STRONGEST ARMOR KNOWN TO MAN!
ADDITIONAL TRANSISTORS FOR MY BUILT-IN RADIO SYSTEM ARE CARRIED IN PADS AT THE SIDES
DUE TO LONG HOURS OF PRACTICE, I CAN DON MY ARMOR IN SECONDS!
CLICK!
AND NOW, IRON MAN IS READY FOR WHATEVER MAY BEFALL!
AND FINALLY, MY NEW, LIGHTWEIGHT HELMET SLIPS FIRMLY INTO PLACE!
THEN, BY ACTIVATING MY BUILT-IN GENERATOR, I GIVE MYSELF A FULL POWER CHARGE...
3

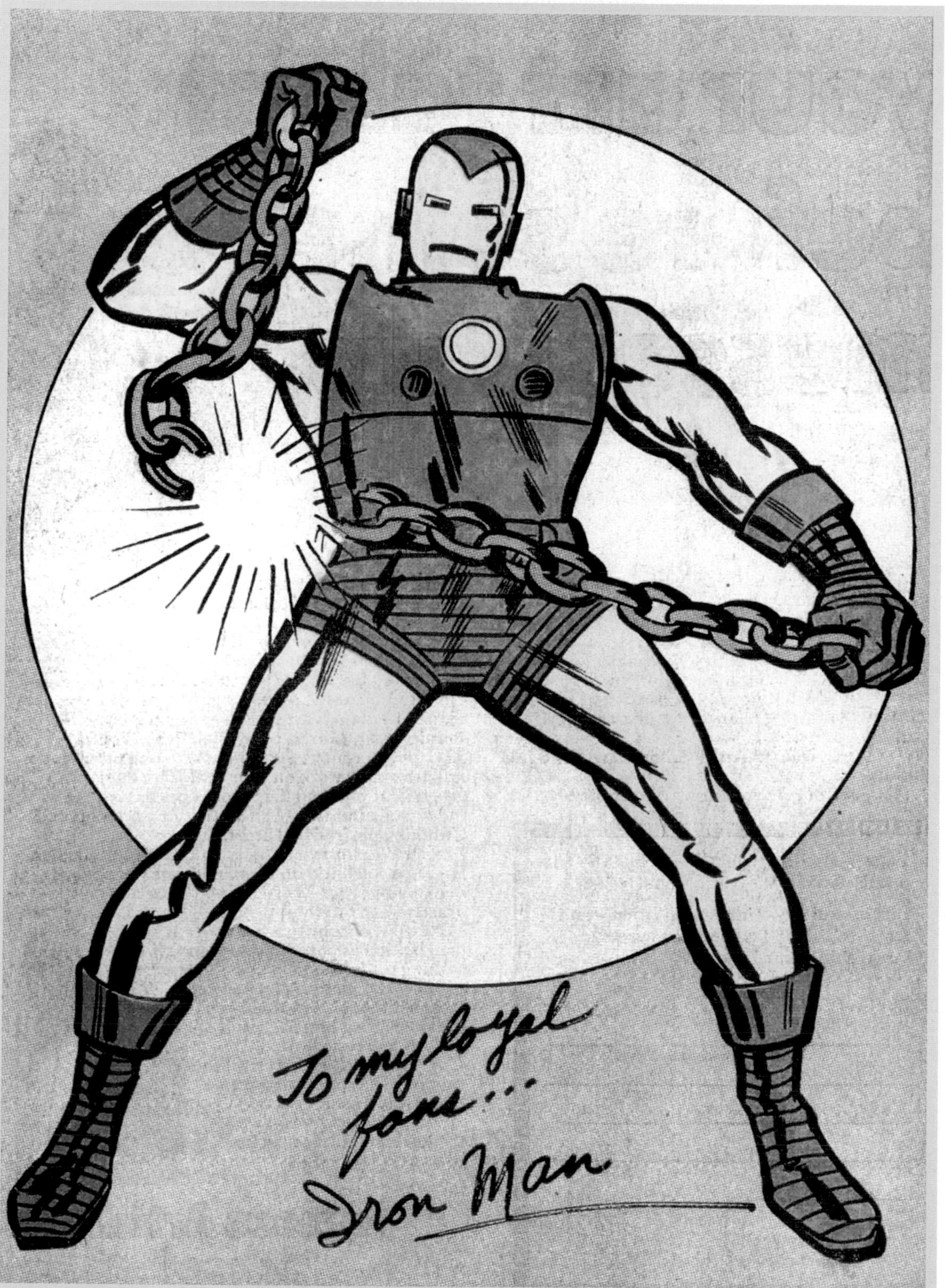
To my loyal fans...
Iron Man

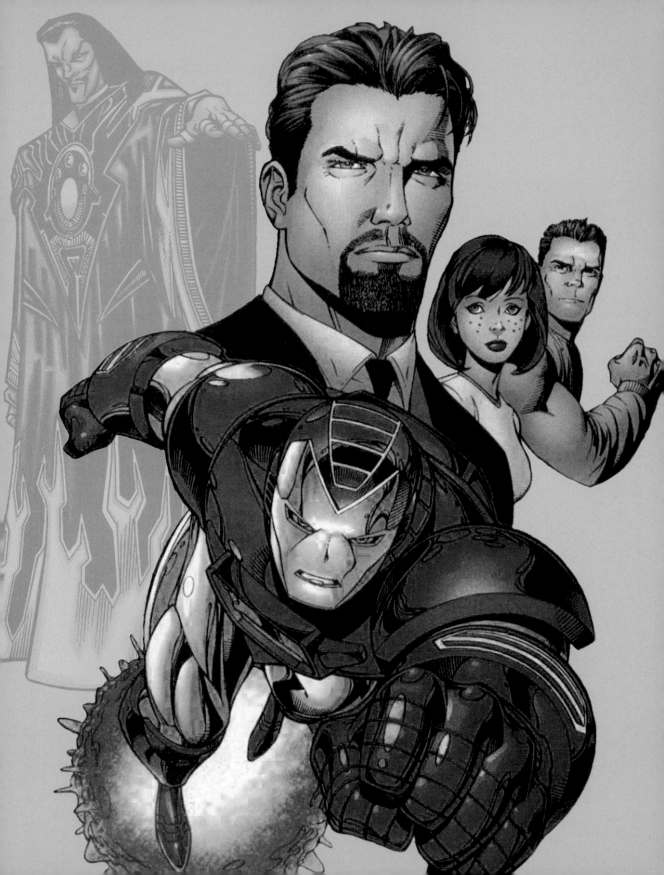

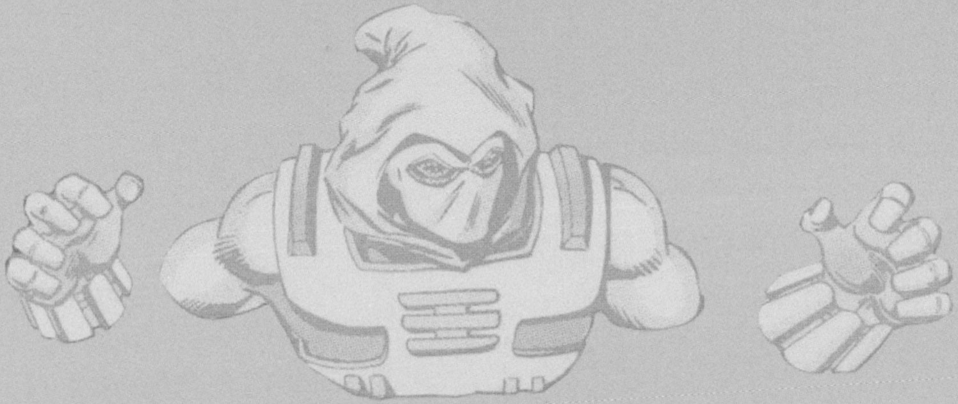

CHARACTER BIOS

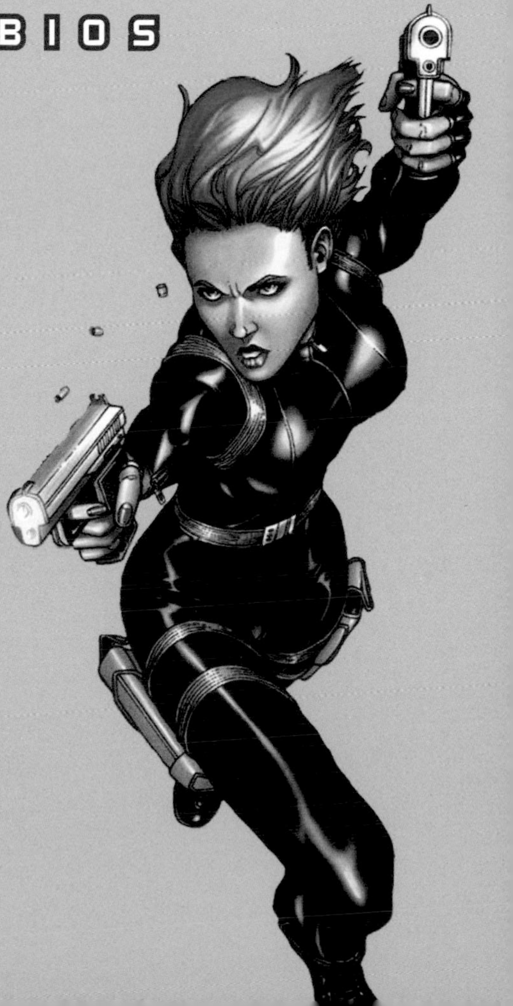

TONY STARK / IRON MAN

Alias: Iron Man

Real Name: Anthony Edward "Tony" Stark

Height: 6'1" (Stark); 6'6" (in armor)

Weight: 225 lbs. (Stark); 425 lbs. (in armor)

Eyes: Blue, **Hair:** Black

Group Affiliation: CEO of Stark Industries; Member of the Mighty Avengers and the Initiative; Director of S.H.I.E.L.D.; Former member of the Avengers, the West Coast Avengers, the Illuminati, the Thunderbolts, Force Works, the Hellfire Club; Former US secretary of defense; Former CEO of Stark International, Circuits Maximus, Stark Enterprises, Stark Solutions

First Appearance: *Tales of Suspense* #39

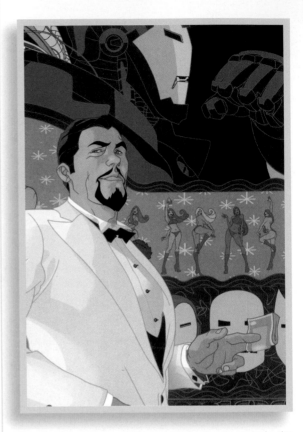

From an early age, Anthony Stark was fascinated by stories of heroes, explorers, and scientists. His mother, Maria, doted on him, but his father, Howard—who ran America's leading munitions plants during the Cold War period—wanted a tougher child to carry on his legacy. Little did either of them suspect that the collision of heroics and science would figure so strongly in Tony's future . . . nor that the amazing armor of Iron Man would enable him to become a figure admired not only worldwide, but on other worlds as well!

Sent to a boarding school at the age of seven due to Howard's hopes that it would toughen up his son, Tony retreated from people and instead read about the exploits of King Arthur and his Knights of the Round Table, and about inventors and explorers such as Marco Polo and the Wright brothers. With his mechanical aptitude and inventive genius, Tony enrolled at the Massachusetts Institute of Technology (MIT) at the age of fifteen. A prodigy, Tony was mentored by Professors Theodore Slaight and Sal Kennedy, and he graduated with a double master's degree in physics and engineering at nineteen. He also fell in love with a girl named Meredith McCall, but because she was the daughter of one of Howard Stark's business rivals, the pair were separated.

Tony began working at Stark Industries but also used his trust fund to travel, romance women, and drink, often with his friends Tiberius "Ty" Stone or his cousin Morgan Stark. Tony also briefly romanced a slightly older woman, Sunset Bain, but it proved an error in judgment; Bain burgled the Stark Industries offices and used stolen technology to start a rival company. It was the first time Tony would be betrayed over technology . . . but not the last.

Shortly after Tony turned twenty-one, his parents were killed in an automobile "accident" that was secretly engineered by agents of rival company Republic Oil (later Roxxon Oil). The saboteurs hoped that the irresponsible playboy would sell his father's company, but Tony soon found purpose running Stark Industries as its owner and chief executive officer. He promoted a woman named Virginia "Pepper" Potts to be his executive secretary, a task at which she proved invaluable, while Tony learned responsibility.

Stark eventually became a strong leader for the company, building it into a multimillion-dollar industrial complex by generating more lucrative military contracts and taking a personal hand in inventing new technology. One such invention was a proposed battle suit that might help protect and enhance soldiers who wore it. Stark also became engaged, to a socialite named Joanna Nivena, who saw him off when he embarked on a trip to one of his international plants in Southeast Asia. Stark was attending a demonstration of some of his military hardware, but during a raid by local terrorists, Stark was caught in the explosion of a land mine.

Stark was taken captive and brought to the camp of Sin-Cong revolutionary Wong-Chu, who explained to Stark that a piece of shrapnel was lodged in his chest. Tony was told that this shrapnel would kill him within a week if he did not get medical help; Wong-Chu promised him that lifesaving help if Stark first built him a powerful weapon. With few options other than death, Stark agreed, soon finding that he was working alongside another prisoner, the genius physicist Professor Ho Yinsen.

Stark and Yinsen conspired to build one of the prototype battle suits that Stark had been developing, creating an extraordinary armor out of the materials available to them in the small laboratory. The armor was powered using magnetism, electricity, and transistor technology, and it contained crude magnetic defense weaponry. A special chest plate contained a miniature magnetic field generator, designed to keep the shrapnel from reaching Stark's heart, while a pacemaker-like device would make certain that Stark survived if it did.

Stark donned the armor and was powering it up when Wong-Chu's men tried to enter the laboratory. To buy Stark time, Yinsen tried to distract the guerrillas and was fatally shot. Moments later, moving for the first time in his clumsy-but-powerful Iron Man armor, Stark avenged Yinsen's sacrifice, tearing Wong-Chu's camp apart and seemingly causing the death of the warlord. Stark made his way into the nearby jungle, trying to escape the enemy territory, and met a military pilot whose helicopter had crashed. Convincing the pilot, James Rhodes, that they were on the same side, Stark repowered his suit using the chopper's batteries, and the two men eventually found their way back to freedom.

Once he had returned to America and safety, Stark began to redesign the armor's chest plate so that he could wear it under normal clothing; he couldn't remove the chest plate or allow it to lose power or he would die from the shrapnel. Although he initially planned to sell the suit's design, after using it to stop some industrial thieves Stark became concerned that unscrupulous wearers of the armor might use it for criminal acts. He told the secret of his escape and the armor to Joanna Nivena, who encouraged him to use the suit to become a Super Hero. It was the dawn of a new age, and superpowered characters were appearing in abundance, after having mostly disappeared following World War II. Stark decided to become the new hero known as Iron Man.

Early in his super-heroic career, Stark began what would become a never-ending set of modifications intended to make his armor more powerful. His first action—inspired by frightened onlookers at one rescue he performed—was to paint his dull gray suit a shining gold. He would soon redesign it in a much more significant way, creating a red-and-gold set of armor that was collapsible enough to put in a briefcase and featured components such as palm-mounted "repulsor rays," boot jets that allowed him to fly, and external power packs—since his armor often ran out of power at inconvenient times. His slimmer mask earned him the nickname *Shellhead*.

Stark also established an elaborate fiction about Iron Man: The armored hero was Stark's "bodyguard," thus explaining why he was often around when Stark was threatened. Whether it was because Stark's inventions and munitions were so tempting, or because they wanted to face the hero Iron Man, saboteurs, spies, and superpowered villains began to attack Stark Industries with regularity. Iron Man faced them all, and while he was often victorious, many of his foes retreated before they could be captured. His attackers were a colorful lot, facing him in powered battle suits and armor, and utilizing such names as Gargantus, Jack Frost, the Crimson Dynamo, the Melter, Mr. Doll, the Scarecrow, the Black Widow, the Unicorn, Hawkeye, the Black Knight, Count Nefaria, Titanium Man, Ultimo, Whiplash, the Crusher, Gladiator, the Controller, Madame Masque, and many more. The foe he faced most often—though he was powerless to fully bring him to justice due to international laws—was the Mandarin.

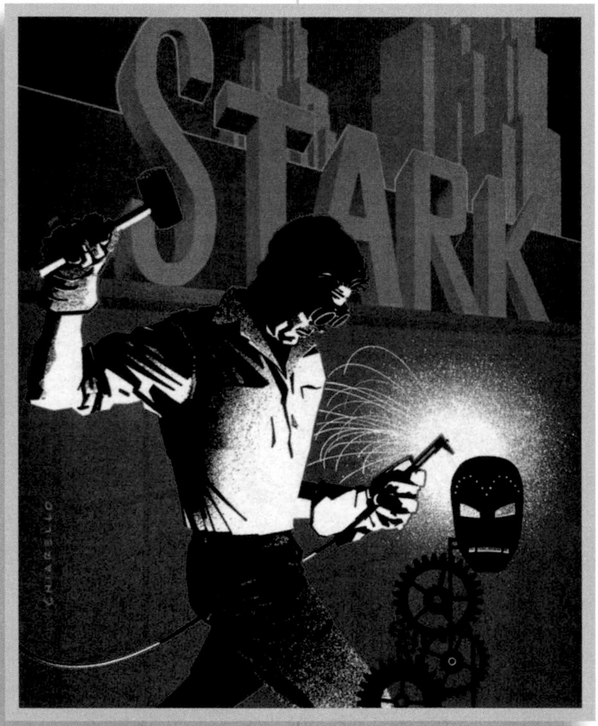
STARK
CHIARELLO

Often put at risk in these battles against bad guys were Stark's closest employees, Pepper Potts and chauffeur Harold "Happy" Hogan, neither of whom initially knew about their employer's dual life. Joanna Nivena was not endangered, however, having called off their engagement. Stark dated many beautiful women over the coming years, from starlets and debutantes to other scientists and even employees. He was even caught in the midst of a love triangle with Potts and Hogan for a time, but he stepped back, and eventually Potts and Hogan eloped.

During his early years as Iron Man, Stark was also one of the founding members of the Avengers, an assemblage of some of Earth's mightiest heroes. He funded the organization through the Maria Stark Foundation and donated the Stark family mansion to serve as headquarters. He also gave members the use of the family butler, Edwin Jarvis, who had been a servant to the Starks since Tony was a child. Although Iron Man would occasionally leave active Avengers membership, he returned just as often, helping them face terrestrial—and occasionally extraterrestrial—threats.

Stark was also instrumental in aiding and arming the international intelligence and law enforcement agency known as S.H.I.E.L.D., and he struck up a long-lasting friendship with its director, Nick Fury, whose appointment he had helped secure. Stark helped design many of S.H.I.E.L.D.'s most important devices, including its hovering helicarrier headquarters, the flying cars its agents often used for transportation, and the android Life Model Decoys (LMDs), which could convincingly impersonate anyone. On more than one occasion, Stark would use an LMD to save either his identity or his life.

Stark's frail heart and health often caused problems for him and Iron Man, and in the aftermath of a battle against Midas and others, Stark suffered a major heart attack. The Avengers helped Stark get to Dr. Jose Santini, who performed a transplant that gave Stark a synthetic heart. In fear for his health if he returned to adventuring, Stark asked boxer Eddie March to take over as Iron Man for him. The change proved impermanent, as it did later during times when Stark was incapacitated or otherwise unable to use the armor and a select few others—including boxer Happy Hogan and pilot James Rhodes—would don it and become Iron Man. Although the mask could synthesize their voices enough to fool the public or villains, the replacements' inexperience with the battle suit meant that Stark had to reestablish his identity as soon as possible.

The armor continued to change, with Stark upgrading or adding features. Although some additions were silly, such as a nosepiece and pop-out roller skates, other armors were specially designed for specific uses including the Space Armor, the all-black Stealth Armor, and the Deep Sea Armor. Stark also upgraded the transistor technology, using microscopic integrated circuitry to replace it and adding weapons such as laser projectors, tractor beams, force fields, and many others to his arsenal.

With changing times came changing politics, and Tony began to steer his company away from munitions contracting and farther into other scientific realms. He eventually changed the name of the company to Stark International to reflect the worldwide expansion he was spearheading. He also brought in trusted new employees such as personal pilot James "Rhodey" Rhodes, who had helped him in his first outing as Iron Man; beauteous bodyguard Bethany Cabe; and no-nonsense personal assistant Bambina "Bambi" Arbogast. He allied himself with other costumed adventurers such as Guardsman, Jack of Hearts, the second Ant-Man, and Madame Masque, but the alliances sometimes proved his undoing, such as when Guardsman's personality disorder made him come to hate Iron Man, or when Masque's loyalties to the criminal organization known as the Maggia overrode her love for Tony Stark.

Stark also began to face ever-increasing attacks from rival industrialists, including the reclusive Justin Hammer, who used his great wealth and criminal connections to upgrade superpowered battle suits for villains (in exchange for 50 percent of their profits) and often had them attack Stark or Iron Man. He once even caused Iron Man's armor to kill a Carnelian ambassador, though the hero was later cleared of the murder charges.

The stress of being both hero and multinational multimillionaire industrialist took its toll on Stark, and eventually his drinking became worse and worse. He developed into a full-blown alcoholic for a time, but eventually faced his demon in a bottle and stoppered it. Later, insane industrialist Obadiah Stane targeted Stark on multiple fronts, triggering battles between Iron Man and his operatives, outbidding Stark for key contracts and buying up the company's debts, and even setting Stark up with a beautiful woman, Indries Moomji, whose job was to make Stark fall in love with him and then break his heart.

Pushed to the edge, Stark began drinking again; in the coming weeks he lost his fortune, his company, and almost everyone around him. Jim Rhodes took over as Iron Man, and eventually, after Stark hit bottom, Rhodes helped him rebuild his life. Along with siblings Morley and Clytemnestra Erwin, Stark and Rhodes founded the Silicon Valley electronics company known as Circuits Maximus. After a period of time in which Rhodes worked as Iron Man, and Tony created a new armor, Stark faced Stane in battle. Stark wore his Silver Centurion armor, while Stane wore a huge battle suit and called himself Iron Monger. The battle ended with Stane's suicide.

Although he did not initially take back his original company, Stark eventually launched Stark Enterprises. He also learned that a past saboteur, the Spymaster, had sold Justin Hammer secrets of his armor design elements and technology. Enraged with the knowledge that dozens of Super Villains were using his technology, Iron Man engaged in an Armor War that brought him into conflict with S.H.I.E.L.D., Captain America, and other heroes in addition to the villains. Having broken international laws, and constantly under attack, Stark faked Iron Man's death with a remote set of armor. Soon thereafter, he announced that he had hired a "new" Iron Man, though it was still Stark beneath the mask.

One of the women Stark dated, Kathy Dare, was psychotic; after he dumped her, she took her revenge by shooting him. Stark survived, but spinal damage meant he could not walk unless he was in the Iron Man armor. He eventually regained his mobility thanks to an implanted microchip, but the chip was hijacked by corporate foe Kearson DeWitt. Although Stark defeated DeWitt, his body was ravaged, and he was forced to wear a lifesaving neuronet suit to be mobile. He eventually was compelled to don the Iron Man armor again, despite the costs to his health, although it seemed to be the thing that was keeping him alive. He also created a silver-and-black weapons-heavy Variable Threat Response Battle Suit, which was nicknamed the War Machine armor, and asked Rhodes to become head of Stark Enterprises and Iron Man upon his death.

A short time later, the world learned that Stark had died, though Iron Man battled on courtesy of Rhodes. What few people other than some key scientists knew was that Stark was in cryogenic storage, with his nervous system being rebuilt. When Stark was revived, however, he was unable to function normally. Worse, Rhodes was enraged at being deceived, and he stormed out of Stark's employ and friendship, although he eventually agreed to take the War Machine armor to fight evil on his own.

Stark soon controlled a new Iron Man, which in reality was the Neuromimetic Telepresence Unit 150, which he remote-controlled from his bedside. During this time, he designed two artificial intelligence computer programs to aid him as he recovered, code-named HOMER and PLATO. The NTU-150 armor was destroyed in a battle with Ultimo, and Rhodes called together a team of past armor wearers

and trusted friends to don many of Stark's old armors as the Iron Legion to fight Ultimo. But it was Stark, wearing a new modular armor, who defeated the robotic creature.

Shortly thereafter, Iron Man cast the deciding vote to disband the West Coast Avengers team, but he soon recruited some of its members to join a new team called Force Works. The team members benefited from Stark's cutting-edge technology, but the group would ultimately disband.

As the Avengers would learn, at some point in the past Tony Stark had fallen under the control of Immortus, posing as the time lord Kang the Conqueror, who was gradually subverting Stark's mind to his will and had been responsible for some of Stark's more questionable acts over the last several years. Horrifically, Iron Man murdered three women, and then faced the Avengers. The team he had helped found brought with them a new ally, however—a teenage Tony Stark from an alternate Earth's time line who now wore Iron Man armor—and although the teen Tony's heart was horribly damaged in the battle against his older self, Stark eventually sacrificed his own life to stop Kang and destroy his temporal transposer.

The teenage Tony Stark operated for a short time, but he was also seemingly killed when the Avengers, the Fantastic Four, and other heroes faced the mutant Onslaught in New York City's Central Park. However, the heroes were actually "reborn" as alternate versions of themselves on a Counter-Earth, where Iron Man and the others had several adventures alongside and against doppelgängers of their friends and enemies. Eventually, the immensely powerful mutant child Franklin Richards brought about the event known as Heroes Return, returning the missing heroes to reality in the form and a time he remembered.

Tony Stark was now both an adult again, and in the peak of health. He designed a new set of armor and helped reestablish the Avengers, but he did not immediately attempt to regain his old company, known as Stark-Fujikawa. Instead, he founded Stark Solutions, a consulting firm, though he did eventually begin to date Rumiko Fujikawa.

After being badly beaten, Stark learned that his body's healing abilities were being severely inhibited by his armor's energy fields, so he created a new set of armor, collapsible enough to fit into a wristwatch! He also discovered that the consciousness of Jocasta—a one-time android Avenger whose programming had become self-aware—was in need, and he installed her in his computer systems as his new artificial intelligence assistant. Unfortunately, part of Jocasta's programming was to bring her robotic creator, Ultron, back to life.

When a bolt of lightning struck Iron Man during a battle, Stark suffered a heart attack, but something wondrous happened to the armor: It seemed to develop its own sentience! Although Tony tried to train the Sentient Armor in aspects of humanity, the armor beat the villain Whiplash to death, and eventually faced Stark down on a deserted island. As Stark's weakened heart began to kill him, the armor ripped out its own power source and put it on Stark's chest. The battery burrowed into Stark's body, saving his life; the Sentient Armor deactivated, and Stark buried it.

I WENT FROM BEING A MAN TRAPPED IN AN IRON SUIT TO BEING A MAN FREED BY IT.

He soon developed a new set of armor based around the SKIN (Synthetic Kinetic Interfacing Nanofluid) technology, a fluidic creation that could form an adamantium-like hyper-resilient flexible sheath around whatever it covered, including Stark. Conflicts with the monks known as the Sons of Yinsen, the revived Ultron, and the Mandarin's son Temugin would plague Iron Man in the days that followed,

as did a further armor redesign. On the plus side, he did regain Stark Industries thanks to Rumiko's machinations. Stark eventually revealed his secret identity to the world—which seemed a good idea at the time but left him even more in the media spotlight.

The most significant change in Stark's life, however, came when he was approached by the military to act as an adviser. He then discovered that a loophole in his past patents was allowing the military to legally use some of his inventions in defense equipment. Unable to stop this use of his technology, and angry that American soldiers were being hurt by misuse of it, Stark made President George W. Bush an offer. Soon, Tony Stark, Iron Man, had a third title: US secretary of defense!

Stark's time in the post did not end well, due to the actions of an insane Scarlet Witch, and the events that followed brought everything down. The Witch's actions caused the destruction of Avengers Mansion—Tony's childhood home—and the disassembling of the team. A corporate rival stole Iron Man's armor and killed the entire board of Stark Industries, as well as Rumiko. In the end, Stark announced that he was not only resigning as secretary of defense but also stepping down as Iron Man. Yet "there will always be an Iron Man," he promised.

A short time later, Stark indeed became Iron Man again to fight Mallen, a terrorist who had been enhanced by the techno-organic Extremis virus. Stark asked Extremis's designer, Dr. Maya Hansen, to inject him with the bio-agent, not knowing exactly what changes it would wreak within him. The Extremis not only rebuilt Stark's organs but also stored itself in his bones, extruding through his skin to create a powerful undersheath on which Stark could layer Iron Man's armored components. Additionally, Stark could now use Extremis-enhanced powers to link to any computer on Earth, along with performing a variety of other astonishing functions!

The new Iron Man refounded the New Avengers with Captain America, housing them in the top floors of Stark Tower in midtown Manhattan. When Congress began hearings on the Superhuman Registration Act (SHRA), Stark initially opposed it, but events that followed the hearings made him reconsider this stance. He eventually became an ardent supporter of the SHRA, convinced that if the superhuman community did not start policing itself, the government would, and things would become very ugly.

Stark again made his identity public in support of the pro-SHRA movement, and he convinced Spider-Man to do the same. The heroic community was sharply divided on the issue, and Iron Man found himself opposing the anti-SHRA movement's leader, Captain America. In the Civil War that broke out between the two superhuman factions,

Stark secretly engineered a number of shady developments, including a war between the United States and Atlantis. Eventually, the SHRA became a reality, though some heroes did not register and found themselves fighting both villains and the government. The Fifty State Initiative was then put into place; registered superpowered individuals were being trained, with the intent of installing a crime-fighting team of defenders in each US state.

Following the departure of S.H.I.E.L.D.'s leadership, Stark took over as director of the organization. He now leads S.H.I.E.L.D., serves as a member of the Mighty Avengers, and oversees Stark Enterprises. Those closest to him are suspicious of the changes that have happened in Stark's life over the last few years: radical transformations in his physiology, his psychology, his technology, and his ideology. Has Tony Stark really transformed so far from the ideals he once supported, or have the ideals become so corrupted that change was both necessary and inevitable?

Having sacrificed his life and his fortune time and again for humanity, whatever his current actions may be, Tony Stark—Iron Man—will always be a hero.

JAMES RHODES / WAR MACHINE

Alias: Iron Man, aka War Machine
Real Name: James Rupert "Rhodey" Rhodes
Height: 6'1" (Rhodes); 6'6" (in armor)
Weight: 210 lbs. (Rhodes); 575 lbs. (in armor)
Eyes: Brown, **Hair:** Brown

Group Affiliation: Base commander at the Initiative's Camp Hammond; Former member of the Avengers, the West Coast Avengers, and the Crew; Former leader of Sentinel Squad O*N*E; Former US military officer.
First Appearance: *Iron Man* #118 (James Rhodes); *Iron Man* #169 (Iron Man II)

Born and raised in South Philadelphia, young James Rhodes was bullied as a child, and became determined to become something better and stronger than those who picked on him. Even in his wildest dreams, however, he could not have imagined that he would take on the mantle of two different Super Heroes and travel the globe and even to other planets and worlds. As he grew, his world did not yet have Iron Man or War Machine . . . though it did have war.

SAY, JACK, I'M YOUR PRIVATE PILOT, REMEMBER? MY ARM'S ALL HEALED UP--

--AN' FROM READIN' THE NEWSPAPERS, I FIGURED YOU MIGHT NEED A LITTLE HELP.

Rhodes eventually joined the US military—early sources indicate that it was the US Army, while later sources cite the US Marine Corps—serving several tours as a pilot in Southeast Asia and studying to become an aviation engineer. Rhodes was haunted by those who were killed in missions he undertook, even if they were enemy combatants, but he followed his duty. On one mission, Rhodes's helicopter was shot down by enemy rockets and he barely landed safely in the jungle. While attempting to repair his chopper, Rhodes was startled by the appearance of a man in a large gray iron suit. Although Rhodes didn't know it, the man inside the suit was industrialist Tony Stark, who had recently escaped from the warlord Wong-Chu by using cobbled-together armor to become a powerful "Iron Man." After proving that they were on the same side, Iron Man recharged his armor from the copter's batteries, and he and Rhodes made their way through the jungle. They eventually found a hidden enemy base, stole a helicopter, destroyed the base, and escaped back to an American encampment.

A short while later, Rhodes was approached by Stark, who offered the pilot a job once his military service was completed. After Rhodes returned to America, he didn't immediately take Stark up on the offer, becoming a mercenary and taking other jobs instead. Eventually, though, he contacted Stark, becoming the millionaire's personal pilot and chief aviation engineer. Stark and Rhodes—or Rhodey, as his friends called him—became close friends, although the pilot was not initially told the truth about the real relationship between Stark and his "bodyguard," Iron Man. Given the numbers of saboteurs and Super Villains that came after Stark or Iron Man, Rhodey's sense of heroism and military skills were often useful.

During the era when Stark was succumbing to alcoholism for the second time, Rhodey tried to be supportive of his friend without enabling him, but that changed after Iron Man suffered a humiliating defeat by the villain

I JUST REALIZED... I'M PUTTING ON THE SUIT. ME-- JIM RHODES!
SOON AS I DROP THIS HELMET ON I'LL ACTUALLY BE IRON MAN!
THEN WHAT?
TO BE CONTINUED..

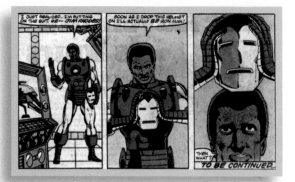

Magma. Stark was too intoxicated to fight, but Rhodes wasn't, and the heroic man donned Tony's red-and-gold armor for the first time to save Stark International from Magma's rampage.

Stark told Rhodes to continue to wear the Iron Man armor, and Rhodes knew he'd need to make some changes. He resigned Iron Man from the Avengers and had technician Morley Erwin help him learn how to use the armor effectively. Shortly afterward, when Obadiah Stane took over Stark International, Rhodes and Erwin cleared out the remaining Iron Man armor tech so that the scheming arms merchant couldn't get his hands on it. Rhodes soon encountered villains such as the Radioactive Man and the Mandarin, and was swept away to another dimension to take part in the Secret Wars with other heroes. As Iron Man, Rhodes eventually joined the West Coast Avengers.

Rhodes continued to act as Iron Man while Tony Stark recovered from hitting bottom. The pair of them soon arrived at California's Silicon Valley to start an electronics firm, Circuits Maximus, with Morley Erwin and his sister, Clytemnestra. During this time of change, Rhodes experienced ever-increasing headaches and grew irritable and resentful of Stark, particularly when he learned that Stark was designing a new suit of armor. Eventually, Stark and Rhodes battled it out—with Stark wearing a version of his early prototype armor—and Stark promised Rhodey that he wouldn't take away the one thing that meant the most to him in life . . . the feeling of being a hero. Stark gave Rhodes the armor and sent him off to find help for his headaches.

Rhodey found the answers during a mystical encounter with Alpha Flight's Shaman: He was giving *himself* the headaches because he both envied Stark and yet felt he was stealing the armor from his friend. (Rhodes also learned that the armored helmet's cybernetics had never been recalibrated for Rhodey's brain patterns.) Finally at peace, Rhodey returned to being Iron Man, while Stark rediscovered the hero within himself in the neo-prototype armor. After Rhodey was injured when a bomb was delivered to Circuits Maximus, Stark donned a new armor—the Silver Centurion armor—and defeated Stane, the architect of the explosion, who was suited up as Iron Monger.

Although he still armored up occasionally, Rhodey stopped being Iron Man for a while, allowing Tony to return to the game. Rhodes still worked with Stark; the two became perhaps even closer due to their shared knowledge of what it was like to be the armored avenger. But even without his battle suit, Rhodes was now a formidable foe, and he disarmed villains such as Blacklash and Boomerang on his own. He still donned the suit occasionally, to aid the Avengers or fight alongside Tony against Mandarin or Fin Fang Foom.

When Tony Stark suffered a total nervous system collapse and was on his deathbed, he transferred control of Stark Enterprises to Rhodes. He also sent his friend a radically different set of armor he had recently developed: the weapons-heavy silver-and-black Variable Threat Response Battle Suit, nicknamed the War Machine armor. When Stark appeared to die, Rhodes became both CEO of Stark Enterprises and Iron Man—as his predecessor had been. He soon faced Spymaster, Blacklash, Beetle, and Blizzard, as well as Atom Smasher and the Living Laser.

Shortly thereafter, Rhodes learned that Stark had deceptively faked his own death in order to reboot his new nervous system. Feeling justifiably angry and betrayed that his friend had lied to him about his own "death," Rhodes walked out on Tony, leaving behind their friendship and quitting his position at Stark Enterprises. Stark later gave Rhodes the War Machine armor and challenged him to be a better hero than Tony was. Rhodes called the West Coast Avengers hours later, joining them for a time as War Machine. Although his relationship with Stark was still rocky, when Stark was temporarily incapacitated Rhodes gathered other past armor-wearers as the Iron Legion to stop Ultimo.

When the West Coast Avengers decided to disband, Rhodes resigned his Avengers membership. Unsure of his place in the world and searching for a cause, Rhodey found one courtesy of his girlfriend, Rae LaCoste. She introduced him to Vincent Cetewayo, an activist for worldwide peace who invited him to join WorldWatch Incorporated, an agency dedicated to exposing injustices and abuses of power across the globe. Rhodes initially balked, but when Cetewayo was kidnapped by a brutal African dictator, the hero reconsidered. Neither the Avengers nor S.H.I.E.L.D. would intervene due to international laws, but War Machine decided the laws didn't apply to him. In his battle to find and free Cetewayo, War Machine encountered the mutant Cable and the cyborg Deathlok, and came into conflict with S.H.I.E.L.D.

Unable to prevent Cetewayo's assassination, Rhodes assumed the role of director of WorldWatch and was nearly branded a criminal by the United Nations for his actions in the country of Imaya. But War Machine gave them a message: If they didn't start cleaning up the misery of the world, he would . . . by any means necessary! Rhodes followed through with his threats on other missions, including the investigation of mass graves in Cortena. But when his armor needed repairs, Rhodes was forced to revisit Stark Enterprises and have a chat with Tony Stark. Unfortunately, it didn't go well—Stark felt that Rhodey "misused the equipment"—and Iron Man used a computer interface to shut down the War Machine armor.

During a confrontation with the Mandarin and Force Works, War Machine's armor was reactivated, and Stark and Rhodes came to a reconciliation of sorts. Shortly thereafter, War Machine revealed his identity to the members of WorldWatch, giving the small team of employees a say in how the armor could be used to further the goals of the organization. Unfortunately, War Machine wasn't able to work with the group for long, as he scrapped with a group of villains named the Rush Club, then got waylaid into a battle involving a S.H.I.E.L.D. strike force, Nazis, and time travel. Thanks to a time paradox caused by Rhodes's actions, when he and others returned to the future the War Machine armor was destroyed.

Haunted by his actions in the past—and without armor—Rhodes took time off for a vacation, leading to a bizarre experience in which he was grafted into a battle suit of Eidolon Warwear armor, the biotechnology of a long-dead extraterrestrial species. Rhodes used the armor for some time, even battling Iron Man in it, but after Stark was killed as the Avengers fought Immortus, Rhodes had seen enough. He soon left WorldWatch, turned down a position with the merged company Stark-Fujikawa, and sacrificed his Warwear armor in order to purge Stark's computers of all the Iron Man secrets they held.

After Tony Stark's homecoming to the Marvel Universe following the Heroes Reborn reality-altering event, Rhodes visited his old friend to help bring down Parnell Jacobs, a mercenary who was using a prototype set of War Machine armor to commit crimes. Jacobs had once been a friend of Rhodes in the army—they had even taken on some mercenary jobs together—but they found they no longer had anything in common, and Parnell jetted away with the armor after smashing Iron Man down.

Although Rhodes wanted to return to civilian life, he didn't have much of one to return to after so long in Stark's employ. He founded a marine salvage company but had to declare bankruptcy due to an unscrupulous accountant. He later turned vigilante in order to bring to justice the drug-dealing 66 Bridges gang who had killed his sister, Jeanette. He was aided in the act by a group of other urban vigilantes: a new White Tiger; a former Secret Service agent named Junta; and a Muslim minister named Josiah X, who was descended from a 1940s super soldier. Calling themselves the Crew, the group brought to justice several evildoers.

More recently, Rhodes has served as a key member of the Office of National Emergency (O*N*E), during which time he became the commanding officer and head combat instructor for Sentinel Squad O*N*E. Wearing armor derived from Sentinel technology, he helped train a group of recruits to pilot the Mark VIII mecha-like Sentinel bodies created by Stark Enterprises to help defend mutants.

Following the events of the Civil War that broke out among super-humans with the passage of the Superhuman Registration Act (SHRA), Rhodes sided with Tony Stark in the pro-registration camp. He was given a new suit of War Machine armor to help train recruits in the Fifty State Initiative, a program designed to train new Super Hero teams for each state. However, recently, during a World War Hulk confrontation, Rhodes began to feel that Stark's actions as Iron Man had become too questionable. Whether those feelings will result in another rift between the longtime armored allies is a question for the future.

Although the War Machine armor was modified and enhanced many times during the time Stark and Rhodes used it, the basic suit gave them both superhuman strength and the ability to fly with jet boots. The armor was loaded with weaponry, which included at various times repulsor rays, a uni-beam emitter, a shoulder-mounted Gatling gun, a wrist-mounted force shield, wrist-mounted cannons, flamethrowers, rocket launchers, a plasma sword, a particle beam discharger, targeting computers and scanning devices, and more. The suit of Eidolon Warwear armor that Rhodes briefly wore was a living armor that reacted to his emotions and thoughts, producing weapons or sensors as necessary.

Historian's note: There have been other James Rhodeses and War Machines encountered in Marvel's alternate universes and on alternate Earths. On Earth-311, where the Age of Heroes began at no 1602, Rupert Rhodes is an accomplice to Lord Iron. On Earth-2149's Marvel Zombies universe, Rhodey is one of the heroes who has, to date, survived the zombie plague. Rhodes has been changed into a near-robotic form by experimental microscopic robots in the Earth-982 time line of Marvel's MC2 project *A-Next,* while on Earth-1610, the Ultimates universe, Rhodey and Stark met in prep school. The designation is unknown for the Earth on which the James Rhodes of the Max imprint's two *U.S. War Machine* mini series resides.

HAROLD "HAPPY" HOGAN

Alias: The Freak
Real Name: Harold Joseph "Happy" Hogan
Height: 5'11"
Weight: 221 lbs.
Eyes: Brown, **Hair:** Brown

Group Affiliation: Employee of Stark Industries; Former member of the Iron Legion.
First Appearance: *Tales of Suspense* #45
Final Appearance: *Iron Man* volume IV #14

Although he had earned his living—and his nickname, *Happy*—as a boxer early in life, Harold Hogan found his true calling as an employee and friend to millionaire industrialist Tony Stark. His dedication to his friend would result in him becoming both the monstrous Freak, an armor-wearing fill-in for Iron Man, and the loving husband of Stark's secretary Virginia "Pepper" Potts.

During his boxing days, Harold would face Battlin' Jack Murdock (father of Matt Murdock, who later became the Marvel hero Daredevil) and Eddie March, but he was too nice a guy to knock out his opponents. His sad-faced demeanor and refusal to smile earned him the ironic nickname of Happy, but his string of pugilistic losses led him to early retirement.

Hogan worked a variety of jobs but seemed ill suited for any of them. One day at a stock-car race, Hogan witnessed the brutal crash of an experimental race car driven by Tony Stark. Risking his own safety, Hogan daringly rescued the millionaire; Stark was so grateful that he gave his rescuer a job as his well-paid personal chauffeur and part-time bodyguard. In Stark's office, Hogan worked most closely with Stark's

MANY READERS HAVE ASKED WHY HAPPY HOGAN NEVER SMILES!? WHEN WE PUT THAT QUESTION TO HIM, THIS IS THE ANSWER WE RECEIVED...

ARE YOU KIDDIN'? I'M SMILIN' RIGHT NOW!

SO HAPPY'S FORLORN EXPRESSION MAY WELL BE ONE OF THE GREAT UNEXPLAINED MYSTERIES OF OUR TIME!

secretary Pepper Potts. He soon fell in love with her, despite the fact that she carried a torch for Stark, and although she initially spurned Hogan's advances, she did eventually begin dating the "big lug."

Hogan became one of the first people on Earth to find out that Tony Stark was secretly Iron Man, and he guarded the secret closely. Later, when Hogan became critically ill, doctors used Stark's experimental surgical device, the Enervator, which was powered by cobalt radiation. Although Hogan's life was saved, he soon mutated into a giant, savage, immensely strong humanoid known as the Freak. After the Freak went on a rampage and abducted Pepper Potts, Iron Man was able to restore Hogan to normal by re-exposing him to the Enervator. Luckily, Hogan was amnesiac about his time as the mindless humanoid. Unfortunately, Hogan became the Freak twice more over the next several years before he was completely cured of the condition.

Eventually proposing to Potts, Hogan was elated when she accepted. They eloped, surprising everyone, including Tony Stark. Both remained in Stark's employ, and Hogan even donned the Iron Man armor for a brief time, to face down the Mandarin. The resulting battle left the armor damaged beyond repair, leading Stark to make an upgrade to the suit once he donned it again himself.

Given the danger that seemed to swirl around those connected to Tony Stark, Hogan and Potts took a leave of absence from Stark Industries for a time. He eventually became a boxing promoter, then later returned to the newer Stark Enterprises to become a personal fitness trainer for Tony Stark. Eventually, when James Rhodes called, Hogan donned an older version of the Iron Man armor as part of the Iron Legion. During a battle against Ultimo, Rhodes's armor was again damaged, but not before he had helped rescue two other members of the armored vanguard.

Hogan and Potts resumed their life, and Hogan worked at raising an adopted son and daughter. Unfortunately, financial and other difficulties eventually led to the dissolution of their marriage, and Hogan began battling alcoholism. During the post-Heroes Reborn era, wherein Tony Stark was reborn, the two had a confrontation about Hogan's drinking, but the ex-boxer agreed to return to work for Stark and even remarried Potts.

Unfortunately, Hogan was attacked by Spymaster and critically injured from a multistory fall. Rushed to a hospital in a vegetative coma and placed on life support, Hogan seemed to have little hope of recovery. Potts told Stark that Hogan had never wanted to end up with brain damage; she begged her employer to turn off the life-support machines and allow their friend to die. Stark initially refused to use his Extremis-enhanced abilities to manipulate the machines—even though only he and Pepper would know the truth—but Hogan's monitor eventually flatlined. Although no funeral or service for Hogan has been held, it would appear that Stark's long-time friend, and Potts's sometime husband, has passed away.

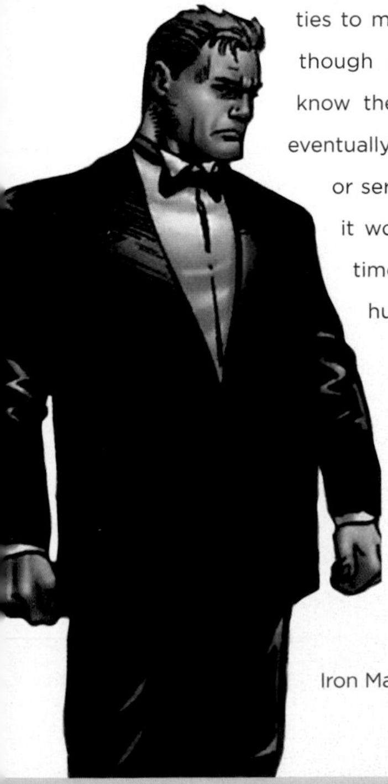

Historian's note: There have been two other Happy Hogans seen in Marvel's alternate universes. In the Heroes Reborn reality, Hogan was Stark's public relations chief. On Earth-1610, the Ultimates universe, Hogan and Potts both assist Iron Man in Stark's control center.

VIRGINIA "PEPPER" POTTS HOGAN

Alias: Hera
Real Name: Virginia "Pepper" Potts Hogan
Height: 5'4"
Weight: 110 lbs.
Eyes: Green, **Hair:** Red

Group Affiliation: Employee of Stark Industries; Leader of the Order
First Appearance: ***Tales of Suspense* #45**

Virginia "Pepper" Potts has risen far from the days in which she was a member of the secretarial pool at Stark Industries (then run by Howard Stark). Whether as Tony Stark's most trusted secretary and executive assistant, as wife to Harold "Happy" Hogan, or as the leader of the millennial Super Hero team the Order, Pepper Potts has brought a strong morality, utter reliability, and sensible attitude to everything she does.

Shortly after Tony took over the business, Potts caught an error that saved the company millions of dollars. Because she understood the day-to-day business of running Stark Industries, she became invaluable to Tony Stark, and he relied on her to keep the company on track when he was distracted or facing other duties. Although Stark was a jet-setting playboy who dated debutantes and celebrities, Potts carried a torch for her boss, wishing he would see beyond her freckled face. After Stark hired Hogan as his chauffeur and bodyguard, and Hogan began pursuing a romance with Pepper, Stark began to notice his assistant in a more romantic light as well. The complex triangle was made more difficult when Potts changed her look, hiding with makeup the freckles that had given her the nickname *Pepper,* and accentuating her natural beauty instead of hiding it.

Initially, Potts deflected Hogan's attentions with caustic rejoinders, but eventually they began dating.

Following a battle in which Hogan aided Iron Man against the Titanium Man—and was nearly killed—Pepper realized that she loved Hogan, and they eloped. The two continued to work for Tony, although both were often put in extreme danger by villains who attacked Stark or Iron Man; Potts was taken hostage multiple times but never badly hurt, whereas Hogan was severely injured and almost killed on a number of occasions.

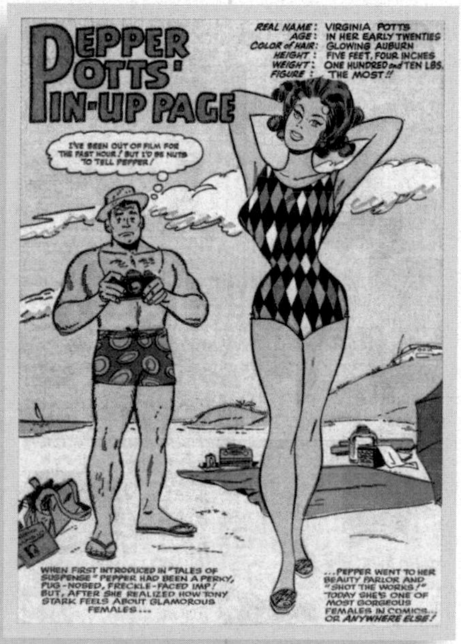
PEPPER POTTS' PIN-UP PAGE
REAL NAME: VIRGINIA POTTS
AGE: IN HER EARLY TWENTIES
COLOR of HAIR: GLOWING AUBURN
HEIGHT: FIVE FEET, FOUR INCHES
WEIGHT: ONE HUNDRED and TEN LBS.
FIGURE: THE MOST!!
I'VE BEEN OUT OF FILM FOR THE PAST HOUR! BUT I'D BE NUTS TO TELL PEPPER!
WHEN FIRST INTRODUCED IN "TALES OF SUSPENSE" PEPPER HAD BEEN A PERKY, PUG-NOSED, FRECKLE-FACED IMP! BUT, AFTER SHE REALIZED HOW TONY STARK FEELS ABOUT GLAMOROUS FEMALES...
...PEPPER WENT TO HER BEAUTY PARLOR AND "SHOT THE WORKS!" TODAY SHE'S ONE OF MOST GORGEOUS FEMALES IN COMICS... OR ANYWHERE ELSE!

Eventually, Potts learned what her husband had known for some time—that Tony Stark was really Iron Man—and shortly thereafter, Potts and Hogan left Stark's employ to lessen the dangers they faced. The couple settled in the Rocky Mountains and then Cleveland, adopting a pair of children since they could not conceive on their own. After a period of time, Hogan returned to work for Stark, and Potts later did as well. Unfortunately, the marriage between the two dissolved sometime before Tony Stark's "death."

During the post-Heroes Reborn era, wherein Tony Stark was reborn, Pepper worked at Stark Solutions. She verbally sparred with Rumiko Fujikawa—whom Stark was romancing—but eventually warmed up to her. Potts and Hogan even reconciled their differences and remarried. Potts surprisingly became pregnant, but lost the unborn child when she was attacked by the cyborg woman Ayisha. Although she never told Hogan about the pregnancy, Potts did tell Stark, and he helped her grieve. He also gave her a fail-safe device that could shut down his Iron Man armor if necessary.

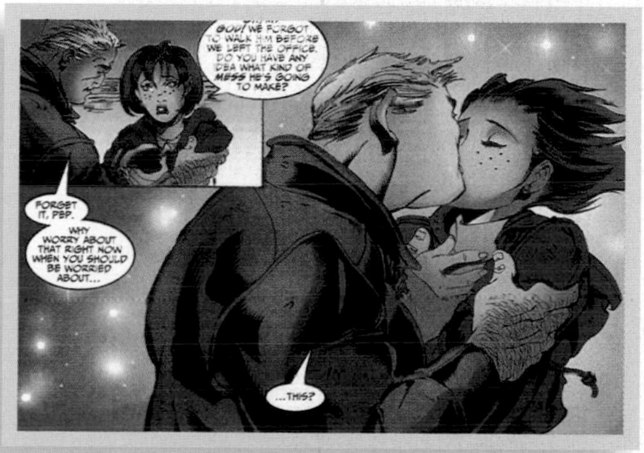
GOD! WE FORGOT TO WALK HIM BEFORE WE LEFT THE OFFICE. DO YOU HAVE ANY IDEA WHAT KIND OF MESS HE'S GOING TO MAKE?
FORGET IT, PEP.
WHY WORRY ABOUT THAT RIGHT NOW WHEN YOU SHOULD BE WORRIED ABOUT...
...THIS?

Potts and Hogan continued to work for Stark for several years, but Hogan was critically injured during an attack by Spymaster, leaving him in a vegetative state. Knowing her husband's feelings on the matter, Potts begged Stark to use his Extremis-enhanced abilities to depower the life-support machines and allow Hogan to die naturally. Stark refused, but later Hogan's monitor flatlined.

Following the apparent death of her husband, and given her involvement with Super Heroes, Potts became involved with a new group in the aftermath of the Civil War that raged over the Superhuman Registration Act. Tony Stark supported the Fifty State Initiative designed to train and redistribute groups of heroes throughout the United States. Headquartered in Los Angeles, a new group called the Order was created, with its members all bearing names and powers associated with the mythical Greek gods. Stark was its figurehead as "Zeus," while Potts took the role of "Hera," the handler and logistics leader who monitored and directed the team from their headquarters.

Historian's note: There have been two other Pepper Pottses seen in Marvel's alternate universes. In the Heroes Reborn reality, Potts was Stark's employee and lover. On Earth-1610, the Ultimates universe, Potts and Hogan both assisted Iron Man in Stark's control center.

BLACK WIDOW

Alias: Black Widow
Real Name: Natalia Alianovna Romanova, aka Natasha Romanoff
Height: 5'7"
Weight: 131 lbs.
Eyes: Blue, **Hair:** Red-auburn (formerly dyed black)

Group Affiliation: Member of the Mighty Avengers; Former member of the Avengers, the Initiative, Marvel Knights, Queen's Vengeance, Champions of Los Angeles, Lady Liberators, and KGB; Former partner of Daredevil; Freelance agent of S.H.I.E.L.D.
First Appearance: ***Tales of Suspense* #52**

Despite the potential conflicts involved in dating a Russian woman during the Cold War, Tony Stark became romantically entangled with Madame Natasha Romanoff early in his career as Iron Man. Little did he know that Natalia Romanova (the Russian version of her name) was really a top Soviet spy known as the Black Widow, who was only using him to recover the defected scientist Anton Vanko and his Crimson Dynamo armor. Shortly thereafter, the Widow deceived Tony again, this time stealing a powerful antigravity device from him and using it against Iron Man.

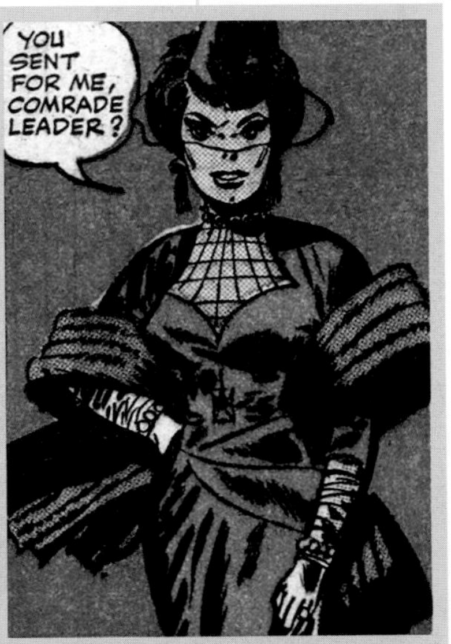
YOU SENT FOR ME, COMRADE LEADER?

The Widow would later seduce Clint Barton, a marksman who took on the name Hawkeye, and convince him to battle Iron Man on her behalf several times. Eventually, however, the spy decided to defect to the United States, and she first became an ally—then the sixteenth member—of the Avengers. Since that time, the Widow has had romantic flirtations with Iron Man and Hawkeye, but became the lover of Daredevil for some time. She also became a member of other Super Hero teams such as the Champions, and often worked as a freelance agent for the espionage agency S.H.I.E.L.D.

Although early stories established Romanova as a highly trained but nonpowered human, later tales revised her origin to include her early days in the USSR's covert Black Widow Ops program, in which she was biotechnologically and psychotechnologically enhanced, giving her a longer life span. The program also implanted numerous false memories in Romanova's mind.

In recent years, Romanova learned that another younger agent, Yelena Belova, had taken on the mantle and costume of the Black Widow. Belova was also trained in the same program in Russia; after many adventures and battles against both her predecessor and the New Avengers, Belova retired to Cuba. In the post-Civil War time, Romanova became a member of the Mighty Avengers, working alongside Iron Man.

Although the Black Widow is an expert martial artist and markswoman, has world-class athletic and gymnastic skills, and has received extensive espionage training, she does not have any innate superpowers. Along with the biotechnological enhancements that give her a longer life span at the peak of human physicality, she benefits from a wide range of specialized equipment developed by Soviet scientists, with later improvements by S.H.I.E.L.D. technicians. The Widow usually wears wrist-cartridge bracelets that fire energy blasts known as Widow Sting or Widow's Bite; the bracelets also contain spring-loaded Widow Line cable and grappling hooks, a radio transmitter, and tear gas pellets. The belt she wears around her skin-tight costume contains plastic explosives and espionage gear, while the fabric of the costume itself has been augmented to withstand temperature changes and even small-arms fire. It is also equipped with microscopic suction cups on the fingers and feet, enabling the Black Widow to cling to walls and ceilings like her arachnid namesake.

Historian's note: There have been multiple other Black Widows, including a World War II heroine, and Widows seen in Marvel's alternate universes. On Earth-1610, the Ultimates universe, the traitorous Widow seduced Tony Stark, betrayed the Ultimates' secrets, and even killed Edwin Jarvis, but Stark immobilized her with nanites and rendered her unconscious or possibly dead. On Earth-2149, the Marvel Zombies universe, the Widow was infected with the contagious plague and is now a zombie. She has appeared in other alternate realities as well.

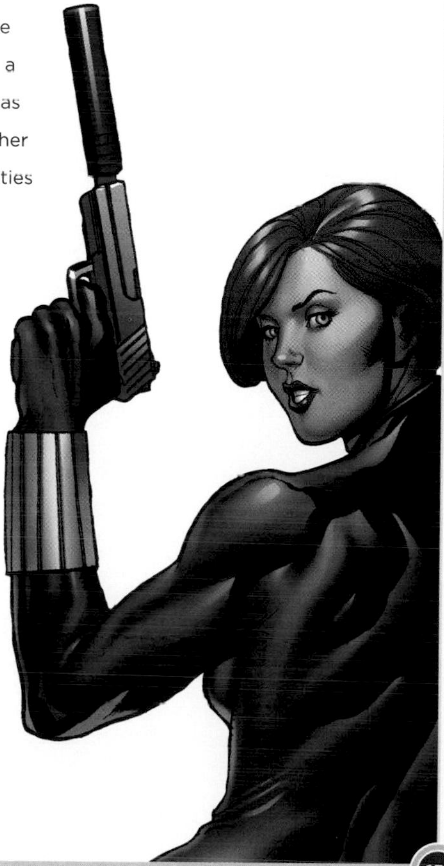

MADAME MASQUE

Alias: Madame Masque, aka Big M, the Director, Kristine "Krissy" Longfellow
Real Name: Countess Giulietta Nefaria, aka Whitney Frost
Height: 5'9"
Weight: 139 lbs.
Eyes: Gray, **Hair:** Black

Group Affiliation: Leader of the Nefaria family of the Maggia; Former ally of the Avengers
First Appearance: *Tales of Suspense* #97 (Big M); *Tales of Suspense* #98 (Whitney Frost); *Iron Man* #17 (Madame Masque)

Although she was the daughter of the Italian Maggia crime lord Count Luchino Nefaria, Giulietta Nefaria never imagined her life would take the horrifying turns that it did, nor that she would forever be trapped behind an iron mask . . . and in love with an Iron Man.

When her mother died in childbirth, Giulietta was sent to be raised in America as the adopted daughter of wealthy Wall Street financier Byron Frost. Named Whitney Frost, she had a normal upbringing; she never knew her true parentage, nor that her adopted father was laundering money for the Maggia. When Frost died, her real father, Count Nefaria, informed her of her origins and manipulated her into coming into her birthright as the successor leader to Nefaria's branch of the Maggia, a "family" that was more technologically based than the other two prevailing families, run by Hammerhead and Silvio "Silvermane" Manfredi.

Nefaria trained Whitney to manage his underworld operations, and she brilliantly mastered many forms of criminal strategy and combat skills. Frost became Big M of the New York branch of the Maggia, and she proved capable, though she refused to get involved in certain illegal pursuits, such as narcotics trafficking. She planned to amass power in a way that could challenge governments through force, and led a raid on Stark Industries headquarters to steal high-tech weaponry. This brought her into conflict with Iron Man and revealed her true identity to S.H.I.E.L.D. agent Jasper Sitwell—whom she had been dating. Frost barely escaped the confrontation with her life.

Unfortunately, Frost's escaping skycraft crashed, and the beautiful woman's face was horribly scarred by burning chemicals onboard. Frost was rescued by agents of criminally eccentric billionaire Mordecai Midas, and the corpulent crook engaged a surgeon to save her life. Frost hid her ravaged face behind a gold mask and took on the new code name of Madame Masque. Midas planned to use Masque as a criminal operative against Tony Stark, but the woman soon became conflicted: Stark not only was genuinely romantically interested in her but also reacted kindly when he witnessed her unmasked visage.

Masque eventually helped Iron Man defeat Midas, but remained torn between her new feelings toward Stark and her old feelings toward Sitwell. Taking on a new guise and the name Kristine "Krissy" Longfellow, Masque became Stark's assistant and, eventually, his lover and confidante about his dual identity as Iron Man. However, the détente ended when the death of Count Nefaria—at Iron Man's hands—left Masque feeling bitter and paranoid. Resuming her criminal past with the Maggia, the woman went into hiding in Las Vegas and had several bio-duplicate clones of herself created; she would sometimes send these clones

out as Madame Masque to do her dirty work or clash with Iron Man or other heroic foes.

One of the clones developed shape-shifting powers and joined the Avengers for a while as Masque, but when Frost abducted the clone, she wouldn't believe that there was still a chance for her to experience happiness with Tony Stark and the side of good. As multiple dead clones of Frost began to surface, raising doubts that Frost was really dead, Count Nefaria was also revived as an ionic super-being who attempted to enslave the entire world! The clone Masque sacrificed her life in a battle between Nefaria and his minions and the Avengers and Thunderbolts.

Recently, following the events of the Civil War brought about by the passage of the Superhuman Registration Act, Madame Masque joined the crime syndicate of Super Villains run by the Hood. However, although she still feels anger at Iron Man for causing her father's death, she has never revealed Tony Stark's secret to the world, nor struck him down without provocation.

The original Madame Masque had no superpowers, but she was a formidable martial artist and markswoman, and a brilliant criminal strategist and tactician. She utilized a wide variety of high-tech weapons, including concussive energy blasters and sleep-gas guns, and wore a lightweight formfitting body armor that protected her from some danger. The bio-duplicate Masque who joined the Avengers could shape-shift to mimic other people, and had empathic and minor telepathic powers.

THE WOMEN OF TONY STARK

As a millionaire playboy—and a handsome man—Tony Stark has become one of the world's most eligible bachelors. Little wonder, then, that with power and opportunity, Stark has dated numerous beautiful women. Unfortunately, many of Tony's romantic entanglements over the years have led to financial ruin, psychosis, attempted murder, and even death! Pepper Potts may have been the most constant female presence in Tony Stark's life, and the Black Widow and Madame Masque may have been the most superpowered, but the following femmes have given our hero love and kisses . . . and bullets and broken hearts.

Real Name: Janice Cord
First Appearance: ***Iron Man* #2**
Final Appearance: ***Iron Man* #22**

One of Tony Stark's insane business rivals, Drexel Cord, unleashed a robot called the Demolisher to destroy Stark. Cord came to his senses when his creation almost killed his beautiful daughter, Janice. After the death of her father, Janice began dating Stark, but she found herself constantly menaced by villains, from the Mandarin to a Hulk robot. Unfortunately, during a battle among Iron Man, Titanium Man, and Crimson Dynamo, Janice Cord was killed.

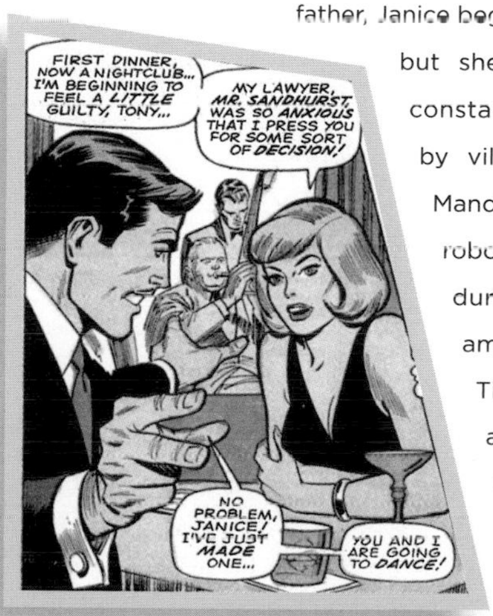
FIRST DINNER, NOW A NIGHTCLUB... I'M BEGINNING TO FEEL A LITTLE GUILTY, TONY...
MY LAWYER, MR. SANDHURST, WAS SO ANXIOUS THAT I PRESS YOU FOR SOME SORT OF DECISION!
NO PROBLEM, JANICE! I'VE JUST MADE ONE...
YOU AND I ARE GOING TO DANCE!

Real Name: Meredith McCall
First Appearance: ***Iron Man* #28**

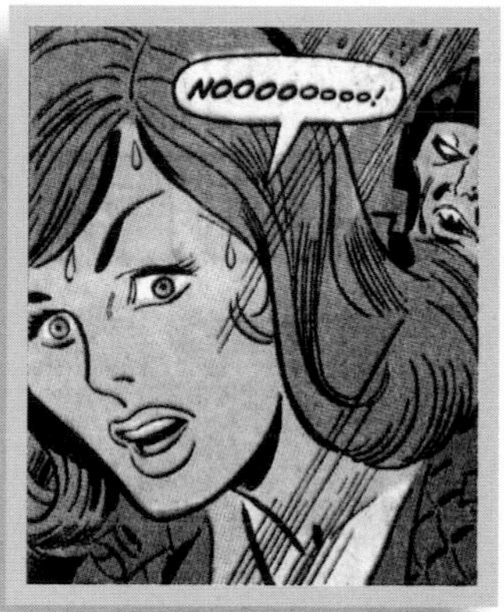
NOOOOOooo!

When he was a teen, Tony Stark was in love with Meredith McCall, but their fathers were rival business owners, and the pair were sent to schools on separate continents. Years later, Iron Man rescued McCall from the Controller, only to learn that she was now married. Later, Stark learned that McCall was divorced and available . . . but also an aggressive member of the ninja group Masters of Silence! More recently, McCall remarried and became a professor at Columbia University, where she encountered the teenage Tony Stark in the pre-Onslaught time line.

Real Name: Marianne Rodgers
First Appearance: ***Iron Man* #36**

Although Marianne Rodgers had strong psychic powers—which even allowed her to learn the truth about Tony Stark and Iron Man—they didn't protect her from Super Villain attacks, nor from eventually suffering hallucinations and doom-filled premonitions. Her actions led to

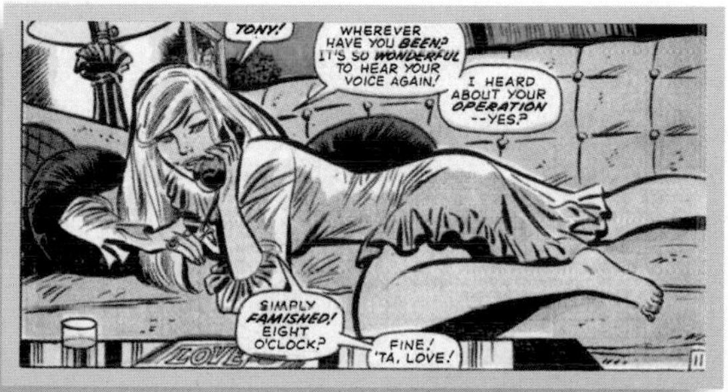
TONY!
WHEREVER HAVE YOU BEEN? IT'S SO WONDERFUL TO HEAR YOUR VOICE AGAIN!
I HEARD ABOUT YOUR OPERATION --YES?
SIMPLY FAMISHED! EIGHT O'CLOCK?
FINE! 'TA, LOVE!

Stark calling off their engagement, and Rodgers eventually had a mental breakdown. After years of therapy in a mental institution, Rodgers regained her clarity (if not her full sanity) and even helped the Avengers to stop Iron Man when he was under the control of time lord Kang. Unfortunately, her aid ended with the first real death of Tony Stark.

Real Name: Bethany Cabe
First Appearance: ***Iron Man* #117**

Probably the greatest love of Tony Stark's life was a woman who was uniquely matched to his dual world. Bethany Cabe was a gorgeous professional bodyguard who found herself working alongside Stark and soon fell in love with him. With Iron Man, Cabe faced villains ranging from Madame Masque to Force, and even deduced that Iron Man and Stark were one and the same . . . though she didn't initially tell *him* that she knew his secret. Cabe also stood by Stark through his first major bout with alcoholism, but their relationship ended when she was forced to return to Europe to deal with her husband—a drug-addicted junior ambassador whom everyone thought was dead. Cabe was kidnapped by agents of Obadiah Stane and had her mind switched with Madame Masque; Masque-as-Cabe tried to kill Tony Stark, but Cabe-as-Masque stopped her, and the two women's minds were switched back again. Years later, Cabe donned a suit of Iron Man armor as a member of the Iron Legion, then returned to Stark Enterprises to act as head of security. Unfortunately, in the time since, Cabe and Stark have been unable to rekindle their romance, although they remain good friends.

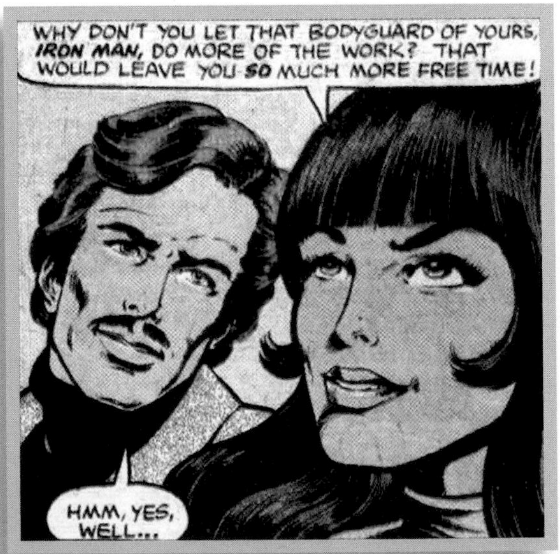
WHY DON'T YOU LET THAT BODYGUARD OF YOURS, IRON MAN, DO MORE OF THE WORK? THAT WOULD LEAVE YOU SO MUCH MORE FREE TIME!
HMM, YES, WELL...

Real Name: Indries Moomji
First Appearance: ***Iron Man* #163**

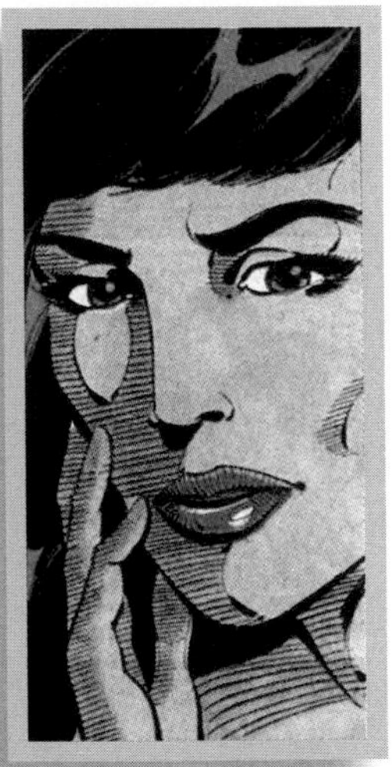

When the exotic Indries Moomji began seeing Tony Stark romantically, she was secretly an operative of Obadiah Stane, who was planning Stark's downfall. Moomji was a member of the espionage group Sisterhood of Ishtar, trained to be the perfectly desirable woman. She manipulated Stark's emotions, then coldly rejected him, sending Stark on a downward spiral that led to a recurrence of his alcoholism and the loss of his company to Stane International.

Real Name: Kathy Dare
First Appearance: ***Iron Man* #233**
Final Appearance: ***Iron Man* #286**

Beautiful heiress Kathy Dare had the most obsessive personality of all Tony Stark's girlfriends, and she would prove to be the most dangerous to his health. Stark saw

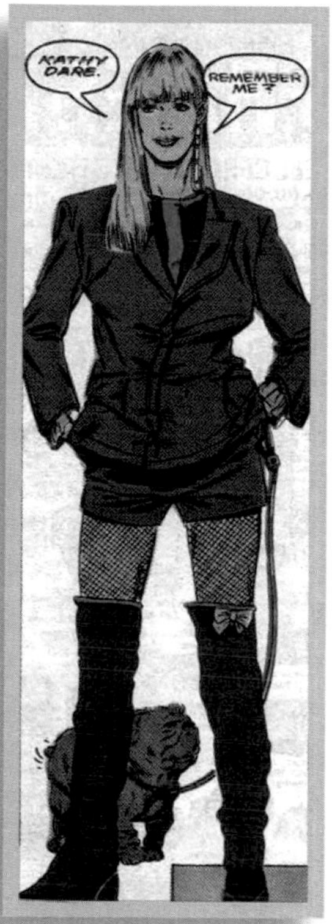
KATHY DARE.
REMEMBER ME?

that Dare was clingy and obsessive, but he was mostly amused by her stalking him and never expected her to shoot him. After he told her that they would have no relationship, Dare snapped and shot him in the spine, temporarily crippling the millionaire. Unfortunately, Dare never quite faced the justice she deserved: At her pretrial hearing, she was declared mentally incompetent and sent to a mental hospital. Following the apparent death of Tony Stark, and in the aftermath of a memorial service and battle between Iron Man (James Rhodes) and the Avengers and a quartet of villains, Dare declared that she couldn't live without Tony, then shot herself and died instantly.

Real Name: Rumiko Fujikawa
First Appearance: ***Iron Man*** **volume III #4**
Final Appearance: ***Iron Man*** **volume III #87**

During the second time period in which Tony Stark was thought to have died, Kenjiro Fujikawa took over Stark Industries. After Tony returned to life in the post-Heroes Reborn era, Fujikawa's daughter, Rumiko, began to date Stark, partially as an act of rebellion against her disapproving parents. Although Rumiko enjoyed the perks of Stark's lavish lifestyle, she soon became frustrated by his obsession with work and his unexplained disappearances (when he was functioning—or under attack—as Iron Man). Her attitude

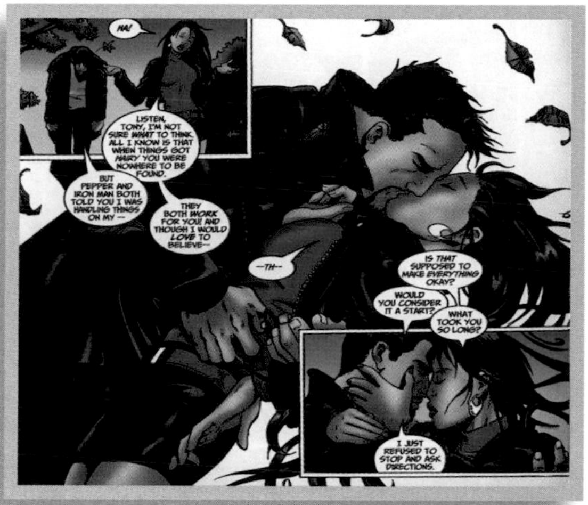
HA!
LISTEN, TONY, I'M NOT SURE WHAT TO THINK. ALL I KNOW IS THAT WHEN THINGS GOT HAIRY YOU WERE NOWHERE TO BE FOUND.
BUT PEPPER AND IRON MAN BOTH TOLD YOU I WAS HANDLING THINGS ON MY—
THEY BOTH WORK FOR YOU! AND THOUGH I WOULD LOVE TO BELIEVE—
—TH—
IS THAT SUPPOSED TO MAKE EVERYTHING OKAY?
WOULD YOU CONSIDER IT A START?
WHAT TOOK YOU SO LONG?
I JUST REFUSED TO STOP AND ASK DIRECTIONS.

became more needy and self-absorbed; at one point, she even slept with Stark's business rival, Tiberius "Ty" Stone, unaware that she has been manipulated by Stone. When her life was put in danger by Stone, Rumiko was rescued by Iron Man, but Stark soon broke off their relationship. Later, Rumiko arranged for Stark to buy the last bits of stock he needed to reclaim control of his old company. Unfortunately, even as she attempted a reconciliation with Stark, Rumiko was murdered by Clarence Ward, an impostor wearing Iron Man armor.

Real Name: Dr. Maya Hansen
First Appearance: ***Iron Man*** **volume IV #1**

An old acquaintance of Tony Stark, Dr. Maya Hansen reentered his life following the suicide of the creator of the Extremis virus. A brilliant scientist, Hansen soon began working with Tony, especially as the heroic inventor used Extremis to repair his own body. Knowing Stark's secret identity as Iron Man, Hansen has been a part of his support

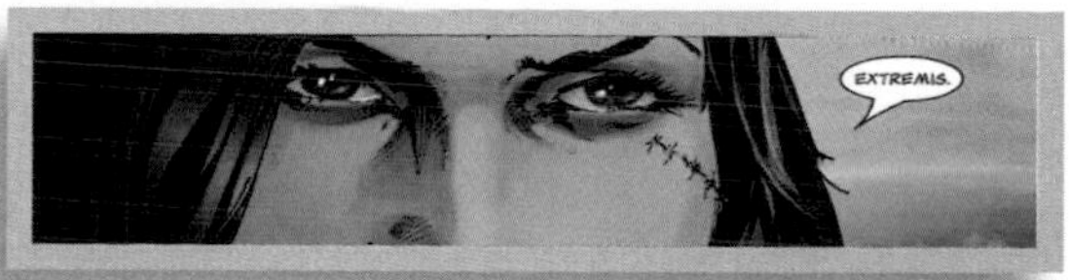
EXTREMIS.

crew—after a brief stint in prison due to her involvement with Extremis—and eventually became romantically entangled with him. Recently, she agreed to continue researching Extremis for the US government, unaware that the head of Prometheus Gentech Inc.—the company with which

AND DID THIS.

she was to work—was none other than old Iron Man foe the Mandarin!

Other women that Stark has dated include teen-temptress-turned-thief Sunset Bain (first appearance: *Machine Man* #17); Stark's first fiancée, Joanna Nivena (first appearance: *Iron Man* #244); political activist Roxanne Gilbert (first appearance: *Iron Man* #59); fellow Avenger the Wasp, aka Janet van Dyne (first appearance: *Tales to Astonish* #44); alcoholic Heather Glenn (first appearance: *Daredevil* #126); hopeful actress Brie Daniels (first appearance: *Iron Man* #222); wealthy beauty parlor owner Rae Lacoste (first appearance: *Iron Man* #223); Chinese neurologist Dr. Su Yin (first appearance: *Iron Man* #270); physical therapist Veronica Benning (first appearance: *Iron Man* #292); and Askew Electronics president Calista Hancock (first appearance: *Iron Man* volume III #42).

THE AVENGERS

Founding Avengers Members: Iron Man, Hulk, Thor, Ant-Man I (Henry Pym), Wasp

Later Avengers Members: Ant-Man II (Scott Lang), Ares, Beast, Black Knight III, Black Panther, Black Widow I (Natalia Romanova), Captain America, Captain Britain II, Captain Marvel II aka Photon, Crystal, Darkhawk, Demolition Man, Doctor Druid, Dr. Strange, Echo aka Ronin I, Falcon, Firebird, Firestar, Gilgamesh, Hawkeye aka Ronin II, Hellcat, Hercules, Human Torch I, Invisible Woman, Iron Fist, Jack of Hearts, Justice, Living Lightning, Luke Cage, Machine Man, Mantis, Mister Fantastic, Mockingbird, Moon Knight, Moondragon, Ms. Marvel aka Warbird, Quasar, Quicksilver, Rage, Sandman, Scarlet Witch, Sentry, Sersi, She-Hulk, Silverclaw, Spider-Man, Spider-Woman I, Spider-Woman II, Starfox, Stingray, Sub-Mariner, Swordsman, Thing, Thunderstrike, Tigra, Triathlon, Two-Gun Kid, US Agent, Vision, War Machine, Wolverine, Wonder Man

Honorary Avengers Members: Aleta, Moira Brandon, Captain Marvel, Charlie-27, Deathcry, Iron Man (alternate-time-line teenage Tony Stark), Jocasta, Rick Jones, Magdalene, Major Victory aka Vance Astro, Marrina, Martinex, Masque (Madame Masque clone), Nikki, Starhawk, Swordsman II, Whizzer, Yellowjacket II, Yondu

Base of Operations: Formerly Avengers Mansion (890 Fifth Avenue, Manhattan); Formerly Avengers Compound (Palos Verdes, California); Formerly Avengers Island (aka Hydrobase); Formerly Avengers Emergency Headquarters (undisclosed location outside New York City); Currently Stark Tower Complex (midtown Manhattan) and Dr. Strange's Sanctum Sanctorum (177A Bleecker Street , Greenwich Village, New York City)

First Appearance: *Avengers* #1

They are known as "Earth's mightiest heroes," assembled together to fight the superpowered villains whom no single champion could defeat. The Avengers is the most prestigious and powerful Super Hero team in the world,

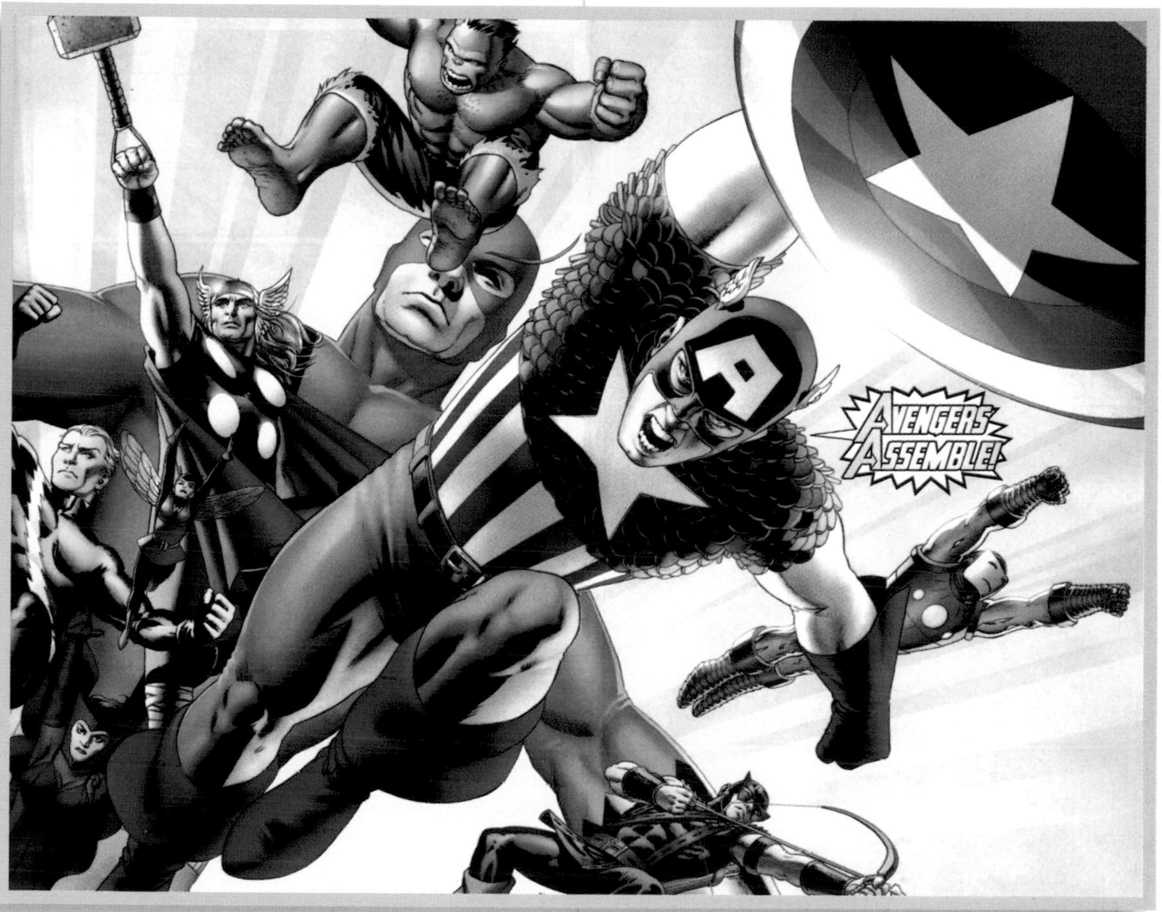
AVENGERS ASSEMBLE!

although its membership is always changing and evolving over time. But throughout most of its long history, the Avengers has had one constant: the support of Tony Stark (as a financier) and of founding member Iron Man (often as a member).

The Avengers first came together when the Hulk's teen sidekick, Rick Jones, put out a call for heroes to help defeat the Asgardian trickster-god Loki; answering his call were powerhouses Iron Man, Thor, and Hulk, as well as diminutive heroes Ant-Man (Hank Pym) and Wasp. It was these latter two who suggested that the group stay together as a team, and the resulting assemblage of Super Heroes and costumed crime fighters protected the planet for the next four decades.

Tony Stark donated his Manhattan mansion to serve as the Avengers headquarters—through the Maria Stark Foundation—as well as the use of his longtime family butler, Edwin Jarvis. Stark also helped to draft the charter and bylaws for the group, and sought security clearance from a distrusting federal government. Following the departure of the volatile Hulk and the joining of revived-from-suspended-animation World War II hero Captain America, the Avengers were granted clearance, and became beloved by the public.

Iron Man eventually exited the group for a time. Captain America stepped in to lead the team, which now included former Iron Man foe and super-archer Hawkeye, as well as former mutant terrorist siblings Quicksilver and the Scarlet Witch. Although there was initial mistrust of the reformed criminals, the new Avengers roster proved solid.

Iron Man and most of the other founding members would have a recurring status on the team, though Pym would develop new powers and identities, calling himself Giant-Man, Goliath, and Yellowjacket. Further new recruits over the following years included the Swordsman (who was eventually expelled), Hercules, the Black Panther, an android known as the Vision, and the sword-wielding Black Knight. The Avengers became involved in the cosmic Kree–Skrull War, allying for a time with alien hero Captain

Mar-Vell. They would also aid Tony Stark when he underwent a heart transplant operation.

Former Iron Man villainess the Black Widow was initially an ally of the Avengers, but she eventually became a member, as did the reformed Swordsman and a strange telepathic woman named Mantis, who had a unique prophesied destiny. Former X-Men member the Beast joined the team; other heroes and heroines became either full or reserve-status members, including Moondragon, Hellcat, Two-Gun Kid, aging speedster Whizzer, the robotic Jocasta, and Ms. Marvel (later Warbird).

The Avengers continued to expand their official ties to the US government, but were restricted for a time by National Security Council agent Henry Peter Gyrich, the government's liaison to the team. Gyrich restricted active membership in the group and instituted screening requirements for admission. During the years that followed, new members included Falcon, Wonder Man, Tigra, She-Hulk, a new female Captain Marvel, and Starfox.

Eventually, Avengers chairman Vision petitioned the US government to approve a second team of Avengers, to be based in Los Angeles at a second headquarters called Avengers Compound. Hawkeye was appointed chairman of the new team, the West Coast Avengers, which included over time not only his wife, Mockingbird, but also Iron Man (James Rhodes, later as War Machine), Moon Knight, US Agent, Firebird, Living Lightning, Spider-Woman, Machine Man, and Darkhawk . . . as well as Tony Stark in his Silver Centurion Iron Man armor. Meanwhile, the eastern team took on a whole host of new members over the years, including Sub-Mariner, Doctor Druid, the Captain (the recostumed Captain America), Demolition Man, Gilgamesh, Quasar, Sersi, Spider-Man, Stingray, Rage, Sandman, Crystal, Thunderstrike (an alternate Thor), Justice, Firestar, Triathlon, Silverclaw, Jack of Hearts, Iron Man ally Ant-Man II (Scott Lang), and Captain Britain. Briefly allying themselves with the team were Marrina, Yellowjacket II, Swordsman II, Magdalene, Deathcry, and Masque (a clone of Iron Man foe Madame Masque). Members of the Fantastic Four also worked with the two Avengers teams.

When Avengers villain Immortus, posing as Kang, fully established his long-planned control over the mind of Tony Stark, the hero turned against his Avengers compatriots and was killed. The Avengers had already enlisted the aid of a young Tony from an alternate time line, and this youngster became the new Iron Man for a short time.

During a battle against the villain Onslaught, however, the Avengers and many of their allies were shunted into an alternate universe where their lives and origins were more contemporary. Eventually, Franklin Richards, the powerful child of Reed and Sue Richards, returned all the heroes to their own reality, although in doing so he reset the time lines for some of them to the point at which he remembered them best. Thus, Tony Stark was not only alive again but also unaffected by Kang's mental tampering.

More recently, the Avengers have been rocked by a series of devastating events. First, in an event known as Avengers Disassembled, an insane Scarlet Witch destroyed Avengers Mansion and apparently caused the deaths of Hawkeye, Vision, Jack of Hearts, and Ant-Man II. With Tony Stark facing his own financial crisis, the founding member was unable to rebuild the team. Later, however, Captain America allied himself with six heroes to rebuild the Avengers: Iron Man, Spider-Man, Luke Cage, Spider-Woman I, Daredevil, and ally the Sentry, though Daredevil failed to stick around. By that time, Stark had regained control of his fortunes, and he offered the top floors of his new Stark Tower skyscraper as the team's new headquarters.

The New Avengers existed for some time, gaining members Wolverine (suggested by Stark) and the mysterious Ronin (secretly Echo, then a no-longer-dead Hawkeye), but a reality-altering event during which most of the planet's mutant population was depowered caused further dissent. During the Civil War that broke out among the superpowered community over the government's Superhuman Registration Act, the team was splintered. Captain America was killed by an assassin of the Red Skull, while Iron Man became the director of S.H.I.E.L.D., fully supporting the Fifty

State Initiative, which was intended to establish and train a Super Hero group in each US state.

Currently, there are two Avengers teams: the government-sanctioned Mighty Avengers (Iron Man, Ares, Black Widow, Ms. Marvel, the Sentry, Spider-Woman, Wasp, and Wonder Man) and the anti-registration underground team called New Avengers (Dr. Strange, Echo, Iron Fist, Luke Cage, Ronin II, Spider-Man, Spider-Woman I, and Wolverine), which operates from Dr. Strange's Sanctum Sanctorum in Greenwich Village. A Young Avengers team of teen Super Heroes also operates in New York, though its future following the Civil War and the Initiative is unclear.

Historian's note: There have been dozens of other iterations of the Avengers seen in Marvel's alternate universes. The most popular of these is on Earth-1610, the Ultimates universe, wherein the core Ultimates team of Iron Man, Captain America, Thor, Giant-Man, and Wasp have faced battles with the Hulk, interstellar invasions, betrayal, assassination, and a massive terroristic superhuman war that resulted in thousands of casualties. There are other popular versions, including the futuristic Avengers seen in the Earth-982 time line of Marvel's MC2 project *A-Next,* the zombie Avengers seen on Earth-2149 in the various *Marvel Zombies* series, and the kid-friendly adventures of an alternate Avengers on Earth-20051 in the *Marvel Adventures* line.

ALLIES OF IRON MAN

Real Name: Edwin Jarvis
Height: 5'11"
Weight: 160 lbs.
Eyes: Blue, **Hair:** Black

Group Affiliation: Employee of Anthony Stark and the Avengers; Former Royal Air Force (RAF) pilot
First Appearance: *Tales of Suspense* #59

No person on Earth has been by Tony Stark's side longer than Edwin Jarvis, who was the butler to the Stark family when Tony was young. To this day he continues his houseman duties, though since the formation of the Avengers, Jarvis has served as their domestic servant, "on loan" from Stark.

Little is known of Jarvis's history except that he had once served in England as a pilot for the Royal Air Force, during which time he was the boxing champion for three years. His mother is still living, and in his private time, he either dotes on her or socializes with a woman named Glory Garsen—or, more recently, May Parker (aunt to Spider-Man). For years, Jarvis also used his funds to sponsor a child in a foreign country; the child, Maria de Guadalupe "Lupe" Santiago, eventually came to New York to go to college. It was then learned that she had become a super-human adventurer known as Silverclaw, and she soon joined the Avengers.

As the chief of staff for the Avengers headquarters—which has been located in multiple places, but was longest at the Stark mansion at 890 Fifth Avenue in Manhattan—Jarvis engages in multiple duties. He not only oversees staff members who cook and clean, but often does those jobs himself. He oversees crews who perform maintenance on the Avengers' quinjets and specialized equipment, and monitors Avengers missions and dangerous situations from the Avengers control room. He also acts as a surro-gate father figure or confidant for many of the members, including Tony Stark.

Although he has been let go during the times when the Avengers have disbanded, Jarvis currently works for the Mighty Avengers team in its skyscraper headquarters atop the Stark Tower Complex. There, he interacts almost daily with Tony Stark, as he has for most of Stark's life.

Historian's note: There have been multiple other forms of Edwin Jarvis seen in Marvel's alternate universes. On Earth-1610, the Ultimates universe, Jarvis is the often sarcastic and openly gay manservant of Tony Stark, but was murdered by the Black Widow. On Earth-2149, the Marvel Zombies universe, Jarvis was eaten by hungry zombified members of the Avengers. And in the alternate time line of Marvel's MC2 project *A-Next,* an elderly Jarvis still serves the futuristic newer Avengers.

Alias: Ant-Man II
Real Name: Scott Edward Harris Lang
Height: 6' (and variable)
Weight: 190 lbs. (and variable)
Eyes: Blue, **Hair:** Reddish blond

Group Affiliation: Former member of the Avengers, Fantastic Four, and Heroes for Hire
First Appearance: ***Avengers* #181**
Final Appearance: ***Avengers* #500**

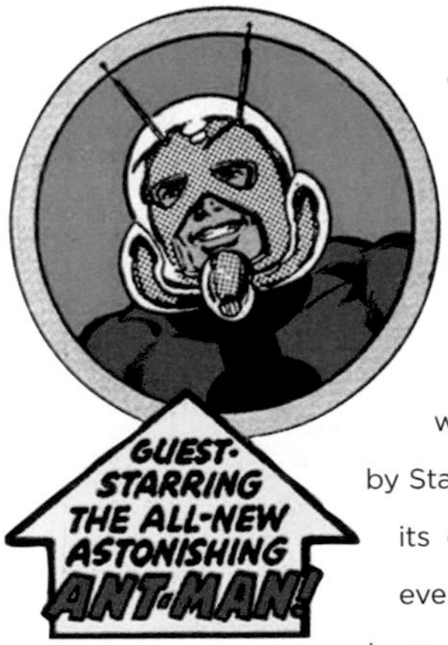
GUEST-STARRING THE ALL-NEW ASTONISHING ANT-MAN!

Although he used his expert electronic skills for burglary, Scott Lang was not a heartless criminal. Apprehended early on, Lang served his sentence and was paroled, whereupon he was hired by Stark International to work in its design department. Lang even installed security systems at the Avengers Mansion.

When his daughter Cassandra was diagnosed as having a serious congenital heart condition, Lang needed help. Unfortunately, he believed that the woman who could help her, surgeon Dr. Erica Sondheim, was being held captive at Cross Technological Enterprises. Lang resorted to burglary again, this time stealing the Ant-Man uniform and shrinking gas canisters from the New Jersey home of Dr. Henry Pym—once the Avenger Ant-Man, who called himself Yellowjacket now.

Rather than immediately capture Lang, Yellowjacket followed him, and the burglar donned the Ant-Man costume and used its powers to free Dr. Sondheim from Darren Cross's clutches. Impressed by Lang's attitude, Pym allowed him to keep the costume, provided he used it for good. The reducing/enlarging gas (containing Pym particles) contained in belt-mounted canisters on Ant-Man's costume allowed him to shrink in size to half an inch or even microscopically small, while the cybernetic helmet allowed him to communicate with and control insects. Riding on flying ants, Ant-Man is thus able to travel quickly.

Lang continued to work at Stark Industries and shared many adventures with Iron Man, even saving his life when Stark became trapped in his own armor. Ant-Man eventually became an affiliate member of the Fantastic Four, then a full-time member of the Avengers. For a period of time, he also dated former Super Heroine Jessica Jones, but they were not a serious couple.

Ant-Man was later killed in the Avengers' battle against an insane Scarlet Witch, but his daughter, Cassie, whose life he had fought so hard to save, took up the heroic mantle as the size-enlarging Stature, a member of the Young Avengers. A third Ant-Man, a rogue S.H.I.E.L.D. agent named Eric O'Grady, has recently been active, but he wears an experimental Pym suit, not the one previously worn by Lang.

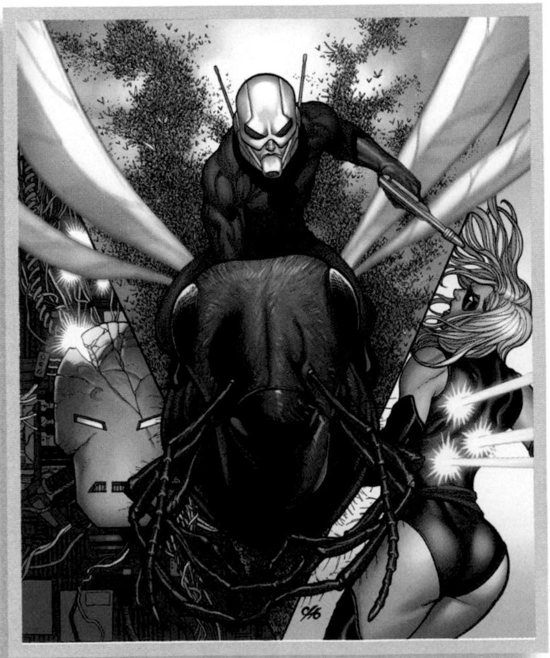

NICK FURY AND S.H.I.E.L.D.

Real Name: Nicholas Joseph Fury
Height: 6'1"
Weight: 225 lbs.
Eyes: Brown, **Hair:** Brown with graying temples

Group Affiliation: Former director of S.H.I.E.L.D.; Former colonel in US Army and agent of Central Intelligence Agency
First Appearance: ***Sergeant Fury and His Howling Commandos* #1**

Organizational Acronym: Supreme Headquarters International Espionage Law-enforcement Division; later Strategic Hazard Intervention Espionage Logistics Directorate
Base of Operations: Floating Helicarrier with satellite offices in all major cities
First Appearance: ***Strange Tales* #135**

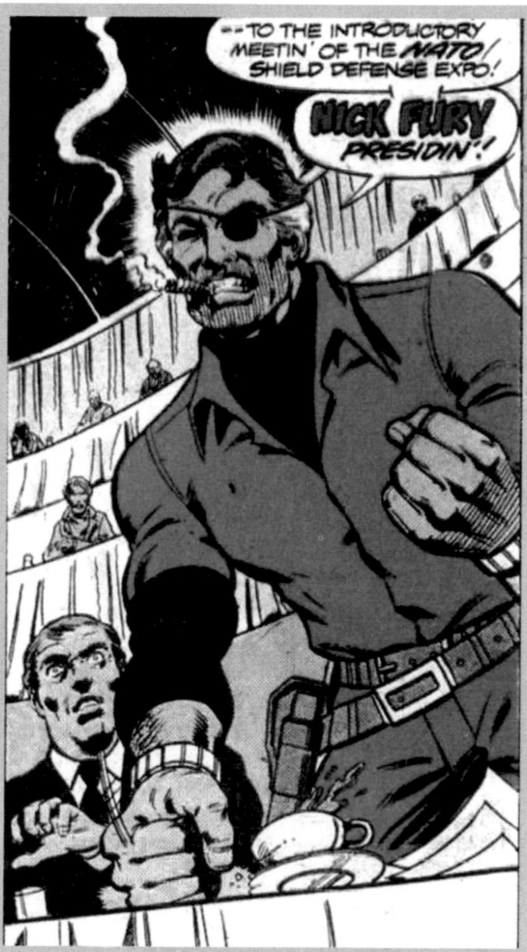
--TO THE INTRODUCTORY MEETIN' OF THE NATO/ SHIELD DEFENSE EXPO!
NICK FURY PRESIDIN'!

The son of a World War I pilot, Nick Fury practically bled red-white-and-blue as he grew up in the Hell's Kitchen neighborhood of New York City. Enlisting in the army as America became involved in World War II, he attained the rank of sergeant and soon came to lead the rambunctious-but-brave Howling Commandos, an infamous band of soldiers fighting in the European theater of operations. Fury remained on active duty during the Korean War, serving as an army intelligence agent and sometimes reuniting the Howlers for special missions. Spy missions he undertook in Vietnam brought Fury a promotion to the rank of colonel and an appointment to the CIA.

One mission that Fury undertook saw him assigned to investigate a spy at Stark International; he was initially unaware that owner Tony Stark himself was involved in organizing Project S.H.I.E.L.D., a plan to introduce a new international extragovernmental intelligence, espionage, and security organization dedicated to protecting the nations and peoples of Earth from all threats, terrestrial, extraterrestrial, or super-human. Eventually, Fury was recommended by Stark to become the director of the newly organized S.H.I.E.L.D. (Supreme Headquarters International Espionage Law-enforcement Division), especially in light of renewed attacks by the terrorist organization Hydra. Fury soon recruited some of his Howling Commandos to join S.H.I.E.L.D. as agents, including Timothy "Dum-Dum" Dugan (his new second in command) and Gabriel Jones. Fury also began ingesting the Infinity Formula, a chemical that slowed the aging process.

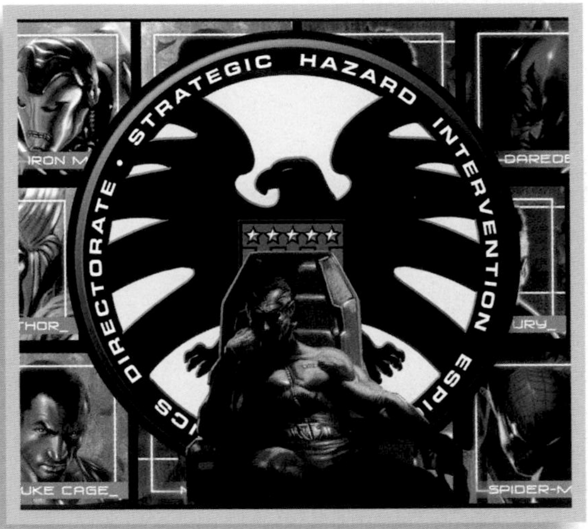
STRATEGIC HAZARD INTERVENTION
DIRECTORATE

Fury and S.H.I.E.L.D. waged a covert war against terrorist organizations and the occasional Super Villain, including Hydra, A.I.M. (Advanced Idea Mechanics), the Druid, Doctor Doom, Yellow Claw, Scorpio, and others. Having worked with Captain America and the man who would become Wolverine in World War II, Fury smoothly became friends with many superhuman heroes over the years, even regularly playing poker with the Thing and members of the Avengers. Despite their friendship, Fury saw some of the heroes as potential future threats, and he tried to balance his duties as S.H.I.E.L.D. director with those of a being a friend. He wasn't always successful at this, occasionally losing friends—or agents.

S.H.I.E.L.D. continued to get technology and support from Tony Stark, including the lifelike robots known as LMDs (Life Model Decoys), which could take the place of any agent in dangerous situations. Stark also aided in designing and building the huge mobile Helicarrier that functions as the organization's sky-high base, as well as technology ranging from the Mark V Flying Cars to jet packs. In the time that Stark chose to steer Stark Industries away from weapons manufacturing, S.H.I.E.L.D. contracted with other companies, but when Obadiah Stane took over Stark Industries—renaming it Stane Industries—S.H.I.E.L.D. once again contracted with the company to design and create sophisticated weaponry.

Following an infiltration of its ranks by artificial life-forms, S.H.I.E.L.D. disbanded and Fury retired to spend time with fellow agent Kate Neville. His retirement was not to last long, though; after a confrontation with ex-Nazi villain Baron Wolfgang von Strucker, a new S.H.I.E.L.D. (now Strategic Hazard Intervention Espionage Logistics Directorate) arose, once again with Fury as its director. The new S.H.I.E.L.D. faced battles with the Red Skull and Hate Monger, as well as Hydra and many others. Fury was demoted at one point, but regained his position as director for a time. However, he found that manipulating his superpowered allies was creating more and more internal conflict, and after a battle-suit-based Secret War, Fury eventually lost his directorship and went into hiding.

While Fury now works underground, his replacement as director of S.H.I.E.L.D. for a time was Maria Hill. Following the Civil War that arose in the Super Hero community as a result of the Superhuman Registration Act, Hill turned the position over to Tony Stark, who had again revealed to the world that he was the hero Iron Man. How long Stark will remain with S.H.I.E.L.D., and what role Nick Fury will play in the proceedings, is as yet unknown.

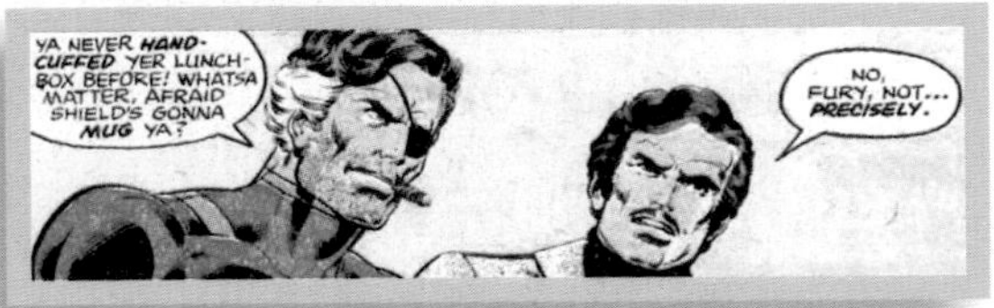
YA NEVER HAND-CUFFED YER LUNCH-BOX BEFORE! WHATSA MATTER, AFRAID SHIELD'S GONNA MUG YA?
NO, FURY, NOT... PRECISELY.

Historian's note: Nick Fury has been seen in a number of forms in Marvel's alternate universes. On Earth-1610, the Ultimates universe, Fury is an imposing bald African American man who closely resembles actor Samuel L. Jackson. In the Marvel Mediaverse, Nick Fury was played in a made-for-television movie by David Hasselhoff.

STARK INDUSTRIES

If you can tell a man's worth by the company he keeps, what would Tony Stark be worth? The multimillionaire inventor is the son of Howard and Maria Stark, and his father originally founded Stark Industries (SI) as a small electronics firm based on Long Island, New York. Stark Industries began to grow as electronics took off, and the company also became a pioneer in the development of computers. It was, however, the decision to begin designing and manufacturing munitions for the US government that put the company into the pages of history and built the Stark family fortune.

Howard and Maria Stark were killed in an automobile accident, leaving their young son to become the company's owner and chief executive officer. Because SI had a number of plants, Stark soon became used to travel. It was on a trip to a plant in Southeast Asia that his life was changed, leading him to become the hero known as Iron Man.

Although Stark Industries was often under attack by Cold War spies or angry business rivals, it was the fact that Stark's self-proclaimed bodyguard—Iron Man—was on site that brought superpowered villains out of the woodwork. It wasn't uncommon for executive secretary Virginia "Pepper" Potts or chauffeur Harold "Happy" Hogan to be taken captive, nor a high number of other Stark employees. Still, the company remained one of the most innovative and technologically forward-thinking places to work in America, even providing the international espionage agency S.H.I.E.L.D. with much of its equipment.

Eventually, however, Tony Stark decided to discontinue manufacturing munitions and

designing weapons, turning Stark Industries into the global leader in technological research and development. Eventually, with branches throughout the world, the company was renamed Stark International. Unfortunately, when personal problems plagued Stark, he was too distracted to see debt mounting in his company. Business rival Obadiah Stane engineered a hostile takeover of Stark Industries, renaming it Stane Industries and returning the plants to the manufacturing and designing of weapons.

Stark eventually recovered from his personal problems and founded the Silicon Valley, California, electronics company known as Circuits Maximus with friends James Rhodes and siblings Morley and Clytemnestra Erwin. The evil Stane would not rest, however, and he attacked Stark again, blowing up the headquarters and killing Morley Erwin before killing himself after a battle with Iron Man.

Stark eventually regained his fortunes and founded the Los Angeles–based Stark Enterprises. With the slogan of "Where Tomorrow Begins Today, " the new company was more of a think tank, where scientists researched chemical and electronic breakthroughs. Stark Enterprises absorbed other companies, including Accutech Research and Development, Barstow Electronics, Centrex, Pendyne, Inc., and eventually Stane International. Unfortunately, when Tony Stark was killed in a battle with the Avengers and Kang—and was replaced by a teenage version of himself from an alternate time line—Stark Enterprises was bought out by Kenjiro Fujikawa of Fujikawa Industries, who renamed it Stark-Fujikawa.

After Tony returned to life in the post–Heroes Reborn era, Stark set up Stark Solutions, a consulting firm, but due to a subliminal message planted in his brain by rival Tiberius Stone, Tony closed Stark

Solutions and took on the name of Hogan Potts to work for the electronics firm Askew Electronics. Eventually he came to his senses, regained his fortune, and reestablished Stark Enterprises. Shortly thereafter, Fujikawa's daughter, Rumiko, sold Stark enough shares that he was able to take control of his company again, and he reopened it under its original name, Stark Industries.

Today SI is headquartered in the three-building Stark Tower Complex in midtown Manhattan. In the main ninety-three-story building, the top floors function as the headquarters for the Avengers, while the ninety-second floor houses Stark's private office. The ninetieth floor is the Major Robotics/Electronics Fabrication laboratory where Stark designs and builds his Iron Man armor components. The lower levels of the Main Tower, as well as the shorter South and North buildings, are dedicated to Stark Industries subsidiaries and offices, as well as the various nonprofit organizations that Stark funds. Sitting atop the Main Tower is the Sentry's Watchtower, a baroque construct that serves as that Avengers member's private headquarters and home.

Over the years, Stark has had many memorable employees, including Edwin Jarvis, Virginia "Pepper" Potts, "Harold "Happy" Hogan, Edward "Eddie" March, Anton Vanko, Bethany Cabe, Scott Lang, and James Rhodes. Other important workers, many of whom are dead or have had their employment terminated, include motherly executive assistant Bambina "Bambi" Arbogast, public relations directors Artemus Pithins and Marcy Pearson, engineer Carl Walker (aka Force), security chief Vic Martinelli, former vice president and COO Felix Alvarez, and former general counsel Bertram Hindel.

First Appearance: *Tales of Suspense* #41 (Stark Industries); *Iron Man* #73 (Stark International); *Iron Man* #188 (Circuits Maximus); *Iron Man* #215 (Stark Enterprises); *Iron Man* volume III #1 (Stark Solutions)

THE IRON LEGION

Although Tony Stark and James Rhodes have worn the Iron Man armor more than any others on Earth, they are not the only heroes who have donned Stark's high-tech suits. At various times, Stark has asked others to become Iron Man for a brief period of time, though never for long. During one particularly dangerous mission against Ultimo, Rhodes asked all of the former Iron Man fill-ins to suit up to rescue Tony. Including Bethany Cabe, the first woman to don Stark's armor, the group wore a selection of previous armors from Stark's armory. Dubbed the Iron Legion, the quintet jetted to the rescue of their old friend. You've previously seen the entries for Happy Hogan and Bethany Cabe (one of the replacements), but here are the other heroic members of the Iron Legion, which appeared in *Iron Man* #300.

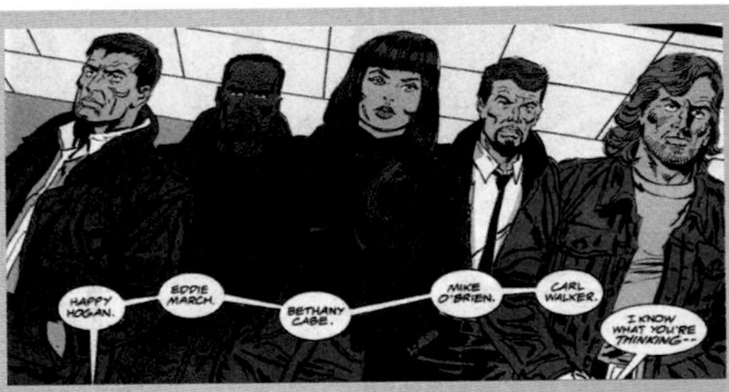
HAPPY HOGAN.
EDDIE MARCH.
BETHANY CABE.
MIKE O'BRIEN.
CARL WALKER.
I KNOW WHAT YOU'RE THINKING--

Real Name: Edward "Eddie" March
First Appearance: ***Tales of Suspense* #21**

A boxer who was once Happy Hogan's sparring partner, Eddie March idolized Iron Man. When Tony Stark got a heart transplant, he ceased to be Iron Man, afraid that the strain would take its toll on his life. He recruited March to take over the Iron Man suit, unaware that March had medical problems of his own. March fought Crimson Dynamo II, but was hospitalized and rushed into surgery shortly thereafter. March wore the Iron Man armor only a few more times prior to making his onetime appearance as a member of the Iron Legion. There he wore a copy of Iron Man's clunky original gray armor.

Alias: Guardsman II
Real Name: Michael "Mike" O'Brien
First Appearance: ***Iron Man* #82**

Kevin O'Brien was a bright scientist and friend to Tony Stark, and the pair built a special set of green armor for the Irishman. Unfortunately, O'Brien's instability and the machinations of others led to Guardsman seriously injuring four civilian protestors. Shortly afterward, he was killed during a conflict with Iron Man. His brother Michael, a New York police officer, believed Stark was the cause of Kevin's death, and stole the Guardsman suit. A battle with Iron Man led to him being placed in the Avengers' custody. Later, in a twist of fate, Stark was forced to wear the Guardsman armor; O'Brien donned the Iron Man armor to battle the Mandarin. When he was a member of the Iron Legion, Mike wore the Silver Centurion armor.

Alias: Force
Real Name: Clayton Wilson/Carl Walker
First Appearance: ***Sub-Mariner* #68**

When Clayton Wilson first encountered Iron Man, he was the villain Force, working for Justin Hammer in

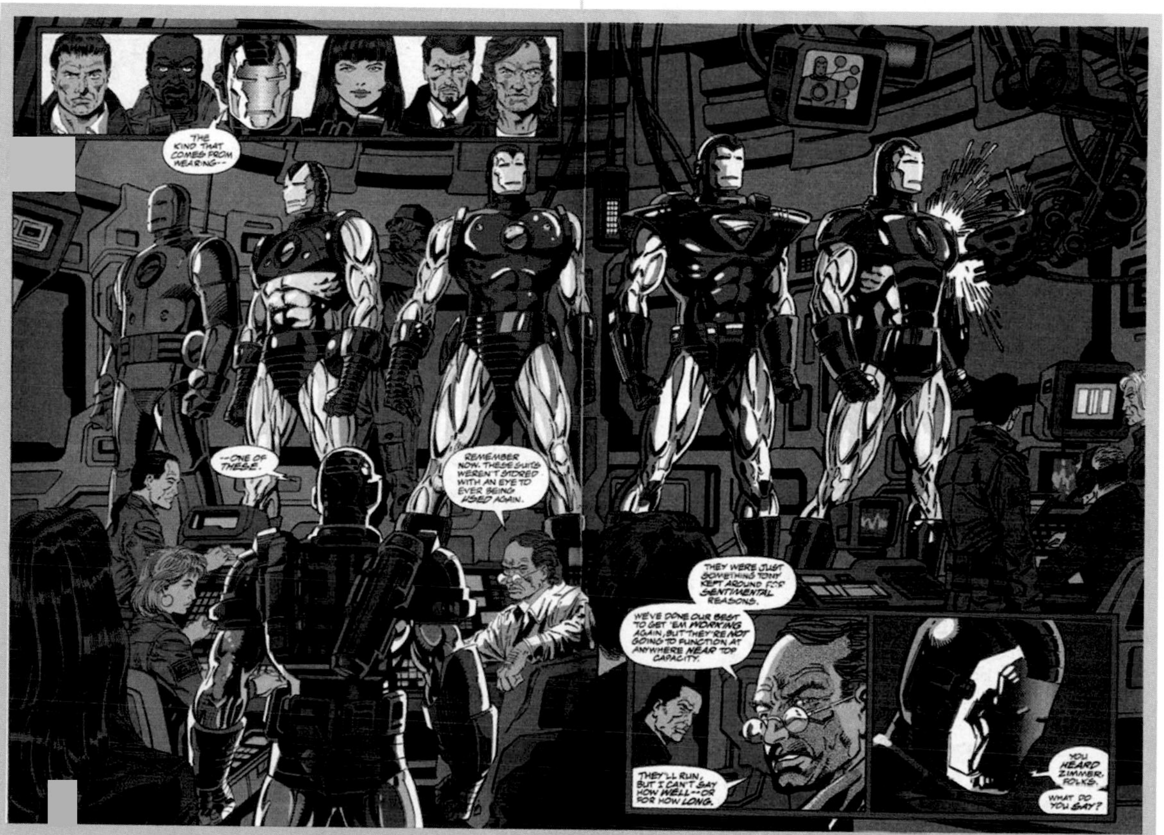
THE KIND THAT COMES FROM WEARING--
--ONE OF THESE.
REMEMBER NOW. THESE SUITS WEREN'T STORED WITH AN EYE TO EVER BEING USED AGAIN.
THEY WERE JUST SOMETHING TONY KEPT AROUND FOR SENTIMENTAL REASONS.
WE'VE DONE OUR BEST TO GET 'EM WORKING AGAIN, BUT THEY'RE NOT GOING TO FUNCTION AT ANYWHERE NEAR TOP CAPACITY.
THEY'LL RUN, BUT I CAN'T SAY HOW WELL--OR FOR HOW LONG.
YOU HEARD ZIMMER, FOLKS.
WHAT DO YOU SAY?

a powerful battlesuit whose force-field technology was enhanced by microchip circuitry. Eventually tiring of his criminal ways, Wilson turned to Tony Stark to help free him from the deadly control of Hammer. Wilson turned his Force technology over to Stark—as well as information on Hammer's activities—and Stark helped him get a new name, Carl Walker, and a job as a technician at Barstow Electronics. Coming to aid Stark as a member of the Iron Legion, Walker donned the classic red-and-gold armor, but was horrified when Ultimo melted it off him!

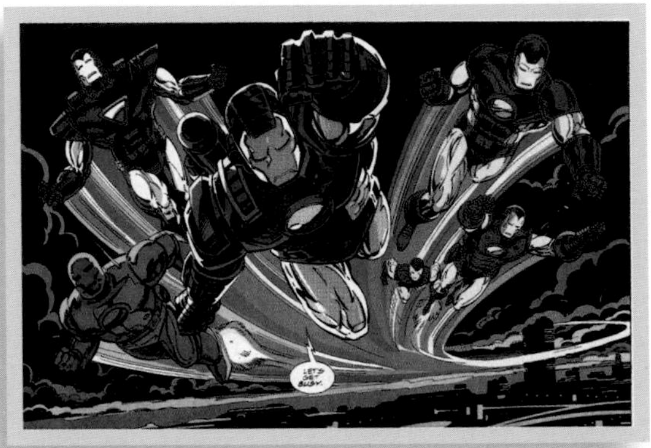
LET'S GET BUSY.

ALTERNATE REALITY IRON MEN

The space–time continuum is full of an infinite number of parallel worlds, many of which develop similarly to the world we know as the Marvel Universe (aka Earth-616), and some of which develop in extraordinarily different ways. Marvel heroes and villains have traversed and crossed over to various alternate realities, sometimes staying continuous with the time stream and sometimes appearing in alternate futures or pasts. Marvel Comics writers and artists have told stories of these alternate universes in the popular series *What If?,* as well as in mini series such as *Earth X* or *1602,* and in the mature-reader-friendly Ultimate line. Here are a number of alternate versions of Tony Stark or Iron Man that have appeared in the last forty years.

Alias: Iron Man of 2020
Real Name: Arno Stark
Group Affiliation: CEO of Stark Industries; Member of the Legion of the Unliving
First Appearance: ***Machine Man* #1**

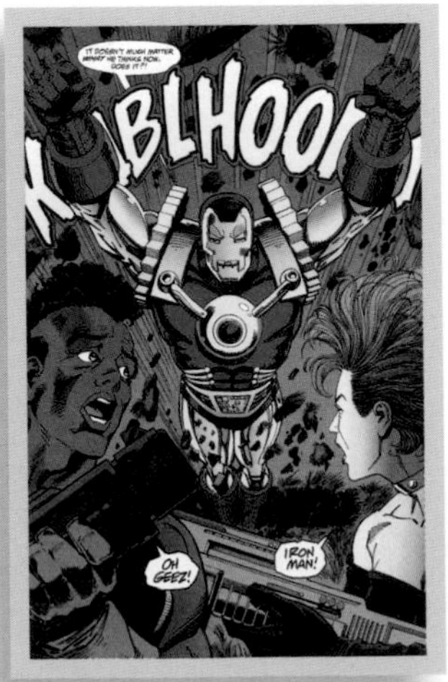
IT DOESN'T MUCH MATTER WHAT HE THINKS NOW, DOES IT?!
BLHOO
OH GEEZ!
IRON MAN!

The cousin of Anthony Stark in an alternate future on Earth-8410 did not have the same moral compass as his relative. Arno Stark inherited Stark Enterprises and eventually updated the Iron Man armor. However, instead of becoming a hero, the Iron Man of 2020 instead became a mercenary, hiring himself out to Sunset Bain to battle her for Machine Man. Over his next several adventures, Arno vacillated between hero and villain, battling the Avengers and Spider-Man in the past, but sometimes performing heroic deeds in his future time line.

Alias: Iron Man of 2093
Real Name: Andros Stark
Group Affiliation: Ally of Doctor Doom
First Appearance: ***Iron Man* #250**

In 2093, Arno Stark's grandson of Earth-8912, Andros Stark, donned the armor and teamed up with the ancient Doctor Doom to wipe out most of the remnants of humanity with neutron weaponry. They were defeated by the unlikely team of the original Iron Man and Doctor Doom, who were transported to the future by Merlin. While the younger Doom slew his older self, Iron Man 2093 was defeated by Stark's Iron Man, who utilized the fabled sword Excalibur to end the threat of future genocide.

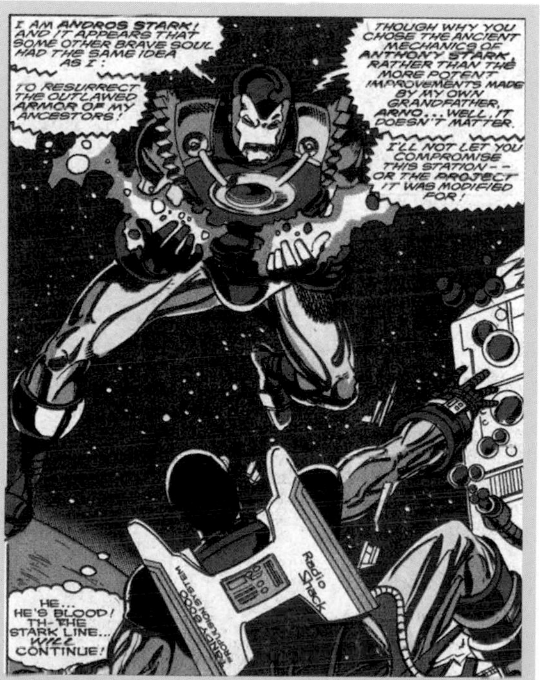
I AM ANDROS STARK! AND IT APPEARS THAT SOME OTHER BRAVE SOUL HAD THE SAME IDEA AS I:
TO RESURRECT THE OUTLAWED ARMOR OF MY ANCESTORS!
THOUGH WHY YOU CHOSE THE ANCIENT MECHANICS OF ANTHONY STARK, RATHER THAN THE MORE POTENT IMPROVEMENTS MADE BY MY OWN GRANDFATHER, ARNO... WELL, IT DOESN'T MATTER.
I'LL NOT LET YOU COMPROMISE THIS STATION-- OR THE PROJECT IT WAS MODIFIED FOR!
HE... HE'S BLOOD! TH-THE STARK LINE... WILL CONTINUE!
Radio Shack

Alias: Iron Man
Real Name: Anthony Stark (as a teen)
Group Affiliation: Ally of the Avengers.
First Appearance: ***Avengers: Timeslide***

The nineteen-year-old Anthony Stark was pulled from the alternate Earth-96020 time line by the Avengers. In their own time, they faced a murderous Tony Stark whose mind had been corrupted by Immortus, posing as the time traveler Kang the Conqueror. Kang's son murdered Tony's parents years before they were to actually have died, diverging the time line, and the newly orphaned Tony went to the alternate future to don Iron Man armor and battle his older self. Unfortunately, the younger Stark's heart was damaged in the battle, and following the death of the older Stark, the younger Stark was forced to use the armored chest plate to keep himself alive in much the same way his predecessor had. "Teen Tony" stayed on the modern Marvel Earth and began attending Columbia University, occasionally aiding the Avengers. His adventures were short-lived, however, as he was seemingly killed during the battle against Onslaught, then wiped from history with the reality-altering events of the Heroes Reborn era.

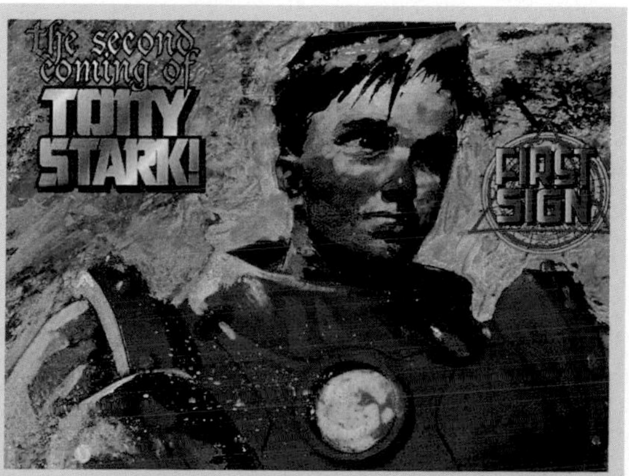
the second coming of
TONY STARK!
FIRST SIGN

Alias: Iron Man
Real Name: Anthony "Tony" Stark
Group Affiliation: Member of the Avengers
First Appearance: ***Iron Man* volume II #1**

Following a battle with the powerful psionic villain Onslaught, many Marvel heroes were warped into an alternate pocket dimension that contained a Counter-Earth much like their own, but with chronological differences. On this Earth's reality, Tony Stark developed the Iron Man Prometheum Armor to sell to the military as a weapon, but he later used the armor to save his own life after a confrontation with the Hulk. Iron Man did join the Avengers but was not its benefactor; the group was funded by the US government and reported to S.H.I.E.L.D. Alongside the Avengers, Iron Man faced Kang the Conqueror and Loki, among others, while in his solo adventures he fought the evil forces of Madame Hydra, Whirlwind, the Living Laser, the Titanium Man, Crimson Dynamo, and more. The alternate Tony Stark and his companions were eventually reincorporated back into the proper Marvel universe through the reality-altering powers of young Franklin Richards—though once they were reborn, they were "reset" to a previous part of the earlier time line . . . essentially becoming amalgams of their Earth-616 counterparts and themselves.

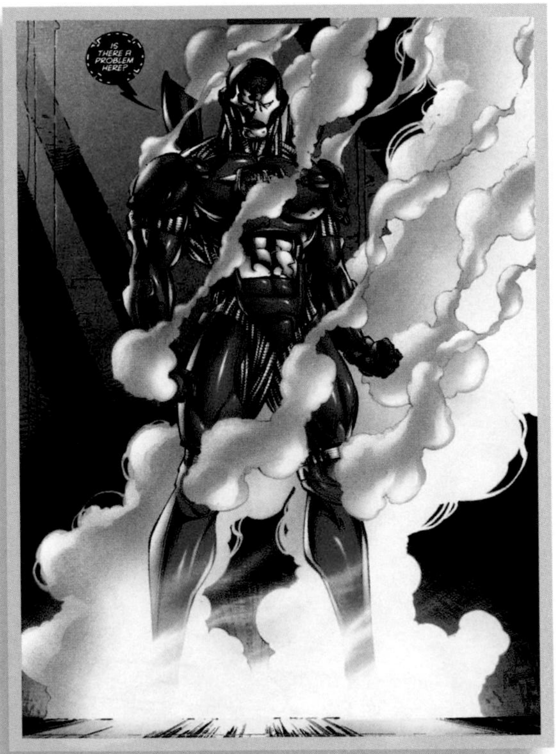
IS THERE A PROBLEM HERE?

Alias: Iron Lad
Real Name: Nathaniel Richards
Group Affiliation: Former member of the Young Avengers
First Appearance: ***Young Avengers* #1**

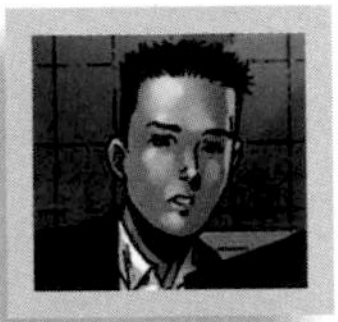

With the most complex history of all of the Iron Man alternates, Iron Lad is actually from the year 3016 of the technologically advanced Other-Earth (Earth-6311). When teen robotics student Nathaniel Richards was rescued from an attack by his future self—the time-traveling villain Kang the Conqueror—he was given a suit of psychokinetic armor . . . and a glimpse of his evil future. Horrified, Richards used the armor to escape to modern-day Earth-616, intending to recruit the Avengers in a battle against Kang.

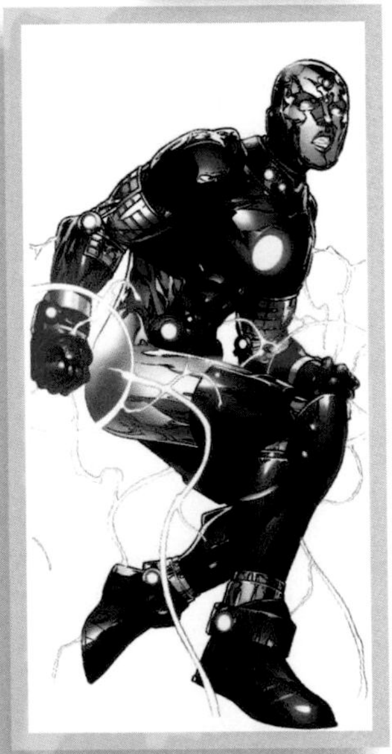

Unfortunately, the Avengers had disbanded, but Richards broke into Stark Industries and used the central processing unit of the now destroyed synthoid hero Vision to pinpoint the next heroes to rise. Calling himself Iron Lad, Richards assembled a group of heroes, most of whom had ties to previous Avengers: Patriot, the African American grandson of an early super soldier program participant; Asgardian, a mysterious boy mage; Hulkling, a shape-changer; Cassandra "Cassie" Lang, the size-changing daughter of Ant-Man; and athlete and markswoman Kate Bishop.

The Young Avengers caught the attention of Captain America and Iron Man, but the heroes assembled were soon faced with Kang, who wanted Iron Lad to return with him to the future to fulfill his destiny. Kang was killed by Iron Lad, but the youth realized that he now had to return to the future, or the time line of events would be altered! With Vision's aid, Richards returned to 3016, leaving behind the Iron Lad armor, which now houses Vision's reincarnated electronic essence.

•

Other alternate Iron Men have appeared on various Earths and time lines. On Earth-2031's Mangaverse, Iron Man fights in a robot-like suit alongside armor-wearing Iron Avengers, while on Earth-9997's Earth X, Tony Stark—one of the few unmutated humans—creates robotic duplicates of fallen heroes as the Iron Avengers. On Earth-2149's Marvel Zombies universe, Tony Stark is now a zombie, while on Earth-58163 of the House of M stories, Tony Stark designed his suit of armor to fight the world's strongest mutants. The mentally unhinged, facially scarred Tony Stark of Earth-5012 had once been a heroic Iron Man, but he devolved into Doctor Doom and then the blue-and-purple-armored Iron Maniac. The more kid-friendly tales of Iron Man in the *Marvel Adventures* line also exist in an alternate universe, on Earth-20051.

ULTIMATE IRON MAN

Alias: Iron Man
Real Name: Anthony "Tony" Stark
Height: 6'1"(unarmored); 7' (armored)
Weight: 225 lbs. (unarmored); 2,000 lbs. (armored)
Eyes: Blue, **Hair:** Black

Group Affiliation: Member of the Ultimates
First Appearance: ***Ultimate Marvel Team-Up #4***

The Tony Stark of Earth-1610 may have similarities to the Marvel Universe Tony Stark of Earth-616, but the course of their lives, heroic careers, and even physical makeup are significantly different. Tony is the son of inventor and Stark Defense Corporation contractor Howard Stark and geneticist Maria Cerrera Stark. Howard was developing a nanotechnology armor that could be adapted for individual use, but the result eventually ate away the skin of its wearer. Maria was developing a virus that could regenerate body parts, but the new neural cells were hypersensitive. After Maria was accidentally infected with the regenerative virus, she discovered that she was pregnant. The virus was killing her even as it mutated her unborn child, who developed additional neural tissue throughout his body. Maria died during Tony's birth, and her child could only be saved being bonded with the nanotech armor developed by Howard Stark. The armor ate away Tony's constantly regenerating neural flesh, keeping him alive but in constant pain.

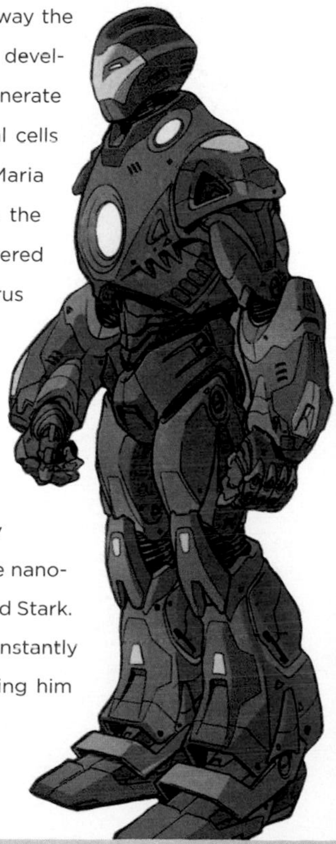

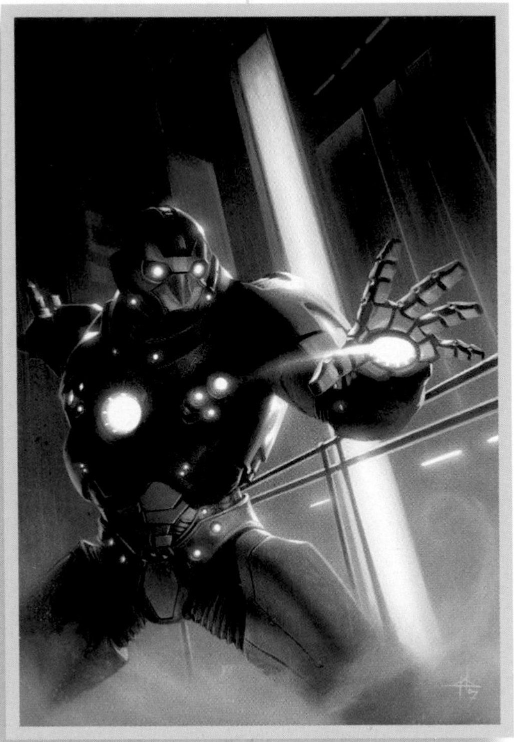

Business rival Zebediah Stane instituted a hostile takeover of Stark Defense, but Howard kept the secret of the armor hidden away. Stane even attacked Tony to get the secret to the bio-armor, to no avail. Now wearing a transparent version of the armor to provide a sense of normalcy, Tony Stark grew to become a phenomenal scientific genius and inventor who was gifted with nearly total recall and a seemingly limitless capacity for multitasking. In prep school, Stark began to design his own ablative "Iron Man" armor technology, along with his friend and fellow student Jim Rhodes.

Later, Rhodes became a part of a government think tank headquartered in the Baxter Building—where he encountered the revenge-minded son of Zebediah Stane, Obadiah—and Tony founded a design and manufacturing corporation called Stark International. Stark would become tremendously wealthy, as well as a womanizer and jet-setting playboy. Because alcohol helped dull the pain his neural body constantly felt—to say nothing of the knowledge that an inoperable brain tumor was killing him—Stark often drank to excess.

Tony also used his self-created armor technology to become the new hero known as Iron Man. He eventually used the new Iron Man armor to save the president from an assassination attempt, thus building his alter ego's celebrity. Still, he refused to sell the secrets of his armor technology to anyone. He did agree to join a S.H.I.E.L.D.-sponsored Super Hero team known as the Ultimates, however, teaming with World War II super soldier Captain America, self-proclaimed Norse thunder god Thor, and the size-changing S.H.I.E.L.D. scientists the Wasp (who could shrink) and her husband, Giant-Man (who could grow to a height of sixty feet).

The Ultimates helped to subdue the rampaging beast known as the Hulk, then saved the planet from the extraterrestrial invasion of the Chitauri. Tony dated teammate Natasha Romanov (Black Widow) and eventually proposed to her, even creating a special suit of nanite armor for her as an engagement gift. Later, when the United States was attacked by a phalanx of super soldiers known as the Liberators—which included a squadron of armored Crimson Dynamos—Stark learned that Natasha was the traitor in their midst. Stark incapacitated—and perhaps killed—Natasha, then embarked on a mission that allowed him to reunite the Ultimates and destroy most of their foreign opponents. Afterward, Stark agreed to privately fund the Ultimates team, although his own future was full of darkness.

Iron Man's original bacterial bio-armor shrouds his body like a second skin, enhancing his durability and inhibiting his chronic neurological pain. The armor he wears over the top of it as Iron Man is known as Iron-Tech, and it gives him super-human strength and the power of jet-propelled flight. He also is equipped with repulsors, force fields, neuro-scramblers, force bubbles to capture opponents, and even a cloaking device.

MANDARIN

Alias: Mandarin (I and II)
Real Name: Unrevealed, aka Tem Borjigin, Gene Kahn, and Zhang Tong (I); Temugin, aka Temujin (II)
Height: 6'2" (I); 5'10" (II)
Weight: 215 lbs. (I); 170 lbs. (II)
Eyes: Blue-black (I); Brown (II),
Hair: Black (I); None (II)

Group Affiliation: Employer of many superpowered villains; Former member of the Hand (I); Former commander of the Avatars (I and II)
First Appearance: ***Tales of Suspense* #50** (Mandarin I); ***Iron Man,* volume III #53** (Mandarin II)
Final Appearance: ***Iron Man* #200** (Mandarin I)

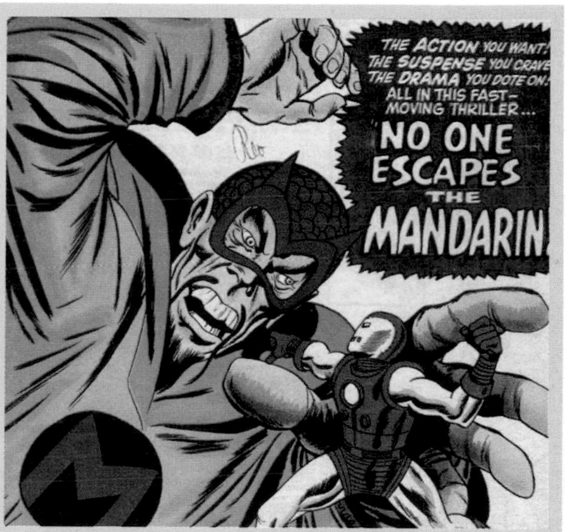
THE ACTION YOU WANT! THE SUSPENSE YOU CRAVE THE DRAMA YOU DOTE ON! ALL IN THIS FAST-MOVING THRILLER...
NO ONE ESCAPES THE MANDARIN!

Iron Man's greatest foe is also his most ever changing. The Mandarin's motivations for conquest morph as often as his accoutrements, but he is always formidably equipped with his ten Rings of Power.

His true name lost to the ages, the Mandarin claims to be a direct descendant of Genghis Khan, and is the son of one of the wealthiest men in pre-revolutionary mainland China and an English noblewoman. Orphaned as a child, the boy was raised by his father's sister, a bitter woman. Highly educated, he had specific aptitude for various sciences, both proven and theoretical. At one point, he was a renowned high government official—a "mandarin" during the Kuomintang Party's reign over China—but he lost his power and wealth during mainland China's Communist revolution of 1949.

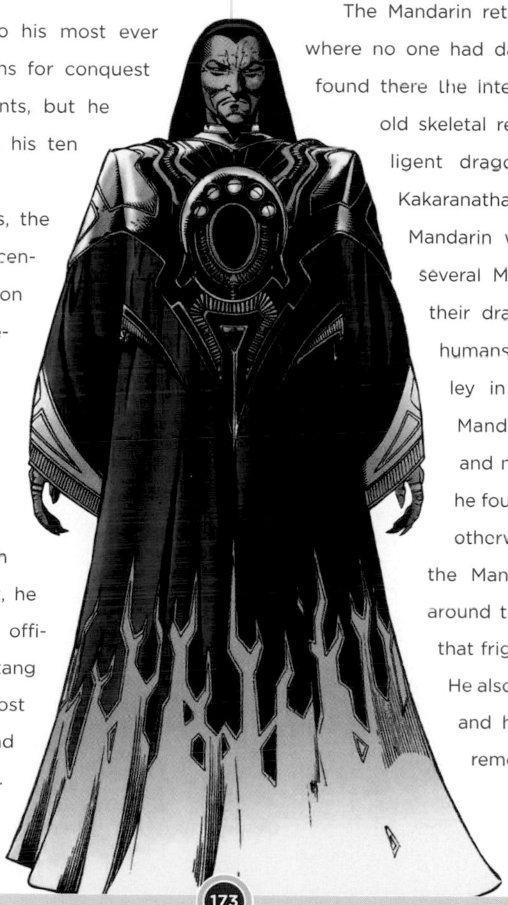

The Mandarin retreated to the Valley of Spirits, where no one had dared set foot for centuries. He found there the interstellar starship and centuries-old skeletal remains of Axonn-Karr, an intelligent dragonlike alien from the planet Kakaranathara (also known as Maklu-IV). Mandarin was unaware at the time that several Makluans were on Earth, hiding their dragon-like selves and posing as humans. From a new home in a valley in the Chinese hinterlands, the Mandarin studied Makluan science and mastered the ten powerful rings he found within the starship. Using his otherworldly knowledge and power, the Mandarin subjugated the villages around the valley and became a power that frightened even the Chinese army! He also fathered a son named Temugin and had the child sequestered in a remote monastery.

One of Mandarin's war-

LEFT HAND

LITTLE FINGER: "Ice blast." The ring emits waves of cold which can be used to stun an opponent. The ring usually causes the air in the path of its blast to turn to ice, and can lower an object's temperature to nearly absolute zero.

RING FINGER: "Mento-intensifier." The ring magnifies the wearer's own psionic energy, allowing him to place one or more people under his mental control and to transmit orders to them mentally. This ring can affect only one person at a time and only at a distance of ten feet.

MIDDLE FINGER: "Electro-blast." The ring emits electricity in amounts and intensities mentally determined by the wearer. The maximum voltage attainable is not known.

INDEX FINGER: "Flame blast." The ring emits infrared radiation, or heat, at intensities mentally determined by the wearer. Usually the heat produces flame through incandescing the molecules in the air in the path of the blast. The heat beam can be used to trigger chemical explosions. The maximum amount of heat it can generate is not known.

THUMB: "White light." This ring can emit various forms of energy along the electromagnetic spectrum.

Over the years the Mandarin has established a strong psionic link with his rings, which was made many times stronger during the period in which his mind / spirit actually inhabited them. One result is that no one who wears the rings other than the Mandarin himself can command them. The Mandarin can now command the rings even when they are separated from him by vast distances, and mentally monitor events taking place around a ring that has been separated from him.

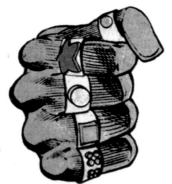

CLOSE-UP OF LEFT MIDDLE RING

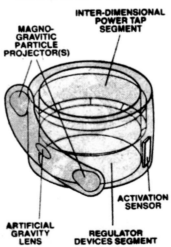

INTER-DIMENSIONAL POWER TAP SEGMENT

MAGNO-GRAVITIC PARTICLE PROJECTOR(S)

ARTIFICIAL GRAVITY LENS

ACTIVATION SENSOR

REGULATOR DEVICES SEGMENT

RIGHT HAND

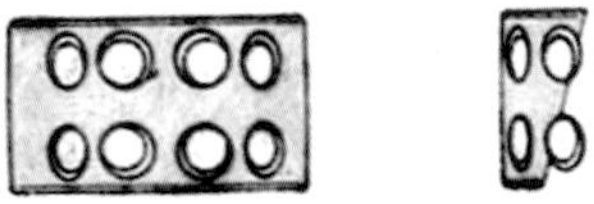

LITTLE FINGER: "Black light." The ring can create an area of absolute blackness that seems to absorb all light used within it. Although "black light" is a term used to refer to ultraviolet radiation, the darkness created by the ring is probably a form of the "darkforce" used by Cloak, Darkstar, and the Shroud.

RING FINGER: "Disintegration beam." The ring emits a beam of energy that destroys all bonds between the atoms and molecules of the object it strikes. This ring needs twenty minutes to recharge after use.

MIDDLE FINGER: "Vortex beam." The ring causes the air to move about at high speed in a vortex. The vortex can be used as an offensive weapon, as a means of levitating objects, or as a means of propelling the ring's wearer through the air.

INDEX FINGER: "Impact beam." This ring can project various forms of energy, most frequently that of fast neutrons with the concussive force of 350 pounds of TNT. The ring has also been used to project intense sonic vibrations and to create magnetic waves to attract or repel objects. The ring may be capable of emitting other forms of energy as well.

THUMB: "Matter rearranger." This ring can rearrange the atoms and molecules of a substance, or speed up or slow down their movement, so as to produce various effects. The ring has been used to condense water vapor in the air to liquid water, to solidify gasses, and to create lethal poison gas from the air. The ring cannot transmute elements. Nor can it rearrange the atoms and molecules of Iron Man's magnetic-beam reenforced armor.

lords, the Sin-Cong revolutionary Wong-Chu, was directly responsible for creating Iron Man when he imprisoned an injured Tony Stark and Professor Ho Yinsen and attempted to force them to build weapons. The Mandarin himself, however, did not encounter Iron Man until a few months into the hero's career. Their clashes soon became semi-regular as the Mandarin schemed new attempts to achieve world domination.

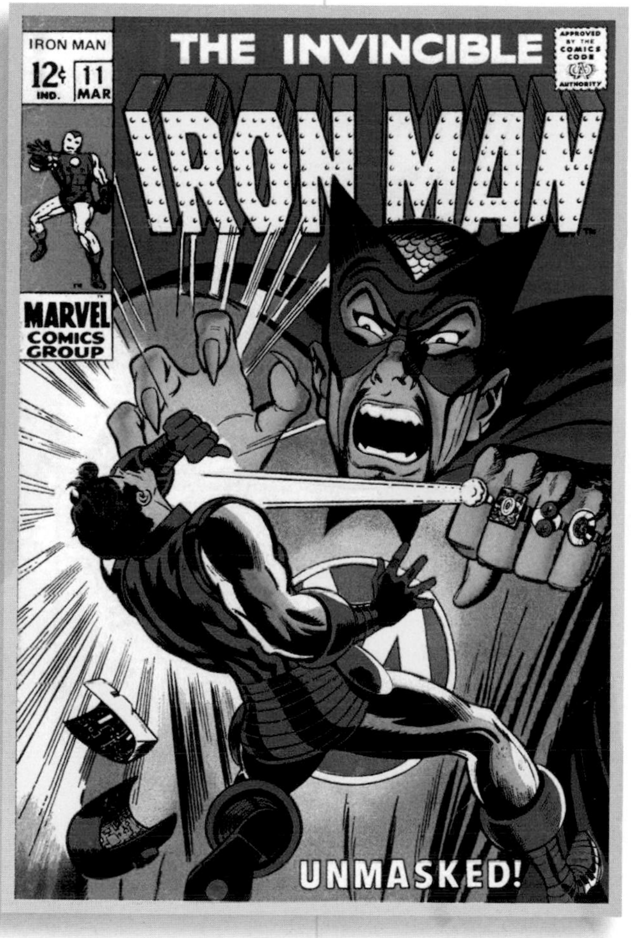
IRON MAN
12¢ 11 MAR IND.
THE INVINCIBLE
IRON MAN
APPROVED BY THE COMICS CODE AUTHORITY
MARVEL COMICS GROUP
UNMASKED!

The Mandarin frequently turned various nations' missiles and weapons against them, including rockets and spy planes built by Stark's plants. The villain also utilized a small orbiting satellite that could fire a "death-ray" toward Earthly targets such as Stark Industries, and he created a thirty-foot android he called Ultimo, which was immensely destructive. He also used Makluan-derived teleportation technology to kidnap people at will or teleport himself to escape threats.

Even though the Mandarin often succeeded in overpowering or capturing Iron Man, the hero always managed to get away. The armored avenger was, however, always unable to bring the Chinese villain to justice due to international laws. In one encounter—when an armored Stark rescued Happy Hogan, who was substituting for Iron Man at the time—Iron Man was able to use missiles to destroy Mandarin's castle. The villain escaped, later facing down the Avengers and the Hulk before using a robotic Hulk to attack Iron Man again. When Mandarin tried to kill Stark's girlfriend Janice Cord, his own betrothed, Mei Ling, saved Cord by sacrificing herself.

Next encountering the Inhumans, Mandarin lost his rings, but he used a technological headband from the Makluan starship to find them again. Afterward, he fought the Yellow Claw for control of his reconstituted castle, but while Mandarin's body was killed, he used the rings to transfer his consciousness into one of Yellow Claw's underlings and transform his new body into a younger version of his old one. Several more encounters with Iron Man and other heroes left Mandarin no closer to his goals, and he eventually took on the name of Zhang Tong, becoming a financial leader in Hong Kong and controlling leaders of industry and government. He used his powers—and minions known as the Hand—to stop Tony Stark from setting up a branch of Stark Enterprises in Hong Kong.

During this time, Mandarin was manipulated by Chen Hsu, the elderly captain of the disguised shape-changing Makluans. Hsu eventually aided Mandarin in controlling the gigantic Makluan dragon Fin Fang Foom, which allowed the villain to seize control of one-third of China. In a conflict that followed, Mandarin was confronted by both Tony Stark and James Rhodes in Iron Man armor, and upon learning that the Makluans planned to rule Earth themselves, Mandarin turned on his allies. Stark channeled his armor's power through the ten rings, which seemed to destroy the dragon aliens—at the cost of the Mandarin's hands, which were burned off.

After growing new reptilian hands and recovering his rings, Mandarin discovered the evil mystical talisman known as Thuviskaroth of Cataphylaxis—the "Heart of Darkness"—and used it to revert China to a medieval, less technological era. The Mandarin and his super-human allies, the Avatars, were defeated by the combined group of Iron Man, War Machine, and the Force Works team, but not before Mandarin finally confirmed Tony Stark's secret identity. The Mandarin appeared to have died, but he later resurfaced with a new belief that the feudal system of the past had merely been transformed into the capitalism of today. Mandarin planned to conquer Russia and faced Iron Man once more in a giant flying fortress called the Dragon

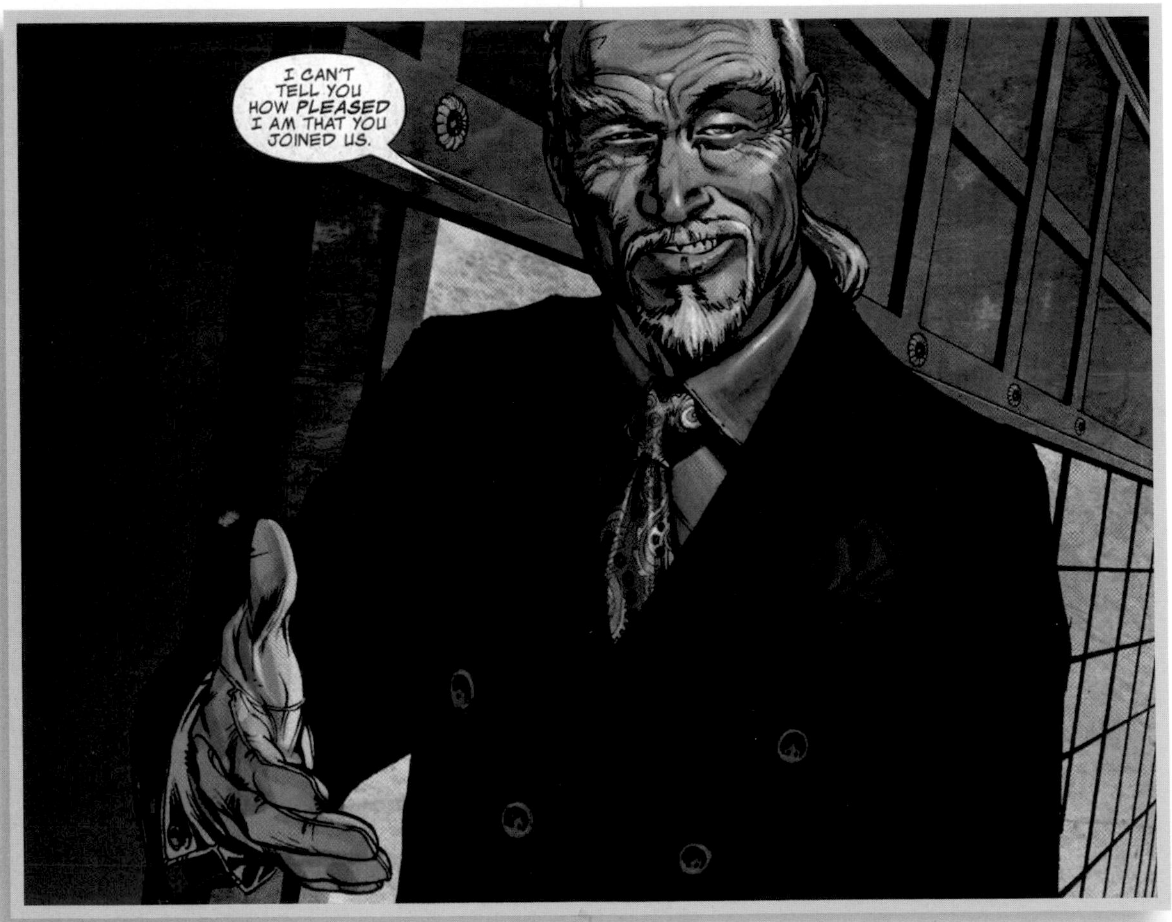
I CAN'T TELL YOU HOW PLEASED I AM THAT YOU JOINED US.

of Heaven. Mandarin again appeared to die.

The severed hands and rings of the Mandarin were eventually delivered to his son, Temugin, along with a message that he should avenge his father's death at the hands of Iron Man, regaining the family's honor. Temugin's first encounter with the hero occurred without the rings, and his prodigious martial art skills—which seemed almost super-human when he focused his chi—allowed him to severely damage Iron Man's armor. But Temugin was unable to take the battle farther when the Arctic base that he and Iron Man battled in was destroyed.

The Mandarin's servant, Po—unhappy with Temugin's interest in spiritual purity over conflict—bombed the Chinese embassy in New York, framing Tony Stark for the crime. Iron Man soon faced Mandarin again, and he might have been killed had he not been able to expose Po's treachery. Although Temugin promised that he would now work to bring tranquility to the world—and that his blood debt against Stark was over—he eventually equipped a criminal named Clarence Ward with a duplicate set of Iron Man's armor, resulting in many deaths, including that of Stark's lover Rumiko Fujikawa. Later, the Avatars, previous servants to the first Mandarin, rampaged in Manhattan following the enactment of the Superhuman Registration Act. A recent scrap between Temugin and the villain Puma may have cost Temugin the loss of one of his hands and some of the rings.

Recently the original Mandarin returned, with the Rings of Power now infused into his spine. By manipulating the Extremis virus, he appears to be creating a technology-powered army with the goal of a full-blown Extremis war!

The original Mandarin had no special super-human abilities, though he was strongly versed in various forms of martial arts, and he also developed a psychic link with his Makluan Rings of Power. Temugin can focus his chi to create near-super-human powerful blows, and has intense speed. Both Mandarins have mastered the use of the Makluan rings, each of which contains powers. The rings of the left hand include the powers to create icy, electrical, flame, or electromagnetic energy blasts, as well as to allow the wearer to psionically control another human at a short distance. The rings of the right hand can create ultraviolet radiation black light beams—which can disintegrate matter—can create a vortex, or use sonic vibrations or other energy as a concussive force. The final ring can rearrange or change the movement of the atoms and molecules of some substances, although it does not transmute elements.

IRON MONGER / OBADIAH STANE

Alias: Iron Monger
Real Name: Obadiah Stane
Height: 6'5"(Stane); unrevealed (in armor)
Weight: 230 lbs. (Stane); 4,230 lbs. (in armor)
Eyes: Blue, **Hair:** None

Group Affiliation: Former president and CEO of Stane International; Former ally of Madame Masque
First Appearance: *Iron Man #163*
Final Appearance: *Iron Man #200*

Obadiah Stane had an unfortunate childhood, but he eventually made himself very rich and powerful. His mistake, in the end, was targeting Tony Stark as the focus of his rage.

When Obadiah was a child, his drunkard father played Russian roulette in front of him, killing himself instantly. Obadiah was sent into foster care, and went bald from the trauma he had witnessed. Ridiculed by children around him, Stane retreated into games of strategy, especially chess, and vowed that he himself would never lose at anything. He soon employed his first signs of psychosis by killing the dog of a chess opponent before their big match; Stane later used blackmail to demoralize an industrialist for whom he worked.

By the age of twenty-five, Stane had turned the industrialist's company into a multimillion-dollar munitions concern, and he cared little who he sold arms to. Like Tony Stark, he created a set of specially powered bodyguards, known as the Chessmen. Stane's aggressive attempts to form an organization of European and Oriental industrialists, led by himself, put him into conflict for the first time with Tony Stark, and Stane soon decided that the brilliant leader of Stark International was his new opponent in the game of life.

Stane embarked on a series of maneuvers meant to destroy Stark, whose weakness, he knew, was his alcoholism. Stane's agent Tattoo brought about widespread sabotage at Stark International's Long Island headquarters before he died from a secret poisoning by Stane. The munitions seller also hired a woman named Indries Moomji to make Stark fall in love with her, then betray him. Iron Man battled several of the Chessmen and was forced to deal with several attempts on the life of James Rhodes. Stark's confrontations with Stane didn't go well, and with no proof against the man, Stark was in despair. Moomji's betrayal sent Stark psychologically spiraling into the alcoholism he had tried to fight.

By buying up back debts and instigating lawsuits, Stane slowly gained control over Stark Enterprises, but a demoralized and drunken Stark hardly noticed. Eventually, Stane took over the company, renaming it Stane International and banning its original founder from the premises. James Rhodes, who now took on the role of Iron Man, made sure that Stane didn't get any of the Iron Man technology, but he couldn't stop Stane from reinitiating the weapons contracts that Stark had moralistically pulled away from in the past.

After spending months as a drunken and penniless derelict, Stark hit bottom and, with the help of James Rhodes, began to rebuild his life. The pair joined with the siblings Morley and Clytemnestra Erwin to found the California-based electronics firm Circuits Maximus. Stane soon found out that Stark was back leading a constructive life. Having already deduced that Stark had once been Iron Man, he knew that his foe was back in the armor when two Iron Men battled Stane's pawns, the Circuit Breakers.

Stane began a series of abductions of Stark's friends and allies, and even bombed Circuits Maximus, killing Morley Erwin and sending Clytemnestra into a trauma-induced rage. Even as Stark donned a new set of armor he created—the Silver Centurion armor—Stane did, too. Some of Stark's designs had been discovered at Stark International, and Stane had his scientists create a giant blue suit of armor. With little battle experience, Stane eventually donned the prototype armor, calling himself Iron Monger, and attacked Iron Man.

Due to his inexperience, Stane was unable to defeat Iron Man, so he took an infant hostage and threatened to kill the child unless Iron Man surrendered to him. Instead, Iron Man destroyed an unoccupied nearby building, in which he theorized that a computer was controlling the Iron Monger armor. His gamble was correct: Stane dropped the baby and barely made a crash landing in his bulky armor. Iron Man caught the falling child, then confronted his foe.

Determined that he would not allow himself to be defeated, Stane removed his helmet and put a repulsor ray blast from his armor through his own head, dying instantly as his father had many years prior. Iron Man was the only witness to Stane's death; Stane's security personnel quickly removed the body from the scene, and the death was covered up from the media. Stane was replaced with a life-like android known as a Life Model Decoy for a short time. Although he didn't immediately do so, Stark eventually recovered his company. Stane International and Obadiah Stane's evil legacy have been effectively erased.

The Iron Monger armor featured many of the same powers as the Iron Man suit worn by James Rhodes. The omnium steel suit (code-named I-M Mark One) gave its wearer superstrength and the ability to fly using boot jets; it featured repulsor rays set in the palms of the gauntlets, and a powerful laser beam mounted onto the chest plate. Following the suicide of Obadiah Stane, the armor has been re-created by multiple others, mostly for nefarious purposes.

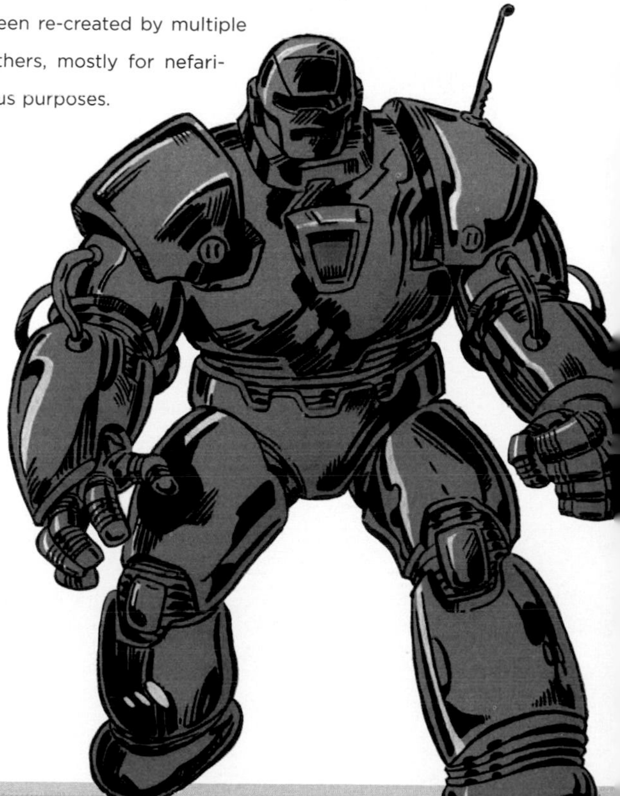

CRIMSON DYNAMO

No Iron Man villain has had as many identities as the Crimson Dynamo, largely because the Russian or Soviet Super Villain wears a suit of armor, and his controllers find him replaceable. To date, at least ten men have worn the armor, most of them clashing with Iron Man during his heroic career. Here are some details about each of them.

Alias: Crimson Dynamo (I)
Real Name: Anton Vanko, aka Anton Vankovian
First Appearance: ***Tales of Suspense* #46**

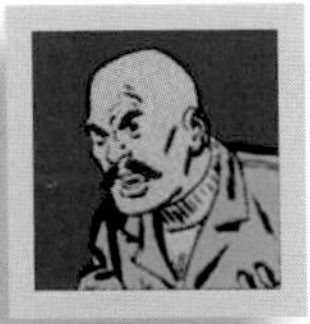

The first Crimson Dynamo was Professor Anton Vanko, a brilliant Soviet inventor who created the armor as part of Project: Krasnii Denamit, wiring it with electricity to become a human dynamo. His battle suit allowed him to control electricity and to fly. Vanko clashed with Iron Man early in the hero's career, but Stark tricked him into believing that his Soviet handlers were planning to kill him. Vanko defected and worked for Stark as one of his chief scientists. However, he was killed during a battle with Boris Turgenev, who wore the stolen armor; Vanko saved Iron Man, but perished in the act.

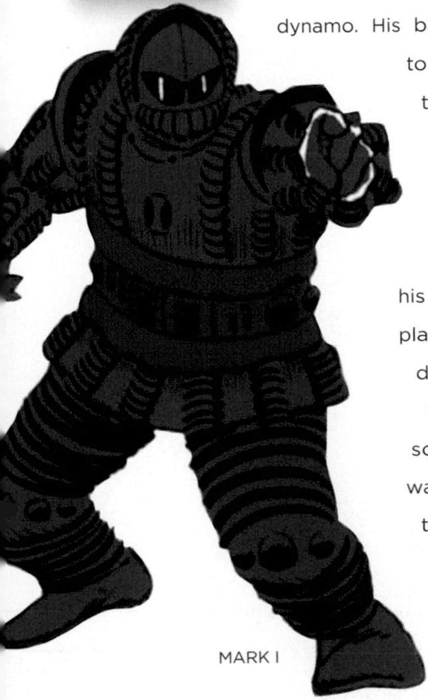

MARK I

Alias: Crimson Dynamo (II)
Real Name: Boris Turgenev
First Appearance: ***Tales of Suspense* #52**

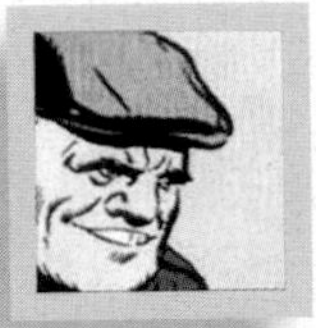

Coming to the United States with the Black Widow, Boris Turgenev stole the Crimson Dynamo armor and almost defeated Iron Man. He was killed by Anton Vanko, his predecessor, who fired an experimental and unstable new laser pistol at him.

Alias: Crimson Dynamo (III)
Real Name: Alex Nevsky, aka Alex Niven
First Appearance: ***Iron Man* #15**

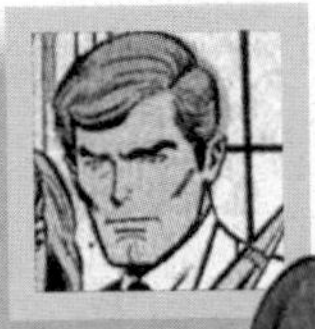

Although Alex Niven appeared to be Cord Industries' hot new scientist, he was secretly Alex Nevsky, the Russian protégé of Professor Anton Vanko. Disgraced when his idol defected, an exiled Nevsky planned vengeance against both Tony Stark and the Soviet government. At Cord Industries, he created improved Crimson Dynamo armor and fought Iron Man twice (facing both Eddie March and Tony Stark in the armor), but the Soviets sent Titanium Man to kill him. Niven blamed Iron Man for the death of the woman he loved, Janice Cord, even though it was Titanium Man who did

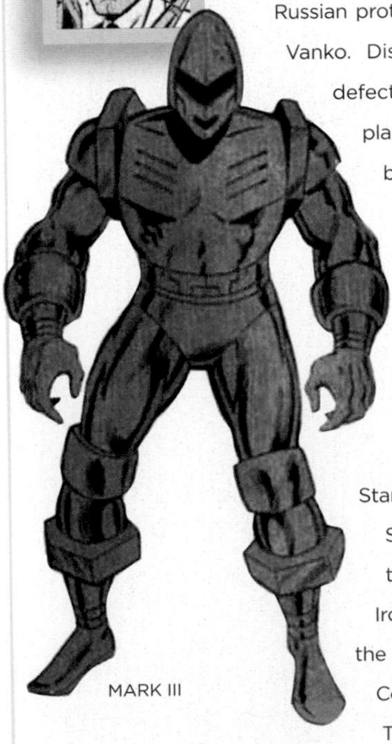

MARK III

the deed. Crimson Dynamo allied with Titanium Man and Radioactive Man as the Titanic Three, and later defected to Vietnam. Although he faced Iron Man again, Nevsky was assassinated by the KGB, and his armor was confiscated.

Alias: Crimson Dynamo (IV)
Real Name: Yuri Petrovich
First Appearance: *Champions #7*

Trained as a KGB assassin, Yuri Petrovich was the son of the Black Widow's partner, Ivan Petrovich. When the Black Widow and Ivan defected to the United States, Yuri was given the Crimson Dynamo armor and sent on a mission to kill them, not knowing that one was his father. Allied with other Soviet "heroes" (Darkstar, the Griffin, Rampage, and the original Titanium Man), Yuri engaged in battle with the Widow and West Coast Super Hero team the Champions. Learning that his father still lived, Yuri went berserk. Back in Russia, he was stripped of his armor and exiled to a Siberian labor camp.

Alias: Crimson Dynamo (V)
Real Name: Dmitri Bukharin
First Appearance: *Iron Man #109*

Dmitri Bukharin was given the Crimson Dynamo armor by the KGB, and he joined the Soviet Super Soldiers for a time, until they discovered he was in their ranks as a governmental spy. He later became a member of the Supreme Soviets, a super-human team loyal to the Soviet government. Following the dissolution of the USSR, the group renamed itself the People's Protectorate, but when his armor was confiscated by the new government, Bukharin took on new armor and the code name Airstrike.

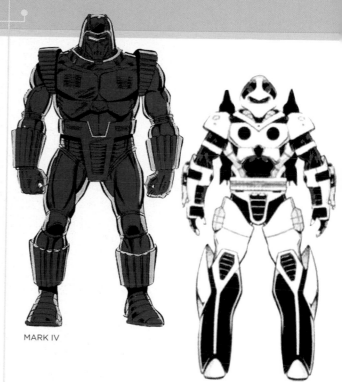

MARK IV

AIRSTRIKE

Alias: Crimson Dynamo (VI)
Real Name: Valentin Shatalov
First Appearance: *Iron Man #255*

Valentin Shatalov was a colonel-general in the Soviet army and a KGB agent who wore Bukharin's confiscated Crimson Dynamo armor. Allying himself with the original Titanium Man, the cyborg Firefox, and the original Unicorn, he fought the Soviet Super Soldiers as well as a team of exiled Russian mutants. He later allied himself briefly with the Red Skull.

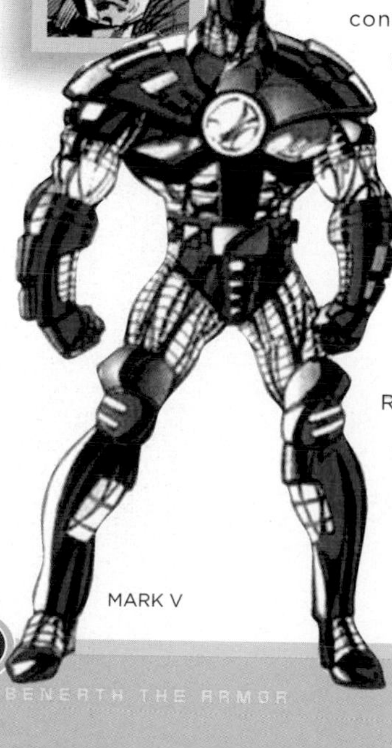

MARK V

Alias: Crimson Dynamo (VII)
Real Name: Unknown
First Appearance: ***Captain America* #42**

The short-lived career of an unknown—and minimally skilled—wearer of Bukharin's Crimson Dynamo armor came to an end after a confrontation with Nick Fury and Captain America.

Alias: Crimson Dynamo (VIII)
Real Name: Gennady Dmitrievich Gavrilov
First Appearance: ***Crimson Dynamo* #1**

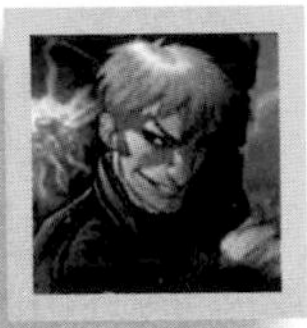

Young Russian Gennady Gavrilov found the helmet of a prototype armor suit designed by Anton Vanko, which allowed him to control the Crimson Dynamo armor. He would utilize it briefly for an accidental battle with the Russian military, as well as a purposeful fight against an agent of the anti-government group known as the Konsortium. Gavrilov still retains the armor, stored in his stepfather's plant, but his plans for it are unknown.

Alias: Crimson Dynamo (IX)
Real Name: Unknown
First Appearance: ***Secret War* #3**

Another short-lived wearer of one of the Crimson Dynamo armors was a Soviet loyalist who worked as an ally of the Answer and Latverian prime minister Lucia von Bardas. The tinkerer had upgraded the armor prior to the Dynamo working with other technologically powered villains to battle the Avengers. He was later captured by Iron Man after the villain robbed a bank.

Alias: Crimson Dynamo (X)
Real Name: Unknown
First Appearance: ***The Order* #2**

Pity the poor unknown man in the armor of the tenth Crimson Dynamo. He and his fellow members of the Alpha Gen Soviet Super Soldiers were put into cryogenic stasis during the Cold War, destined to awaken only if a nuclear explosion was detected. The base they were stored at abandoned and forgotten, the Alpha Gens weren't awoken until a battle between the Order and the Infernal Man caused an explosion that registered as a nuclear blast, activating the Soviet Super Soldiers. Crimson Dynamo was apparently killed in a later explosion.

Although each Crimson Dynamo armor contained its own technology and weaponry, many elements were similar. In addition to the protection that the armor itself afforded them, the wearer was often given superstrength and the ability to fly using boot jets. The gloves or gauntlets often contained energy blasters, and the helmet generally contained communications devices and tactical equipment. Other weaponry on the armors include missiles, guns, and a fusioncaster.

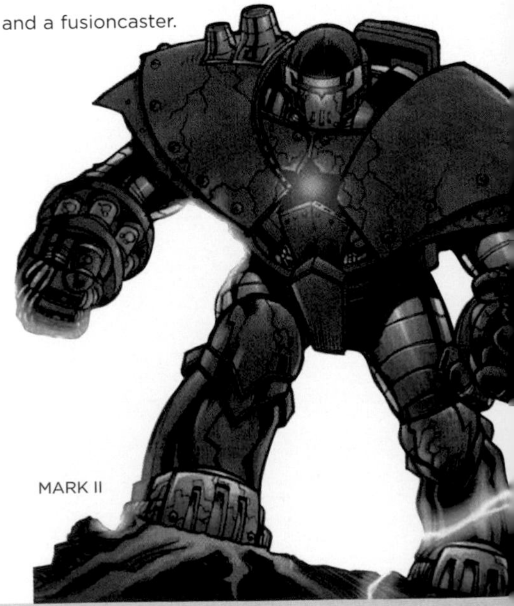

MARK II

A.I.M.

Organizational Acronym: Advanced Idea Mechanics
Base of Operations: Secret
Group Affiliation: Agent of Mind
First Appearance: ***Strange Tales* #146**

A.I.M. (Advanced Idea Mechanics) is a criminal organization comprising brilliant scientists who are dedicated to using technology for both the acquisition of power and the overthrow of all governments. The group was organized during World War II by Baron Wolfgang von Strucker; it initially developed weaponry for his subversive organization Hydra. Although Hydra was defeated during the war, like its mythical namesake it proved hard to destroy.

Publicly, A.I.M. was believed to be an international cartel that developed and marketed new technology. It even supplied the US government with hardware and weaponry. But when a revived Hydra was defeated and A.I.M. members set out to publicly discredit S.H.I.E.L.D. director Nick Fury, A.I.M.'s true nature as a subversive organization became known to intelligence agencies.

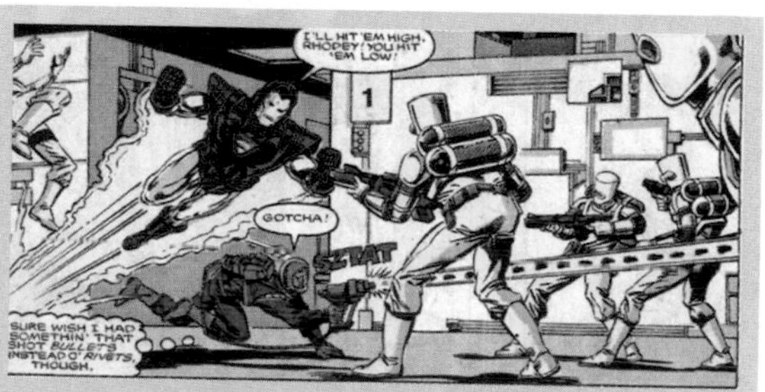
I'LL HIT 'EM HIGH, RHODEY! YOU HIT 'EM LOW!
1
GOTCHA!
SZTAT
SURE WISH I HAD SOMETHIN' THAT SHOT BULLETS INSTEAD O' RIVETS, THOUGH.

Following the deaths of Baron Strucker and most of the principal members of Hydra, A.I.M. fell under the leadership of Modok, who severed all ties with Hydra and put A.I.M. in place as an independent agency. The organization clashed with the Avengers and Iron Man many times, including confrontations in which its members were able to scan and analyze Iron Man's armor. A.I.M. sabotaged satellites and space stations, and threatened the United States with nuclear attacks, but despite the efforts of the Super Hero community, S.H.I.E.L.D., and the crime syndicate known as the Maggia, A.I.M. has never been erased.

Although A.I.M. has hired or utilized superpowered agents to do its bidding, average A.I.M. soldiers and scientists have no specialized powers. They do, however, get to wear the bright yellow jumpsuits and beekeeper-like helmets that have brought them much sartorial scorn from the intelligence and super-human communities.

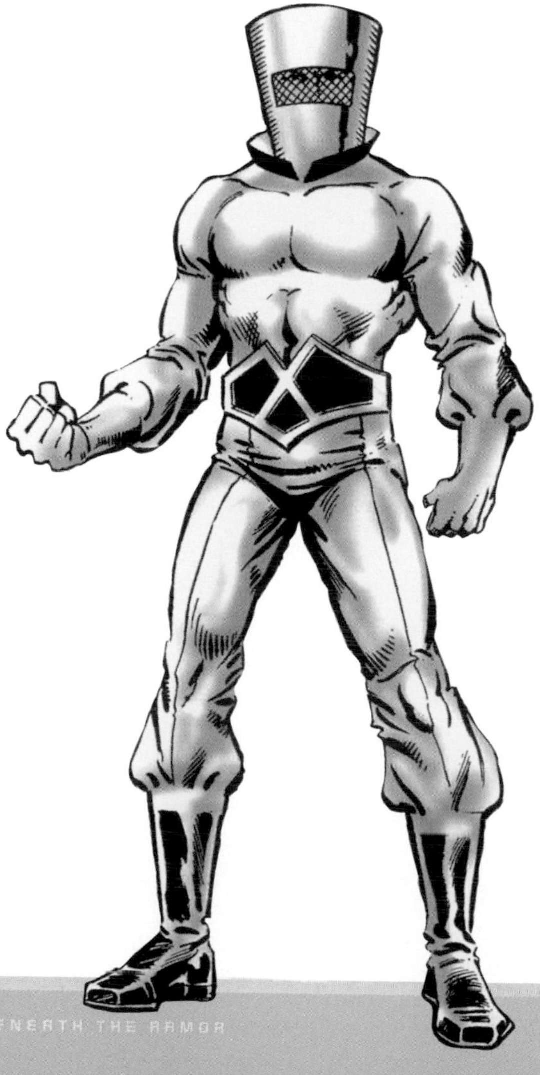

BLIZZARD

Alias: Jack Frost, aka Blizzard (I); Blizzard (II)
Real Name: Gregor Shapanka, aka Donald Gill
Height: 5'6" (I); 5'9" (II)
Weight: 165 lbs. (I); 170 lbs. (II)
Eyes: Brown (I and II), **Hair:** Brown (I and II)

Group Affiliation: Former partner of Whiplash and the Melter (I); Former employee of Hammer Industries (I and II); Former member of Thunderbolts (II)
First Appearance: ***Tales of Suspense* #45** (Jack Frost); ***Iron Man* #86** (Blizzard I); ***Iron Man* #223** (Blizzard II)
Final Appearance: *Amazing Spider-Man Annual* #20 (Blizzard I)

Gregor Shapanka was a Stark Industries research scientist who was also privately researching a way to achieve physical immortality. Planning to sell Stark's micro-transistor designs to finance further research, Shapanka tried to rob his employer's private vault. Shapanka was captured and fired, whereupon he donned an experimental suit he had created that could create intense cold. Nicknamed Jack Frost by the media, Shapanka embarked upon a crime spree to finance himself, and then attempted vengeance against Stark and his closest staff. Frost was captured by Iron Man and sent to prison.

Years later, Shapanka escaped confinement and donned a more powerful cold-generating battle suit, rechristening himself Blizzard. He first attempted to steal Stark's weather-altering climatron device, but was again defeated by Iron Man. Blizzard later allied himself with multimillionaire Justin Hammer, partnering with other costumed criminals Blacklash and the Melter to take down Iron Man. Blizzard was repeatedly defeated, first by the armored avenger and later by Hulk and Spider-Man. Blizzard was eventually vaporized by Arno Stark, the Iron Man of an alternate future.

Justin Hammer utilized a battle suit design similar to Shapanka's to outfit Donny Gill, a young thug who was working for him and became the new Blizzard. Hammer used him several times to attack Iron Man and Force. Although he was given several chances to reform, the Blizzard always returned to a life of crime. Eventually, however, Gill ended up joining the Thunderbolts, a team of ex-villains who operated as Super Heroes.

There was a third Blizzard who donned the costume only once: Randall "Randy" Macklin used one of Shapanka's spare battle suits, but was defeated by Iron Man. Macklin became an employee of Stark Enterprises shortly before Christmas in the *Marvel Holiday Special* (1992).

Although Shapanka accidentally developed some impermanent powers during his time as Jack Frost, the majority of Blizzard's powers were created by his battle suit, which was laced with micro-circuited cryogenic units (micro-cryostats). Using the circuits and water-filled tubing on his costume, he could project intense cold or create mist, sleet, snow, icicles, even ice darts. He could also encase victims in a layer of frost, form an ice barricade, or even create an ice slide on which he could travel. Gill wears a battle suit that has been modified by the Beetle and the Fixer.

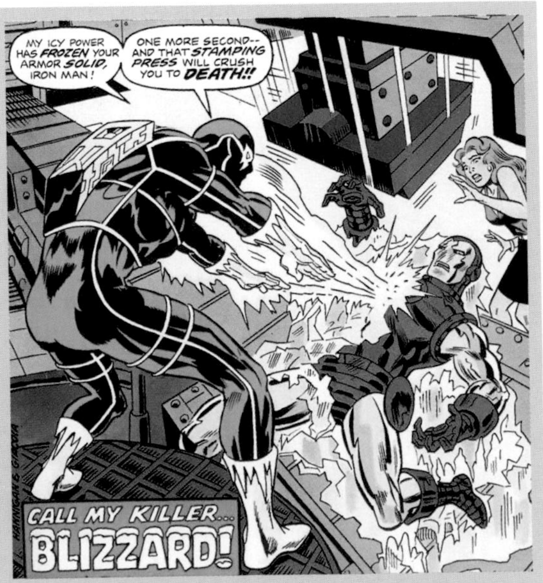
MY ICY POWER HAS FROZEN YOUR ARMOR SOLID, IRON MAN!
ONE MORE SECOND-- AND THAT STAMPING PRESS WILL CRUSH YOU TO DEATH!!
CALL MY KILLER... BLIZZARD!

CONTROLLER

Alias: Controller
Real Name: Basil Sandhurst, aka Alexander Basel
Height: 6'2"(in exoskeleton)
Weight: 565 lbs. (in exoskeleton)
Eyes: White, **Hair:** Black

Group Affiliation: Member of Crossfire's Mind Control Gang; Former agent of Thanos; former agent of the Red Skull; former agent of the Master of the World
First Appearance: *Iron Man* #12

An electromechanical and chemical research scientist at Cord Industries, Basil Sandhurst had a reputation for unorthodox and unethical theories and experimentation, which left him almost unemployable. During a scuffle with Vincent, his visiting brother, Basil was caught in a chemical mishap that left him scarred and paralyzed. Vincent embezzled funds from Cord to set up a private laboratory for his brother, who eventually created a mental-wave absorbatron that could leach cerebral energy away from others and transfer it to an exoskeleton that allowed Sandhurst motility . . . and more!

Using "slave discs" to gather the energy from human victims, Sandhurst christened himself the Controller and enslaved a small town. The act put him into conflict with Iron Man, and he became comatose; a second battle against Iron Man left him similarly defeated. Later, the Controller was aided by the interstellar entity known as Thanos, who used Titanian technology to augment the slave discs and allow the Controller to leave behind the absorbatron technology.

The more powerful Controller battled the Avengers and Captain Mar-Vell, and later upgraded his exoskeleton with stolen Stark technology provided by Justin Hammer. He encountered Iron Man again and again, then worked with the Red Skull to enslave Namor the Sub-Mariner and

the trickster-god Loki, but he was defeated by Captain America. Since then, the Controller has clashed with Iron Man, the Avengers, and Heroes for Hire.

The Controller has a stainless-steel exoskeleton that was micro-surgically attached to his body. Stealing cerebral energy from others and converting it into superhuman powers through the body armor, the Controller gains immense physical strength; if he taps into a person with psionic abilities, he can also gain the power of levitation and the psychokinetic ability to project mental bolts of pure force. He gathers the cerebral energy by attaching slave discs to his victims, whom he can also control and communicate with telepathically. At one time, he channeled the energies through a mental-wave absorbatron, but now he does so directly through his exoskeletal circuitry. He also once utilized a weapon known as a Molecular Negatizer, which shot a powerful beam that could cut through virtually any material; he has used other technology as needed, including boot jets to fly, image inducers, and stun mists.

DREADKNIGHT

Alias: Dreadknight
Real Name: Bram Velsing
Height: 5'8"
Weight: 160 lbs. (without armor)
Eyes: Blue; Red (Dreadknight)
Hair: Blond; None (Dreadknight)

Group Affiliation: Former ally of Morgan Le Fay and Modred
First Appearance: ***Iron Man* #101**

Although he was once a patriotic young scientist serving his country of Latveria, Bram Velsing had higher aspirations than serving the schemes of his monarch Victor von Doom, also known to the world as Doctor Doom. When Velsing's ambitions became known to Doom, the villain had a metal mask fused to Velsing's face, scarring him forever. The wounded Velsing was sent to the Balkan wilderness to perish.

Velsing fled Latveria and eventually found his way to Castle Frankenstein, where he came under the care of Victoria Frankenstein, who was also tending the genetic creations of her great-grandfather Dr. Victor von Frankenstein. Victoria nursed Velsing back to health, but the scientist plotted his revenge against Doom. At the castle, Victoria had also attempted to restore to normal the winged horse of the twentieth-century hero the Black Knight, but she had only succeeded in giving it bat-like wings and other horrifying mutations.

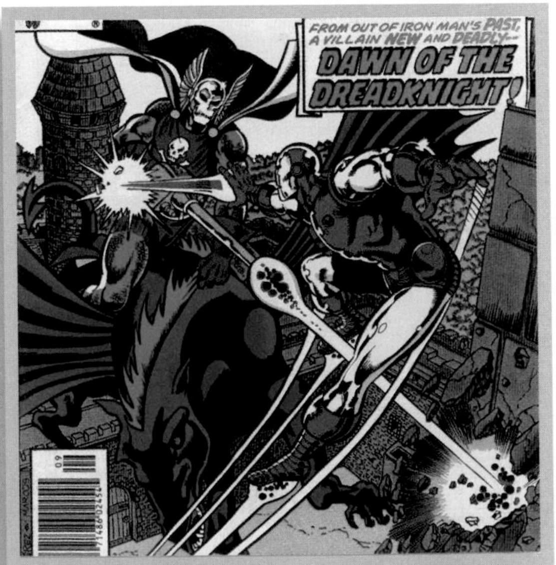
FROM OUT OF IRON MAN'S PAST, A VILLAIN NEW AND DEADLY--
DAWN OF THE DREADKNIGHT!

Taking on the armored identity of Dreadknight, Velsing mounted his steed, Hellhorse. He planned to use Dr. Frankenstein's secret research journals to create monsters to destroy Dr. Doom, but his plans were thwarted by the original Frankenstein monster and Iron Man. Returned to the care of Frankenstein's "Children," Dreadknight recovered and later returned to imperil the world again, fighting against the Black Knight III, plus Spider-Man and Silver Sable. Although his hatred toward Doom seems undiminished, Dreadknight has not resurfaced recently, though his accoutrements were once worn by Avengers member Hawkeye in an infiltration scheme.

Dreadknight wears a full suit of chain mail, which protects him against projectile impact but does not grant him any specialized powers. However, he has constructed a power lance that is equipped with multiple forms of technological offensive abilities: Twin force-blast pods project a concussive electromagnetic beam of charged alpha particles; two spools of electrically conductive steel cable can be magnetically fired at enemy combatants; and two small missile launchers can shoot rocket-propelled penetroshell explosives. As a sidearm, Dreadknight carries a CO_2 pistol that can stream a highly concentrated nerve gas capable of causing near-instantaneous unconsciousness or even respiratory paralysis. Dreadknight rides astride his Hellhorse to fly through the skies, but the beast has no powers other than flight.

FIN FANG FOOM

Alias: Fin Fang Foom
Real Name: Basil, aka Basel
Height: 44' (including tail); 32' (without tail)
Weight: 20 tons
Eyes: Red, **Hair:** None

First Appearance: *Strange Tales* #89

An enormous dragon, Fin Fang Foom was a legend of ancient China that was based in reality—but that reality was extraterrestrial in origin. Foom is a sentient alien from the world of Kakaranathara (also known as Maklu-IV) in the Maklu system of the Greater Magellanic Cloud. Although their homeworld was peaceful, not all of the Kakaranatharans were; eleven of them departed their planet on a ship powered by ten Rings of Power, intent on conquering other planets.

The dragonlike aliens eventually crash-landed on Earth, in ancient China, and the ten surviving Kakaranatharans (or Makluans, as they came to more commonly be known) used their shape shifting powers to mimic the human form. They felt they could study the society better before conquering it if they blended in. Fin Fang Foom was the only one who didn't change; he was placed in an artificial catatonic state in a tomb, held in reserve for the battles that surely were to come.

The Chinese land that held the tomb became known as the Valley of the Sleeping Dragon, and Fin Fang Foom awoke only once—in the eighth century—before he was awakened by teenager Chan Liuchow, who tricked the dragon into fighting the Chinese Communist army. Foom was awakened again in the twentieth century, and controlled by the Mole Man to fight the Fantastic Four. Foom returned to hibernation until he was awakened by a scientist named Dr. Vault; shortly afterward, Foom aided the Living Colossus to repel an alien invasion. Foom, after all, intended that the Makluans would conquer Earth at a later date.

Unbeknownst to the hidden Makluans, a Chinese man discovered their Makluan vessel, whereupon he stole the ten rings that powered it. In time, the man became the villain known as the Mandarin, a foe of Iron Man. Years later, the Mandarin was led to the Valley of the Sleeping Dragon by Chen Hsu, who was really the shape-shifted dragon-like captain of the Makluan vessel. Mandarin awoke Fin Fang Foom and used the dragon to threaten the Chinese government. However, when the other Makluans began to shed their human forms to begin their conquest of Earth, the Mandarin was forced to join with Iron Man and his allies to defeat the dragons.

Although it appeared that Fin Fang Foom was destroyed along with the other Makluans, it proved hard to keep a good dragon down, and Foom has reappeared at numerous times since, battling Iron Man again. He later converted to Buddhism and forswore his world-conquering ways.

Fin Fang Foom has superstrength, wings that allow him to fly at great speed, and the ability to breathe a fire-like combustible acid mist. His skin is tough, but if injured, he can regenerate. He is thousands of years old, and has the power to shape-shift into a human form—or a much larger nonflying dragon form—as well as the ability to communicate telepathically.

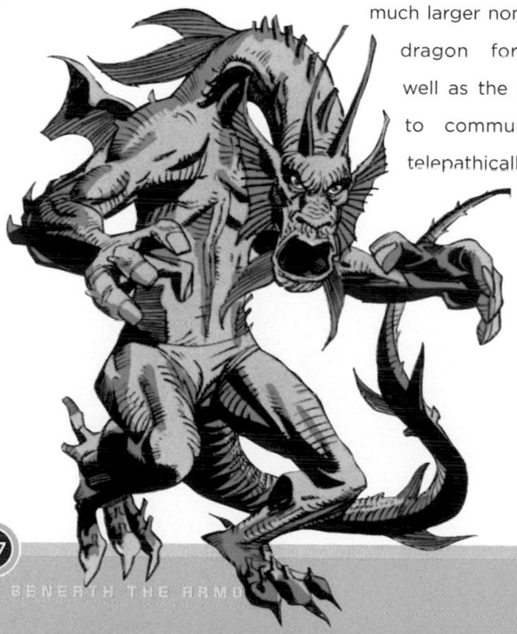

GHOST

Alias: Ghost
Real Name: Unknown
Height: 5'11"
Weight: 175 lbs.
Eyes: Blue, **Hair:** Brown

Group Affiliation: Former agent of Roxxon and A.I.M.; former ally of Spymaster and others
First Appearance: *Iron Man #219*

As a freelance industrial saboteur, the man known as the Ghost is one of the most difficult-to-stop mercenaries that Iron Man has ever encountered. Even his motives remain unclear—he has taken on jobs without compensation. One thing seems constant, however: The Ghost loves to attack and destroy those companies that deal with electronics and technology. It seems an odd vendetta for a man who is himself an inventor, and one who wears a high-tech cybernetic battle suit that allows him to become intangible, invisible, and undetectable to most scanning devices!

The Ghost first encountered Iron Man when the saboteur took on the job of driving Accutech Research and Development into bankruptcy so that it could be bought out by the Roxxon Oil Corporation. Roxxon wanted to get to its scientists' work on a beta particle generator, but Tony Stark bought out the company first. Iron Man encountered the Ghost and drove him away, but the villain swore revenge. Fearing that the Ghost had gone rogue, Roxxon hired Spymaster to kill Ghost, but Spymaster was killed instead. In a near-fatal confrontation, Iron Man used the experimental beta particle generator to trap the Ghost, but the villain still managed to escape.

Reappearing in Italy, the Ghost attacked Electronica Fabbrizi, a company owned by Justin Hammer. The rival industrialist tried to sell the company to Tony Stark, even

agreeing to join forces to stop the Ghost, but Hammer's forces—Blacklash, Blizzard, and Boomerang—could not be trusted. Later, Hammer was confronted by the Ghost, but while both men emerged relatively unscathed, there would be no peace between them. The Ghost didn't immediately strike back at Hammer or Stark, however; he next worked for the Kingpin against Roxxon, then targeted energy research company Tricorp, where he ran afoul of Spider-Man.

Later, the offices of a number of electronics corporations were bombed, with devices hidden inside personal computers. Tony Stark, undercover as a regular employee

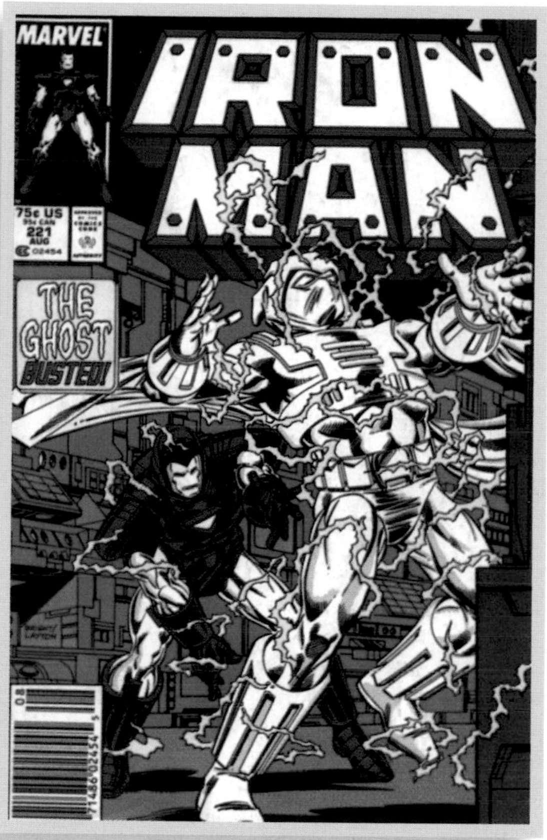
MARVEL
IRON MAN
75¢ US
221
AUG
THE GHOST BUSTED!

at the time, tracked down the attacks to a shell company of A.I.M. He soon learned that A.I.M. had hired the Ghost to eliminate the other businesses. In battle with Iron Man, the Ghost was actually defeated and arrested, but his identity and any information about the man behind the mask were not forthcoming. The Ghost apparently escaped before his past could be revealed.

More recently, the Ghost has reappeared, wearing a new costume and working with the third Spymaster to free the Living Laser from Stark Industries. The Ghost once again attempted to kill Iron Man, but was unsuccessful. He remains at large today, ready to strike again.

JUSTIN HAMMER

Real Name: Justin Hammer
Height: 6'
Weight: 170 lbs.
Eyes: Blue, **Hair:** Gray

Occupation: Industrialist; Employer of many superpowered villains
First Appearance: ***Iron Man* #120**

Although Tony Stark has had to deal with a wide variety of unscrupulous business rivals, the one who plagued him the longest is Justin Hammer, the reclusive industrialist and criminal financier who headed various international design and manufacturing firms. Hammer was pleased when Stark Industries ceased to manufacture munitions and weaponry, rushing to fill the lucrative void, but he would also come into conflict with Tony Stark over the building of an electronics plant in the small Communist country of Carnelia.

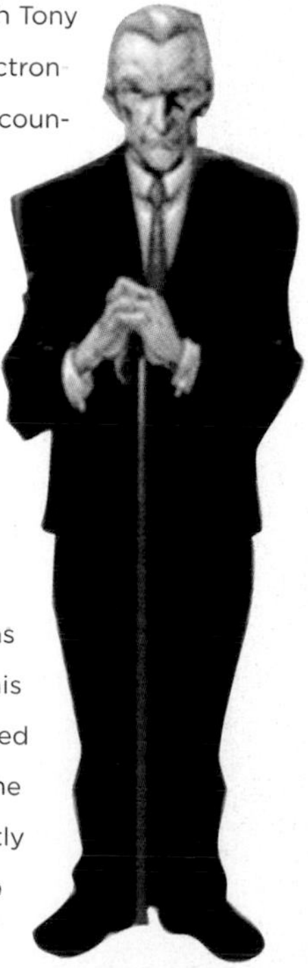

Because Iron Man was an essential part of Stark International's image—and security, of course—Hammer assigned his top engineers to create a way to override Iron Man's armor. The resulting hypersonic device proved troublesome, as some of Iron Man's weapons systems would fire against his will. Hammer eventually activated Iron Man's repulsor unit, killing the Carnelian ambassador and perfectly framing Iron Man! Unable to use his impounded armor, Stark traced Hammer to the Mediterranean Sea, but was taken captive by Hammer's mercenaries.

Stark soon learned that Hammer was providing financing and technology to a variety of super-criminals—including Blacklash, Blizzard, Melter, Man-Killer, Beetle, Spymaster, Leapfrog, the Porcupine, Water Wizard, and the Constrictor—in exchange for 50 percent of their profits. Wrecking the hypersonic device that made his armor unstable, Stark became Iron Man. He soon battled a small army of Super Villains and found evidence to clear himself from the charge of killing the ambassador. Unfortunately, he was unable to prove Hammer's complicity in any crime.

Hammer later bought the secrets of Iron Man's armor technology from Spymaster I, using it in his super-criminal technology. He also kidnapped Stark's girlfriend Bethany Cabe, but while Iron Man was able to severely damage Hammer's huge submarine in his rescue of Cabe, he was again unable to apprehend the man. The billionaire villain would later try to have the criminal Force killed when he decided to leave his life of crime behind; Force was aided in his reformation by Tony Stark.

Hammer then hired Super Villain trainer Taskmaster to help train a second Spymaster to perform industrial spying for him. He also worked with Roxxon and other companies to abduct Super Heroes for study, and to have the Masters of Silence attack Stark Enterprises. When Hammer learned that he was dying, he assigned Spymaster to inject Stark with nanite "rogue cells." The cells made Stark irritable and dangerous, and James Rhodes had to step in to keep Iron Man from doing anything too damaging. Iron Man eventually confronted Hammer at an orbiting space station—on which the man intended to live his final days—but the resulting battle caused the destruction of the station. Hammer's body was frozen in suspended animation in a block of ice, which now orbits the Earth!

LIVING LASER

Alias: Living Laser
Real Name: Arthur Parks
Height: 5'11" (now inapplicable)
Weight: 185 lbs. (now inapplicable)
Eyes: Blue (now inapplicable)
Hair: (now inapplicable)

Group Affiliation: Former member of Batroc's Brigade and the Lethal Legion; Former agent of Mandarin
First Appearance: *Avengers #34*

As with many of Iron Man's foes, the Living Laser was once a brilliant research scientist whose work on weapons technology went awry. Arthur Parks was researching lasers as offensive weaponry, and he eventually fashioned two wrist-mounted laser projectors and a gaudy costume to exact revenge on his ex-girlfriend's fiancé. Shortly afterward, calling himself the Living Laser, Parks became infatuated with the Wasp and abducted her, thus picking a fight with the Avengers.

Imprisoned in New York, the Laser escaped with the help of the Mandarin, and his life as a criminal henchman began, bringing him into conflict with Iron Man, Captain America, and other heroes. Eventually, tired of being defeated, Parks attempted to ramp up his powers by implanting an array of miniature laser diodes in various places on his body. Unfortunately, when he agreed to have his powers augmented by the Maggia's Count Nefaria, the Living Laser found that he could not shut down the energy-gathering diodes . . . he had to expel the energy he absorbed or he would explode!

Parks made a deal with Communist East German agents of the group Heaven's Hand; he would power their laser-armed Russian satellites in exchange for them siphoning off sufficient amounts of his excess energy. But all did not go as planned, and when Iron Man destroyed the siphoning machine, the Laser exploded. Only Parks's corporeal form died in the explosion, however, and he continued to exist as a sentient energy being composed purely of laser light.

Able to create photonic laser blasts or light-based holographic illusions by drawing from energy in the air itself, the now inhuman Living Laser found that he could also create a semi-corporeal body and a three-dimensional holographic image of himself—or any human being. Captured by Iron Man and James Rhodes, the Laser was sent to the West Coast Avengers compound, where Henry Pym attempted to restore his normal form, but the Laser eventually escaped. He encountered Iron Man numerous times afterward—even impersonating the dead Titanium Man and Tony Stark—but despite the aid that Iron Man tried to give the villain in returning to a corporeal form, the Laser remained vengeful. He was later trapped by Iron Man; he remained in a containment unit at Stark International for a while before escaping to continue his half-life of crime.

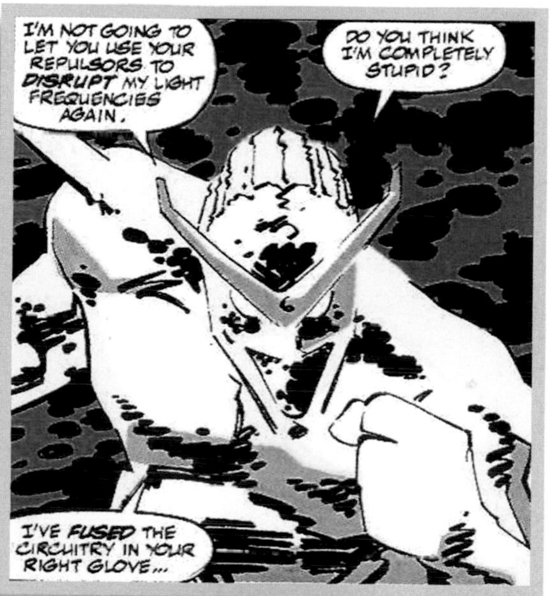
I'M NOT GOING TO LET YOU USE YOUR REPULSORS TO DISRUPT MY LIGHT FREQUENCIES AGAIN.
DO YOU THINK I'M COMPLETELY STUPID?
I'VE FUSED THE CIRCUITRY IN YOUR RIGHT GLOVE...

MODOK

Alias: Modok (Mental Organism Designed Only for Killing)
Real Name: George Tarleton, aka Gerlach and Damocles Rivas
Height: 12'
Weight: 750 lbs.
Eyes: White, **Hair:** Brown

Group Affiliation: Leader of Modok's 11; Former member of A.I.M.; Former associate of the Headmen
First Appearance: ***Tales of Suspense* #93**

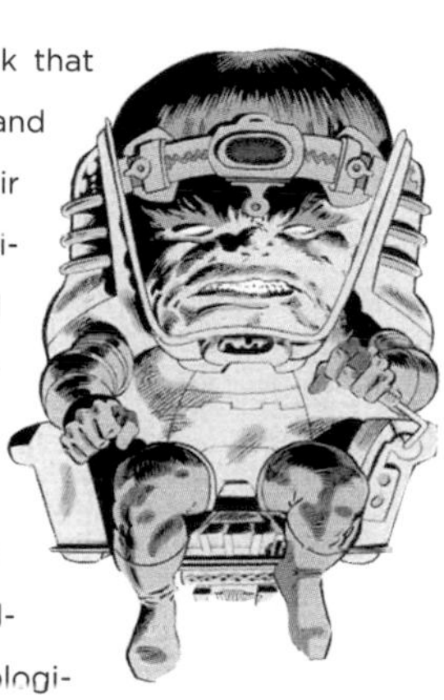

Although one might think that being a twelve-foot-tall head and atrophied body in a hoverchair might get one all the happiness in the world, Modok would be content to tell one otherwise. Modok was once an average technician for A.I.M. (Advanced Idea Mechanics), a criminal cabal comprising brilliant scientists whose technological creations were used for evil. Plucked from the crowd randomly by the Scientist Supreme of A.I.M., George Tarleton was subjected to numerous experiments and bio-engineered mutations in an attempt to create a "living computer" that could explore the mysteries of the powerful Cosmic Cube.

The experiments changed Tarleton into a being whose massive head possessed super-human intelligence and extraordinary psionic powers, but the process drove him insane as well. Although he had been given the designation of M.O.D.O.C. (Mental Organism Designed Only for Computing), once he had slain all those who mutated him and declared himself the new Scientist Supreme, the thing that had been Tarleton changed his acronym to Modok (Mental Organism Designed Only for Killing—although in some appearances, *Mental* has been designated *Mobile*).

The hero Captain America and S.H.I.E.L.D. Agent 13 were the first to confront Modok, but as the giant brain-creature began to control more and more of A.I.M., he also came into conflict with Doctor Doom and the Sub-Mariner, the Hulk, and, eventually, Iron Man. Defeated by the Yellow Claw, Modok was deposed as leader of A.I.M., but he soon allied himself with one faction of the group to attack another faction. Eventually, however, A.I.M. united itself against Modok and put out a hit on him. The Serpent Society killed Modok, and his corpse was returned to A.I.M. for use as a form of living computer. One agent sent Modok's body into battle against Iron Man via remote control, but the mutated corpse was completely annihilated.

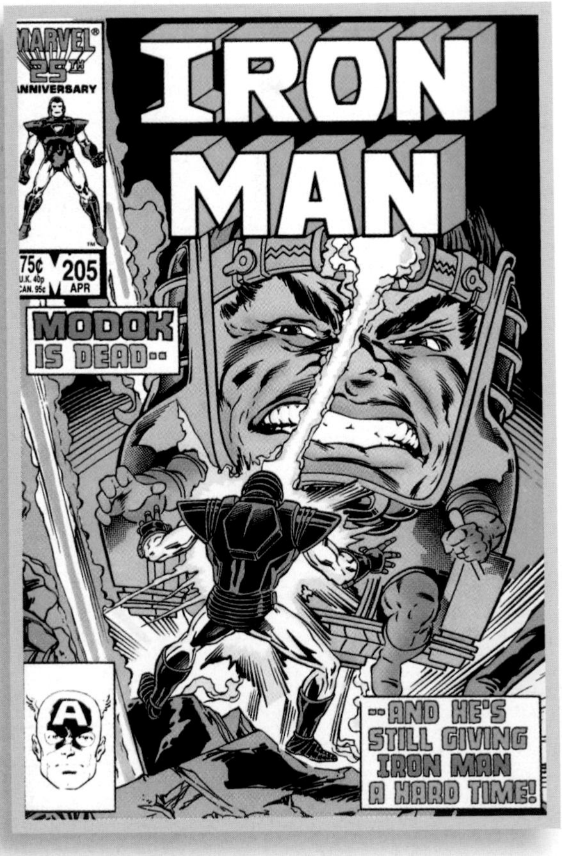

MARVEL 25TH ANNIVERSARY
IRON MAN
75¢ 205 APR
MODOK IS DEAD--
--AND HE'S STILL GIVING IRON MAN A HARD TIME!

Years later, A.I.M. used the Cosmic Cube to restore Modok to life, in an attempt to restore reality, and Modok once more seized control of the organization. Under his command, A.I.M. explored not only scientific research but mystical powers as well. Modok battled many Marvel heroes other than Iron Man over the years, including Alpha Flight, the Defenders, Captain America and the Falcon, Hulk, Deadpool, and even Squirrel Girl. Today he is no longer in control of A.I.M., but Modok recently formed a team of current and former Super Villains—including Armadillo, Chameleon, Nightshade, Living Laser, Mentallo, Puma, Rocket Racer, and Spot—called Modok's 11, which has engaged in various criminal acts when its members aren't struggling among themselves.

Years after Modok's creation, Dr. Katherine Waynesboro was briefly transformed into a female Modok counterpart called Ms. Modok. The giant woman nearly married Modok until she turned against him, escaped A.I.M. control, and was returned to her normal form. Later, an unnamed woman was mutated into a large-headed creature nearly identical in appearance to Modok. Designated S.O.D.A.M. (Specialized Organism Designed for Aggressive Maneuvers), her name was later changed to M.O.D.A.M. (Mental Organism Designed for Aggressive Maneuvers). She remains at large.

Despite his grotesque and bizarre appearance, Modok is a formidable foe. His magnetically powered hoverchair has dozens of built-in weapons, and although his near-atrophied body is useless, Modok's mental powers are vast. In addition to his unparalleled intellect, he can project force fields, produce blasts of heat and psionic energy, telepathically probe minds, and even decorporealize himself and transmit his energy form as raw data through the Internet! In the past, he has also used a forty-foot robotic body that is proportionate to the size of his head.

SPYMASTER

Alias: Spymaster (I, II, III)
Real Name: Unrevealed; Nathan Lemon; Sinclair Abbot
Height: 6' (I); 5'11" (II); 6' (III)
Weight: 195 lbs. (I); 190 lbs. (II); 198 lbs. (III)
Eyes: Blue (I); Brown (II); Blue (III), **Hair:** Brown

Group Affiliation: Former leader of the Espionage Elite (I) and the Espionage Elite II (II); Former employee of A.I.M., Justin Hammer, the Maggia, Roxxon Oil, S.H.I.E.L.D., Zodiac I, and others
First Appearance: ***Iron Man* #33** (Spymaster I); ***Iron Man* #254** (Spymaster II); ***Iron Man: The Inevitable* #1** (Spymaster III)
Final Appearance: ***Iron Man* #220** (Spymaster I); ***Iron Man: The Inevitable* #2** (Spymaster II)

The original Spymaster's true identity has never been disclosed, but he first came to Iron Man's attention when he led an industrial spy cadre called Espionage Elite to raid Stark Industries at the behest of the subversive organization Zodiac. In the process of sabotaging Stark's Long Island complex, the Elite were captured in the battle with Iron Man, but Spymaster escaped after shooting S.H.I.E.L.D. agent Jasper Sitwell. Shortly afterward, Zodiac sent Spymaster on another raid with some of its own superpowered members, putting them in conflict with Iron Man and Daredevil.

Later, Spymaster was assigned to assassinate Anthony Stark by four S.H.I.E.L.D. agents who were acting without the knowledge or permission of director Nick Fury. Spymaster bombed Stark's penthouse, then destroyed an android Life Model Decoy of Stark, which he believed to be his real target. Invading Stark International's main computer center to steal computer records, Spymaster was confronted by Iron Man, but escaped again.

Over the following years, Spymaster would encounter Iron Man repeatedly, but the costumed criminal always managed to escape. At one time, he managed to steal Tony Stark's briefcase, which contained his armor. During one of his raids against Stark, Spymaster stole the designs for many of Stark's inventions, which the hero had incorporated into his Iron Man armor; Spymaster then sold them to criminal financier Justin Hammer, who used the technology in battle suits worn by various criminals he sponsored. Spymaster appeared to also have learned that Stark was Iron Man, but he did not sell that secret to anyone. Still, his leak of the armor secrets would eventually lead to the Armor Wars.

On a mission to kill the Ghost, another super-criminal, Spymaster again encountered Iron Man at Stark Enterprises; attempting to escape with his fellow criminal, Spymaster was double-crossed by the Ghost, who materialized Spymaster's body halfway through a wall he had been phasing through. Spymaster was killed instantly.

A second Spymaster was trained by the Taskmaster at the behest of Justin Hammer, but his identity was also a mystery, although Iron Man would later deduce that he was named Nathan Lemon prior to becoming the Spymaster. Iron Man encountered this new criminal several times—as did the Avengers, She-Hulk, and Silver Sable and her Wild Pack—but it was the armored avenger who eventually sent Spymaster to prison. There, Lemon was attacked and killed by an agent of Sinclair Abbot.

Abbot, a rich man who contributed to charitable causes through the Abbott Foundation, had a great contempt for Tony Stark. He would become the third Spymaster, teaming with the Ghost to take

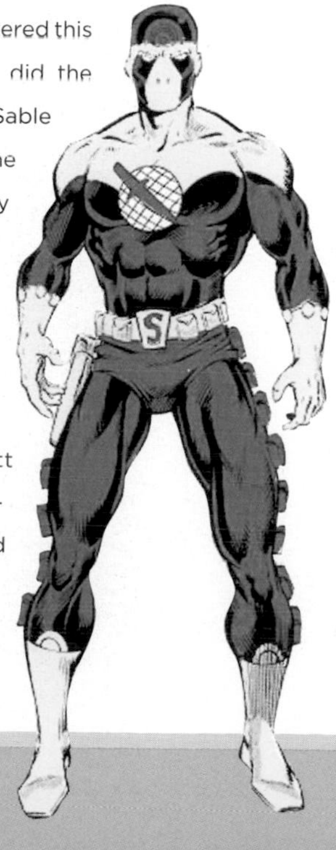

down Stark and Iron Man. He escaped during a battle between Iron Man and the Living Laser, though it appeared that his wife, Greta, was killed either by the Living Laser or during the destruction of Abbott's mansion. Spymaster later attempted to use Harold "Happy" Hogan to lure Stark to his death, but Hogan attacked Spymaster, and they both fell several stories from an airport hangar scaffolding to hit the tarmac below. Hogan was left comatose and eventually died, but Spymaster's whereabouts are unknown.

None of the Spymasters has ever had super-human powers, though they have all been trained in various forms of hand-to-hand combat, weapons usage, and espionage. They have all been outfitted with Kevlar bodysuits that protect them, as well as a wide variety of high-tech weaponry, including energy-blasting gloves, electrical nets, razor-sharp discs, energy siphoners, and stun guns. Abbott's helmet is equipped with a voice-masking system and an image inducer, which apparently disguised him when Iron Man unmasked him in battle.

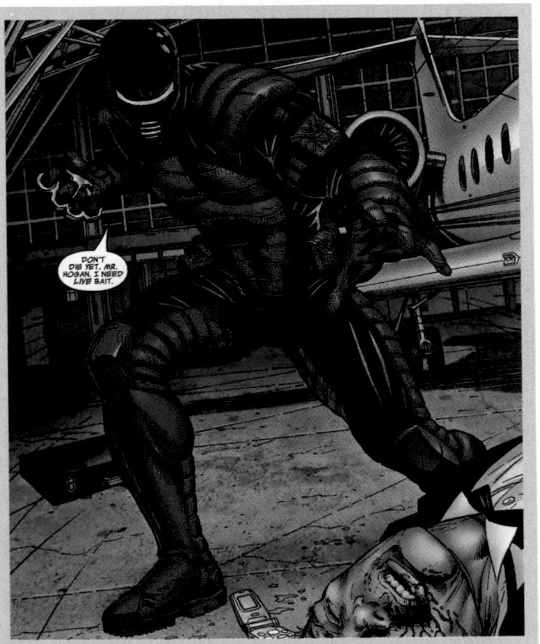
DON'T DIE YET, MR. HOGAN. I NEED LIVE BAIT.

TITANIUM MAN

Alias: Titanium Man (I and II)
Real Name: Boris Bullski (I); Topolov (first name unrevealed), aka the Gremlin (II)
Height: 7'1" (I); 4'6" (without armor, II)
Weight: 425 lbs. (I); 215 lbs. (without armor, II)
Eyes: Blue (I); Blue (II), **Hair:** Black (I); None (II)

Group Affiliation: Former member of the Hammer, Remont 4, the Green Liberation Front, and the Titanic Three; Former partner of Black Widow, Secret Defenders (I); Former member of Soviet Super Soldiers (II)
First Appearance: ***Tales of Suspense* #69** (Titanium Man I); ***Incredible Hulk* #187** (Titanium Man II)
Final Appearance: ***Iron Man* #229** (Titanium Man II)

Once a high-level official in the Communist Party during the Cold War, Boris Bullski was known as Boris the Merciless for his intimidating size and uninhibited ambition. Nervous Kremlin officials decided to inhibit him by transferring him to administrate at a work camp in Siberia. The sadistic Bullski ruled the camp ruthlessly, but came up with a plan: He forced the scientists at the camp to create an immense suit of green superpowered titanium armor for him. He reasoned that if he could beat the American hero Iron Man, he could prove that Communism was better than Democracy . . . and he would be made premier of the Soviet empire.

The Titanium Man armor was created in the same laboratory as the original Crimson Dynamo armor had been, but the new battle suit was nearly twice the size since the scientists did not have the micro-transistor technology that Stark had used. It gave Bullski incredible strength and the ability to fly, and was equipped with an impressive weapons system. As Titanium Man, Bullski challenged Iron Man to a televised battle, and—knowing he couldn't allow the United States to be mocked by a Communist—Iron Man agreed.

Thankfully, after a tense battle, Iron Man defeated

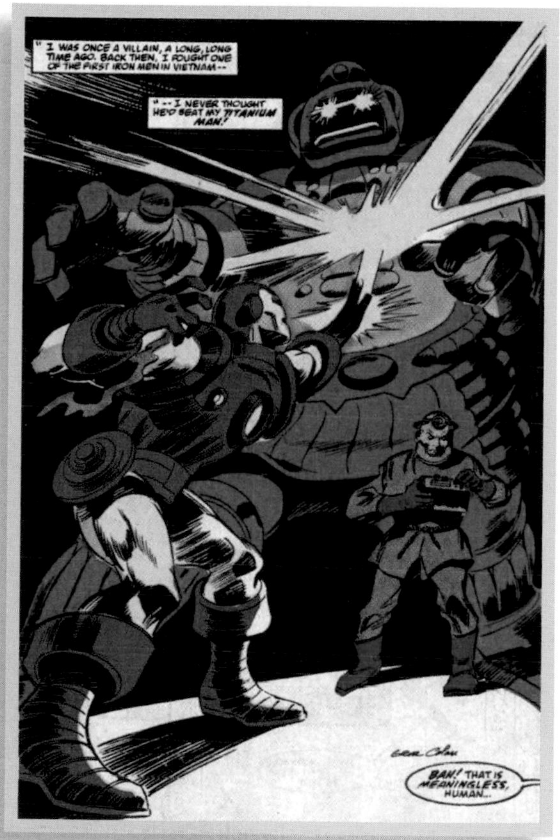
"I WAS ONCE A VILLAIN, A LONG, LONG TIME AGO. BACK THEN, I FOUGHT ONE OF THE FIRST IRON MEN IN VIETNAM--
"--I NEVER THOUGHT HE'D BEAT MY TITANIUM MAN!"
BAH! THAT IS MEANINGLESS, HUMAN...

Titanium Man, taking his helmet as a souvenir. Bullski returned to fight Iron Man soon, in Washington, DC, wearing an even larger suit of armor equipped with more weaponry, including a paralysis ray, force blasters, and more. Despite the improvements, the armored Avenger beat Titanium Man again.

The cycle of battles between Titanium Man and Iron Man became regular, with the Communist villain often upgrading his armor—adding an Ocular Destructo-Beam, flight rockets, and a device that magnetized his armor—but never managing to best his foe. Titanium Man sometimes worked alone, though he later teamed with the Crimson Dynamo and Radioactive Man as the Titanic Three.

Bullski has died and come back numerous times over the years, being resurrected through mechanical and biological means, and even through the cosmic powers of Thanos, but every time he faced Iron Man, he lost. Meanwhile, a diminutive man known as the Gremlin became the second Titanium Man, serving for some time with the Soviet Super Soldiers. During the Armor Wars, the Gremlin lost his life in battle with Iron Man, when Iron Man's boot jets accidentally ignited the Titanium Man armor and it exploded.

Recently, a possible third Titanium Man appeared, attacking Stark Enterprises; later, a Titanium Man who identified himself as Andy Stockwell was revealed to be an agent in the Communist sleeper cells of the Hammer. Titanium Man also appeared during the recent Civil War among super-humans that followed passage of the Superhuman Registration Act. Whether any of the new sightings of the Titanium Man are really Boris Bullski in disguise has yet to be revealed.

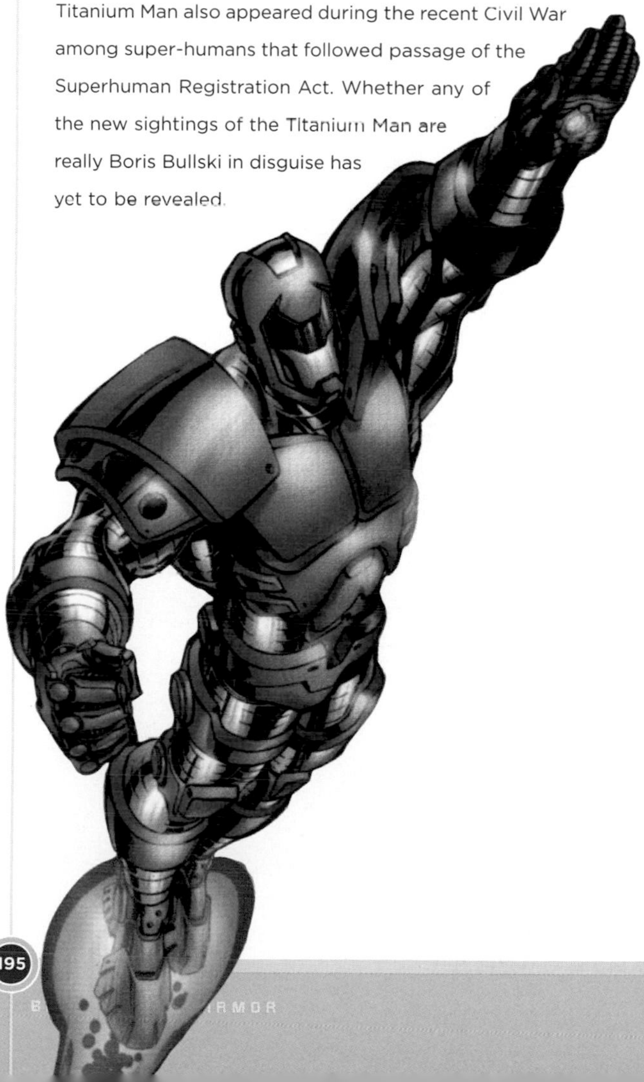

WHIPLASH

Alias: Whiplash, aka Blacklash
Real Name: Mark Scarlotti
Height: 6'1"
Weight: 215 lbs.
Eyes: Blue, **Hair:** Blond

Group Affiliation: Former agent of the Maggia; Former partner of the Melter, Man-Bull, and the Wraith; Former associate of Justin Hammer
First Appearance: ***Tales of Suspense* #97** (Whiplash); ***Iron Man* #146** (Blacklash)
Final Appearance: ***Iron Man* volume III #28**

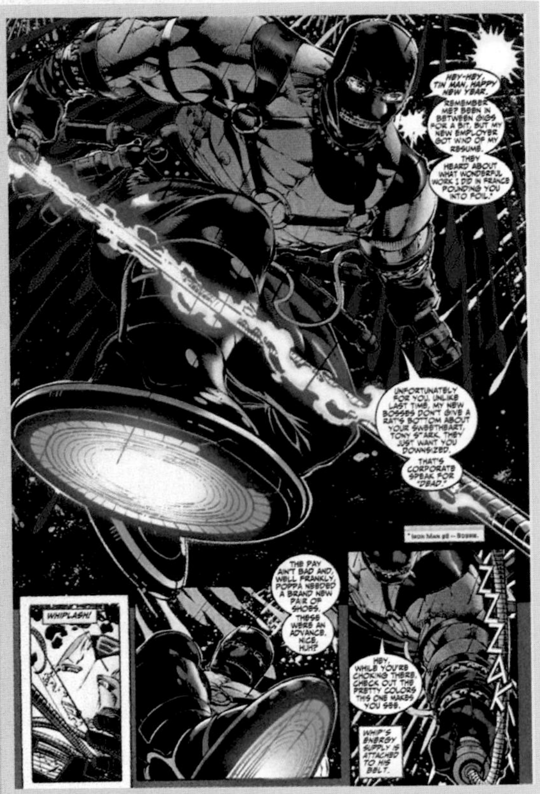
HEY-HEY, TIN MAN, HAPPY NEW YEAR.
REMEMBER ME? BEEN IN BETWEEN GIGS FOR A BIT, BUT MY NEW EMPLOYER GOT WIND OF MY RESUME.
THEY HEARD ABOUT WHAT WONDERFUL WORK I DID IN FRANCE POUNDING YOU INTO FOIL.*
UNFORTUNATELY FOR YOU, UNLIKE LAST TIME, MY NEW BOSSES DON'T GIVE A RAT'S BOTTOM ABOUT YOUR SWEETHEART, TONY STARK. THEY JUST WANT YOU DOWNSIZED.
THAT'S CORPORATE SPEAK FOR "DEAD."
WHIPLASH!
THE PAY AIN'T BAD AND, WELL FRANKLY, POPPA NEEDED A BRAND NEW PAIR OF SHOES.
THESE WERE AN ADVANCE. NICE, HUH?
HEY, WHILE YOU'RE CHOKING THERE, CHECK OUT THE PRETTY COLORS THIS ONE MAKES YOU SEE.
WHIP'S ENERGY SUPPLY IS ATTACHED TO HIS BELT.

Engineer Mark Scarlotti worked for the Maggia crime syndicate as a weapons designer, creating technological weapons. His best invention was a steel-fiber whip that was capable of piercing three-inch steel. An expert with this whip, Scarlotti decided that he could make more money as a costumed agent for the Maggia, so he created the costume and name of Whiplash. Early on, he battled Iron Man to a stalemate, winning himself a reputation in the underworld.

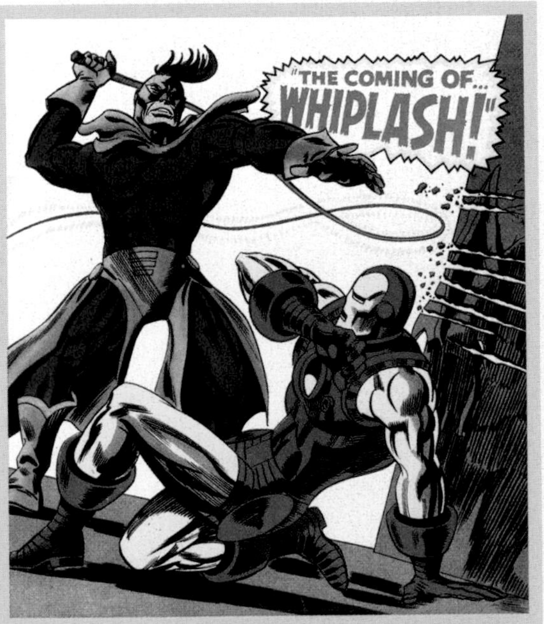
"THE COMING OF... WHIPLASH!"

Later, the Maggia assigned Scarlotti to infiltrate Stark International's Cincinnati plant to steal its secrets. The assignment eventually brought him into conflict with Iron Man again, and Whiplash again escaped unscathed. But after Whiplash joined with the Melter and Man-Bull to work for the extradimensional Black Lama, he was defeated and jailed. Later, Whiplash was driven almost insane by an ally of Iron Man called the Wraith.

Once he recovered, Whiplash was approached by criminal financier Justin Hammer. His sponsor promised that he would help upgrade and finance Whiplash for 50 percent of his profits; Hammer was already working in the same manner with dozens of other costumed criminals. Scarlotti renamed himself Blacklash and upgraded his weaponry, then returned to the life of a freelance mercenary. Later encounters with Iron Man—sometimes in partnership with criminals such as the Beetle and Blizzard II—never ended well, however, and Blacklash's reputation went downhill. He married and tried to leave his life of crime behind, but his wife was brutally attacked by an assassin called Shatter-head.

Recently, Scarlotti changed his name back to Whiplash and used his newly upgraded weapons against Iron Man again, this time while sporting a chest-baring all-leather fetish-style outfit. They clashed twice—resulting in Tony Stark's identity being revealed to the world as Iron Man—but the third time, Whiplash was facing the Iron Man armor that had gained its own sentience. The sentient armor beat Whiplash to death in midair, then dropped his corpse into a river. There have since been others using the code names Scarlotti employed, including a female member of the Femme Fatales as Whiplash, and a fetish-costumed husband-and-wife team of Whiplash and Blacklash who have been members of the Thunderbolts.

Whiplash's weapons included two cybernetically controlled whips housed in his gauntlets that could be converted into nunchakus or vaulting poles, spun fast to create a wind, or cracked in the style of a bullwhip with the power to cut through steel. His armament also included an electrically charged necro-lash, antigravity or heavy gravity bolas, a kinetic whip, a cat-o'-nine-tails, and a whip made of superconductive filament that channeled lightning or energy blasts offensively. Later in his career, he also used a flying platform and jet discs for midair combat, and a cybernetic flying harness so that he could wield multiple whips at once.

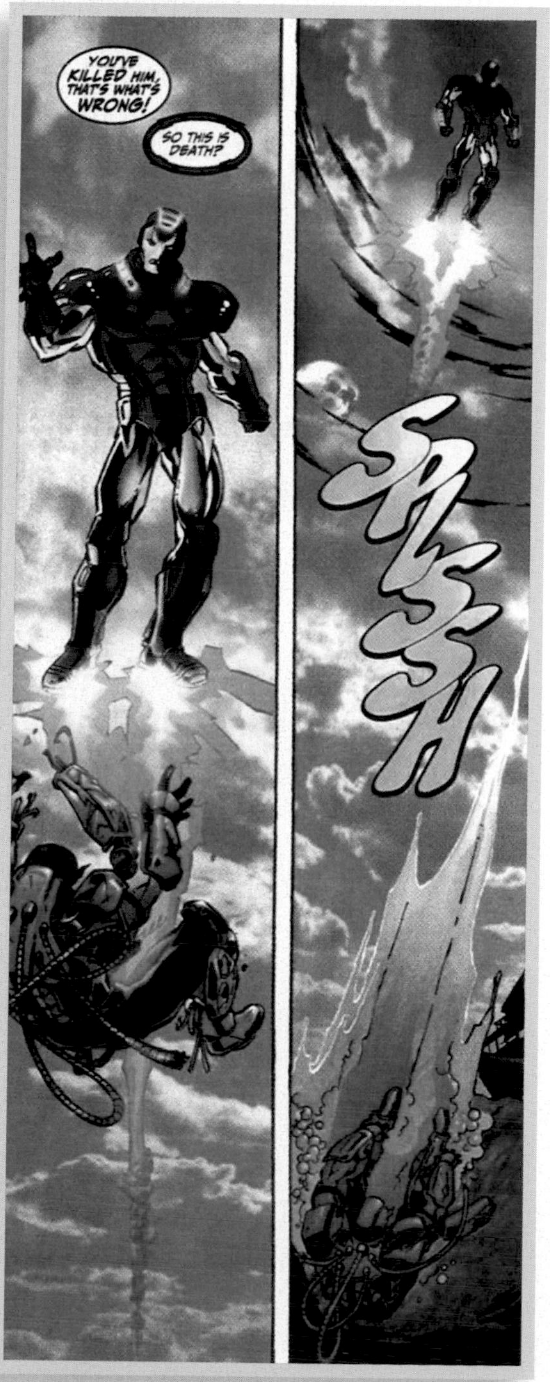
YOU'VE KILLED HIM, THAT'S WHAT'S WRONG!
SO THIS IS DEATH?
SPLASH

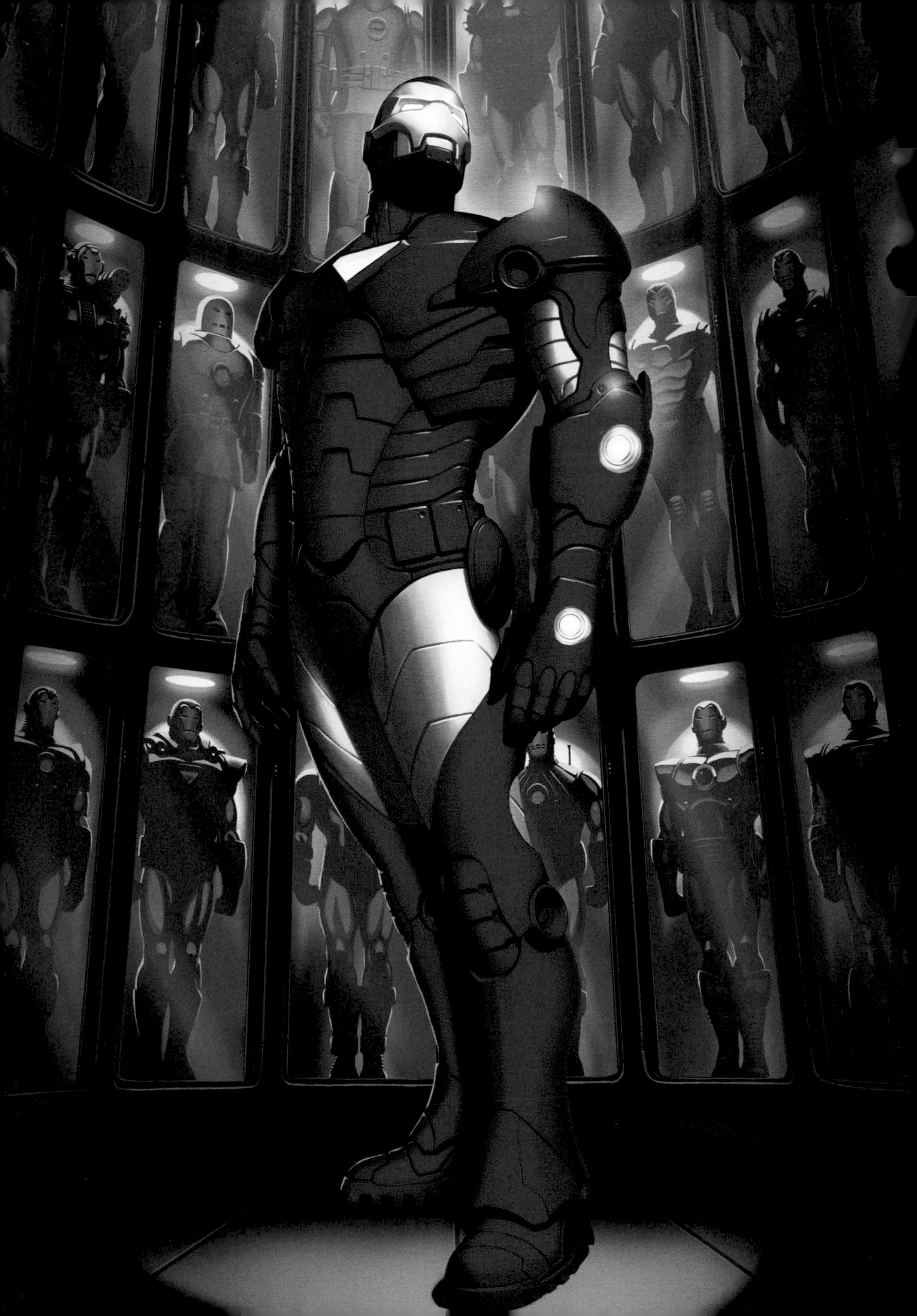

ARMOR GALLERY

ARMOR ILLUSTRATIONS BY IAN FULLWOOD

GREY ARMOR

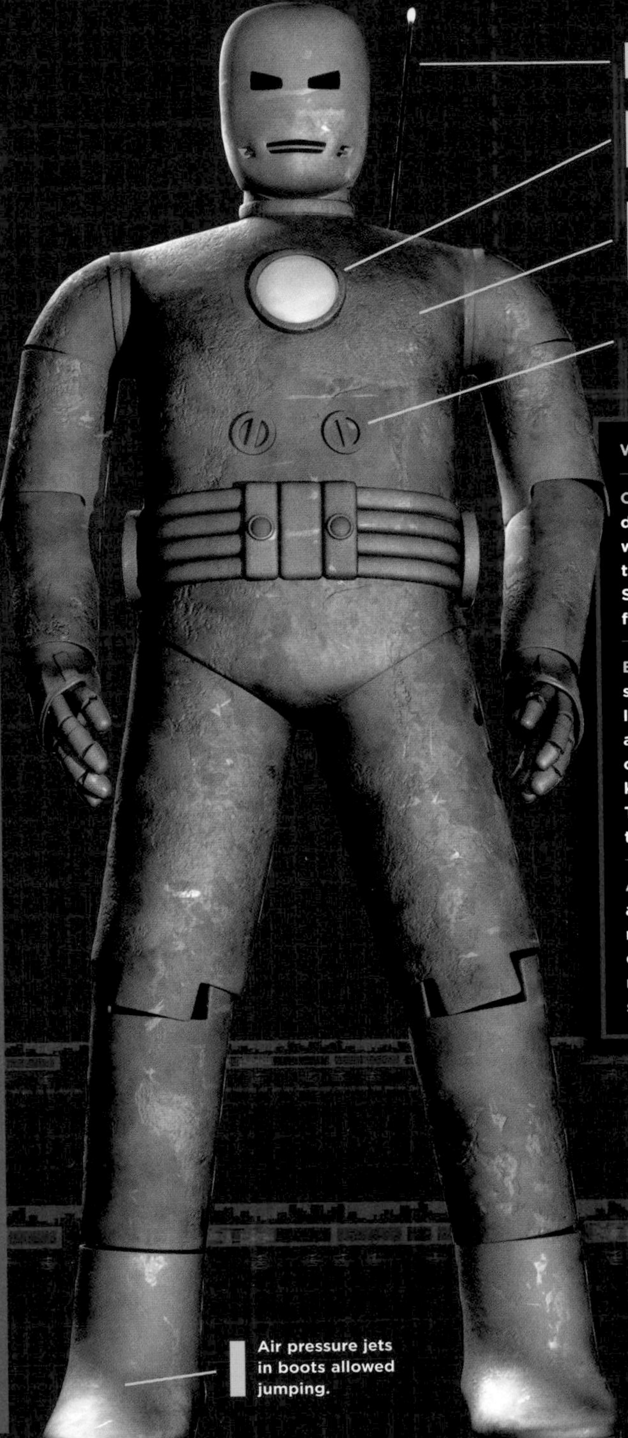
Telescoping antenna enhanced two-way radio communication.
Chestplate contained a Monobeam, and later, a Proton Beam Generator and heat beam.
Chestplate could be worn independently under clothes to act as life support for Tony Stark.
Recharging plugs could be connected to wall outlets or other energy power sources.
Air pressure jets in boots allowed jumping.

WORN BY: Tony Stark, Eddie March

CREATION AND VARIATION: This armor is the first design created by Tony Stark and Ho Yinsen, and worn by Tony Stark. It originally appeared only a few times, before being painted gold. Over the years, Stark would re-create this original armor in similar forms, and would wear it into battle.

BASICS: Created from a variety of metals, this bulky suit was a significant form of powered body armor. It was resistant to heat, cold, energy, and acidic attacks, as well as small-caliber projectiles. The chestplate also contained a pacemaker, designed to keep Stark's heart from being stopped by shrapnel. The armor was powered electrically by miniature transistors, which had to be constantly recharged.

ABILITIES: Stark would regularly add technology to all of his armors. Some of his additions included a miniature finger-mounted buzz saw, transistorized electromagnets to allow magnetic attraction or repulsion, suction cups to adhere to walls or ceilings, short-wave radios, and more.

First Appearance:
Tales of Suspense #39

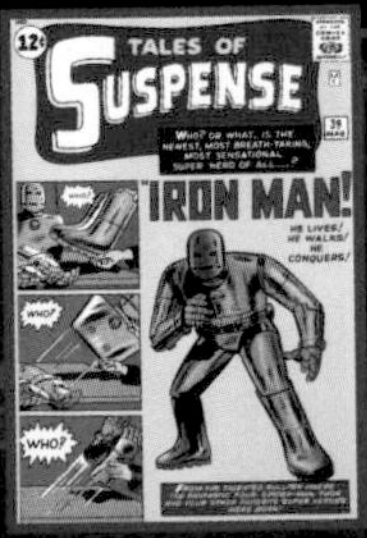
12¢
TALES OF
SUSPENSE
39
IRON MAN!
WHO?
WHO?
WHO?

CLASSIC ARMOR

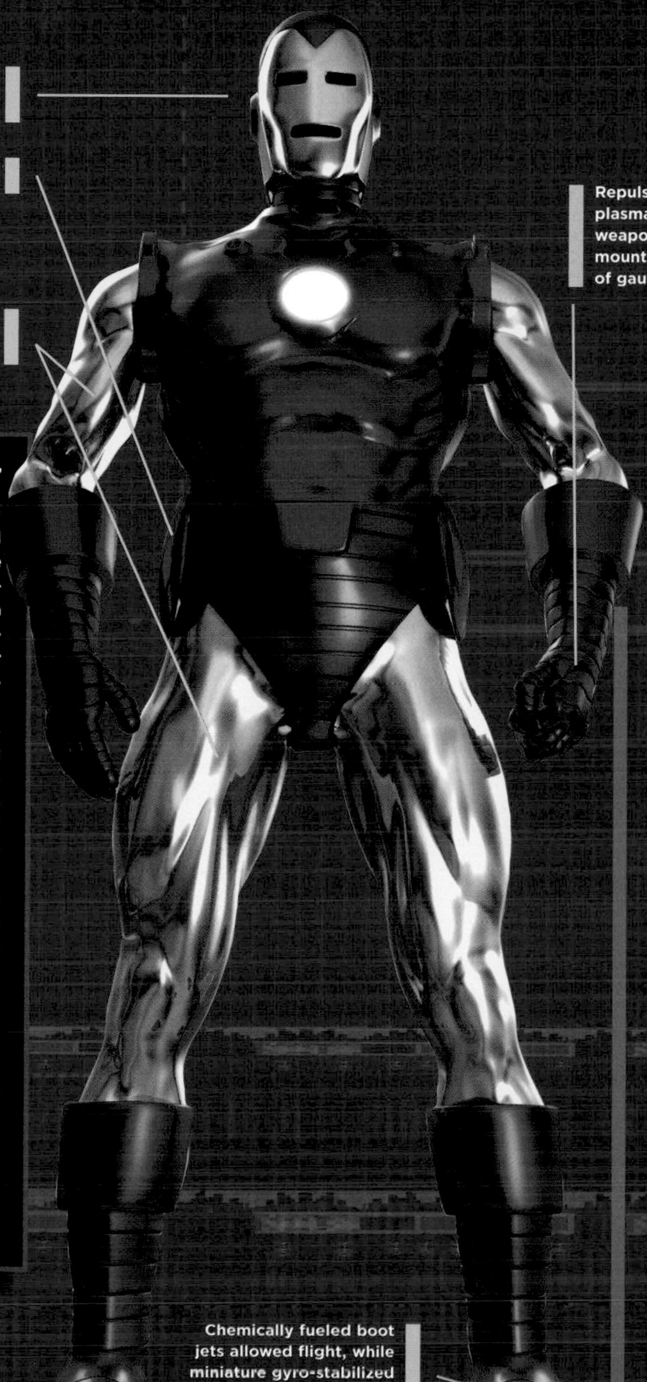
Cybernetic interface controls mounted inside helmet could be controlled by tongue, or later, by voice command.
Energy pods allowed wearer to recharge batteries.
Flexible molecular-scale chain mail could be folded into briefcase, then activated by a magnetic field to create a rigid armor.
Repulsor ray plasma-projecting weapons were mounted in palm of gauntlets.
Chemically fueled boot jets allowed flight, while miniature gyro-stabilized turbines enhanced maneuverability.

WORN BY: Tony Stark, Happy Hogan, Eddie March, James Rhodes, Michael O'Brien, Carl Walker

CREATION AND VARIATION: This red and gold armor was created and worn by Tony Stark. The armor shown would go through cosmetic and technological changes, resulting in the design shown here. Early versions included stripes on the chest-plate, rivets on the faceplate, and a lack of power pods, while a later version saw a nose added to the faceplate.

BASICS: This streamlined suit significantly ramped up the power and comfort level of its wearer. The armor was still powered electrically, with chargeable batteries, but was eventually modified to absorb and utilize solar power. The exterior was a flexible iron alloy that could harden to resist attack, but allowed a full range of movement. The integrated circuitry control systems for the armor and its weapons were mounted inside the helmet and on wrist-mounted controls on the gauntlets.

ABILITIES: Over the two decades that Stark wore this armor and its variants, many changes were made to it. Additions included collapsible jet-powered roller skates in the boot soles, weapons such as the Vapor Ejector and Variobeam Tracer, and defensive devices including force fields, fire extinguishers, and holographic image emitters. The most significant new weapon was the "repulsor ray," which was initially slipped on over the glove, and eventually mounted in the palm of each hand.

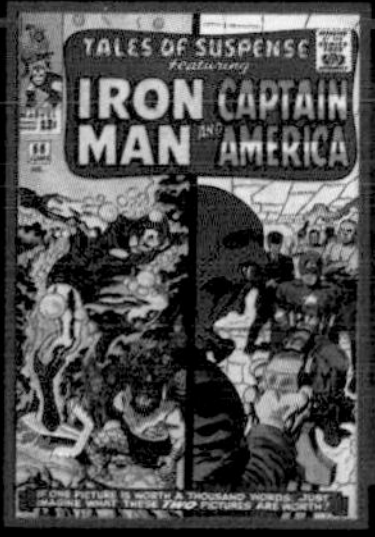
TALES OF SUSPENSE
IRON MAN
CAPTAIN AMERICA

First Appearance:
Tales of Suspense #66

SILVER CENTURION ARMOR

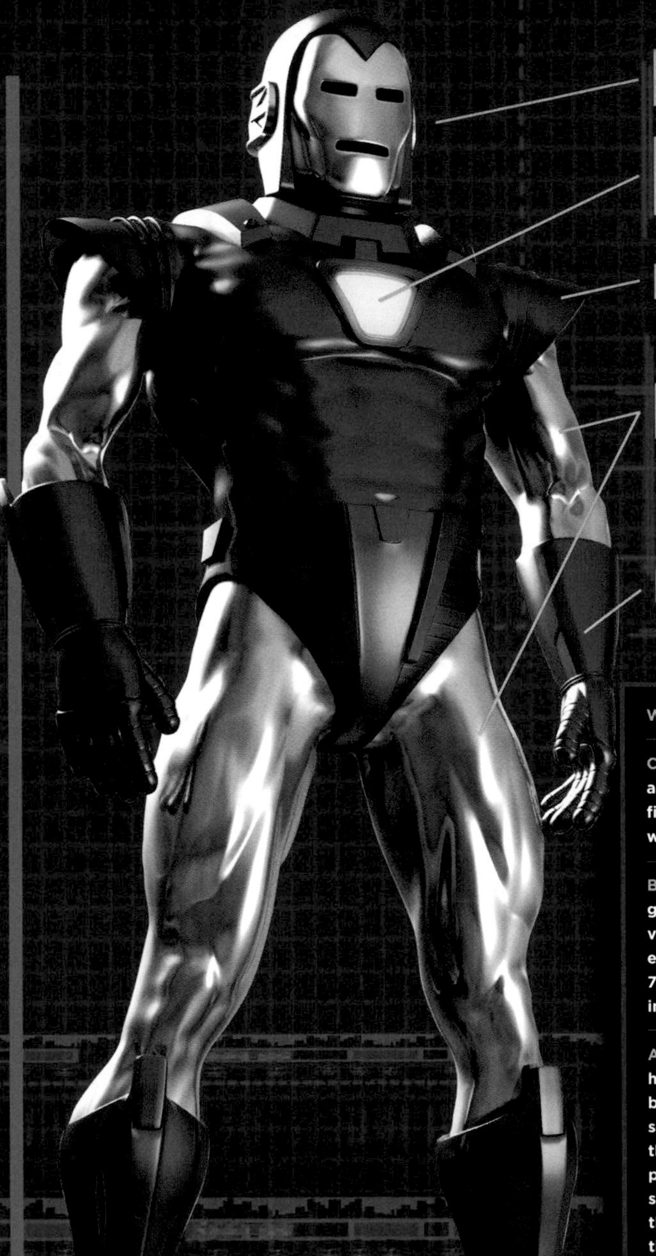

Mouth and eye slits could be sealed for life-support purposes, while the suit could recycle air.

Chest-mounted Unibeam used light and energy to emit a search light, heat beams, tractor beam, lasers, image inducers, and ultraviolet light rays.

Reinforced shoulder-mounted solar power converters.

Sensors in the body of the armor could measure magnetic fields, and allowed the suit sonar, radar, and infrared capabilities.

Gauntlets contained computerized navigation interfaces and displays.

WORN BY: **Tony Stark, Michael O'Brien**

CREATION AND VARIATION: **This red and silver armor was created and worn by Tony Stark. It was first worn into battle against Obadiah Stane, who was wearing a giant suit of armor as Iron Monger.**

BASICS: **With more powerful computers and stronger weapons, this suit of armor improved on all versions to date. It also contained a separate twin engine rocket system, able to attain speeds of 750 mph in the air, or 180 mph when submerged in water.**

ABILITIES: **New weapons included gauntlet-controlled high-energy plasma discharges known as "pulse bolts," and devices that created a disruptor field, sonic distortion, and heat beams. For a short time, the suit also featured a "chameleon effect," which projected holograms of a background across the surface of the armor, rendering it nearly invisible; that feature was dropped because it interfered with the wearer's nervous system.**

First Appearance:
***Iron Man* #200**

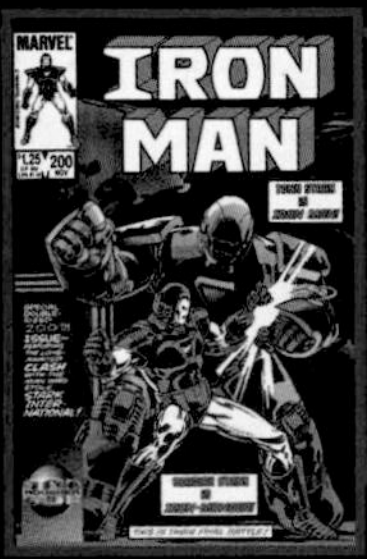
MARVEL
IRON MAN
200

MODERN CLASSIC ARMOR

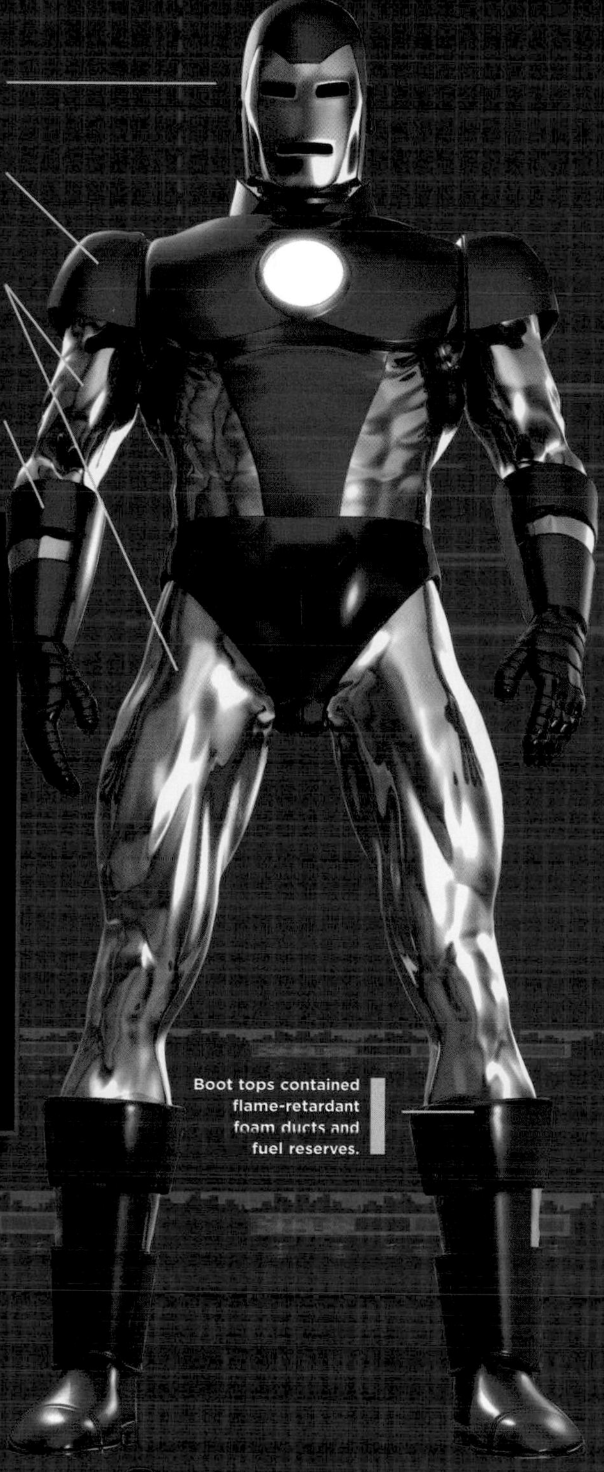

The helmet contained ear protectors to baffle incoming high-decibel sounds, while automatic polarized lenses in the eye slots could protect the wearer from blinding lights.

Shoulderpads contained a Beta Particle Generator to power the armor.

The surface of the armor contained an embedded absorption grid, which collected and redirected energy from attacks or outside power sources.

In addition to repulsor circuitry, the gauntlets contained pulse bolt and energy shield generators.

Boot tops contained flame-retardant foam ducts and fuel reserves.

WORN BY: **Tony Stark, Bethany Cabe**

CREATION AND VARIATION: **Following the events of the first "Armor Wars," Tony Stark created this new red and gold armor, reminiscent of his longest-lasting suit. After Stark was shot and partially paralyzed, he used a remote-control version of this armor, then wore an electro-mesh bodysuit underneath the armor to enhance his mobility.**

BASICS: **This was the first set of armor to incorporate the Beta Particle Power Supply, although it did convert solar power as a backup energy supply. The armor's surface could also absorb energy from attacks or other power sources to recharge itself.**

ABILITIES: **An electromagnetic pulse (E.M.P.) weapon was powerful enough to knock out electrical systems for a one-mile radius, but the pulse also shut down the Iron Man armor for a six-minute reboot. The suit's computerized system also gained a translation matrix, which allowed Iron Man to translate multiple non-English languages, and the helmet's visor contained an L.E.D. tactical display.**

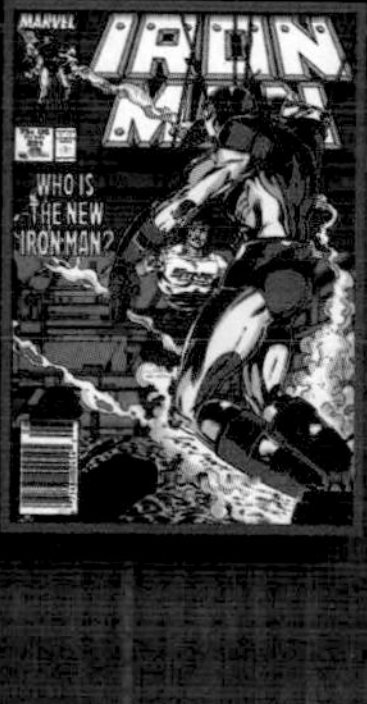
MARVEL
IRON MAN
WHO IS THE NEW IRON MAN?

First Appearance:
Iron Man #231

WAR MACHINE ARMOR

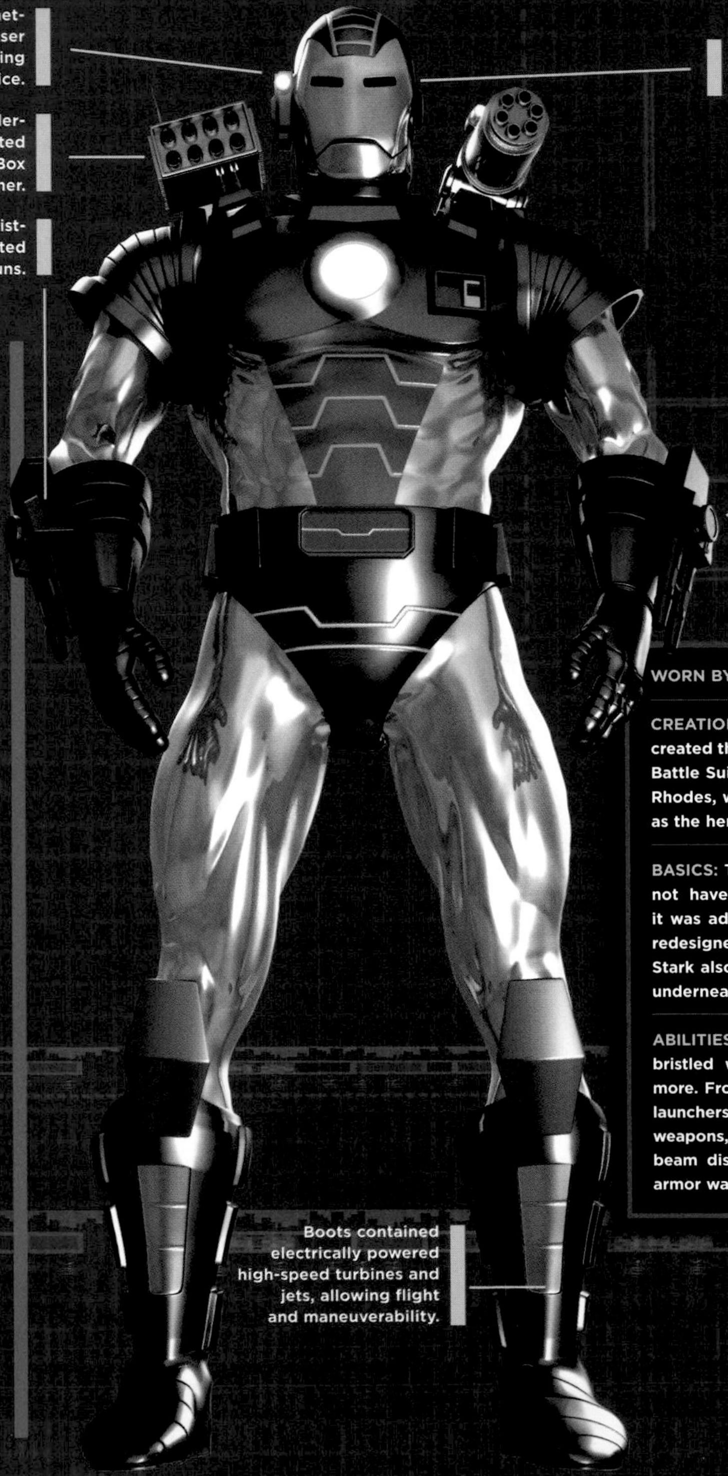
Helmet-mounted laser targeting device.
Shoulder-mounted Missile Box launcher.
Wrist-mounted guns.
The helmet contained ultrasound sensors and scanning data that was displayed within the visor.
Wrist-mounted flamethrower.
Boots contained electrically powered high-speed turbines and jets, allowing flight and maneuverability.

WORN BY: Tony Stark, James Rhodes

CREATION AND VARIATION: Although Tony Stark created this heavily armed Variable Threat Response Battle Suit, it is most closely associated with James Rhodes, who wore it for a significant period of time as the hero War Machine.

BASICS: The original suit created by Tony Stark did not have the usual chest-mounted Unibeam, but it was added back to the armor when the suit was redesigned for Rhodes. Due to mobility problems, Stark also originally wore an electro-mesh bodysuit underneath the armor.

ABILITIES: From its first appearance, the War Machine bristled with weaponry, and over time, it gained more. From a shoulder-mounted gatling gun, missile launchers, lasers, flamethrowers, and other projectile weapons, to wrist-mounted laser blades and particle beam dischargers, the wearer of the War Machine armor was able to blow up just about anything.

First Appearance:
Iron Man #282

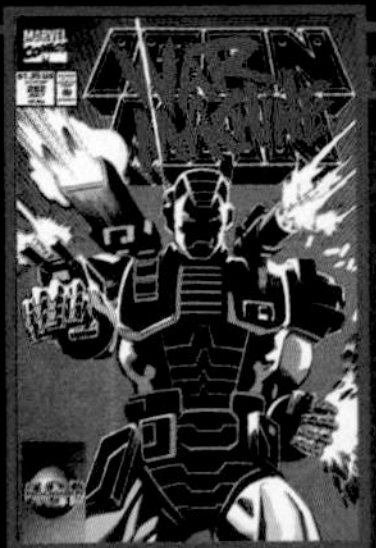

MODULAR ARMOR

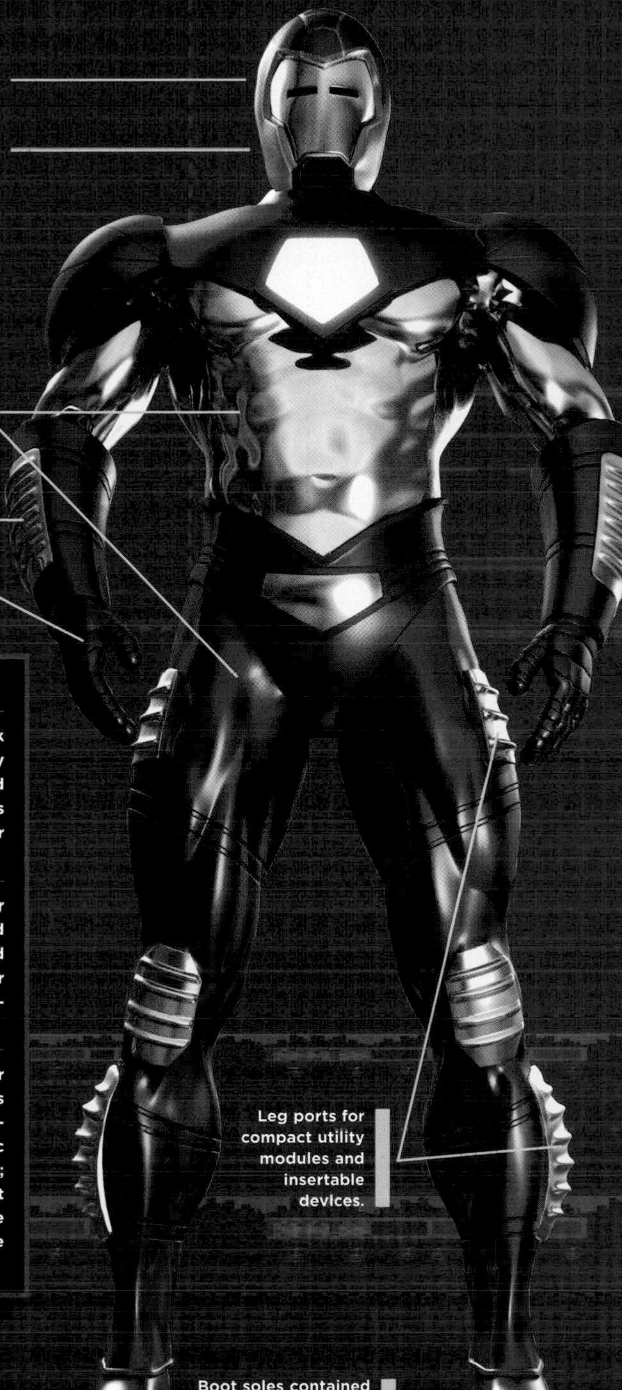

The helmet originally featured a vented "no ears" style, but later was modified to include earpieces.
This was the first Earthbound helmet that did not feature a mouth opening.
The surface of the armor is a refractive coated "flex-metal," which allows the armor to be condensed.
Gauntlet ports for compact utility modules and insertable devices.
Palms contained strong magnets.
Leg ports for compact utility modules and insertable devices.
Boot soles contained strong magnets.

WORN BY: Tony Stark

CREATION AND VARIATION: After Tony Stark received a new artificial nervous system, he initially used a robotic "telepresence" armor that followed his mental commands. When Stark regained his mobility, he created a new Iron Man suit of armor unlike any he had designed before.

BASICS: Although Stark had altered his armors for over three decades, this suit was actually designed to be modular, allowing its wearer to attach and detach special weaponry or technology needed for specific missions. The suit was otherwise tremendously sleek and flexible.

ABILITIES: The cybernetic interface of the armor was directly connected to the artificial nervous system of Tony Stark. Some of the modular equipment employed by Stark included: Magnetic Tractors and Repulsors; a Full Spectrum Scanalyzer; a Magnogravetric Field Generator to cancel out gravitational effects; a Cryogenic Compact Module to freeze targets in liquid nitrogen; and a gluelike Polybond Adhesive Compound.

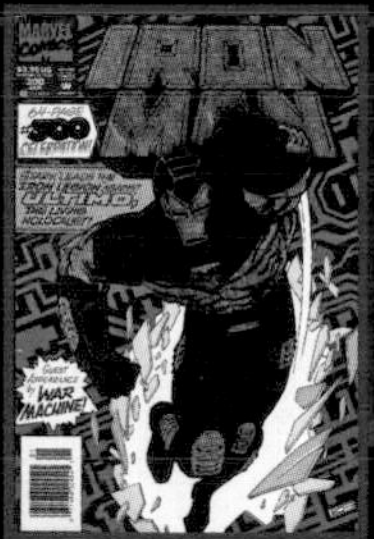

IRON MAN

First Appearance:
Iron Man #300

PROMETHEUM ARMOR

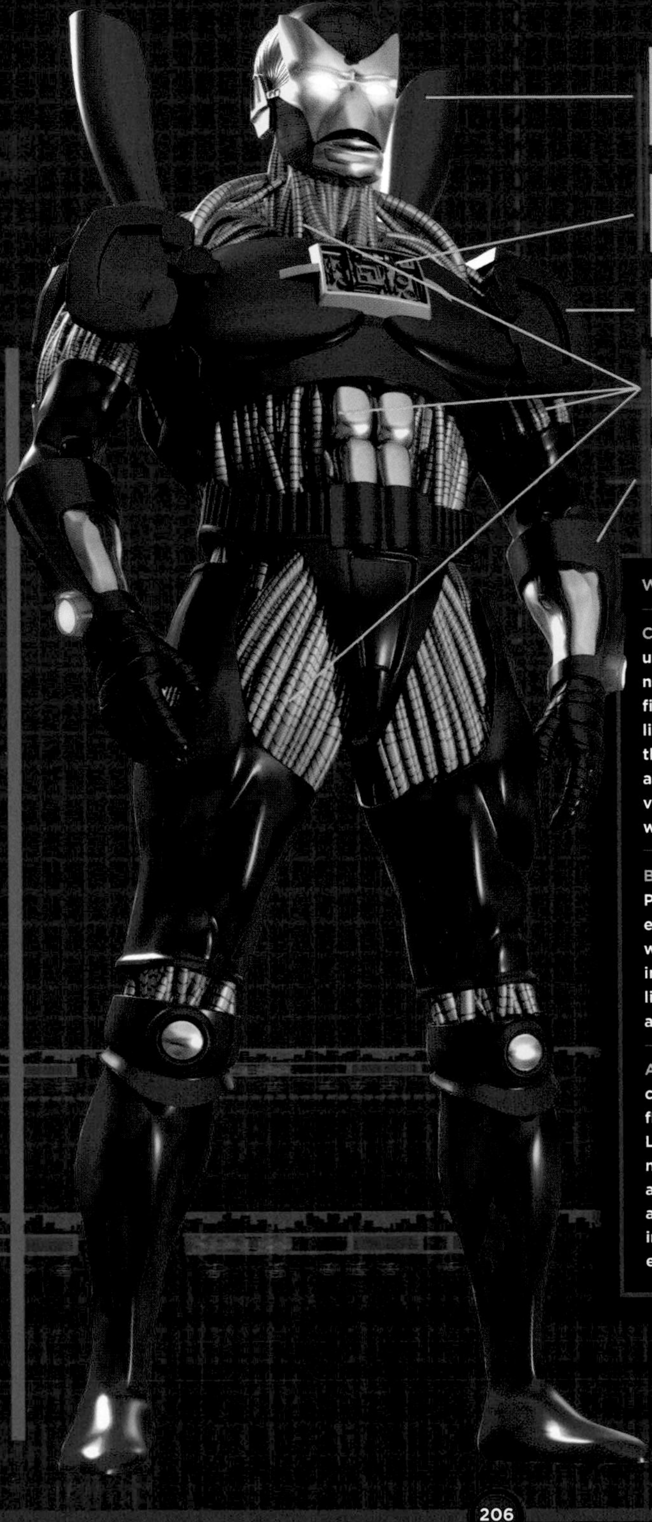

The Heat Extraction Tubes (HXT) were smokestacklike pipes that allowed Iron Man to eject steam from the suit's internal power sources, and to create vented plasma blasts from redirected energy attacks.

The chest module contained a holographic projector, communications devices, a scanning laser, emergency controls, interface ports, and power input terminals.

Called the "autocloak system," LED coating built into paint allowed the armor to reflect color, or turn "invisible" when armor was removed.

Tubes throughout armor contained breathable air supply, computer conduits, and nanobots, which repaired damage done to the armor or Stark.

Gauntlets contained a variety of weapons, including palm-mounted energy emitters, scanning sensors, and control computer devices.

WORN BY: Tony Stark, Connor "Rebel" O'Reilly

CREATION AND VARIATION: In the alternate pocket universe of the "Heroes Reborn" timeline, an alternate Tony Stark created a powerful suit of armor to fight the Hulk, but its creation became tied to his life. As with the earliest days of the original Stark, the alternate inventor was also forced to wear the armored chestplate to keep himself alive. But this version of Iron Man was jagged and rougher than any who had come before...

BASICS: Utilizing cutting-edge nanotechnology, the Prometheum Armor was composed of multiple layers, which included a base layer of tubing, atop of which a layer of titanium alloy armor was coated in Carbon Nitride, energy-resistant Aero-Gel, and a light-refracting LED coating. Stark could control the armor psionically, with mental commands.

ABILITIES: When Stark pressed a button on his chestplate, the armor was magnetically activated and flew to him; due to the autocloak elements of the LED coating, the armor pieces were invisible when not activated. The armor could be worn underwater, and had flight capability. Its primary capabilities and defensive weaponry were energy-based, utilizing beta particles, electromagnetic fields, thermal energy, and other power sources.

First Appearance:
Iron Man volume II #1

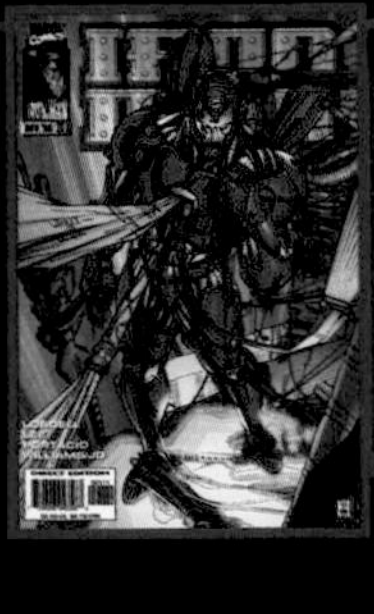

RENAISSANCE ARMOR

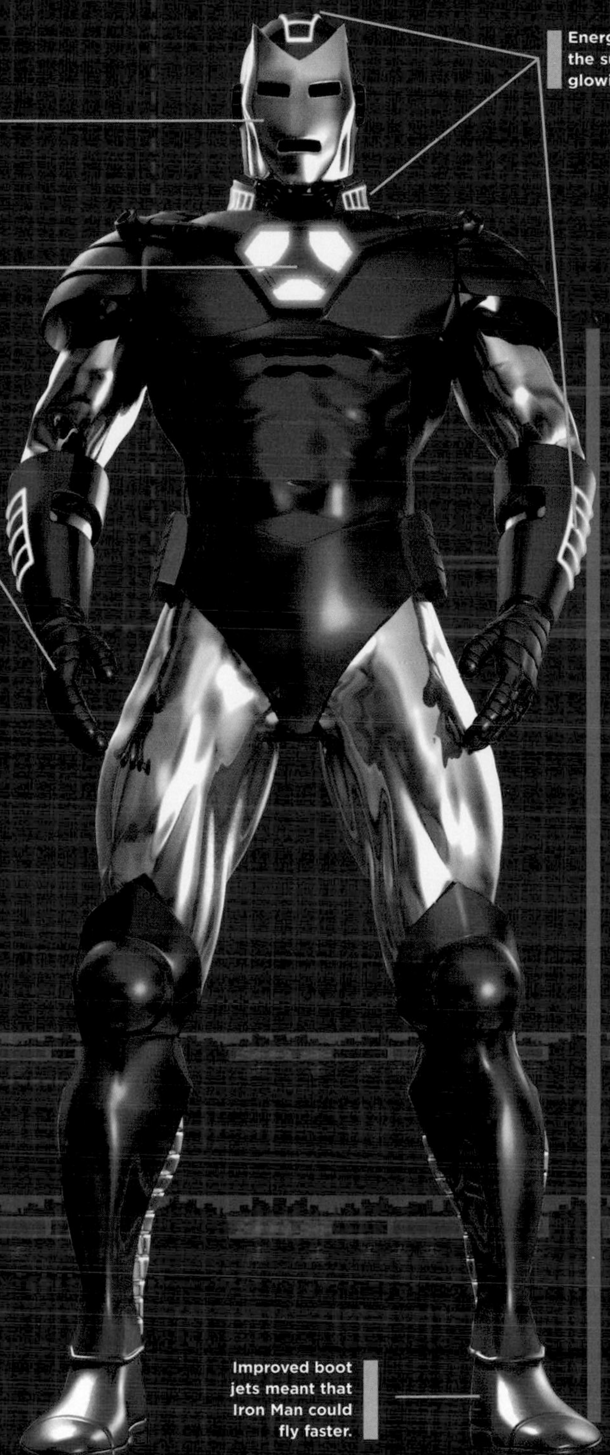

Energy from within the suit created glowing elements.

Faceplate could be lifted up or removed completely.

The latest model of the Unibeam emitted force beams, a search light, heat beams, a tractor beam, lasers, holographic images, ultraviolet light, and electromagnetic pulses.

Repulsor rays in palms could be of varying intensity; they were strong enough to blast through concrete or turn falling glass into powder.

Improved boot jets meant that Iron Man could fly faster.

WORN BY: Tony Stark

CREATION AND VARIATION: Having returned to life due to the cosmic alterations of the "Heroes Reborn" and "Heroes Returns" incidents, Tony Stark soon created a new armor that had visual similarities to his original armor designs, but that included state-of-the-art technology. When overexposure to the suit's energies began to threaten his health, Stark was later forced to completely rebuild this model to be servo-powered.

BASICS: The steel mesh armor and its technology are solar-charged, with energy induction grids that create power from heat. This, combined with built-in cooling units, allowed Stark to face explosions and even a volcanic blast! An intertial dampening field on the armor protected bystanders from ricocheting bullets if Iron Man was shot at.

ABILITIES: The cybernetic command system can be controlled by Stark through mental, vocal, or physical commands. Circuitry even allowed Stark to sleep while in flight, and to withstand psionic assaults. The armor eventually became sentient, due to the plans of the robotic Avengers villain, Ultron.

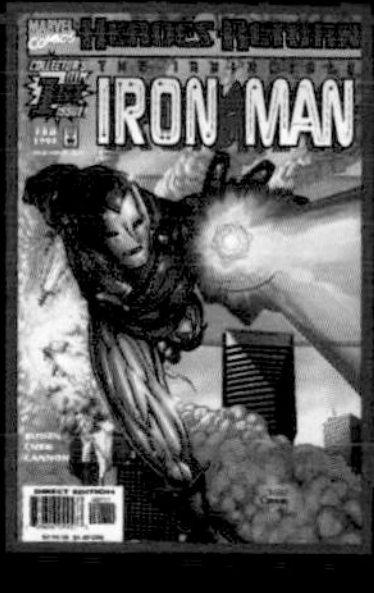
HEROES RETURN
IRON MAN

First Appearance:
Iron Man volume III #1

EXTREMIS ARMOR

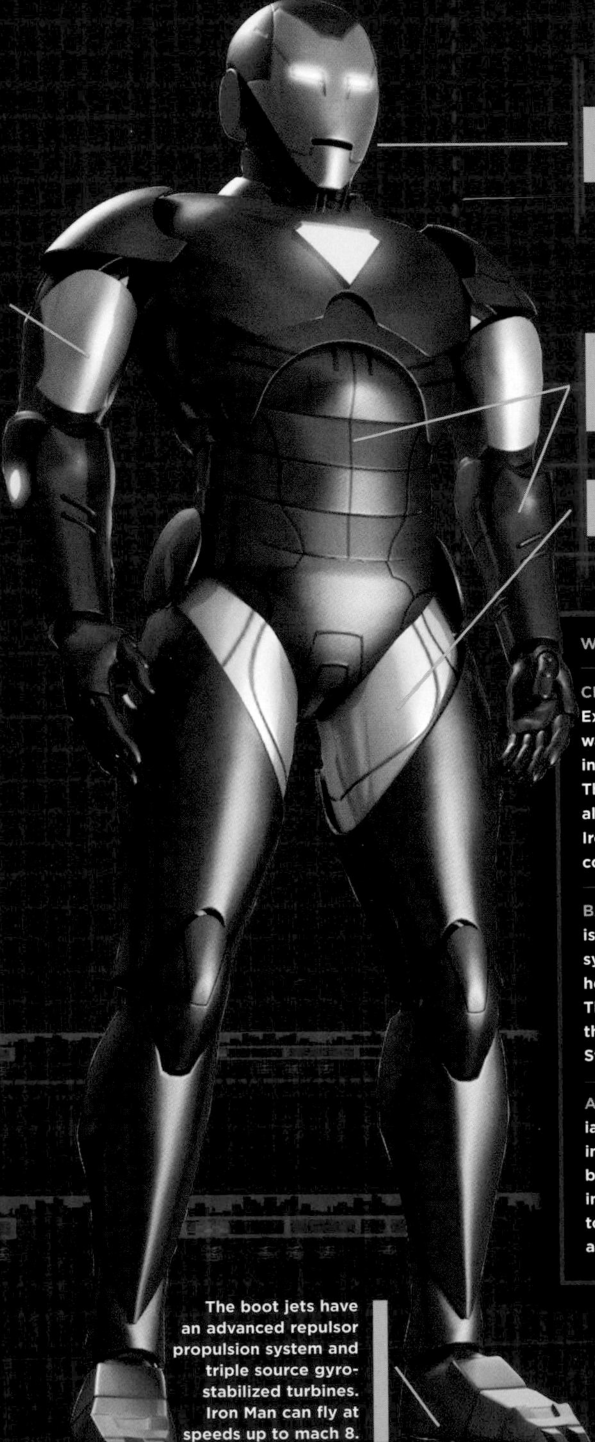
The armor can be sealed for underwater, low-oxygen environments, or brief outer space excursions. An internal air supply lasts over an hour.
The armor's exoskeleton gives Iron Man superhuman strength level of Class 90, allowing him to lift 100 tons!
A cloaking effect that utilizes chameleon-like visual adaptability can give the armor the illusion of invisibility and radar resistance. This effect cannot be maintained during combat, and is a massive energy drain on the armor.
Gold-colored undersheath is contained in Stark's bone marrow and extrudes to protectively cover his body.
The boot jets have an advanced repulsor propulsion system and triple source gyro-stabilized turbines. Iron Man can fly at speeds up to mach 8.

WORN BY: **Tony Stark**

CREATION AND VARIATION: **During a battle with the Extremis-enhanced villain named Mallen, Tony Stark was critically injured. To save his own life, Stark also injected himself with a modified version of Extremis. The techno-organic virus fused with Stark's body, allowing him to store the inner undersheath of the Iron Man armor in the hollows of his bones and to control the armor through direct brain impulses.**

BASICS: **The Extremis armor's operating system is directly connected to Stark's central nervous system, giving him both superhuman speed and a healing factor that can regenerate entire organs! The "memory metal" armor is magnetically drawn to the undersheath once it has been extruded, allowing Stark to become Iron Man within seconds.**

ABILITIES: **The exterior armor is outfitted with familiar equipment, though it has been updated. This includes repulsors, pulse bolts, the Unibeam, and boot jets. Using his Extremis-enhanced cybernetic interface, Iron Man is also able to remotely connect to satellite communications or computer systems across the globe.**

First Appearance:
Iron Man volume IV #5

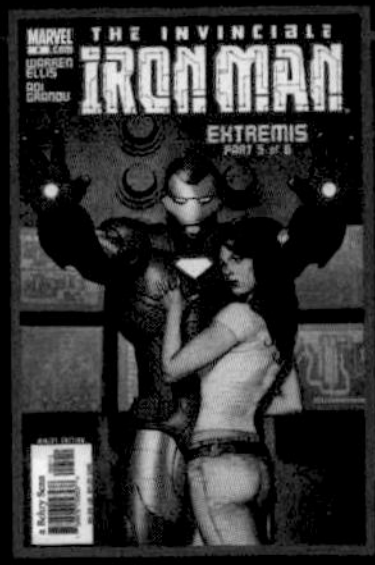
THE INVINCIBLE
IRON MAN
EXTREMIS

ULTIMATE ARMOR

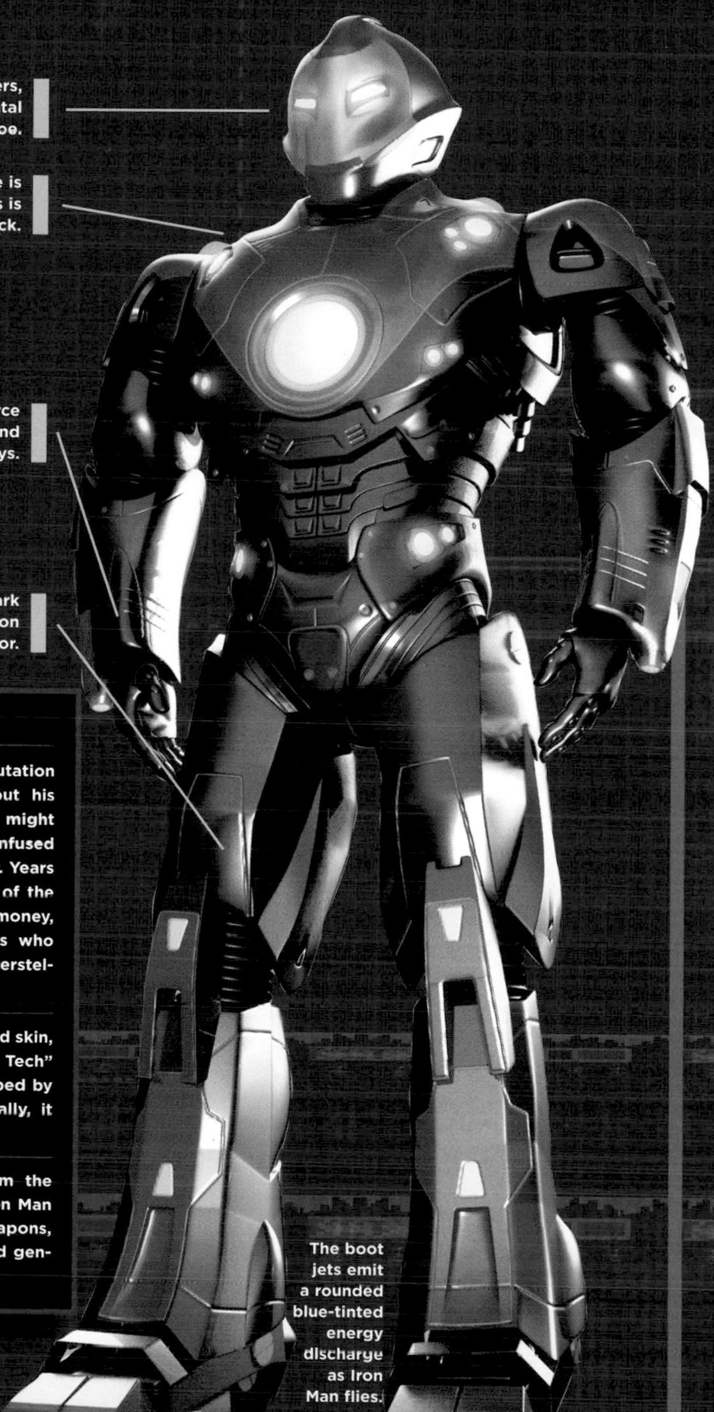
The armor contains neuro-scramblers, which can cause disruption of mental capabilities when directed at a foe.
When Stark emerges from the armor, he is often covered in a greenish coolant. This is stored in two containers in a backpack.
Weapons capabilities include force field generators, pulse blasts, and palm-mounted repulsor rays.
Because of its bulk and size, Stark often requires assistance to don the Iron Man armor.
The boot jets emit a rounded blue-tinted energy discharge as Iron Man flies.

WORN BY: Tony Stark

CREATION AND VARIATION: Born with a mutation that created excess neural tissue throughout his body, the Tony Stark of alternate Earth-1610 might not have survived had his scientist father not infused him with an experimental bacterial bio-armor. Years later, Stark would create various prototypes of the Iron Man armor, using them to gain fame, money, power, and girls...and to fight those villains who attempted to destroy democracy, or those interstellar invaders who wished to conquer Earth.

BASICS: Stark's bio-armor is literally his second skin, though it is invisible at most times. The "Iron Tech" technology of the Iron Man suits was developed by Stark when he was in prep school. Essentially, it functions as a powerful exoskeleton.

ABILITIES: Although visually distinctive from the Iron Man armor of Earth-616, the Ultimate Iron Man battlesuit contains many of the same weapons, including repulsor rays, a Unibeam, force field generators, and boot jets.

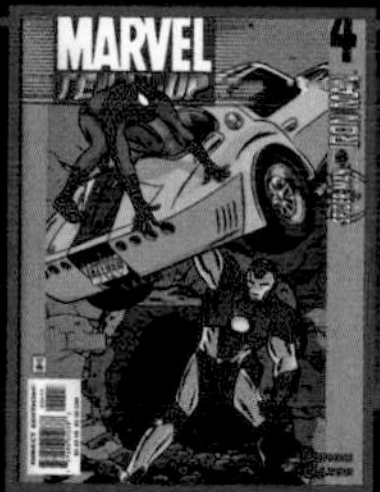
MARVEL
4

First Appearance:
Ultimate Marvel Team-Up #4

SPACE ARMOR

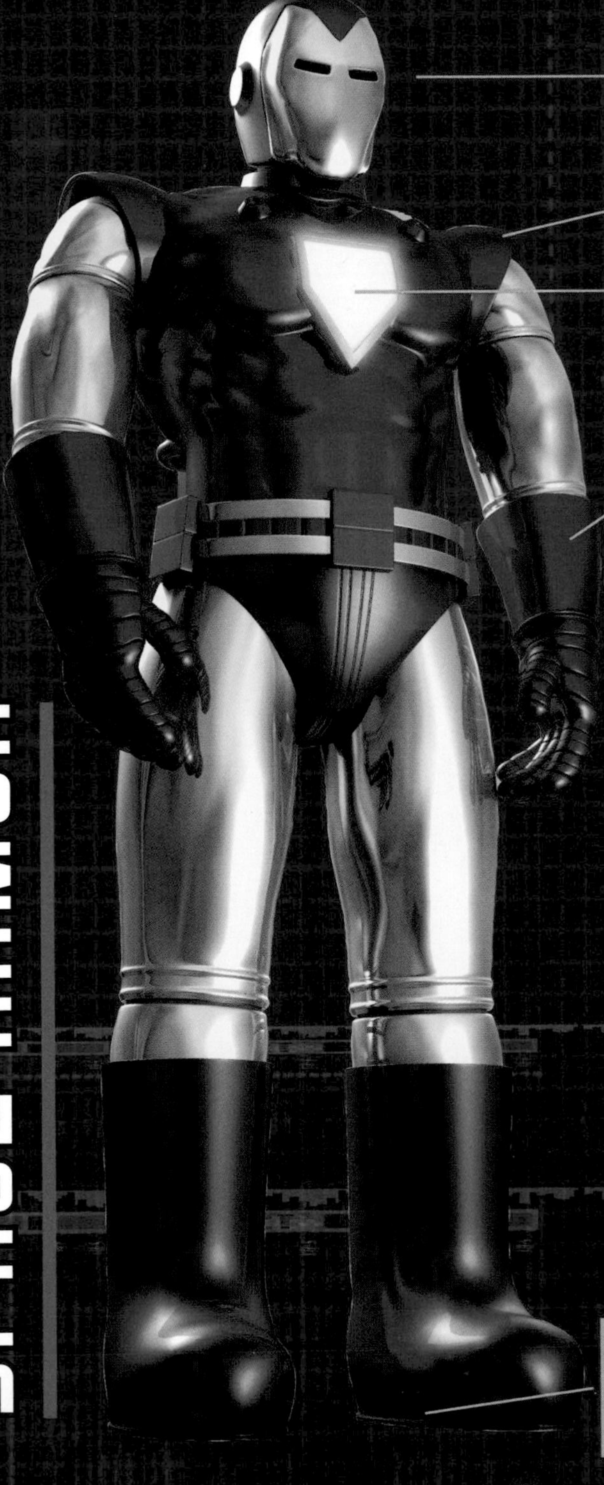

The helmet was completely sealed, and the armor contained a two-day supply of air, as well as water and nutritional supplements.

The epaulets held within them concussion-burst cannons.

Instead of a Unibeam, this battlesuit was equipped with a protonic Pentode Chest Beam. Ideal for use in space, it contained a vario-beam spotlight, lasers, and a deflector beam.

Iron Man could launch Exo-Unit long-range grapplers to attach to satellites or other objects. The "hands" on the grapplers were fully articulated.

Short-range boot jets allow Stark to launch himself into the atmosphere, while nuclear-powered thrusters give him the power to break away from Earth and into orbit...or beyond.

WORN BY: Tony Stark

CREATION AND VARIATION: Realizing that Iron Man would need to undertake missions in outer space, Tony Stark created a specialty armor suited for the rigors of null-gravity, extreme cold, and lack of atmosphere. He would later modify his space armor designs as he undertook missions away from Earth...including trips to other galaxies!

BASICS: Large and bulky, the Space Armor did not function well on Earth due to the gravitational pull, but was necessary for the extreme conditions of outer space survival. Due to internal life support devices, Stark could survive in the void of space, unaided, for at least forty-eight hours.

ABILITIES: The Space Armor contained many defensive systems that were designed specifically for outer space environments, including grapplers, magnetic units, and targeted lasers. Although the boot jets contained nuclear thrusters to reach escape velocity, the fuel was a safe form of liquid oxygen.

First Appearance:
Iron Man #142

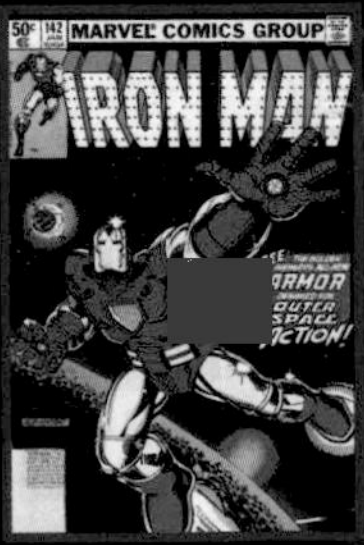
MARVEL COMICS GROUP
IRON MAN

DEEP SEA ARMOR

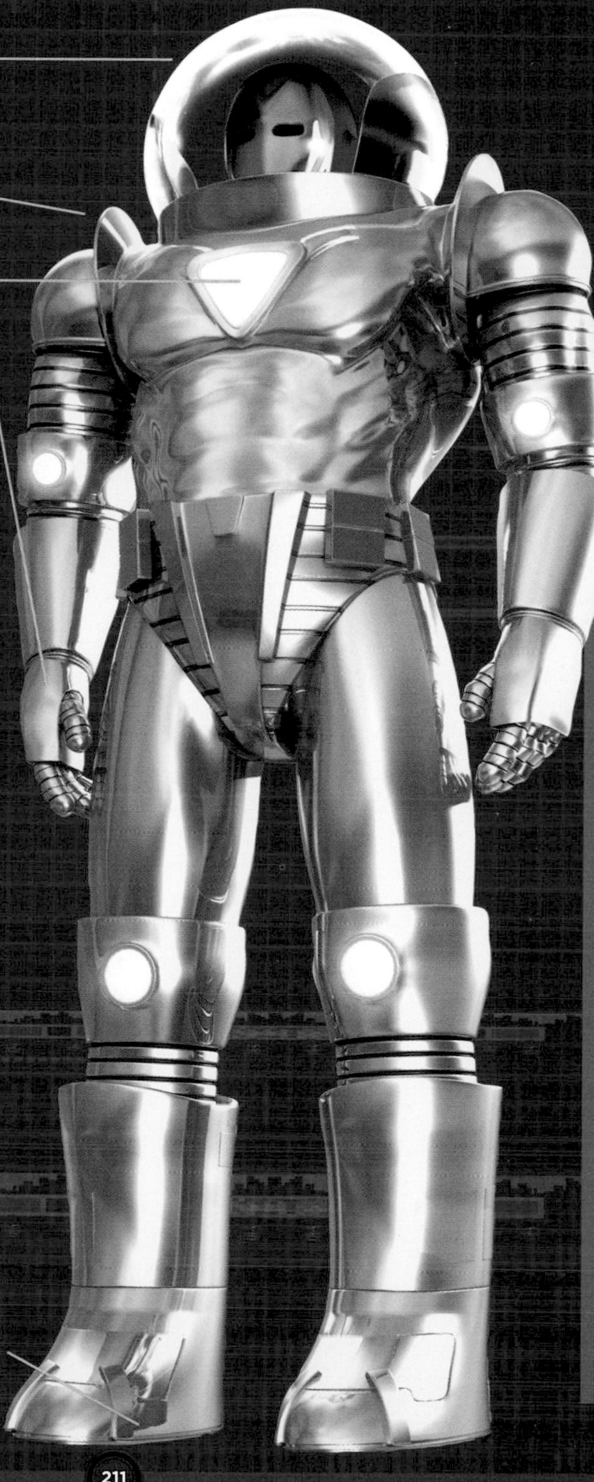

The dome atop this battlesuit was a transparent crystal quartz visor that provided a full oxygen environment and safety from incredible aquatic pressures. Iron Man wore his traditional helmet underneath the dome.

Two launchable minitorpedoes were mounted in the shoulder epaulets.

A chest-mounted Tri-Beam housed an advanced halogen lamp spotlight, as well as a tunable laser.

In addition to repulsor rays, the gloves of the suit contained advanced micro-hand articulation to enable Iron man to grasp things properly.

The aquatic propulsion jets are dual mode; in the air, they allowed Iron Man normal flight, but underwater, they utilized silent micro water impellers to propel the armor both silently and swiftly. The boots were also immobile, and did not flex.

WORN BY: Tony Stark

CREATION AND VARIATION: Also known as the "Deep Submergence Suit" or the "Hydro Armor," this specific battlesuit was created by Tony Stark for salvage missions in which he'd have to submerge deep into the ocean depths. His regular Iron Man armor was watertight, but did not function well in great depths, or for long periods of time. Stark rarely wore this suit, but has utilized elements of it to enhance the underwater capabilities of later armors.

BASICS: The battlesuit was created to function as a diving suit as well, and was thus composed of thick, composite material with redesigned joints and high-pressure ring seals. The suit is rated at 8,000 lbs. per square inch, and can submerge to depths of up to three miles. It is powered by a micro-nuclear supply pack.

ABILITIES: The battlesuit is actually two sets of armors; a secondary "Inner-Escape Suit" is a more compact set of armor that allows Iron Man to eject the outer suit and surface quickly. Heavy pressurization keeps him from getting "the bends." In addition to weapons mentioned above, the suit featured an octopus-inspired chemical smokescreen, and an electrical field generator to allow transmission of energy blasts based on the jolts of an electric eel.

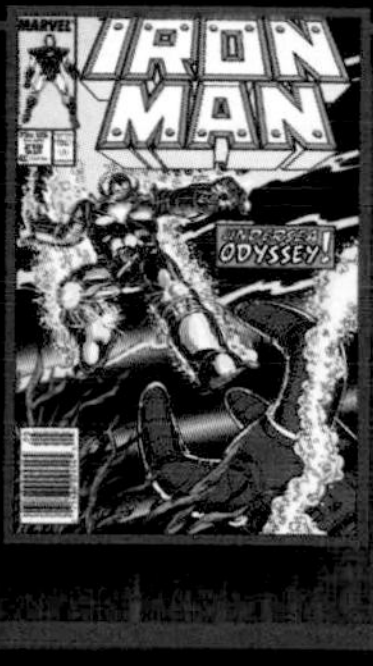
IRON MAN
ODYSSEY!

First Appearance:
Iron Man #218

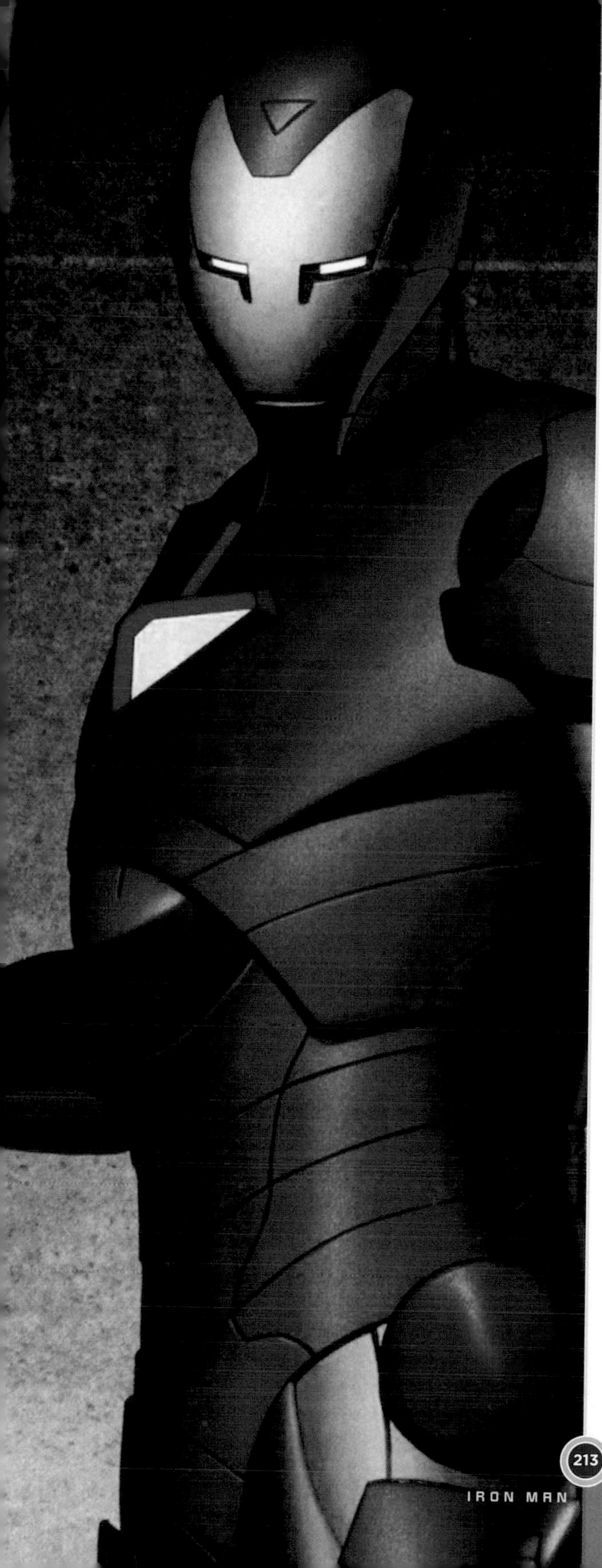

ACKNOWLEDGMENTS

The author would like to thank the following people, without whom this book would not have come together as quickly and smoothly:

For interviews by phone and e-mail, appreciation goes to Iron Man co-creator Stan Lee, as well as Gene Colan, Adi Granov, Bob Layton, David Michelinie, Denny O'Neil, Frank Tieri, John Jackson Miller, John Byrne, Jorge Lucas, Kurt Busiek, Larry Lieber, Luke McDonnell, Mike Friedrich, Mike Grell, Paul Ryan, Robin Laws, Roger Stern, and Tom Brevoort.

For research help and materials, thanks go to Patty Jeres and Mark Evanier, as well as Jon Ingersoll, Snard, Bob Cherry, and Yoc. For invaluable secrets of the *Marvel Super Heroes* show, gratitude is given to Vince Oliva, while the title of "Mego Master" must go to Benjamin Holcomb, author of *Mego 8" Super-Heroes: World's Greatest Toys.*

For their Modok-sized brains full of Iron Man knowledge and trivia, their essential input and corrections, and time-intensive interview transcription work and photos, a hearty "Excelsior!" is shouted to the masters of *Advanced Iron,* John B. Comerford and Roger A. Ott II.

For the stupendous job in making this book look so great, thanks go to artist Ian Fullwood, production manager Erich Schoeneweiss, production editor Crystal Velasquez, and the talented designer Brad Foltz of Foltz Design. Editor Keith Clayton was a breeze to work with, and thanks are also due to VP Scott Shannon for recognizing my moustache from across a crowded convention hall and inviting me to rejoin the Del Rey family with this project.

A special thanks to the team at Marvel Brand Assurance: Adam Levine, Mitch Montgomery, and Robert Shatzkin.

CREDITS

Grateful acknowledgment goes to each artist whose work is included in this volume. Each of them made Iron Man strong!

Ian Akin

Mike Allred

Darren Auck

Chuck Austen

Dick Ayers

Mark Bagley

Chris Batista

Mark Bright

Eliot R. Brown

John Byrne

Ralph Cabrera

Jim Calafiore

Eric Canete

Eric Cannon

John Cassaday

Sean Chen

Jim Cheung

Mark Chiarello

Dave Chlystek

Frank Cho

Dave Cockrum

Gene Colan

   (aka "Adam Austin")

Hector Collazo

Vince Colletta

Johnny Craig

Alan Davis

Roberto de la Torre

Brian Denham

Marcelo Dichiara

Steve Ditko

Don Drake

Kieron Dwyer

Pam Eklund

Steve Ellis

Mike Esposito

   (aka "Mickey Demeo")

Pasqual Ferry

Seth Fisher

Ian Fullwood

Rey Garcia

Brian Garvey

Joe Gaudioso

Gabriel Gecko

Frank Giacoia

Michael Golden

Adi Granov

Keron Grant

Mike Grell

Jackson "Butch" Guice

Gene Ha

Scott Hanna

Ed Hannigan

Don Heck

Bryan Hitch

Dave Hoover

Kevin Hopgood

Don Hudson

Rob Hunter

Frazer Irving

Reggie Jones

Rick Ketcham

Jack Kirby

Scott Koblish

Alan Kupperberg

Yancy Labat

Andy Lanning

Salvador Larroca

Bob Layton

Ron Lim

Jorge Lucas

Larry Mahlstedt

Alitha Martinez

Luke McDonnell

Mark McKenna

Steve McNiven

Gary Michaels

Al Milgrom

Steve Mitchell

Jim Mooney

Tom Morgan

Paul Neary

Hector Oliveira

P.L. Palmiotti

Sean Parsons

Andrew Pepoy

George Pérez

Rich Perrotta

Joe Pimental

Whilce Portacio

Joe Quesada

Rodney Ramos

Bill Reinhold

Ivan Reis

Robin Riggs

Patrick Rolo

John Romita Jr.

William Rosado

Michael Ryan

Paul Ryan

Mike Saenz

Tim Sale

Javier Saltares

Jonathan Sibal

Walt Simonson

Barry Windsor Smith

Paul Smith

Karl Story

Larry Stucker

Rob Stull

Philip Tan

Thomas Tenney

Robert Teranishi

Tim Townsend

George Tuska

Adam Warren

Bob Wiacek

Anthony Williams

Scott Williams

Mike Zeck

Patrick Zircher

PHOTO: PAUL SMALLEY

ANDY MANGELS is the *USA Today* best-selling author and co-author of more than a dozen novels — including *Star Trek* and *Roswell* books — all co-written with Michael A. Martin. Flying solo, he is the bestselling author of several non-fiction books, including *Star Wars: The Essential Guide to Characters* and *Animation on DVD: The Ultimate Guide*, as well as a significant number of entries for *The Super Hero Book: The Ultimate Encyclopedia of Comic-Book Icons and Hollywood Heroes* and its companion volume, *The Super Villain Book: The Evil Side of Comics and Hollywood*. His forthcoming books include *Lou Scheimer: Creating The Filmation Generation* and *The Wonder Woman Companion*, and a story with Martin for the *Tales of Zorro* anthology.

In addition to his publishing work, Andy has produced, directed, and scripted documentaries and provided award-winning Special Features for more than forty fan-favorite DVD box set releases, ranging from *The Secrets of Isis* to *He-Man and the Masters of the Universe*, and *The Archies* to *Dungeons & Dragons*.

A member of the International Association of Media Tie-In Writers, Andy has written licensed material based on properties from Lucasfilm, Paramount, New Line Cinema, Universal Studios, Warner Bros., Microsoft, Abrams-Gentile, and Platinum Studios. Over the past two decades, his comic book work has been published by DC Comics, Marvel Comics, Dark Horse, Image, Innovation, and many others. He was the editor of the award-winning *Gay Comics* anthology for eight years. Andy has also written hundreds of articles for entertainment and lifestyle magazines and newspapers in the United States, England, and Italy.

Andy is a national award-winning activist in the gay community, and has raised thousands of dollars for charities over the years, including more than $43,000 raised for domestic violence shelters during his October "Wonder Woman Day" event. He lives in Portland, Oregon, with his long-term partner, Don Hood, and their dog, Bela.

Visit his website at www.andymangels.com

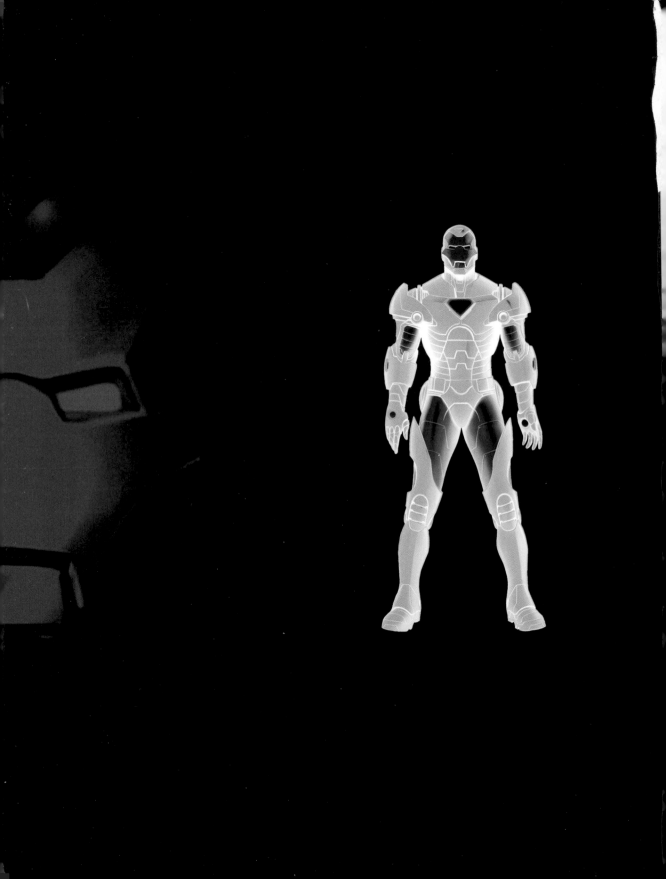